OTHER ISLANDS

BOOK THREE OF
THE *HOOK & JILL* SAGA

ANDREA JONES

REGINETTA PRESS

Copyright © 2017 by Andrea Jones

The Reginetta Press
www.reginettapress.com

www.HookandJill.com

Interior design by Celia Jones
Book jacket designed by Erik Hollander
www.ErikHollanderDesign.com

LCCN: 2017946862
ISBN: 0-9823714-1-1
ISBN-13: 978-0-9823714-1-1

Printed in the USA

The *Hook & Jill* Saga
by Andrea Jones:

Book One

Hook & Jill

Book Two

Other Oceans

Book Three

Other Islands

For those who walk in two worlds.

For Nancy —
May you find
your Island

Andrew
Jones

Contents

OTHER ISLANDS

Harsh Mistress

David didn't get to the Island in the usual, unusual way. He didn't fly, like the other boys— and the girl— with arms flung wide, squealing with glee to see the mountaintops shining under a bulbous sun, the cerulean seas glimmering over the shores. David didn't get there like those earlier children did, by choice or by guile.

He arrived on the Neverland in the same way he did everything: by necessity. He drifted ashore like the remnants of his splintered craft— soaked, swollen, beyond repair. Magic had nothing to do with it, or so he believed.

Except for the beauty, there was little of magic to be seen when he opened his eyes. A long C-shape of sandy beach, thick forest behind it and lush tropical foliage on either side. Bright exotic birds screamed in the trees, taunting him. Once, when he thought he heard a lion roar, the sopping hair at the back of his neck rose stiff. The air he inhaled was fresh and clear, except for a streak of red smoke away off over the trees. David rolled himself out of the surf and closed his scratchy eyes. The tears, when they came, helped to wash the salt from his stinging lids. David was young, but he was not quite a child. He knew no magic could wash away the sorrow.

Alone and alive. He understood it was a blessing, to be alive. The alone part saddened him. Those he'd left behind were not alone in their watery tomb. All his mates, his four officers. And his uncle. For all their fears, it wasn't the pirates that finished them. It was the sea. As his uncle had declared with his last, labored breath— all sailors served a harsh mistress.

The words sent a flash of memory through the young man's mind. An emerald green gown and golden, flowing hair. A laugh like drops of diamonds, a sound that sparkled over even the darkest gloom. David could only think of the woman in terms of jewels. Eyes like sapphires. Even her teeth were set like pearls. Yet she hadn't seemed harsh. And she wasn't a mistress any more. She was a wife, and David had witnessed her wedding. But it was her fault that David languished on this beach. Her fault that all the merchant sailors whose pulses had quickened as they watched her, so avidly, were pulseless dead men now. She was like a sea siren. She was a temptress, presaging disaster.

Red-Handed Jill.

Her image sent a jolt through his body, fighting the chill of the ocean. If she hadn't captivated David with her charm and her beauty, he never would've given up his shamrock, his lucky piece. Not even if those pirates shot him for it. He was just a cabin boy, but he was a sailor. He knew the necessity of luck. Yet, like the men, David was unprepared— blindsided— by the force of her loveliness. She'd reached out that hand, vividly crimson with bloodstain, and, unscrupulous though she was, David had yielded to his need to touch her, setting his hand upon hers and settling his silver charm in her palm. Unlike the pirate she proved to be, the lady had squeezed his hand, smiling, and thanked him. Then she leapt into the arms of her lover, her new-made husband, that gold-plated gypsy brute of a captain, and soared away across the chasm between ships. Pain had stabbed at David's heart as she disappeared under the sign of the grinning black flag. Pain, and worry.

His uncle had believed the trouble was over then. But just as hope returned to his breast, within only an hour, Jill's vultures descended to pick the helpless *Unity* clean. Boarding with the promise of succor, the Frenchmen had robbed even the old surgeon of his instruments. That second assault proved too much for David's ailing uncle. He died before the storm reached its full intensity, leaving his shaken mate to contend with the tempest. The temptress had vanished, taking with her not simply David's shamrock, but the *Unity*'s fortunes as well. Tasting the bitter brine in his teeth, David spat in the sand.

He only hoped she was gone forever.

Superstitious like all sailors, David blamed his luck. But he had felt the power of enchantment already. It had changed what was left of his life. He just didn't know about the magic yet. He didn't understand the usual, unusual way it worked— like a woman. By choice, or by guile.

A Family Man

White Bear looked to the pale light seeping at the edge of the tepee door. His heart felt heavy, his body unsatisfied. Raven lay raised on one elbow, clutching the blanket to her breast. Her black eyes watched him, full of caution. He knew she wasn't afraid. Her courage annoyed him. Under her submission, she wasn't cooperative; she was simply careful. White Bear's growl of a voice spoke softly so as not to disturb his wife, nor awaken the others slumbering in the encampment.

"Tell your sister when she wakes. I am hungry."

Raven understood him, but chose to answer literally. "I will cook your breakfast."

"You do everything I need. But you do not allow me to approach you."

"You are a patient man, White Bear. When the right day comes—"

"The right day came yesterday. And the day before. You turned away."

"I am sorry. It is not easy for me." Raven didn't look in her brother-in-law's hard, gray eyes. She wished to avoid challenging him, but she had to make her point. "There has been no ceremony."

"No ceremony is necessary. It is custom. A good man cares for his family."

"You are a good man. You care for my sister, and I am grateful. But she is near her time. I am respectful of her feeling."

"It is because her time is near that she sent me to you. It is she who asked, so many moons ago, that I provide for you."

Raven kept her eyes cast down. She beheld his leggings and moccasins, made of soft-worked buckskin, elaborately beaded with designs of her sister's making— the finest beadwork in the camp. Willow's pride in her husband showed plainly in her work. She was a skilled woman and she loved her husband. Why should she not? White Bear was a fearless warrior, a plentiful provider. He was not a young man, but already he sat upon the council, its youngest member. And, as Raven had reminded him, he was patient. White Bear had chosen Willow among all the other girls, then waited for her to come of age. At the time they spoke their ritual vows, he hadn't known her older sister would need a husband, too. No one had known.

Raven blinked back the tears before White Bear might see them. He might mistake the reason for them. She laid the blanket aside, gently, rising without a sound. Without a sound, she served him his morning meal. Using her hands to useful purpose lessened the sadness.

When he finished, she received his bowl. He reached out to thank her, the way he so often did for her sister. But before his fingers could touch her cheek, his arm stopped in midair. Raven's words hung there, too.

"You are welcome…Brother."

His eyes narrowed. Raven saw the muscles on his lean body go taut.

"I hear you," he said. He rose and flung open the tepee door. Stepping into the morning air, he turned to stand straight and tall. The bear claws on his necklace gleamed ivory-white, and an early breeze stirred the feathers that Raven herself had woven into his scalp lock, where the long hair was gathered at the peak of his shaven head. The slanting sunlight highlighted the battle marks on his copper skin. Raven wondered if he knew how her eyes were drawn to him. The drum of her heart beat faster. White Bear was a formidable man. A man any other woman might desire. And she had called him 'Brother.'

When he dropped the door flap, Raven shoved her hand through her close-cropped hair and considered her sweet, sleeping sister.

Willow lay on her side under the prized white bearskin, dormant in the exhaustion of late pregnancy, her legs drawn up beneath her swollen belly, a trace of a smile curving her pretty lips. Even with her hair shorn, Raven knew herself to be handsome, like her sister. But she was not as openhanded as Willow.

Today, Raven addressed her sister's husband as 'Brother.' What would she call him tomorrow?

Fair Warning

The old oak near Peter Pan's hideout bore more battle scars than a fortress. The arrowheads had chipped away at its bark so that a wide, bare, notched spot lay exposed, like a shorn patch of skin on a bison hide. A target showed there, painted and repainted in diminishing sizes of bloody red circles. Every so often a breeze kicked up and the oak would rattle its branches at its assailants in a threatening sort of way, withholding the sunlight and casting its mammoth shadow over those boys. But the oak was hardy. When the breeze died down, the tree settled in again to grit its leafy teeth and endure. It bled a bit of sap to blend with the blood of its target, then scarred itself over in gnarly scarlet lumps. Even Peter's treatment couldn't kill it.

Most of the old oak's wounds were inflicted by Peter himself. Today his boys were doing their part, but still he crossed his arms and shook his unruly head; marksmen they were not. Only one other boy could zing an arrow straight on target. He was a chip off Peter's block, right down to his appearance, and that's what Peter had named him.

Peter smiled with pride as he watched Chip stand posed, commanding every inch of his four-foot height, his back straight, one green eye squeezed shut. His arm strained to stay the bowstring. Chip was almost as smart as Peter. He had adopted Peter's customs, all of them, beginning by sporting a bright sharp knife in his belt. Like Peter, Chip exhibited the air of a champion. Habitually, he tossed his head of wild golden hair and crowed in a bold little voice.

Chip hadn't been a Lost Boy very long— one season, Peter guessed— but already he'd absorbed Peter's genius and could shoot the wings off a dragonfly. Peter was proud to be Chip's father. Or his chief, his king, or his captain, depending what game they played at the moment.

Today they were playing Indians. The four of them had foraged in the forest and rounded up a parcel of sturdy sticks. The earlier part of the morning was spent hunched over with tongues between teeth, attaching tips and feathers. Peter had relished impressing his boys over breakfast. With a flourish, he had opened his Wendy-pocket to reveal a cache of arrowheads he'd confiscated as he prowled the People's hunting grounds. He could shape his own arrowheads of course— no one did it better— but at times like this he missed the Twins, who used to perform the labor for him, even experimenting with innovations and improving all his weapons. But today, and every day now, the Twins, too, were Indians.

Peter didn't like to think about the Twins. It brought a sour taste to the back of his throat. The Twins had broken his law. They'd grown up. Now they were known on the Island as the Men of the Clearing, and they were big and bronzed, considered to be real Indians by the outcast native ladies who had taken them in. Peter got a feeling he wasn't used to feeling— a writhing in the pit of his stomach— when he remembered that the Twins and their ladies lived in the house Peter had ordered built for his Wendy. Like everything the Twins touched, the little dwelling had been reinvented by the pair, and now it comfortably held two men, three women, and four children. Or Peter supposed it was comfortable. He wouldn't know. He wasn't welcome in that house. Nor did he wish to be: it held too many grown-ups.

Chip's arrow sped away with a spitting sound to strike the oak in a 'Thunk!' A shout followed from Chip himself. Not to be outdone, Peter threw back his head to discharge his signature crow, drowning out the other boys' voices. Bertie and Bingo dropped their bows and joined hands to circle round, celebrating Chip's superiority. Their bare feet thumped the forest floor. "Hurrah, huzzah, for the prince, the warrior brave!"

Two less-competitive boys didn't exist, in the Neverland or not. Full of the joy of living, Bertie and Bingo embraced the world. Peter smiled at them, approving as they cheered. These boys were the perfect foils for his own perfection, and for Chip's rising star. They followed their leader's commands and applauded everything he accomplished. Unenterprising if left to themselves, yet they entered into Peter's every scheme with enthusiasm.

A few weeks after Chip was discovered in the park in London, Jewel's cousins there, the park fairies, had found these two little boys after Lock-out Time. One was dark and chubby, the other a hungry carrot-top. They now wore cast-offs the burly boy Tootles had outgrown, rapidly, during his tenure as a Lost Boy, and they swam about in Tootles' oversized shirts and breeches. Once he'd named these children, Peter could never remember which was Bertie and which was Bingo, but they answered to either. If Peter stopped to think about it, he believed the three boys of his latest band were created specifically for his benefit, just like the plot of one of Wendy's stories. Sooner or later, her tales always came true. No doubt she invented these two as she told his legend to the pirates she'd run off with when, true to her story, she stained her hand with blood and changed her name to Jill. Peter hadn't liked that idea at first, but now he preened to think how her tales of Peter Pan must impress those scummy buccaneers. He doubted they'd trouble him again soon. The pirates had sailed away with Jill and two of Peter's boys, and they'd tried to filch his fairy, too, a while ago. But Jewel couldn't live without Peter. Even before he swooped in to rescue her, she escaped to fly home to him. He was her wonderful boy.

"Peter," Chip's eyes glowed green, like his own. "You're thinking of a story. Tell it to us!"

Bertie and Bingo jumped up shrieking, "Yes!" then plumped down cross-legged on the damp, grassy earth of the forest. "We're listening."

"You two need more target practice. The story I'm thinking of is about pirates, and you never know when they'll attack."

Bingo, the carrot-top, piped up, a note of disappointment in his voice. "But they're off sailing the high seas. We haven't spied a single pirate since we got here."

Chip suggested, "We only *suppose* they're off on a voyage. They could be making use of a ruse to catch us off guard. Right, Peter?"

Nodding wisely, Peter put on his best father face. "Exactly right. You've been paying attention." He unslung his quiver and bow to drop them on the ground. With a bound, he leapt to the low, bench-like branch of the old oak tree. Here he perched with one knee under his chin, ready to hold forth with his own variation of one of Wendy's stories. It was a pirate story on the surface but like all the best tales, it was, in fact, about himself.

"Red-Handed Jill is a Pirate Queen. Fearing nothing and no one, she dares to sail the salt sea beside the Terrible Captain Hook, spreading terror in her wake."

Scenting adventure, the boys scooted closer, leaning toward their leader.

"Her pirate moniker comes from a deed she accomplished. She slew a tiger all on her own, tugging its tail and slashing its throat. Because it was her first kill, she underwent the blood-rage—" Peter's voice hushed with reverence, "a mystical union between the hunter and the hunted."

"Did *you* undergo the blood-rage, Peter, with your first kill?"

"Of course I did, Chip. I went wild, and whooped and danced. I'm sure it lasted a week."

"What did you kill? Or...*who?*"

Peter shrugged. "I forget them after I kill them." He was never one to dwell on the departed, even if he'd been able to remember them.

Appropriately impressed, Bertie croaked, "But why is she called Red-Handed Jill?"

"Because after her kill, she dropped down on her knees and plunged her right hand in the blood of the beast that had stalked her. It stained her skin forever. Her handprint flies from the *Roger*'s mast now, blood-red on a pure white banner, next to Captain Hook's. Jewel says it's a mark of initiation. *I* say it shows her ferocity. But the best part is...Red-Handed Jill wasn't *always* a pirate." Peter pulled back with an enigmatic expression, looking from face to face. "Once upon a time, when she was just a girl, she dared to fly beside *me*. She was my Wendy."

The boys expelled sighs. "Ahhh!"

"But I'm sorry to say that girls grow up to become ladies." The boys grimaced, just like Peter. "And you know what ladies like…" Four shudders shook the foliage. "Kisses."

Only Chip had the grace to blush. He once liked kisses himself. He'd given a peck on the cheek to Peter when Peter first adopted him. Chip held a deep, unlikely secret under the cover of his leafy tunic. He knew from Peter's stillness at the time that, far from despising that kiss, Peter had taken it to heart. Watching Peter with a sly look now, Chip felt just a bit wiser than his 'father.' Peter knew more forest lore than his two newest boys could ever hope to grasp. But where his emotions were concerned, Peter was green as a seedling. Even Bertie— the dark, chubby one, as Chip continually reminded Peter— owned a better understanding of friendship. Bingo on the other hand was like a puppy; he held a soft spot for anyone who bothered to feed him. But, young as he was, Chip himself was clear on the subject of feelings. He loved Peter, he loved adventure, and he loved life as a Lost Boy. He wasn't ashamed to show his emotions, but he was shrewd enough not to.

He was also dutiful enough to move Peter's agenda along. "Did you have to kiss her like she wanted, Peter?"

Disapproving, Peter angled his head. "If you know anything about chivalry, Chip, you know that a knight never discusses his lady." He smiled, cunning now, and slipped a lacy cloth from his pocket. "But I *can* tell you that I carry her kerchief!" Peter dangled the handkerchief over his nose, inhaling loudly with an appreciative grin, "Scented with all the oils of Araby!" Admiring their leader, Chip, Bertie, and Bingo laughed, and Peter sat back. "She granted me this token one afternoon, as I set off upon a quest. And one day I expect I'll have to do battle in tournament over it. As soon as Red-Handed Jill's villainous captain gets wind of it, he's sure to come to collect it." A determined look settled over Peter, sharpening his patrician features. He tucked the handkerchief away and fingered the tip of his knife. "And I'll be ready for him."

As if in answer to the challenge, a thunderous boom exploded in the distance. A flock of parrots squawked in alarm, swooshing from the trees. The very Island trembled at the blast. Peter sprang up to balance on his bough, tense and alert. "Long Tom!" His eyes opened wide as he stared at his boys, then he shoved off to soar up through the branches, ignoring the sting of the old oak's revenge. A shower of leaves flickered, swirling downward in the spot where he roosted a moment before. He was in the air and overlooking the bay in time to see white smoke erupt from a row of cannon before the roar of the second barrage reached his ears.

"*Two* discharges?" Chip exclaimed. He darted up through the treetops with the other children at his heels.

Peter hovered, a look of disbelief on his face. But quick as mercury, his expression changed to glee. For the first time in months, his heart banged against his ribs, double-time.

"Hook and Jill are back!" he exulted. "You'll get your fill of pirates now, my boys! It's the *Jolly Roger*…and she's taken a mate."

All the boys beheld her now. Chip's pulse raced; Bertie and Bingo swallowed hard, feeling their insides go hollow.

The *Roger* flew from the east. With rays of morning light behind her, she glimmered like a sunrise on the horizon of Neverbay. A far more beautiful vessel than these boys had imagined, more handsome, even, than Peter had described, she was fierce— a forty-gunner— graceful but substantial. Gold paint glinted on her deck and rails, white sails arched like wings. Her only dark spot was the black flag, streaming proud at her mainmast. And gliding along behind her, newly embraced by the arms of the bay, was a lithe, lovely ship, smaller and more modest. A fighter, but every bit as trim.

And both ships swarmed with pirates.

Peter punched the air and crowed. Not to be outdone, Chip dove into a somersault, flung back his head, and joined his voice with his chief's. Below them, the oak tree agitated in the breezes, and leaked its sap to mend the morning's wounds.

But it didn't stir a leaf of warning when a lonely, tattered figure crept beneath its cover. A moment later, the arrows were gone, yanked free of the target, and Peter's best bow disappeared in the underbrush.

The Men of the Clearing paddled through Neverbay in record time. Slick and sleek, the canoe parted the waves to run alongside the *Roger*, just as the twins had designed it to do. Swimming light like a fish, it also carried two of the Men's ladies. Lily's braves put their broad, tan backs to their task. They knew how anxious she was to greet her sailor man. He'd been away three moons and more, and for the last weeks she'd been gazing seaward, listening for the sound of the cannon. The twins grinned to see the look on Smee's rugged face as he hailed Lily from the rail; clearly, he too was eager for reunion. In two shakes, the big red Irishman had shed his boots, thrust his knife and spectacles inside them, and tossed them to the twins. Then, to the cheers of his men, he hurdled to the rail and dove into the sea, the splash of his robust build creating a wave that thrust the little craft bouncing from the hull of the *Roger*.

"Smee!" Lily and Red Fawn laughed as the boat rocked to the slap of bay water. Lily reached for her soggy sailor, displaying a fine golden bracelet and nearly swamping the canoe as she leaned over the side for the salty kiss on his lips.

"Ah, lass, I'm that glad to be setting my weary eyes upon you!" Smee rolled aboard as the twins leaned to balance their craft and the ladies shifted to make room. He embraced Lily thoroughly, pulling her full, pleasing figure into his arms. Inhaling her fragrance, he reveled in the woodsy scent of her black braided hair. When he released her, he gathered himself to turn a respectful regard toward his commander. Smee saluted, waited for a nod, then turned to the twins. "Go on and take us to shore, lads. Your brothers send their greetings. They've a job to be doing for the commodore, and then they'll be joining us this evening."

Lily registered surprise at Smee's choice of titles. But, mindful of her Men, she subdued her curiosity, asking before the twins could reply, "Our young men wish to speak with their mother, Smee. What of the Lady Jill?"

Smee's face turned a shade redder than his customary complexion. "She'll be along when she can, Lily. Let's not talk of her 'til then."

"My Irish Smee, not talking?" Lily smiled, but not quite as openly as before. More had changed during this voyage than just his captain's rank.

Her slate-gray eyes had already noted Smee's fine white shirt and the new neat trim of his beard. "Well, man, I am sure we will find something else to do."

"A woman after my own heart!"

"Yes, Smee. One of them." But she held him, dripping as he was, firmly against her best beaded tunic.

The twins winked at one another. Lily was a woman after their hearts, too. A lovely, welcoming woman. For the thousandth time, they thanked the stars they'd had the sense to abandon Pan's hideout and grow up. A glance at Red Fawn inspired them to paddle with swifter strokes. She blew her kisses to the ship's crew, the dazzling smile in her dark, graceful face surrounded by dimples as she issued her invitations. There'd be little opportunity before the onslaught. Lily would be occupied with Smee, but Red Fawn always found time for her providers. And so did Lelaneh. The twins looked up to position the sun; the children would be napping soon, in the cool, shady nursery of their house in the Clearing. The young men's loincloths grew tighter. Their hearts beat faster.

As the twins turned their craft toward shore, they scanned the colorful crowd of pirates hanging over the rail. Among the rowdy sailors calling after the women, they searched for their brothers. High in the rigging clambered Nibs the Knife in his orange kerchief, and Tom Tootles, still straining the seams of his breeches. The Men of the Clearing paused only a moment to wave their paddles and shout, "Welcome home!" But they took a long, lingering look at their mother.

At the end of her very first voyage, Red-Handed Jill, the pirate queen, reigned from the quarterdeck, a match for the arrogant captain who had swept her away. She wore a gown of sapphire blue— the hue of the gems circling her throat, the same color as the jewels studding Hook's wide-brimmed hat. The wind tugged the waves of his black hair as he stood posed beside her. It stirred one golden lock of Jill's hair, too; the remainder was twisted in an elegant knot. A superior sword shone at her lover's side, like the sword in the sash at Jill's own waist. Protruding from his blue velvet cuff was the notorious end of his arm: a deadly, barbarous hook.

The sun of Neverbay reflected sharply in its curve. Jill's arm ended in a delicate hand decorated with rings— a hand blood-red on the inside, from palm to fingertips— and a band of sapphires around her wrist. Linked arm in arm, the pirate pair stood aloof and erect, flanked by their officers, observing the homecoming with identical smiles of satisfaction. The sails aloft folded obediently, like wings of a hawk, as under Hook's orders men hauled them up to furl them. The image of the *Roger*'s rulers embedded itself in the Men of the Clearing's minds. Any doubts they harbored over the past several moons evaporated like morning mist in the certainty of sunrise. Red-Handed Jill belonged with that legendary pirate.

And even if she didn't, a man would enter hell trying to pry her away.

Two such tormented men existed; only one was present in the company. But the twins didn't see that man at the moment, nor did he take notice of their women. In his own personal purgatory, Captain Giovanni Cecco stood staring at Jill, a cable's length behind her, astride the bowsprit of his ship, the vessel he had named for her. His exquisite *Red Lady*.

"Creature of the woodland, I revere your sacrifice." White Bear followed tradition, withdrawing his arrow from the deer with ceremony. He stanched the flow of blood with a handful of moss, another gift from the forest. With this custom performed, he rose from his knees and slung the carcass across his shoulders, impatient to return to the encampment. Squinting against the light, he looked up toward his companion in the treetop.

He called, "Have you satisfied your curiosity, Lean Wolf?" He knew Willow would be anxious. The thunder of the guns must have set the entire village scurrying. White Bear could hear the defiant beat of the drums in the distance. The women would be pulling children into tepees. The elders would be gathering in council. Even at this distance, in the moist air of the wood, White Bear whiffed the stench of gunpowder. For every member of his tribe, that smell evoked recent and frightening memories.

Memories of the Black Chief, He of the Eagle's Claw, the pirate whose presence now was certain. He called again, urgently. "Tell me what you see. I must return to meet with the council."

Lean Wolf took one last leer and slid his tough, muscular body down the maple trunk to drop soundlessly to the forest floor. He was a silent hunter. His prey never heard him stalking.

"You want to tell the elders what I see?" Lean Wolf spat on the ground. "I see a faithless woman. A pass-around woman, selecting her patrons." His sharp black eyes narrowed as he mocked his companion's frown. "You do not approve of my words. Yet I challenge you to find them false."

"It is said that those women do not sell themselves. You are wrong to assume it; more so to speak it."

"You are wrong to chastise me. Red Fawn is wrong to abandon me." Lean Wolf secured the hunting knife strapped beneath his knee.

White Bear glanced at the beaded marriage bracelet on Lean Wolf's wrist, but kept his face impassive. "We will not debate it again. Take up your deer and speak as we travel. What happens in the bay?"

"Oh, White Bear! The report you carry to the council will set them trembling." The smirk Lean Wolf had adopted in recent months marred his comely features. "Wait until I tell you. Lily and Red Fawn and Lelaneh will have their hands full. Ha! Did I say their *hands?*"

White Bear halted as if to cast down the carcass. "Very well, Lean Wolf. I will climb the tree myself."

"No, no, brother Bear. I will tell you and you can run home to your flock of old men. You won't want to disappoint your crone, either. The Old One appointed you to the council so her ancient eyes will get some exercise!" Lean Wolf laughed as he easily flung his own kill, another doe, over one shoulder. The strength of his arms was well known among the fairer members of the tribe, and except when a woman was watching, a fully grown doe's weight meant nothing to him. "And that shows how badly her old eyes need entertainment. Scarred and sinewy as you are, you are hardly a maiden's dream. But an old woman's, certainly."

"I have asked you before, Lean Wolf Silent Hunter. I ask you again, respectfully. I would have you show more deference to our ancestors.

They are the guardians of custom, and it is custom that keeps us unified. I need not remind you that only as a tribe can we prevail against the white devils."

"And yet you defend my wife, who breaks with custom and runs off to oblige those very demons." Lean Wolf shook his head, his lengthy black hair, bound only by a leather headband, falling over his unburdened shoulder. "You do not see how you yourself have broken with tradition. And in one other respect, as well."

Quickening his steps, White Bear hoped to outdistance the familiar comment coming next. Sun and shadow filtered through the leaves, alternating against his eyes. Light and dark, like his feelings for his longtime friend.

"You share your tepee with two women," Lean Wolf called, sprinting to catch up. "Yet you wear only one marriage bracelet. Why not reconsider and give Raven to me? You know how badly I need women."

"So badly that you drive your wife away."

"Red Fawn need not have run to the Clearing. I can provide for the requirements of two. Like you, White Bear." Lean Wolf's clever smile lit his face. This smile was the one that had won an old man's little bride. "And believe me, that second girl required me."

"That girl's father gave her, too young, to a man too old. You had a wife. The fault was not yours to correct. Nor were you responsible for soothing a certain sister's grief when her brother died."

Lean Wolf shrugged. "You would not say so if you yourself had—"

"The sun moves in the sky," White Bear growled. "Tell me quickly. Why should the council tremble over the pirates?"

White Bear could run all day, and few braves of the tribe could match him. Lean Wolf toted the carcass easily but panted to keep up. Yet he made his voice obey, striking a tone of intrigue worthy of his news. "There comes today not one ship— but two."

Abruptly, White Bear stopped to turn and stare. "Two ships? Twice the number of warriors?" He dropped his eyebrows, and his gray eyes hardened. "Then it is well we have prepared. Surely this is a sign that the Black Chief of the Eagle's Claw wishes to finish what he started."

"He started nothing. He only chased us up the mountain. Rowan Life-Giver has testified to his motives. The Black Chief only wished to count coup and impress his female, to lure her from the Golden Boy. And he was successful! I saw her. She still stands at his side." Lean Wolf's hunger showed plainly on his long, narrow face. "I would like to impress that woman, myself."

"The man who impresses many women impresses none."

"*Your* philosophy. Not mine."

"And what else did you see?" With a gesture, White Bear urged his companion to move homeward again.

"The Black Chief; his woman; two ships full of wild men. The Golden Boy peeping from the treetops, as usual. I counted three in his band."

"It is to be hoped that the boy will engage the pirates and leave our people in peace."

"But think, my friend, what a favor that child performed for you! He slew Raven's husband, and now the prize is yours."

"You speak too lightly of tragedy. Ash was impulsive, but he was a good man."

"He was a fool to challenge the Golden Boy alone. A show-off."

"Ash had seen that boy do too much harm. As I say, he was impetuous, but he was a true brave. In my tepee we honor Ash's memory. Did you see anything else of importance?"

"Oh, no. Nothing of importance to the council. Just the shaggy-haired twins, canoeing with all their might to get Red Fawn alone before—"

"I have heard enough." Hiking the deer higher on his shoulders, White Bear backed from Lean Wolf. "I will make haste now. The People must know." He turned and jogged away, gaining speed with every stride. Even with the warm burden bouncing on his neck, White Bear fell easily into his lope. Keeping his head high and his breathing regular, he covered the distance in half the time another warrior, even a younger one, would need.

He was glad of an excuse to leave Lean Wolf to his brooding. Once ignited on the subject of his runaway wife, Lean Wolf would smolder for hours, varying only to insist that White Bear alleviate his single status with the gift of his sister-in-law. Whenever possible, White Bear avoided that question. In spite of Willow's wish that he shelter her sister, his position of provider to Raven grew increasingly awkward. The more she withdrew from him, the less the elders would consider her his. She exhibited no inclination to go to another brave, but excuses to keep her were becoming difficult to find. Unless the irksome woman capitulated soon, White Bear must reconsider Lean Wolf's petition. Lean Wolf might pretend to despise the council, yet he was not above using it to get his way. But how to tell a woman, a grieving woman, that she must submit to one man in order to avoid another?

Maybe he wouldn't tell her. Maybe he would simply manifest his will. Willow would agree. It would be best for everyone's sake if—

A jaybird screamed above him in a white birch tree. Like a spear, its cry violated White Bear's reflections, interjecting another— an unthinkable— thought. The thought of the taboo that Red Fawn, Lean Wolf's unfortunate wife, had broken. Suddenly, White Bear understood his old friend's bitterness. He felt the venom seeping into his soul, the gall that poisoned Lean Wolf's spirit. It was a tightening of his gut, a wrench of his honor, more shocking in its vulgarity than the call of the blue jay.

Looking past the bird to the sky, to the west, White Bear eyed the plume of red smoke. It hadn't abated since those shaggy-haired twins had kindled it, moons ago. Willow, his wife, never caused his thoughts to veer that direction, but now, Raven flew him there. Unlike Willow, Raven was headstrong. Already she demonstrated a lack of respect for herself. Look how she had mutilated her hair. If she was pushed too far, might she, too, run away to live outcast at the House of the Clearing? A house ordained by the Black Chief himself. A place in which men of any shade, of any persuasion, were made welcome. Just to contemplate his sister-in-law in that situation made White Bear feel dirty, dishonored. The woman vexed him for simply inducing the idea. The raucous jaybird, so wanting in circumspection, could be an omen.

White Bear realized he was standing still, his breathing no longer regular, his eyes staring at the moccasins his wife's loving hands had crafted for him. He shook his head to clear it. This inaction was no way to serve the People. He started up again, running faster to recapture the time. As the din of the drums attested, the presence of pirates only made the circumstances more urgent, for the People— and, perhaps, for Willow's stubborn sister.

Setting his teeth, White Bear determined one thing for certain. This matter was one of pride as well as practicality. He was a responsible provider. An honorable husband. He would not allow a member of his family, a female under his protection, to shame herself as an Outcast. Never.

Tradition must be upheld. Willow's sister would do as she was told.

Willow's sister watched after White Bear, her feet making stirring sounds in the underbrush as she crept from her hiding place back to the path. She had heard him coming— not his footsteps; they fell like the wind's— but the even whoosh of his breathing. Once again, she observed, his hunt had been successful. The game he carried so lightly would feed his family for months. And when his son was born, the soft fur of the deer's breast would line a cradleboard. Willow's sister would prepare it.

Bitter as it felt to Raven to shed her individuality, she understood she was better off in the background. Aunt to his children. Sister to his wife. A shadow woman. Her husband, Ash, who had truly known her, waited at the Dark Hunting ground. Considering the manner in which White Bear looked at her, Raven, too, might as well reside in the land of Dark Hunting. She was only a burden to him, like the weight of the carcass that crowned his shoulders. He had condescended to offer his body, but he never offered to call her his wife. Raven, the Shadow Woman, approved. It was better this way.

A short while ago she had jumped to hear the cannon fire. She had snatched up her berry basket and started running back to the village. The drums were pounding. Willow would be needing her. Now that White Bear had passed by, Raven prepared to hasten away again, but she gasped instead. Berries tumbled from her basket as a strong grip encircled her waist. She smelled blood.

"Lean Wolf." Dragging his arm from her body, she spun to see his powerful frame unbent by the weight of his kill, his lips smirking. Clutching the basket, she backed from him. "Silent Hunter."

"That is one pronouncement the Council of Elders made properly. My name." His prey never heard him stalking. "Are you running from the pirates, Raven? Have no fear. I will protect you from those devil men…if you say yes to me." He plucked a berry from her basket.

"And who will protect me from *you?*"

"I think it is I who need protection— from that barbed tongue. But I am daring. I am fearless enough to overlook your faults. No, don't go. I am only trying to make you smile." He held the berry up and offered it to Raven, but she declined. Shrugging, he squeezed it. The dark juice oozed along his fingers. He bit the berry and rolled it between his lips to swallow it. "You should smile again, Raven. You were beautiful not so long ago, with your lovely laugh and your long, long hair." He sucked the juice from his fingers, savoring the syrupy taste. "You never laugh any more, but I see that your hair is growing."

Raven's hand flew to her temple. She tidied what little hair she had. "A woman in mourning has no need for beauty."

"Not according to the man who would be her next husband. Raven, it is clear to all the People that White Bear rejects you. I am not so foolish. Tell him you wish him to accept my offer."

Swiftly, her black eyes rose to meet his, surprised.

Lean Wolf laughed. "So that is it? White Bear is more crafty than I suspected! He has not told you of my suit." He enjoyed the confusion on Raven's face. Thanks to White Bear's obstinacy, he had caught her off guard. He seized his advantage. "So now you are aware of my proposal. And to make certain you remember, I give to you two gifts."

Unaccustomed as he was to revealing his feelings, Lean Wolf did so with grace. He knelt down on one knee and slid the weight of the doe from his shoulder. Laying it at Raven's feet, he stroked its coat smooth and looked up at her. No trace of mockery remained in his eyes. "To prove to you I am an able provider." He stood. He took the basket from her hands and set it in the grass, then guided her to step carefully over the carcass. A smear of blood trailed down his wide, naked chest, thick near his shoulder, more watery where it mixed with his perspiration. "To prove to you I am an eager lover." He leaned down and, gentle as the doe, he took her cheek in his hand, and he kissed her.

Raven's heart rebelled. She hadn't wanted to be kissed. She dreaded desiring to be kissed. As she had feared, the touch of a man set every nerve alight. The body whose urges the Shadow Woman had damped in a river of sorrow resurfaced to propel her once more into the physical realm, the world of life, of which she had so lustily partaken with Ash. And, surprisingly, this philanderer's kiss was tender, lingering, still flavored with the sugar of the berry. Like his other women, her blood was up, her desires aflame. With only one touch, Silent Hunter had driven her from her hiding place.

Reasserting her will, she pulled back before the doe's blood stained her dress. "Lean Wolf." She shook her head. "I am not thinking again of marriage."

"Then think of me. I will not stand on ceremony."

Raven searched his face. She saw the angular features that used to be handsome, before disappointment made him hostile. He wasn't hostile now. His face was set in caution, but she read the sincerity there. Raven perceived that she must use caution herself. She couldn't afford to make an enemy of White Bear's friend.

"I thank you, Lean Wolf, if what you offer is a compliment. But word of your actions causes me to wonder. As you have said, you are willing to do away with ceremony."

"Now you speak like your brother-in-law. Always clinging to custom."

"Do not be offended, and I, too, will forgo offense. Let us leave the matter here."

"So you do not answer me?"

"My brother-in-law must answer for me." Truly, she thought, he *was* a lean wolf. His hungry smile had appeared.

"You fish for more gifts, then." He moved toward her, and leaned closer. The strength of his arms was well known among the fairer members of the tribe.

When, a few moments later, Raven emerged, alone and panting, from the forest at the edge of the encampment, she held her basket in front of her breast. She stole to the river's edge to kneel down on its bank. As her knees slid toward the water on the cold, hard pebbles, she scrubbed at the blood upon her dress.

Silent Hunter had caught her, and she'd never heard him stalking.

Stolen Pleasures

Hook's pirates boarded the Island, not to plunder this time, but to partake of the pleasures of shore leave. Far from looting, an advance party had trudged ahead bearing gifts— casks of wine, rounds of cheese, a crate of poultry, even a goat for roasting. The Men of the Clearing, anticipating, had already propped up the spits. Less practical but more impressive were the offerings of earrings in silver, copper, and gold, one pair for each of the hostesses, as well as a coffer of sparkling Venetian beads. For the hosts, a cask of brandy, pouches of tobacco for trading, and two shining axes with Spanish leather grips. Though not in attendance tonight— to the disappointment of the ladies— Commodore Hook was a generous man.

Executing an order to act in the master's place, Mr. Smee took charge before the festivities that evening, doling out the largess. "Compliments of himself, Lily. He commands more sailors now, but he won't be letting them eat you out of house and home." Relaxing on a wide-striped blanket with Red Fawn nearby and Lily in his arms, Smee leaned against a log and glanced at the fine residence the twins had constructed. A tidy, two story abode, white with green vine shutters, it mightn't have looked out of place on an Irish country estate. The original structure, the hut that had been Wendy's, still stood adjoining it, dwarfed but welcoming, its leaves sighing in the breeze and its quaint little chimney puffing out that distinctive red smoke signal. The bones of a rising workshop stood off in a corner of the Clearing, like fingers waiting to be gloved.

Above the song of a brook, the surrounding forest rang with the night sounds of crickets and tree frogs, while a glow from the bonfire illuminated the arches of treetops, tinting them orange. The Men of the Clearing tended the fire as deftly as they tended the women— all as the master, Hook, had contrived when he first waylaid Wendy in this very spot.

Lily filled her eyes with her brawny Irishman, well content. Smee was first mate and steward to a commodore now, and still ship's bo'sun with two new mates to assist him. But in spite of his rise in rank, he still proved as strong and as sweet as rum. And even if he talked less, he loved more. She answered him slyly, "It is not the house and home that concern me." Deep in the woods, a commotion could be heard. Eagerly, her eyes turned toward her impending guests. "But how will we accommodate so many?"

"They'll not be visiting all at once. The commodore and the captain agreed—" Peering over his spectacles, Smee sent Lily a significant look, "agreed, at least, on *that* point."

"But you said that the two captains made truce."

"Aye, when the commodore returned from his absence to take the helm, a truce *was* struck. He was wise enough to compromise. The men were relieved, at first, to see their officers settling their differences— or should I be saying, their similarities? But once those storms knocked us off course and threatened our shore leave, everyone's tempers warmed up. And then we had to be mending sails, and running up the spare mizzen for *Red Lady*, too. It felt as if we'd never be finding this blessed Island, and the *Roger*'s men began to wonder if the place was warding off the *Lady*'s sailors, seeing as they're strangers here. Eight days of foul and eight days of fair. Our fresh paint and polish only just dried before the Island called us home."

Lily rested her head on Smee's shoulder, comforted by his presence. "After you sailed away, my dreams told me that your homecoming would be delayed. I dared not look for you too early, and it is well that I did not. I knew you might face storms of the waters, but I did not foresee these storms between your officers."

Smee held her, relieved to unburden his heart. "It's a time I've had, trying to keep the peace between the two of them. Clashing over every little thing, two mighty men, for protocol's sake avoiding the fight they're both itching to battle out. It's true what people say. There's no conflict so consuming as the struggle over a woman."

Red Fawn piped up, and her dimples, so pronounced as she had put on her silvery earrings, now disappeared. "It is a dangerous manner in which to live and to work."

"Aye. The men watch. They feel the tension, and they react to it. Commodore Hook knows it wouldn't be seemly to appear to be bearing a grudge. But the danger lies mostly for Captain Cecco. He can only be showing so much resentment. Nothing that smacks of mutiny. Instead, he vents his ire on whatever else may get in his way."

Lily's brow creased. "You must take care not to incur his wrath, Smee. You yourself are a symbol of the commodore's power."

"May be, Lily. Captain Cecco was fit to be tied when he learned I was appointed personal steward to—" Smee stopped and stroked the unfamiliar cut of his beard, "…to the commodore."

Lily divined the meaning that Smee hoped to spare her. To lessen her lover's discomfort, she gazed toward the fire. "Is that not the trouble you face? Captain Cecco himself cannot approach the Lady Jill, and yet he must smolder to think of you alone with her…touching her each morning, and each night."

Employing his new reticence, Smee tipped his head, but made no reply.

"But is there no resolution?"

"Ah, Lily, lass." Smee sighed, the burden of Hook's welfare heavy on his heart. Jill's well-being, too, although he had downplayed his devotion to her in recounting the ship's last adventure. Smee had come within a hairsbreadth of ruling the *Roger*, and it had taken every ounce of his integrity to deny himself the full enjoyment of Jill. But he judged it best to gloss over these details; Smee and Lily were a match, and while not an exclusive pair, they trod lightly on each other's affection. "It's a right mess the three of them are in. That Doctor Hanover caused more trouble than even *he* knows, kidnapping the commodore and paving the way for Mr. Cecco's captaincy. If the commodore hadn't sent that blackguard packing back to Austria, I'd have roasted the man on a spit myself, like yon ruddy goat."

Red Fawn inched closer to Smee, her large, dark eyes wide. "Are you certain the handsome commodore has recovered from his ordeal? Shackled for weeks, drugged, and nearly starved to death!"

"Aye, I'm keeping an eye on him. Hale and hearty now, but leaner." Smee grinned. "And stronger, as any who witnessed his resurrection can tell you."

"Stronger, you say? You must ask your commodore chief to honor us with his presence." Red Fawn's dimples returned. "We will welcome the opportunity to assure ourselves of his good health. And I hope our dashing Mr. Cecco will not neglect us now that he is an important officer. I admit I have missed him, and his exotic accent." The twins' parrot squawked high in the fringe of trees, calling its warning. Red Fawn turned an ear toward the forest. "Listen, your comrades are approaching. But ah! The poor fellows who have to stay behind!"

Sitting up, Smee chortled. "The 'poor fellows' will get their turn. Tonight they'll be rigging their hammocks above decks, staring up to the stars and gulping down the ale. The Commodore knows what he's about."

"Indeed," said Lily. "He is wise to post guards. Our Men have been watching the Golden Boy. He has assembled a new band of youngsters. They are bound to wish to prove themselves against the pirates."

"You're wise yourself, Lily, to catch on to the commodore's purpose. How I missed you while at sea!"

One of the twins looked up from turning the spits. "We think maybe Pan's pack has been prowling. Several times we've found things missing from our stores, although nothing of importance. Some food, some clothes."

Frowning, Smee said, "I'll be looking into it, then. We can't be having that nuisance of a lad taking food from the ladies' mouths. Or from the children's."

"We're not certain, though, that the culprit is a Lost Boy," said the other twin. "Pan and his brood have no need to steal food, nor clothing. And we've seen tracks along the stream. They're larger than Pan's, and since Jill's brothers returned to London, he has no older boys."

Smee lifted his eyebrows. "Do you say, now? The commodore will be interested to hear it. Mayhap he'll feel an inclination to go hunting." He turned to Red Fawn. "And has that husband of yours given up trying to steal you back?"

Looking down, Red Fawn blushed. "No, Smee. He still bears my marriage bracelet. I never know when he will show himself. Lean Wolf the Silent Hunter stalks like a panther."

"It's a shame he can't be leaving you in peace." To the Men of the Clearing he said, "Let me know if you're wanting a hand in dealing with that one."

The twins nodded. "We will."

"Lean Wolf is one of the reasons we trained our Scout," the second twin said, looking toward the parrot's roost. "His sharp eyes don't miss much in the forest."

Coming from the house, now lit with a nightlight that fell through viney shutters to speckle the ground, the third of the outcast native women, Lelaneh, glided through the cool, dewy grass. She entered the circle of logs around the bonfire and sat beside Smee, nestling against his shoulder. She brought with her a fragrance of honey. As Smee and the women watched the twins at work over the spits, Lelaneh's waist-length hair swept over the arm Smee circled around her. A bright colored shawl, loosely clasped, barely covered her abundant breasts, and she wielded liquid brown eyes that might make even a strong man weak. "The children are asleep. Your angel, too, Smee. She looks more like her mother every day, except for her hair."

"Aye. The red locks are mine, but I bless Lily for the rest." Smee lowered his lilting voice. "And Lelaneh, have you more of that herb tea you sent along before we sailed?"

"I made up a packet as soon as I heard your cannons." She produced a pouch from under her shawl and gave it to him, revealing a morsel more of copper skin.

"The lady sends her thanks. You've no idea…"

"But yes. I do." She smiled at Smee's discomfiture and exchanged a knowing glance with Lily. "And so, also, do the women of the tribe. But now that I am an Outcast of the Clearing, only the most daring among them venture to visit me, when they have need of my medicines."

Feigning indifference, Smee tucked the packet away. "The lady herself will be visiting you soon. She wrote a lovely story for the children— happy endings for all of them. And here, Lelaneh, the golden pair is for you, from himself."

Lelaneh fingered the earrings, her voice inviting. "Please give your commodore my gratitude. You, too, may collect my appreciation, a little later, when you are free."

Lily giggled and, clearing his throat, Smee found it necessary to shift his lower regions. But no one would be free for a while; bouncing beams of lantern light could be seen now, like fireflies, in the forest. The voices had started vague, but grown steadily more distinct. The parrot beat its wings and screeched again, dancing along its branch while a rowdy sea chantey swelled to fullness. As the men neared the Clearing, they bellowed it out, their different accents rich with anticipation, and caring not a whit for stealth. Safety lay in numbers, even in the perilous woods of the Neverland, and numbers there were of hardy seamen. Some sported the gaudy shirts customary aboard the *Roger*, others the French blue of her mate. Soon more earrings glinted in the firelight, above weapons and tattoos. Ponytailed, pigtailed, clean-shaven or bearded, the pirates entered the Clearing, snapping branches and rustling leaves, and the ladies laughed at them— rule breakers, even on dry land.

No rules interfered tonight. The roasts rotated on their spits, turned by the skilled bronzed arms of the twins and dripping fat to sizzle and hiss in the fire. Bottles changed hands as often as the women. Pipes, drums, and song filled the air; the bonfire flung up its arms in pagan dance.

One more theft in this gathering of thieves would hardly be noticed. Drawn like a mongrel to the feast, the ragged remains of a cabin boy lurked on the periphery. His clothing, caked with dried mud, blended with the night. He kept downwind, hiding the rancid smell he'd acquired from his dwelling place. Gnawing hungrily at discarded bones still warm from the roasting, David crouched outside the ring of logs, watching for his opening. And when the moment was ripe, a blanket slid from the circle. A bottle, when reached for, went missing. Even a French blue jacket found its way to the shadows.

Stealing glimpses too, David witnessed the degenerates at their orgy— the men, the women— some couples sinuous in silhouette before the fire, black shapes that fascinated him, exhaling gasps and sighs. Some appeared vivid in the firelight, more and more of their warm skins bared to glisten in it. But all were touching, kissing, laughing, dancing. David, also, felt the heat of the flames, the cool sweat breaking out on his brow. He breathed, too— more heavily every second— and knew now what he'd never learned at sea. David opened his eyes, a thief himself, prostrate in the darkness, and the true meaning of shore leave surprised him, in a rush of stolen pleasure.

In the commodore's quarters, the morning sea shifted the tapestries of the four-posted bed. At the windows, too, curtains swayed, still closed on their three sides of the luxurious cabin, yet the fragrance of the Island, lush with green growth, wafted within. The commodore himself, although a prickly growth of whiskers darkened his neck, was as fully dressed as his single hand could accomplish. The collar of his shirt would have to wait to be tied. It lay open above his waistcoat now, to reveal a V of black fringe beneath his throat. His long coat and his breeches boasted a burgundy hue, complementing the lady's garment of scarlet that waited on the daybed. Jill's two hands had readied the clothing the night before, laying out his suit, smoothing the folds of her frock. Hook had watched her as, in the absence of Mr. Smee, Jill brushed her own hair before retiring, the golden sheen of its strands shining like treasure. He had run his few fingers through that treasure, then locked her up safely, hoarding her behind his cabin door. Behind the bed curtains.

Hook gazed upon her again, then moved to the desk to turn the glass and set the sands sifting downward. He'd grant her another hour's rest, while the Island prepared for their first day's adventure. After a harrowing voyage, Hook and Jill were at leisure. Today a visit to the Clearing, a stroll in the Fairy Glade; tomorrow, perhaps, a picnic at the waterfall.

A rapping sounded. Hook squinted at a seam of light between the drapes; Mr. Smee couldn't have returned so early. And Smee would use his key. Hook strode over the Oriental carpets to throw the bolt and open the door, widely at first, then, upon identifying his company, he narrowed the opening. "Captain Cecco."

"Commodore. I give you good morning." Cecco's face as he bowed appeared guarded but determined. His dark hair was tied back with a leather lace, his strong chin shaved smooth. As always, his bare arms jingled with bracelets; loops of gold adorned his ears. He had donned his gypsy regalia as well: a heavy mesh of coins crowned his forehead, draped over a crimson kerchief, and a necklace thick with linked medallions circled his throat. His Mediterranean accent fell pleasantly, but not too softly to carry within the commodore's quarters. "I have come to call upon *Signora* Cecco."

"Your wife is sleeping." A note of satisfaction seeped into the velvet voice. Above almost anything, Hook prized victory. "In my bed."

Cecco maintained his pleasant expression. Showing offense to his superior would get him nowhere. "As I am aware. But I will be happy to awaken her." Setting one boot inside the opening, he smiled, showing even white teeth. He hadn't become a captain through timidity.

Hook looked askance at Cecco's boot. A lesser man would lie dying by now, savaged by the claw. But this offender was Captain Cecco, the man who, in Hook's recent absence, had preserved the *Roger*, raked in a fortune, defended Jill…and married her. The lady's husband was a worthy officer, deserving of lenience.

Limited lenience. Hook stood tall. "What is the nature of your business, Captain?"

"No business. Only pleasure."

Hook stepped forward, compelling Cecco backward onto the companionway. With his claw, Hook gestured toward the land. "We have arrived, after much tribulation, at the Island. You have leave to seek your pleasure ashore."

"If the *signora* will join me there, I will be able to do so." The lethal look in the commodore's eyes gave warning. Cecco had pushed too far.

He shrugged. "My apologies, Commodore. As you can appreciate, our lady's loveliness has a way of steering a man into perilous waters. In truth, I seek only a word with her, for the moment."

"I have shown my appreciation for your service to the *Roger*, and for your— temporary— care of my lady. You received your rewards."

"It is as you say. But I am not satisfied." Cecco's brown eyes brooded as he cast them down and splayed his fingers to stare at the band of gold there. He clenched his fist. "I am a married man, with no rights to my wife."

"You agreed to her terms."

"Yes. I agreed. And yet I cannot turn my back on her."

"I advise you *not* to turn your back, Captain. On your commodore."

Cecco's ear heard the threat in the smooth-as-silver voice. His eye caught the hook's glare in the sun. "Surely we can come to terms, Commodore, some kind of peace. You love her; you understand. Red-Handed Jill is your soul." He placed his hand on his chest. "She is my heart, as well."

"I have never thought of dividing my soul with you, Captain. Still less my woman."

"But…with your first mate?" Cecco's eyes tightened. His dusky hand moved to rest, ever so lightly, upon the knife in his belt. That knife had earned him his notoriety and set a bounty on his head. Not long ago, that blade almost murdered Mr. Smee.

"My mate, like you, has demonstrated his loyalty. Unlike you, Mr. Smee does not presume upon my gratitude." Hook jerked his chin toward the Island. "All the pleasures of the Neverland await you, Captain. I suggest you enjoy them, while you are healthy enough to do so." Stepping back, he began to close the door.

"All the pleasures?" Cecco shook his head. "All but the one I most desire." Then, as if his wish had been granted, his gypsy smile lit up his face. "Madam!"

Silently, Jill had stolen to Hook's side. The sunlight nestled in her hair. Her sky-blue dressing gown draped her body with a soft brocade, outlining the curves of her femininity. A gemstone bracelet sparkled on her ankle. On her toes gleamed silver rings. Fresh and welcoming as the new day, her smile shone upon Captain Cecco.

"Giovanni! Good morning." Her clear voice did not falter, but spoke out unashamed. Offering her left hand, she allowed Cecco to clasp it. His grip was as fervent as she remembered it; so also was his kiss upon her fingers. Immediately it drew the memory of other kisses, deeper intimacies. Her heart skipped a beat as she savored his familiar touch, only to sink in sorrow. How much more did his own heart feel upon this contact? Only just restraining herself from squeezing his hand, Jill inclined her head instead, managing to preserve her composure. As Cecco's smoky eyes clung to her, she slipped her hand away and turned to her commodore. Her fingers slid up the embroidery of his waistcoat. Her tone grew intimate.

"Hook. Good morning to you, too." Deliberately, Jill took Hook's face between her hands, and the man she called husband ceased to smile. Lurching back a step, he spied her blood-red palm as she engaged her lover, stroking the trim whiskers of his beard. Petite as she was, she had to arch her neck to look into the commodore's eyes— eyes of deep, dark blue that exactly matched her own. Her voice softened with seduction as she uttered to Hook his own endearment, "My love…" It was the most delicate of blows, but one aimed, with precision, to bore into a festering wound. Captain Cecco sucked in his breath.

"Jill." Hook allowed her to draw his face down to hers, and she kissed him. As he responded, their embrace grew in intensity and when the lovers pulled apart to look again, Captain Cecco was striding over the deck, hailing a sailor and gesturing toward the gangway. They saw the leather vest that concealed the cut of the cat-o'-nine-tails on his back. They observed the golden armbands that dazzled with morning sun. But neither Hook nor Jill divined the tidbit with which Cecco fed his starving heart.

For the captain of *Red Lady* had seen something, too, a sight that raised his sodden spirit. In the weeks since their parting, Jill hadn't allowed him near enough to be sure. But just now, one stolen meeting informed him. Despite the fact that Jill declined today to extend to him her crimson hand, the signal that meant she welcomed his embraces, Cecco suspected that the most desirable woman on the

Seven Seas did, indeed, harbor him in her heart. She had staged a display of her affection for Commodore Hook, a performance that carved as skillfully at her husband's gut as his notorious knife. As ever, she was faithful to the loyalty she'd sworn, first, to Hook. But although Red-Handed Jill lived in the commodore's quarters, even though she slept in the commodore's arms and granted to him all the pleasures her Giovanni remembered and relived night after night in his dreams, she remained, in whatever degree, *Signora* Cecco. Whether or not she was aware of her gesture, Cecco's gypsy eye was drawn to shining metals. He had plundered meaning among her adornments.

Cecco turned for a last look at his ideal woman. Framed by the gilding of the magnificent companionway, standing sky-blue and burgundy in the quarters he once called his own, his Jill and her lethal lover watched him. Cecco snatched the cable Hook's sailor swung to him and, kissing his fingertips, he sent a farewell flying to his wife. Then he leapt across the waves to board his own vessel, anticipating a day his lovely one might beg release from her oath and join him, joyfully, there. Knowingly or not, she had revealed to Cecco a hidden treasure: the knowledge that, on the fourth finger of her precious hand, Red-Handed Jill, still, wore his wedding band.

Jill didn't perceive how Cecco buoyed his sunken heart. She felt a sting of moisture beneath her eyelids. The sunshine diminished, the door clicked closed, and a warm, strong arm supported her. The touch of Hook's fine linen handkerchief swabbed the tears of her grief. Then, perversely, came the pang of being understood— transparent— in the most private of moments. When close to her like this, the commodore read her heart as easily as one of her stories. Even if she chose to do so, Jill could hide nothing from his perception. Like Pygmalion's, her art had created him. Captain Cecco claimed her hand; only Hook held her soul.

"Hook."

"My love?" He always allowed her the courtesy, the illusion, that words might be necessary.

But she said nothing. Leaning upon him, she dragged a knuckle along her dampened cheekbone.

"A loving wife you are, Jill. Administering torture to ensure your husband's survival."

"To ensure you both."

"Such devotion." Hook raised an eyebrow. "An admirable ruthlessness."

"Like your own." Jill's jaw set in determination. "I will do what I must— whatever I must— to keep you from killing one another."

"Defying destiny?"

"I learned from you. When one cannot escape one's chains, one must embrace them."

"I hardly embraced the good doctor's chains, Jill. Nor his daughter's charms. Let us say that I worked within them."

"And I work within my own. I decided on the day you returned from the dead, the day we reclaimed one another. I cannot be a wife. But I will not be a widow."

"Yet your method of preserving your husband may drive him to hasten his demise. Be warned, my love." Hook's features grew stern. "He knocked at doom's door this morning."

"Please, Hook—"

"He dared even to threaten Mr. Smee."

"He speaks rashly, but I won't allow him to harm Mr. Smee."

"No, Jill. *I* will not allow harm to Smee."

"Surely he wouldn't be so reckless. He is simply distracted with heartbreak."

"Your affection cannot change his jealous nature."

"But the circumstances will change. We lie in the best possible port for him. Giovanni— Captain Cecco— is sure to find consolation here."

"My dear. I myself can attest that among its innumerable species, the Island nurtured only one flower as flawless as yourself. No. You would do better to yield to the man one last time…then slip your knife beneath his ribs."

Shocked, Jill pressed the back of her hand to her mouth. Hook's expression, so loving as he complimented her, had grown as cold as his reasoning. Turning away, she felt the prodding of her honesty, which, as ever, she was unable to ignore. She considered, then lowered her hand and faced him again. "That strategy, I believe, is exactly the one I just executed."

Hook surrounded her with his arms, he pressed his chin against her temple. "As you remember, I once suffered from the curse of solitude."

"Aye. I remember." She knew his story too well. It was a story she herself had begun.

He breathed deeply, scenting the sea in her hair. Whatever pain she had put him through, Jill was his jewel, beyond price. "Now that I have won you, I shall never submit to my former state of loneliness."

Jill sheltered in the fortress of his arms. She anticipated the sentence that was forming, like a thunderhead, and she dreaded it. The thought was abstract, but once captured in speech it might never be banished. Knowing how often her own words came true, she had refused to utter it. Yet, like her commodore, Jill possessed plenty of courage; she armed herself to face the facts.

Hook laid them bare. "You are afflicted now, my love, with a curse of your own."

"I haven't wanted to admit it."

"Our advantage lies in confronting the difficulty. It would seem, Jill, that before we set your other husband adrift— our dear, departed surgeon— the act of wedding him cursed you splendidly. Not with the plague of loneliness, but with an excess of..." he bent his head to speak it in her ear, "...alliance."

Touched by truth, she didn't deny her emotion. Her shoulders shuddered within his hold.

"Be comforted," Hook said. "Even now your vengeance is at work. As one of your husbands, Doctor Hanover lives tormented." Her lover smiled, half-way, as he held her. "With all respect, my pirate queen, marriage to Red-Handed Jill brings an anguish all its own. I thank the Powers that I do not suffer from it."

With an artful smile, Jill dabbed her nose with his handkerchief. "Perhaps one day you shall. I may just decide to take another husband. After all, why stop at two?"

"Before committing, I shall await the outcome of your current alliances."

Jill looked down at the costly carpets. With his humor, Hook had roused her from her sadness, but only for a moment. He was shrewd enough not to allow her to forget her trouble, her curse. "Alliance," she repeated. And, submerged beneath that notion, a spectre threatened to rise, like a waterlogged corpse, to the surface of her consciousness. Bleary and bloated, it was a horror substantial enough to demand consideration. And although Jill sensed that Hook discerned her apprehension, that he wished her to deal with it, she had managed to push all thought of the rendezvous with her other husband away— a year away. She rested her head on her lover's velvet chest and felt the tickle of his beard at her forehead.

"My beautiful storyteller," he murmured against her hair. With his hook, he toyed with its strands. "Tied to one husband you despise, one you love too well. Both haunting you beneath the shadow of my sword. You are caught in a tidy trap, Jill. How ever will you pen a happy ending?"

Then his smile lost patience and, with a firm hold, Hook forced her chin upward. He gazed into her eyes, wet and blue as the sea, irresistible to a sailor, be he swab or commodore. He declared, "I am persuaded you shall not escape— from *me*." Hook didn't speak again, but Jill, forsaking the thoughts he had read so precisely, heard his question as he swept her to his embrace.

And would you wish to do so?

Spoken or unspoken, her answer was unequivocal.

In the commodore's quarters, the single hand of a single man disturbed the tapestries of the four-posted bed. Hook shed his velvet and Jill laid it, not so neatly this time, near her garments. The hook on its harness thumped down to pierce the Persian carpet. The sky-blue dressing gown lay huddled where it fell.

This couple had learned in recent weeks: however durable their union, their circumstances lent it a fleeting quality. Hook's legend was immortal, but only days ago and by a narrow margin, the man himself evaded murder. Jill knew her devotion to him to be eternal, yet she had lavished love on his successor. Remembering, they gazed at one other with sharpened perception, taking in every detail as if for the very last time. Thieves they might be, but they didn't dodge the truth; like the skull on the black flag that flapped high above them, Hook and Jill's fate hung balanced on the blades of crossed swords.

Yet there was nothing tenuous in their lovemaking. Seizing one another, Hook and Jill pitched to the bed where they rolled together to thrust and parry, grapple and hold, dueling to the death. Pleasure so near the edge of agony honed their ecstasy. Aggression lay in the offing, awakened by the lady's husbands, and it urged a ferocity between these lovers that they'd never indulged— like the infamous hook, a razor-sharp passion with a mortal point. Bloodlust, once aroused, demanded battle.

But the first foray couldn't quell it. Though her breathing still shook, Jill's hands tangled again in Hook's hair, angling his throat for her lips' assault. Scored by his whiskers, her face burrowed in the blackness there. Jill thrilled to his power, and it vibrated right through her core.

Like claws, her fingernails strafed his shoulders, raked his arms, trailing a path of scratches. Stinging, Hook gathered her wrists to pinion her, holding both her bloodied hand and her pale one hard against his chest.

She struggled in the pinch and in the pleasure of his grip. Unable to free herself, she raised her head to pursue him in hissing whispers. An inch apart, they fired vows of unconquerable constancy. Then he stopped the words, kissing her cruelly. On the edge of submission, ecstasy at hand, still Jill pushed to prolong her struggle.

He knew what she craved; he forced her down upon the mattress, his teeth bit upon her mouth to leave it throbbing. Biting back, she kicked and countered, then caged him with her legs, hugging as if to cleave him in two. The sense of his vigor, the heat of his body within her limbs stirred her barbarity to fever.

Hook gloried in the pressure of her grip around his thighs. Her brutality excited him. But it was just another of her weapons and, firm in his practice, he used it against her. With the stump of his arm— like her own scar, the wound from a prior hostility—

he shoved at the bedding to lever himself on his back, his one hand pulling her by the wrists to lie atop him. Now her legs were pinned, and, rigid to the point of misery, he found his entry, still heated from his earlier incursion.

The more they fed their aggression, the hotter their ardor. They stormed one another and, fair fight or foul, all the while he raged inside her, waging war from within— civil war, at the end of which no victor conquers, no vanquished lies alone. With the weapons of love, the pirate pair engaged in their skirmish, and neither yielded until their fury flamed to the highest pitch…to hold there, glowing, until it burnt at last to ash.

As Jill lay on her commodore, exhausted but exhilarated, the Island breeze slid within the curtains, carrying the pacific sounds and scents of her home— water, palm, and pine. Under its influence, the fervor of their bodies began to cool. She administered kisses to the scar of his manacles, raw around his wrist. Tears stung again, pricked by the memory of how near he had sailed to oblivion. She pressed her lips against his own, tenderly this time, and inviting.

But he resisted, pulling away to observe the rose of her face, and musing, "Really, my love, I must arrange to be kidnapped and killed more often. The prospect of death appears to heighten your passion."

"It isn't death that does it, Hook." Jill always kept a smile near to hand; she had used it many times. "It is life."

"Ah. Life." He lulled her with a moment of counterfeit security. Then, abruptly, he shifted, careening her over and rolling his long, sculpted body above her.

She could barely breathe beneath her burden, but his next words, with a velvet edge, halted any attempt.

"Is it blackmail you practice, Madam, or bribery?"

Not daring even to blink, she lay still.

He clicked his tongue. "How low you do stoop to win your way." He lowered his chin. "Your *husband's* way." Finally, easing his stance, he allowed her to draw breath. "But perhaps the blame lies with the company you keep." His fingers, armed with rings, traced the throbbing artery along her throat, from her jaw line to her scar. Infused with sudden cold, she shivered, and he mocked,

"I have been known to stoop, myself. Even lower." His eyes signaled with a smoldering look, and, descending upon her, he retreated to the tender trenches of her thighs.

With strokes that tingled, the waves of his hair caressed her there. And then his lips. Above the gentle pulsing of the bay water came the sounds of her sighs, surging, slowly, in crescendo. As his mouth laid siege to her, he exacted his price. Unresisting this time, she surrendered it.

Thus it happened that the sands of the hourglass passed, precariously at first, then more pleasantly by the moment, before the commodore, a superb tactician and a thief of the highest order, drew on his garments again and caused his collar to be tied. In this duty his mistress— the wife, not widow, of two defrauded men— obliged him, having purloined from her lover's attentions her own cache of pleasure…and for another hour at least, prolonged her husband's life.

Dispossessions

Mr. Yulunga feared no thing and no man. Ordinarily he would tread the forests of the Neverland alone, with only his dark coloring for cover and his boarding ax for protection. He'd done so, many times, when serving under the direct command of Captain Hook. But after the ship's careening to scrape the bottom clean of barnacles, on this third day at anchor he led a party inland.

These men were Frenchmen, the pick of the hands on *Red Lady*, on which at Hook's behest Yulunga now served his friend Captain Cecco as first mate. Both commanders had earned Yulunga's deference, and he showed them due respect. Although largely immune to the hazards of the Neverland, he had learned to approach the Island, too, with deference. He'd warned his men of the resident perils of beasts, boys, and Indians, and when one of his sailors stumbled with a jingle of weaponry, Yulunga turned to him, raising a stern finger to his lips. "Keep quiet."

Immediately the sailor nodded acquiescence, his eyes wary, awed by more than just the Island. Yulunga was a giant of a man, an African king, tall, broad, and fearless. The colors of his homeland, fiery orange, yellow, and red, brightened his ebony throat on a triple string of beads. His story was whispered among *Red Lady's* crewmen; with his cruelty he had betrayed his native people. Betrayed in return, he bore the scars of slavery on his wrists and his ankles. From his shoulder to his naked back a lighter streak of flesh indicated the more recent judgment of Hook's claw. Yulunga deferred to the commodore as the only man who had never flinched at the power embedded in Yulunga's immensity.

It was, therefore, his woman for whom he brought the protection of the escort, a diminutive little thing, with brown hair and bare feet, and a figure just beginning to show her child. Even with his back turned, Yulunga was aware of the jostling taking place as the sailors competed for positions behind her saucy backside. Over his shoulder he ordered, "The scenery is agreeable, but keep your eyes on the forest."

Mrs. Hanover was his property. Because she was unburdened by a heart and overburdened with bodily appetite, she made an apt partner for her master. A handful to handle, herself. With a dash of irony, Mr. Yulunga wondered as he trudged through the wilderness whether he and his men guarded Mrs. Hanover, or if they protected her potential assailants. Nearly everyone feared Mr. Yulunga; only the enlightened were wary of Mrs. Hanover.

Keeping the enlightened to a minimum was Yulunga's job. He had witnessed the damage she'd caused. In her hunger for Hook, this little woman had started off a chain reaction that deposed two ships' commanders, overset the order of both crews, and propelled Mr. Cecco to his captaincy. The commodore placed a load of responsibility on Yulunga's shoulders when he trusted him to tame this virago. Speculation ran rampant, but no one under the rank of first officer really knew what transpired between the girl and the commodore as he'd lain a prisoner in her bed— not even the girl herself. Yet the result was understood. Hook had nearly died of her.

Yulunga inhaled the perfume of the Neverland's greenery, not as heavy but just as fertile as that of his birthplace. The grassy turf underfoot seemed oddly solid after months of pitching decks. This new path through the forest would become more negotiable with every expedition. Seeing puzzlement in the Frenchmen's faces as they navigated, Yulunga slowed and spoke in an undertone.

"The Clearing was established only recently as a gathering place for Hook's pirates. But don't worry. The shortest route from Neverbay will soon be beaten smooth." Amused by the men's enthusiasm, he reckoned that the foliage stood little chance to re-root itself until the *Roger* and her mate, *Red Lady*, upped anchors and went about their lucrative business on the sea— or until the rest of the sailors learned to fly, like bo'sun's mates Nibs the Knife and Tom Tootles. As youngsters, the two had infested these woods among the Island boy's pack. That first day the ships lay in port here, they had cruised around the Neverland, reporting back to Hook before joining the festivities at the home of their twin brothers. The Frenchmen of *Red Lady* had been amazed to see a pair of pirates airborne, soaring toward shore, and the new buccaneers grew eager to experience the magic of this place. All the more so now as Hook's fairy, Jewel, zoomed past.

"Sacré coeur!" cried a sailor, forgetting caution while he clutched his cap and pointed at the pixie. Chiming, she fluttered her fingers toward Yulunga, then trailed a comet tail of glitter in her hurry. She had answered her master's summons to the *Roger*, and after an invigorating visit, she was off on his errands. The men's eyes rolled toward Yulunga when she'd gone, as if bracing to see the massive mate, too, jump up and streak through this enchanted air.

Yulunga chuckled at the thought of his own bulky body borne upon the winds, then he regarded his slender girl. She, too, exhibited astonishment at the fairy's apparition, yet she didn't dare open her mouth to exclaim. But where Yulunga demanded silence from his men, he frowned on reticence in the woman. "No word from you?"

She only looked down.

Yulunga grunted, and the party struck out again. "One more voyage, Mrs. Hanover, before you must stay behind to be tended by Lily and the others— if they accept you." Once her brat was born, she could return to *Red Lady* and continue her duties. For now, her bare feet felt their way along, padding over roots and brambles, her ankles exposed as she raised her fine maroon skirt to negotiate the flora. Bred in a European city, she was unaccustomed to woodlands, and Yulunga could tell by her ashen face that the strange sight of the fairy had unnerved her. The dress he had given her was becoming, with a neckline cut low above a cream-colored triangle that set off her figure, but her only ornament was the golden ring that matched its mate in Yulunga's ear. She had earned that piece and, one day, if she behaved, he'd reward her with its partner. Then he'd get a larger pair, thick with gold, and wear it, just to taunt her. He had no doubt she'd find a way to win that pair, too. Yulunga smiled to himself, then in a low tone admonished his men.

"Look sharp there, and keep an eye open for natives in these parts. You don't want to be surprised by an arrow in your heart. Watch for the Lost Boys, too, as I warned you. They are smaller, but no less deadly."

"*Oui, Monsieur.* Yes." The party's voices were obediently hushed, their English spotty, but by the hands on their weapons and their guarded faces as they looked around, Yulunga knew they understood.

Mrs. Hanover, too, sharpened her lookout. She threw a glance at Yulunga before inspecting the forest. She had heard the tales of Indians dwelling on the Neverland, but she never could tell when Yulunga was teasing and when he was serious. The rumors conflicted; Indian warriors killed pirates, yet their women were known to offer hospitality. Three of the Lady Jill's adopted sons lived among them. As for the 'Lost Lads,' or whatever they were called, to such a sophisticated girl the idea of grown men on guard against a ragtag passel of boys seemed ludicrous. Still, she was wary. Yulunga might be in earnest. In Mrs. Hanover's few weeks as his mistress, she'd learned many of his ways, but no matter how she delved, he always seemed to harbor another depth to plumb.

He confused her sometimes, but she drew satisfaction from the fact that Yulunga had, conversely, tapped only the surface of herself. If she played her hand correctly, he might take years to discover her depths. By that time, by the time he grew tired of her, she would hold a position of her own— ship's surgeon— and she could stand on her own two feet as an officer. Every day she studied her father's medical tomes, beginning with the chapters concerning childbirth. One day she would be as skilled a physician as her sire, indispensable to her commander. Mrs. Hanover smiled to think of it, then gasped in pain as her toes tripped over a knobby root.

Yulunga's huge black hand caught her. So did another, lighter hand that was never far away. Mrs. Hanover sent a quick, grateful look to the china blue eyes and the Gallic smile that shone so disarmingly upon her. Yulunga grunted an acknowledgement to Pierre-Jean, and from then on he guided her, half pulling, half lifting, and the blond sailor fell back a step. Mrs. Hanover felt Pierre-Jean watching, as always, but she took care to ignore him now, leaning on Yulunga's arm instead.

With no effort, her African lover bore her along until the red smoke in the sky coiled overhead and a parrot could be heard screeching its heart out. The sound of children's voices surprised her, and she hesitated on the damp clay of the path, staring through the thinning branches until Yulunga's tug pulled her from the woods.

Two nearly naked men approached, one bearing the parrot, now bobbing and lurching, on his shoulder. He laughed and propped a nut between his lips, and the parrot retrieved it with a kiss. The two men were identical, tanned to bronze and boasting shaggy blond hair streaked with darker shades. Their bodies obviously understood and, just as obviously, relished hard labor. From the tools and lumber scattered round the Clearing, Mrs. Hanover surmised that these twins were building the structure rising from the earth in one corner of the Clearing. Behind the men tagged three children with black hair and a minimum of clothing that looked to be sewn from animal hides. Unsure whether she was within her rights to stare at the men, Mrs. Hanover studied the children instead. Perhaps her own child would play here and be dressed like this. A slim chance existed that it would have dark skin like these children, or darker. But...more likely...

"Mrs. Hanover," Yulunga commanded, "show your respects to the lady's sons, the Men of the Clearing. If they agree, they will one day be your providers."

Mrs. Hanover plucked up her skirt and curtsied. The twins grinned, responding in turns.

"You're welcome here."

"One more child won't make any difference. Come, everyone, and meet our ladies."

Having been a child herself until recently— she was only fourteen— Mrs. Hanover wondered if the man referred to herself or to her baby, but she kept quiet and followed Yulunga. He introduced the Frenchmen, who shook hands politely but whose avid gazes rummaged the open space, like wolves scenting prey. Clearly, they sought the women of whom they had heard from the previous nights' celebrants. Only Pierre-Jean still watched Mrs. Hanover, his long blond pigtail lying over his shoulder, blonder still in the sunlight that lit up his French blue jacket. His eyes engaged her, but his hands remained at his sides. All the sailors knew that as Mr. Yulunga's property, Mrs. Hanover was untouchable. For now.

A tall, buxom native woman emerged from a hut. She clapped her hands and the children ran to her like a flock of black-downed chicks. As the Frenchmen spotted the female, Mrs. Hanover felt electricity ignite the air. Too much time had passed since they'd sailed into any port, and Mrs. Hanover knew exactly what these men craved. She had made a study of sailors, spying and eavesdropping since her first days aboard the merchantman on which her father took employment. Evidently the tall woman understood sailormen, too. Shooing the youngsters inside, the lady sent a knowing smile toward the pirates, then flicked a glance at Mrs. Hanover before disappearing into a fine white house.

This house astonished Mrs. Hanover. Whereas she had expected a wigwam or some sort of lodge built of mud and sticks, the House in the Clearing was very like the home she had known in England, an odd contrast to the tangled wilderness all round it fairly bursting with birdsong. And from the scent of lavender wafting through the air, she determined some kind of garden was cultivated behind it.

Through the polished oak doorway, a second, very curvy, woman appeared. Yulunga strode toward her. His low voice rumbled with pleasure and his wide dark face split in a smile. "Lily!"

"Dark Prince." Lily opened her arms. Yulunga snatched her up, planting a kiss on her full brown lips. She returned it, heartily, and without haste. The sailors shuffled in the grass. Mrs. Hanover blinked.

Still clasped in Yulunga's arms with her toes dangling over the earth, Lily exclaimed, "How good to see you again." She beamed as he set her down. "And who have you brought to us? Your new men, I see." She turned to face them. "I welcome you to the Clearing. Please, take off your boots and be comfortable as we become acquainted." She indicated a ring of logs around a fire pit. A wisp of smoke still rose from a second night of festivities, and Mrs. Hanover recognized the acrid smell that accompanied her stab of jealousy to be the remnants of the fire. The men hurried off to sit and pry at their boots.

"Red Fawn," Lily called, "our company has arrived."

The third woman stepped from the house. Balancing a tray on her hip, she bore a flagon and wooden cups. Immediately, Pierre-Jean moved to her side to assume her burden. A fine display of dimples greeted him, and Red Fawn relinquished the tray, taking Pierre-Jean's elbow in her shapely hands and guiding him toward the fire pit. Mrs. Hanover's brow wrinkled until Yulunga spoke her name. At the sound of it, she indulged in a full-scale scowl.

Her name was hateful to her. Hook himself had condemned her to its use. And she had earned it— was earning it still. Some nights she woke in a fit of perspiration from dreams so carnal she was compelled to shake Yulunga awake to indulge them. Dreams of her former lover who, even thousands of miles away by now, set her afire with his skill. Doctor Hanover was a man who studied love, researched it as a science. The art of desire was, in fact, his life's work, his genius. In his hands he held an intimate knowledge of a woman's body— and he had used it to seduce his daughter. When he'd found no other way to master her, he mastered her passions. As much her father's prisoner as the pirates', she hated him. And she adored him.

"Lily, this is Mrs. Hanover. I am her provider. As you can see, she will be needing care in the coming months."

"If you ask it, I cannot refuse." Lily's eyes were tranquil as she observed Mrs. Hanover. "Please, Miss, make yourself at home."

"No." Yulunga placed a heavy hand on Mrs. Hanover's shoulder. "I thank you for your good manners, Lily, but the commodore has given strict orders. My woman is to be addressed as Mrs. Hanover. Nothing else."

Lily noted Mrs. Hanover's grimace, but her tone remained neutral. "I see."

Mrs. Hanover saw Lily's gaze strengthen upon her, but felt no judgment. Whatever this native woman knew about her she kept hidden. Mrs. Hanover relaxed her posture. Evidently what she had heard of the Women of the Clearing was true. Outcasts themselves, they accepted all who came to them. Mrs. Hanover's relief showed on her face, and Lily greeted it with a smile.

"Sit, and take something to drink. We will discuss your needs."

Yulunga stared at Mrs. Hanover, waiting. With an effort, she responded to Lily with the proper words. "Thank you." Her voice could be low
and lovely; right now it was coarse from lack of practice. Her accent
was strange, but she never spoke enough for a listener to recognize it
as the Austrian of her father, the English of her mother, or the African
of her master. And her quick ears had already picked up a smattering
of French that would be useful. Mrs. Hanover was a chameleon,
adopting whatever characteristics would serve her best, and betraying
them without a backward glance if better opportunities arose.

Yulunga nodded approval of her words. He had a rich, fluid
voice that Mrs. Hanover loved to hear. Especially when, in intimate
moments, he poured it into her ear. He did so now, standing pressed
against her back, wrapping his large, warm hands around her, and
caressing her hips.

"Listen to Lily. She knows how to make a man happy."

Mrs. Hanover's too-responsive body began to melt. She wondered
how, when the time came, she would live without Yulunga's hands.
Her gaze wandered toward Pierre-Jean, then played upon Lily's near-
naked men. Bearing armloads of firewood, they laughed with the
Frenchmen as their bodies bent and flexed with the labor of laying
the fire. No flame could be seen as yet, but Mrs. Hanover felt it
flaring already.

And then she stiffened. Yulunga had turned to Lily, and his
mesmerizing voice broke faith with its victim.

"Be on your guard, Lily. If fear meant anything to me, I would
fear this woman."

Lily's gray gaze stared at him, somber.

With his matching ring gleaming on his ear, Yulunga pinched
Mrs. Hanover's one empty earlobe. The pain started tears in her eyes.
He looked at Lily and shook his head.

"Don't trust her."

"Sister, I do not claim that any man, even White Bear, can take
the place of Ash in your heart." Willow's words, soft as they fell, grated

on Raven's sensibilities. "Our tribe boasts no other brave like Ash. He was a fiery man, full of flash and valor."

Raven set her sewing aside and held her shorn head high. "My husband died in the manner of his choice. Nobly, in battle."

Willow nodded and shifted her position on the floor of White Bear's tepee. With the birth of her baby impending, she found it difficult to sit in comfort. The plush fur of the albino bearskin was her favorite refuge. A patch of mid-morning sunlight illuminated her beadwork, slanting in cheerfully from the open door on the east. It lightened Willow's worries. "Ash was a true warrior, and you have shown your respect for him."

"I do not believe White Bear understands why I cut my hair."

"He understands that you mourn."

"I followed the ancient custom."

"And rightly, Sister. But remember that White Bear came to us from the People of the Other Island. Some of our customs, especially the older ones, are not familiar to him." Willow smiled in her gentle way. "I remember how strange he looked to me, that first time I saw his long scalp lock. You must have appeared just as strange to him, after you cut your hair."

"You were a tiny girl when he underwent his naming ceremony and caused all but his lock to be shaved."

"Now the young braves imitate him." Willow couldn't hide her pride. It shone in her face. "Once a stranger from a sister tribe, he has carved his place as a leader in our own."

Raven held silence, letting the warmth of the morning rays penetrate her back. Sometimes she could feel Ash's passion in the sunshine, as if he stood, not in the land of Dark Hunting, but behind the sun itself. Until Lean Wolf's kiss reawakened her body, the Shadow Woman had hidden from the sun, refusing to indulge in this fantasy. But this morning, Raven found relief from her anxiety in memory. Lost in her daydream, she allowed herself to drift from her sister's discourse.

"Raven! You must listen to me."

Opening her eyes, Raven attended her sister.

"Since the day the pirates arrived, he is most concerned about you."

"I told you then, Willow. I can still run like a deer. And I was not assail-ed by bears or pirates in the woods. Not even by the hateful Golden Boy."

"But something happened to you. You came home breathless and disheveled."

"Everyone was breathless after the guns went off."

"But your dress was drenched. Whatever happened to you, by walking out alone you made yourself vulnerable to it. In the old days, I would have accompanied you."

"If I cannot walk when and where I please, I am no more than—" Raven stopped, dissatisfied with herself. Until the day before yesterday she was resigned to her role as the Shadow Woman. Twice now, she had defied it. Difficult as it was, she must discipline herself. Already she had aroused the unwanted attentions of a warrior— if the stories were to be believed, a less than honorable warrior. Raven admitted that her young sister's advice was sound. With Lean Wolf on the prowl, she would require White Bear's good will more than ever. She looked down at the albino fur on which Willow rested. "Please assure White Bear that I will be more cautious."

"You must assure him yourself. He wishes to counsel you, today."

A flash of panic leapt from Raven's stomach to her throat. "No! You must speak for me."

"He has already decided. But Raven, you are pale! If I didn't know of your courage, I would think you are afraid of White Bear."

Raven looked at her generous sister, whose heart made room for so many. "Of course I do not fear him." She tried to smile, but could not force it through her lie. How could her sister be so blind to danger? Raven was older, more experienced. She understood the ways of men so much better than Willow. She felt her heart thundering; she had good reason to fear White Bear. And now he wanted to speak to her— alone.

In a milder tone, Willow soothed her sister, "Surely, and soon, you will recognize White Bear's goodness. He will care for you, as a woman needs to be cared for."

Raven turned away. She couldn't bear for Willow to see the turmoil such a thought stirred in her. The thought of White Bear… touching her.

"Is it Lean Wolf Silent Hunter? Do you wish White Bear to accept his suit after all?"

"I have told you many times, Willow. I will not marry again."

"Yes, but now that a formal declaration has been made, a gift bestowed…"

"His gifts change nothing."

"Gifts? Were there more than one?"

Raven met her sister's gaze with a stubborn stare, and lied again. "No."

Willow's pretty face smoothed. "I am glad. Since Red Fawn ran away, I have doubts about Lean Wolf's suitability." Willow would not betray her husband's confidence by divulging his friend's indiscretions. "And of course I am happy you wish to stay with me."

"I will help you raise your children. I do not require much 'care' from your husband."

"You have always been an independent spirit, braving the forest all alone, running for the fun of it. But you may find, when your mourning-time is over, that you *do* need more."

Protesting, Raven opened her mouth, but Willow interrupted. "But for today, White Bear seeks only to remind you that his rules are for our family's safety. I know you will listen to him. If we are guided by his wisdom, his burden as our protector is lightened. And please, remember that it is I who asked him to assume that burden. Now, with the return of the Black Chief and his pirates, he has the welfare of the tribe on his mind as well. The council rely on him."

"You need not remind me of White Bear's importance!" Then, ashamed to see the surprise on Willow's face, Raven relented. "I know very well that he has earned it." Her hand fell to stroking the precious white hide on which Willow sat. The pelt was dense, both soft and tough, and full of comfort-bringing warmth. White Bear prized it. Each night as he lay down beside his wife, he wrapped her in its sanctuary, a token of his affection.

Willow smiled and ran her fingers through the fur. "Only a great hunter could slay a beast as fierce as this one." Taking Raven's silence for agreement, Willow went on, more confidently, "With our son so near his birth, I look forward to seeing you settled." She hesitated, then plunged ahead, her eyes aglow. "Raven, you don't yet know the peace the prospect of a child brings to a woman. White Bear can give you a son of your own to cherish." She laid her hand on Raven's arm. "Please, do not turn away from life. Embrace it."

The shock Raven experienced would not be subdued. "Sister." She backed away. Her voice trembled with intensity. "You do not know what you are asking."

"You could bear a boy to White Bear, to fill the hollow of Ash's passing."

Heat flushed Raven's cheeks at the same moment a chill struck her back. A shadow blocked the sunshine, and Willow looked up, smiling. Raven held still. From the corner of her eye, she saw White Bear's feet in his beaded moccasins, stepping into the tepee. She listened for the timbre of his voice, to determine his mood. It was gruffer than usual. Raven sat straighter.

"You must leave us, Wife." White Bear stood tall, his scalp lock nearly brushing the upward slope of the tepee. "It is time for your sister to hear my words."

Willow accepted Raven's arm, to rise ungracefully to her feet. Her docile voice answered, "I understand you, Husband." Turning to Raven, she encouraged her with a smile. "White Bear has your best interests at heart, Raven. As does your sister." Unable to bend down in her pregnancy, she bent her knees to gather up the leathern water pails, then slipped through the tepee door, closing the flap behind her.

Raven guessed that her sister was tempted to linger to overhear her husband's advice, yet she knew Willow was too proud to eaves-drop. And Willow trusted White Bear. Raven imagined Willow turning from her door to walk in her swaying way toward the river, relying on her husband to settle her sister's hurt.

At the moment, Raven felt anything but settled. As the tepee flap fell to, the darkening space encroached upon her spirit, its soft sides enclosing her. The hides that flexed to keep out wind and rain now felt smothering to Raven. The stoic presence of its headman was the one uncompromising element in her sister's home.

White Bear stepped closer. He knelt down at her right to lean back on his heels. Raven could smell his man-smell, a mix of sweat and sun and muscle. Her every instinct told her to flee, to run as desperately as she had run from Silent Hunter.

But to whom?

She cast her gaze down. Her spirit ran; the Shadow Woman took her place.

Except for one couple, the mountain camp lay deserted. Cold cooking fires sat waiting, surrounded by colder stones, for the people of the Indian village to move with the seasons. They'd move upward, and homeward, to populate the empty tepees and crowd the long lodge at feast times, filling the air with savory flavors. The Black Chief had driven the tribe to the mountain camp early this year. A few days later, the People migrated down again, as he and his pirates sailed away. The village rhythm was disrupted, but except for the singeing of the totem pole, the Black Chief had caused no lasting harm. Rowan Life-Giver had testified: He of the Eagle's Claw had merely counted coup at the expense of his enemies. His valor was proven and he had won his woman. In a final thrust much more to the People's liking, the Black Chief had slain the terrible crocodile. Then he, in turn, had deserted his island berth.

Rowan Life-Giver emerged from the one warm tepee with his old friend, his tomahawk, at his thigh. He held the flap for his other companion, whom the elders had named in ceremony at the last new moon. Lightly of the Air was a lucky brave. He had been adopted twice in his short life, once by the Golden Boy's girl, once by Rowan's tribe. The natives were not a diverse lot, had even cast Rowan's mother out— not for bearing his redheaded sister, but for consorting with pirates, a transgression of taboo made obvious by his sister's coloring. Yet the People were wise enough to welcome Lightly, whose appearance was as different as could be. He had been born in London, and found by the Golden Boy in the park. Whoever his natural parents were, they were blond-haired and blue-eyed, for so was Lightly. Tall and rangy, Lightly topped his companion by a hand-span as he straightened and stretched outside the door. "Will you come along, then?" he asked.

"I will accompany you, Lightly, but judging by our first meeting with the Black Chief, we must use caution." Rowan Life-Giver was a stolid young brave, eyes like chips of glass and cheekbones so pronounced as to seem carved into his face. His nut-brown skin contrasted with his partner's, his tightly braided hair as black as Lightly's was blond. Rowan had been taught by his mother's example. Like Lily, he was observant of custom, yet unafraid to think for himself. Even in his choice of partner, he declared his independence.

"Yes, we'll have to be careful," Lightly agreed, "And consider that one entire ship's company of those pirates have never seen us before. They're bound to be hostile— after they get over the shock of seeing Indians fly like birds."

"We shall travel by canoe, this time," said Rowan.

"Maybe we should do like the twins and bring some women along."

Rowan smiled. "One would believe you were nurtured by a pirate, Lightly. And in truth, you were. Although your mother was not yet aware as she raised you that she was destined to become a pirate matriarch."

"The word's 'queen,' Rowan."

"Yes. An unnatural concept. But one that succeeds in the society of wild men in which she dwells."

Laughing, Lightly flung an arm around Rowan. "It is amusing to walk in two worlds. Both my clans think of themselves as civilized, the other as wild. In truth, I think, civilization has yet to be achieved. The closest to approach it are the fairies. They dance and feast all day, welcome anyone, large or small, who cares to join them, and then they make love together among the flowers. And even they have their uncivilized element, Jewel being the prime example."

"Fairies!" Rowan scoffed. "Next you will sing praise of the mermaids."

"There is no question of mermaids. Not one of them would save a drowning man, as the stains on Marooners' Rock can show."

"Still, plenty of men take the risk."

"Better to leave the mergirls to Pan. He and his lads are too young to harbor expectations, and so are not disappointed. Or drowned. But let's get going. It's time we did our duty for the elders. And I'm eager to see Jill again."

An unusual pair in several ways, these men served the tribe with their power of flight, a holdover from Lightly's childhood as a Lost Boy. This rare capability had made them Messengers for the council. Speeding about the Island as the need arose, they reconnoitered, delivered messages, collected herbs for medicine from the garden in the Fairy Glade and, most importantly, kept an eye on the wild boy. Indeed, Lightly knew the Golden Boy better than did almost anyone else. He advised the council in all that concerned that minor menace. The boy's ally, the crocodile, was dead and skinned now, but during the nightmare of its reign, Rowan and Lightly had paid each other life-service, rescuing one another from its jaded jaws. Since that day, the two formed a curious couple, so curious as to violate taboo.

Handing Lightly his quiver, Rowan said, "Let us go to the mountaintop to survey the situation in morning light."

Lightly yawned and slung the quiver over his bare shoulder. "The bonfire in the Clearing burned long and hot these last couple of nights. And as I predicted, nothing occurred in all that time to alarm the council. And no sign of Pan, either. I'm glad we stayed here to sleep. No children or dogs to disturb us too early."

Rowan laid a hand on Lightly's arm, cautioning, "I too find delight in our privacy. But remember the warning of the Old One. We must use discretion. We cannot retire here as often as we might wish."

"The People won't close their eyes forever, Rowan. One day, when neither of us takes a wife, they'll understand."

"When that happens, my mother and your brothers will welcome us to the Clearing. Until then, we are trusted with responsibilities. We will serve the People."

"On that day, we may truly learn which of our worlds are civilized." Lightly flashed a grin. "But don't forget our other option. We could run away to London and erect a tepee in the park."

"Where the Golden Boy will find us."

"He'd think we were Lost Boys, and he'd bring us right back to the Neverland. I guess we can't escape our fate, after all. For us, there is no other island!"

Bursting into laughter, the lovers fell together in a tumble of mirth. Only after indulging their humor did they rise again, dusting off their divergent skins of brown and white, to snatch up their bows, quivers, and tomahawks, and they leapt into the air toward their lookout perch on the high, breezy summit of the Indian mountain.

Speaking in their amusing accents, the Frenchmen enchanted the Women of the Clearing. The ladies discovered that the newest pirates often abandoned language to communicate, quite fluently, with their hands. As promised, Lily talked with Mrs. Hanover, too, whom she found self-conscious and shy. Mrs. Hanover, like her shipmates, relied on gestures to express herself, as if she were not unable, but afraid to use her voice. Mr. Yulunga hovered over them all like a huge disciplinary hen, keeping the men respectful and the girl civil. And for all her machinations, the women recognized that Mrs. Hanover, even laden with her ponderous name, was little more than a girl. As implausible as Yulunga's warnings sounded, they arrived on top of Smee's, and the women prepared themselves.

Still, Lily's open heart went out to the creature, so young and so alone in her world of primitive men. But Lily was not fool enough to allow youth to hoodwink her sense of character. She studied the girl. Mrs. Hanover was in the early stage of her pregnancy, but her roving eye, her restless hands, indicated that she might be difficult to keep occupied during the final term before birthing. Nor did Lily miss the concern on Lelaneh's face as she gleaned what sparse information she could, evaluating the state of the baby. Something in Mrs. Hanover's reticence seemed to speak to Lelaneh. Clearly, as an herbalist, she sensed the birthing would be difficult. But, in the end, Lily, her companions, and their providers agreed to accept charge of the little mother when her time came, for Yulunga's sake.

After an hour of conversation and a measure of sweet ale, Yulunga ushered Mrs. Hanover and the new men away, having arranged for their return the following evening. The most courteous sailor, Pierre-Jean, held the shrubbery aside for Mrs. Hanover, bowing as she passed. Lily watched as Mrs. Hanover slid him a secret look. She noted, too, that Mrs. Hanover did not acknowledge his gesture, nor did he appear to take offense. Then the party jingled off into the woods, frightening the finches and causing a squirrel to claw its way up a tree, chattering in indignation. Lily smiled to hear Yulunga chastise his sailors for their carelessness. In their pleasure at socializing with females, they had plainly forgotten their awe of the Island. The scream of a panther in the distance quickly reminded them, for, from then on, Lily heard no more clamor from the pirates. The restless fauna quieted.

The steady, rhythmic rasp of sawing emanated from the growing structure in the corner. It had ceased at the sound of the panther, and one of the twins stepped out for a look around with his shining new ax in hand. Assured of the women's safety, he returned to his workshop and the noise of saws resumed, until, shortly afterward, the parrot squawked again.

Captain Cecco emerged from the forest bearing a brace of pistols and his famous knife in his belt, looking more commanding, more dashing than ever— but with an air of melancholy he'd never before exhibited. Lelaneh and Red Fawn ran to greet him with enthusiasm, but Lily read his mood. She approached with more reserve and, under the vigilant eyes of the Men, soon escorted him to a private place, the patch of garden behind the house. Here he sat on a stump, and with a cool drink in his hand, relaxed enough to breathe the zesty scent of Lelaneh's herbs, and to confide in Lily.

Lily's eyes softened as she listened, standing behind her visitor and looking down on him. When he subsided to silence, she said, "I find you much changed, Captain. I speak not only of the marks upon your back." Cecco had allowed her to slide his leather vest away and, slowly, her capable, comforting fingers massaged his shoulders. She had winced when his scars were revealed. He bore ugly gashes, inflicted months ago by the commodore's cat-o'-nine-tails, in the hands of Smee. Cecco was just a common sailor then, and the *Roger* about to embark on the recent voyage that ended in his promotion. Cecco was punished for allowing himself to be distracted, watching Jill when he should have guarded Hook against the crocodile's attack. Lily had seen such blemishes before, but not so many, and never so deep. Yet she understood. In the odd fashion of fate, the barbarity unleashed upon Cecco measured Smee's feeling for Hook.

As Cecco turned his head, his bound-back hair shifted to reveal more damage, and the medallions on his headdress chimed. He granted her the ghost of his gypsy smile. "My punishment was not so unbearable, when I considered that it came of love for my lady." His smile faded. "But perhaps you are unaware of the impact your Mr. Smee can deliver."

"I confess it. He is a strong man, but the gentlest of lovers." She cajoled him, "Unlike you, when you are inspired." She leaned down to lay a kiss upon his ear, just above a sizable loop of earring. "I cannot but believe that you need some inspiration now."

"Inspiration I have in full. *Signora* Cecco is the perfect woman. Not only is she beautiful; she is the bravest, the most loyal. I cannot fault her...and I cannot hold her."

"Truly, your patience is tried."

"And let there be honesty between us, Lily. Your patience, also, is tried." The wound of Cecco's resentment broke open. His words bled with passion. "While I am forbidden to touch my wife, your Mr. Smee has the commodore's permission."

Lily's voice lost pliability. "The commodore's permission is irrelevant. It is the lady who makes the choice."

Cecco reached across his chest to capture her wrist as she rubbed his shoulders. He turned to face her, and his brown eyes smoldered. "I warned her once. Now you may warn your Mr. Smee. I can barely endure the commodore's claim on her. Any other man who seeks to have her, I vow to kill."

Lily cast a haughty glance at the grip on her wrist. Her eyes rose to challenge him. "It is well, perhaps, that '*my*' Mr. Smee does not make similar threats."

Cecco stared at her, then, shaking off his temper, he loosened his grip. "I am sorry, Lily. My frustration makes me less than chivalrous." Tenderly, he lifted her wrist again and kissed its circumference. "I am grateful for your company."

"I accept your apology. Not everyone owns a heart that can stretch as far as mine. Nor as far as your lady's." Cecco's face darkened again, and she slid her wrist from his hand. "But Captain. I will not tolerate such threats at the home of Smee's daughter. And if you must quarrel with him, I expect you to do so honorably, with equal advantage on each side."

"You, too, are a courageous woman. How do you and the others fare here, in exile?"

"Thanks to the commodore's kindness, we are safe and content. Our Men love and provide for us, our children thrive. We cannot ask for more."

"You miss living among your tribe?"

"As deeply as you miss your own, my gypsy captain."

"Aye." Heaving a sigh, Cecco gazed far into the woods. "I may never set eyes on my tribe again. We are a band of wanderers. I would not know even how to seek them now. In any case, the bounty on my head prevents me from returning to my homeland."

"Your mother is blessed with many sons, and by now, no doubt, grandsons. I am sure she is well cared for, even though she must grieve for you."

"Lily, I believed, when I married, that I would at last have a family again. A wife, many *bambini*." He shrugged his mighty shoulders. "You laugh, and well you might, to imagine a pack of gypsies aboard a pirate vessel. Yet this was *la prima speranza*— the fondest hope of my heart. When I lost my Jill, I lost also this beautiful dream."

"This, then, is the change I have found in you. Once you were cheerful, reconciled to your loss. Now you have lost not one family, but two. It must be difficult to bear."

Cecco didn't answer. The sorrow in his eyes spoke for him. Lily knelt at his boots to take his hands between her own.

"You now walk like a man possessed. The spirit of the volcano dwells within you. Even I have felt it scorch me today. Please, Captain, for your own sake, and for the sake of my daughter, do not allow yourself to vent this anger upon one who cannot help feeling as you feel."

With an ironic smile, Cecco snorted. "Your Mr. Smee. The commodore's Smee." The smile vanished. "Jill's Smee."

Lily squeezed his fingers. "It is well that you are here now, on the Island. You must spend time with us. And with your fellows. Comradeship, affection, will be balm for your injured spirit. Red Fawn, especially, has asked after you."

"I thank you, Lily. And I thank Red Fawn. But I must model myself after my commodore. Even as a captain, he never mingled with the men. Not until…Jill."

"The commodore is a different man entirely. His solitude defined him. You are a man to whom companionship gives life its meaning. Family, friends…"

"And wife. No, Lily, I will not insult my lady by flaunting my favors before my men."

Cecco found himself being pulled to rise. Once on his feet, he faced Lily. She exerted a gentle pressure, drawing him closer. Her curves were pleasing in his arms, her lips warm and welcoming. Cecco pressed against her softness, a familiar feeling stirring his loins, the stimulation this engaging woman had never failed to rouse in him. His golden bracelets tinkled as he moved to appreciate her figure.

Lily closed her eyes and loosed a sigh. "Your men are not among us now, Captain. Come. Come with me." She tugged him toward the house.

But Cecco's body went rigid. His eyes opened fully, his face, so mellow a moment ago, hardened, and he whipped his arms from Lily to seize his knife. In a flash of silver, it was poised in his fist. He glared at the path to the stream.

Lily spun just in time to see a blaze of French blue dive into the brush. "Oh! It must be he! Our bandit."

Cecco was striding toward the wood, swatting branches from his path. "*Ragazzo!* Boy!" he bellowed, "You do not skulk around this place. Go back to your hole in the ground!" Having lost sight of the intruder, he stopped to scan the forest. Once he was sure that the spy had fled, he returned to Lily. "You have seen him before?"

"No. We saw only his tracks, and afterward we missed things he has taken."

"I see that he has robbed one of my men. Now I know how Flambard lost his jacket. I thought he had gambled it away."

"The boy steals only food and clothing. I think he must be hungry, cold, and frightened."

"That is like you, Lily, to have sympathy for one who would steal from you." With a grim look, Cecco thought of Red-Handed Jill's plunder of the heart of Lily's Smee. "But you must beware of this thief, if he is a member of Pan's pack."

"His footprints are always alone. And I daresay he would have flown away from you just now, if he could. All the Golden Boy's flock do so. And they steal only weapons. A few days ago, one of the braves from the village lost a number of arrowheads to them."

"We will identify your bandit soon enough. The commodore intends to smoke him out. But...I can't help feeling he seemed familiar."

"You recognize him?"

"I cannot be sure. I caught only a glimpse, and mainly his back-side. Most likely he is a Lost Boy."

Lily's voice changed, subtly. "Lost, indeed." Laying her hand on Cecco's arm, she crooned, "Now let us see if we can find where *you* belong."

Cecco covered her hand. "Thank you, Lily. I know where I belong. I have only to be patient. I have reason to believe...one day..."

"One day. In the meantime, be good to yourself. Your Jill wants you to take care."

For the first time, his eyes brightened. "You have heard her speak of me?"

"Every woman speaks of you. But yes. She confided to me this morning what you already know. She loves you. I would not be in her position for all the gold in your treasure chests. To choose between two warriors, both handsome, both skilled and powerful. But, as you say, the lady's loyalty decides. Her first love and allegiance are for the Black Chief."

"I could wish, Lily, that the Black Chief's heart might stretch like your own."

"That he might share her?" Lily smiled. "Commodore Hook is, after all, a generous man. You have said so yourself. He might have killed you; instead he rewarded you."

"As he admits, a ship is not an even exchange for a woman. Not—not *our* woman."

Lily paused. Her gaze lingered, searching deep within his eyes. "If he loves her, Captain, he will grant to her the deepest wish of her heart."

Cecco's eyebrows drew together as he considered.

"Can *your* love do the same for her, my dear?"

"Lily…"

Placing two fingers on his lips, she shook her head. "Hush, my fine gypsy captain. Remember, you are on the Island now. Magic dwells here. Mysteries of a nature that can occur no other place."

Unable to speak, Captain Cecco, like his Frenchmen, communicated with his hands. He took Lily's face in his fingers. He laid a thoughtful kiss upon her lips. Then he took up his vest and his weapons, saluted her, and, all alone, walked into the woods.

In the darkened tepee of the warrior White Bear, Raven watched her hands. They lay clasped on her lap, her knuckles white. She felt the grip of White Bear's hard, gray eyes. His voice was harsh.

"I have spoken with Lean Wolf Silent Hunter, to thank him for his gift. But I refused his offer."

"Yes, Brother."

"He holds affection for you. But I speak no slander, only truth, when I say that his affections have no bounds."

"I am grateful for your farsightedness."

White Bear hadn't known what reaction to expect. Always, his sister-in-law puzzled him. "In this matter you show good judgment. You were right to withhold an answer. Now Lean Wolf can hold no resentment toward you."

"I hope no ill feeling has arisen between you and your friend."

"None that need concern you." White Bear became graver. "But *I* have concerns. Had you kept your place, Lean Wolf would have found no opportunity to press you."

"This I concede, Brother." Facing straight ahead, Raven turned only her eyes to look at him. The claws on his necklace loomed lustrous in the half-light. "If I had been forewarned of his offer, I would have been more circumspect."

White Bear drew himself up. "You question my judgment, when it is shown to be well-founded."

"I am not a child to be shielded, to be given rules to obey. Give me truth, and I am armed."

"My protection serves you. If you stray beyond it, I cannot pledge your well-being. Nor can I uphold my honor."

Raven wondered at his utterance, and she looked directly upon him. "Have I damaged your honor?"

White Bear held silence, considering. He must make this woman of headstrong ways see the effect of her actions. Everything of value to White Bear rode on her submission. She must be made to comply. At last he spoke, his tone more solemn than before. "You know the answer better than I. Reflect on Lean Wolf's words."

Searching White Bear's inflexible face, Raven read his meaning. As she recounted what she had heard, she tried to deny its wider implication. "He contradicted himself. He said that you are foolish; that you are cunning."

"It is thus that the People perceive me, where my wife's sister is concerned."

"But he also observed that you honor tradition. Surely, this is also perceived."

"That is the heart of the difficulty, Raven. I honor tradition. You disdain it."

"I—"

"If the People see it, so also do the council. The elders will not long respect a man who cannot come to terms with a woman."

Her voice diminished as she asked, "What terms?"

"What terms did Lean Wolf suggest to you?"

Her color deepening, Raven turned her face away.

"I have known Lean Wolf since we were boys. He is a hunter, Raven. The thrill of pursuit runs hot within him. He will not lose the trail of his quarry. Now that you have eluded him, he will employ every skill he knows to run you to ground." White Bear's scar-marked chest rose as he drew a deep breath. "The challenge you present has only made him hungrier. If I hold firm in my rejection, I foresee that Lean Wolf will not scruple even to importune the council."

As the dimensions of her dilemma became apparent, Raven's forehead creased. White Bear's message was clear. His power to protect his sister-in-law was great; it was not limitless. She remembered the force of Lean Wolf's embrace, the strength of his arms, so celebrated among the People. She now understood how inescapable was the snare of Silent Hunter. With effort, she kept her voice from quivering.

"What can I do?"

Slowly, White Bear rose from his haunches and stood before her. Refusing to look in his eyes, Raven remained seated and focused on the sinews of his wrist, the wrist bearing her sister's marriage bracelet. As he had done before, only to meet rejection, he approached her with his hand. This time she allowed him to settle it on her upper arm. With the smallest movement, Raven flinched. Inclining her body ever so slightly to the side, she tried not to pull away from his touch.

White Bear tensed as she shied. His grip on her arm tightened, and he growled the answer to her question.

"Woman: you will grow your hair. You will be guided by my judgment. When the sun deserts the sky, you will be permitted to lie upon the furs I provide you, in the tepee I have made."

Raven's gaze rose gratefully to his face, her arm relaxing beneath his grasp. Then her muscles clenched, for with a look in his eyes as inescapable as Lean Wolf's pursuit, White Bear continued.

"And *this* night, you will not turn from me."

Knowing the Foe

The picnic hamper lay pillaged, overturned. A few drops of claret dampened the dirt at the mouth of the bottle where it lay, making heady mud for the bees beginning to buzz around it. Only a scant patch of mud could form, however, as another tiny being beat the bees to it, lapping up the wine. Jewel leaned against the bottle's mouth, her elbows up as she thrust her face in, her iridescent wings of peacock blue folded for the moment, but ready to flare in flight. She didn't hear Peter descend to the grass beside her. Above the roar of the waterfall, lesser sounds were hard to heed.

"Here I am, Jewel. I've been following you."

Jumping backward, the fairy jingled. When she saw that the speaker was Peter, she smiled slyly; it was she who had performed the 'following,' but the bottle and its contents had lured her from the cover of the woods. Remembering her mission, she shot a quick glance toward the water.

Peter's foot righted the hamper and he rummaged inside it. "Nothing left." His eyes narrowed and shifted to study the waterfall. He spied the weapons and clothing on a high, dry rock close beside it. Resentful, he said, "Red-Handed Jill must be showing Hook our secret spot."

The river that poured from above fell heavily onto an outcropping, then flowed in a glossy green sheath, a perfect panel until it stumbled over another shelf of rock. From there it fell crazily in a froth of billowing white, plunging to the pond. Behind the curtain of rushing water, as Peter knew very well, a cave opened in which the rivulets pooled like a bath, warmed earlier on the mountain above, where the river basked in sunshine. His bold voice puzzled, "But how did Hook get up there? Even I can't climb behind the waterfall, and I have two hands. Too steep and slippery, unless you're flying."

Jewel had drunk up another drop of wine as he talked, and the mention of her master spurred her to duty. Quickly, she darted into the underbrush, beckoning Peter to follow. Her plumage struck a brilliant blue, vivid against the green of the forest, reflecting her anxiety to ensconce Peter in its safety.

"No, Jewel! I haven't gotten a proper look at Hook yet. The mermaids say he promoted himself. Commodore! Ha!" Peter kicked the grass. "He thinks a big title and another ship full of men might make me fear him."

Jewel frowned through the purple stain on her lips. Grasping Peter's belt, she heaved, signaling her urgency with her music, but he wouldn't budge. True to form, Peter relished this peril.

"I don't hide from Hook." Peter's green eyes flashed as he patted his sword. "If he wants to come out and fight, I'm ready for him. Right now I'm scouting before laying plans for attack. I left Chip and the others at the Lagoon."

Jewel interrupted her impatient reply, spinning to scan the woods. She thought she had caught a movement at the corner of her eye, the stealthy slinking of an animal. Flitting up and down, she searched, but saw nothing out of the ordinary. Listening, she heard only the crash of the waterfall. Then she turned to Peter, stern, and crossed her arms. Her music box language held a note of irritation.

"Jewel, we've been waiting all this time for Hook and Jill to sail back to the Island. I promised Chip, Bertie, and Bingo a tangle with pirates. My boys are eager for action! The sooner the better."

A shrewd look passed over Jewel's face. She'd learned how to handle her boy. Her luxurious wings stroked as she hovered over Peter's shoulder and dropped to settle there. His muscles were firm and strong, but not as developed as those upon which she had reclined this morning. Peter was Jewel's boy— but Jewel's man, after long months, had returned to her.

Her task this time was much the same as before. Jewel was commanded to repeat to her master all that happened on the Island in his absence. Next she was instructed to keep an eye on Peter. Hook had honored his word to Jewel last time, and today he promised he would endeavor not to harm her boy; it stood to reason that he needed to spy on Peter's plans and whereabouts. Jewel understood. The more the commodore knew of Peter, the better he could preserve him. Jewel never doubted her master's intentions. He had taken the Wendy away. He had given Peter back to her. She was Hook's creature and, willingly, she gave to him all that he asked. Even Peter's secrets.

And in return, Hook granted his affection. Peter was just a boy. He could never understand how to handle a female, much less a fairy. Jewel remembered the striving she'd witnessed as the Wendy attempted to ensnare him. A girl's needs were negligent compared to a fairy's, but Peter hadn't responded even to requirements as elementary as the Wendy's. Thanks to her master, Jewel didn't have to hope any longer that Peter would discover her mysteries. The commodore knew them all, and, of all humans, his fingers alone delivered the touch his creature craved— the long, light caresses that lit up her wings and made her body sing. Through Hook's tutelage, Jewel had banished the bitterness of her jealousy. With the expulsion of such an enormous emotion, her heart made room for two kinds of love— the companionship she felt for Peter, and the passion that burned for her master. Unless Peter blundered beyond expectation, Jewel would never have to choose between them.

The Wendy had had to choose, and now she was Hook's woman, Red-Handed Jill. But in Jewel's opinion she was far more acceptable these days, thanks to the master's influence. This morning Jewel carefully applied her thistle, brushing out her flaxen hair to a fine-spun cloud, then slipping on her greenest, gauziest dress. She had even scented her throat with a drop of lily of the valley, straight from the stalk. When she twinkled through the great cabin's doorway, Jill had greeted her warmly, even treated her to tea. After that, the lady set off for the Clearing, leaving the commodore and his fairy to commune in private. Hook had poured a honeyed nectar in a thimble and, with tenderness, laid his fairy upon her velvet cushion.

Jewel's cheeks had glowed pink as he caressed her. Her pulse beat heat through her veins, her wings burst into radiance unrivaled by the brightest gem in Hook's coffers. Reliving the strokes of his fingers, she understood why Jill preferred sailing on the *Roger* to her old life in the hideout under the ground.

But Jewel was more practical. Peter lived in the woodlands, and the woodlands were Jewel's home. Much as she hated to admit it, some of the Wendy's carefulness had rubbed off on her; where before Peter had adventured at will, Jewel now took upon herself the responsibility of guiding him from risk. And despite the fact that Hook had already wreaked his vengeance on Peter, he warned Jewel this morning: for Peter, pirates remained a danger. Her master trusted that, for her own happiness' sake, she would outwit her clever boy. As she nestled now on Peter's shoulder, she followed the sensible course and executed her scheme.

Kneeling near his ear, she chimed a reminder.

Peter's brow wrinkled as he considered. "But Wendy was different from Chip and the others. She was a girl."

With newfound patience, Jewel waited for her idea to become Peter's.

"But...Nibs and Tootles were boys...and they're pirates now... just like Wendy!" With a shocked expression, Peter pivoted. Jewel took to her wings, floating as he faced her. "They were *my* boys, and they learned all the glories of piracy— from *me!*"

Sympathetically, Jewel wagged her head.

"I can't let that happen again. What if Chip—" Here a look of horror struck his face. After a moment, Peter straightened. He squared his shoulders. "No. I have to protect my family." Peter jumped up to hang in the air above the picnic hamper. "Well, hurry up, Jewel! We have to get to the Lagoon. I've got to guard my boys against pirates."

With a smug smile, Jewel made to fly after him, but Peter had come to a halt. Hovering, he stared over her shoulder. Jewel registered the look of wide-eyed surprise on his face, then whirled to follow his gaze.

Commodore Hook had emerged from the cavern. He stood on the ledge before the falls with the water foaming at his feet. Having walked through the downpour, his body dripped and shone with moisture.

Jewel soon understood why Peter's face, usually confident, even arrogant when observing his nemesis, now displayed confusion.

Hook stood poised against the background of the green, glassy falls. His hair hung thick against his head and chest, the curl dragged down but unconquered by the weight of the water. A man who typically dressed in formal attire, the commodore devoid of clothing cast an equally elegant impression, his tall frame fleshed and honed—except for his wound. The infamous hook was absent, leaving his stump and his scarring exposed. As he raised his arms to stretch, the wrist Peter had mutilated glided in the air, looking not so much part of a human body as it looked like a serpent. The ink of an intricate tattoo stained the forearm all around it, increasing the likeness to scales on a snake. Peter's face contorted as he observed. Although he himself had inflicted this wound, it repelled him. But it wasn't the wrist on which his gaze fastened, in the end.

Through his revulsion, Peter laughed aloud. Then he shouted, "Hook!"

Instantly, the man found him. Hook's eyes glittered as he stared, and his relaxed pose of a moment ago vanished in a battle-ready stance. Hook held no weapon, yet in the sheer shape of his naked body, he waxed fierce.

Peter's face looked baffled, his voice incredulous. "You…" He used the only words he could find to express his meaning. "You're pointing the wrong way." He gaped, then forced his laugh to ring out again. "You must have a terrible time in the privy!" Amused at his witticism, Peter clutched his middle to roll in the air, hooting with mirth.

Jewel drew closer to the boy, sending a look of apology toward her master. Her light flickered in uncertainty, and she was relieved to see Hook remain impassive.

He called back to Peter, "Your ignorance is charming, boy, if not your wit." Striding to the dry side of the falls, Hook snatched up his sword. "Shall I sharpen it for you?"

Jewel was tugging at Peter's hair now, willing him away. He brushed her off. "Now I see how deformed you are." He smirked. "Jill must like you better after dark."

"A lucky guess, Pan. I'll not bother to enlighten you. Begone now, and see to your boys before the mermaids turn them to men," Hook looked down toward his well-primed privates, then rolled his gaze upward again. "Like me." With an ironic smile, he waved Jewel off.

Peter stopped grinning and turned toward the west. He didn't demand to know how Hook knew the whereabouts of his boys. Jewel surmised that he was preoccupied with the grown-up doom of Nibs and Tootles again and sensing the threat to Chip, for without ceremony he called, "Come on, Jewel. You know how aggressive those mergirls can be." With no further banter with the enemy, Peter sped away.

Watched from the waterfall, Jewel tagged behind the blur of Peter's trail. Before slipping out of sight she turned, raised her fingers to her lips, and flung her hand toward her master. Hook bent his head in a graceful bow, saluting her with his sword. He replaced it by his clothing; Jewel indulged in one last eyeful and a long, satisfied sigh, and then she blazed after Peter, toward the Mermaids' Lagoon. Neither master nor servant was aware of the eyes that observed them.

Eyes black as coal, that kindled when the object of their search appeared at the cavern mouth. Merely a wavy haze behind the water at first, Red-Handed Jill stepped through the downpour into the commodore's arms, and a silent hunter came to attention behind his tree.

Like the Black Chief's, Jill's hair was drenched. It parted into long, sleek ropes. The dampness made it darker, the shade of buckskin. Lean Wolf had never touched hair that color except to seize and slay an enemy. Never had he reached out to stroke this hue in peaceable acts of attraction. And this woman's coloring differed in other ways. Even from his hiding place, the hawk eyes of the predator spotted the blood on her hand. The sign intrigued him. He wondered what it symbolized, but, knowing her band to be brutal, Lean Wolf held little doubt. That kind of paint meant the mystery of initiation. A double intrigue, signifying both birthing and murder. Clearly she was marked by the headman. A woman with a red hand matched a Black Chief with only one.

Also unlike the native women, this European wore a delicate undergarment. But Lean Wolf wondered why. The saturated clothing only served to enhance her nakedness, clinging to her curves in a manner more provocative than bare flesh. Her pink skin glowed through the garment. Lean Wolf saw the indentation of her waist, the cleft between her buttocks. Restless, he waited, watching her lover's single hand rove up and down her backside. His stomach sickened to see the tattooed stump of the other wrist roam her body too, in a parody of its partner's embraces. Lean Wolf's lips twisted.

What kind of female wouldn't flinch at that disfigurement? Clearly this pirate woman wasn't squeamish. Quite the opposite, she pressed against her lover, and when they drew apart her fingers pulled his hand— and the mutilation that was his wrist— to her lips. Even as he shuddered, Lean Wolf felt a respect for the woman from the sea. Her crimson hand spoke truth. She must indeed own the courage the stories attributed to her.

Lean Wolf speculated whether the other wild men had possessed this pretty piece. The thought reminded him of his runaway wife, outcast at the Clearing and delivering herself into their arms. As he imagined it, a shock of outrage shot through his body. Perhaps Red Fawn also accepted the damaged Black Chief as her lover. Had she felt his grotesque touch? Had she taken payment to endure him? Disgust entered Lean Wolf's soul, leaving a taste of rancor in his throat. Twisting the marriage bracelet that wrapped around his wrist, he mastered the rage. Surely, with a woman like this in his power, a woman of his own people with skin like the blush of the rising moon, the Black Chief had no need to dally with pass-around women. The gossip of the tribeswomen claimed that the Outcasts were no such thing, but to Lean Wolf's mind, they were little better. He swallowed the bitterness and returned his thoughts to the vision before him.

The couple had stepped back into the waterfall. It fell full upon them as they embraced, the water rolling off his head, off her upturned face. The lovers broke apart to smile up into it, drew the droplets into their mouths and kissed again, greedily. Then, turning Lean Wolf's direction, the woman clasped the man's arm and pulled him along the ledge where their clothing lay waiting by their weapons on a dry, quiet rock. Water coursed from her hair and her underskirt, her smiling face looked radiant. Her shift hugged her body like the skin of a grape— barely containing the lusciousness of her fruit. Lean Wolf found this fallacy of fabric maddening to watch. He wanted to rip that cover away, to expose the pulp and devour her goodness, from her rigid tips to her rounded breasts. He could taste her sweetness as he imagined it. Salivating, he licked his lips. Once more, and much more urgently, he hungered for this woman.

So strong was his compulsion for her that he turned away. Had White Bear not denied his suit, Lean Wolf would have run to Raven now, claimed her by betrothal and the strength of his arms to carry her to his trysting place. But as yet, without her consent and in the sight of the People, he held no rights to Raven. As he still hoped to wed her one day, he must make at least a show of respect toward Raven's provider. White Bear was an old friend. A foolish friend, to be so obstinate over a sister-in-law he didn't relish. Lean Wolf had turned his back on tradition, but he was grounded in it enough to long for the comforts of a wife, and to understand that, as a suitor, he must keep his distance. Nor would it be fitting at this point to couple with either of the willing women he'd already preyed upon, for to persuade the council to counter White Bear's protection, he must be discreet. Tales of dalliance would fly like larks to Raven's ears. And even if he got past the Men of the Clearing, waylaying Red Fawn was out of the question for the time being. The tribe would hear of that kind of connection, too. Silent Hunter could do nothing to satisfy this craving until he got the cause of it— the sea woman— alone.

Stealing back through the woods, Lean Wolf trotted toward his hidden lair. The caves were only an arrow's journey from the falls. He followed a path up an incline toward the honeycombed hills, each with its own hollow. Some of these caverns were unsuitable, some unsafe, occupied by bats or by beasts. Lean Wolf hiked over the gravel that prickled through the soles of his moccasins until he came to the rock that marked his own entrance. No other animals made this cavern their home. The boulder kept them out, and kept Lean Wolf's secrets in.

He hunkered down and, with the remarkable strength of his arms, pressed the boulder. He grunted, his biceps corded, and gradually it budged, then it rolled under the pressure of his muscles, crunching over the pebbles. Once he'd opened a slot large enough for his body to thread, he crawled in and flung himself down on a bed of furs. Here he settled under phosphorescent moss in the tomblike silence, inhaling its earthen smell. Envisioning the woman from the sea, he lay feeling the fiery touch of her blood-red hand, stoking his lust for her with visions of the future.

Snaring Red-Handed Jill would be a task, with a tantalizing reward. Lean Wolf's once handsome features smoothed as uncertainty left him. He was equal to the challenge. Like that picnic hamper from which she and her lover had indulged their appetites, her existence would be pillaged. Overturned.

Silent Hunter had scented his prey.

Deep in thought as he left Lily at the Clearing, Captain Cecco traveled a path he'd never followed before. It led him through the forest, a narrow track of earth just visible between long grasses. Made by the Indians, it was wide enough for only two feet to walk, as if those who trod upon it were reluctant to claim more than their share of forest floor. As natural to the wood as the underbrush, it snaked along according to the shifting landscape, and, like Cecco himself, always heading toward the sea.

Cecco whiffed the smell of salt when he approached, a vitalizing tang. The sound of breakers on the shore grew steadily more insistent. To the left and right other paths intersected from time to time, but stealthily, so that Cecco didn't detect these tracks until he came upon them. He knew the trails to the left would end at the beach of Neverbay. The tracks to the right he must avoid, as they led surely to the Indian encampment— and certain death.

Even armed as he was, Cecco preferred to meet with the beasts of the forest than with the natives. One crack from a pistol would send a pack of animals fleeing; used against a warrior, it would serve only to incense the People. Even if he encountered a single brave, even if he killed him, the tribe was sure to hear and hunt Cecco down. And to wield his dagger would bring no better. Skilled as Cecco was, the warriors of the tribe, too, lived by their knives. A fight between sailors might be child's play compared to battle with a brave.

Cecco remained cautious, weaving his way between the trees in the soft green glow, and treading as lightly as his boots allowed. He had pushed his bracelets tight upon his arms to still their music. No longer a gypsy boy, nor yet a brash young sailor, he felt responsibility weigh upon his shoulders. His men depended on him; his commodore relied upon him; his wife…Cecco shook his head. His wife had plenty of men to protect and adore her. She needed him less than anyone, yet it was she who would grieve, if he met with Fate. That thought alone caused him to guard himself. On no account would Cecco bring pain to Jill.

Pain was, however, the very thing Jill brought to her husband. Lily's words confirmed his faith in her affection. That first morning at anchor, Jill had injured him— with deliberate intent. She had drawn Cecco close only to shove him away, wounded, in an attempt to satisfy Hook as to her loyalty. Yet Cecco recognized that she had acted out of love for him. Her rejection was his shield. Death, after all, did not lie only in the hands of the natives.

How brave she was, how valiant, to dare to wear his ring. How Cecco longed to capture that ring and kiss it, to clasp her red hand, too, and bestow upon it more gold than she could hold. Until that time, Cecco must endure the cuts she dealt him, the watching from afar, the tension in his gut, the jealousy that ate him alive…

An incline brought him up short. Looking around, Cecco concluded that the sea lay just over the ridge. A cluster of spruce trees stood sentinel, as if guarding the forest from a tumble over the cliff. He spied a track on either side of the trees, indicating that his trail converged with that path, in view of the ocean. The steady shush of the shore sounded beyond those trees. Silently, Cecco approached. Between blue-green arms of spruce lay a shelf of rock, a cliff top, white, wide and bare. Seeing no one, he slid between the firs, their needles scratching his neck and arms and shedding a spicy scent of resin.

Before him lay the ocean. The myriad peaks of its ripples glistened in the sunshine. No beach graced the shore here, but rather a rocky wall against which the waves lapped far below him. At an angle to the left, the waters of Neverbay bounced against the coast. The *Roger* stood out, magnificent, and *Red Lady* behind her, dancing in the gentle swell. Protected by the arms of the bay, the ships rode at anchor as if embraced by the Island.

Cecco could make out the lookouts in the maintops, more vigilant here than in any other place, for near the Island peril might move in the air, and swiftly. In the distance, the longboat floated beside Cecco's ship. Yulunga's party of Frenchmen scaled *Red Lady*'s side, and Yulunga himself leaned over the gangway handing up his woman. Immediately behind Mrs. Hanover, Cecco recognized Pierre-Jean's blond streak of pigtail. Pierre-Jean helped her place her feet on the steps, poised to react if she slipped. Cecco snorted. No danger there. Mrs. Hanover had her situation well in hand— Yulunga before her, Pierre-Jean behind, so that should she require a new champion, she had only to turn to him.

Cecco understood that Mrs. Hanover modeled herself after Jill, whom she had served until Hook's resurrection. But except for a resemblance in dress and demeanor, Cecco brooked no comparison. Jill was by far a superior woman. The lady was independent, Mrs. Hanover clinging. Jill was loving, Mrs. Hanover grasping, and where Jill schemed for the greater good of the company, Mrs. Hanover's intrigues had at heart her own advancement. The girl had been known to act unselfishly only once— when faced with the decision to preserve her child or abandon its fate to her father. Yet none could blame her for her defects. Doctor Hanover had molded her every day of her life, through neglect on the one hand and unseemly attention on the other. At the outset of the *Roger*'s last voyage, that man and his daughter had presented a peril no lookout, however vigilant, could perceive.

Jill's husband wondered again as he remembered Yulunga's generous gesture. Seeing Cecco's dejection persist after the loss of his wife, Yulunga offered the comforts of his own mistress. Jealousy was unknown to Yulunga, but how he could imagine Mrs. Hanover might satisfy Cecco's needs was a mystery. It was she who caused the *Roger*'s tangles in the first place. Cecco longed for Jill from the moment he met her, but Mrs. Hanover's plotting had compounded his misery; had he never known the joy of union with Jill, he would not have plunged into purgatory at its passing. Still, while declining Yulunga's offer, Cecco appreciated his mate's sense of fellowship. He only wished that another man, of higher rank, might prove so openhanded.

A lone alder leaned over the rock on the left, its roots wedged into the cliff top like toes in sand. Under its shade grew a mossy patch, a sort of cot rimmed by the roots themselves. Here Cecco lay down, his back supported by the tree, the massive root between him and the cliff. A light, warm breeze buffed his face. To feel it better, he drew off his headdress and kerchief, setting them aside. He closed his eyes and listened to the whisper of alder leaves, and the song of the sea. Now his thoughts, not his feet, traversed a foreign path, a course they'd never traveled before.

Cecco knew Lily to be a wisewoman. He respected no one so well in matters of the heart. Still, her words had astounded him, feeding both his hope and his fear.

If he loves her, he will grant to her the deepest wish of her heart.

But the nature of Hook's feeling for Jill was unclear to her husband. Did Hook cherish her, or did he simply possess her? Cecco's heart had at first leapt up at Lily's wisdom. Whether or not the commodore loved his Jill was immaterial. If he did not, surely Jill would do as Mrs. Hanover prepared to do— fall back on another champion. And if Hook did love her, he must grant to Jill her wish.

The question was, then, did Jill wish for Cecco? With his heart in his throat, Cecco hoped the answer favored him. If so, in time, an opportunity would arise. Jill would follow her feeling. All the men knew Hook took pride in the fact that he never forced a woman. And Hook esteemed Jill, certainly. Surely his dignity would lead him to release her when she asked. If she asked.

But Lily's words had not stopped there. They led Cecco deeper into unknown territory, the murky depths of his soul.

Can your love do the same?

Should Jill's deepest desire be, after all, for Commodore Hook, could Cecco grant what he himself so hopefully expected Hook to give? Her release? This path was, indeed, a painful one, and one whose steps he dreaded. With an acid bile beneath his tongue, Cecco brooded.

With the sea's splendor beneath him and the bounty of the forest on his right, Cecco saw nothing. He remained at the brink of his own personal precipice, teetering, and only looked up when he heard a sound— a very human sound— of running footsteps. Snatching a pistol from his belt, he sprang to his feet.

From the forest path, a native woman burst through the trees. With a look of terror on her face, she ran as if a demon pursued her. Beyond that, Cecco had time to glimpse only her beaded tunic, her bare feet and legs as they pumped toward him along the cliff. He lurched forward to seize her round the waist and roll to the mossy ground, covering her body with his own. Then he twisted toward the wood to aim his gun in his outstretched arm.

As the hammer clicked, the woman gasped, struggling in his grasp. Her panting surged but, although she fought like a feral thing, she made no cry. Cecco held her down with his body weight, his pistol poised, waiting to kill whatever emerged from the forest.

Urgently he asked, "What is after you?"

She only fought more fiercely. Cecco gripped her tighter in his one available arm, but he didn't dare take his eyes from the forest. He couldn't tell what pursued her. Her panicked breaths masked any sound from the wood. His shoulder hurt where she shoved at him. From her desperation, he deduced that she was just as frightened of him as of her hunter.

"Lie still, woman. I will kill it."

At last she understood. Her body went limp beneath him. Now Cecco listened, but his ears detected nothing. Still, he kept his eyes on the path and his pistol cocked.

"Is it beast or man?"

"Neither."

Cecco shifted to look at her, then quickly returned his gaze to the forest. "I hear nothing."

"There is nothing to hear."

"Something chased you toward me."

"My own cowardice. You can put your weapon down."

"So your brave can shoot his arrow through my heart?" He shook his head. "No."

The strained quality of her silence brought his head around again. He gazed into her eyes, black eyes, as black as his sorrow. After a moment, she looked down.

"I have no brave."

Something in her voice echoed home to him. His heart was pulled, as if she spoke his very own feeling. Carefully, he disengaged the hammer of his gun. "I believe I understand." He laid the pistol down, drew the second from his belt and set it next to the first, out of the woman's reach. She began to strive again, trying to push her way out from under him. Rolling to the side, he took both her wrists in his hands, pulling her to sit up. "You need not fight with me. I will do you no mischief."

"You are one of the boots. A wild man."

Cecco grunted in amusement. "May be."

"I have heard what your kind do to mine. I have seen it."

"I have seen yours do the same." Relaxing his grip, he softened his voice. "Now, tell me why you run."

"I will not."

Smiling now, Cecco studied her. In her defiance, she reminded him of Jill. Her black eyes and high cheekbones were set in a face no longer in the bloom of youth, but handsome in maturity. Her dress was skillfully made, with fringe and modest beadwork, belted at the waist. Her manner was marked with an air of sadness. But none of these features was the first Cecco noticed.

"Lonely woman, for whom do you mourn?"

The look of rebellion fell from her face. She stared at him, and at last she asked, "How do you guess?"

Cecco shrugged. "You have cut off your hair."

"But…you know of this?"

"Certainly. It is an ancient sign of mourning. For my tribe, too. I watched my grandmamma do this, on the day my grandpapa died."

Her eyes attended him; she was listening. Feeling he had struck a chord, Cecco ventured, "Did you cut your hair as she did, to honor a fallen husband?"

With the slightest of movements, she nodded. A wince of pain flickered over her face.

"Ah. I grieve for you." After he said this, Cecco realized that she no longer struggled in his hold. He released her, but she didn't seem to notice. She simply sat looking at him. When she spoke, it wasn't quite a question.

"You will not harm me."

"I swear it. But I *will* dust you off." Keeping himself between the woman and his pistols, Cecco brushed the leaves and soil from her dress. "I apologize for throwing you down. I believed you were in danger."

Raven knelt there on the mossy cliff, astounded. She was astonished not only by the stranger's attack and his sudden switch to courtesy, but by herself as well. Why did she allow this barbarian to touch her? Why did she not run?

Staring at him, she absorbed his alien appearance. He was big and broad and solid, not tall, but compact; he had nearly crushed her as he threw himself upon her. His teeth were white against his olive skin, his body decorated with shining gold at every point— earrings that bobbed as he moved, bright armbands, a heavy, layered necklace, and bracelets that made metallic music, clear high notes she rarely heard except in tribal rites. His hair was tied back with leather and it was dark brown, not black. It was a most unusual shade, like hickory nuts. A shade that, she now realized, she was tempted to touch, as if its color might affect its feel. Yet his eyes, a matching deep, soft brown, were as familiar to her as many of her tribe's.

His dress seemed outlandish to Raven, a mixture of what was proper and what was not— a leather vest that gave his arms and shoulders freedom to move and allowed his comely chest to be displayed, yet he wore noisy jewelry, bright trousers that shone against the woodlands, and the confining boots by which the pirates came by their Indian designation. And those boots, Raven knew, would prevent him from catching her when she ran.

But just as she permitted his hands to tidy her tunic, Raven allowed the anguish in his eyes to persuade her to delay. Pirate though he was, the man had understood— instantly— the circumstance that had driven her into his arms. She, too, recognized a similar spirit; this man mourned. Still, she remained cautious. She kept her voice low and, once she had examined him, dropped her gaze.

"You also grieve," she said.

"Aye. It is no secret. Perhaps I should follow tribal custom, as you do, and cut off my hair to honor my lost one."

"No!" Already, she had raised her eyes again. She almost raised her hand to catch his hair.

"It would be shame to shear such beauty."

"And this was said of you, was it not?"

He spoke openly, with frankness, and Raven's modesty made her look away. She remembered Lean Wolf's compliments, just as blatant. But this so-called wild man didn't leer. His eyes showed respect. They seemed to know her, and she felt it pleasant, even nostalgic, to be seen for who she was. Always, White Bear's eyes looked upon her with irritation. They never understood, never yet encompassed her the way this man's did, with such intensity, with esteem. His eyes seemed to view her almost like Ash's eyes had done. But that recollection was painful, and she redirected her thoughts. "I was not aware that your people come from tribes."

"I am a gypsy. We are unlike the others."

"From another island?"

"From another tradition. One similar to yours, I think. My grand-mamma was a wisewoman. You put me in mind of her."

"I am not wise. If I were, I would not speak to you." And Raven was reminded of her precarious position. In an attempt to mend her indiscretion, she summoned the Shadow Woman. She let her face go blank, and, starting up, took two swift steps toward the forest, back the way she had come. Surely to return to White Bear's tepee, to endure the ordeal that awaited her, was preferable to finding herself outcast.

Over his shoulder, Cecco called, "Her hair was black as a raven's wing, like yours."

Raven halted. He stood up to face her. She turned to fix him with her eyes, puzzling as if she didn't quite believe in him. "I, too, am the Raven." But why did she reclaim her identity? Why not submit, once and for all, to the role of the Shadow Woman? Some living chord vibrated within her, as if the stranger plucked it with his unfamiliar speech. It roused her, made her all too aware of the flesh she tried to deny.

"Raven?" Cecco took a step toward her. "Is this your name?"

Suppressing the vibration in her heart, she backed away. "I must not be found with you."

"Found by whom?"

"It does not matter. It is taboo." She turned to run.

"Raven."

His accent was strange to her, and yet appealing. At his odd artic-ulation, she stopped, somehow anchored to the earth by the speaking of her name.

He asked, "Do you not wish to know how I am called?"

"I know how you are called." She faced him, and her dark eyes pierced his soul, like the scavenging of a raven's beak. Now she was certain of him. "You are Another Island." She took a step backward. "And a forbidden one."

"I like the name. It suits better than you may guess." But Cecco scuttled his smile. "Your intuition reminds me of someone I know."

"The someone you would reclaim." A flash of kinship lit her eyes.

"Yes. A storyteller."

"I do not tell stories. I do not believe in them, any longer."

"I do not know if I should believe, either."

Her voice fell kindly, drawing Cecco's heart again. "For whom do *you* mourn?"

Cecco said simply, "My wife. My family."

"The more I hear you, the more I wonder…"

"Wonder what, lonely woman?"

"Why the elders forbid it. Surely, it is well to know one's enemy."

"In spite of your denial, you *are* a wisewoman." He hesitated, then he realized with a sinking of his spirit that when she left, he would stand alone on this barren cliff top once more. Suddenly, he rebelled against his solitude. He asked her, "will you be wise enough to come here again?"

She turned her face from him, but not her eyes. "I cannot say."

"I will come tomorrow. When the sun sails high overhead, as now." He stood waiting, hopeful of he knew not what. She closed her eyes and raised her face, as if communing with the sunshine that penetrated her flesh. On impulse, Cecco reached both hands out to her.

"Raven."

She opened her eyes and her gaze settled on his hands. He had already taken greater liberty than this touch that he offered. He had clasped her close, pressed his body upon hers. He had ministered to her needs, even guessed her heart. Now her own hands surprised them both, fitting into his, full of warmth. In that moment of contact, Raven and Cecco stood on the cliff above the ocean, two islands from two different seas. Between them passed a look of recognition, deep, and startling.

She gave a gasp, and then Raven ran. And as she ran— back to White Bear's authority— like Cecco, she measured the outside of her courage, traveling in her mind a path she'd never followed before.

Cecco gazed after her, until she blended like a deer into the forest. Turning to the bay again, he looked upon the *Roger*. He flexed his fingers, tempted to peer into his palm, to read the fortune written there beneath the wedding band. But he squeezed his hand shut instead.

"Another Island. And a forbidden one." He heaved a great sigh. "My lovely wife. May you sail your way to it." And then he recalled Lily's voice, comforting.

Magic dwells here...of a nature that can occur no other place.

"Well, Jill. This Raven, I feel, is an omen. But if she has come merely to pick my lonesome bones, she is welcome to them." Cecco smiled, sadly, replaced his pistols, collected his headdress, and followed the narrow path to the left. Toward Neverbay, and desolation.

Boy! Go back to your hole in the ground! The pirate's shout rang in David's head as he dashed along the muddy stream bank toward his hideaway. He knew of nowhere else to flee. But did he dare to enter there? If the man's words were to be trusted, he was aware of the hole in which David had believed himself safe. It was so very secluded, so dank and disreputable a place, surely David's first hunch was correct. No one had entered there in a long time, nor would anyone desire to enter it, even if it were known or found. By virtue of its nature, it must be protected. A fouler place David could hardly imagine.

Yet that spot was where he sped when the captain routed him from his spying place. David turned tail, never stopping until he reached the stagnant end of the stream. Here he paused only long enough to decide, then he shinned up a tree to hide high among its rattling leaves. He waited, watching to see if the pirate would follow, if he would seek David in his den. The dry brown leaves scratched his cheeks, bristly bark cut into his skin, but David didn't stir. Nor did the willow branches clinging to the rock wall at the end of the path below, concealing his grotto.

The cavern was another of the incomprehensible elements of this Island. A certain mysteriousness hung like a fog wherever David wandered. Rules of nature, immutable in the parts of the world David had sailed, were blatantly broken here. Waters that fell from snowy mountaintops were warm. Dressed like savages, white men lived with Indian women— in an English house. Tiny beings whizzed through the air sometimes, much too large to be fireflies and much too mobile to be pegged for certain as fairies. Animals that in the wider world would eschew each other's company here banded together to hunt and howl in packs. Most disturbing of all, David had seen with his own eyes a crew of boys, looking as dirty and unkempt as the 'fairies' were fey, jumping into the atmosphere and hanging there, for all the world as if they could fly.

After the experiences he'd endured— the pirates, the privateers, the storm and the shipwreck, the days lost at sea in a sinking, shrinking boat— David didn't trust his senses any longer. In the same way he denied the magic of this place, he delayed the conclusion that the one hospitable spot on the Island was too disgusting to shelter him. His need for sanctuary outweighed the evidence of his corrupted intellect. Surely the decay underfoot and the stench in his nose were only his faculties overreacting to all he had suffered?

Three days ago he heard salutes fired from a fleet of ships as they sailed in, but he hadn't yet traveled to the bay to view them. A sailor himself, David knew several days must pass before these vessels made sail again. He hoped to secure passage on one of them, but he'd been too hungry to hike that far, opting first to put the stolen bow and arrows to use. And in any event, he'd have to tidy himself up before approaching ship's officers to beg favor. His hair and his mud-caked shreds of clothing reeked. The pool by his dwelling place was ideal for catfish; as a wash pond it proved less than satisfactory. David could imagine the revulsion a layer of green scum would fetch him, even from a slack ship.

The arrival of the vessels cheered him, until that first night at the bonfire. At that point, an unspeakable dread descended upon David. He stared at the men making merry, and understood that these people were pirates. And worse, David thought he recognized them. Yet as he blinked the dimness of despair from his eyes and his heart's banging calmed, only one man seemed familiar. The burly redheaded seaman. But this man didn't dress like the *Roger's* sailor had done. Instead of the striped shirt that pirate had worn, this man sported a fine white blouse with ruffles, and his beard was trimmed close and neat, like those of David's uncle and the other officers of the *Unity*. He wore spectacles, but David couldn't remember whether that pirate did; a protective officer had shoved David under a cannon during the boarding and, later, his vision had been taken up entirely with— well, David hadn't paid attention to the *men* after that.

The foreigners speaking French that night certainly reminded David of the privateer crew that boarded after the pirates, but he reasoned that blue jackets such as his assailants had worn were common among sailors, French and English alike. He assured himself that the pirates who attacked the *Unity* were worlds away. Surely the *Roger* would anchor in one of the rowdy, more populated ports such ruffians enjoyed. David set his mind at ease on that score. He had determined that, after all, no matter what the sailors chose, this place was far too much of a wilderness for the jaded tastes of— of Red-Handed Jill.

David didn't trust the quirkiness of this place. Naming the woman might cause her to appear at his elbow, magically, like one of those birdlike beings he thought of as fairies. He hesitated to conjure her, even in his thoughts. He despised her. His emotion was all the more vehement because he despised himself for falling stupidly, embarrassingly in love with her, at the first moment of impact. He was just a boy then, prone to the traps such vixens laid for their victims. But in the following weeks he'd learned. *Beauty is as beauty does.* The truth lay in the homilies his widowed mother quoted four years ago as she kissed him goodbye and sent him off to earn his keep on his very first voyage. *All that glitters is not gold.* But along with David's immature, ungovernable body member, his hatred rose, threatening to choke him. He'd been a ninny. He hated himself. He hated the passion he'd leaked at the sensual rites of those revelers that night.

He hated Jill.

But he had believed himself to be rid of her. He'd thought with the arrival of those ships that his bad luck had blown, like mist off the mountains. Pirates or no, he could stow away, or even work his way back and jump ship in some civilized port. Then, this morning, just as David had begun to believe he could escape this Island, his confidence was shattered.

Captain Cecco cinched it. David could not pretend that that ostentatious Italian was anyone other than who he was. Those big, braceleted arms had seized David on the *Unity*. He had questioned David, forced him to take him to his uncle's quarters. David had waited on him, served wine. He had witnessed the wedding, seen the bride and groom's signatures mark the logbook. How could he ever forget the man Red-Handed Jill had chosen for her mate? The man she'd kissed so provocatively, in the same breath with which she'd flirted with a cabin boy. David had felt only envy burning then. Now the circle of Fate was closing in on him, a crushing darkness, blacker than the inside of his cavern. Ill luck returned with a vengeance. Those pirates were *here!* David hadn't broken free of them. Nor had he a prayer of escaping this Island.

Exhausted by his turmoil, worn out with watching, David slunk down the tree. Searching the path by the stream one last time, he allowed his shoulders to slump. Clearly, Captain Cecco was not in pursuit. No doubt he judged a cabin boy too negligible an adversary with which to bother.

David brushed aside the crippled willow branches that hid the mouth of his lair. Then he shrugged off his overlarge jacket and tossed it inside. Holding his nose, he got down on his dirty belly to slither under the wall of rock. Chilled air greeted him, raising gooseflesh. He slipped his jacket back on but didn't wipe the mud off his feet; the layers kept out the cold. Creeping on the frigid muck of the floor, he felt his way toward a mat to collapse upon it. Its woven branches were smooth, and warmer than the ground. It kept the blankets from seeping with dank. Whoever made this bed must have had a similar use for it. David wondered if that person, too, had sought this grotto as a refuge. Had he reclined on this mat and, closing his eyes against the blackness, lain beset by visions of a golden-haired harpy?

It seemed he was safe for the moment. David thought of the bundle secreted in a fissure at the back of the cavern. Captain Cecco might send his best men to search, but he'd never find David's most precious possession. Wrapped in oilcloth, it would withstand the dampness of the cave as long as necessary. At first, David had set the packet on the shelf at the cave's right end, next to the bowl of teeth and the lion's paw, and by the shell full of scorched-smelling powder. But then on one of his ventures he'd found the hand mirror. It had an ivory handle, carved in scrollwork. An odd object to lie abandoned— unbroken— on an untamed shore.

David discovered it at the far western end of the Island in a sunny lagoon. Sunny, but eerie. He'd glimpsed the lagoon from a cliff top and, finding no entrance on land, he'd had to swim in order to enter it. Once within its secret confines, he splashed along through its rock pools with a feeling of self-consciousness, as if he was watched. But he'd seen nothing but rocks and seaweed, the rippling clumps of which held an uncanny likeness to human hair.

Curious to view his dwelling, on returning to it he had propped the mirror against a rock outside the opening to direct sunshine into the cave. From the doorway he'd seen moss and mud and confirmed his theory that the crunching underfoot came from bones. Of these he avoided closer scrutiny. He'd also found the secret fissure. Only an intense beam of sun could reveal the cleft and, since that time, David had hidden even the mirror for fear some unknown person might employ it and discover his bundle. Now, in spite of the carrion, he felt more secure.

The mirror's light had also revealed a painting of mud above the shelf. A crude drawing of a clock. David decided that someone long ago, attempting to live here, had tried to make the place more homely. But what purpose the collection of teeth served was beyond his imagination, and left him with a queasy feeling, an even queasier sensation than the rotten odor had given him, which, unbelievably, David learned to tolerate. When he got back to civilization— here tears scalded David's eyes— when he was delivered from this hellhole, David would place his oilcloth packet in the proper hands. His duty to his uncle would be done, and, maybe, with this final act of obligation, the curse of the *Unity* would lift from his shoulders. Rolling his eyes toward the spot where he knew the mud clock loomed in the darkness, David pretended to hear it ticking away the minutes he was doomed to spend here.

But with the feeling of safety came the leisure to wonder. His own luck had washed out, but Captain Cecco's should be in full spate. Why was the pirate alone this morning? Or rather, not alone, but keeping company with the females at the clearing? He had been fondling that woman, just as his men had made love to her at night. Like the impostor clock, David had lost track of time. Yet he knew Jill and Cecco's marriage to be only recent. How did it happen that even a buccaneer would neglect such a wife to play the rake with another? David's experience in such matters was so limited he could attribute the act only to the immorality ingrained in pirate life. No doubt Captain Cecco sought women just as blatantly as Red-Handed Jill trifled with a cabin boy.

And, in his heart, David was glad. He hoped Jill was hurting. Maybe Cecco had taken David's shamrock from Jill; maybe her luck was sinking, too.

In the timeless dusk, David counted the few possessions Jill and her company had left to him. Mostly they were goods he'd stolen since the shipwreck, and nothing even pirates would pilfer. A bow and arrows, two blankets, moccasins that fell off his feet, a relatively clean blue jacket, an empty rum bottle, deerskin leggings he'd blushed to find he couldn't wear without a loincloth. Catfish bones. He wiggled his fingers and felt the weight of his one great find.

Mined from his hole in the ground, it was a magnificent gold and ruby ring.

David smirked. Let Red-Handed Jill feast her eyes upon *that*.

But the smirk soon slid from his face. He swung his head to dart a look toward the smudge of daylight at the cave mouth, covered by willow boughs. Distinctly, David heard footsteps approach.

A single pair of boots.

Predatory Creatures

The boots halted just outside the grotto. David held his breath, his eyes wild in the darkness. He didn't move for fear of a noise that might prompt an investigation. The dim aura at the entrance became dimmer, and David's heart pounded, waiting for a hand to sweep aside the willow boughs. While the filter of light shifted in flickers, he heard a shuffle of foliage. With raised hackles, David endured this torment for some minutes, then all became still. After a pause, the boots could be heard again— retreating.

Nearly faint with relief, David let out his breath, hearing his echo hiss. He had been certain Captain Cecco had come with torches to roust him out. He'd heard of other boys being pressed into service, by naval captains and by pirates. David felt no love for this cavern, nor for this evil Island, but he far preferred to remain here in its bewildering wilderness than to serve that bully and his bewitching wife again. Dizzy from fright and foul air, David dragged himself to the opening.

He poked his nose out for a deep and reviving inhalation. Pushing the willow aside, he was surprised to find the air full of a dusky, sweet aroma, the scent of flowers. As his eyes adjusted to the light, he observed, arrayed on either side of the entrance to his cavern, armloads of roses— red, pink, yellow, even blue and purple— all of them big as his fist, and perfect. David had spied a glade toward the end of the Island growing an abundance of such blooms. The fragrance there had been pleasing, like the promenade of a palace, only three times as strong. He recalled that the scent of roses in that garden had mingled with apple blossom, and, sure enough, the same blossom mixed with these roses, arranged with artistry next to the opening, as if laid in tribute at the mouth of a tomb.

David shuddered. He didn't like to think of his shelter as a tomb. He always tried to ignore the skeletons, passing them off in his mind as animal remains, hunted and discarded by the cavern's earlier inhabitant. But now, with growing trepidation, David understood that his dwelling might not be so innocent, nor was it unknown on the Island.

He calmed himself with soothing thoughts. No doubt this place was a mystery to the natives, too, a place spawning superstition, and held in reverence. Perhaps the bowl of teeth was meant as an offering, just as these flowers must be today. But David remained uneasy. He had invented a fine theory…but it didn't explain the boots.

The boy saw no one about. Thinking to splash some water on his face, he slid from the opening, taking care not to dirty his stolen coat. Under the shade of a willow on one side and the dead-looking tree in which he had hidden on the other, he knelt at the bank of the stagnant pool. He shoved up his sleeves and, dipping his hands, sent a patch of scum whirling away, then scooped some tepid water for a rinse. He kept his lips pressed tight, knowing from experience the swampy taste of this pool. The ruby ring on his finger glowed in the softened sunlight, a pleasure to see.

David became aware as he relaxed that the birds, no doubt as startled as he by the boots, had begun to call again. Mourning doves with their lugubrious coos. He knew a nest of them to be wedged in the lower branches of the tree above him. Waiting for the ripples to still, David focused on the tree's reflection in the pond. Gnarly brown leaves, branches like broken bones. Then, with his skin still dripping, he gasped.

Reflected in the water below was a face. It stretched and distorted as the water undulated, but it didn't disappear. Looking hurriedly up, David spied an Indian hanging in a branch above, watching, a bow slung over his shoulder and a knife at his knee. In a flash of time David wondered two things— why did the doves sing with this intruder so near? and how came a native on this Island to be fair? Then he bolted.

But as soon as he spun, another fair face confronted David. The fairest he'd ever seen, more lovely now in this woodland setting than it had appeared upon the *Unity*. With her hair damp and curling, her body sheathed in topaz, the deadly beauty of Red-Handed Jill stood smiling at David, regal, fierce, and commanding. The knife and pistol at her sash completed the effect. David staggered back, jumping as a rose thorn pierced his heel. He stumbled into another native who blocked the entrance to the cavern, this one with hair like ebony, and a tomahawk at his thigh. The Indian shoved him forward to stand facing Jill.

With her clear voice, so well remembered, she caressed David. But, as if stroked by a tiger's paw, he felt the graze of her hidden claws.

"David. How pleasant to see you again. And how surprising. Almost...magical."

He caught his breath and, too late, plunged his hand in his pocket.

Far too late. Jill purred, "Welcome to our Island. I see that you have made yourself at home." Still smiling, she shifted her sapphire eyes to consider his pocket. "But you are an honest boy, are you not? I happen to know to whom that ring belongs."

David backed from her, shaking his head.

"Come. We will return it together." Half turning, she indicated with her blood-red hand a man standing in the glossy greenery farther down the path. The glitter of a silver sickle made David's stomach twist, and he knew, at once, whose boots had stalked him. And why Captain Cecco walked alone.

Mrs. Hanover enjoyed her sewing. The occasional prick of a needle didn't bother her. She was accustomed to pain of many kinds, willing to tolerate it. Her pins and needles as she worked made no noise in her fabric, but she listened to the shirring of her scissors. Because she used her voice so infrequently, the sense of sound brought her special pleasure.

The fabric between the scissors' teeth felt nice, too— a rich material, cool and crisp. It wasn't topaz, like Red-Handed Jill's, but it was close.

Canary yellow, perhaps. Like one of those birds she saw flitting through the woods this morning. The color would complement Mrs. Hanover's brown hair. She had twisted her hair up and pinned it this afternoon, just as she'd helped Jill to do on her father's wedding day. She liked the nakedness of her neck.

Mr. Yulunga had allowed her to take this linen from a chest in the hold. He, too, appreciated the feel of it, and he bought it for her from ship's company. Under Mrs. Hanover's hands, the scissors, needles, and threads would soon produce a garment to rival the lady's. Raising her head a notch, Mrs. Hanover envisioned herself flaunting it.

If only Mr. Yulunga would grant her a necklace to go with it. He was wealthy enough to spare some jewelry for his mistress. Gold, like their earrings, would look well with this yellow. And bangles. Mrs. Hanover bit her generous lips as she thought of the bright, wide armband and the many bracelets Captain Cecco had tempted Jill to remove from his body, whenever they were intimate. Maybe Mrs. Hanover would win that same opportunity. Such presents wouldn't come cheap; as used to ill-treatment as Mrs. Hanover was, she recognized that the captain, in his high state of emotion, would subject his next carnal partner to a volatile encounter. She had eavesdropped to overhear Yulunga offer her to him. Even as she listened for the captain's answer, quaking at the idea of placing herself in that angry man's arms, she had hoped to gain by it.

A greedy look sharpened Mrs. Hanover's features, a look that receded as she remembered the jewelry in which Doctor Hanover had adorned her for similar purposes. Her father had bejeweled her in private, of course, because at his insistence she had purloined the treasure from Hook's own sea chest. She delivered it into his hands, and his hands had enhanced her. Rings, earrings, chokers of emeralds, ropes of pearls he strung across her belly— when it was flat.

Looking down at her figure now, Mrs. Hanover ceased to smile. He'd left a seed pearl there, in her womb. Only time would reveal if it was flawed. By now Mrs. Hanover had studied her father's medical texts enough to understand. Her child— his child— had little chance of escaping its heritage. In a few months' time, the Women of the Clearing would deliver her of the new life inside. Mrs. Hanover was accustomed to discomfort. She would take charge of her child, then she would do what she had to do. Resolutely, she took up the scissors.

Mr. Yulunga's footsteps made no sound, but when she heard him open the door, Mrs. Hanover looked up. Squeezing through the frame, he stooped under the ceiling, shoved the door closed, then dropped lazily to his haunches beside her. He looked around to determine whether she'd tidied the place. She had done so, but he eyed the yellow fabric spread over the rug.

Until recently, this cabin bunked the two skinny mates of the ship's former captain, the French privateer DéDé LeCorbeau. The room boasted four windows, two to starboard and two to stern, and it was cheerful when the maroon paisley curtains hung open. Captain LeCorbeau was a man of very different tastes than his successor, and Mrs. Hanover had seized upon his discarded furnishings. She'd spread an Oriental carpet on the floor. A petite but ornate chest of drawers held court against the bulkhead. Over it Yulunga had hung a beveled mirror for his mistress. She kept her sewing box and her books on a shelf over the claw-footed table and two satin-padded chairs. Yulunga's weather-beaten sea chest, locked, reposed by the folded paisley comforter at the foot of the bunk. A matching bolster supported the pillows. Yulunga had the carpenter tear out the two mates' cots and build a bigger bed under the portholes against the starboard side, but nothing could be done to raise the ceiling. Although cramped for a man of his size, these quarters were Yulunga's first private lodgings since his abduction from Africa, and he enjoyed them to the fullest. His tastes were simple, his woman small. Her ambition, he found, was boundless, yet he managed thus far to confine it to his quarters.

He could see it would be a round-the-clock job. "So your new dress is not a dress after all."

Stealing a glance at him, Mrs. Hanover shook her head.

"Turkish trousers and a tunic." Yulunga folded his arms. "Just like the lady's."

She shrugged, but laid one hand on her unadorned throat.

"Like the lady's, but without her jewels. Maybe I can find you some trinkets to sew onto it."

The smile with which she rewarded him made him laugh, a deep, liquid laugh that bounced the beads of his necklace and turned Mrs. Hanover's bones to jelly. She dropped her scissors and flung herself upon him.

He caught her. "No, no. You haven't studied your books yet today." He gathered her hands and pulled them from his neck. "And you will tell me, with words, how you found the Clearing."

Mrs. Hanover frowned. Her body was more expressive than her voice, but always, Yulunga insisted upon words. They came out huskily, "Good women."

"Good women. And they will care for you when your time comes. Unless you'd rather remain aboard, sailing. It's your choice. Mr. Smee can deliver you."

As her gray eyes showed panic, Mrs. Hanover pulled away.

"Use words."

"Mr. Smee hates me!"

"Most of the *Roger*'s company hate you. *Red Lady*'s men don't yet know you well enough." His big hands squeezed her wrists. "Don't give them the chance."

Mrs. Hanover looked down. She thrived on this rough attention. It made her feel alive. Resisting just enough, she caused him to increase the strength of his hold.

Laughing again, Yulunga humored her, yanking her close. "I know all your games, little girl. But I tell you now, so you understand. Ship's discipline demands it. No one touches you but me. Or the captain." He waited for a reaction. Receiving none, he was certain. "You've been eavesdropping again. All the better. Now you know what the captain thinks of you. You know what to expect when he takes me up on my offer."

Her gaze flew to meet his leer.

"Yes, he refused you. But I know Captain Cecco. He's a gypsy. Hot-tempered, hot-blooded. A time will come when he needs to work off that temper. No. *Say* what you think."

"You won't let him hurt me."

"I let him do what he needs. He needs Red-Handed Jill. You make yourself look like her....You handle the consequences." Yulunga snatched the pins from Mrs. Hanover's hair so that her thick brown locks tumbled down below her shoulders. "It looked nice on you. It looks nicer on *Signora* Cecco. Find your own way."

"Cruel!"

"Good. A useful word. See what you get when you speak without prompting?" And now that she was angry at him, now that he had wounded her, Yulunga forced his kisses upon her. She fought him, turning her head and thrusting away. She ended on her back on her fabric, her skirt flung above her waist and the cold steel of the scissors pressing her buttocks. Naked now, Yulunga shoved his breeches away. Lowering the mass of his body down, he made her feel the heat of his sable skin. He pressed it against her, rubbed her thighs with his own, and, easily, as she had known he would do, he pushed his way within her. She had been craving him this last hour past. And he knew it.

All the same, he took the scissors from her reach and tossed them to clatter against the door. He ignored the needles. They didn't bother him.

The color drained from David's face. He took one long look at Hook. Then he turned on his heel.

Only one path lay open to him. He dashed to the pool and, seizing a willow branch, vaulted over the water. Clinging to the bough until the very last moment, he hurtled across, splashing only ankle deep on the far side. He felt his heart stop as his feet sank in the mud. With agonizing slowness, he dragged them up, one by one, to launch himself into the forest. Terrified that the barbarous hook might snatch him, he didn't look back.

But Hook did not pursue him; Jill flung herself on his trail. Her feet spurned the ground. She flew across the pool to follow David into the woods, keeping low. If he glanced back at all, he would believe her to be running. Hook always cautioned her to maintain the advantage of surprise. No need to waste her secrets on this boy.

But in the weeks since washing ashore, David had been a victim of this danger-filled Island. He was familiar with this ground, and quick upon it. He dodged low branches, skipped fallen limbs. The underbrush grew thicker as he left the stream behind. To move silently was hopeless, but invisibility was possible. He turned sharply under cover of a thick tree trunk, hightailing it on a slant from his original course, toward a less lethal territory.

Jill reached the tree and straightened to stand, casting her gaze about. She caught a glimpse of French blue and took off again, speeding after him.

David wondered that he heard no pursuit. No boots, no thumping feet or moccasins. At the next dodge— an enormous moss-covered rock— he stopped to pant and check behind him. His eyes grew round as he spied Jill running toward him, her arms flung out at her sides and her long topaz tunic flying. He caught the gleam of her pistol, and he set off again, angling to the left to take up his original direction. He hoped he'd lose her before he covered enough ground to reach the end of this wood. He had no wish to blunder into the Indian camp. Between pirate and native captors, David would be hard-pressed to choose. Burrs pricked at his ankles. His lungs gasped for air as he pelted through the forest.

Still on the wing, Jill swooped around the rock. Listening, she heard nothing but the silence of the birds where David had passed; scanning, she detected no trail. She peered up through the treetops. Lightly hung there, pointing the way. David was headed toward the Indian village. Signaling to Lightly to keep following the boy, Jill flew.

David clutched at the stitch in his side, wondering if he dared stop to rest. A few more paces and he knew he had no choice. His gut ached with a stabbing pain. Weeks of scant food and unhealthful air had weakened him. He threw himself down on the ground and rolled to stretch alongside a fallen tree. Torn from the soil, its roots propped up its trunk. Squeezing beneath it, David listened again and heard only the buzzing beetles on its surface. A shadow passed overhead— some bird of prey, no doubt— and David looked up too late to see it. When he returned his gaze to the earth, he grimaced.

Red-Handed Jill stood there.

David's breath came in spasms, but except for the light in her jewel-blue eyes, Jill showed little sign of exertion. The gems sewn to the bosom of her tunic winked in the spangles of sunlight. She reached her scarlet hand out to him.

"Come now, David. You trusted me, once upon a time."

"Once upon a time," he spat, "I was a fool."

"All children are foolish. But they learn." Her bare feet stepped closer. David caught the glow of gemstones on her ankle, below the tight cuff of her trouser. "Have you learned, David?"

He waited a moment, gathering one last gulp of air. Under his hand he felt something hard, a nut of some sort. He clasped it, then twisted his hands together, pretending to yank off the rubies. Hiding his ring hand, he pitched the nut past Jill. He watched her tense, turn, and trace it, heard it drop behind her in a crunch of leaves. Nimble now, he rolled under the log and doubled back. He let loose a howl— he couldn't help himself— and thrust deeper into the woods.

For once David felt some relief. If Jill meant to catch him, she must choose task over treasure. Nor had he heard any sound of men on his trail. Jill seemed to seek him alone. That meant he couldn't move too far in this direction; it would bring him back where he started— at the boots of Captain Hook. Aboard the *Unity*, David had listened with alarm to the legends of the pirate king. Beyond many another horror, he dreaded that monstrous man. He felt stupid he hadn't thought of it before— naturally a pirate like Red-Handed Jill would join the blackest of buccaneers. But he saw no sign of Hook now. With luck, David could pull ahead of Jill and find a likely tree to scale. Even if she abandoned the phantom rubies, she couldn't hunt him forever.

As he ran, he kept his hands clenched to secure the ring. David's arms pumped. He became aware of a flash of his blue sleeves with every movement. It gave him an idea. He searched for just the right spot and, flinging a fast look behind him, he halted on the crest of a ravine. A row of prickly bushes lined the top. David knelt by one and, with frantic haste, broke branches near its base. The skin of his hands got rubbed raw, but the overlarge jacket slid easily from his shoulders. He stuffed the coat through the opening and discarded it on the other side of the bush, then backed and ran to the left, down the hill in a direction he knew would lead to the river. Jill might believe he'd crawled through the hedge and rolled down the opposite side of the slope.

David didn't see the darker Indian dive from a branch of a nearby oak to snatch up the jacket.

Swift as the girl of her childhood, Jill caught up to Rowan and drifted upright. She smiled when Rowan pointed to the broken bush, holding up the coat. With his eyes, he indicated the route toward the river. Jill adjusted her garments and streaked off after David. Tossing the nut was a clever stunt; the jacket showed more desperation. Together, she and Lightly had followed the 'ring's' progress and quickly unearthed it, amused. The Neverland never disappointed Jill. It was treating her to another adventure. She found the chase invigorating; the fragrance of the Island filled her lungs. Her heart was at home here, in the thrill of a hunt. She felt even happier now, more complete, than in the days of her girlhood. Laughing, she let the wind tousle her hair. If any boy needed a mother, surely, that boy was David. The Wendy within her hadn't vanished.

Nor had the boy. The earth sloped downward here. In time the trees thinned, and smaller plants pelted Jill's skirt and trousers. A trampled trail led her onward. At last she spied the tatters of David's white shirt ahead, as he plunged in the river. A cloud of heron rose flapping from the shallows. Jill crossed a narrow Indian track at the foothill of the mountain and lit upon a rock. The green waters rushed by at her feet, bubbling over boulders. Wary of the natives, Jill glanced about before concentrating on David again.

He was swimming, his streaming sleeves flashing as he fought the current, which was strong here at the head of a rapid. Halfway across, he tossed the wet from his eyes and treaded water to look back. In his surprise he gulped a mouthful of river. He coughed it out, then filled his lungs and bobbed beneath the surface.

Jill stood on her rock, shaking her head. As if on an afternoon jaunt with all the time in the world, she wiggled her toes in the water. It felt cooler than the waterfall, and just as refreshing.

She couldn't hear the gasp as David sucked air again, but she saw him surface some distance upstream. He dragged himself to the shore, lay panting for a moment, then, walking backward, staggered among the rushes. Unsure of Jill's intentions, he kept moving but spared his energies. Jill allowed him time to recover his breath. She marked his direction. Then she pulled her pistol.

David froze. Abruptly, he turned to bound into the woods. With his dripping rags plastered to his skin, he headed through the thin fringe of the forest. He had to find a hiding place, and soon. The sea lay only a short way off, more foothills straight ahead. Before long no avenue of escape would lie open. He was exhausted. His ruse at the bushes hadn't shaken Jill off his trail, but surely the river would delay her, if not stop her altogether. He must find just the right tree and scamper up for shelter. Not a large tree— she might look for him there. A slender one, just hardy enough to hold him, but with leaves enough for cover. David's feet stung from the rocks and sticks he'd trodden. The parts of his body not numbed by cold ached instead. He'd have to climb immediately, before he lost control of his limbs. And he'd wedge himself securely among the branches, in case he fainted.

Finding a young maple, David seized a bough. With dogged determination, he hauled himself upward. He scraped his knees and knuckles, but at last he jammed himself in the crotch of two flimsy branches, ten feet above the earth. He clung there. Fatigue caused his muscles to twitch, but he clamped on, gritted his teeth, and waited.

David had, however, forgotten something. As his breathing slowed, his ears awakened. Within minutes he heard someone else breathing, too, someone walking in the grasses. A sniffing sound followed, and in that moment, with his stomach flipping, David remembered.

He paled as the notion came to consciousness. The river water made his clothing sodden. The damp also strengthened the stench. He understood that, no matter where he hid, the reek of his cloister clung to him. Shielded from sight, still he perched unprotected, for, screened by the foliage that hid him, whoever smelled him edged closer. Was it Captain Hook with his claw poised to carve? The two Indians aiming arrows? Or more natives, perhaps, bearing tomahawks, from the village downriver. Then he forgot other enemies, as into the grass beneath him stepped a set of substantial feet.

David's hunter stood revealed. As his blood pounded in his painful head, David clutched his branches and sat perfectly still. He dared not descend; he couldn't climb higher. Already his sagging perch threatened to snap. He held no weapon to defend himself. The chase was at an end.

Jill hadn't caught him. But if she kept searching, she would find him. Or, at least, she'd find his remains.

A thought struck David. He gaped down at the tigress staring up at him with her unforgiving eyes, her striped sides shrinking and expanding with every pant, and David knew he belonged in that cairn of a cavern after all, with flowers marking the mouth of the tomb where this afternoon he lay among bone and sinew— the remnants of his fellows, the other helpless victims.

Victims of a predator. This lethal Island itself.

Idolatry

The tigress spared Jill the effort of searching for David. Jill couldn't see the boy, but the animal stood at the base of the maple, her large, fierce head turned up to gaze at him. The black tip of her tail curled, and its rigidity told Jill she hadn't much time. The beast was about to spring.

In silence, Jill crept closer. A strip of David's white shirt showed between the maple leaves, within striking range of the tiger's claws. The wind from the west served Jill; she caught the odor of the boy's clothing and the frowzy taint of the cat, but her own scent flew downwind. At twenty paces, she halted. She braced her legs apart, raised her pistol, and aimed it in both hands. The ring on David's finger had been swallowed once, when the crocodile devoured Hook's hand. She swore she'd not allow *this* creature to ingest it, too.

With what was left of his life, David was praying. His eyes were wide open. He wanted to pray to his god, but all his mind could conceive was what he saw— the bestial face, the green eyes nailing him to his cross. He prayed to his pagan predator instead, begging her to be merciful, to kill him quickly. He felt the sweat pouring from his skin, the warmth of liquid at his crotch where his fear took fluid form. In the humiliation of defeat, David begged his huntress, "Don't. Don't hurt me." If he could have fallen to his knees, he would have done so, to encourage the hot breath to smother his neck, the blades of teeth to strike swiftly. Anything to assuage that ferocity, to submit, to offer Fate her due with a minimum of pain.

"Please…please." He moved his lips in supplication; his voice broke, as it had broken the last time he'd met with a killer.

He'd been braver on his ship that day, the day the *Roger* attacked. Then he was an extension of his uncle's authority, a member of ship's company among officers, facing pirates. Those enemies were men. This threat was Nature herself. David knew he could offer no battle; he had already lost to Nature. He'd been devoured by her, his soul eaten up, that first instant he set eyes on Red-Handed Jill.

The woman he loved.

No: the goddess.

David leaned outward, relaxed his grip on the tree. Serenity evened his features. Welcoming the end now, he gazed into the eyes of hell— the damnation his blasphemy deserved— and, gently, he fell forward.

Peace flew to pieces at the blast of a gun. The jaws of death, open to tear David's sacrifice, ejected a shriek instead. In a violent twist, the black and yellow beast spun to the side. A spurt of blood from her eye striped David's face.

The boy hit the ground with his shoulder, blinking to clear the gore away. The blended smells of blood, grass, and gunpowder confused him. Was he in hell, or in heaven after all? No, not heaven, for pain shot through his arm, and worse, a vibration beat through the earth, Mother Earth, as the tiger's pads pounded— away from him. And David prayed again, horror stitching up the patchwork of his tattered soul, to the only god who might listen, "No…no! Take me! Take *me!*"

His idol, his Jill, was dropping her pistol, seizing her knife. It sparkled in the sun; quite clearly, David saw the colored jewels glowing below her fist. She bared her teeth, she lowered her jaw. Her eyes flashed before they narrowed, and she waited for the tiger's lethal bound.

The animal sprang. Her hiss of a growl terrified David. Her long, sleek back mounted up, her hind feet left the ground. The tiger rose upon Jill, her leap reached its zenith, and Jill vanished beneath the mighty frame.

Closing his eyes at the very last moment, David listened: a sickening slice, the sound of rending flesh. His imagination saw Jill's beauty torn to shreds, her long bright hair matted and mauled— and all because of his cowardice. Gagging on vomit, he awaited her scream.

"Jill!" The shout came hurtling down, as if from the treetops. A male voice, strong, confident, but tinged with care. "Use your bows, men— shoot it!" The hum as arrows stung the air, and a ghastly roar of pain. David opened his eyes.

Three men surrounded the slaughter. The black-haired captain stood there in his boots, his sword drawn but useless. The two Indians cocked fresh arrows, their spent darts sagging from the tiger's side. Jill stretched out behind the animal, rolling on the grass, still clutching her knife.

Blood covered her arm and coated her dagger. David guessed that instead of falling backward, she had dived beneath the tiger as she attacked. The cat, not yet tamed, lumbered around to face her. Lying on the ground, David could see a long, gory gash along her underside, from her forelegs to her groin. Already the slippery insides were spilling out. The men around Jill watched, their eyes wide, unwilling to prod the beast to violence, unable to shoot for fear of hitting Jill.

The animal stumbled, Jill jumped to her feet, and before the tiger could gather to charge, Jill leapt to her back— a flying leap. She grasped the beast's neck in the crook of her arm and dug her heels in her sides. Locking the head in her elbow, Jill hoisted it high. She grimaced and, swift as thought, slashed her blade across the tiger's throat. Holding the pose, she waited as the lifeblood poured to the forest floor. The tiger snarled, her whiskers jerked as she wrinkled her snout, and David watched, disbelieving, until, at last, the beast convulsed and collapsed, with Jill still hugging her back. For a moment Jill lay at rest upon her wild, exotic couch. Her left arm, encircling the throat, was pinned beneath the carcass.

Hook rushed to her side and threw down his sword. He knelt in the grass and heaved the head up by the scruff. Jill withdrew, still clutching the dagger. Fresh red blood painted her arm. It splotched her face and spotted her tunic. She looked ferocious, more savage than her tigress, and her eyes as she beheld Captain Hook held a passion David couldn't identify. Hook returned it with a mixture of pride, adoration, and outrage. David had never fathomed such scope in a man so vile. He was amazed as, with tenderness, the pirate opened Jill's fingers for her and removed the knife, lifting her to her feet.

Jill lingered, looking down, triumphant, at her kill. When she turned her gaze upon David, he was on his knees, worshipping. Swaying a little, she walked toward him. Much as he wished to adore her, he dropped his eyes to stare at her bloody feet. She stood before him like a Titan, and took his chin into her hand. She raised his grateful head, and, to David, her wicked eyes reflected the divine.

"Now," she commanded, her cheeks flushed beneath the blood-stains. "Give me my due."

She stretched out her scarlet hand. Unhesitating, this time, in the face of Fate, David pulled the bauble from his finger. As he had gifted her with his shamrock that day upon the *Unity*, today he presented her with the ring. The red of its rubies looked garish next to the ruby of the lifeblood on her palm. She turned to Hook, who had never left her side. Taking his hand, she slid the ring on, to join the other jewels among his fingers. She didn't flinch at the color she smeared on him, nor did Hook. He merely watched her, tensed as if to catch her if she faltered.

Jill didn't falter yet. With the grace of an angel, she stooped down to David where he knelt, so that from the bounty of bosom she revealed, beyond the rusty smell of blood, he whiffed her perfume— her foreign, familiar perfume, that together with her nearness stimulated his loins. Placing a firm crimson hand on his cheek, she kissed him full upon the lips.

David tasted the tang of life, Jill's life, his own life hard-won for him. He accepted the transfer of vigor, reverenced the throbbing in his body, and when the warmth of her lips deserted him, his cheek was damp where she'd stained it. Red-Handed Jill had touched him, and he would never be untouched again.

Loath to return to his loneliness, to the privation and the treachery of this Island, David prayed to his goddess, "Take me with you."

She didn't answer. She spoke to her Indians. "Bind my captive and bring him to the *Roger*." Weaving on her feet now, she turned to Hook, and although her agitation grew, her voice lost power with every syllable. "Hook…My first kill." Her gaze rolled toward the carcass, to the scarlet pool in which it lay. "You know the story. You know…what I'll do." She uttered the words hoarsely at the end, gutturally, as if discarding her humanity.

"I know the legend, my love. I will attend you." With his arms around her, Hook guided her toward the site of her victory, waiting only long enough to direct the natives, "To the *Roger*— by water. You understand."

The light-skinned one said, "We understand, Commodore, and we'll deal with the carcass, too. But what about Jill?"

"You may leave us alone. And alert Mr. Smee."

"Yes, Sir. We'll take a canoe, as you say."

The braves slung their bows on their backs and seized David by the arms. He dragged his feet, reluctant to leave his protectress. Supporting him, the pair marched him down the river. David balked, divining that their destination was the Indian village, then he surrendered in fatigue as the blond one bound his wrists behind him. He'd have to have faith in her. He looked back over his shoulder to see Hook and Jill on their knees by the tigress. Hook, too, was watching Jill, with intensity.

Jill's eyes closed, her head tilted as if in trance, and her hands worked in the grasses by the kill, circling, conjuring. She might be casting some spell, some arcane charm. In the lengthening distance, her voice rose in long, unintelligible shouts. Twenty paces behind her, a bough of David's maple tree bent, crippled forever by a boy's initiation. Next to Jill, the beast lay vanquished.

Once more, David felt the power of enchantment. David's spirit rose, drawn back by her chanting, to her rites, to Jill, and somehow his body mixed in the mystery, too. His cheek burned hot where she had touched him.

He only hoped she would touch him again. Because, by choice or by guile, David was learning about the magic.

The magic was strong, Hook observed. Stronger this time than the last, and rightly so. Then she had merely drawn blood from her enemy. Hook himself had performed the killing, with her consent, when he had 'murdered' the girl Wendy— not in cold blood, but hot with passion and purpose, and Red-Handed Jill had sprung to life to take her place. A rite of passage transpired, death and rebirth.

Now Hook knelt with Jill, watching as, crazed with her victory, she plunged again into blood-rage. This conquest— her *first* kill— affected her strangely. She had understood the process, ordained it, long ago when she spoke the story; Hook understood it of old. This ritual united hunted with hunter, beast and human, breaking the bonds of bodies and melding their spirits. Voice was granted to the speechless, humanity drained from the victor. The song of Jill's kill echoed through the wood, the paint of its blood swirled around her fingers, creeping down her forearms as she raised her hands in triumph to the skies.

Hook caught her excitement, felt a wave of desire for her surging inside. He lived for victory, and, in this moment, Jill was victory incarnate. Her hair spilled on her shoulders, her color heightened. She was wild and beautiful, like a goddess of the forest. No chaste Diana's, Jill's lips were tainted with the taste of experience, her breath as she expelled it thick with the spirit of the animal, making the grasses quiver where it stalked. Earthly and unearthly, Jill had never appeared more seductive.

Hook held himself back, guarding her, respecting her rite yet anticipating the moment when he, too, could partake of it, when he'd indulge his senses in the pleasures of her flesh. He searched her face, past the tangle of her hair, and saw the emerald of the animal's eyes beyond the sapphire of her own, and in that moment he loved her with a fierceness he had never felt before. More than ever, she was his counterpart— the woman who had brought him into being, who conceived and then healed his maiming, the woman who tore antagonists without qualm. Destroyer and creator, no other mortal could command his heart. She, alone, was Jill.

Yet of her many mysteries, none surrounded the reasons men sought to possess her. Hook realized as he won her from Pan that rivalry must accompany his claim on her. It was a circumstance he'd come to accept, if not to relish. He remembered the look on the new boy's face, the pup she called David. Hook had watched as, fearful at first, the youth yielded to Jill's powers. Another set of antlers for her mantel, albeit budding ones. Surely Jill would dismiss the lad, once she'd reaped his worth in service. But who could blame the boy?

Hook himself stood transfixed as she butchered a tigress five times her size, not in desperation, not to save her own life, but to preserve this foolish David's. In one stroke, she'd conquered beast and boy. Sooner or later, those who sought to hold her found that Jill herself was the one who took possession.

And the men she had married— Hook discounted them, too. They were serpents in his paradise. They were nothing more than tempters, arrogant fools believing they could domesticate her, two who walked knowingly into her snare, there to languish in suffering. True marriage, Hook reflected, took place in the woods in sacraments like this one, or upon the font of the sea, in rites of passage, blood ritual, magical transference such as only he, who inhabited her soul, could share with her. Hook and Jill were joined with unbreakable bonds, yet those bonds were as flexible as the willow boughs that trailed in the river nearby. He and Jill were as united as a man and a woman could be.

But now he saw her weakening. Her shouts died, her shoulders drooped, and, still kneeling with her, Hook supported her. While her body lost tension, she raised her bloody hands as if in wonder. The green of her pupils flickered out and, dark blue once more, her eyes searched for his. But as he hooked her hair to draw it from her face, she became distracted, focusing on his claw instead. It was a weapon, and in her madness it became the object that she craved. Within his arm, her body tensed again.

The night Jill came to life, the night she'd stained her hand, he hadn't worn the hook; in primal lust, she'd lunged for his knife, easily held above her reach. Now, though, in her blood-drunk delirium, she seized his wooden wrist, unknowing or uncaring of the danger. This moment, Hook knew, was the most lethal time, as the huntress forgot what she'd achieved and shifted her obsession. Incapable of reason, she struggled to command the hook, drawing its shining, sharpened point too near to her flesh.

He had promised to attend her; his duty lay in keeping her safe from herself. Nevertheless, he couldn't remove his hook. To do so required that he shed or shred his shirt, impossible while she clung to his wrist. Nor would it be wise to denude himself of his most potent defense. Hidden hazards lurked within the Neverland.

As quickly as his single hand allowed, he unbuckled his belt. Straining to keep control, he held the hook upright and out of contact with her body, his one arm braced against her two. But, as she fastened on this mania, Jill's strength rebounded as if she were her tigress, risen from the slaughter and reawakened to life. Hook could swear he heard the animal purring, deep in her throat. The sound of her power stirred him, even as he fought to subdue her.

He flung the belt over her wrists, he tried and failed to thread its end through the buckle. They tussled, and the effort to protect her from the claw caused his fingers to bungle. He tried again, and again, until he managed to pass the belt through the hasp. Then he yanked its loop tight, cinching her hands together. He regretted that he must burn her with the leather's binding as, with a twist of his wrist and a pull on the belt, he drew his arm from Jill's grasp. Exhaling in relief, he found footing to stand. He wound the belt short around his knuckles, then he hauled her up with him, and lowered the hook from her greedy view. Stimulated the more by this struggle for dominance, Jill's lover fought his own compulsion, too, a burgeoning impatience to take her. But the time was not right. A kiss was all he might risk right now, and he bent to her, burning like the leather on her flesh, to take her mouth within his own.

The verdure surrounding them felt sultry as a jungle, and the air rang with cicada song. The huntress' eyelids were heavy with wanting. As he came to her, she opened her lips to snatch at his, to devour him in a kiss both aggressive and agreeable. Close by, the river raged into froth, as unsettled as Jill's disposition. They mustn't linger here. Possessed by gods, they were only mortals, and danger walked in these woods. Hook resisted the drive to lay her down and love her, forced himself to pull away from her instead. He soothed her, "Soon, my love. Soon." With only one hand, and that one obliged to hold her, he left their weapons where they lay near the carcass, and led her on her tether toward the water.

One more ritual to perform, and then he could fly her to safety.

He paused and lifted his head, listening; was that noise the throb of Indian drums, or just the pounding of the water? Jill took advantage of his hesitation to lunge for the hook again, and he lurched away and tightened the belt. With the help of his teeth, he tied it in a knot below the buckle so that she could not escape him if he slackened his grip. He moved more quickly now, dragging her to the river, hoping to the Powers that her magic might last, if only a little while longer.

"Grandmother! Come quickly!" The black-lashed girl ran to her grandmother, to lay her hands in her lap. "Rowan and Lightly have brought us a captive! Oh, Grandmother, Rowan looks so brave."

"Cease this chatter, girl. Take me to them." Stiffly, the Old One accepted her staff from her granddaughter and rose on the arm of the girl. Before setting foot from her blanket, she took care to straighten. Tilting her face to the sun, she let its rays fortify her frailness with heat.

The drowsy camp of midday came awake. Dogs barked and skipped, the children howled, rushing with their relatives toward the river, and the drums pounded their welcome. Grouping around the council members, the warriors cleared a path among the People, for the elders. The Old One stood in the center with her son, her granddaughter's father, behind her, and three council members on each side. Tallest of all, White Bear took his place among them, the claws of his necklace pale against his skin. A stone's throw from the river, they waited with dignity as the People whooped and cheered the approach of the braves.

Three figures forded the river, waist high here at the end of the rapids. As was his habit, Rowan displayed no emotion as he and Lightly slogged across the rush of water, supporting the boy whose hands were bound behind him. David stumbled over a rock and plunged face forward into the stream. His captors hauled him up again as he sputtered and shook water from his face. The children laughed to see it, mimicking his mishap.

Lightly's fairer features showed hints of concern. At this time of afternoon, it should have been a simple matter to slip ashore and glide away in silence in a canoe, and the young men had hoped to do so, avoiding notice from the tribe. Looking at the assemblage on shore,

Lightly identified the reason for it. The Old One's granddaughter stood on tiptoe, her hands at her heart, viewing Rowan with her eyes a-sparkle. She must have been watching for Rowan's return, as she had taken to doing of late. Her father, too, stood among the People, smiling in approval. Lightly of the Air's heart burdened down. As he'd suspected, this girl presented the first step on the path to exile.

Lightly slid his gaze toward Rowan. Rowan nodded, but displayed no other sign of awareness. He avoided the eyes of the girl. Ayasha must not be encouraged, and this business of prisoners was man's domain. Had not even Lightly's mother so indicated when she called upon her son to remove her captive? Like the Old One, the pirate queen was a leader, understanding her role among men. Not even Rowan's admiration for her kill shifted him from this certainty. And since the day his mother and sister were cast out from the tribe, Rowan claimed his place within the wider world of men.

The young ones hooted, jeering at the boy as the two braves dragged him up the bank. Several children snatched sticks from the shore, to dash up and strike him, counting coup to etch in tally marks, and boast of their bravery. David cringed at each sting, his fear on his face, but, feeling no slackening of his captors' grips, he trusted in his mistress' judgment. He belonged now to Red-Handed Jill; she would not suffer him to linger in this adversity.

The Old One murmured to the other elders, then raised her staff for silence. As the drums ceased, she declared, "Our brother White Bear is the tongue of the council. He will speak for us."

White Bear stepped forward. Before he spoke, his iron gray eyes inspected David.

David shrank back from the sight of this warrior. The man called White Bear epitomized everything he dreaded in these natives. He looked impressive, lean and hard, with scars to show his valor in battle. His mostly shaven head revealed a fierce face, sharpened further by an absence of sympathy. He spoke in a deep, harsh voice.

"Rowan Life-Giver; Lightly of the Air. Why do you bring us this boy, who is marked by the red-handed woman of the Black Chief?"

David's face flushed, and the spot where Jill's hand had rested scorched his cheek. Apparently his dousing in the river hadn't washed away the blood. Equally clear was the fact that his mistress' reputation was established upon this Island. Everywhere he went, he heard talk of her— from the gang of boys, from the pirates and their women, and now from the Indians. Pride ballooned in his chest as he considered her fame, and his posture unbent.

At White Bear's question, Rowan turned to Lightly, allowing him to answer.

"We bring respect to the council, White Bear, but we do not bring this boy to the tribe. As you have seen by his mark, he was captured by she who raised me from a child, Red-Handed Jill. We are on our way to deliver him to her keeping."

"He is one of the Golden Boy's band?"

"No. He is a thief."

David jerked in surprise. He hadn't expected to be described with this epithet.

White Bear became wary. "He has stolen from the Black Chief?"

"Your perception shines, White Bear. Yes, he has stolen from the Black Chief. And..." Lightly hesitated, "also from the Outcasts."

"The tribe no longer thinks of the Outcasts."

"The tribe does not think of them, but my blood brother Rowan Life-Giver and I, Lightly of the Air, think of our relatives."

"You have gone among them, then."

"Family ties are strong. They pull us together."

"The council will consider this." White Bear's scrutiny ranged over David again. "And from whom did the thief steal the blood that paints his face?"

"My mother, the valiant huntress Jill Red-Hand, slew a tiger to save him from its jaws." The people gathered around exclaimed in interest. "The thief owes her life-service. I will find it an honor to tell the People of my mother's deeds, when the sun slumbers and the moon is listening."

White Bear paused to consider. He did not seek concurrence from his fellow council members; the Old One had voiced their trust in him. "Take him, then. We observe your duty to your mother."

Lightly relaxed. He hadn't realized how tightly he'd been holding his stomach.

"And did your valiant mother hunt among her warriors?"

Lightly had relaxed too soon. He only just stopped himself from glancing at Rowan. "Yes, White Bear. Although the most courageous of women, she is cautious to protect herself. She hunted in the company of the Black Chief himself."

Disapproval met Lightly's words. One of the elders grunted.

At the mention of the pirate, David watched the children staring with round, dark eyes. He understood their fright, and it prodded the terror that coiled within him. Soon he might face this 'Black Chief' again.

White Bear crossed his arms. "Go, and rid your shoulders of obligation. The Council of Elders will consider, in your absence, your forbidden fellowship with pirates from the sea."

The Old One struck her staff upon the ground, and when its thumping ceased, the drums broke forth again. As the children circled the two braves and their prisoner, Ayasha's father strode smiling toward them, too. "Rowan." He reached out to clasp Rowan's arm. "Glory flies with you."

Rowan accepted Panther's greeting, but his face remained sober. "Perhaps the council do not agree."

"Do not concern yourself. My mother understands the homage owed by a son. She never lets me forget it!" And, still grinning, Panther clasped Lightly's arm next. "All the People will hear your words tonight, Lightly of the Air, and you and Rowan will sit in places of honor. And I invite you both, tomorrow, to feast with my family in my tepee."

Lightly observed Ayasha. The situation was just as he had feared. The girl was smiling at Rowan, her face turned coyly away, and her black lashes blinking.

Lightly read the signs. Before long, Rowan would be offered a bride. Lightly felt a pain in his chest, a stab of homesickness for this camp and its inhabitants. He'd lived among his adopted people for only a season. Against all reason, perhaps, he had hoped to grow old here.

The river was chilly; chilly enough, Hook hoped, to shock Jill from her trance. Grateful for his tall boots, he pushed against the rush of the water and pulled on Jill's tether. She entered the river with reluctance, but kept her eyes focused on his hook, still with that animal gleam that warned Hook not to trust her. As her tunic and trousers became sodden, he tried to support her with his right arm, but she turned to watch the claw, and he understood that this effort would be useless. Her desire to possess his weapon had not abated. He kept his damaged arm behind his back after that, and, wading backward into the water, he drew her by the belt, into the deeper flow at the middle of the stream.

He could hear nothing but the roar of the water, this place being the head of a length of rapids that ended, as Hook was too aware, at a site even he loathed to dare. Sticks and leaves hurried by them, bobbing and turning on their journey downstream. Each step was more difficult than the last, and Hook watched Jill with concern as she battled her garments, the current, and her madness. Finding footing between the slippery rocks, he stopped and pulled her up to his chest. Her face remained rosy with emotion, spattered with blood, but her eyes flickered with reason. Slowly, Hook turned her away from him, then wrapped his arm around her waist. This time, she didn't seem to notice the hook; she leaned against his chest.

He bent his knees to bring her lower, submerging her up to her neck. Her skirts bloomed upon the surface of the water, her hair fanned like lily stems, straining to float downstream. The ring she had collected for him radiated a ruby tone under water, and its sticky residue dissolved. Murmuring in her ear, he said, "Feel the water's touch, Jill. The river rinses this bloodlust away." She shivered. She closed her eyes. Hook raised her up and immersed her, three times. Strands of blood swirled from her hands and her arms, from the fabric of her tunic, to dissipate into ruddy clouds as it eddied toward the sea. The water running from her face turned her eyelashes to stars. "There, my love...there now." If she heard she gave no sign; she leaned limp against his strength. The river foamed and bubbled around them. From it, both Hook and Jill drew energy.

As Hook had hoped, Jill's ferocity washed away. Her shivering calmed and her respiration came deep and natural. With relief in his heart, Hook held her close, his own tension fading. He scanned the surroundings once more, alert for enemies, but he spied only the base of the mountain on one side. On the other were the yellow of the tiger's pelt and the glints of the weapons lying near it. Taking command of the situation, he unfettered his emotions now, leaning his chin against Jill's hair, pressing kisses upon her neck. She responded, tilting her head as she always did when a lover caressed this sensitive spot. Hook felt his effect upon her, and both his mind and his body mirrored her feeling. A tingling; a tempting throb below the belly.

Freed of anxiety, Hook allowed her to draw him to her Eden; she arched her back and tugged at the belt that imprisoned her. He unwound it from his knuckles and let it go. With hands still bound by the buckle, Jill grasped his fingers and pulled them toward her abdomen. As her skirt floated before her, she reached beneath it, then nudged his hand within her clothing, to trace her flesh. Soon she pushed him lower, into her center, and trembled with the pleasure of his touch. With her fingers covering his, the lovers stroked the softness at the entry to her womb, warm and warmer against the chill of the water. Her hands remained tied; the belt that bound them slithered in the current, like a serpent in the stream.

A twitch tickled his lip. Hook sensed that Jill had not yet returned from the wilds, but he reveled in her untamed sensuality. He and Jill lived so constantly and so closely intertwined that, in spite of the river, in spite of the risk, he joined in her sensation. He knew from the first occurrence of her bloodlust that, at this moment, she burned for him; his ardor partnered hers. He had held himself back before, to preserve her. Now he indulged in her. He allowed her to guide his fingers, penetrating her womanhood. Holding her firm against his chest, he provided what she craved, while, irresistibly, his own arousal mounted. Her respiration grew harsh again, the purring of the tigress just audible until, finally, in a burst of rapture, she threw back her head in a visceral cry. Hook himself went giddy with it.

And then, just past the pinnacle of sensation, she turned on him. Hook caught the tiger's green in her eye before she lunged for his claw. She flung her weight against him, toppling him backward into the foaming river. She lost her footing and fell upon him. As the wintry water closed above their heads, Hook thrust her from him and yanked his right arm hard, free from her grasp.

He knew at once that he had erred. No matter the bloody consequences; he should have let her hold the hook, for as it slipped from her fingers, Jill slipped from his reach. The force of the river caught her up. He glimpsed the flutter of cloth as her body, so much lighter than his own, swept downstream. He swiped at her clothing, trying to snag it with his claw, but already she'd drifted too far to catch.

Hook flailed against the river. He bobbed to the surface. For long, precious moments, his boots stumbled over the riverbed, searching for purchase. Upon finding it, he stood, gasping for air. He shook the dripping hair from his eyes.

Immediately, he spotted the topaz of her gown. Jill lay face downward, half submerged by the weight of her garments, writhing, tumbling away among the rocks and the crests and the rage of the water— with her hands locked together. The belt, the cold, the river itself— the tools Hook had used to save his love— now conspired to kill her.

He launched himself downstream, stroking with all his being to reach her.

Solitary Practitioners

Hook was unaccustomed to fear. For many a year, he hadn't felt it on his own behalf. As Jill faced her tigress, he'd felt anxiety, yet his confidence in her abilities left only an edge— a sharp, raw vulnerability— for his courage to conquer. The dread he felt now rose up to slap him like the chilly surface of the water. His fear stemmed not from man nor animal, but from world-wise experience, from his knowledge of the Neverland. Hook struck out on his course downstream, fighting the Island's perils, and afraid as only a strong man can be afraid, that the dearest part of himself, the woman for whom he pledged his protection, might perish in spite of it.

He cursed the boots that slowed his progress. As he glimpsed Jill struggling to raise her head above the surface, his blood ran as cold as the liquid streaming over his skin. When she gasped for air, her sodden hair covered her face. Her body rolled one way and then the other as the current rushed her downstream. Rocks lay treacherous in her path, ready to dash her skull. Tied together, her hands were useless. The hurry of the current swept her on, and Hook cringed as her shoulder slammed into a half sunken log. But ahead of him lay another, and as he shoved himself away from it, it hurled a dash of water at his face. He shut his eyes and lost sight of her. Water gushed noisily into his ears. The muddy taste of the river flooded his mouth, and he spat it out.

His heart nearly stopped when, upon opening his eyes again, Jill was nowhere in sight. Kicking and slipping against the streambed, he twisted his ankle with a twinge, but he won a glimpse of her yellow garment.

She had rolled onto her back, and her bound hands were locked as if in prayer. Perhaps now she could breathe, but Hook was certain her new position left her little command of her direction. She passed another cluster of rocks, narrowly, and Hook felt the hairs rise up on his skin.

For a man of action, this helplessness was torture. No enemy could wreak the havoc on Hook that losing Jill would cause. Spurred to new effort, Hook increased his exertions, stroking his arms, pumping his legs, blinking his eyes open to track that bit of linen, the bold, blazing streak of topaz that signified everything he loved about Jill.

It seemed to Hook that he'd drawn closer. Her arms formed an angle, weaving to balance her motions, but still she could not guide her course. If she called to him, the roar of the river drowned her voice. Nearer now, Hook cast about as he swam, searching for a branch he might reach out to halt her progress. Among the flotsam around him, he found no useful item, only more hazards ahead, obstacles to injure her. A fallen tree…a derelict raft wedged drunkenly between boulders…and a pile of stones, directly in her path.

With no time to think, Hook submerged to speed forward. He didn't waste time looking up again until he was sure she must be near. When he did raise his head, the disaster was about to happen. Jill tumbled headlong toward the rocks. Too exhausted to float, she sank in the stream. Then, at the water's whim, she bobbed up again, heading all the while for that nasty, jagged mass.

Hook shot out his arm. The iron of his hook struck the rock, ringing. It jarred his stump, but didn't slow him. He curled his elbow about her and hauled her sideways, just as the two of them passed the outcrop. The water gurgled against the stone, toying with its inflexibility, cuffing its surface with a harmless note, a sound deceptively different from the ghastliness he had dreaded, the splinter of bone, the crack of death. As warm, blessed relief poured over him, Hook held onto Jill. He clasped her chill, drenched body, and inhaled for what seemed the first time since he let her go, so far up this lethal stream.

Holding her face above the water, he supported her. His one hand moved to shield her head. They hurtled down the rapids, together, gasping for air, clutching one another. Hook guided their course, dodging the hazards, and allowing the river to carry them. In time, the current grew milder, gentler, slowing their progress. Soon they floated as effortlessly as if they were bathing in the Mermaids' Lagoon. Drifting with a sense of deliverance, Hook felt for the bottom. He found a stable spot, planted his boots and, at last, stood erect, with Jill within his arms. He closed his eyes and filled his spirit with the living, vital feel of her.

Her perfume had washed away; Hook smelled damp cloth and the savor of her skin. She hung limp at first, barely able to stand. He ignored the pain shooting up from his ankle, and pressed her against him, willing his strength to enter into her. With every breath she gained stability. As he chafed her back, she pressed her lips to his chest, and his heart nearly burst to feel her nestling there. Wanting to hold her forever, yet he yielded to concern, pulling away just enough to examine her.

"Jill…" Seeing the redness of her wrists, he lost no time. With the blade of his hook, he sawed at the leather of the belt. Water dripped from his hair to his eyes, but he blinked it away and didn't cease his labor until her hands broke free. The belt slunk into the water, to lazily follow the current. Once again, he drew her close. "You are unharmed."

"Hook." Exhausted as she was, she managed a smile. Free at last, her arms wrapped around his waist. Hook had never been so grateful to feel a simple touch.

With a trusting look, she gazed up into his eyes. "I…" But her gaze slid from his face. She looked beyond his shoulder, and her loving expression changed to apprehension. "Oh."

Only now did Hook become aware of where they stood. The rapids had ended. The water here, waist deep, slipped agreeably past his boots, holding none of the menace of its earlier course. Trees lined the bank, their branches swaying in a breeze, their woodland host to game. The smell of sunbaked wheat drifted on the wind. Just audible above the burbling of the water, birds chirruped, and crickets crooned. Not far from this point, the river met the sea, full of fish, and opened to a route for trade with other islands. And, he knew, a beach of pebbles lay behind him, and beyond that, a pleasant plateau, fringed by forest. A homey site, and a welcoming one. A perfect place to host a village.

Reading Jill's eyes, Hook discerned that the Indians were assembling behind him, staring at the strangers in their stream, and laying plans for the capture of intruders. Although he had rescued Jill from the peril of the river, she was not yet out of jeopardy. He must save her, again.

Hook didn't turn to see the natives. He spoke low, to Jill. "Swoon."

Still watching the people on the opposite shore, Jill understood, too. She rolled her head backward and sagged into Hook's ready arms. He bent down, lowering her to the water as if to revive her.

"You must swim under the surface, as deep and as fast as you can. Get out of sight, and when you have rested, fly." He paused only to lend emphasis to his final command. "Go *directly* to Captain Cecco." She drew a breath, then he immersed her, not in stately ritual this time, but in stark necessity.

Hook held his pose as long as he dared, and he did not turn to watch her. He feigned to cradle her in his elbow and hold her body submerged, until in the corner of his eye he saw her topaz trail fade away.

An arrow dashed the surface of the river, spitting contempt at him. Hook had waited for it; now he snatched up the arrow to hold it like a dagger. He straightened.

Then he turned. With an expression of indifference, he confronted his enemies. At a guess, he saw forty braves nocking forty arrows, and each of them aiming for his heart, to liberate his soul.

But Hook knew better. With the time he had bought her, his soul had escaped, downstream. What fear he had felt fled with her.

Hook faced his fate, alone— and, for once in his career, he was pleased to be solitary.

"So it's you, is it?" The bo'sun studied the lad through his spectacles. "Let me place you now....Cabin boy...on the *Unity*, was it?"

David knew now that this man called Smee with the fine new shirt and the beard trimmed and tamed was indeed the redheaded sailor he'd seen with the other pirates, attacking his uncle's ship. Reluctant to cooperate, he barely nodded.

"Where're your fancy brass-buckled shoes now, boy?"

"You ought to know."

Before David could blink, the back of Smee's hand struck him, viciously. The boy reeled backward on the deck. The ache in his cheek began, bone deep, and intensified. His hands were still bound behind him, and he could not clutch his face if he wanted to. But he had no wish to show this ruffian he was hurting.

"I'll be having none of your cocky lip, boy. You're lucky the commodore didn't strike you down dead, after the danger you put the lady in."

David felt the man's fury, boiling hotter than his words. Plainly, this Irishman, too, was in love with Red-Handed Jill.

"I'd gut you myself, soon as look at you. So mind your manners. You may be marked by the lady, but you'll soon learn. She'll not allow disrespect."

David was puzzled again. Marked? That Indian had said much the same.

"Now get you down those steps." With brute force, Smee grabbed David's shoulders and shoved him toward the *Roger's* hatch. David couldn't see much in the sudden dimness, but Smee's grip bore into him as they descended, turned, and descended again, startling a crateful of chickens that squawked and fluttered, and eventually ending in a hold smelling of bilgewater and straw. Smee threw David into a cage with flat iron bars, then drew his knife. Alarmed, David recoiled. As he realized his mistake, his face seared with embarrassment, and he turned to present his bonds to his jailer.

The sailor cut him loose. A set of keys jangled as Smee pulled them from his belt. He left the cell and slammed the door. "I'll be sending you a dry set of britches. And some soap, to scrub that stink off your carcass. When the lady sends for you, you'd better be looking— and smelling— presentable." The key turned, and the lock snapped irritably.

Even after Smee stamped up the steps, the man's anger filled the brig. Once David's two Indian escorts dragged him aboard, the

Irishman had stood aside with them to listen to their story, told with accompanying gestures. Smee's face had turn redder and his eyes blazed with indignation, but David didn't know if he himself was the cause of it. Now he was certain. And to judge by the way the man issued orders to the crewmen, David guessed Smee was a high-ranking officer. Touching the swelling of his cheekbone, he decided it would be wiser not to rile the man further. And he'd be grateful for a wash.

David's heart beat faster as he anticipated nearing Jill again. *The Lady*, they called her. He wondered what use she might make of him. He hoped she had enough able seamen to work the ship; David could read and write, he could cipher a little. Or maybe she needed a cabin boy. The thought of entering her quarters, of waiting on her personally, made the heat travel from his throbbing cheek to his groin. David was infused with the same giddy pleasure he'd felt aboard the *Unity*, when he held the book for his uncle as he conducted her marriage, when he'd served her wine to toast the union. She had granted David a sip, from her own cup. He'd touched his lips to the rim where her lips had drunk, and the warmth of the spirits had spread all over him. He would gladly serve her again, in any role she required. He owed her his life, his rescue from that evil Island, deliverance from those warriors. But whatever she needed now, David needed her more.

He peeled off his ragged shirt and his filthy breeches, casting them from him, forever, through the bars of his cage. Despite the confinement of his cell, he was liberated. Fresh, clean sea air bathed his body. He filled his lungs with it. He felt as shameless as those sailors he'd watched with the women in the clearing. He spread his arms and circled, spinning south, west, north and east. Then, as honest and naked as the day he was born, David got down on his knees in the sweet-scented straw to fold his hands, as his pious mother had taught him to do, and offer up a prayer for his future. This time, he had no trouble addressing the proper deity.

When the soap arrived, he would scrub his skin pink to be acceptable to Jill…to be touchable. Above anything he'd ever wanted in his whole young life, David wanted his goddess to answer his pagan prayer.

Hook stared straight ahead at the Indian forces. A canoe slid from the bank, its birch bark shushing over the pebbles, to glide downstream. Once in mid-river, the warriors within it turned it broadside to the current and held their paddles firm, anchoring their craft and blocking escape in that direction. But Hook never considered swimming; the rapids lay above him, and fleeing downstream would lead the braves to Jill. He'd never reach the far bank before an arrow pierced his back, nor for the same reason might he take to the air. With no alternative, Hook began wading, leisurely, toward the Indian shore.

The canoe paddled closer. The People's tension swelled as he drew nearer to their homes. A slope behind them leveled into a plateau, where a totem pole loomed, dark with images carved long ago, and singed black in places by Hook's own order. Also there, in the center of the encampment, a bonfire smoldered low, wafting smoke toward the heavens. Beyond the fire stood many tepees, their hides painted bright with symbols so vivid they seemed to move like the creatures they represented. A canopy of green leaves spread its roof on either side of the dwelling place, and other trees grew here and there, uninhibited by the village.

In front of Hook, the people on the beach formed ranks. Warriors, still threatening with their arrows, stepped to the fore; women and young ones moved uneasily backward. A gaggle of elders remained between these groups, all save one appearing aged but proud, some with colored blankets wrapped about their shoulders, their only movement from feathers in their hair, twitching in the wind. Facing this tribe, Hook felt like the solitary he was, entering an atmosphere open to Nature in every way, but stifling to a prisoner.

No children counted coup with this captive. Even the littlest knew He of the Eagle's Claw to be too much of a legend. His scalp was proclaimed by the council to be taboo. Coveted as it might be, it exuded too much power. The elders in their wisdom understood how a trophy of such magnitude might divide the tribe. And now, as the man himself walked among them, the situation called for words, not war.

Still, some celebration seemed in order. The People had trapped a potent foe, and jubilation danced on their faces. The older boys who had not yet earned names ran to stoke up the fire, and the pop of igniting tinder soon mixed with the triumph of their ululations. The children beat their tom-toms, lending rhythm to the ritual.

While Hook approached the encampment, the braves in the canoe pulled their paddles from the water, and the craft turned downriver. Hook's heart jumped with the drums. Beyond doubt, the natives meant to hunt Jill down. If they caught her, if they killed her, the Indians would at last hold sway over the Island. The celebration just beginning would mount to full pitch, then.

Hook knew his legend alone kept this fearsome people at bay. Now that the Black Chief had taken a mate, to eliminate her, and thus eradicate the Black Chief's line— his 'family'— would emasculate his threat. With Jill in their hands, the council could tip the balance of power. Although Hook's attack on the village had produced no enduring damage, he understood the rancor it caused, and the zeal it engendered in the warriors to prove their mettle. For that very reason it had been a bold move. Hook knew it to be a risk, had known it when he designed that assault to win his way to Jill. Now the supremacy it gained him might destroy them both, for, once giving Hook a reason to wreak vengeance in blood, the tribe must rise up to slay him before he took it. A lethal eagerness seethed in every soul who watched him. He felt it beating in the tom-toms.

As for Jill herself, she had cunning enough to hide from the scouts— if she wasn't too wearied by her ordeal. For his own sake Hook would have to stall, keep the Indians debating, to allow her time to reach the ship and alert Captain Cecco to his capture. He hoped that if Jill eluded the natives, if they could not exterminate Hook's clan in a single blow, they would decline to eliminate Hook himself. But, as the light of victory burned in the warriors' eyes, Hook could not be certain.

Yet displaying no trace of anxiety, Hook took his last stride from the water. His boots crunched on the beach, one step each, and stopped. He looked only at the Old Ones. He held his hook at the ready, the arrow in his left hand raised waist high. Unflinching, he watched the council as the warriors began to dance to the drums, still aiming their weapons.

With every step, their lithe, oiled figures gained momentum. Soon they leapt up high, yelping, twisting, then hunched low to point their arrows at him, creeping forward as if stalking game. They whirled and crouched, and ended each pass with their arrowheads menacing, closer to their prey. Their mouths set in ferocious grins. More drums took up the cadence, throbbing inside the captive's chest. A harsh kind of rattle joined in, and before long Hook was surrounded by a dozen leering men, a dozen arrow points dancing about him, always circling, always drawing nearer to his vitals. The yells that accompanied these movements rang through the forest, long, loud, and savage enough to wither the stoutest heart. Hook endured it, and hoped Jill was far enough away not to shudder at the sound.

Hook guessed the meaning of this rite. It was a test of his courage, and that of his captors. To the warrior who provoked him to fight, honor would accrue; to the warrior who wounded him, likewise. But if Hook stood firm, if he failed to show fright, the honor would be his— and he would win a better basis for his bargaining. He guessed, also, that because he was a prisoner in their home camp and not at war upon the battlefield, the man who wounded him without provocation would suffer discredit. Adhering to this conviction, Hook continued to gaze straight ahead, his expression haughty, and his eyes upon the elders.

Even for a man of Hook's experience, the situation proved harrowing. With every war cry, he felt the hair rise up on his scalp. He recognized that the Indians practiced the same tactic he exhorted in his men: before boarding any ship, his pirates hollered as horribly as possible, to intimidate their victims and thus reduce resistance. Only now did Hook fully appreciate the effectiveness of his ploy. Strengthened by the thought, he stood unwavering. And with every brittle moment, Hook understood that Jill might travel farther, and his deliverance move closer. For this reason, he did not begrudge the Indians their harassment. He welcomed it.

Another spine-shattering yelp erupted from behind him, nearly knocking him off balance. The ankle he had wrenched in the riverbed began to ache under his weight. If it gave way beneath him, he might never recapture his dignity. The dancers' arrow tips flitted a hairsbreadth from his body now. Their breezes brushed by as they nearly scored him. Standing in his damp shirt and breeches, he could not allow himself to shiver, trying instead to summon the sun's heat. The elders watched, and witnessed as he held steadfast.

At last, when the warriors had proved themselves as bold as their prisoner, the tallest of the elders stepped forward, a sinewy, hawk faced man, younger than the rest but one who carried himself with importance. The white and silver hair of the others blew loose or hung braided; he alone wore a scalp lock of long, dark hair. He was dressed in fringed leggings and moccasins, exquisite with beading. The string of bear claws at his neck spoke as fiercely of his courage as the scars upon his chest. Hook waited and kept silent. The further his enemies prolonged their formalities, the better.

The Indian raised his hand, and the braves ceased their torments. As the dancers stilled, the drums by the fire halted. Rattles hissed as they hit the ground, and the warriors uncocked their bows. Hook found the stillness nearly as ominous as the frenzy, as, no doubt, it was intended to be.

The tall man dropped his arm.

"White Bear speaks for the Council of Elders."

"Hook speaks for himself," he retorted. He relaxed his hand on the arrow. All through his ordeal, he had held it poised to strike.

"Come." White Bear gestured to a patch of sun, several yards from the shore. Clearly, the natives had no desire to bring this pirate into their village. Not taking his eyes from the captive, White Bear sat down, settling cross-legged on the beach. The elders, too, dropped their blankets and seated themselves. A few females assisted them. In the center of the group, the only woman among the council attended the commodore with blue-hazed eyes and blue-veined ears, eyes that, no doubt, resented the ostentation of his victory, ears that surely echoed with the arrogance of his commands. When the elders were still again and the younger women had retreated, the crone nodded to White Bear, and he spoke.

"The People show respect to a noble captive. Courage earns our enemy the right to sit among us."

Hook, too, held his adversary's eyes. He disguised his limp, taking his time. He lowered himself to sit opposite White Bear, the river to his right, the council to his left. Higher on the slope, the young ones knelt to listen, their backs to the fire that crackled high with fuel, its smoke now curling thick into the sky. The smart of his ankle faded as he eased his weight off of it. Slowly, he laid the arrow before him, to point in a neutral direction, toward the stream. Water still dripped from his hair, his beard, and his clothing. White Bear took notice.

"My tepee holds many blankets. You will accept one?"

Unhurried, his captive spoke without emotion. "I will."

White Bear looked to the women who had assisted the elders. To one, he shook his head. To her neighbor, he jerked a silent command. Hook paid no attention to the movement within the crowd. He betrayed neither curiosity nor trepidation. Understanding the scrutiny to which he was subjected, he kept his eyes on the warrior before him.

When White Bear turned back to face his captive, he remained silent until Hook's needs should be tended. Soon Hook heard a light step on the pebbles behind him. He smelled a woodsy scent; he sensed a woman.

White Bear gestured his approval. With her eyes lowered, the woman stole to Hook's right. Silently, she held out a woven blanket in offering. Hook turned to her, and felt instantly drawn to this woman. He beheld a lovely creature, well proportioned, past the age of marriage but bearing no bracelet. She was slim and handsome with, surprisingly, a head of close-trimmed, raven-black hair. He sensed her discomfort; she disliked calling attention to herself, and she dreaded the copper-skinned brave who commanded her.

Hook raised his arm to accept the blanket, but the metal of his claw shone severe in the sunlight, an obvious hazard to the fabric. The woman gasped at his gesture, stepping backward. Hook permitted himself a half-smile at her distress, then, with evident pleasure, he allowed his eyes to linger over her figure. As always, he sought his enemy's weakness.

White Bear uttered a command, "Woman, attend the Black Chief of the Eagle's Claw."

She obeyed, quickly composing herself and spreading the blanket open. She approached Hook again, and this time she bent to hang it over his shoulders. Glad as he was to block out the chill, Hook did not reach to secure the mantle. He waited for the woman to pull it together for him, her cool hands grazing his chest. When she finished, he turned to look again at her, and, with his fingers, he brushed at one side of his hair.

The woman shot an inquiring look to White Bear. He gave a nod, and she knelt beside the commodore. Then, delicately, as if she was afraid to handle it, she gathered up his dripping curls, pulling them free to hang outside the blanket. She squeezed the moisture from the thick mass of his hair, so that the droplets ran down her arms and dampened the sand.

Knowing that to acknowledge these ministrations would indicate weakness, Hook did not thank her. He looked into White Bear's eyes as she worked, then he reached to the back of his neck and placed his hand over the woman's, trapping her fingers for the breadth of a moment. Her breath caught, White Bear's eyes narrowed, and Hook released her. She stood, her slender shadow falling over him, and at a glance from White Bear, she hurried to a position out of Hook's sight, ready to return if White Bear called.

Having asserted some power in his helplessness, Hook straightened his back and waited for parley to begin. He noted that White Bear wore one marriage bracelet. This woman he dominated wore none. She may be some relation, but she was not his wife, nor was she his weakness.

Perhaps because she wasn't, White Bear had not risen to the bait. He showed no disapproval, but kept his words to the point.

"Black Chief of the sea men. Days ago, your boats carried twice as many warriors to the Island, yet today we take you alone."

"Today's visit is unintentional."

"Last time you came to the People in great numbers, in stealth and with hostility."

Hook merely acknowledged the statement.

"Now the tide is reversed."

In no hurry, Hook drawled, "Tide is a changing force."

"Today, advantage lies in the hands of the People."

"You will not win the promise of that advantage, without loss."

"Brave words. But the People find no honor in overpowering a single man."

"Then your honor is useful to me. But I shan't be alone for long. Even now, my men march on the warpath." Hook leaned forward to grasp the arrow. He turned it to point toward the elders, then, with emphasis, set it down.

White Bear's gravity showed the significance of Hook's gesture. He lifted an arm to indicate the braves all around them. "You see our warriors. We are ready to fight."

"I have never doubted it. This is the reason that, the last time I called, I took care to surprise your People." Hook paused to underscore his words. "Today, no surprise will hinder either side."

But the Indian, too, probed for his enemy's weakness. "When we track down your mate and hold her scalp by the golden hair, you may change your opinion." Assured of his advantage, White Bear sat back.

"I claim no mate."

White Bear seemed taken aback. "Your white wife, then."

Hook waved toward White Bear's wrist. "Your custom upon marriage is to wear a bracelet. Ours, a ring, a simple circle of gold." He spread his hand and rested it on his knee. "The Black Chief bears no woman's binding. I wear ornaments only to demonstrate my wealth."

White Bear's brows lowered. "We saw her in the water. Your woman."

"What you saw was a mermaid. I hear that you are wise enough to avoid them, but surely you know one when you see her."

"When our braves drag her back, a prisoner, we will 'know' and 'see' the truth."

"She'll have slithered to the sea by now. You are welcome to try to catch her; I find it helpful to offer gifts. Precious jewels are especially effective." Raising his hand, Hook smiled and rotated it to display his several rings to the People. Among the other gems, the recovered rubies burned red in the sunlight. When the women whispered, his smile turned to a smirk. "As I say…most effective."

White Bear stiffened, and the whispering stopped. "Enough talk of women. Why do you lead more warriors to our shores?"

"I won these new warriors from an enemy. They are pledged, now, to serve me."

White Bear sat quiet, thinking. A single tap from the scout's drum caused him to look toward the river. In the distance, the white form of the canoe was returning. As it neared, it was seen to bear the two braves— and no captive female, mermaid or otherwise.

Hook's chest rose with a lungful of air, but beyond that movement he showed no trace of his encouragement. The magnitude of his relief was as great as before, when he'd snatched Jill from the roiling path of those rocks. Jill had won her freedom. Still uncertain of his own chance of survival, Hook found it didn't much concern him. His 'family' was safe— even if other men must guard it for him.

White Bear stared at the arrow on the ground, where it spoke a threat to the People. After contemplating, he asked, "And for what purpose do your warriors ride two boats into the bay?"

"We come— as we have always come to this island— to improve our vessels and rest from our labors on the sea."

"You lie about the red-handed woman. Why will I believe what you say about the men?"

"I need no lies. Nor do I need your trust."

"It is well. You will not receive it." The People stirred around them, but held silence as White Bear assumed his most formidable posture.

"Black Chief of the Eagle's Claw. White Bear speaks for the council. We release you today. Do not approach our home again." White Bear stood. "Tell your warriors. Another venture toward our village will start the war drums pounding."

Hook stood, too. "Agreed." He threw off the blanket. "Your warriors will find no welcome in the bay. But…one point I must declare." Hook seized the arrow. "I have established a House in the Clearing. Those who abide there live under my protection. All who enter the Clearing must enter under truce. Men..." Here Hook turned toward the lovely female who had waited on him, his blue eyes piercing into the deep black eyes of the raven-haired one. He stared until she blushed. "...And women."

Hook spun to eye the council. He raised the arrow, he raised his claw, and with one vicious slash, he severed the shaft. The feathered end fluttered to the ground. "Any harm to those who dwell in the Clearing will earn my retribution." He flung the tip of the arrow to his feet and, standing tall before the outrage of the elders, he ground it into the gravel with the heel of his boot.

The drum at the edge of the water burst into warning, and all heads turned toward the scout. Instantly, the warriors readied their bows again. On the river, an armada of longboats approached, their oars rising and falling in quick, precise rhythm, up, down, and under, and flashing in the slanting sun. Each boat held as many sailors as it could carry, all armed with guns, swords, and knives.

At the fore of the leading boat stood the figure of Captain Cecco, one boot on the prow, his golden armbands shining, his weapons glinting. He held a cutlass in one hand and the other rested on the ax at his belt. Within moments, his company was skimming toward the beach. He searched the shore, sizing up the Indian forces and appraising his commodore's condition. At his signal, his blue-jacketed men beached his boat, and the other vessels closed in around the black flag flying at the stern.

"Commodore Hook," Cecco called. "We stand ready for you to embark, Sir."

Hook aimed a dark look sideways at White Bear, a challenge. When the Indian remained motionless, Hook turned to his man. "Aye, Captain Cecco. I join you anon."

Hook collected the blanket he had thrown aside. Deliberately, he walked toward White Bear's woman. The braves tensed, crowding closer, but made no move to lay hands upon the mighty chief the council had released. When he stood before her, he rubbed the blanket against his cheek, and then his chin. As he did so, he trained an insinuating smile on her. He watched with interest as her eyes darted between him and Cecco, as if she half expected Hook's own officer— not White Bear— to intervene. The pregnant woman standing next to her wrapped an arm about her and pulled her close. Hook held out the blanket.

"I am grateful for your hospitality."

She didn't move, she didn't speak. She simply stared with her handsome black eyes. Hook read those eyes, sensing both fear and rebellion. He glanced at the other female, who was big with child, and he determined by their likeness that they were sisters. This younger sister wore a marriage bracelet. As Hook held the blanket toward the first one, the older sister, she shifted her feet as if to back away, then seemed to think better of it. Stoically, she held her position as he draped the blanket over her shoulder. Before releasing it, he squeezed her shoulder, then slid his hand up her neck, to brush her jaw, the touch of a connoisseur, appreciating.

Then Hook bowed to her, his most elegant bow, flourishing the hand that sparkled with jewels. He ignored the flash of pain at his ankle. "Fair lady. May we meet again."

He turned to make his way to the longboat. Cecco jumped into the water, relinquishing his position to the commodore. His sailors shoved the boat from the shore and they all leapt aboard. The pirates eyed the natives, ready to repulse attack, but no aggression followed. As the distance between them lengthened, each army eased its stance.

"Commodore," Cecco said above the creak and dip of the oars and the celebratory whoops of the Indians, "I am pleased to find you uninjured."

"And Jill?"

"She is weary, but well. She waits for us aboard the *Roger*." Cecco paused. "Your steward is attending her." Preferring not to dwell on the thought, he turned to behold a certain someone on the shore.

The direction of Cecco's gaze was not lost upon his commander. "Very well, Captain. I commend you on your swift and thorough action."

"*Grazie*, Commodore. I could do no less, and face my determined wife again."

"Aye. I am familiar with that dilemma."

The two rivals stopped short of smiling at the image of Jill that Cecco had evoked, and indulged instead in a rare sense of camaraderie. Unused to amity, they simply stood, considering the phenomenon and evaluating one another. As the strain of the past hour had mounted, so too their opposition seemed to dwindle. Cecco pulled a flask from his pocket and opened it.

Hook stared at the hand that proffered that flask. A simple circle of gold confronted him— and reminded him of the words he'd sworn to the council.

The Black Chief bears no woman's binding.

Hook accepted the flagon and drank deep, strengthened as the fire of spirits burned its way down his gullet. Propelled by the muscle of their men, the officers' boat rounded a bend in the river, and the chaos of the Indian drums receded.

When Hook lowered the flask, the camaraderie had dissipated with the danger, for, according to custom, the dusky eyes of the captain challenged the commodore. But, as usual, amity and enmity gave way to protocol. Cecco averted his gaze. Inwardly, both admitted the truth: they were too much alike. Given the opportunity, one day, each of these men would kill to claim all the other man cherished.

And on that day, no surprise would hinder either side.

Invigorated, Hook hoisted the flask for a toast. "To your raven-haired beauty, Captain. As I say, you are to be commended...on your swift and thorough action."

To Cecco's startled face, Hook returned a shrewd look. Then, with a laugh rich with victory, Hook tipped up the flask again and drained the potent contents, leaving not a drop for another man to savor.

Escapes and Escapades

The celebrations began before the pirates rowed out of sight, and Lean Wolf looked forward to the revelry. He felt very much alive, and too unsettled to sleep this night. He and Panther listened to a hasty account of the Black Chief's detainment, and as the two scouts returned to the beach to secure the canoe, the yells of their fellows matched the uproar in Lean Wolf's spirit.

With little effort, he inverted the canoe next to the others to lie like ribs along the shore, and Panther tucked the paddles beneath it. Lean Wolf stretched his muscles to relieve their tightness.

"Thanks to the Black Chief's interruption, this long day is turned to an interesting evening." After his spying this afternoon, and the dissatisfaction that followed, Silent Hunter had welcomed the urgency of the trip downstream to hunt for the pirate woman. He longed to see her, and he dreaded to see her, all at once. Her image burned like summer sun in his mind. And now, after the events in the village, he had an excuse to show his excitement, to move and to dance, to release the pent-up energy that churned within him ever since his eyes had drunk their fill of that red-handed female, bathing in the waterfall.

"You are more restless than usual, Lean Wolf." Panther was a well-built brave, competent and fair-minded. His nature was easy and confident, only in part because of his mother's influence among the elders. Through his long braids a lock of white hair reminded everyone of his relation to the Old One. Panther was a jovial comrade, but even he had not been able to cajole Lean Wolf into talking this afternoon. He thought he had an inkling of the cause of his companion's mood.

"The People are saying that you have spoken for Raven. Is this the reason for your impatience?"

Lean Wolf studied Panther's open, friendly face, but found no disapproval there. "I have spoken for Raven, but speaking is not the cause of my discontent."

"Ah." Panther nodded in sympathy. "White Bear has decided to keep her, then?"

"In my opinion, White Bear has decided nothing. He delays to consider his choices."

"I cannot blame him. It is a heavy responsibility to determine what path is best for a sister, or for a daughter. I have had my own reasons to delay Ayasha's marriage." Panther smiled. "But, I think, my dreams have led me at last to a wise decision."

Lean Wolf raised his eyebrows, and the handsome grin that had found no reason to appear all afternoon emerged at last. "So...you will give her to me?"

Laughing, Panther clasped Lean Wolf's shoulders and steered him to sit on a fallen tree trunk along the riverbank. The arms of a silver maple spread above the two braves, sheltering them from the late afternoon brightness that speckled the river. "I am sorry, my friend. You are too old for my daughter. Not in age, but in outlook! Remember, I witnessed your younger years. I know you are advanced beyond the imagining of a young girl."

"So you will marry her to a greenling, like Rowan Life-Giver, whom I suspect to have no experience with women at all! So be it. I have seen how Ayasha moons over him. They can grow up together."

Panther laughed again. "It is obvious, Lean Wolf. Raven is the fitting bride for you. She was Ash's wife. She knows how to handle a hot-blooded man. Raven is the answer to your restless spirit's call."

Disinclined as he was to sit still, Lean Wolf welcomed a chance to secure an ally in his cause— and one who might sway the old woman on the council. He settled his rangy frame on the log in the cool of the maple's shade, and conquered his agitation. "Then you favor my suit, if only to protect your daughter. It is enough of a reason. I could wish that White Bear would show such sense." He picked up a handful of stones and pitched them into the water, making a dry, miniature rain storm.

"White Bear's judgment is clouded these several moons past, like the river where your pebbles have muddied it. But only where his family is concerned. The People are fortunate that he traveled to us over the water from the Other Island. My grandmother, from whom my mother the Old One suckled wisdom as a nursling, was farsighted to urge the council to accept him, even though he was only a boy and as yet unnamed. Today, without question, he demonstrated his sageness in tribal matters. Not one of the elders could have handled the Black Chief more skillfully."

"I never said White Bear is not clever. He is a worthy opponent."

"And a worthy friend. But in recent months he has risen in authority, he has accepted a second woman into his tepee, and, most daunting of all, he will at any moment become a father. This last is the weightiest burden a man can bear. Even your strong arms will tremble at the effort of raising a boy to manhood, Lean Wolf. You must trust me on this matter. I am a father five times. I know well of what I speak."

"Excuses. White Bear has been my friend, but his new life sets us apart."

Panther's face grew serious, and his resemblance to the Old One more pronounced. "Lean Wolf. It is not only White Bear's life. Remember that you have led your own, and not always successfully."

"If you speak of Red Fawn, you speak unfairly. Until I am granted a new wife, I will wear her token."

"I know in my heart that you love her still. You would welcome her return. Even so, any provider would question a suitor whose first wife chose to leave his tepee…to become an Outcast." Panther's voice had dropped low in spite of the noise of the People's singing, and he glanced around to be sure no one listened. Higher up, on the plateau, the tribe circled the bonfire, making music and abandoning their bodies to the rhythm. "Hear me, Brother. Some have reason to think Red Fawn ran…from your heavy hands. No, I do not believe it, nor did Red Fawn claim it. But the talk of the women says she sometimes bore bruises."

"And so a husband must accept the blame for his wife's failure." Lean Wolf's bitterness rose again to taint the back of his throat.

"And thanks to your words, I see clearly that no father will trust his daughter to me. If I desire companionship, I must wait for White Bear to come to his senses."

"Now I suspect you of deception. You are moody because you do not *want* any other woman. Truly, you are in love with Raven. And if this is so, I see all the more reason you should marry her." Panther rested his hand on Lean Wolf's forearm. "I feel the beat of your pulse. But I counsel you to be patient, my friend."

As the drums throbbed faster and louder, Lean Wolf felt his body fill with need. He faced Panther, shaking his head. "You feel the blood surge in my arm. I felt it surge in my spirit today. We held the Black Chief in our power. Like the rest of the People, I craved his killing."

"You have scoffed at his threat before. Why do you now take it seriously?"

"Today he came strolling into our village, as if he created it."

"He has done that once before."

"But…" Lean Wolf sought a reason to explain his vehemence. If he wished to retain Panther's support in this battle for Raven, no flicker of passion for the pirate's woman must be perceived. "But now I see that the mighty Black Chief wraps his only vulnerability in lies, believing us too stupid to discover it. As if we were dogs, he thinks to put us off her scent."

"And his attentions to Raven? How he dallied with her? I would think this the first reason you revile him."

"Yes….Of course." Grimly, Lean Wolf reflected that his reasons for resentment were far more personal than those of the People. Perhaps no older reason existed for one man to murder another.

But Panther seemed to accept Lean Wolf's motives. "His behavior would show that he does not value his woman above any other. If this is the case, my heart softens toward her. But I cannot understand how she escaped us. Our eyes are sharp as the hawk's, and we traveled like eels down the river."

"I reminded you then, Panther. If the female he raised from the river is the one we believe her to be, she once flew with the Golden Boy's flock. No doubt she became a bird again."

"A bird with wet feathers. We should have spotted her in the waterway, or hiding along the banks."

"Well, perhaps she became a mermaid, as the Black Chief claimed."

"If she did, he is welcome to her. I know better than to tangle with those creatures. No man who swims with sea-maids returns with his spirit intact."

"Many times as a boy I fished for them in the Lagoon. Only once did I come close enough to touch a sea woman." As he remembered her, Lean Wolf's yearning returned in full. "She had flowing yellow hair, and sea-green eyes. And the veil of her tail was so filmy, I thought I could spy legs beneath it. Her tail was golden and shining, with scales so delicate I believed I might breathe them away to see her bare."

"How did you get so close, Lean Wolf?"

"I did as the Black Chief claims to do. I brought jewelry, to tempt her. I searched the shores for a cycle of seasons, saving up the most unusual shells. All shapes and colors— coral, eggshell, brown like a yearling, striped and speckled. I polished them until they glowed, and I strung them on braided threads."

Panther's expression was one of amazement. "And?"

"And one day I sat on the big boulder in the Lagoon, stirring the water with my toes and wearing that necklace. The white clouds reflected in the sea, and drifted past my eyes many times before I saw her rising from them. Her hair was yellow, as I told you, but under the water it looked green as a spent leaf turning in autumn, and rippled when she moved, like seaweed in the current. I watched her circling around and around that rock, each time swimming a little closer. She was just as beautiful as the legends say, and she displayed everything...everything but shyness at her nakedness.

"You can imagine how, as a boy, I became dizzy staring at her. I was thrilled to see that she kept looking at me, too, admiring my necklace. I pretended indifference, all the while the green-gold of her tail flashed the light of the sky at me from under the water. I was dazzled, but I would not show her. I sat and waited. Finally, when I made no move, she slithered right up on the rock beside me."

"Then?" Panther's eyes were circles of brown.

"I felt her hair dripping water on my elbow. I smelled the salt on her skin— oh, Panther…such a fragrance! Ever since, the smell of the sea bewitches me. And then I felt her soft, damp hand upon my chest. Not a clammy hand, as you might expect, but warm, like the waters that fall from the upper river. The golden scales on the back of her hand reflected shards of sunlight, but her palm was smooth, like a girl's. I was already aroused, but just to feel her touch on my breast nearly unmanned me, and my eagerness became my downfall."

"She fled?"

"No! She swished her tail in the water, to tickle my feet, and then she leaned closer, and she kissed me— with lips soft and moist as a willing woman. A trickle of liquid flowed from her mouth to mine. I lost control. I tasted the brine on her tongue, I seized her in my arms, and of course I had to caress her breasts. They were full, but not heavy, with lovely blue veins showing just beneath her skin— skin so pale above the surface, but blue-green in the water. I bent to press my lips to her nipple, perfectly round and pointed, the most solid thing about that soft, soft mergirl, and it was a shade of purple you could not conceive. She pushed close, as if she enjoyed my nibbling. She blew gentle breaths in my ear, like sighs of pleasure. When I raised my face, she took hold of my necklace and slipped it over my head to slide it over her own. I didn't care about the necklace, it had done its work, but I reached for her hair so that I might feel the color of the sun, and the next thing I knew, I sat aching and alone on a wet rock, my mouth empty, my fingers bereft, and my branch as hard as the surface on which I perched, with no relief in sight…only the foam bouncing where she'd splashed. I swam through the cool waters to one of the caves in the cliff, and in the darkness there, I listened to her crooning in the distance, and conjured the feel and the taste of her long enough to end my torture."

"Lean Wolf. How do I believe such a tale? Surely you would have told this story long before now, if it is true."

"Ha ha! Oh, no, Panther. Not I. I was young and proud. I boasted only of my successes…and this was the fish that got away!"

Panther slapped his thigh and guffawed. "And, I think, the only one! But you were wise to bring her a gift, and lucky to have pleasured her. Otherwise she might have drowned you."

"I do not doubt it. Under such enchantment, a man thinks nothing of his need to breathe."

"It's true! I myself stopped breathing as you described her."

"I learned a lesson. I am no fisherman. I am a hunter. Since that time I limit my pursuits to solid ground. I find creatures of the dry land much easier to catch." Lean Wolf's narrow face grew determined. "Still, I enjoy a challenge. Perhaps I can coax a bird woman, like the Black Chief's, to fly to my hand."

"Or a raven, maybe?" Smiling at his joke, Panther stood to eye the festivities. "Come and dance now, Lean Wolf. She is watching the celebrants. You will have an opportunity to show off your plumage."

"Yes. I will come." Waiting for the prerogative of indulging in Raven's body was an annoyance, but Lean Wolf knew the remedy. And as he strutted with Panther toward the bonfire he thought again: how to catch a bird? How to clip her wings? He would need to use his strength; he would use persuasion; he would need a cage to keep her. And, mostly, he would need his cunning. Today he allowed her to escape. The next time he hunted, she would be his. He would hold that hair and, at last, feel the color of the sun.

For he had tracked her down this afternoon. His hunter's eyes had spotted the broken reeds where she'd dragged herself from the river. He had seen her disappearing behind a boulder in a shady, shallow bit of marsh, a doe's leap from the stream. His eyes had locked in a stare with her startled, sea-blue gaze. She knew she was found.

But she hadn't moved, she hadn't shied from him. She knelt stock still, exhibiting no trace of panic. Lean Wolf had glanced at Panther to make sure his friend had not glimpsed her, but Panther was searching the opposite bank. Lean Wolf steered the canoe toward the far shore. When he looked behind him, the red-handed one was sitting, panting, her head leaned back against the rock in a posture of exhaustion and relief. She wore a tunic of golden yellow, the exact same color as the tail of that intriguing creature in the Lagoon so many years ago, and just as clinging; he thought he could see her legs through it. The jewels at her breast twinkled topaz in the sun, like that sea woman's scales, and her nipples rose from her breast, just as soft, just as solid. The human had proven nearly as elusive as the sea-maid, but the Silent Hunter had stalked her. The moment to lure her from hiding had not yet arrived. Lean Wolf wanted to take her captive, but, unlike the tribe, he didn't want to harvest her scalp, and he didn't want her dead.

Silent Hunter wanted the Black Chief's woman very much alive.

"He saw me. I looked directly into those wolf-like eyes." Jill's gaze was intent on Mr. Smee as he finished tying her dressing gown. She was safe once more in the commodore's quarters, dry and warmed by a brisk toweling and the cup of broth Smee insisted she drink. But the images of her ordeal kept flashing before her vision. "He had such a hungry look, like a half starved predator."

"The hungry look I can understand. The mystery is why he let you go free."

"I was sure he'd come after me. And I was so tired, and my clothing so heavy with water. It was all I could do to pull myself from the river. I had no strength left to cover my tracks, even if I'd had time." She shivered again, and Smee refilled her cup. Gratefully, she wrapped her hands around its heat. "But why didn't that warrior capture me?"

"There's no way of guessing, Lady. In all my dealings with those Indians, I've never known a brave to show mercy to a man. But to a woman now, that might be more understandable."

"Then why did they hunt for me at all? Surely the People are eager to take Hook and his mate together. What a prize we would be to them!"

"I shudder to think how readily they'd have murdered you, once they'd trapped you both."

"I wish I knew what is happening to Hook." Jill's eyes strayed to the hourglass sitting on Hook's desk. How long had Cecco and the men been gone? It seemed to her that the sands dropped slowly, as if freshly dredged from the Indian river bottom. After her own troubles, Jill's resistance was low, and she had to blink the weary tears away. "If only I could save him, as he saved me, twice over, this afternoon."

"You're knowing as well as I am, Ma'am. He's content just having you safe here with me."

"Conor."

Smee responded to her cue; she had called him by his given name. "Jill," he gathered her into his arms. She needed him, and Hook counted on Smee to watch over her. Smee would do anything the commodore commanded, but this obligation was no chore. He was accustomed to the silky feel of her dressing gown. With her body inside it, though, it felt like heaven.

Jill sought reassurance in his hold. "Do you think Captain Cecco can free him?"

"I'm thinking he can." Smee peered over his spectacles. "But it remains to be seen if he did."

"You don't doubt that Cecco would fight for Hook? You saw how quickly he ordered the boats and rallied the men."

"Aye, I saw him. But he'd have to make a show if he wanted to be keeping you, now wouldn't he? Cecco's no fool. He's aware you'd be turning your back on him if he shirked his duty in any way— let alone throwing the commodore to those bloodthirsty natives."

"He saved Hook from the doctor."

"That he did. But time's been passing, and he's had long enough to brood over that decision. Time he didn't have *before* he made it."

"Hook tested him then. He trusts him now. And so do I."

"Then it's up to me, isn't it, Lady, to keep a protective eye on you both?" Smee drew the cup from her fingertips to set it down, then he took off his spectacles and pulled her closer. "Now I'm duty bound to be following the commodore's orders. He'd brew to a fury if I let you stand here fretting, and neglected to remind you of his love. So kiss me, lass."

A smile wavered on Jill's face. "I'll kiss you, Conor Smee. We'd neither of us disobey his orders." Her spirit drew strength as she thought of the constancy of her lover's consideration. He had arranged that she should never be left wanting for his affection. "Hook always knows what I'm needing. He's an insightful man."

"And a generous one." Smee lingered a finger's width from her lips. "And you're just like him...with one important difference." Smee was accustomed to strong concoctions, but, hardy as he was, he got the heady feeling he always got when Jill stood close. His great heart ached, and the room seemed to turn. He'd felt something like this years ago, the first time he laid eyes on the commodore, so fine and so capable. To serve such a man had given Smee's drifting life direction, a purpose to fulfill. Smee felt needed. He planted his feet more firmly and, with tenderness, he drew Jill to his embrace. The blood rushed to his head again. She was Hook's woman. She was Hook himself. In Smee's mind, his duties to the two were inseparable.

But the kiss was brief. It lasted only long enough to steady them both. Grounded once more— as Hook intended— in the comfort of their companionship, they addressed the concern that never left them: Hook's safety. Smee retrieved his spectacles and threw a glance at the sluggish hourglass, then guided Jill to the cushioned window seat that ran from port to starboard under the stern windows of the commodore's quarters. Here they sat, framed by the elegance of the woodwork, and held each other's hands. Together, they gazed anxiously toward the Island.

Jill said, "I'd never caught the Indian war cry so close at hand. It's a ghastly sound. Exhausted as I was, I nearly dropped when I heard it."

"Don't upset yourself, Lady. The commodore has heard it before. It'll not be fazing him." But Smee's worry wasn't easy to hide. In spite of the lilt in his accent, his voice betrayed it. "You're sure he wasn't injured in the rapids?"

"I really don't know. He seemed all right when he sent me away, but I had no time to inquire."

"I'll see to him when he gets back. Your shoulder will be tender for a week or so, but that poultice will soothe the bruising. It's as well you took a dip in cold water. Keeps the swelling down. Washed the bloodstains right out of your tunic, too."

"I'm glad. Hook loves to see me wear it. He says the color matches my spirit."

"Aye, it does. Bright and bold. But why ever were you bold enough to go swimming in the first place, and right there at the head of the rapids? And how the commodore could leave every weapon but his hook behind is beyond me."

"I do wish you had allowed me to see Lightly and Rowan, to thank them for collecting our things. I see you've cleaned them already." The swords and pistols hung in their places on the cabin wall, waiting for the next adventure. Jill's jeweled dagger slumbered beneath her pillow, where she herself had declined to lie, knowing rest would elude her.

"You were in no condition to receive visitors, Ma'am."

Shouts from the quarterdeck caused Jill and Smee to sharpen their watch. Soon the lookout hailed Captain Cecco's return. Boots stamped overhead as men ran to the taffrail, and Jill held her breath, scanning the mouth of the river. She snatched up a spyglass.

Across the bay and past the cliff, the boats were returning. Their oars pulled at the water in regular rhythm, and all seemed orderly, as if no struggle had taken place aboard them. Jill let out her breath. The boats appeared to be returning at least as many men as they had carried to the encampment.

Squinting, Jill tried to distinguish the figures. The setting sun cast the river's mouth in shadow, and at first the boats were shaded by the Island. As the lead craft pulled into the sea, left of the cliff face, the light fell fully upon it. Jill saw two familiar figures standing at the prow. Her husband's jewelry twinkled brightly now. And then, Hook's white shirt took precedence, seeming to bloom as the sun illuminated it.

"Smee, look! He's safe! They're both safe." She squeezed Smee's arm and gave him the glass.

"Aye! Thank the Powers."

Jill didn't need to hear the sailors' cheering to confirm it, but she relished the sound. Her heart felt light again, and hardly required the following boom of *Red Lady*'s cannon to buoy it. Hook lifted his arm to return his sailors' salute, the metal of his claw bright against the shadows from which he had emerged, unbeaten. Another round of "Huzzah!" rolled forth from the ships.

Jill jumped up, preparing to race to the deck, but Smee held her back. "No, Lady. It wouldn't be fitting to go among the men in just your robe. Best to wait here. I'm sure the commodore will want to greet you privately, anyway. Come and sit you by the window again."

"Yes, you're right." She knelt on the pad of the window seat to lean out the casement. Smee held her waist to secure her. She'd been so tired when Cecco brought her home. Wet and bedraggled, she'd barely managed to fly to *Red Lady*, and Cecco himself had carried her to the *Roger*, swinging across on a cable with the lady in his arm. He'd spoken strictly to Smee, instructing him, unnecessarily, to get her into dry clothing and lay her down to rest. Her face had been white with anxiety and fatigue. Smee was encouraged to see her color returned with the commodore…and with the captain. Smee's hold on her waist tightened.

As the parade of boats entered the arms of the bay, two men looked eagerly toward the *Roger*. A patch of blue at a window of the master's quarters set their minds at ease. Jill waved to them, blowing kisses from her scarlet hand. Both officers smiled and returned her greeting, until one of them stopped abruptly. The longboat floated near enough now for him to see, quite clearly, the possessive arms of the bo'sun clasping her waist. Captain Cecco leveled a malevolent stare at Smee. He watched, darkly, as his wife turned without thinking, and hugged him.

Without thinking, Cecco felt for his weapons.

A restraining hand covered Cecco's.

"We have left the enemy behind, Captain." Hook released him. Darting a glance to the rowing sailors, Hook reminded Cecco that he was observed.

Cecco showed only as much animosity as he dared. "That is your opinion. Sir. It may not be mine."

"Perhaps you will listen to the *signora's*, then. And, no doubt, you would like to assure yourself of her welfare. Come to my quarters, Captain. I owe you a drink, after all."

"Aye, Commodore." Cecco muttered only to himself, "You owe me."

Hook, as Mr. Smee had stated, was a generous man; as Jill asserted, he was an insightful one. While the gypsy captain anticipated a meeting with Jill, Hook watched his features smooth. But haunting those dusky eyes was a hungry look. Like a half starved predator.

Once again, Hook experienced that fleeting sense of brotherhood, an awareness of shared desires. Further, Hook himself was once condemned to solitude, just as Jill's husband was a lone man now. Thoughtfully, the commodore considered the captain, and, as he did, he resolved to call upon the occupants of the House in the Clearing. It was time he paid his respects to Lily.

And Hook was curious. He found it useful to familiarize himself with all that transpired on the Island. Hook's association with Jill had stirred in him a thirst for stories. In more ways than one, his thirst was stimulated this afternoon. He and Cecco, indeed, shared common desires.

Lily was certain to know the story of the raven-haired beauty.

Secrets of Unity

Hearing boots on the steps, Jill opened the door to her men. She flung herself into their arms, Hook on her right, Cecco on her left. After her concerns, their double embrace felt wholly satisfying. "I am so glad to see you— to see you both." She kissed each one, receiving fervent returns, and when she pulled away, a damp patch darkened the right side of her dressing gown. "Oh, but you must get dry, Hook. Come in! Mr. Smee, please see to the commodore."

Smee smiled wryly to hear a second unnecessary command today, but he merely nodded and shut the door. "Aye, Madam. I'll do that."

Hook gestured to the dining table. "If you please, Captain, seat yourself. Jill, will you do the wifely thing and pour your husband a drink? The cognac, I believe."

"Of course I will. Giovanni," Jill waited while Cecco removed his weapons, then she took possession of his arm and accompanied him to the dining area at the aft starboard corner of the cabin, bathed in the light of a setting sun. It was here she settled with Cecco when he was first elected captain, when she dined with him, pretending to eat but grieving for Hook, second-guessing her decision to become his successor's mistress. So many meals they had shared together, so many plans laid, here in the glimmer of the silver candelabra on this round, polished table. And on the window seat, just behind it, she had proposed to become Cecco's wife. Avoiding his eyes, Jill drew out a cushioned chair for him, then skirted away to the sideboard to find the finest bottle of cognac.

Cecco delighted in watching her. He sensed she was remembering, as he, too, was doing. "On the lower right, Lady. As I recall." He smiled.

"Yes." She caught the nostalgia in his gaze, then looked away. Having located the bottle, she set out four snifters.

Cecco stood to draw the cognac from her hands. Along with the emeralds Hook had given her, he saw the luster of his own ring on her fingers. "Allow me."

"Thank you. Thank you for everything." Her eyes looked deep into his. "I can't begin to tell you…"

"Then do not attempt to." He uncorked the bottle and poured, salivating as the burnt wine aroma of cognac rose to their noses, and then he seated her. Neither lifted a glass; both turned toward the commodore, waiting.

Smee had stripped the shirt, boots and breeches off his master, and the soggy garments now huddled at the foot of the wardrobe, giving off a smell of mud, while Hook supported himself with a hand on the carved back of the couch.

Smee pronounced, "You look to be undamaged, Sir. But I see you're favoring that right ankle."

"Yes. I wrenched it in the riverbed. Nothing serious."

"I'll be making up an arnica dressing for it. Lelaneh gave me a fresh supply of her herbs. Keep the weight off it, now."

Cecco observed as Smee released a clip and, cautiously, disengaged the leather harness from Hook's arm and shoulders. The Irishman picked up a towel and rubbed it vigorously over the commodore's honed, muscular body. Cecco was reminded of classical statues he had seen when he was a gypsy boy wandering the Italian countryside. Some of those marble bodies, too, were broken but beautiful, their limbs or faces nicked by time.

Smee gathered Hook's hair in the folds of the towel to press the water away. "It's a good thing you wore your second-best boots today. Tom Tootles will have a job to do, drying them out. And I'll be tending your hook right away, Sir. A fair piece of oiling it'll need, after the soaking it took this afternoon."

Cecco found himself staring at the harness where it lay upon the carpet, the gleaming, wicked hook inert at last. He had viewed it once before when he presumed the commodore dead, and it had filled him with gypsy superstition. But he had never glimpsed the workings of the commodore's weakness as the man lived and breathed beside it. For many long years, only Smee had witnessed that sight.

Nor had Cecco laid eyes on the crippled wrist since the day his commander— known as Captain James in those days— fell to his knees in agony, baring his teeth and clutching his arm to his breast as it bled. The Island boy, aided by a blinding ray of sun on his blade, had severed the captain's hand from his arm. Cecco remembered the horror of that moment. With his fellow members of Hook's crew, he was stunned to behold the maiming of his leader— his heretofore unbeatable leader— at the height of his manhood. The crew were shocked by the shrill, joyous laughter of the child, as he hovered with a gory sword in one hand, and a gory hand in the other. When he tossed it, the lunge of the crocodile as it consumed the captain's hand seemed tame compared to the violence of that child. The suddenness, the senselessness of his act laid Hook's men low, too.

Cecco recalled the gloom that reigned on the *Roger* in the following days: the groans that rose from the captain's quarters, the harried voice in which Smee sent Noodler scurrying to fetch this and that. For days, no one spoke of the captain's wound, even below decks in their hammocks. Two other men had been killed outright as the wild boys took advantage of the chaos, and Cecco and his mates sewed them into their hammocks, weighted with shot at their feet, consigning their remains to the waters. Smee had ordered Mullins to set a course for the nearest mainland and, grimly, the men put to sea, with none of the eagerness, none of the songs or ribaldry that usually accompanied the turning of the capstan and the raising of the anchors. Like a phantom ship, the *Roger* had slipped from her mooring and ghosted toward a moonless sea. Unable to catch sight of their captain, the men's imaginations filled his ship with speculation. Rumor had it the captain was feverish, was mad, was dead. But Smee kept discipline, barking orders and shoving bowls of blood and bandages onto the companionway, for Noodler to carry away.

Smee's doctoring saved Captain James; the ingenuity of a harness maker salvaged him. Another visit, to a blacksmith, and James was never seen again. Captain Hook took his place, a man more volatile, more bitter, and more determined than even his former incarnation had been. Where he was once strict as a disciplinarian, he was now vindictive. And he was demon-driven to conquer his crippling. When the pain receded to a slow, constant throb, the captain took up his cutlass— in his left hand— and fought every man aboard, day in and day out, until no one could best him. Once he'd mastered the cutlass, he handled his rapier, fighting duel after duel with Gentleman Starkey, the finest swordsman afloat. To this day, Starkey's scar-marked face bore witness to the captain's progression.

Hook had never cultivated the society of his men, and his maiming widened the distance. When he wasn't fencing, he retired to his cabin. Sometimes the men heard the harpsichord singing, plaintive songs, bawdy songs, stormy symphonies— but all missing some fundamental dimension. One-handed music. Silence might ensue, but when the captain emerged from his lair to stalk alone upon the quarterdeck, blots of ink stained his cuffs. Months churned by like the sea, then years. Hook regained his abilities, but— until Jill— he never found his civility.

Beholding the bald, mottled stump that caused so much suffering, Cecco wondered about his own civility. Confronted by the mutilation that the harness disguised, by the helplessness of the stub so cleverly cloaked by that claw, Cecco debated. Did he have the right to steal Hook's hand from him, again? Jill was everything the commodore had lost in that battle. She restored him, body and soul, to wholeness. Cutting her from Hook's side might amount to a second mutilation.

Cecco looked at Hook's face, and was startled to find the dark blue eyes intent upon him, as if Hook read his thoughts. That wily intelligence was seldom hoodwinked. Cecco had studied his commander for years. He owed his own success to the lessons he had learned from Hook. By now, Cecco was canny enough to appreciate the man's manipulations. And all at once, Cecco understood why Hook had invited him here. His rival had seized the opportunity today's misfortune provided, and used it. Hook designed this scene for Cecco's edification. Exposing his weakness, Hook cemented his strength. In a physical demonstration, he reminded Cecco of his needs. Hook needed Jill— and he needed Smee. Cecco squinted into those eyes, acknowledging the lesson, admiring the man's method while begrudging his victory. Without a doubt, Hook still stood as master.

And Jill, as his mistress.

Abruptly, Cecco turned away and grasped his glass. No longer waiting on courtesy, he hoisted the cup in salute to his wife. "To the Lady, our lovely one," Cecco swiveled his gaze toward Hook, "who, most fortunately, possesses *two* hands." Jill blinked in surprise, and Cecco drank.

He wasn't certain, but through the bevels of his snifter, he thought he saw Hook's half-smile. Yet when he set the glass down, no trace of amusement remained.

"Do have another drink, Captain." Hook slid into the dressing gown Smee held open for him, a handsome affair of maroon, silk, and velvet with a rich ruby sheen and buttons like jewels. Smee worked the buttons, then gathered up the harness and the clothing and excused himself from the commodore's quarters.

"No, Mr. Smee. Send my things away, and join us at the table. We've matters to discuss."

"Aye, aye, Sir. Right away." Smee left, quickly replaced by Noodler, who touched his tricorn to the officers before swabbing up the puddles on the floor. The sailor exited as Smee returned to sit with the commodore, the captain, and the lady. Smee's busy hands began rubbing oil into the hardened leather of the hook's harness.

Raising his glass, Hook proposed his own toast. "To Captain Cecco. My thanks for your commendable performance."

Cecco nodded, and the others drank to him.

"You may put it about, gentlemen, that I intend to show my gratitude to the company, as well. I shall host a celebration of our success."

Smee looked up from his work. "That's right good news, Commodore. The lads will look forward to it."

"Aye, Sir, they earned a reward," affirmed the captain of *Red Lady*. "Every man tended his duty, and speedily. Even my Frenchmen."

"Agreed." Hook said. "I am satisfied with the new sailors' performance. Today's incident was a test of their courage, not to mention their loyalty. Facing the natives in battle fury is never easy, even when one is accustomed to their methods." Hook sipped and savored his drink, as if the harrowing affair of this afternoon had happened to some other man. "The festivities will take place in a few days' time, on the beach of the bay. I'll allow the men to anticipate the revelry, and by then Jill's strength and my ankle are certain to be improved. I trust you have satisfied yourself as to the lady's health, Captain?"

Cecco gazed upon Jill, glad of an excuse to do so, and lingering on her loveliness. With her loved ones restored to her, she appeared wan, but recovered in spirit. Cecco replied, "Aye, Commodore. But please, Madam, to me your well-being is *primo*— my first concern. You will rest yourself."

"I will. You needn't be anxious for me."

Hook set down his cognac, laying his hand and his stump upon the gloss of the tabletop. "And now to business. I am not displeased with today's misadventure. It gave me the opportunity to accomplish my aims. First, we have solved a mystery, apprehending the thief who preyed upon our ladies."

"Oh," Jill exclaimed. "I'd forgotten. Giovanni, you'll remember him. It is David, the cabin boy from the *Unity*."

"David? Ah, yes. That is his name. I thought I had seen him before."

Smee snorted. "He's a cheeky lad. You'd best keep a short leash on that one, Ma'am."

"Not to worry, Mr. Smee. I believe David worships me."

"As do we all." The Irishman grinned.

Cecco sent a black look to Smee. "I see no need for my lady to entertain worshippers. Surely two husbands and two lovers are enough."

Hook bridled, and Smee's hands ceased their labors over the hook. His ruddy face turned redder, but he didn't dare retort. Smee might be Hook's first mate, bo'sun, and steward, but Cecco was a captain.

Jill's expression grew sober. "I possess only one true husband, Giovanni. And one true lover."

"*Signora,*" Cecco shook his head. "So loyal— to *all* the men she loves." Murmuring, he said, "Fortunate men." Cecco huffed in Smee's direction, then turned to Hook's disapproving eye. "But how does this David come to be on the Island?"

"Jill will question him tomorrow to discover his story. Tonight he lies a prisoner in my brig. The twins forewarned us, and we waylaid him, of all places, at the crocodile's grotto."

"Yes," said Cecco, "When I frightened him at the Clearing this morning, he ran that direction. But what were you doing in that foul place?"

Jill answered, quietly, "We laid flowers from the Fairy Glade at the tomb of the Lost Boys. It was my first opportunity to pay my respects. But I never dreamed we'd find another lost boy there."

Hook said, "Judging by his appearance, I should say your David is as lost as any. Possibly more so."

"Yes, the poor dear. The Island certainly confused him. He seems not to have arrived here by choice."

"Magic, then," Hook replied. "No wonder the lad is baffled. I predict he will be even more mystified before he leaves the Neverland. I gather he possesses a limited imagination."

"Except where his idol is concerned." Jill smiled.

Hook returned it. "Indeed, my love. Now to the next order of business. The second of today's accomplishments is the establishment of truce for the Clearing. The native people now understand that I will punish violation of the peace there. I expect that the ladies, and Jill's twins, and even my sailors will be safe in that sanctuary. Captain Cecco, Mr. Smee— you will inform the company of this truce. On no account will I allow my men to disturb the tranquility of the Clearing. I vowed to protect *all* who visit there, Indians of both sexes included. I will brook no excuses of drunkenness or provocation. Any violation of my decree will meet severe penalty."

Smee asked, "With what punishment, if you please, Commodore?"

"I shall abandon such an offender to the justice of the natives."

"Aye, Sir. That should do it." Smee nodded. "You've set my mind at rest for Lily."

"A harsh penalty, but a just one," Cecco agreed.

"Third," Hook continued, "as is my policy before any enemy, I cast doubt on my devotion to our lady. You must understand this tactic, Captain, and lend credibility to my misinformation. I learned at the village what I have heretofore suspected: the Indians are keen to capture Jill. They were, perhaps, more eager to scalp and kill my 'wife' today than to dispense with me."

Smee's eyes enlarged behind his spectacles. "But why, Sir? What's the lady ever done to them?"

"It isn't what she's done. It is what she might do."

As Hook's thoughts communicated his meaning to her, Jill paled. "No."

"As a single man, I pose less of a threat. Once I head a clan, the natives will seek to emasculate me— through my offspring. You must faithfully follow Lelaneh's instructions, my love, and continue imbibing her tea. My disinclination to father children is no longer the primary factor. It has never been more important to deny me a son."

Cecco's brow creased. "Commodore, how is this? How do you forbid Jill what every woman—"

"I forbid Jill to place herself at risk. Should she honor me with progeny, she would only produce new scalps for the warriors' trophies. Her own, and her children's."

Jill's pulse seemed to pump ice through her veins. "But what of our grown sons?"

"Nibs and Tom are not sons of my blood. The Indians know me to be their foster father, and they know that I only recently became so. And, of course, their mother is another man's wife."

"And Lightly? Might they turn on him because of me?"

"If I deny your importance, there is little chance of his suffering for your sake." Hook turned to Cecco. "So, once again, your marriage to my mistress proves useful. The gossip will spread among the Islanders, throwing doubt on Jill's value as a vulnerability."

Cecco's dark eyes smoldered. "I will be happy, at any time, to make our marriage *completely* useful, and take my wife to live upon the *Lady*."

"As always, Jill holds that option." Hook's voice had turned wintry. "She may seek release from her oath— should she wish to do so."

Jill watched Cecco, in silence, then turned her gaze. Gently, she reached her red hand out, to lay it upon the scars of Hook's wrist. It seemed to Cecco that she spoke to Hook, though her words were inaudible. At her touch, Hook dropped his bristling posture.

Stung, Cecco subsided, gripping his glass again. He clutched, also, at the words Lily had spoken to him. His task was now clear. Only one choice would serve in this matter. For everyone's sake, he must discern the deepest wish of Jill's heart— and find, within his own, the power to grant it.

Becoming aware of Smee's scrutiny, Cecco snapped out of his reverie. He shot the bo'sun a murderous look, then refilled his own cup with cognac.

Smee sought to ease the tension with a change of topic. "Commodore, Sir, you'll be glad to be knowing that the lady suffered no worrisome injuries. Not a scratch from that cat, thank the Powers, and only a nasty bruise upon her shoulder. She tells me you saved her from worse, but I looked her over to be sure. Held the poultice to the hurt myself, as her poor chilled hands shook too much from exhaustion."

"One bruise is too many." Hook slid his hand in the collar of Jill's robe to expose the blue-green flesh of her upper arm. "I regret that I was unable to prevent it, my love." Softly, his ringed fingers touched the discoloration.

Cecco stared. As his wife's robe opened to show her shoulder, the curve of her breast appeared as well. He now saw that she wore no nightgown, nor a shift. Her bosom lay open to view— a view Mr. Smee could see. A view Mr. Smee had seen, without doubt, in his ministrations.

Cecco remembered the order he gave, in haste, to the commodore's steward, the command to remove Jill's wet clothing, to warm and dry her, and to lay her down upon her bed. Until now, Cecco had not given thought to the consequence of his own commands. Smee's casual discussion of the lady's condition, his entitlement in regarding her now through those ever-observant spectacles, brought home to Cecco the reality of his wife's circumstances. Hook was not the only man who looked upon the tempting flesh of his wife. Hook was not the only man who touched her, intimately. Watching the three of them together, Cecco felt the truth, which until this moment he merely suspected, crashing upon his consciousness like a falling yardarm. The commodore was too free with his favors. Jill belonged to Hook, and whatever was Hook's, be it clothing, table service, or mistress, fell naturally into his steward's fingers. No doubt Smee tended Jill's person like he tended that harness this minute: dutifully, lovingly, and thoroughly. Cecco knew for certain now what he had hoped was only the jealous conjecture of his imagination. Plainly, Hook *did* grant to Smee what he withheld from Cecco. Jill's husband might not lay a hand on her. Hook's steward touched her every day.

Unable to repress his resentment, Captain Cecco allowed his lip to snarl as he remembered that once upon a time, these quarters and all they encompassed had been his. The cognac, the furnishings…the lady. A wave of bitterness rose within him, threatening to engulf his heart. Cecco gritted his teeth, calling upon his common sense, his loyalty, to stop himself from jumping to his feet and overturning the table. Given his will, he would seize his knife and, before the company could blink, he'd slash Smee's Irish throat. Hook was unarmed at the moment, but Jill…

With a steadying breath, Cecco let his gaze dwell upon her again, forcing himself to calm. For such an act, Jill would never forgive him. Smee was one of the several men Jill loved. She trusted Cecco to honor her wishes. Her deepest longing was as yet a mystery to her husband, but he knew she wished for accord among her company of pirates.

And, for the present, Jill's wishes ran parallel to Hook's. Hot as Cecco burned to defend his wife from intruding attentions, he must keep a cool head upon his shoulders. His oath to Hook, too, insisted. For the time being, the commodore's orders must be obeyed.

Wishing to escape this torment, Cecco stood. "If we have covered everything, Commodore, I will take my leave."

Jill had adjusted her dressing gown to cover her bruise, and now she looked upon Cecco with disappointment. Did she regret his leaving, he wondered, or did she regret the threat he posed to her lovers? She wouldn't allow him to speak with her privately. How could he know her feeling?

Hook scrutinized Cecco. "Only one more point, Captain." He indicated that Cecco should reseat himself, then paused to collect his subordinates' attention. Grudgingly, Cecco sat.

True to form, Hook minced no words. "The warrior White Bear is a member of the Council of Elders. I gather he wields a great deal of influence within the tribe. Pray, Captain, be discreet in your relations with his delectable sister-in-law."

As with his first insinuation regarding Raven, Hook took Cecco by surprise. Cecco shot from his seat and stumbled backward, upsetting his chair. Smee leapt up to secure it. Cecco's jaw dropped open in protest. He stared at Hook in disbelief, then looked to Jill to determine her reaction.

She sat still, locking eyes with her husband, then, cloaking her emotion, she dropped her gaze to her lap. Cecco caught a whisper, perhaps it was the waves on the hull, perhaps it was her own heart speaking to his. It echoed his dilemma. *Beware, or you may acquire your desires.*

"Madam...Commodore..." Cecco gathered his wits. "Believe me— I assure you. I would not make a move that might endanger my shipmates. Nor do I diminish my marriage." Cecco stretched his hand across the table, toward his wife. "I wish only for unity."

"*Unity.*" Hook smiled in irony. "The ship on which you were married, Captain."

Jill beheld Cecco's outstretched hand. Her own wedding band beckoned to her, shining on his finger. She repeated, "Unity. Yes." She turned her eyes up to Cecco.

He tried to smile. "Your deepest wish, Lady, is the one that I must grant to you."

Cecco watched as Jill raised, not her pale left hand, the insignificant one she had extended since Hook's return, but her crimson hand, the hand that signaled engagement. Hook's emeralds sparkled on her ring. For a moment she looked upon that bloodstained hand, then she lowered it to the table and slipped it under Hook's.

Cecco felt his heart sinking. The old, unbearable disappointment rushed upon him, weighing him down. And then the feeling lightened, for Jill coaxed Hook's arm toward her husband's. She laid both of their hands atop Cecco's. When Cecco's flesh met Hook's there, warmly surrounding her own, Jill looked to her husband. Above the gentle slap of the waves of Neverbay, her voice came low, but clear.

"Like you, Giovanni, I wish for unity." She raised their three hands together, and kissed first Hook's fingers, then Cecco's. Just as she had done when she embraced her two officers at the door, she shed her apprehension. As at that time, for one luminous moment, Jill appeared wholly satisfied.

The three men surrounding her did not.

The next thing Cecco knew, he stood on the companionway with the commodore's door clicking closed behind him. The taste of cognac lay upon his tongue, his desire for his wife felt solid within his breeches, and Mr. Smee, more quiet than usual, descended the stairs ahead of him, the lethal hook and its harness in hand. And down below decks, Cecco now knew, the *Roger* contained a witness to a marriage: David, the *Unity*'s cabin boy.

Unity. The hallmark of a successful company.

The essence of a marriage.

How to grant a wish so profound and so impossible? Cecco could not imagine. He turned to gaze toward shore. In the darkening landscape, among the fertile clumps of drowsing greenery, he spied the white, ghostly outline of the cliff top where— when the sun sailed high and the world was real— lovely, lonely Raven had run into his arms.

He had forgotten, until that moment, that he had arranged an assignation with Raven. Tomorrow, at noon, his empty arms might hold her again.

Forgotten in his cell, David lay down upon the bench. Reluctant to muss his new clothing, he had resisted even sitting until now. He was determined to appear neat and spotless when summoned to the sacred presence of Red-Handed Jill. But he waited and he paced, and that summons never came. Now the sun was long abed, and only the dim lantern on the stairway lent light to David's disappointment.

He had heard the excitement, the huzzahs and cannon fire close to sundown. He didn't know it meant that the commodore had escaped a hideous execution until an odd, repulsive man with gold teeth and a tri-cornered hat brought him some supper and told him about the Indians. David listened in shock to the story of Red-Handed Jill's danger and deliverance, but he was too sickened by the messenger's hands to ask any questions.

The sailor introduced himself as Mr. Noodler, and he was grotesque, another ghastly show of the Island's quirks. The hands that bore the supper tray were backward, as if someone had chopped them off and sewed them back again on the wrong wrists. Those hands had set the tray down, but David was too nauseated by the sight of them to eat anything they had handled. When Noodler left, David shoved the food aside and continued his pacing, the brittle straw chafing underfoot.

According to Noodler, Jill was unscathed, but still recovering from her ordeal. That must be why she left her captive languishing here in the brig. Sorry as he felt for himself, David's heart cringed to think of Jill in peril. This afternoon she had shown that she could handle the Island itself. In David's opinion, she was its queen. But no one could expect her to prevail against a pack of savage men. And what would happen to David if harm came to Jill? He didn't hold much hope that Commodore Hook or Mr. Smee or even Captain Cecco had any use for him. Only Jill cared for David….Jill had kissed him.

Soaring at the memory, David's spirit bounded further as he contemplated the idea that Hook, who loomed so large and commanding on the Island this afternoon, might have perished that very evening. The Legend was mortal after all! David thought it a shame that the natives hadn't rid his horizon of that menace. No doubt Captain Cecco felt the same. It was a wonder Cecco troubled himself to rescue Hook. David couldn't fathom why a man would lift one little finger to serve the blackguard who had stolen his wife. The boy shook his head. No doubt it was just another demonstration of the depravity of pirates. Honor and decency didn't exist upon this ship.

Still thinking of Cecco, David looked up, and he gasped. There the man stood, his powerful hands wrapped around the bars of David's cage, his dusky eyes glowering at him. He was darker, his bare chest broader, his arms more muscular than the cabin boy remembered. He looked as if he could tear the iron bars asunder. His countenance was hostile, as though he would sooner strangle David than not. In the feeble orange lantern light, the cutlass and the dagger David remembered from the attack on the *Unity* gleamed at Cecco's waist. His earrings and bracelets also shone, and, for one blessed moment, David thought of the matching jewelry Jill had worn on her wedding day. The image of her in her finery did not sustain him for long. David shrunk back, suddenly glad to feel the protective bars of Hook's brig enclosing him.

Cecco's Mediterranean accent was too familiar to David, with the same words he'd heard that morning at the clearing, this time uttered with contempt.

"*Ragazzo.* Boy."

David swallowed.

"You were too swift for me, but my lady hunted you down. Did she not?"

The prisoner nodded.

"I am told that you worship her."

David's eyes bulged. Remembering the ritual he had performed hours ago, flagrantly pagan and naked in his cell, he reddened with humiliation.

"I pity you, boy. You will never receive what you pray for."

Offended, David dared to speak at last. "What could you know of me or my prayers?"

"I know everything. My Jill is a never ending story. Only striving and heartbreak await the man who seeks to hold her." With burning eyes, Cecco continued to stare between the bars. "But you are not a man."

Unsure how to deal with his visitor, David stood and craned his head toward the top of the stairs, hoping to see someone, anyone, come down them. The light of the lantern revealed the left side of his face.

Cecco laughed a cruel, mocking laugh. "Ah! I see!" He gestured to David's cheek. "Jill has marked you. And you believe this mark signifies success."

Covering his cheek, David glared. "You're jealous, Captain. And not just jealous of me. But I bet you don't dare to talk to your commodore that way."

"I have more sense than to challenge the commodore. Do you? Boy?"

"He's the only one I'd bother to challenge. You seem to have lost your wife to him."

"Pitiable soul. Are you arrogant— or ignorant? A bit of both, I think."

"Do pirates take prisoners just to insult them?"

"A prisoner is an item of value, or a prisoner is dead. Mark my words, my Jill will use you. Then she will discard you."

"What did you come here for?"

"At last you ask an intelligent question." Cecco sneered. "I came to use you, too."

David recoiled. He wanted to be used, in every conceivable way— by Jill. But this…this idea was a nightmare. David had heard tales of depravity among sailors. Beastly things might happen on the high seas to boys who shipped out with men. Up until now, David's uncle had shielded him from the urges of seafaring queans. David looked sideways at Cecco, uncomfortably aware once again of the man's physical superiority. The boy's panic took over, as he imagined what it would be like to be imprisoned in those arms, to be the object of craven desires, and violated by that…body. David even imagined he could smell the man's skin on his own, afterward. The cold of dread settled in the bottom of David's stomach. More disturbing still, he felt a twinge of arousal at his privates, and shame invaded his soul. He tried to forbid these images to linger in his thoughts. At Cecco's next words, however, relief made cold sweat break out all over David's flesh.

"What happened to the *Unity?*"

David exhaled. His sense of deliverance made him brash. "Why do you care? You did your best to ruin her."

"Your captain and your surgeon. Do they live?"

David sulked in silence.

"Dead, then." Cecco performed his gypsy banishing gesture,

down from his forehead and across his chest. "I do not come to speak of the dead. You are alive. You are the last surviving witness to my marriage. Are you not?"

Sensing he might gain leverage by Cecco's need, David nodded. "I am. The *only* witness."

"And what proof exists? Do your captain's papers remain?"

"Nothing remains. The ship broke up in a storm."

"You did not aim for the Neverland. The Island called you here." Cecco leaned his forehead against the bars and peered at David. "How?"

David's brow contracted. This question had never occurred to him. "I…I just washed ashore."

"In a boat?"

"In what was left of it."

"With only the clothes upon your back."

David blinked. "That's all."

"Your uncle entrusted no packet to you?"

"No, nor valuables, either, if that's what you're looking for." Defiantly, David tipped his chin toward Cecco. "You'll remember that Jill took my own silver shamrock."

"Your good luck piece. Yes. She hung it on a necklace. I kissed her bosom beneath it, many times."

The look of loathing on David's face confirmed that Cecco's dart hit home. David retorted, "That shamrock was the *Unity's* good fortune. Jill took everything when she took that charm."

Cecco observed Jill's branding on the young man's cheek. It had darkened, to resemble the vivid crimson of Jill's hand. The boy was lying. "What from the wreckage did you manage to preserve?"

David dodged Cecco's eyes. "Nothing."

"Nothing. I have killed men for less."

David backed against the bench. As his knees buckled beneath him, he sat down hard. He felt ill and dizzy. He had the sensation that if the door to his cell opened, that moment would be his last.

"Let me tell you a tale, cabin boy, a story that is real as these iron bars.

"A dangerous man lurks across the ocean. He is a physician, a profession that commands respect in all circles, on land or on sea.

He believes himself to be Jill's husband. He holds papers that seem to prove his claim. When he catches up to her— and he will catch up to her— he will exercise his legal right to possess her. He will pry her away to a place far from her Island. A 'civilized' place, where only the law dictates right and wrong. A place where, because of the law, I cannot go to save her, nor can the commodore, nor any of our men. This man will convince the authorities that she belongs to him. He will keep her as much a prisoner as you feel tonight in this cage. He has money, he has influence, and he has tools to use against her. Tools more subtle than her sword, her whip, or her pistol— and far more treacherous. He will lock her up, he will drug her, he will brutalize her, until she submits to his rule."

David heard the fear in the captain's voice. Strange fear, in a man so raw with physical might. David could not doubt that Cecco believed this story, nor could he doubt that Cecco, pirate though he was, loved Jill with ungovernable force. Ashamed of his lie, David waited to hear more truth.

"Young David. This is how to serve the woman you worship. You can save her from hell. You can turn this evil man's morality against him. So I ask you again." Cecco grasped the bars and steadied his voice.

"Where is the *Unity*'s logbook?"

And at that enlightening moment, the succor for which David had hoped arrived. Someone tramped down the steps. When Mr. Smee reached the brig, he peered over his spectacles and shot a look between the two of them. Judging by the expression on his face, their tension was palpable.

"Why, Captain Cecco. Whatever would you be wanting with the lady's boy, and at this hour of the night?"

David jumped up from his bench. "Mr. Smee! Thank—" David faltered, then chose the orthodox form, "Thank God you've come. Captain Cecco says he wants me to warm his bunk— and I won't do it! I won't! Not if he rips me apart, like he's been threatening to do this half hour past!" Jill's handprint flared upon his cheek now.

Cecco saw it. He stared at David for a long, brooding moment, then turned away. Under Smee's quizzical regard, he headed heavily up the steps.

David watched him go. Keeping up his pretense of outrage for Smee, he smiled only to himself. He felt an optimism he'd never hoped to attain since the *Unity* went down, since he dragged his waterlogged body from the brine.

David wasn't helpless any longer. Captain Cecco had a use for him. The man wanted David alive and well. The legendary Commodore Hook must come to value him, too, eventually. And Jill couldn't help but be swayed when at last she realized how desperately she needed her David. After all, the insignificant cabin boy held more than a rubied ring in his hands now. He held Jill's very life.

When Cecco's boots disappeared through the hatchway, David plunked himself on his bench, and wolfed his cold dinner down.

Love Birds

The smoke of the bonfire drifted upward to cross the clouds, trailing an acrid scent where the revelers celebrated. Much had transpired within the village today, and its toll could be seen in the lines around Willow's mouth, and in the hand she pressed to the base of her back this evening as the People danced, sang, and feasted by the fire.

White Bear hadn't needed to charge Raven with her sister's welfare through the festivities. Raven had stayed by Willow's side. She studied Willow now, saying, "You must tell me if you tire, so that I can take you home. You and your baby need your sleep."

"Very well, Raven. I admit that I am weary, but I would not sleep with this noise, and I'd like to watch a little longer. It is good to see the People so proud tonight."

"Truly. The tribe is glad of victory."

Willow patted her middle. "Soon I will be able to join in the dances again." The merriment carried on while the sisters sat on the periphery. Men and boys perched with their drums before them, the meat of their arms jolting as they beat in rhythm. Their cadence was sometimes simple, sometimes complex, forming hollow, resonant measures. Women sang in spirited chorus, shuffling, bending, stepping, and rising up again to reach toward the moon. Raven and Willow only smiled and watched. Willow was too advanced in her pregnancy to participate further. Raven was too distracted.

Against Raven's inclination— against the Shadow Woman's— she felt the drums vibrate in her vitals; the dancers' movements enlivened her. The line of women snaked around now to circle the fire, chanting, while the men danced about them in the opposite direction, working off the energy that their unfought battle had aroused. One by one, the women left the circle to kneel down and watch with Raven and Willow, but the men carried on, turning away from the ring to show off their nimbleness, each on his own. The men would perform their celebration far into the evening, until the thunder of the drums ceased to rumble.

Raven recognized that both exultation and relief fueled this evening's fervor. The talk, the songs, the dances— they all spoke of the People's feelings.

The tribe rejoiced in release from anxiety, but they also felt a fresh sense of power. The pirates won the advantage in the previous encounter, on the night the Black Chief drove the People up the mountain. Now the Black Chief had been captured. Today, He of the Eagle's Claw was tried and freed by the People, and no dishonor could be counted on either side. True, the Black Chief had spoken insolently, had issued threats. But had not White Bear prevailed over him, in judgment and in restraint? Had not the chief of the pirates exposed his weakness for women when he lied to protect his paramour, and when he lingered to speak to Raven?

Raven suffered a twinge of dread, as sharp as the pirate's claw, when she remembered how the Black Chief singled her out. The skin of her jaw burned as she recalled the brush of his fingers, and how he dared to touch her. Reflecting upon White Bear's reaction, though, Raven believed she had acted properly. The Shadow Woman did not desire attention. Even her brother-in-law could not suppose she invited the pirate's regard.

And, surely, the wild man had behaved as expected. All the People knew the pirates to be uncivilized. No one reproached Raven with a word or with a look.

No, Raven thought. The new anxiety she carried did not center around the Black Chief, but around another matter— a matter that distressed her beyond even her impending coupling with White Bear. Here Raven did experience the reprimand of her conscience. After White Bear counseled Raven this morning, commanding her submission, he left her alone. She had dashed from the tepee and flung herself into the woods, where she ended in the arms of the enemy.

Befriending pirates was taboo. Raven shuddered at the consequences if White Bear discovered her familiarity with an adversary. Unlike the Women of the Clearing, who knew too well the punishment for consorting with sea men, Raven would be lost living in exile. To exist on the outside of tribe and tradition would, to Raven, feel like a breathing death. Even Lightly of the Air faced the council's disapprobation tomorrow, and he had good reason to break with custom: his obligation to visit his mother. Raven, on the contrary, made no excuse for her behavior. She had disobeyed her provider. She had defied the elders. Even Willow wouldn't understand her conduct. Raven wished she could understand her reaction, herself.

As if she intuited Raven's thoughts, Willow gasped, startling Raven in the midst of self-reproach.

Willow apologized. "White Bear's son is awake, my sister. I felt a powerful kick! He must know his father to be a great warrior, and he, too, wants to dance in celebration."

Soothingly, Raven said, "His father will teach him, when the seasons bring the proper age."

"Our family is proud tonight. White Bear confirmed the council's confidence in him."

"The People honor him for his dealings on their behalf. But we know White Bear's character, Willow. It is he who is proud to serve."

"It pleases me to hear you praising White Bear." A warrior howled and Willow's gaze followed the sound. "Oh, see how Lean Wolf struts!" Her voice mocked, gently. "He dances for you, I know."

"Yes. He dances for me."

"He preens in a courting ritual, like the cock birds in the forest."

Silently, Raven agreed. As she observed the dancers, Lean Wolf frequently positioned himself in front of Raven, next to White Bear. When he moved his taut, athletic body, he demonstrated skill and control, while his endurance could not be questioned. He had removed his hunting knife and his leggings to dance in his breechclout, and his muscles flowed like water under the flesh of his arms, his legs, and his thighs. His enthusiasm was contagious; the young braves mimicked his movement, ducking and spinning and throwing their heads back to shout to creation. The fervency of Lean Wolf's courtship was apparent in his unceasing motion. As the moon rose and the dance wore on, the younger warriors began to drop out of the circle, but as long as the music played, Lean Wolf persisted.

Raven's were not the only eyes that watched him. All the women admired Lean Wolf this evening. She felt their sidewise gazes upon her. She saw the sly smiles cast her way, and those smiles gave her pause. As Lean Wolf pranced in the firelight, Raven noted that he allowed sincerity to shine through his face again, as when he proposed to Raven to join him in marriage. Once again, she wondered at Lean Wolf's twofold nature, at his friendship and rivalry with White Bear, at his ability to charm...and betray.

But all the while her black eyes followed her suitor, Raven recalled the sound of the breakers as they poured themselves upon the base of the cliff; she remembered the noise of metal bracelets chiming, and her name pronounced in exotic accents. Yet when White Bear, her provider, danced before her, Raven immediately returned to the present, banishing thoughts of forbidden islands. She disciplined her features, and drew herself and her secrets a little farther from her sister.

In this effort, she succeeded. Willow trusted Raven, and caught no hint of impropriety. She sighed, relaxing as the baby's kicks at last subsided. "Sister, I tease you, but I agree with White Bear. You do well to show no sign of interest to Lean Wolf. You are better off in our tepee."

Discreetly, Willow studied Raven to gauge how she reacted to White Bear's more traditional approach. Raven did not acknowledge her hopeful face, so Willow plucked up her spirit and continued, speaking low to avoid being overheard by the other women, "I am certain, too, that Ash would want his widow to settle safely under the wing of a dependable warrior. You must remember how Ash and White Bear respected one another. And consider that today White Bear won the right to exult, yet he remains levelheaded during this excitement."

Both sisters approved of White Bear's dance this evening. He stepped with confidence, displaying his battle scars, the bear claws dancing, too, upon his chest. His copper skin glowed in the light of the bonfire. His arrow-straight frame seemed supplemented by a new kind of pride, earned this afternoon in his pow-wow with the pirate. His dance was slow and steady, not flamboyant like Lean Wolf's, but constant in its purpose. He, too, was courting. But Raven knew; unlike Lean Wolf, he was not seeking Raven's love or admiration. In wooing Raven, he was courting Willow's peace of mind, and the esteem of the elders.

Reminded of her sister's condition, Raven wished to set Willow's mind at rest. "You must never be uneasy for me. You have a more important matter to dwell upon. Let me take you home to lie down now. The camp will soon calm, and you and your little one can sleep."

Willow consented. Raven rose, supporting her sister as she struggled to stand, too. Raven gathered up their blankets, and, receiving a nod of acknowledgement from White Bear, led Willow through the cool, dew-wet grasses to his tepee. She braided Willow's hair, fetched a drink of water for her, and tended to her comfort.

Before closing her eyes, Willow looked earnestly at her sister. "I understand that you are anxious about lying with White Bear. But I do not doubt that, in the morning, you will begin to learn contentment." Then Willow settled, snug beneath the blankets, and soon she drifted into doze.

Raven readied herself for slumber, also. Yet, once Willow dreamed, Raven felt the impulse to burst from the tepee and seek solace among the trees beyond the dwelling place. She wished to run deep into the wood, as she had done this morning.

But White Bear's decree, at last, restrained her, as tightly as Willow's papoose would one day soon be wrapped. The afternoon's events had served to reinforce his supremacy. White Bear— brother-in-law, provider, speaker for the council, decider of the enemy's fate— had spoken.

The hide of the tepee seemed to tighten, pressing in upon Raven as it did this morning when White Bear spoke his ultimatum, as if it meant to force her out to face a new life, like a woman giving birth. And, in truth, a birth *was* imminent. Kneeling to check on Willow, Raven found her safely in slumber after the long day's events. To Willow, this tepee was a place of peace.

A wise-bird hooted in the branches above the village. Raven listened, wishing she could interpret its message. By its invisibility, the bird reminded her to seek shelter as the Shadow Woman, but its very boldness— crying out in the center of the camp— contradicted. Who should she be? Whom should she please?

Raven slipped out the door, and only her gaze wandered among the trees that fringed the camp. Her fingers still felt the silk of Willow's lengthy black hair, so like her own used to be, before she hacked it away with Ash's hunting knife. It was almost, but not quite, as fine as the long curls she had handled this afternoon, at the Black Chief's command. With a sudden vigor, she rubbed her hands together, to rid herself of the reminder.

Since her childhood, stories of the Black Chief were impressed upon Raven. Today she witnessed in reality the frightful, deadly claw at the end of his arm. In perfect clarity she remembered the appreciation in his outlandishly blue eyes, his insinuating smile. She could not deny he was a man of compelling power. Although He of the Eagle's Claw eyed her with admiration, Raven was certain he was motivated, in part, by cunning. Still, she would never forget the imprint he made upon her spirit. It was not unlike the imprint White Bear made, every day that she lived within his tepee.

Along with her thoughts, she turned her gaze toward her brother-in-law, where he and a few remaining men, Lean Wolf among them, squatted by the fire, smoking the last celebratory pipes. Like the People's, the bonfire's sounds were mild now, compared to its earlier roar. The drums lay silent; the night noise of crickets and creatures prevailed.

The owl startled Raven, hooting directly above her this time, and this time Raven caught the bird's meaning. *Who...who woos you?*

Who, under his sorrow, was her stranger-friend? Who was Raven? Would she go to him, to learn these answers? Was she valiant to risk her existence, as barren as it was, or was she cowardly? Would she venture out of the camp again, at midday, not to run this time, but to walk with purpose into his company?

She did not know.

Her empty heart leapt as she considered his invitation. All her soul cried out for the kinship they'd discovered between them. All her mind instructed her to refuse her feeling. She must not bring disgrace upon White Bear, nor compromise his standing among the elders. Neither Raven nor the owl asked who White Bear was. He was known. She must not ever forget.

In spite of her logic, Raven's heart flew away from the village again, to perch upon the cliff top overlooking the sea. To alight, once more, on the dark-haired sea man whose arms sang with bracelets, whose voice held tenderness, who uttered Raven's name before she had spoken it, and whose own name she'd refused to hear.

But she *had* heard his name, this afternoon, in this very camp. His was a strange name, harsh to her ear, and made up of hard sounds, like a command. *Cecco.* The Black Chief had called him 'Captain Cecco.' And now that Raven had seen the two white men together, she understood that her acquaintance, this Captain Cecco, was an important man among the pirates. He stood second only to their chief. His name was a name of power.

Instinctively, Raven had called upon Cecco's power. Yet she had done so at her peril. In her distress this afternoon, she looked to Cecco for assistance, instead of turning to her brother-in-law. A foolish mistake, and still, in that time of discomfort, it felt fitting to appeal to the offender's fellow. What, after all, might White Bear— or even Ash if he were still alive— have done to relieve her of the Black Chief's beguiling?

Her reaction was a natural one. But it was not an acceptable response for a woman who did not know this pirate. At any moment now, Raven must lie at White Bear's mercy. Did he notice her blunder? Did he guess her deception? Would he censure her? Or would he choose to remain aloof, ignore the question, and assert his dominance in a physical manner— tonight— *now?*

Whatever White Bear's sense of honor led him to do, Raven knew that she could no longer resist him. Just as she was stirred by the dancers leaping about the bonfire, she would be moved against her inclination. Soon, Raven's emotion would steal upon her, whether she willed it or no. She foresaw what White Bear did not divine, and what Willow could not grasp. To surrender to his touch would bring another natural reaction. Trouble would dance its way into their tepee.

She found herself pressing against the dusty bark of a tree, her fingernails gleaning its grit. It was too late now to run away, to flee to the Clearing, or even to her pirate. Too late; with a fresh rush of panic, Raven detected White Bear's stride as he approached his dwelling, a black, sinewy silhouette with the orange of embers behind him.

She had no strength left to wrestle his will. She backed from the tree. She stepped into White Bear's tepee, to the furs that he provided her— to submit to his authority, in whatever manner he chose to enforce it.

When White Bear threw open the door flap, his figure dark against the dusk of the sky, two women lay under the skins he had hunted. One woman smiled in her dreams, loving and obedient even in slumber.

The other watched as he covered her sister, not with his body this night, but with the token of his protection, the albino bear pelt. Raven saw him stroke the hair at Willow's forehead; the bear claws on his necklace dangled over Willow's breast. He left her sister and removed his beaded moccasins. As he lifted her blanket, Raven was chilled by a draft of evening air. His long, unyielding body slid beside her, and beneath the scent of tobacco smoke she smelled his man-smell. Her sister's marriage bracelet skimmed over her belly as his arm reached to enclose her. The smooth, cool feel of those beads caused her to shy, but her courage remained to sustain her. The Shadow Woman lay silent, and, too soon, the unwelcome weight of obligation pressed down upon her.

"Woman," White Bear said, in a gruff, quiet voice, so that his wife lay undisturbed, at peace with his son in her womb.

Warily, Raven held her body still, watching him.

"I still hunger."

She felt the tepee shrinking, bearing down on its inhabitants, threatening to give birth to a new— and a malformed— family.

Pierre-Jean cast a cautious glance around the galley of *Red Lady*, as he had done twenty times in the previous half hour. The lanterns shone yellow, softening the casks and barrels of provisions, illuminating the onions, garlic, and beets swinging from the beams, but in their light no one lounged at the tables that hung at intervals around the room. The cannon ranging along the hull averted their snouts, nosing toward the sea through their gunports, as if making a point of not listening.

The girl who appeared in the doorway, now, was listening.

Pierre-Jean's face brightened. "I am wait for you." He spoke low in his clumsy English, adding quickly, "*Madame* Hanover." He shrugged apology, "I hope no offense to make?"

Mrs. Hanover conducted a fast, panicked search of the deck behind her, then entered the galley and shut the door without a sound. Her gaze fastened on the Frenchman's china blue eyes, questioning.

He said, "I see you each night. Each night you enter here."

The girl tilted her head to study him, a line of suspicion drawn upon her brow. Pierre-Jean blushed, then got up his nerve to stride toward her. Mrs. Hanover backed away, her maroon skirt swishing.

He stopped, his hands empty in the air, signifying harmlessness. "No, *s'il vous plaît*, I…I…Here." He reached for the flagon in her fingers. "I pour for you, tonight." Venturing another step, he drew the vessel from her grip.

Mrs. Hanover wondered as the Frenchman filled it from the cook's cask of grog. This job was one she performed most evenings, drawing and serving for her master. Since her abduction by pirates, no one waited upon Mrs. Hanover. She had forgotten how special she felt when pampered by her nurse, and now she experienced a resurgence of that gratification. She could not fail to be flattered by the constancy of Pierre-Jean's attendance to her needs, but he had never before been so daring as to contrive to talk with her alone. They both knew the danger in which, by doing so, he placed himself. Both Captain Cecco and his mate Mr. Yulunga took a serious view of discipline, and these officers knew better than to trust Mrs. Hanover in the company of men.

The flush remained to tinge Pierre-Jean's cheek, showing that he, too, was pleased by his gamble. His work was quick but neat, and he soon stood before her again, settling the flagon in her hands. "Now you go, no madness from Meester Yulunga."

Mrs. Hanover allowed herself a moment of amusement. Pierre-Jean caught the light in her eye, and his Gallic grin lit up his face.

"Ah! You are please to see manners. In France, I am most manners."

Mrs. Hanover chortled, then stifled the sound for fear of being overheard. Such a precaution was not one with which she was familiar. Mrs. Hanover almost never made noise, and rarely with her voice. Still, she indicated the drink in her hand and, as Mr. Yulunga insisted she do, she tried to articulate her thanks.

As she opened her lips, Pierre-Jean shook his head. "No, not to speak. I see you. I see you enjoy not to speak."

As her shoulders relaxed, Pierre-Jean knew he'd hit upon the way to slip into the lady's graces. He didn't care about the soft swell of the child below her waist. Most sailors wouldn't. Most were relieved to keep company with a woman *enceinte* by a man long gone. No blame would accrue to them, nor could another liability be conceived. And little Mrs. Hanover had months to go before the bulge got in the way. But Pierre-Jean's infatuation ran deeper than convenience. Despite her condition, Mrs. Hanover wasn't common like a fishwife. She was born a lady. She looked dainty, pretty in her own way, and even at her young age she handled a hard life. Daily, he loved her from afar, intending to watch and to wait. But he was young, he was French, and opportunity urged him to make the most of this privacy. He pressed his point, "I, too, enjoy not to speak, because I am no good to English."

The boy was tall and slender, and Mrs. Hanover found herself looking up into his earnest face. Only then did she realize how close he stood. She saw him every day, felt his interest and his courtesy following her. She even searched for his long blond pigtail wherever a cluster of sailors gathered, but she'd rarely had leisure to really gaze into his adoring countenance. With a flutter in her heart, she discovered the sensation to be pleasant.

His sailor's hands were calloused. She should have shaken them off, but in spite of their texture he touched her so subtly, so lightly, that he was stroking her face before she realized it. She melted, just a little.

Pierre-Jean held her gaze. "I am no good to English, but I know why you enjoy not to speak."

Her eyes grew round.

"He...your papa..."

Mrs. Hanover, named for her liaison with her father, nearly dropped the drink. Only her cognizance of the consequences preserved it, and kept her from spilling as she turned on her heel and dashed away to serve Yulunga.

Pierre-Jean appreciated her pretty figure as she hastened from him. He smiled, and he didn't fret. In his twenty-two years, he had never mastered conversation, even in French. But he had always been good with his hands.

"It is as well, Lightly, that you were not among us when your foster father was captured and your mother pursued." Panther's face in the firelight was kind, but shadows danced upon it, showing Panther's savage side, the side that craved the enemy's blood.

"I thank you for your understanding, Panther, and for telling us what happened this afternoon while we were dressing the tiger's hide. Although I want what is best for my adopted people, I rejoice in my mother's safety."

Rowan said, "I believe White Bear himself understands. If the People of the Other Island found a reason to make war upon us, he would walk the same path Lightly treads today."

Lightly nodded. "Sometimes, it is useful not to conquer, but to maintain equal footing with one's foes."

Gazing with surprise on Lightly, Panther asked, "How did you learn such an old lesson in such a young life?"

"My mother of the Red Hand possesses an old one's soul. When we were children she counseled peace in the Golden Boy's hideout. Not only to protect us, but also, I think, because she knew that if our pack routed the pirates, the bond of peril that united us might be so much the weaker. Perhaps the elders believe the same."

"You are both worthy braves," Panther said. "But even if the council free you of blame tomorrow, I advise you to heed my mother's warnings." He unfolded his legs to stand, and his long, streaked braids fell forward. "The fire is dying and the dances are done. I go to my slumbers now, but tomorrow, before the sun hides his face, we will feast together at my tepee. I look forward to hearing the tale of your hunting."

Rowan and Lightly rose in respect, wishing Panther good night. Only a few braves remained by the fire, chatting and smoking their pipes to the dregs of their bowls, the warm, sweet tobacco smoke curling round their heads. When Panther left, Rowan spoke quietly.

"Panther is right. We must listen to the Old One's words. We violate the same taboo that banished my mother. If we wish to remain among the People, we must keep our distance from the pirates."

"I'd have been sorry to miss seeing Jill conquer that tiger. I'm glad we were able to hunt with her today, and to return her weapons to her when we found them. But from now on, I'll arrange to see her when she's alone."

"And your brothers, Nibs and Tom?"

Lightly flashed a grin. "We can meet them at the Lagoon, where the People rarely venture. My brothers will appreciate an excuse to dive after mermaids."

Rowan smiled. "We will bring enchanted moss from the Fairy Glade, to stuff our ears against the siren song."

"And against Tom's vocal chords. His voice has become booming since he went to sea. He'll make an excellent captain one day, bellowing orders to his men."

"Perhaps he will rise to commodore, like his foster father."

"Yes, although I understand that Hook never bellows. He's much more subtle. I notice that Nibs has taken after him."

Rowan grew serious. "Using subtlety. As the Old One advises *us* to do." He and Lightly exchanged a sober look. "From her hints tonight, I gather that Panther has spoken to her of his hopes for Ayasha's marriage."

In his new life as a brave, Lightly had learned self-discipline. His pale skin rarely blushed anymore. But now, he felt his cheeks begin to burn with emotion. He couldn't help it. "Rowan."

Rowan motioned toward their tepee on the outskirts of the dwellings. The two young men stole away from the bonfire. The chill of evening descended upon them as they left the social circle to enter their private space. Once inside, Rowan pinned the door flap closed and wrapped his arms around Lightly. A glow from the smoke hole illuminated their tepee, and the weakening firelight seeped through the tawny sides. Feeling one another's chests swell with their breathing, they stood together in the soft light, two men forming a single entity. A partnership.

"Lightly. I feel your heartbeat. I know it beats for me." Rowan laid his head on Lightly's shoulder. "When Panther speaks to me of his daughter, I will find a way to refuse her, without offense."

"But should you refuse her?"

"What do you mean?"

Lightly waited for his spirit to calm. He had considered the question all afternoon, but time had not made the answer easier. "Ayasha adores you. That much is clear. She will make a devoted wife. And if you decline to accept her, she will be only the first of many brides who will be offered to you."

"It is your affection that speaks, Lightly, not the voice of my conceit."

"But Ayasha will bear you sons, and joining her family will assure you of a place on the council, some day."

"A place on the council. Instead of the revilement that one day, you and I, as lovers, might encounter."

"It would be better for you, after all, to follow tradition. To live the rest of your life in the certainty that you have a home among your people, in the knowledge that you have won and kept their respect." Lightly swallowed, and lifted his chin. "Rowan. This is my counsel. You must take Ayasha to wife."

They stood quiet for a long time. Even the tree frogs hushed their trilling. Finally, Rowan asked, "And what would you do if I married, Lightly of the Air?"

At stake lay the future of the person who meant existence itself to Lightly, the fortunes of the brave aptly named 'Life-Giver.' Lightly took command of his voice so that it would not falter.

"I will always be as I am. Your friend and blood brother, who wishes the best for you." But even as he said it, Lightly knew he spoke a lie. Not in his intentions toward Rowan, but about himself. If Rowan married, the elders would have to choose a new name for Lightly. He would no longer be Lightly of the Air. He would never fly again.

Rowan stayed silent. For the first time since their meeting, Lightly was unsure of Rowan's feeling. The dim light on Rowan's eyes revealed only their smooth charcoal surfaces. Did relief lurk there? Did gratitude? An owl hooted in a tree high above the tepee.

Rowan released his companion. "The wise-bird tells us to sleep." He stepped to the blankets, untied his leggings, and knelt. "In the morning, Lightly, when the sun no longer hides his face, you will know how I answered you." He stretched out his hand.

The owl hooted again, asking Lightly, *who-woo, who-woo?*

Who might Lightly be, when, in the morning, the wise-bird folded its wings and closed its eyes to the air?

The evening had cooled, but White Bear was not cold. He was a temperate man. Only tonight, while he danced the dance of a suitor, did his waiting body come awake. As Willow's pregnancy advanced, he knew the aches of abstinence. And when charged by the Old One to speak for the council, White Bear felt his physical being take on new dimensions, seeming to grow in girth and in greatness.

White Bear understood the power that flowed under his feet as the Earth Mother manifested her force, in her pouring waters and in her budding fruits. But not until he allowed himself to dance, preparing to claim Raven, had Earth's energy transferred itself to his body. He hadn't looked at the woman; he hadn't needed to do so. The culmination of this day's events was incentive enough. He had asserted himself as master of his home; he judged wisely in the case of the boy captive; and, trusted by the council, he established his shrewdness as a negotiator in the face of the Black Chief. White Bear; Black Chief. These opposites were now known to the tribe as a balance of power. White Bear's spirit, measured as he was, possessed much in which he could take pride tonight.

And, after tonight, no foolish rumors regarding his sister-in-law would cast doubt on the warrior White Bear. This slim female with her hair too short to catch a man's fingers now submitted to his authority. His companion and competitor Lean Wolf, who had done his best to delay this union right up to the moment of White Bear's entry to the tepee, must stop his badgering. All the People would resume their proper roles, and the elders would approve.

The People had honored White Bear today. Now, as he lay with Raven upon her pallet, he set tribal concerns aside and turned his mind to the command of domestic matters. A feeling of contentment made him patient. A feeling of triumph made him impatient, to conquer the pride and the problem of his wife's older sister.

The warrior White Bear, temperate and tempered, turned toward his sister-in-law— unpredictable as a comet. Disposed for their roles or no, the two must join, tonight.

Raven lay alert. She felt she could hear every sound the world was making, beginning with White Bear's breathing and ending with the songs of the stars. The smoke of the bonfire lingered in her hair and on her skin, and the musk of the man who lay covering her, as if she were his wife, mingled with the scent of his victory. With an abundance of stimulation, and only this single moment to wrestle her body into submission, Raven's spirit dwindled to the form of Shadow Woman.

White Bear's weight pressed her down. The solidity of his branch against her abdomen shocked her, urging Raven to stir from hibernation, to reawaken her wifelike role, rouse herself to the pulse of the seasons. She closed her mind from the present. She turned to her inner woman, and hid away, as she had in reality fled this morning from the men who wished to tame her wearied heart.

Denying impulse— to push and claw or to succumb to desire— Raven lay immobile. Her wide eyes stared in the darkness. She perceived the ghostly bear skin that covered her sister. The darker form of White Bear loomed above her. She looked beyond his shoulder to the tepee's skin, and, in her mind, she looked far beyond its enclosing wall…to the cliff, to the sea. To an island.

Another island.

When White Bear gripped her shoulders, his manhood hard in anticipation of the conquest just to come, he was surprised at the change in Raven's manner. She seemed restless no longer; an air of serenity surrounded her. White Bear was even more surprised when, graciously, she rolled on her side, guiding him likewise, as if to grant equal claim to her pallet. With a dubious look, he settled himself to face her, aroused anew by her changed, yielding attitude, and by the warmth of her wrappings. He watched her face.

"Brother," she said, in a conciliatory tone. With her hand she traced his arm to his wrist, lingering on his marriage bracelet. "Brother. If you and I are to share a blanket, if I am no longer to call you my brother, then," Raven hesitated. Her eyes, in the dimness, acknowledged his power, and appealed to him. "Please tell me, White Bear. Tell me about the home of your birth. Speak to me...of the Other Island."

Like sands in a stream, White Bear's patience trickled away. "The Other Island lies far from our village, and even farther from my thoughts, this evening. Headstrong woman, I will not travel there tonight."

Raven knew his hands upon her, she closed her eyes and shrank her being into shadow. High above them, as if it felt her anguish, the wise-bird hooted in alarm and flapped away. Raven tried to hear nothing, to see nothing, inhale nothing, feel nothing.

She knew her efforts had failed when the whoop of a warrior rent the night, above the dwellings. The mocking voice of Lean Wolf Silent Hunter called from the branches, "If I could fly tonight, old wise-one, your feathers would fletch my arrows tomorrow!"

As White Bear stiffened in anger, laughter rose from tepees far and near. Dogs barked. Willow woke, and turned to sigh aloud, calling to her husband.

The Shadow Woman rose, to clothe herself and stir the embers of the cooking fire, and to warm a soothing broth. She still wondered about the Other Island, but a welcome— a wondrous— feeling of contentment made her patient.

Somehow, she would join her stranger-friend again, on his cliff top. *Tomorrow, when the sun sails high overhead.*

A Pilgrim's Progress

When David ascended to the glory of the morning, his desire to make pilgrimage to Jill's private quarters was dashed. Smee steered him astray toward the quarterdeck, and just as quickly David lost hope of talking with her alone. Though he genuflected before her, a worshipper, he knew he stood no chance of coming close enough to kiss the hem of her skirt, let alone to win a kiss from her lips again. The space in his chest where he'd cherished these aspirations felt hollow.

Across the bay, David recognized the stretch of sand where he washed ashore, and he was relieved to feel ship's timbers beneath his feet again. But once he got his bearings, David devoted his full attention to Jill. She asked for his story, and he confessed it— most of it. He summed up his narrative as a penitent.

"...and please, Lady, accept my apologies for keeping the commodore's ring, and for running, and for taking you into danger. I'm so very thankful that you found me and rescued me from that wilderness." Short of breath by now, David concluded, "If you hadn't, I'd be dead within days, murdered by the natives or eaten by beasts, or just plain starved, with my bones laid to rot in a foul, stinking crypt."

As David had answered Jill's inquiry, the silver shamrock he gave her upon the *Unity* twinkled at her breast. He'd avoided looking that direction, in order to relate his trials in a coherent manner. Now he allowed himself the bliss of watching the shamrock shimmer with her breathing. He felt that any dizziness that resulted would be perceived as the effect of his misadventures.

To David's adoring eye, Jill looked heavenly. She wore her deep green gown today, the one he remembered from her wedding day, sewn of satin whose sheen rivaled her hair. The color was perhaps intended to complement the shamrock, or maybe to match the hues of the Island lurking on the horizon behind her. She sat enthroned under a canopy of sailcloth rigged for shade. The pirate flag streamed high on the mainmast, and below it played a banner of white, displaying two mismatched, blood-red hands. David guessed what that flag symbolized: Jill Red-Hand's union with her pirates. How strange, and how...*magical*, David thought, glancing at her hands, that this woman could appear at once so saintly and so savage.

She reached up to touch the talisman, hiding it beneath those ruby fingertips. David's eyes returned to her face.

She said, "I accept your apology, David, although you stole from the People of the Clearing when you might have asked for their help. But I know that you possess a more selfless side. This shamrock you kindly gave to me brought luck to us both, yesterday."

The boy cleared his throat, but his voice cracked anyway. "Yes, Madam." A sour comment from Mr. Smee reminded David of his presence, and he felt the throb of the bo'sun's blow again.

"I'm thinking you'd have caught the lad before meeting up with that tiger, Ma'am, if you'd had your whip along." Smee stood straight as a staff against the taffrail, damning David with his eyes. A set of manacles dangled over his shoulder.

Smee's two young bo'sun's mates looked daggers at David, too. They manned a post next to the ship's bell, by the stairs that descended to the main deck. The one with the orange kerchief bound about his head was tall and dark complected, the other barrel-chested and beefy. Hostility radiated from both of them. Obviously, none of Jill's crewmen absolved David for the peril in which he'd placed her. Even he condemned himself, for the purple bruise on her shoulder, the sight of which rebuked him more severely than the bo'sun's mates' glares.

Yet David had faith that, now that he belonged to her, Jill herself commanded the generosity to answer his prayer. And, maybe, she'd answer it before he need describe how he might become her savior.

"No doubt you are correct, Mr. Smee. My whip might have snared David, as it once snagged another youngster." With her smile fading, Jill turned back to the cabin boy. "The Neverland is a paradise, but it is not a place with which to trifle, I dreamed of coming here when I was a girl. Once arrived, I discovered its dangers. I also learned how to deal with them."

David nodded. "I surely admire you, Lady. You proved yesterday that you can handle the hazards."

"As you might learn to do, David."

"You mean that you'll teach me, Madam?"

"I mean that I'll see that you are taught."

"With respect, Lady, now that I'm aboard, I hope you'll allow me to serve you on the water. I can read and I can write, and do sums. I'm trained as a cabin boy, if it pleases you, but I could work for the quartermaster or the sail maker, and even run powder."

Jill's doubting look disappointed him. "I will consider not only what I require, but what is necessary for you. From your account of your time on the Island, I gather that self-sufficiency is not your strong point."

"I thank you, Lady, for your consideration. But I never want to brave those wilds again." In truth, David had one last errand to run there, unpleasant but unavoidable— yet he kept to his plan, delaying the moment that he'd have to give his secret away. "I pray that I've been delivered from that dreadful isle for good."

Ignoring David's supplication, Jill said, "I am sorry to learn that the *Unity* went down, taking all hands with her."

"Aye, Madam. The storm did us in, but the seal was set on her destruction after the Frenchmen boarded."

"Then you'll be pleased to know that Commodore Hook broke up *L'Ormonde*'s company, and put that ship to our service as *Red Lady*." Jill nodded in the direction of the sister ship, a cable's length beyond the *Roger*'s bow.

At the mention of the commodore, David looked over his shoulder, as apprehensive of meeting him as of the devil himself.

But Hook did not materialize, and David calmed enough to recognize the former *L'Ormonde*. He was reassured about another anxiety, as well. "Then the French captain wasn't working for you?"

Jill laughed. "Certainly he works for us. But he isn't a willing partner."

"And you didn't look for the *Unity*'s destruction?"

"On the contrary, David. I treasure the memory of my time aboard her."

"The memory of your marriage." David glanced away to say, "Your first marriage, I mean. The sacred one."

Smee squinted his disapproval, but Jill guessed at David's intent. "You are wise to discover all you can about the people who hold power over you." She studied him. "It is a virtue not to judge what you don't understand. Another lesson you'd do well to learn."

Diplomatically, David changed the subject. "I'll be pleased to learn how you plan to put me to work, Ma'am."

"Just a boy, and so eager to work! Sent to sea so young, you must have been allowed only a limited childhood. Did your mother tell you stories?"

"She wasn't much for whimsy, Ma'am. My father died, leaving her to shift for me and my brother and sisters. She read to us only from the good book."

"So you remember nothing of Peter? Nor dreams of the Neverland?"

"Peter? Isn't that the name of a boy I saw over there in the forest?"

"Indeed. It is the custom for Peter to escort the children who are meant to come to the Island. Yet *you* arrived…and in a most unusual manner."

"Not so unusual. I washed ashore. But do you mean that the children I saw were *sent* here?"

"A few lost ones are sent. Others are invited, tempted, or seduced." Jill smiled, reminiscing. "Sometimes all three."

David lowered his voice to reach only Jill. "I'm a lost soul, too, Lady. And from what I've learned of the Island, I think I was sent here to be saved…by an angel." David's face went pink. He expected a denial. Her answer surprised him.

"That explanation *is* the most likely," she said. "What you would call 'Providence' takes many forms."

David gazed at her, and, neophyte though he was, the devotion he pledged with his look might have kindly inclined another woman. Jill remained cool as an icon. She asked, "But can you tell me why you and I have met again?"

David shook his head. "No, Madam." His left cheek began to burn.

"Why, David," she observed, "You are lying to me."

"Madam?"

"My blood-mark. It's as vivid as if I'd just this moment touched you. Mr. Nibs, fetch a mirror."

"Aye, aye." The kerchiefed sailor bowed in obeisance, then departed.

"But I washed, twice...and with the soap that Mr. Smee brought. Did I not scrub it away?"

"I understand that you are bewildered, David. This Island holds magic. But you must have noticed signs of it before today."

Remembering his enchantment as Jill kissed him— the transference of her life force in a rite that set his body to throbbing— David's ears grew heated. His cheek blazed hotter still as he said, "I don't believe in magic." He'd told another lie. He believed in his goddess.

Smee snorted. "Here's a stubborn one, Ma'am. No use to try teaching this lad."

Mr. Nibs dashed up the steps, returning with a shaving mirror. Jill reached with her scarlet hand to take it, and held it up at David's level. "Do you believe your eyes?"

Glad of a reason to approach her, David stepped closer. He was blessed by a whiff of her perfume, which went straight to his head, like liquor. Soon he sobered to catch his reflection. He brought it into focus, and inspected himself.

After weeks forced to fast on the Island, David looked gaunt. His eyes had sunk deeper in their sockets. On his right cheekbone a bruise had bloomed, from the wallop Mr. Smee delivered. His skin had lost the tan he acquired while he sailed his uncle's ship, but, as yet, his chin showed only peach fuzz, although his hair, light brown again now that it was clean, hung some inches farther past his neck. He decided that, once he assumed duty for Jill, he'd tie it back and club it, like a gentleman. Then David turned to view the left side of his face.

He looked up fast, appealing to Jill. "Your…your hand…I can see your handprint!"

"I captured you, and claimed your life as mine. The Island's enchantment worked the rest."

"So that's what that Indian meant, and Mr. Smee, and Captain Cecco, too."

"It also tells us if you're speaking truth. I'm known for my honesty. My mark, therefore, can label you a liar. When the color deepens and burns, your duplicity is obvious."

David stepped back, covering his cheek— not to hide it, but to treasure Jill's token. "But— how long will I keep it?"

Jill laid down the mirror. "I expect that at the proper moment, my mark will fade. Whether one propitiates it or not, Time may work its way on the Neverland."

The boy stood dumbfounded, a pillar of salt.

"Now, David, I ask again. For what reason were you brought to me?"

He delayed for a time, trying to think of a way not to answer. "If you please, Lady, I can't see how reason enters into it." He shrugged. "I was shipwrecked."

"In a disaster that only you survived. And you ended here, a place you weren't invited, that you don't remember from nursery tales, and which you never once held a longing to see."

Mr. Smee leaned forward. "Captain Cecco told you about the doctor, didn't he, boy? The lady's second husband."

"The…the doctor?" Still attempting to prevaricate, David turned his face aside.

Jill's eyebrows raised. She gripped the arms of her chair. Deadly serious now, she stood, strode forward, and grasped David's jaw. He didn't fight her; it was heaven and hell to feel her touch. His heart kicked, then began to thump in double time. As she pulled his left cheek toward her, her fingers firm with authority, the crimson stain revealed David's falsehood.

She dropped her hand. "Dishonesty is a trait I will not tolerate."

She gestured, and Smee clomped forward, dragging the manacles from his shoulder. Next he reached for his keys.

Desperate to remain in Jill's company, David sorted his options. He couldn't bear to disappoint her, and, clearly, subterfuge was impossible. When he'd knelt before her by the carcass of the tigress, he'd vowed to serve Red-Handed Jill. For her benefit, he must protect the secret he safeguarded, bundled in oilcloth, concealed in his cave. He had to use it himself, and use it before his devotion to her forced him to sacrifice it on the bloodstained altar of her palm, just as he'd surrendered his shamrock that day he first succumbed to Jill's spell. But he remembered what Captain Cecco had warned— *a prisoner is an item of value, or a prisoner is dead.*

At last David gasped, "Yes, then. Yes, my lady. Captain Cecco told me about that other man you married. I know how corrupt the doctor is, and how worried he's made you. I want to help. I know something that can protect you."

Contrary to David's expectation, Jill's expression remained fierce, with no hint of relief. "I won't abide foolishness. Mr. Smee, explain what I mean."

In an instant, Smee was gripping David, and the chill of iron wrapped his wrist. David struggled, crying out, "It's no lie! You can see it! Look at my face, the mark will prove I'm telling the truth." He tilted his head for her to see.

Smee had both of David's hands cuffed by now. Jill turned her back. She processed toward the taffrail, her posture regal, her frock fingered by the impious wind. Her profile against the Island appeared, to her disciple, both wonderful and wicked.

David's reverence for her surged through his body and his soul. He dropped to his knees and pressed his shackled hands to his heart. "I swear to serve you, Lady, for all my days if you so command. But I owe one last duty to the *Unity*...to my uncle."

Smee retorted, "You've a duty to your mistress, boy, who risked her life to salvage your sorry hide." He rattled David's chains. "You'd best come clean before she orders you overboard."

"No! No, I'll do anything for her! I promise I'll answer, Madam— I think I know now why I'm here— but I can't explain it— not yet."

She remained aloof. "An act of generosity on your part, David, might ensure your well-being."

"I have to sail back to London, just one last time. I need to go there to defend *you*. And it's a matter of principle, too. My family's honor."

"A liar with honor." Jill turned only her head. Her frame remained aligned with her Island. "A pretty story."

Contrite and confused, he begged, "All right— I'll answer what you ask. Only pledge to me first that you'll get me home."

"You feel you're in a position to parley, David?"

"Aye, I am."

"Tell me everything. *Then* I'll decide."

"But if I tell you the secret, I'll only help you halfway. And my duty to my family might be sacrificed."

"If you tell me, or if you don't tell me, I cannot grant safe passage to London. We are pirates, David. We won't be docking in the Thames."

The three sailors laughed, and this time David didn't blame them. Like any martyr, he felt the absurdity of his position. Jill didn't mock him, but she did regain her smile. This time it was catlike, and calculated. He was reminded of the tigress.

"I understand, David. We're discussing serious matters, and you're still just a boy. How ever and why ever you arrived here, you are now a guest of the Neverland. Perhaps, before you grow up, you must learn how to play."

Smee cocked his head toward her, his question unspoken. Jill answered, "And since David insists on returning home to best serve his mistress, he might ask to be guided there…by someone else."

Smee's rumbling chuckle held an ominous note.

The weight of David's chains made his arms sag. The weight of a terrible dread dragged his spirit. He listened, frightened, for his lady to pronounce penance for his sin.

Red-Handed Jill seated herself, and spread her emerald skirts. Commanding David to settle on the deck before her, she signaled for the bo'sun and his mates to sit, too. Then she leaned forward, a radiance in her eye, an eagerness in her manner. And David, the boy who had rarely heard a fairy tale, waited, enraptured, for a story.

"Take heed, David…liar, lover, and lost one. Now I'll weave you some magic. This day is young, but when the hourglass turns to midnight, by choice or by chance, you'll believe."

Her sentences descended, like a gentle benediction…

"The figure of a boy sails high against the clouds. He rarely flies at night, but this evening he feels the lure of adventure. The sensation is strong— so strong that he brings his fellows. He wants witness to the valor he's about to display. His hideout under the ground awaits his return, sighing through root-woven walls, grateful for some silence. It's the sky's turn to host him, and the sweet-scented night welcomes him to her breast.

"Peter promised his boys pirates, and pirates have arrived. More pirates than he's ever seen here on the Neverland. Too long he's avoided a skirmish, and his blood fires to prove his courage now that not one, but two companies of buccaneers lie afloat in Neverbay. The more hopeless the odds, the more glory's in store for the Wonderful Boy.

"While Peter soars above, his flock glides through the woods. The damp of dew cools their faces. Their knives bolster their belts. Arriving at the edge of the wood, they gather together, then dive down a cliff. As they round a craggy bend, they spot the glow of ships' lanterns.

"Peter leads his boys nearer, keeping close to the Island, his home and domain. His sword tugs at his side, but he knows he won't wield it. The air that hums past his ears sings of subterfuge, tonight. Sunlight is bold, but starlight calls for subtlety.

"Peter ducks behind a boulder, peering into the bay. The swells are gentle this eve, warmish, and they slosh around his feet. His boys tend to chatter and splash, and he hushes them. Immediately they obey. These boys don't know quite enough yet to question. Questioning is for grown-ups.

"The boys look up when Peter points. The second ship, the smaller one in the distance, burns more than the usual lights, stem to stern. Through her casements, her cabins glow, and strings of lanterns illuminate her deck. Strains of music float to Peter's ears, with voices pitched for a party.

"Yet the larger ship, the *Roger*, lies dim. The only hint of light is from a cabin, and curtains contain it— in the commodore's quarters. Peter's instincts prove true. Tonight's the night to raid the *Roger*.

"But Peter is clever. He knows something's suspicious, even though Hook, his mortal enemy, seldom posts guards here in Neverbay. Hook is confident to the point of arrogance: the mere whisper of his name protects his ship. At this distance, Peter discerns no sailors on deck, and none in the crow's nest. Long Tom lies unattended. But is a trap set to be sprung? Is Hook inviting a skirmish? Yet how could Hook know Peter's boys would fly tonight? Peter has told no one, not even his fairy, to whom he confides all. He didn't know what he'd do tonight, himself, until it happened.

"His courage wins.

"Peter scoops up some mud, and daubs his face for camouflage. His followers do the same. Disregarding the odor, Peter rubs more muck on his head for good measure. It hides his golden hair. The youngest boy, with similar coloring, follows suit. Some confusion ensues, as the dark-haired boy smears the carrot-top with mire, too, and the carrot-top flings it back in protest. The muck falls plopping in the water until Peter springs to his feet and towers over them, his hands on his hips. The tussle stops. Then, with a grand sort of gesture, Peter Pan leads the Lost Boys toward danger.

"Flying fast with their bellies to the brine, the four figures keep the *Roger* between themselves and *Red Lady*, remaining invisible to her revelers. Confidence swells as the band nears the *Roger*; the festivity on the *Lady* grows louder, but here, not a soul is seen. Not a voice is heard.

"But wait! Peter's ears are keen, and he *does* hear someone. A muffled yelp. Peter swivels his eyes around, searching for the source. And soon he spies it— a net hangs down from the prow, bulging with what looks like a body.

"A thrill skitters up his spine, and he drops below the lowest portholes. One is open, but dim. In a bold move, Peter thrusts his head and shoulders in. A hammock hangs moored there, covered with a blanket. Seeing no weapons to snatch, Peter pulls himself out again, to the relief of his boys. Then he braces up against the hull, its wood scraping his elbows. He signals his band to follow. One by one they press against the ship's side, hiding behind their leader. Rolling their eyes upward in dread, they expect a gunport to swing suddenly open. Their ears anticipate the jingle of steel. But they're mistaken.

"It's the whimper off the bow that freezes them with fear.

"For Peter, nothing else could make that sound. A cry for help, suppressed by a gag. Peter pulls his dagger. The net swings now, as the body inside it thrashes, seeking to be seen. Who could it be? Not a grown man; the body's too small. Is it an Indian princess? A girl? Or… is he a boy?

"Peter edges closer to the figurehead. Hook's mermaid holds her right hand high, grasping a sickle, while her left hand beckons toward the sea. The net that traps her catch is dangling from her elbow. Her tail loops down to the water. In the daylight, she looks like Red-Handed Jill without her clothes on, but now, in the gloom beneath the bowsprit, Peter sees her as a sea witch, condemning the wretch who hangs upon her to his doom.

"And inside the net, balled up and chained, is a boy. He's shaking his head, flinging his hands as if to ward Peter off. The links on his wrists rattle, the noise begins bouncing off the water, and Peter places a finger to his lips to warn the boy to silence.

"Perhaps it's Peter's mud-caked head that puts the prisoner off, but the captive pays no heed. He keeps up the struggle until Peter reaches through the mesh and seizes the chain. Now Peter climbs aboard the net, and the rope stretches and groans. With his new-idea look on his face, Peter holds up a hand, signifying that the lad inside should wait.

"Peter sends his smallest boy to the open porthole, to fetch the blanket off the hammock. Following instruction, each boy holds a corner, and Peter directs them to hover beneath the captive. Peter hangs upside-down now, and saws at the bottom of the net. It's taut with the boy's weight, and every thread cut yields a 'Twang!' that fills Peter with delight. Each member of his band is swollen with joy to be snatching the pirates' victim— without becoming one himself.

"Less elated, the captive clings to the mesh, looking dubiously down toward the blanket. His hands are too sweaty, his bare toes weave round the strings as he tries to hold fast. Inevitably, the net falls open. He plummets. The wool of the blanket itches his skin, but, contrary to expectation, he sits bundled, seeking vainly for a handhold, suspended by mere boys. His fingers give up, and he's forced to trust to his rescuers. He sees nothing as they carry him to their hideout under the ground, but the motion makes him sick, rocking and swaying as they haul him— miraculously— through thin air. Overcome with alarm, unaware where he's going, he can't taste relief; he sniffs no freedom in the night air, but smells only the fug of the blanket.

"Peter Pan and the Lost Boys will feast, boast, and swagger for a week. With no mother to guide them, they sport their mud masks for almost as long. Their newest companion— swiped in an audacious adventure right out from under Hook and Jill's nefarious noses— believes for a time that he'd rather remain with the pirates. He can't figure, quite yet, how his prayer has been answered. Because, of course…questioning is for grown-ups."

Jill sat back, and in the reverent silence that followed her story, she clapped her hands. The bo'sun's mates jumped up, then hauled David down to his cell.

He didn't resist. He was too amazed to find himself in daylight, so caught up in the narrative that he expected to be, already, in the midnight maleficence of the hideout under the ground.

In the brig under the decks, he sat in limbo, waiting in chains for the next circle of hell: torment, in the form of adventure.

Odds—and Ends

At midday, Raven stepped from the wood. The fresh breeze welcomed her to the wide, white cliff top, but Cecco had not yet arrived. Upon leaving the encampment, Raven had told Willow she'd go walking, but she withheld further information, slipping away before questions might be asked. Raven had questions enough of her own.

She wandered to the edge of the cliff. On one side, she viewed the shelter of the bay, calm waters lapping the beach, and the pirates' ships at rest. On the other side, Raven saw the vast expanse of the sea, with the horizon beckoning, leading her eye toward the unknown. Out of sight, and part of that unfamiliarity, lay the Other Island. Years ago, White Bear must have studied a similar view, and made up his mind to venture from the shelter of the familiar.

Raven felt a flutter of nerves in her stomach, yet she looked forward to Cecco's company. Her intuition told her that he could be trusted. After all, the moment he saw her, he had leapt to defend her, not knowing what foe he might be challenging. But, Raven realized, whatever comfort she took from her pirate must be fleeting. He was a man of the winds, blowing in and swirling over the Island, making his impression on its inhabitants, then rushing away again to sail off toward his life upon the sea. It was that motion on which she pinned her hopes, last night, as White Bear loomed above her. Maybe Raven could trust Cecco to protect her, again.

She turned, hearing Cecco shouldering his way between the arms of the spruces that stood guard around their trysting place. He gained the open space and halted. Raven's pulse quickened to see him again. Oddly, for Raven, just like the scent of resin he brought from the spruce, he was now part of the 'familiar.' She noted his dark, sad eyes and his bright, glittering adornments. Instantly she returned to yesterday, and the memory of his body shielding her— so much heavier but just as insistent as White Bear's, last night. At the sight of her, Cecco conveyed welcoming, as she, too, welcomed his presence.

Neither party uttered a greeting. They moved together to sit on the moss beneath the old, lone alder. Its trunk held their backs while its roots formed a barrier from the precipice. They listened for a time to the breakers below. The water battered the foundation of the rock on which they reposed, but distance reduced the sound to a murmur, and made the impact feel merely a tremble.

Cecco observed, "Neither water nor woods. A fitting place for two opposites like us."

"I no longer believe us to be opposites," Raven confessed. "I understand you better today. I have seen you with your people."

"I can say the same to you."

"And now," Raven said, "I have heard your name. I witnessed that Captain Cecco is a man of power. But he is also a man of feeling."

His bracelets tinkled as he moved to lay his hand on her arm. She did not pull away, but, instead, she welcomed this contact, reassured by his strength, and warmed by his touch. Kindly, he said, "Raven is still a wisewoman. What else does she see?"

"I sense the contrast within your spirit. You are a creature of the wind and sea, strong, bold— but..."

He nodded. "But, like you, I lack the anchor of family for which I pine. We are much the same. Islands in a sea of loss." His voice softened. "Tell me Raven, if you will, about your husband's passing."

As if resisting the burden of her grief, Raven sat straighter. The fringe on her tunic quivered with her movement. "Ash saw an opportunity to strike at the Golden Boy, who has harmed so many of our people. He taught me that if the enemy sees your weapon, it is too late to use it." She bowed her head. "But always, Ash was impetuous. In his haste, he showed his arrow. The Golden Boy's knife is quick, and so was Ash's death."

"And you have no children of Ash, to comfort you in your loss."

"I have only the comfort of knowing that my husband died a warrior, in defense of our people. And you, Captain? What can ease your grief?"

"In my country, I am a hunted man. I will never be united with my gypsy tribe again. My brothers, my father, my mother...they are lost to me. When I married I was consoled. But now, although I am certain of her love for me..." Cecco selected his words, mindful of the commodore's command to protect Jill using the cover of their marriage. "She is a woman of independent spirit. Were I to bind her too tightly, she would no longer be the woman I admire."

"Then you own a generous heart. But where is your woman? Does she dwell on another island?"

"You have seen her. She came of age on *this* Island. She is Red-Handed Jill."

Raven's eyes opened wide. "The Black Chief's mermaid? She who eluded our warriors— yesterday?"

"Yes." Raven's allusion to Jill as Hook's woman rankled. Cecco did not subdue the bitterness in his voice. He stretched his fingers and gazed at the golden band upon them. "As your people found, my Jill is a difficult woman to catch. Harder still to hold."

"Yet even so you wear her token. I see how she wounds you. Loving someone who loves another, too— it is more than I would be able to do. My sister is more openhanded than you or me. She offers freely to share."

"I find I have little choice. But, lonely woman, does no other brave seek your heart?"

"Yes. The hunter Lean Wolf, and my brother-in-law judges him untrustworthy. But White Bear is a man of standing in the tribe. It was he whom you saw speaking for the council when we captured your chief. White Bear promised my sister he will provide for me, as his second woman."

"What I saw of White Bear impressed me. He appears an honorable brave."

"Can a man be *too* honorable?"

"Why can you not love him?"

Raven blanched, and she looked away as if to hide her face, and her emotion. "I have said that I am not like my sister." Collecting herself, she faced Cecco again. "And I will do nothing to lower Willow's status in White Bear's tepee. If I accept White Bear, a son might result."

"A son, surely, would secure your position."

"Willow's first child will be born any day now. She is certain she carries a boy. But if a girl arrives, what then? Surely, if a son from my body follows, Willow would lose importance in her husband's eyes, and in the People's."

"I understand." Cecco remembered Hook's objections to fathering children by Jill. That decision began to take on aspects Cecco had not yet considered. It was a subject to which he must give further thought.

Raven continued, "Since Ash's death, I feel that my life is no longer my own."

"Shall you leave the village, then, to live at the House in the Clearing?"

"No. I would be lost there, turning my back on tradition. And, as Red Fawn's experience proves, running from a provider's protection brings shame upon him. This is one reason Lean Wolf is resentful. Red Fawn was his wife; now she is an exile, one whom our people shun as an Outcast."

"If the Outcasts are shunned, how is it that I have seen the younger braves visiting them?"

"How would you not? The young are ever adventurous. We women visit the Clearing only discreetly, when in need of Lily's counsel or Lelaneh's medicines. I intend to go there, as soon as I can manage it...to consult Lelaneh. Although I dare not disobey White Bear, I can act to safeguard my sister's status."

"As you heard Commodore Hook command, you will not be harmed there. His decree forbids our men, like your own, from mistreating anyone who enters the Clearing."

Relieved, Raven said, "I am glad to learn this rule for certain. Now that I know, I will wait only until Willow is delivered to visit Lelaneh. Then, I can truly become the Shadow Woman."

"So you have taken a new name, along with your new life?"

"Along with my abandonment of life. I will retreat to the shadows, and linger there until the time arrives to join Ash in the land of Dark Hunting." Raven gazed into Cecco's eyes, and, for the first time, she entreated him. "Unless…"

Touched by this appeal, Cecco took both her hands within his. Her fingers were small but strong, and Cecco felt her gripping him, as if she were clutching at hope. He vowed, "Lonely woman, if it is in my power to help you, I will do so."

"White Bear came to us from the Other Island. His people dwell there still," with her chin, she indicated the direction, "to the southeast."

Cecco followed her gesture, looking off toward the sea.

"I believe you command your men and they obey. I believe I can trust you. I ask that you carry me there, in your ship."

Cecco sat silent, the surprise on his face obvious, and growing. Raven shifted to face him straight on, kneeling as a petitioner, and yet presenting to him the wealth of her handsome features. Her hands still clung to his. "If you instruct me how to behave, I will cause you no trouble. And, I promise, I will bring you what comfort I may, during the voyage."

Cecco shook his head, puzzled. "But why will you leave your sister behind? Are you not the last of her relations? She will miss you, and you will long for her."

"Here, I will do my sister more hurt than good. There, I may begin anew, yet remain within tribe and tradition. And surely White Bear's first family will accept me, as his obligation. They will know me only as the Shadow Woman, and hold no expectation that I must be other than I am."

Cecco answered, "You must remain true to yourself. This I know to be right. But, with regret, Raven, I must refuse."

Disappointment filled her eyes, but she did not slacken her hold on his hands.

"If I had only myself to consider, I would sail with you, happily, anywhere you wish to go. But to steal away a woman of the People— such an act will bring war. Many men will die, both my men and the People's."

"But if I leave the village secretly? I might hide until your departure. The People need not know that I travel with you."

"And their assumptions will lead to turmoil. All your tribe witnessed the commodore's attentions to you. He will be the first to be accused of your abduction."

"Oh!" Appalled at her own lack of foresight, Raven pulled back. As she considered the idea more fully, the shock of Cecco's prediction paralyzed her.

"So you see, Raven, even if we could smuggle you away, I will not risk upsetting the peace our chiefs achieved, and achieved only yesterday. Nor may I endanger the master I swore to serve."

She could not bring herself to meet his eyes. "I did not consider the welfare of the People, nor the consequences to you. My grief makes me selfish, and I am ashamed."

"Do not feel shame for seeking passage through your difficulty. But, lonely one, be guided by my advice. My own exile teaches me. If I had a daughter, I would counsel her the same. Remain with the people who love you. Do not bring them pain by your absence."

Cecco had kept her hands, and he pulled them flat to his chest, where she felt his strong heart beating, and the vitality of a life force she'd chosen to deny.

"But, Raven. Before you retreat into the Shadow Woman, I do accept your offer. Do, if you will, bring what comfort you may to me, here, on this cliff top. And I will return comfort to you." Slowly, he brought himself closer. He brushed her lips with his own until they tingled, and then he moved even nearer, to lay a kiss on her ear. He whispered to her, "Lonely woman; lonely man."

Raven answered, caressing his cheek with hers to stir an intimacy she hadn't known since Ash. "We are no opposites, at all."

The old alder shaded them on the mossy bed between its roots. Cecco released her hands at last, to gather her tightly in his arms. They embraced, within view of the sea, within scent of the wood, and, for a brief and beneficent moment, the impact of their loneliness felt merely a tremble.

Then Cecco rose, and offered his hand to raise Raven. His arms went round her again, still ardent, but holding her steady.

"I am sorry to disappoint you, Raven. You may be right. The Other Island may hold hope for the Shadow Woman to heal. I will take you there, if your council and my commodore consent. As for your consolation, as much as I crave it, I'll remain true to my marriage. Even if it proves, finally, my doorway to the land of Dark Hunting."

"My dear Captain Cecco. I thank you for your care of me." She laid her hands on his chest once again, beneath his shimmering gypsy necklace. "I feel the fire that burns within your breast. You are wise to keep me at a distance, for here is more life than I have heart to hold."

It was Raven who had come to him. It was the Shadow Woman who turned from him. She walked toward the path, and at the edge of the trees she looked back to say, "I will think on your words. One more time, I will join the Man of the Lonely Winds. At the next noontime, here, at neither water nor woods."

"He will welcome you. You and I are at odds, but, I sense, we are not yet at an end."

As she disappeared, he turned to the sea, to the southeast. His thoughts blew before him, snatched by the winds for which Raven named him, far and away, to another island, where, undoubtedly, some worthy brave lived in ignorance of the good fortune drifting his way.

Raven ran again, reassuming her cares as she covered the ground to meet them. They flew at her one by one. She may have stayed away too long; perhaps Willow had need of her sister; maybe her labor had begun; what if White Bear suspected her forbidden friendship? Raven dashed over the narrow path, the grass blades nicking her ankles. As the green of the forest blurred past her vision, Cecco's counsel echoed in her ears. Wise as he was, he could not end her difficulties.

She admired Cecco, all the more, for rejecting her. He had chosen a woman. He loved his wife, even when he did not hold her. Raven felt the same way. She loved a husband. She simply could not hold him. And the man she might hold, if she allowed herself to do so—

A shudder shook her, and she stumbled. Halting her stride, panting in the humidity of the wood, she closed her eyes to block out emotion. It followed her into the blackness. She had explored every option, yet not one thing had changed.

Lean Wolf succeeded last night in delaying White Bear's suit. But within this night, she would learn all she dreaded to know about her sister's husband. And, afterward, when he lay sleeping with the coarse hair of his scalp lock across her throat, then she would understand, without a doubt, how much or how little he regretted his responsibility for his wife's older sister.

If he enjoyed her, would Willow be diminished? Would he be moved to offer ceremony, to make Raven his wife? If he did not take pleasure in her, how could Raven's pride suffer her to reside, unwanted, in his home? More than she resented ignorance, Raven shrank from learning, for certain, her exact standing in White Bear's estimation.

Raven's eyes opened, and, gradually, her feet moved her forward. Too soon the forest path ended, and the encampment spread out before her: the children, the old ones, the tepees, the totem pole, the rising smoke, the slope descending toward the river, canoes on the beach, gray squirrels tumbling through the trees and the swift waters' gleam in the sun. And there, at the end of her path, where she'd dwelt all her life, Raven's struggles ended, too. She vowed to herself, and she vowed as the Shadow Woman.

Willow's sister would do as she was told.

A glimmer of light flared in the air above Raven. The fairy, Jewel, kept high and out of sight, trailing the native woman as she traveled toward her home. Both females paused at the edge of the camp. One hesitated, to find her resolution. The other hovered, waiting for resolution to be met.

The master's instructions rang clear in Jewel's mind. Follow Captain Cecco's paramour; identify her tepee; learn how to find her again, speedily, in any kind of light, at any time of night.

Jewel hadn't visited the Indian encampment since the day she'd rushed off in despair to plot revenge on Peter and the Wendy. That urge had been a bleeding need, staunched only by the commodore's care for Jewel. Today, his fairy acted only as an observer.

Revenge, should any be required, belonged to Hook.

"Lightly of the Air," Panther said, "I am pleased that the council saw fit to dismiss your dealings with your mother as filial duty. I, too, was nurtured by a strong woman." He looked outside the tepee, following the Old One's departure. "We would not be honorable sons if we neglected to pay such mothers the homage they deserve."

Panther's wife, a pleasant-faced woman with long, beaded earrings, smiled at him. "Well said, my husband. Every day, I remind your sons of that sentiment." She had already sent their grown boys to the common, and as she cleared the remains of the feast, she shooed her two younger daughters out of the tepee, too, to clean the cookware in the stream. They went giggling, whispering to each other as they surveyed Rowan and Lightly one last time.

The matriarch, the Old One, had enriched the family's gathering with tales of her generation's hunts and battles. She had left with one hand on her staff and the other on Ayasha's arm. The camp was becoming quieter as evening fell, and the fire reflected in Panther's round brown eyes. His pungent pipe smoke twisted upward in the air, giving the illusion of intertwining with the white streak in his braids. Over the dew cloth that brightened the tepee's inner wall, his shadow wavered among the painted figures behind him, like the shades of which his mother had spoken— warriors of a time long gone.

The company and the atmosphere were all that could be wished, but now that the feast was consumed and Lightly, too, had enthralled the family with his account of yesterday's tiger hunt, he and Rowan sat uneasy, waiting for a question to be asked.

Although the food was delicious, Lightly felt his stomach resisting the little he'd been able to consume. He swallowed again to dislodge a lump in his throat and answered, "Rowan and I appreciate the elders' acceptance. We can't change the fact that our relatives are unusual. And in return for the council's understanding, we'll make sure that our loyalties don't conflict with the People's interests."

Panther lounged now, puffing out a mouthful of smoke. "The elders have come to depend upon the pair of you, enough to give you freedoms that other young braves might not be granted. Your virtues are rewarded, but your knowledge of the Golden Boy, alone, is worth their indulgence."

Rowan sat in his customary posture, rigid and proud. He said, "We feel the distinction of the council's trust. It is a privilege to serve as Messengers." So that his knee could nestle into Lightly's, he had settled cross-legged in front of the fire. He felt his partner's anxiety, and wished to end his suspense as soon as possible. His answer to Panther's question was ready— but still, his jaw ached from clenching.

"And Rowan," said Panther, "how do Lily and your little red-haired sister fare at the House in the Clearing? I could not ask before, without the council's sanction, but are they well?"

"They are flourishing. Lightly's twin brothers, the Men of the Clearing, are fine providers. Strange as it may seem to the People, they are all grateful to the Black Chief for arranging their situation. My mother and the others miss the village, it is true, but now that their pirate benefactors have dealt with the boy thief, their worries are few."

Panther's wife had finished fussing over the men, and Panther gestured to her that she should sit down beside him on his mat. "Our laws are made to protect us. As I counsel my three daughters, breaking with custom can lead one, especially a woman, into danger." He leaned toward the fire to relight the remnants of tobacco in his pipe. After enjoying his smoking for some time, he continued, "Lily and your sister are lucky to be protected by men who, as I can guess from knowing their brother Lightly, are worthy."

Rowan and Lightly exchanged glances. The gloom they detected upon each other's features wasn't cast only by the firelight. The young men's tension increased as Panther led the conversation toward the subject on everybody's mind.

Ayasha's mother smiled at them, and Lightly thought how kind she was, a generous hostess, a good cook, and, no doubt, an excellent model for her oldest daughter. The girl, too, had behaved in a seemly manner, keeping her black-lashed eyes sober tonight instead of flirting. She had assisted her mother, and made polite conversation throughout the meal. As Lightly narrated the story of Red-Handed Jill and her tigress, Ayasha had appeared fascinated, and her comments showed intelligence. She'd displayed proper respect for her parents, and waited graciously on her grandmother, the Old One, whom she was now attending as was her duty. Ayasha was pretty, and bright, and loving. Lightly could not come up with one reason why Rowan should not marry her.

But, after all, reason was not why people married. Reason lived in the head. Love lived in the heart. Lightly's heart felt on the brink of decease. No matter how Rowan answered Panther, some kind of ending must ensue. If Rowan accepted Ayasha, Lightly of the Air would be the odd man out. If Rowan did not accept this woman, or any woman, but instead adhered through the years to his lover, banishment could bring the end of their life among the People. Only one conclusion was clear and inevitable to Lightly: the end of the life he loved, here, among his adoptive tribe.

Panther sat up, tapped out his pipe, and settled his arm around his wife. "We have devoured a fine dinner; we have relived exciting histories. Now, let us talk of a hopeful future."

With only their knees touching, Rowan and Lightly sat as still as the totem pole. Rowan's features looked as mask-like as the faces on the totem pole, too.

"Rowan, it is no surprise to you that my eldest daughter, my Ayasha, has cast her eye upon you." Panther smiled and raised his hand. "No, you need not find something polite to say yet. I will make my speech and get it over with. Rowan Life-Giver. Can you accept Ayasha as your wife? Can you love her, can you provide for her, and, as my daughter's husband and the father of my grandchildren, be welcomed to our family?"

Panther and his wife gazed hopefully at Rowan. Lightly turned his head only slightly, enough to witness Rowan's answer. Rowan still sat unbending, and his charcoal eyes did not blink.

The fire popped, and three sparks leapt from it. One landed on Rowan's arm. Without haste, he brushed it back into the fire. Another landed on Lightly's leggings. He let it smolder, smelling the singeing deerskin and welcoming the sting as it burned toward his thigh. The third spark simply disappeared, burning out in midair. Panther's wife poked the fire with a stick, to settle the flames. The night noises of the camp came soft through the tepee door— the snap of a blanket being shaken before bedtime, a mother's voice calling to her children.

Next came Rowan's voice.

"Yes, Panther." Rowan's chest rose as he inhaled, deeply.

Lightly felt his own chest collapse.

"Yes, I will be honored to be welcomed to your family, and to accept Ayasha's affection."

Lightly of the Air felt dizzy. The remains of Panther's pipe smoke made him gag. As he forced himself to sit with his knee next to Rowan's, he looked straight ahead, but blindly now. He'd reached the end of his vision. Only his hearing continued to function, and what he heard next was so odd, he could not believe his ears.

"But, Panther," Rowan resumed, "because you trust me with the care of she whom you raised to a woman, I will be truthful with you."

Panther's face dimmed. His wife pushed her hair behind her ear, as if to hear better, and her beaded earring dangled alone by her cheek.

"Rowan Life-Giver and Lightly of the Air are closer than brothers. We two are as one man. So sworn, we can enter into no pledge, one without the other."

The couple waited, silent, trying to understand. Appreciating their stillness as he searched for words, Rowan went on.

"You already know that Lightly and I live not strictly within tradition. Only today, the Council of Elders deemed us worthy enough for leniency toward our circumstances."

Rowan opened his hands and held them out, as if to accept a gift from his would-be father-in-law.

"When you entrust your daughter to Rowan Life-Giver, you entrust her also to Lightly of the Air. We will both feel the honor of bearing Ayasha's marriage token. If you resolve that she will make for us two bracelets…we will make for her two husbands."

Lightly closed his eyes. He heard the fire pop again. Then, finally, came Panther's voice, sounding older.

"Two husbands, where I looked for merely one." Ayasha's father found the grace to chuckle. "Well, Rowan; Lightly….Of any other pair of braves, I would ask that you take *two* of my daughters." Panther paused as if to consider, purchasing time to weigh the young men's reactions. At length, he learned his answer. "As I perceive, however, you are not other braves." He adjusted himself on his mat. "You are both of you your mothers' sons."

He looked to his wife. She had paled, but, after a moment, she nodded. Her husband spoke again, managing to deliver his words with a neutral tone.

"I will consult Ayasha herself. Her father will inquire if she will accept the two hands of an honorable son of an outcast, and the honorable son...of a pirate."

The honorable sons breathed again. It was an odd sort of ending, but, as Rowan intended, no question remained to be asked.

In the quiet of the commodore's quarters, Jill lifted the hourglass in her crimson hand. As the last grains drained from the bulb, she tapped it with her fingernail, then turned it over to count the next hour. Setting it down at its post on her lover's desk, she smiled and murmured, "Midnight. David's story is done."

Hook reclined on the cushions of the window seat, the jeweled buttons on his dressing gown, like his claw, glinting in candlelight. His strained ankle lay wrapped and raised on a pillow before him. He laid down his book. "Douse the light, my love."

Jill did so, and joined him at the window. With the cabin in darkness, they pushed the drapes aside, then leaned out, together. The lush and living scent of the Island greeted them. They peered, but in the starlight no sign of movement could be distinguished, on land, sea, or air.

Mr. Smee's knock sounded at the door, and he entered with a lantern. "Good evening to you, Commodore, Lady. All's well, Madam, it's just as you were telling us. Pan's pack have come and gone, trailing their parcel behind them."

"Thank you, Mr. Smee," she said, "And so begins an adventure. For my true believer, who shall serve me all his days."

"Begging your pardon, Ma'am, but how will David free his hands from his chains?"

"Pan will try to break them, but in the end he'll ask the twins for help. It'll be a good excuse for him to make peace with them. And while they're at the Clearing, David will make amends for his thefts."

Hook said, "Thus assuming responsibility for his actions. The boy is already maturing. I gather that he is as you were, my love. 'The kind that likes to grow up.' "

"As all children, except one, are meant to do."

"And, Ma'am," asked Smee, "will I be getting my shackles back?"

"Yes, Mr. Smee. We'll send the key to the twins. No damage will be done to our property, but they'll put on a good show for the Lost Boys, with hammer and tongs."

"Odds bobs, Madam!" Hook laughed, "A fitting end to the story. Well, Mr. Smee. Jill has settled her boys. Now, what of our men?"

"Tom Tootles is calling them home from the *Lady*, Commodore."

"We shall say good night, then."

"Aye, Sir. Let me be helping you to bed now, so you're not putting strain on that ankle."

"It is much improved, thanks to your ministration. In the morning I intend to visit the denizens of the Clearing, where I shall deliver that key, and a cordial invitation to our celebration. Prepare my chair and assemble an escort, if you please. You will take my compliments to Captain Cecco, and request that Mr. Yulunga and a few of his Frenchmen accompany me."

"Mr. Yulunga?" Jill turned in surprise. "To inquire how Mrs. Hanover is behaving?"

"How shrewd you are, my love. Indeed. In order to command two ships' companies, I must maintain a vigilant eye upon each."

Smee nodded. "Right you are, Sir. That vixen can't be trusted." Nor, thought Smee, might Captain Cecco. But Smee said nothing of the latter opinion, and he ushered Hook to the bed, where he turned down the covers and drew the dressing gown from his commodore's shoulders. Next he unbuckled the hook's harness and hung it at its mooring place close by the bunk. He asked, "And will the lady be joining you on your jaunt to the Island?"

Jill answered, "Not this time, Mr. Smee. I'll be stationed at my desk tomorrow. I've my new story to set down."

"An history, rather," Hook said, gazing at Jill, and in his eyes shone admiration.

"Aye. An history." Jill returned his gaze, and smiled her tigress smile.

Smee sensed the charge in the atmosphere, and, expeditiously, he turned the lantern low, excusing himself from the room.

As the door clicked closed, Hook settled under the bed linens. "And pray tell, my love. What happens next in your story?"

Jill slipped off her dressing gown. The rays of the lantern cast an intimate light upon her, kissing the tresses that fell curling down her arms, and tinting her figure a golden hue. She stood, unashamed, enjoying the sensation of her lover's gaze upon her nakedness. When she answered, her voice came low and clear.

"A pirate queen retires to her chamber. There, her loved one waits. Her bed is warm, her lover warmer, and, although he possesses only one hand, it is an open one.

"She lies down beside him," Jill sank into the bed. "The glimmer of his rubied ring is almost as lustrous as her eyes." Smiling, she lifted his hand to her face, so that he could compare his several jewels.

Hook filled his eyes with their glow, then turned his hand to cup her face. "Aye. As always, my queen, you speak the truth."

Her eyes fell closed, and she nestled her cheek in his palm. The intensity of his attention never failed to excite her. Ripples of pleasure coursed through her body. "If you continue to touch me so, Hook, I'll not be able to finish the story."

"And yet you yourself placed us in this circumstance. But there is no need for you to continue. I shall complete the narrative."

He resumed the tale, "The pirate queen, whose taste for treasure is legendary, knows a greater craving still. All the day, she longs for evening with her king. Now, at last, their moment is upon them."

Gently, he brushed the gemstones of his ring along her face, stroking, "watching her lips open as if to taste the rubies, like cherries." He pulled the gems away then, but, "so that she might not go hungry," he delivered in their stead a satiating kiss.

And yet, "A kiss is never enough for the pirate queen." Hook turned the ring around on his finger, so that, next, when he stroked Jill's bosom, the satin surface of the gems circled round her breast, teasing the tip, rousing her nipple to a peak, its color a paler version of the rubies. She pressed closer, her breaths becoming faster, shallower. Yet again, he drew the jewels away.

She sighed in regret, but her flesh thrilled again as her lover slid his jeweled fingers beneath her breast and downward, leaving a burning trail. Over her ribs he moved his rubies, down her torso, and, irresistibly, toward her point of desire. She indulged in the pleasure as he toyed with it there, rubbing the rubies' gloss against the fire of her loins. As his adornment stroked his adored one, the sensation penetrated her center, bringing her closer, and closer yet, to rapture. It was then, at the edge of her ecstasy, that Hook sought his own. He slid his burning ring behind her, while he pressed himself into the wealth of her womanhood. And still the story did not end.

"To slow the midnight hour for their lovemaking, he takes up the hourglass, and tosses its sand in the sea. He fills the vessel up again, to dazzle his mistress, with golden grains he has stolen from the stars."

Thus beguiled, Jill's senses filled, grain upon grain, with rich impressions— gems and gilding, beauty and bliss, and, not the least, with love for her consort, both physical and mystical. With words, with wealth, or with passion, he was, as she had described him, an openhanded man.

The lovers eluded the boundaries of time, but the hourglass, whether seething with sand or trickling with treasure, measured each instant of intimacy. Counting, counting, steadfast and stealthy, the nighttime carried Hook and his Jill as it carried lesser mortals, inevitably, toward trial.

Of Mers and Men

Lean Wolf Silent Hunter felt the old, familiar craving incite his vitals. He wanted a woman. In the long term, his hopes hinged on Raven. He'd done all he could to prevent a joining between her and White Bear. At the People's celebration, he had danced before her, his chosen one. He'd felt his sincerity shine like the fire, and, as he observed her, he was certain that she saw it, too. He'd sensed a kindling in her spirit as she watched him, just as his kiss inflamed her that day in the woods. But her urge proved elusive, for she quickly subdued it. Still, Lean Wolf felt one step closer to winning her, knowing that he had roused Raven, too, to feel the craving. She needed a man.

Later, when his old friend White Bear puffed up with the day's successes, Lean Wolf watched him retire to his tepee. He saw that White Bear expected to triumph again there, with his sister-in-law. But Lean Wolf had hunted the owl as an excuse to disrupt the quiet, hoping to interrupt any exploits taking place under Raven's blankets. Judging by the irritation on White Bear's face this morning, Lean Wolf's strategy had worked. Plainly, White Bear had not yet enjoyed the delights of his sister-in-law, and his too-pregnant wife could be no consolation. For White Bear, the victories of the day had not fathered the night's.

Lean Wolf could see the question of Raven weighing like a stone around White Bear's neck, dragging at his patience. He smiled his cynical smile. Perhaps White Bear didn't recognize that Lean Wolf, not

Raven, might be that stone. Perhaps Raven was grateful for Lean Wolf's intervention, and found that she was drawn toward her suitor. At this thought, though, Lean Wolf discovered that he shared some frustration with his old friend.

Imagining Raven lying under the skins, waiting naked for a lover's embrace— not quite submissive and not quite rebellious— made firewater burn in his blood, as it had when he'd once found a half empty bottle on the beach of the bay. Even as he gained ground toward changing Raven's mind, marriage to her felt too far away. His hankering for a woman increased in urgency every hour. But here he held an advantage over White Bear. Lean Wolf, the Silent Hunter, need not be as patient as White Bear, the Speaker for the Council. Lean Wolf's longings could be eased outside the confines of the tribe.

And Lean Wolf held a second advantage. If Raven wasn't ready to surrender to her hunter, she was, at least, too busy caring for Willow to tend to White Bear. Time was both his enemy and his friend. The aching days he must wait for Raven could be spent profitably, providing him with opportunity to pursue another bird. The black-haired widow-bird was caged. She would keep. If the wild, yellow-haired bird was to be netted, she must be netted now, before time turned her ship in the bay, and she flew away on its wings of white, heading seaward.

To deliberate upon his situation, the hunter hid himself in his secret cave. He wasn't concerned about leaving the encampment tonight. No disruption was now necessary at White Bear's tepee. As the sun met the mountain, Raven had taken Willow by the arm, and, halting every few steps while the pains nipped Willow's womb, guided her to the birthing lodge. By the time Lean Wolf departed the village, the wisewomen had purified White Bear's home. White Bear took up his position, sitting cross-legged in his open doorway, prepared for a vigil. He would spend this night, the night of his first offspring's coming, deliberating in his own fashion, facing east and burning sweetgrass, the hair of the Mother, to welcome the spirits of birth and regeneration.

The spirits visited Lean Wolf Silent Hunter, too, in his cave. He lay on his pallet under the phosphorescent glow of the ceiling, absorbing the chill that shrouded his body. Soon he slept, and, during the night, he dreamt of a third creature, a fawn, brilliant as war paint in a coat of red fur. The dream drew heat to his flesh, diffusing the cool of the cave, its color clashing with the dim greenish light beyond his eyelids. He awakened at morning with a plan in place. Revitalized, he crawled from his cavern.

He stretched his arms and inhaled the crisp early air. After breakfasting at his leisure, he rolled the boulder back to cover the cave's entryway. Dusting the grit from his hands, he sauntered the short distance to the river, where he washed himself and drank his fill at the pool below the waterfall. There, he revived his memory of the sea woman bathing, damp and ripe for lovemaking. There, the vision of her, the vibration of the earth, the thunderous sound and the swirling of the waters combined to stir his virility. With his resolution renewed, Lean Wolf strapped his knife near his knee and headed through the forest. His being rejoiced to be on the prowl again.

He looked down to view the tiny red beads on his marriage bracelet. Held captive on his wrist by stitches of sinew, the beads formed the shape of a fawn. His hunter's instinct set him in the direction of the Clearing. He traveled rapidly, and, cautious, listened to the voices as he neared. He wasn't surprised when he glimpsed his former wife, Red Fawn, standing on the path with her comely back to him, blowing kisses to a burly, dark-haired European. Lean Wolf had known he would find her. With bright feathers in her hair and a nature too tame for dissembling, locating her was no task. She had always been easy to catch.

Lean Wolf bent down, disappearing sideways into the underbrush. He smelled mint where his moccasins crushed the greenery, but he made no sound where he stepped. With huntsman's eyes, he assessed the area. All clear here, except for the pirates Red Fawn was bidding goodbye. A pack of them was departing, carrying the poles of a carved and enclosed wooden chair on their shoulders.

Lean Wolf had spied this contrivance before. He knew the Black Chief rode inside. He knew also that the pirate was satisfied, for his men were jingling and joking as they marched, showing no sign of apprehension either of their chief or of their position. Even the giant black pirate with the ax at his belt grinned as he herded the men forward. He strutted as if confident that their weapons were sharp and their reflexes ready. But Lean Wolf had no business with white men or black men today. It was the woman he was after, and *his* weapons were ready, too.

Silent Hunter stretched his neck now, to discover the whereabouts of the People of the Clearing. They were all there, men, women, and children, chattering as the devil men departed, withdrawing to their various occupations. The Men of the Clearing looked warily around before they relaxed, their brown eyes alight and their bright hair unkempt, but Lean Wolf shielded himself from their gazes. Thanks to the pirates' visit, the parrot they had trained to guard the Clearing squawked away in a treetop, its warning unheeded.

As the sea men's footsteps faded, peace settled upon the woodland. The hunter moved closer, edging near Red Fawn, hoping to cut her off before she rejoined her people. Unaware of danger, she straggled in their wake, picking Neverlilies as she retraced her steps. She bore no weapons. Still slender, she wore a deerskin dress, silver earrings, and a smile of contentment that softened her dimples.

Lean Wolf, too, was pleased. His dreams had led him to his target, straight and true as an arrow from his quiver.

And, as quickly as an arrow, he ran toward her, snatched her up, and covered her mouth. Before she knew what happened, Lean Wolf, with the strength of his arms, had carried her almost to the pirate band, where any noise he might make would go unheeded by the Men of the Clearing. He ran boldly to the pirates' very heels, then ducked into a thicket. Once secluded by foliage, Lean Wolf settled on a stump and set his former wife on his knee, imprisoning her in his grip.

As she recognized her abductor, her large, dark eyes filled with fright. With a look, he warned her to silence. She stared at him, clutching the remains of the flowers. Rust red petals spattered her dress. Lean Wolf had only moments to act before her absence would be noticed at the Clearing. Only moments to secure two things: information, and a vow of secrecy. He knew how to get them. He used her fear.

"Red Fawn, once wife. You see how easily I take you. If you wish me to go, you will do as I say."

What could she do, but agree? Anxiously, she nodded. Lean Wolf took his hand from her mouth, and no trace of her dimples remained.

"What did the Black Chief say?"

A few seconds passed as Red Fawn recovered her wits and began to think beyond the threat of the hunter's presence. "He…He told us that the Golden Boy will visit us."

"Huh! They are enemies. How would he know?"

"The Lady Jill. She foretold it."

"The Golden Boy does not interest me." But the Lady Jill did. He prodded, "What else did he tell you?"

"He said— he came to— He asked about Raven."

Unprepared for this answer, Lean Wolf gaped, relaxing his hold. Red Fawn lunged for freedom, and he had to seize her arms to prevent her flight. "No," he said, keeping his voice down. "You will stay until I command you to go, and you will answer my questions. What is the pirate's interest in the widow of the warrior Ash?"

"He asked Lily for her story. He didn't say why." She twisted, trying to pull away. "Now let me go!"

Covering her mouth again, Lean Wolf squeezed her jaw, admonishing, "Quietly now."

Red Fawn stilled, as if recalling old bruises, and watched him from the edges of her eyes. The sight of her marriage bracelet, still tied to his wrist, seemed to haunt her. When he allowed her to inhale again, she gasped for air.

"What more did he say?"

Obedient, she answered, "He invited us to a celebration."

The hunter's black eyes lit with mischief. "Ah, I see. When?"

"The fourth night from tonight."

"On the ship?"

"On the beach. But, Lean Wolf, no harm will be done! It is only a party. The pirates will not attack the People."

"You trust those devil men, but you do not trust me." He smiled at her, bitterly. "Truly, Red Fawn, you earn the name of Outcast."

"Set me free now. Oh, please, Lean Wolf, set me free!"

"You know what you must do next, if you don't want me to return."

"Yes." She dropped her gaze from his face. "I know."

"I am the Silent Hunter. I can penetrate the Clearing, and no one— not the braves nor the babies— will hear me stalking."

"Yes, Lean Wolf. I am aware."

"And?"

"As always…I will tell no one that you caught me. No one will know that we spoke."

"No one but Red Fawn the Outcast, who has too much sense to spill secrets."

"Yes, Lean Wolf."

"Where have you been just now, to make you late returning to the Clearing?"

She looked solemnly into his eyes. "I think…I ran after the pirates, to give Flambard my flowers…?"

Lean Wolf picked a straggling blossom from her bosom. It was crushed, and even its scent was sickly. His lips twisted with jealousy— jealousy that would die with the foreigner. *Flambard.* "That's right. Flambard, the husky dark one. And you wanted to kiss him, one final time."

The word escaped in a whimper. "Yes," she said, paling.

Lean Wolf could smell the fear on her skin. It made him want her. He pulled her toward him and pressed his mouth to the chill of her lips. Out of fright, out of habit, or out of greed, she opened her lips to accept his own. *Like a pass-around woman*, he thought, and, repulsed, he shoved her to the ground.

"Woman, you are not my wife." He stood, and pulled her up by her hair. "You are *everyone's* wife. Now go back to your patrons, and do not, by word or by action, dare me to hunt you down again."

He watched her run away from him, while a mixture of emotions danced in his breast. Her backside undulated as she hurried, exciting his lust again. And yet he abhorred her, as she rushed back to her life without him, to the degradation she'd chosen over life as his wife.

He didn't need her now. In two minutes, she had opened his path to the two women he *did* need. In the long term, his hopes flew with Raven.

But on the fourth night from tonight, he'd cast his net for his yellow-haired bird.

Not a soul sought the shade of the tree on the cliff top. Not a creature crept on the chalky ledge. The sun had ascended to its mid-afternoon post, and only one thing was positioned on the place described by Captain Cecco as neither water nor woods: his spyglass. Cursing, he shoved the telescope closed, and threw it on the padded locker beneath his window.

Cecco himself had visited the meeting place. Eager to see Raven again, he'd arrived early for their assignation. A jaybird scolded from up in the branches as he waited, and the surf teemed below. By noon, their trysting time, his mind was full of questions to ask Raven, notions to impart to her. He imagined conversations with the lonely woman, who shared, if not his culture, then his experience. His heart felt lighter this morning than at any time in the weeks since Jill deserted him.

As the noon hour had passed and afternoon encroached, Cecco was deserted, again, by the words he'd imagined he would speak with Raven. With his hopes disappointed, he'd trudged back through the forest toward his boat, seeking the darkest paths, only to be blinded upon reaching the beach, by the brilliance of the sun. While his men rowed him home to *Red Lady*, plowing through the swells of the bay, his heart transformed again into a weight as dull and as burdensome as lead.

While he watched the cliff top from his cabin, still Raven did not come, nor did Cecco sense even the shade of the Shadow Woman. He could think of any number of reasons why she might break her promise. As she had told him, her life was not her own. Her sister's needs must be met, and her brother-in-law obeyed. But reasons didn't matter. Cecco was alone, and, somewhere, so was Raven.

Begrudging, he admitted defeat. He tore his gaze from the Island and strode to his cabin door. Yanking it open, he surprised Mrs. Hanover, tucked into an angle of the companionway. She gasped, but didn't cry out. Swiftly, she slid from the sailor who stood leaning over her, then snatched up her skirts and pattered down the stairs. Cecco surmised that Mrs. Hanover had believed him to be ashore, and, presuming no one would wander near the captain's precincts, she had seized her opportunity to corner Pierre-Jean.

Frowning, Cecco noted that the girl wore her hair swept up and her feet bare, in imitation of Jill. Her stature was petite like Jill's, too, but, with a jolt, Cecco realized that the rounding of Mrs. Hanover's belly was something that might never happen for Jill. A sting of even deeper disappointment turned Cecco's countenance fierce— fiercer than was warranted by the transgressions of his subordinates.

Facing the wrath of his captain, Pierre-Jean stared with his china blue eyes as he backed and stuttered, "*Mon Commandant*...it is mistake, I am fault. *Pardonnez-moi.*"

"I know Mrs. Hanover. No man is safe with that woman."

"No, no, Captain. You and Mr. Yulunga, excuse little *Madame*, excuse— please." Saluting, Pierre-Jean made to depart.

Cecco stopped him, dropping a heavy hand on the sailor's shoulder. "You will be frightened of what Mr. Yulunga will do with you, and well you should be. But," Cecco glared at Pierre-Jean, his white teeth bared. "Be warned, my boy. If you tangle with that girl, she will be the death of you." Cecco's grip on his shoulder tightened. "*Comprenez-vous?*"

Pierre-Jean winced at the pinch of his captain's conviction. He nodded. "*Oui, Monsieur.* I hear it— Sir."

"Send Mr. Yulunga to me, then get on with your duties."

"Aye, aye, *mon* Sir." The sailor touched his hand to his forehead, then his pale pigtail flew behind him as he tore down the steps.

Cecco shook his head as the Frenchman rushed away. If he had any room in his heart, he would pity Pierre-Jean, an ill-fated fool attracted to trouble. Like a siren, Mrs. Hanover lured the lad toward his ruin. In recent days, Cecco had witnessed his pining. Now Pierre-Jean, like Cecco himself, had succumbed to forbidden trysts. Cecco understood his sailor too well. But, he thought, a struggle was pointless, for either of them. What use to resist? Every breath a man drew dragged him closer to the last. Once one unique woman got a hook in your heart, you were a doomed man anyway.

Cecco turned, slowly reentering his quarters. He dropped down on the locker to sit, elbows on thighs, and contemplated the spyglass. His impulse was strong, but he restrained himself, for a time. Yet the siren's call was compelling, too, and, at length, he snatched up the telescope. He yanked it open. This time, he positioned it on neither water, nor woods, but, rather, on the place he described as heaven.

He cursed again.

His wife's window was curtained.

Worse, the Irishman knocked at her door, his red face smiling, and entered without a pause.

Cecco's spyglass shattered as it hit the bulkhead. His hands, empty but for his wedding band, squeezed into fists.

"You know, Guillaume, you're a kind of Lost Boy yourself. That's why I thought you'd feel at home on the Neverland." Tom Tootles lay basking on Marooners' Rock alongside his friend, second officer of the *Red Lady*, with whom he shared a brief but binding history. Tom and Nibs had obtained shore leave this morning, to enjoy a reunion with Rowan and Lightly, and to show Guillaume the wonders of Mermaids' Lagoon.

The other three were swimming like mermen, but Guillaume had not mastered the skill, and, at the moment, Tom felt too lazy to dive in. Both men looked relaxed on the outside, but they kept alert for a flash of fins on the horizon. No female creatures had surfaced as yet, but the men's hopes were high.

Guillaume replied, "Lost or not, this boy sailed a long way from where he started, in the gutters of a little port town."

"I've seen how you've progressed since leaving LeCorbeau. And Captain Cecco trusts you with responsibility." Guillaume usually dressed in his dapper red and blue uniform, and Tom hadn't seen him appear so informal since the night he stabbed Guillaume's hand and pinned him to the deck, and then kissed him to make up for it. This morning they'd all left their clothes in their boat, which was tied to one of the rusted rings driven into Marooners' Rock, grisly evidence of executions here, death by tide and time.

Its notoriety notwithstanding, the Lagoon was a smiling place too, and Tom felt that, like the Neverland itself, this outing was beneficial to the skinny young Frenchman who, despite the scar Tom inflicted on his hand, had chosen freedom and friendship over subjugation to his former captain. So far, the newcomer was delighted with the unusual nature of the Island and its inhabitants. Guillaume was awed by the beauty, and astonished at his first introduction to a fairy. As Tom let his glance rove around the Lagoon again, he grinned in anticipation of Guillaume's response to the mermaids.

Lightly and Rowan had no eyes for mergirls. Their relief at Ayasha's recent refusal to marry buoyed them up, and they splashed with Nibs in the opal-green waters of the Lagoon. The young men played like boys, ducking and racing, the sound of their games echoing off the rocks. Even Nibs submerged his gravity today. The crease between his dark eyebrows relaxed, and he smiled as they dove for sport, and for the odd pearl that might have settled on the sea bed, dropped by a mermaid. For all their high spirits, each man's scalp bristled as mysterious eyes watched from secret spaces.

Around them loomed the towering walls of the Lagoon, emerald with moss and too slippery to climb. A series of crevices opened off the shelf of rock at their base, caves waiting for the wash of tides at sunset, when no mortal man might survive here. At the cliff top, birds of majestic proportions circled with their wings spread wide, as if surfing the currents just for fun.

Lying on his back, Tom explained, "Mermaids' Lagoon is a powerful place, Guillaume." He pointed skyward. "See those eagles up there? When Nibs and I were boys growing up in Pan's hideout, we watched Wendy fly the very same way in the very same spot, the day Hook first set eyes upon her."

Guillaume wagged his head as he imagined a girl flying among eagles. "Another instance of this Island's magic, *non?*"

"*Oui.*" Shifting his sturdy frame, Tom looked earnestly at Guillaume. "The Lagoon often alters men who visit here, but no mermaid changed anyone as drastically as Wendy changed our commodore, even before she became Red-Handed Jill."

"Was *Monsieur* so very different then?"

"Hook was a pirate captain, and a damned successful one. But before Jill, he was like a monster, living only for revenge. We boys were terrified of him." Tom rubbed the mark at his temple, a relic of Hook's discipline. "Even his own men had to keep their distance. I hate to think what he'd become if he lost Jill now."

In spite of the warmth of the morning, Guillaume shivered. "I hate to think what Captain Cecco will become, if he does not win her back. *His* men must keep their distance, too. His temper has worsened even, in these last few days. Since visiting the Island, he has broken his spyglass and damaged his cabin. Mr. Yulunga and I handle him with, how do you say? The gloves of a goat."

Tom laughed, and the walls of the Lagoon tossed his merriment back. "You mean you have to handle him 'with kid gloves.' Aye," he said, more soberly, "I respect Captain Cecco, and I surely regret the misery he must feel. Let's hope the Island makes some magic for him, too."

With a passing cloud, a breeze kicked up, but the sun burst out to cheer the air again, and soon after, arching from one end of the Lagoon to the other, a rainbow bloomed, as if painted by an invisible brush.

Watching it, Guillaume gazed in wonderment. "Is there no end to the marvels of this land?"

"If you dream it, it can happen here," said Tom. "Nibs and I got our wish to be pirates. Lightly met up with Rowan, and got adopted by the Indians. Your dearest wish might be granted, too, once on this Island."

Climbing onto the rock, Lightly had overheard. He smiled as he tossed his wet, fair hair from his face and said, "After our experience this week, Rowan and I can testify that wishes come true here." The others clambered up, too, heaving themselves on the rock to join Tom and Guillaume, shaking off seawater and flopping down to dry on the sun-warmed surface. Now that their games had ended, the sound of the sea prevailed, licking the rock and peppering the shore.

Tom inhaled a lungful of the breeze, relishing the place again, then his hearty voice broke the tranquility. "Finish the story you started, Lightly. Are you getting married or not?"

Lightly obliged. "Panther kept us in suspense for three days, taking time to consider Ayasha's wishes and determine her future. After weighing the portent of his dreams, he delivered a gracious refusal on her behalf. So now all the tribe know that wherever Rowan goes, I follow. Fathers will think twice— literally— before asking one of us to marry their daughters again."

"Our own mother took two husbands," Nibs said, "but I don't suppose your tribe sees Jill as an example their marriageable women should follow."

Lightly sighed. "My heart stopped when I heard Rowan say yes to Panther."

Nibs returned, "But Rowan was wise to answer Panther as he did. Neither father nor daughter could be offended, but neither was likely to accept such an unconventional counterproposal."

Rowan looked grave. "Yes, Panther and his family seem satisfied, but I now read disapproval on the faces of the elders, especially Walking Man. As the Old One warned us, change is frightening, and tradition is not easily breached. Pledged to one another, Lightly and I risk our place among the People. We may even be banished." Rowan made a wet handprint on the rock, and watched as it began to evaporate.

Lightly said, "If it comes to leaving the People, I'll regret it mightily. But if I'm with Rowan, I'm at home." Lightly set his own handprint next to Rowan's, resting his head against his partner's while the two prints vanished together.

Guillaume shrugged. "I do not understand this trouble. When my papa abandoned his children, 'tradition' did not feed me. But Captain LeCorbeau did. Conventional or no, his affection offered survival."

Tom said, "You were loyal to LeCorbeau, Guillaume, and that's commendable. But we could see that your captain wasn't always good to you. I'll never forget that he ordered you into the sea to sabotage the *Roger*, knowing full well that you can't swim."

"Aye," Nibs said, and the crease between his brows returned. "LeCorbeau tried to do to me what he did to you. He took what he needed from you, pretending to love you like a son."

"I have no father," shyly, Guillaume smiled, flexing his hand to see his scar stretch, "but I am lucky now, to have friends." He gestured to Rowan and Lightly. "As of this morning, I count the two of you among them. May I invite you to dine with Mr. Nibs and Mr.

Tom and me on the *Red Lady* this afternoon? Our chef's cooking is superb."

"Believe it, mates." Tom rubbed his tummy. "When I served on *L'Ormonde*, Guillaume smuggled officers' fare to me. I can't wait for lunch."

"Thank you, Guillaume," Lightly replied. "We gladly accept your friendship, but we mustn't visit the ship. We've promised the council that we'll keep our distance from pirates, family excepted, and meet only at neutral locations like the Lagoon. While the elders are granting us their trust, we won't take chances with it."

"Then stay clear of the beach tomorrow," Nibs warned. "It'll be awash with pirates. Hook's hosting both his crews, and the People of the Clearing, too."

"My mother will like that," said Rowan, his brown lips smiling at last. "Maybe Lightly and I will host a smaller party at the Clearing then, for my baby sister and the other children."

Tom snorted. "Do you two even know which end of an infant is up?"

"Of course," Lightly laughed, "I was one myself once, back in London. And I just saw a new baby at the village. White Bear is the proud papa of a girl-child. She's three days old, and I saw him smiling for what I believe to be the first time ever when he showed her off to the People."

"Lean Wolf is cheerful, too," Rowan interjected, more seriously. "He hopes White Bear will give his widowed sister-in-law to him, now that the baby is born. Red Fawn was distressed when we told her. As Lean Wolf's former wife, she says Raven would do better with White Bear, even if she must become only his second woman."

Lightly nodded. "I've never seen Red Fawn so upset. But I don't blame her for feeling that way. Lean Wolf seems conceited, to me. Almost as cocky as Pan."

"Pan can be managed," Tom replied, "now that Hook's appointed Jewel to keep him out of mischief. I'm sure that, as the council's Messengers, you and Rowan keep an eye on him, too."

"Yes," Rowan said. "And after you sailed, we saw three new boys join his band."

"Four, now," corrected Nibs. He fished his orange kerchief from the boat and knotted it round his head. "You've probably seen the lad Jill sent to him. That cabin boy from the *Unity*. I saw them all diving off the cliff near Neverbay yesterday, trying to teach him to fly. Jewel looked almost dim, she'd sacrificed so much fairy dust."

Tom rolled onto his barrel chest, still scanning the surface of Mermaids' Lagoon for inhabitants. "David's nearly too old to be a Lost Boy. He'll outgrow the entrance to the hideout before long, and Pan will deliver him to the House in the Clearing. And I'm guessing that that was Jill's plan from the start. It's obvious that David adores Jill, but he's too young to be of interest to her. After the eight of us, I think she's had enough of mothering boys."

Guillaume had heard the story of the tiger hunt. "Why did the lady trouble to rescue that boy from the beast? The tiger might have mauled her!"

"It was an adventure, wasn't it? *And* David was wearing Hook's jewels. That's our Jill."

Nibs looked suspicious. "Take it from me, she's got some use for David. She's sure that the Island washed him ashore for a reason. David himself says so, but she sent him away before he could explain."

Guillaume said, "The *Roger* has a boy to deal with, the *Lady* has a girl. As you predicted, *mes amis*, Mrs. Hanover is causing the troubles."

Nibs' countenance darkened. "Who's she after now?"

"Poor Pierre-Jean. Mr. Yulunga was to whip him, but, after discussion, he and the captain decided, best not to make a romantic figure of him in Mrs. Hanover's eyes. He is confined to the brig, on bread and water."

Tom smirked. "It's for his own good, Guillaume. I speak from personal experience," he tapped at his scar. "Pierre-Jean will be safer locked away from that— *Guillaume?*"

Guillaume's jaw had dropped all the way open. As he gawked at the foot of the cliff, everyone spun to see what he saw.

Without a sound, a dozen mermaids had slipped from the water to perch upon the rock shelf. Little pools of damp spread around their hips. They sat in various attitudes, leaning back on their hands, trailing tails in the water, or resting on their elbows, relaxed in their own environment regardless of intruders. Some of the sea-maids smiled, others just angled their heads, but all of them stared with large, liquid eyes at the naked men who goggled back at them from the islet of Marooners' Rock.

Like a painter's palette, the mergirls presented an array of color. Their tails were as varied as glints of sunshine on the sea— rose, gold, gray and green, turquoise and indigo; their hair fell over their shoulders in lush, wet locks of yellow, auburn, chestnut, black, covering their bosoms only so far as to make those bosoms more evident. Scales of a delicate tissue rose from fins to midriffs, with V-shaped dips at the front, leading the men's eyes toward mystery. Smaller scales, like sequins, bedecked the backs of their hands and arms, as if they wore gloves that ended near the elbows. A few of the maids consulted mirrors. They wore necklaces of seashells, pearls, and even of gold gleaned from sailors, with gems that winked in the light. One or two exposed shell-like ears where they'd pinned their hair back with combs carved from mother-of-pearl. Each of these beings comprised a sailor's dream, so exquisite, so perfect, that it was painful even to view them.

The men on the rock held still, soaking up the vision. They salivated, their stomachs gnawed with hunger, and their loins began to pulse. Those who, as boys, had met up with mermaids were no more prepared to meet them than their fellows. They had underestimated the creatures' effect upon grown men. With blood rushing to their heads, Nibs and Tom forgot Guillaume and the hopes they'd held of witnessing his response. They were entangled in their own reactions. Rowan and Lightly clutched each other's arms and held their breaths, astonished at the wealth of beauty displayed along the shore, and stunned by its physical effect. Guillaume, utterly aghast, forgot every English phrase he knew, yet his words spoke for his friends. *"Mon Dieu,"* he uttered under his breath. *"Mon Dieu. C'est vrai, mais ce n'est pas possible."*

The company descended to a primitive level of consciousness, and, slowly, Nibs and Tom slid into the water. With their eyes fastened on the row of mermaids, they stroked toward shore. Rowan and Lightly followed, still holding one another, to tread water at a distance of discretion, panting to draw enough oxygen. None of them spared a thought for Guillaume. He sat as if petrified where he'd begun.

Petrified, until a motion at the edge of Marooners' Rock made him jump. Two hands emerged from the water to grasp the stone. No delicate hands these: they were large and strong, attached to muscular arms that easily hefted the weight of a man dripping with water. He swung himself upon the rock. Yet this entity proved to be no man. As he beached his body, a tail of silver flashed in Guillaume's eyes. When the being had settled, he breathed in, expanding a noble chest. He flung his wealth of silver hair over his shoulders to cascade down his back, dripping seawater over the rust streaks on the rock. His hair was plaited, lifted from his face by many little braids, knotted with seaweed. The merman transfixed the landsman with intelligent eyes, so bright a gray as to match his silvery tail.

Those eyes cast a glance at the swimmers, then, benevolently, the merman smiled at Guillaume. His voice flowed, fluid and musical.

"Your friends are in the sea. Why do you not join them?"

Guillaume gulped, and fumbled for his power of speech. He'd been warned not to trust mergirls, but this encounter with a mer*man*, so unexpected, confounded him. "I— I—" He blinked, he swallowed, then he tried again. He felt as if he were addressing a creature from a dream. "I cannot swim."

"You are a sailor?"

Nodding, Guillaume answered, "Yes. Yes, *Monsieur*, I am."

"And," the merman gestured to the uniform lying slack on a bench of the boat, "an officer?"

Guillaume's cheeks pinkened as he became aware that this merman had observed him shedding it. "Indeed. Yes…second mate of *Red Lady*."

"Ah, the beautiful newcomer lying moored in the bay. We've heard quite a bit of gossip about her. Now, perhaps, I shall discover the facts. It is the merfolk's boast that we learn all that comes to pass upon the Island."

In a trance, Guillaume watched and listened. This male of the species was as compelling as the females. In self-defense, Guillaume clung to the courtesy that his faux father, Captain LeCorbeau, had instilled in him. "Of course, yes, I am most happy to oblige." He couldn't keep his gaze from roaming the handsome physique.

With his silver-gray eyes, the merman observed Guillaume. "You are not like the other landsmen."

"Monsieur?"

"The others, when my daughters appear, become unable to speak." He smiled. "Of course, my daughters do take pride in their capacity to stop men's speech." His smile faded. "I will caution you. My daughters also take pride in their capacity to stop men's breathing."

Realizing that his own breath had stopped, Guillaume refilled his lungs. "Thank you, *Monsieur*. I will remember what you say."

"What is your name, my son?"

"I am called Guillaume."

"Well met, Guillaume. I am Zaleh. But tell me, isn't it odd that a sailor and an officer, who spends his life upon the sea, should be unable to swim in it?"

"If you please, *Monsieur*, it is no more odd than a man of the land living his life upon the water."

Merrily, the merman laughed. The sound pealed out like the trumpet of a conch. "Indeed! Not only are you polite, my boy, you are clever. Come," Zaleh said, and he stretched out his hand. Where men's arms might have hair, the merman showed iridescent scaling, reflecting the sky. "Come with me, my son, and I will teach you."

Hesitant, Guillaume reached out. The merman took his arm firmly in his grasp, and coaxed the young man toward the edge of the rock. Guillaume was surprised to find that Zaleh's touch matched the temperature of the air. His grip was wet, indeed, yet neither cold nor soggy. But, as a sailor, Guillaume had been cautioned. "Zaleh?" he questioned.

"You may call me 'Papa,' as my daughters do. We'll soon have you diving like a dolphin. Just keep hold of my shoulders. I won't let you sink."

"But, your daughters? They will drown me?"

"They're much too busy with your friends."

"I do not want my friends to drown, either!"

Zaleh laughed again. "Sea folk are judges of character. I perceive that you are a good man, Guillaume."

"And my mates are good men, also. Please, will you protect them?"

The merman frowned. "It is not our nature to care for human life. We play or we punish, as the whim comes upon us. Our moods are as changing as the moon." He studied Guillaume, registering his concern. "But we do admit to self-interest. What will you give me, if I agree to your request?"

Dismayed, Guillaume sought for an answer. Self-interest had motivated LeCorbeau, too. But Guillaume owned nothing that could be of value to this denizen of the sea. He owned nothing valuable at all. He held only one treasure, which Tom Tootles had given him when he first offered friendship. Guillaume valued it enough to hope that this merman might value it, too. If Mr. Tom and the others perished under the spell of sea sirens, Guillaume would lose that treasure anyway.

He looked Zaleh full in the face and answered, "I will give to you what I have given to my mates. I will give you my trust."

"Then you are not just a good man. You are a generous one." Zaleh nodded. "I accept your trust, Guillaume. Since you wish it, I will see that your friends remain above the surface."

Smiling at last, Guillaume answered, "Thank you, *Monsieur*."

"Bah!" Zaleh looked stern again. "How did I instruct you to address me?"

"Thank you...Papa."

Guillaume looked up into Zaleh's eyes. He liked who he saw there. He took a tight hold, and, trusting, plunged into the depths, under the protection of...Papa.

Mr. Tom was right, Guillaume decided as the bubbles swarmed up beside him, tickling his ears. Mermaids' Lagoon was a powerful place. The currents pressed around him as Zaleh's tail pushed the sea aside, forcing the two of them upward, toward the surface and the sun-blessed sky. Guided by a father's arm, Guillaume's trust in Tom Tootles deepened, too. He believed what Mr. Tom had told him.

This Lost Boy's wish was coming true.

Tonight's dance at the Fairy Glade was no formal occasion. The Queen had not decreed a ball and no invitations had gone out, but when Jewel flitted in with Hook's proposal, of course her kindred jumped at the idea. Over the years, generations of the creatures had advanced sybaritism to a fine art. Like all who are obsessed with the practice of their virtuosity, the fairies seized any excuse to perform it.

Nor did the fairies care who participated. Anyone might enter the ring of toadstools that marked out their territory, as long as 'anyone' was merry. The question of whether Hook and Jill joined the party was academic— a condition in which woodland creatures held no interest at all. The point was the *party*.

With no objection from the inhabitants, therefore, Jewel oversaw the installation of Hook's bequest. Scented with a dab of lily of the valley and flaunting her finest fairy gauze gown, she joined Wittles, the *Roger's* carpenter, at the edge of the forest.

For Wittles, shore leave took some time to get underway. In the week and odd days since dropping anchor in Neverbay, he'd followed new orders, peculiar as they'd seemed. With his broken-nailed hands Wittles had done his best. He didn't appreciate people telling him his business, but as the commodore had sweetened his outlook with silver, it all evened out in the end.

Yesterday he'd put the finishing touches on the piece and disassembled it for transport. Now he supervised Smee, Mason, and Noodler as they helped him deliver it. "Easy lads," Wittles scolded, looking askance at Noodler's backward hands. "On your heads be it, if the commodore complains that the glass broke."

Burdened with their baggage, the four sailors traipsed behind Jewel with their loads. A few hours away from David's training had revived Jewel's flow of fairy dust and, in the excitement of the occasion, she felt like her old self, and better. As she darted about the woods, the fairy's effervescence glowed bright and blue, even in late afternoon light.

Wittles was envious. "You're welcome in my shop, Miss Jewel. I could use a light like that, below decks."

Jewel looked back, rolling her eyes and emitting an exasperated little pinging noise. Between her master and her boy, she had enough duties. And tonight, her spirit held only space enough to anticipate the dance.

"All right then," Wittles huffed. "But if you've a cousin with a yen to go roaming…"

The other men chortled, and Noodler teased the sprite, "Our Miss Jewel's a rare fairy. Only she be daft enough to go to sea!" Jewel circled his head and tugged at his tricorn. Chummy as she and Noodler had become in the months since he'd trapped her for Hook, it was clear that she'd forgiven him.

As the group drew nearer to their destination, Wittles felt the air become charged. They all hushed their banter. Noodler alone among the *Roger's* sailors had ever spent time in the Fairy Glade. He had only acted on the commodore's orders, of course, as Wittles was doing now. Still, the place made the nails in Wittles' boots vibrate. The others followed his example as he shucked off his footwear before entering the magical ring.

In their own uncanny way, Hook and Jill arrived at the Fairy Glade ahead of them. A practical man like Wittles, who worked with wood and with iron, could never get used to their skylarking. As for the other creatures, the pixies did not dare to show themselves with sailors lumbering about, and Wittles was just as glad not to deal with their interference as he labored. Like the mermaids, whether in friendly mood or foul, fairies could be a nuisance. The sooner he assembled the love seat, the sooner he could get back to his workbench, and ship's routine.

But Jewel was not to be rushed. Wittles joined the pieces; then, in their stocking feet, the men shunted cautiously this way and that, their hands full of furniture, following the fairy's direction while Hook and Jill looked on. Once, then twice, they set the seat down, wiped their brows and flexed their shoulders, only to roll up their sleeves again after Jewel stared at the chair for a time with her chin in her hand and her head at an angle.

By the third move she was beaming, and chimed her delight like the silveriest of bells. Wittles wiped the fingerprints off the surface, and whisked away a speck or two of glittery dust before stuffing his polishing rag in his pocket. He stood back to accept the commodore's compliments.

No longer favoring a sprained ankle, Hook stood erect, and approving. His fairy perched on his shoulder while her luxuriant wings fanned his hair. "Well done, Mr. Wittles. I trust you'll enjoy your reward."

As Wittles knuckled his forehead, Jewel fluttered down to prance before the glass, and the lady herself looked enchanted. "Aye, Mr. Wittles. 'Tis a true work of art."

"My thanks to you, Ma'am." The carpenter nodded in satisfaction. Following his instructions, Wittles threw a tarpaulin over the bench. Glad to be done with it, he and the men hurried to pick up their boots and hustle back to the *Roger*, where he would clean his tools and hang them in their places, to rest through happy weeks until the commodore ordered preparations for sailing. With his cracked, carpenter's fingernails he scratched at his chin. Feeling the weight of the coins in his purse, he mumbled, "Now to start shore leave in earnest."

Once the sailors departed, Jewel's kinfolk appeared, popping from flowers and hollows, curious. They buzzed about, peeking under the dust cover, but Jewel chased them off, refusing to allow the wrap to be stirred until Hook gave the signal. In truth, Jewel became a bit intense about it all, causing her relatives to recollect why they avoided her. Even the Queen, Jewel insisted, must tap her pointed toeshoes, waiting to behold the gift Hook had bestowed upon the Fairy Glade.

When she felt Hook's eye upon her, Jewel skipped to a halt, subsiding to sit on his claw. He could guess what she was thinking, and he smiled his approval of the reticence he'd taught her to observe. She refrained from expressing her opinion, but held firm in the conviction that her master and his lady, in their velvets and silks, rivaled the royalty present.

"Oh, the lovelies." Jill's eyes danced as her gaze followed the creatures, who dashed about flouncing their costumes and plucking at their coiffures. She had often visited the Fairy Glade as a girl, and even frolicked here in the company of Pan, but the sight of the creatures *tous ensemble* never failed to enchant her.

At last, the Queen and her entourage gathered and approached, floating in a glowing group, all ribbons, color, and current. Their gauzy garments flowed about them, and they looked like bouquets of the flowers that grew in abundance in their garden just by.

Poised upon Hook's claw, Jewel spread her green gown and bobbed to the Queen. She then plucked at Hook's cuff, a dark shade of jade that he had chosen to harmonize with the woodland. He hoisted Jewel like a lantern, and she lit up to cast her glow over the tarpaulin.

"If I may. . . A gift for Her Majesty." Hook took up a position beside the wrap, set Jewel to hover, and said, "Pray accept this offering, with our compliments." Hook bowed and Jill curtsied. With his hook and his hand, the commodore snatched the dust cloth from the bench, and flourished it. The waxy woodwork gleamed in the light of the fairy horde, and the fresh, spicy scent of cedar wafted up. "A token of our esteem for our hosts and our hostesses."

Like a choir of hand bells, the air pealed with the fairies' delight. The Queen and her consort were the first to alight on the seat. As a bench, it would be useless to them, but quite handy for humans. Yet, when the creatures stood upon it, their reflections looked back in beauty. Where a person's back would rest, a series of mirrors were framed in the decorative woodwork. Gazing at themselves, the royals turned this way and that, unfurling their sleeves and tilting their heads. The mirrors redoubled their loveliness and filled up their senses with pleasure.

The dance was delayed then, so that every one of the Fae could admire his or her or its reflection. Some sillies did somersaults, others pulled faces, but even the littlest clapped their hands in happiness. Jewel herself floated, aloof, buffing her nails on her shoulder. As usual, she felt somewhat superior to her kin. After all, mirrors were nothing new to *her*. She kept one in her niche in Pan's hideout, crafted for her by the twins, and while these pieces were fine, Jewel's was the handsomest looking-glass on the Island.

Hook bent in obeisance. "Now, Your Majesty, not only the mermaids reflect the beauty of this land."

The Queen, justifiably flattered, condescended to dangle her fingers to him. As he kissed them, a little flutter juddered through her wings. Quickly, she joined hands with her handsome consort, and, at last, the musicians finished tuning and turned out a melody. The fairy revels began.

Gratified by the royals' response to their offering, Hook and Jill settled in to enjoy the concert. For tonight, they squeezed together on one end of the love seat, in order to allow the dancers to glimpse themselves whirling. It was no hardship for these lovers to crowd so close together. Like all who are obsessed with the practice of their virtuosity, Hook and Jill seized this reason to perform it.

Mrs. Hanover slammed the book shut. The force of it made the bed bounce. With her lips in a pout, she glared at Yulunga's back. He sat on the edge of the bunk, paying no heed. His big hands continued to mend his sword belt. As always, Yulunga's presence crowded the cabin.

"You tell me to talk," she said, her low voice rusty from the silence of the past three days. "But you won't talk to me."

He said, without turning, "So you've had enough of silence? Good."

Mrs. Hanover liked silence. She was used to it; she was used to using it. "I've had enough of being ignored."

Yulunga smiled his wide, malevolent smile. "And now I know your limit. Three days without a tumble." He looked at her. She lay on the stiff paisley coverlet, in her shift and nothing else. Every curve of her womanhood lay visible. "And you'll wait another three days before I touch you."

"I did nothing."

"You wanted to be caught. You wanted to be punished, and you wanted Pierre-Jean punished alongside you. But much as you crave them, there will be no bruises on either of you. Pierre-Jean doesn't deserve them, nor does your baby."

Once again, Yulunga's insight frightened her. She dropped her stare, revising her strategy. If Yulunga wouldn't satisfy her, she knew who would.

But Yulunga knew, too. "Pierre-Jean won't be joining the party tomorrow. You should already know that *you* won't be allowed there, either. Hook's orders stand. You're to go nowhere near the commodore. Or Captain Cecco. He doesn't want you— yet."

She lay still. She was counting on missing the party.

"Nor will you roam free aboard *Red Lady*, while your young Frenchy is in the brig and only two men on watch." His eyes narrowed. "Say what you're thinking."

"You'll lock me in? Tie me down?"

"No such luck. You'll get some practice with babies. Lily asked that you help watch the children in the Clearing while the ladies are away."

"With those twins who are master there?" The hint of hope in her voice betrayed her.

"No. With Rowan and Lightly. They have no interest in you, and they can swiftly fetch me from Neverbay if you give them any reason."

She nodded, averting her eyes from his body. It was all she could do to restrain her hands from stroking his chocolate-colored skin. No doubt he sat so close to torture her. The coverlet felt coarse under her bottom. She felt it rubbing when she moved, through the flimsiness of her shift. Her gaze wandered over her lover's physique once more, and a current of pleasure pushed through her vulva. She'd been studying her father's medical books, and now she knew the proper terms for her woman's parts. This word felt just right when she mouthed it: vulva. It was a voluptuous word, for a voluptuous vicinity.

Three more days of denial? No. She'd think of a way to slip down to the brig. If she succeeded, Pierre-Jean would soothe her longing. If she failed, Yulunga would have to punish her. Either way, she'd feel a man's touch again, and soon.

She smiled, absently, as though her thoughts were with someone not in the room with her. Such imaginings weren't unwelcome to

Yulunga. He watched her running her fingers along her breasts. With his cock pricking, Yulunga almost forgot his promise. He controlled his impulse, opened her book, and put his hands to work on the belt again. "Get back to your studies."

He looked forward to her next maneuver. Mrs. Hanover was an endless source of stimulation. He'd miss her at the party.

The Forest Fleet

The old oak braced itself, but Peter had no interest in target practice today. The bloody circles painted on its trunk remained arrowless. Instead, Peter leaned on the low, bench-like branch, favoring his 'peg leg' and commanding his crew. He wore a scowl, and squeezed one eye to a slit. Jewel sat on his shoulder, pretending to be a parrot. She didn't feel colorful enough, but Peter imagined the colors for her.

In David's case, no one had to make-believe color. Red-Handed Jill's handprint remained blatant on his face. On the other cheek, the bruise from Smee had altered from purple, to green, to yellow. Trying to fit in, he'd daubed mud on his face, like the others. It felt cool on the bruise, but it didn't ease his embarrassment. Ever since that first night, Peter and the boys called him Paleface, for fun.

For the Paleface, newest member of the band of Lost Boys, the last four days had been wearing. He'd endured Peter's efforts to break his manacles, then was ushered to the Clearing, where, by a mix of magic and manhandling by the identical men there, the chains had fallen off. Instructed by Peter, David had tried his skill at hunting. He'd dueled Peter and the others, capered in the starlight of the Fairy Glade and, steered by Jewel toward the riper ones that wouldn't put him to sleep, snatched apples from its moon-silvered trees. They'd all doused each other at the waterfall and tracked Indians through the woods. But as for flying, the new lad had taken so long to grasp the basics that the Lost Boys were sick of it. This morning, Jewel's peacock glow had faded again, to a feeble baby blue, and Peter felt it time to initiate an entirely new pastime. This game involved the use of arms and legs to reach the treetops, no fairy dust required. Not surprisingly, the idea first belonged to David, but, by now and a little worse for wear, the plan had become Peter's.

"Avast, you swabs! We set sail for the high seas today."

Bertie, Bingo, and Chip fell into pirate personae. They grinned with broken teeth, they smoked pipes, and if you looked closely, you could tell that, in their souls, they were swearing. Jewel yawned. David rolled his eyes sideways to observe the other boys, seeking guidance.

The fact that he'd met up with pirates, real pirates, and more than once, didn't help. He'd already learned that— although Peter couldn't tell them apart— reality and fantasy were two different animals. Among the Lost Boys, fantasy was the game for gaining acceptance, even if it meant going hungry while devouring your dinner. Now that the fabled Wendy had forsaken the hideout, as often as not meals might be imaginary. Pirates could fit into either category, and Peter would fight an illusory enemy with the same zeal he applied to battling the real thing.

Since Red-Handed Jill had thrown David to this pack, he was desperate to fit in. He trusted her judgment, and she'd been confident of the outcome. The lady meant for him to learn something; of that notion he was sure. But the other boys were younger than David, in age and in seasoning. For days, David listened intently to Peter, and he now understood that what he himself called 'experience,' Peter named 'adventure.' At last, David was shedding his dread of Jill's scheme. He'd gained an inkling of what she intended, and David intended to benefit.

He'd been taught that the prime factor in flying was happiness. The other boys seemed carefree, but events in David's previous life made it difficult for him to toss caution to the winds. He couldn't revel in boyhood the way the others could. They were orphans or runaways who never missed their families, while David had a mother at home who worried about him. He'd witnessed death, and the destruction of his ship. He'd barely made it to the Island alive, and he'd become a thief and a sneak to survive here. Above all, love and lust had claimed

David, and pretending they hadn't took all the energy he owned. His best guide in flight was Peter, of course, who brought a certain heartlessness to the sport. David found that he could accomplish the feat of flying only by emptying his heart. He had to approach it like swimming; survival was the only goal. He closed his eyes, held his breath, and paddled to stay afloat. Thus, he discovered, Jill's judgment was sound. He was old enough to see the symbolism, and young enough to make it work. And, once it worked, his happiness increased.

Now Peter petted his parrot and bawled at his men, "Chip, you're my bo'sun. Bertie, Bingo, and Paleface, you're for the crew. Look lively, you scum! Run up the shrouds and trim the sails!"

The younger boys looked confused at first, but David understood. Out of habit, he saluted his captain, and in a flash of inspiration, he thrust a stick between his teeth. He seized the low bough and hiked himself onto the ship's rail. Leaping to the next branch, he rapidly gained the yardarms, leaving the other boys in his wake. Even after they grasped the idea that the old oak was the ship's mainmast, Bertie, Bingo, and Chip lagged behind. Habituated to flying, they'd lost the knack of climbing trees. David's experience at sea served him, and he reached the high, thin branches of the maintop before they met the middle. He grinned as he peered from the heights. Rejoicing, he felt that, at last, Peter demanded a skill that David possessed. And the knee-jerk salute had been brilliant. David could see by Peter's posture that the gesture gratified his captain.

Peter remained below, pacing the quarterdeck with his hands locked behind him. The boys caught glimpses of his golden hair between the boughs. Every now and then he raised his spyglass to scan the horizon, then hoisted his chin to bellow orders.

"Hands to the braces! Now haul away, lads— with a will!"

Spurred by success, David swung from branch to branch, tugging ropes on command. While maneuvering in the rigging of a real ship was easier than dodging clumps of shrubbery, he proved more agile than the lubbers. Peter cursed the company, but praised David for his quick and efficient obedience. David swelled with pride, and threw himself all the more eagerly into the game.

Soon the captain ordered his men, "Hit the deck and man the cannon!" Here again, David excelled. He appointed himself gunner, shouting orders to the crew. He named their cannon Deadly Dinah, painting its moniker on the log with mud. Handing Chip a long, leafy branch, he taught the boy to swab the bore, then sent his powder monkeys, Bertie and Bingo, scavenging for rocks to use as shot. He himself tamped the wadding and powder down, and, closing one eye, squinted along the barrel for aim. Arming the gun crew with 'handspikes,' he made them set the proper trajectory. The muscles of their arms bulged as they toiled, and they wiped their brows with kerchiefs.

"Dinah's primed and standing by, Sir!" he hollered, and Peter strutted over, grasped the line of ivy David handed him, and yanked. As the gun exploded with thunder from five children's throats, David heaved a stone into the distance, kicking up soil where the shot came to earth. He'd sprinkled a dash of fairy dust on the ball, which completed the effect by lighting up the spray. The crew cheered. David was certain he smelled gunpowder, and a haze of white smoke hung by the bow. The captain roared, "Silence, fore and aft!" then it was time to tack the ship for a broadside, with all hands clambering back up the rigging.

David burned with excitement, and so did his captain. By the end of the afternoon, he'd been promoted to first mate, bo'sun, and master gunner. Peter elevated himself, as well, and halfway through the battle he changed sides from buccaneer to British Navy. The crew held David in awe, and although the admiral was shorter than he, he looked down his aristocratic nose at David, buffing his epaulettes and beaming approbation.

In the whole of his young life, David never had so much fun. When Peter tired of the play, all his boys moaned in disappointment. David lifted their spirits by promising to teach nautical knots by the light of the fire in the hideout that evening. He hoped he could find some rope, though. His imagination was improving, but even the simplest of knots wasn't easy to pretend. He opened his mouth to suggest a raid on one of the pirate ships, to steal some.

The parrot's beady gaze stopped him dead, and Jewel looked like a fairy again— a fairy who knew what was what. David shut his mouth, tight.

Reality and fantasy were two separate animals. Survival, David realized, was no longer his only goal. As the boys rose in a flock to head homeward over the forest, he closed his eyes, held his breath… and floated on happiness.

Behind Peter's band, a long shred of David's shirt streamed in the breeze, anchored at the peak of the proud old oak. It wasn't colorful enough, but David imagined that it was. And so, to the tree's relief, the sailors sought shore leave on the Neverland, while the admiral's pennant adorned the flagship of the formidable forest fleet.

The sun reached its height over Neverbay, and as it ebbed toward its bed in the western heavens, preparations for the party neared completion. Two ships' companies, divided while aboard in the bay, united for a night of leisure on the shore. Still on board the *Roger*, Smee tended the final tasks for the commodore.

"I'll tote your pistols and swords myself, Sir," he said, "though we've prepared so well, doubtless you'll not be needing them." He knotted a deep blue scarf about Hook's head, confining his long black hair. Then he nodded. "All set for the Island, Commodore."

Jill sighed, "How handsome you look, Hook. I adore your more formal attire, but you do steal my heart away in just a shirt and breeches." She had finished dressing for the revels, and now she stood admiring her lover.

Reflected in his shaving mirror, Hook's gaze met her own. His voice was smooth, and amused. "Don't forget to breathe, love." Hook and Jill smiled as his words reminded her of their first assignation. He turned to observe her. "You are a vision yourself, my love. Bright and bold."

She spread the skirt of her tunic, posing for his inspection. "I chose the topaz in your honor, since you like it so well. And it brought us luck the last time we ventured to the Island."

Jill touched her hair to make sure she had captured every wisp in its twist. Although she dressed simply, she'd applied a dab of scent behind her ears, her exotic, expensive perfume, a reminder of her position as the commodore's queen. Her crescent earrings dangled free, and she wore the opal and diamond necklace Hook had bestowed upon her, symbolic of the color and complexity of the Neverland. The first jewels she'd ever owned, they glowed at her throat, just beneath the red line of her scar. Her feet were bare under the narrow ankles of her Turkish trousers, be-ringed and ready to dance in the sand.

"Mr. Smee," she declared, "you look quite fine this evening. Like me, Lily is sure to appreciate you."

Smee grinned with gratification. "Too kind you are, Lady." He'd tended his own appearance with a close shave and new duck trousers, and he'd tucked a gift for his Lily in his pocket. "But I admit, the woman has never complained."

Hook inquired, "Is my pavilion erected on the beach, Smee?"

"Aye, Sir, well up from the tide line, complete with rugs and furnishings. The camp bed is made up and ready there, whenever you and the lady decide to retire."

Jill said, "Thank you, Mr. Smee. I believe you and the commodore have thought of everything to make this party a success."

"Yes, Ma'am. The lads have outdone themselves preparing. They're ready for a night of it."

"I'm as eager as the men for tonight's festivity." Jill filled her vision with her pirate king. "And I am many times more grateful than they, Hook, to celebrate your escape from the Indians."

He bowed in acknowledgement. "The men performed worthily in the crisis. This reward is well earned."

"The thought of that day will forever remind me not to take you for granted." Standing near the hourglass, Jill rested her scarlet hand upon the brass of its casing. "Every moment we spend together, every grain of the glass, is precious."

"I am no slave to time— except, my love, where you are concerned. Then I count the seconds like a miser." Hook touched her cheek and caressed her, then took up the hourglass, handing it to

Smee. "As discussed, we shall need this on the beach. Wrap it up and bring it along."

"Aye, Sir. There'll be no complaints about shifts on watch tonight. Every man'll serve his turn of the glass." Smee headed for the cabin door. "The lads are all ashore, Commodore. Your boat's ready to launch when you are."

"My thanks to you, Mr. Smee. We shall join you presently." As his officer closed the door, Hook's aspect became serious. "Since you speak of gratitude, Madam, I'll inform you now that I will make a speech, praising the men for their conduct as they fetched me from the village."

Puzzled, Jill answered, "Of course, Hook. I'd expect nothing less."

"I shall make a point of commending Captain Cecco, as well."

"Oh....Yes. I see." Jill dropped her gaze from his. Three heartbeats later, she met his eye again. "Hook. You should know before we begin that, this evening, I intend to dance with everyone."

"By 'everyone,' you mean to say...your husband."

"I mean to say, everyone."

"Will his hopes not be raised by this attention?"

"What I hope to raise is a sense of unity. Tonight we celebrate the fact that, even faced with the fiercest of enemies, our two ships' companies work as one. You yourself are setting the example. Our leaders must, all of us, demonstrate the same kind of accord, whether fighting or at leisure."

"Have a care," Hook warned, and his visage darkened. "The captain's temper is unimproved. By all reports, his Island beauty has not tamed him."

Thrown just a bit off balance, Jill steadied herself on the desk. Her cheeks heated in a flush. "I..." She stood straight again. "I do not favor tameable men." A part of her heart was glad of Cecco's constancy. Another part regretted it.

"And yet you aspire to reach some accord. Of the three of us, not one is liable to yield."

"I require your patience, Sir. It is my wish that, tonight, we'll find some kind of footing."

"Make no mistake about your aspirations. Or Captain Cecco's."

He placed the tip of his hook on her breast, pressed against her beating heart.

She didn't wince as the cold of the point met her flesh. She waited to feel its prick, knowing even as she did so that Hook would not cause her hurt— not today, and not ever. Yet the power he exuded was so potent that, once again, she ceased to breathe.

But he passed that power to her. "You hold his life in your red hand."

"And you hold my heart on your hook."

"I know your heart. Your love pours, like the hourglass, from one end to the other." Dropping his hook to his side, he drew himself up to his full, imposing height. "I have forewarned you, Madam. With you, I am a miser."

"You are...a commodore." She smiled at last, cajoling him, yet noting the gleam of his claw in the corner of her eye. "I am the commodore's soul."

"See that your husband minds his manners."

"Aye, Commodore." Bold as she was, standing her ground, her pulse beat cruelly behind her façade. She arched her eyebrows. "And shall I see that my lover minds *his* manners, too?"

"I keep command of myself." Deliberately, he bent to her breast, and kissed the place his blade had rested, bringing warmth to chase the chill off her skin. His face remained close to hers as he cautioned, "Bear in mind what you assert: do not take our union for granted."

"Never."

"Then let us fly, to the Neverland. An excellent idea, in fact." He stepped away, to arm's length, enticing her only with his eyes.

It was enough. With just a look, he took possession of her senses. Hook, her lover, became all she could feel, hear, or see. He spoke low and slowly, and the nectar of his voice filled her ear. "As you aim to partner everyone, *I* claim your first dance."

Through the sixth sense that vibrated between them, his desire for her stirred her. She'd have felt his effect no matter where she stood, just as, not long ago when he was a prisoner, Hook perceived her own arousal when she lay with her husband, while he, her lover, lay in chains. Indistinct at a distance, the sensation when so near overwhelmed. And, at any distance, Hook's longing echoed her own. Once again, discord sharpened their ardor. As happened so often since Hook's abduction, uncertainty brought urgency, and it spiced the taste of their embrace.

Afterward, he opened the door and guided her, light-headed, down the stairs of the companionway. When the pair arrived amidships, Hook leaned over the gangway to call to the waiting boat.

"You may shove off, Mr. Smee. We shall meet you ashore."

Smee saluted. "Aye, aye, Commodore." He shouted the command to the oarsmen, and the boat pulled away from the hull.

Above the creak of the boat and the cry of the gulls, music drifted from the beach of Neverbay. A balmy breeze buffeted the couple's garments. Together, they pushed from the deck to rise upward, through the sleeping rigging. Higher and higher they ascended in the early evening sky, eggshell blue speckled with bright white spots, as the stars in the east blinked awake.

When they reached the topmost masthead, Hook pulled Jill with him, leaning backward until they hovered just above it. The Jolly Roger flapped below them, its motion black as shadow. Their banner swirled beneath it with two blood-red handprints. Swimming in the wind, it showed now one hand— Hook's— now the other— Jill's— then both hands, reunited, to divide in the breeze once again.

Setting one boot on the mast, Hook gathered Jill in his arms as if for a waltz, then thrust away toward the Island. Together, they circled and swirled to the melody that grew louder as they neared it. Like the sun before them, they reached their height over Neverbay, and descended to settle, finally, at the wooded edge of the beach. They strolled left hand in right on the sand among their sailors, as eager as every other reveler.

The Indulgence of Divergent Forces

In Chef's estimation, Captain Cecco's appetite had waned with his marriage. In the weeks since *L'Ormonde* became *Red Lady*, the little Frenchman huffed and fumed, feeling that his talents went unappreciated. He'd suffered the frustration of the artist in search of a patron. Tonight, at last, he relished the opportunity to exhibit his culinary *savoir-faire*.

Leaning toward the embers, he basted the boar. His face glowed pink in the heat of the pit. Beneath an apron, his belly extended, at risk of braising, too, but Chef's soul was satisfied as he prepared a feast fit for kings upon the shore of Neverbay.

He kicked his galley mate, encouraging him to rotate the spit. "Come, Jacquot, we must exert every effort tonight. For the sake of my reputation, the crew of the *Roger* must be regaled. And *Red Lady*'s men deserve our indulgence."

Except for the commodore and his lady, Chef didn't expect the ignorant Englishmen to perceive the nuances of his talent, but he was certain his countrymen would smack their lips and gaze toward heaven. He sighed, nostalgic at the thought of his former captain's gusto. "*Monsieur* LeCorbeau would sob at a taste of the fare denied him tonight, *hein?*"

Jacquot shrugged boney shoulders. "*Oui, Monsieur,*" he replied, like an automaton. He wiped the sweat from his brow and kept turning the spit.

But Jacquot's indifference could not diminish Chef's *bonhomie*. "I bless this Isle for its salubrious properties." The meat had been hunted in this forest and seasoned on this magical shore. The very fuel of its firewood bestowed flavor. Chef's only lament at this *fête* concerned his suspicion— the fear of all great artists— that he might never surpass tonight's triumph. He licked the taste of clove from his greasy fingertips and admonished Jacquot, "You are not cranking water from a well, you fool! Turn the spit slowly." Then he looked up the sandy slope, to beam upon those whom, fondly, he termed the royalty of the Island.

Commodore Hook and the Lady Jill appeared tranquil in the radiance before twilight, standing at ease on Persian rugs in front of their pavilion. They sipped from one goblet the wine Chef had selected for them. With every manifestation of cheer, they greeted their guests. Hook stood regal, his hook half hidden by the snowy cuff of his blouse, his scarf a dash of blue over his raven hair. Jill's garment glowed golden in the sunset. Her opals and diamonds dazzled at her throat. Colorful stripes on the tent behind the two-some added gaiety to the tableau. With a silken tie, its flap swagged open to show a net-covered camp bed, lanterns, chest and table, towels and a basin— all the furnishings necessary for the couple's comfort. When not gesturing, they joined their hands together. To Chef and to the company, no hint of tension was evident.

Mr. Smee, however, knew better. He loitered nearby, hoping to forestall ill feeling before it materialized from any quarter, the usual causes being drunkenness, rivalry, or women. Tonight Smee was wary of all three combined, in the single person of Captain Cecco.

He watched with an eagle eye as *Red Lady*'s ruler approached the Island in his boat. Upon arrival, Cecco's rowers raised their oars to slide into shore. The captain sprang from his craft and splashed up the beach, the medallions jangling on his headdress, and the man rolled in like a dark, discordant cloud.

His own first officer, Mr. Yulunga, immediately joined him. Smee had conferred with Yulunga, and he knew that Cecco's mate, too, was prepared to be vigilant. Employing all the power of his presence, the African took up a position opposite Smee, flanking his captain.

Mr. Smee and Mr. Yulunga exchanged nods of accord; amity must rule over even the highest ranks, tonight.

As for external threats, the captain and the commodore had organized precautions. Their officers secured the beach early on. Because the succulent odor of roast boar attracted both men and beasts, Smee and Yulunga ordered torches to be planted along the circumference, and they'd assigned sentries to watch through the night. The perimeters of the party— forest and shore— were lit, armed, and guarded. Each team served a turn of the hourglass, which stood on a post by the commodore's pavilion. At every rotation, Smee signaled the change with a blast of his bo'sun's pipe. At that time, too, a fresh pair of sailors rowed out to *Red Lady* to relieve the watch aboard. As the noise level rose, prowling beasts shied away. The men, however, drew nearer, their mouths slavering and their stomachs rumbling in anticipation.

Among the anticipators were Nibs the Knife, Tom Tootles, and Mr. Guillaume. They sauntered down the shore, Tom shuffling sand before him and squeezing it in his toes to filter its grains between them. He nudged Guillaume. "Going for a dip tonight, now that you've learned how to swim?"

"I think not, Mr. Tom. I prefer the warmer waters of the Lagoon."

"Aye to that," said Nibs, recollecting their expedition to the mermaids' lair. His orange kerchief flapped loose in the breeze, and he re-tied it over his forehead. "I found this kerchief while on scout duty for Wendy, the morning after another party Hook held here. Curse me for a lubber if I lose it in the very spot that Bill Jukes did."

Tom chuckled. "Since Jukes lost it chasing Lelaneh, you might change your mind, mate. As *he* tells the tale, he never missed it."

"And what about you, Guillaume?" Nibs asked, slyly. "You've left off your brass buttons tonight. Afraid you'll lose your uniform in a similar scuffle?"

Guillaume blushed, but shot back good-humoredly, "No, no. Unlike my friends, my wits are not addled in the presence of beauty. If you remember, I am the only man who could speak to the mer-ladies."

"*Touché,*" Nibs conceded.

"You're not afraid of men, either?" Tom grinned. "Of losing your subordinates' respect?"

"I hold little fear that my men won't behave, Mr. Tom. They see Pierre-Jean locked in the brig for disobedience. He looked forward to this *fête* as much as the rest of us, yet there he sits. No one wishes to spoil this opportunity."

Nibs gazed across the beach to scrutinize Cecco. "Aye, the crew are the least of our worries." The wrinkle between his eyebrows sharpened, and he and Tom glanced at one another, then turned to study Jill as they neared her.

The young men were welcomed at Hook's pavilion, and took their places among the officers. As bo'sun's mates, Nibs and Tom were charged with discipline, as was Guillaume, second of *Red Lady*. In or out of uniform, all three were prepared, this evening, to keep their backs straight and their brains clear.

The pitch of the merriment rose higher once the People of the Clearing arrived. Lily, Lelaneh, and Red Fawn, escorted by the bronzed and brawny twins, carried armloads of fruits, breads, and drink. The ladies' attire displayed various gifts of the sailors. They wore their soft native skirts with fringe dangling down their legs, and flowery European shawls were tied provocatively about their hips or flowed from their shoulders. Their bracelets and their new earrings shone mellow like the wakening stars. They smelled of wood smoke, honey, and home. Smiles trailed them, as men turned to admire.

The Men of the Clearing had tucked their new axes in their belts, and strapped bedrolls onto their backs. Judging by appearances, they'd attempted to tame their bright hair, no doubt in token of their respect for Jill. At the commodore's pavilion, they paused to set down a handsome rocking chair. "A gift for our mother," said the first twin.

"A throne for the Storyteller," said the second, and they both smiled at her. The chair's frame was of cedar, still redolent of its zest, and it was overlaid with mesh woven of willow strips, supple enough to require no cushions, yet strong enough to hold her secure while immersed in her tales.

"It's perfect," Jill replied. "The very thing I required for tonight."

With pleasure on her face, she accepted the hands of her sons as they ushered her to her seat of honor. "Your craftsmanship surpasses itself," she murmured, laying her fingers on the chair's arms, fondling its smooth, bumpy finish. It creaked companionably, welcoming her weight. "This seat is inspirational. I feel a story brewing already."

"We're eager to hear it," they said in turns, "Just as eager as we were in the hideout, growing up."

"And now that you're grown, I'm no longer obliged to sweep up your sawdust."

They all laughed. Having accepted her gratitude, the Men of the Clearing made their compliments to Hook and the officers, and excused themselves. They stowed their burdens; then, drawn to the roast's aroma, they soon took the grip of the spit in their own hands. Chef's galley mate flopped on a cool patch of sand, panting in relief.

Wittles, the ship's carpenter, had been busy, too, knocking together some rough wooden tables, now covered in cheery cloths and burdened with serving dishes. The native women laid out their victuals with the feast there, then crowded round Chef. "Such a beautiful boar!" they exclaimed, embracing him soundly.

His plump face creased into smiles at their attention. Jacquot stared openmouthed, and regretted leaving his post. But, nostalgia or no, Chef did *not* regret leaving LeCorbeau. The French captain had his virtues, but he'd never admitted females to his amusements. Between Hook and LeCorbeau, Chef thought, *vive la différence.*

The pirates kindled the bonfire farther east on the beach, nearer the ships, which were fading to silhouette. The vessels dipped in the swells that rolled landward to lap at the shore. With a clatter, Mr. Noodler dropped an armload of driftwood near the flames. Alf Mason jumped back.

"Blast your backward hands, Noodler. You've shattered my toes."

"Apologies, mate," said Noodler, tipping his tricorn, and Mason waded into the surf to soothe the sting.

"Fill my tankard, and I'll forget it." Mason threw Noodler his cup.

Kegs and casks formed a line not far from the fire, and so did the men, filling their flasks and relaxing to the rhythm of the revels. Each man kept his eye on the pavilion, and, quiet but curious, exchanged observations with the others. The French crew, too, had bonded enough with the Rogers to share in ship's gossip.

To roam the Island without weapons was madness, and Hook never forbade arms at his merrymakings. Each man kept his steel close to hand. Still, the sailors noted the famed knife tucked in Cecco's belt, over his scarlet sash, and they witnessed his fingers caressing it. On his biceps, he bore both of the golden armbands he'd once shared with Jill. He was seen to accept the wine that Jill offered in her only white hand. He was not seen to taste it.

With a flourish, the fiddler concluded a jig, and the concertina oozed into music. The seamen sang along, some cavorting, some clapping, all waiting for the women. When Noodler returned with the tankard, Mason swigged a gulp, then pitched his voice over the noise. "I wish the ladies would finish fawning over Chef. That little dollop of lard is arrogant enough."

"With good reason, Alf. I might kiss him myself for a slab of that boar." Noodler lifted his face to the sea breeze that blew up the beach and swayed the surrounding woods. His gold teeth gleamed as he grinned. "Ah, 'tis good to be anchored on the Island again. Land, ladies, green grass, and vittles. No port in the world be more restful."

"Maybe so, but best to take your pleasure quick. I'm keeping a weather eye for sparks, tonight. And I don't mean from the bonfire."

"How's that?"

Mason leaned closer and lowered his voice. "There's embers alight. It won't take an effort to fan them to flame."

Noodler was an able seaman, but not much for metaphor. Seeing his vacant look, Mason explained, "I'm talking of the bad blood between the commodore and the captain." He jerked his head toward the pavilion, where Jill leaned back in her rocking chair. She watched the festivity, and Captain Cecco watched her.

Noodler nodded. "A good man is our Cecco."

"He deserved his fair fortune. The commodore did right by him, giving him the ship."

"Aye, but 'twas a cruel hard blow to lose the lady, so it was."

"A test of his temperament," said Mason. "We've yet to see how he'll weather it." As the squeezebox wheezed to an end, Mason sealed his mouth with his tankard, but like every man present, he and Noodler kept their eyes wide.

Commodore Hook offered his arm to raise Red-Handed Jill from her seat, and she took her place between him and Captain Cecco. To their right ranged Nibs, Tom, and Mr. Smee; to their left, Mr. Yulunga and Mr. Guillaume, all coming to attention. Hook signaled to Smee, who hailed the sailors. At the sound of the bo'sun's roar, the company turned their backs to the bonfire and gravitated toward the tent, forming a throng before the cluster of officers. Expectant grins bloomed on their faces.

"Belay there, mates!" called Smee, and the crowd quieted. "We've a night of carousing ahead, thanks to our commodore. Let's be raising our glasses, with three cheers for our host. Sing out hearty, now, lads. To himself, to Commodore Hook!"

The assembly joined in, hoisting their drinks to shout as one man, their voices uniting in low, vibrant chant:

"Hip, hip…huzzah!"

"Hip, hip…huzzah!"

"Hip, hip…huzzah!"

The cheer shook underfoot and rumbled round in their chests. They all smiled to hear the echoes rebound from the forest. They drank deeply then, savoring their draughts.

Cecco, too, drank to the commodore. He was seen now to empty his goblet.

Next the commodore strode forward, raising his arm, and his cuff fell back to reveal the wicked, gleaming hook. He addressed his guests. "I return thanks to you, men of the *Roger*, and men of *Red Lady*. Our first engagement as a fleet met success. I commend your quick action. I praise your courage in confronting the enemies who held me captive."

Gratified grunts met his words, and nods and winks between seamen. Hook's sapphire eyes glittered in the light of the torches, reminding his pirates of prizes.

"Each member of my company earned tonight's indulgence. As has Captain Cecco, who led you to my rescue." Hook paid his tribute to Cecco in a bow. With dignity, Cecco inclined his head, accepting the gesture. Then Hook faced forward again, his scarf falling over his shoulder. Flourishing his claw, he saluted his men.

"My sincere thanks…*merci beaucoup…*" And, facing Cecco, "*Grazie mille.*"

Gleeful, a volley of voices rang out. Cecco was seen solemnly to applaud.

Hook waited as the crest of enthusiasm broke over him and settled, then said, "But both the Lady and I exult in more than my personal safety. Tonight, we rejoice in accord. Confronted with a ferocious foe, our band stands steadfast. Undaunted, our divergent force fights as one. Let us combine in celebration as we combine in battle. Gentlemen; ladies: I give you 'unity!' " Smiling half-way, he looked sideways at Jill.

The men hollered their approval. Appearing pleased, Jill smiled and kissed her scarlet hand to the commodore. Turning, she curtsied to Cecco. Smee waved to the players, and the fifer piped up with a ditty. The whistle was joined by fiddles, and next by the drums, and as music burst forth, the party started in earnest.

Formally, Hook shook Cecco's hand, then Smee's and then Yulunga's. Jill followed suit, saving Cecco for last. He clasped her hand, looking grateful to do so although she offered her left, and not her marked and more meaningful hand. And then, as the men observed under cover of their revels, he appeared startled, for as the melody swelled, Jill pulled him to the sand to lead the dancing. In a daze he followed her, while Hook reached out for Lily. And, suddenly, Captain Cecco was seen to be smiling.

The chef smiled, too. Although he was vain, he was not a man who denied his mistakes. As the moon appeared low on the eastern seascape, distorted as it waned from the full, he watched the royalty dance, and he learned that his appraisal was mistaken.

His captain's appetite had never waned. Like the fleet before the foe, it stood steadfast.

Knowing Red-Handed Jill, Mrs. Hanover should have prepared to find her imprint on this Island. But until today, she didn't realize how thoroughly the lady left her mark. Mrs. Hanover encountered evidence of Jill's presence— even her adolescent presence— everywhere. Aboard ship, Mrs. Hanover was subservient to Jill. Ashore she was subject to Wendy. The lady's dominance reinforced Mrs. Hanover's resolve to limit the time she must spend here. No matter what Mr. Yulunga commanded for tonight, Mrs. Hanover had designed her own exploit.

Preparing her plan for action, Mrs. Hanover showed only obedience this afternoon. She now stood before the hut she'd been told was the Wendy House. Approaching the door with her bundle under her arm, she peered around the Clearing. The little shack's chimney puffed out the red smoke that rose to the sky, a perpetual portent sending various messages to various beholders. Mrs. Hanover had not made up her mind as to its meanings. This smoke signal was one of the mysteries of the Island. In some way, she felt, it promised satisfaction.

Rowan, Lightly, and the children could be heard laughing and splashing as they washed at the nearby brook. Weary from assisting with the little ones' games, Mrs. Hanover set her envy aside and entered the Wendy House, to lie down on a cot. For a moment she was tempted to make use of the china tea set. On a second look, though, she realized that the sugar bowl was missing, and, closing her eyes to Wendy's relics, she soon dozed off. The wind sighed through the leaves that formed the walls, and when afternoon waned outside the viney window, she rose refreshed and aflutter with excitement for this evening's escapade.

She shook out her skirts. Smiling, she calculated by the slant of the light that the time to shed this dress drew near. She re-rolled her bundle, making sure it was ready, then brushed her brown hair and twisted it into a knot, pinning it in place. Touching her one golden earring, she checked the strength of its catch. She couldn't afford to lose her only ornament in the woods. She knew Yulunga. Tonight's play might cost her its mate.

The trees dwarfed her when she emerged, their massive limbs

catching the breeze. In the treetops, a patch of plumage caught her eye where the sentinel parrot stood guard. But the toys and games had been tidied, and no one else was about. She pricked her ears as, from within the larger structure, childish voices rose above the birdsong. She followed them.

The oaken doorway stood open for her, and Mrs. Hanover slipped into the home and stole up the stairs. Peeping into the nursery, she discovered Rowan and Lightly sitting cross-legged on the floor, each with an infant on his arm and a youngster on his lap. While Lightly narrated a bedtime story— attributed to Wendy, of course— Mrs. Hanover entered and surveyed the room. Before too long, she would have to fashion her own nursery, of sorts, but she very much doubted it would feel quite like this one.

It contained a curious combination: native rugs and blankets on the beds, the walls, and the floor, shot through with bold colors. European drapes to dress the window, a brocade of deep green, like the surrounding forest. The window itself as large as a door, open to admit the fragrance of the garden. A tiny fireplace. A cradleboard. A pendulum clock on the mantelpiece, with pinecones and acorns; dolls made of cornhusks; a wooden ship. The furnishings soaked up the sound, and softened Lightly's voice. No echoes rang in this room, to make one feel cold. Through its mix of cultures, the one constant of this nursery was coziness.

The fire wasn't kindled this temperate evening, but Lightly and Rowan had lit the nightlights. Burning on shelves in the corners, one light shone for each child, little seashells that glowed golden. Mrs. Hanover was drawn to examine one. As she moved closer, she inhaled its scent, like baked apples. For a brief space of time, she was transported to a flagstone kitchen in England, long ago, as the cook pulled scones from the oven. She remembered how the sweet, flakey taste stung her tongue. Like other young ones brought here from that world, Mrs. Hanover felt a pang of homesickness, and then she forgot it.

Lightly ended his tale to happy hoots from the children, and he looked up at Mrs. Hanover. "There you are, just in time to tuck in our sleepyheads. Can you give us a lullaby?"

The sense of well-being abandoned Mrs. Hanover. She had no notion of tucking in children. As for lullabies, she couldn't recall one, nor did she feel she could sing if she did. After years of silence at her father's command, she could only just manage to speak. Song was beyond her capabilities.

"No," she blurted. But these young men had treated her civilly today, and, not wishing to alert their suspicions, she felt she should make up for her inability. "But I'll lay the babies in their cribs." She lifted Lily's redheaded daughter from Rowan's lap and looked around again, and her face showed a growing confusion. The two bigger children climbed onto cots, like the little bed in which Mrs. Hanover had slept as a very young girl. But no cradle could she find.

The men chuckled at her bewilderment, and Lightly pointed to a basket on the floor. Mrs. Hanover had mistaken it for a hamper. As he showed her how to swaddle the baby tight in her wrappings, Lightly explained, "The cradle basket began with Wendy. She made shift with very few resources in our hideout under the ground. We had only the one big bed, you see, and we all tossed and turned through the nights. Michael was so small, Wendy appointed him to be the baby. She judged that placing him above the fray was the most careful course." He waited while Mrs. Hanover arranged Rowan's sister in the basket, then helped her swaddle the littlest boy-child, too.

"When the twins built this grown-up house here in the Clearing, the only crib they could remember was Wendy's invention. And so the tradition continues." Lightly nestled the boy beside the girl, and, employing a system of ropes and pulleys attached to the rafters, he raised the basket to suspend it well above the floor. Giving the cradle a nudge, he started it rocking. He turned to see Mrs. Hanover's astonishment. Smiling, he reassured her, "The twins have refined the design, of course. It's perfectly safe."

Mrs. Hanover blinked. Safety was not a condition she connected with childhood. The Wendy, after all, had not been *her* mother.

Amid drowsy babbles, the men settled the youngsters in their cots and drew up the blankets. In the end, Rowan lulled the little ones to slumber himself, his chiseled features easing as he chanted.

His song was one Lily used to sing to him in their tepee. Being familiar to these children, the melody was comforting, and soon their breathing steadied.

Mrs. Hanover leaned by the window as she listened to Rowan's croon. Little stars twinkled, as if chatting to one another in a language of light. Even ears as sharp as hers couldn't catch their voices. She understood, though, that time was short, and she roused herself. She must make her escape before the lullabies ended, before night blacked her path.

"Good evening," she whispered to Lightly, and signed her intention to retire. She slipped down the stairs and out the front door. Her bare feet scurried through the dew, and she flung herself into the hut. Stripping down to her shift, she tossed her dress on Wendy's cot, and snatched up the bundle.

A twinge of excitement plucked her insides. Almost trembling, she closed the door, and she fled. The clement air met her skin. A feeling of freedom dashed with her. She was released from clothing; unbound from duty, she dared to assert her own will. This rushing was almost as titillating as what she was rushing to meet.

In her flight toward a pirate ship, she couldn't know that, once, Wendy played this same game.

Filled with eagerness, Mrs. Hanover moved so swiftly that the sentinel parrot, unsure of himself, gave only the briefest of screeches. The Wendy House, where she was thought to be sleeping, stood silent in her wake. Rosy smoke surged, urgent, from its chimney, signaling to any beholder, this time, a single, simple message. Upon reading it, Wendy in her day would have flown into action. With the ladies away, though, no one witnessed its warning. Not one caught its mark of alarm.

Just beyond the parrot's purview, Lean Wolf hunkered in the wood, watching the girl run away. His clever smile crossed his face.

He knew what she sought. The signs were painted all over her, and her pregnancy was proof of her fervor. Given opportunity, he himself would gratify that appetite. But a finer prospect beckoned, and the time was ripe to catch her.

Keeping low, he turned and started his trek through the forest. He skirted the plot that the Women of the Clearing had cultivated. He smelled the Neverlilies that Red Fawn favored, and it brought the memory of her skin to his fingertips. All in good time, he assured himself. Red Fawn wasn't going any farther than this garden.

As he crept past the far side of the house, hidden from view, Lean Wolf spied two silhouettes at the window. Familiar with those shapes, he squatted down again, curious to learn more about them. On the edge of the garden, he peered through the tangles of an arbor.

The young men spoke softly. Obviously the children in the room behind must be dozing. Lean Wolf couldn't make out the couple's words, but their actions could not speak more volubly.

The tall, spare figure of Lightly bent toward his companion. Lightly's forehead bumped gently on Rowan's. And, suddenly, their mouths pressed together as if lapping up honey, and their two bodies followed, entwining. With golden light behind them and green vines framing the casement, no lovers could appear more idyllic.

Satisfied as one whose suspicions are confirmed, Lean Wolf whistled to himself. No need to waste further time. His quiver of knowledge was full, with as pointed a weapon as he could wish.

He held nothing at all against Rowan or Lightly. Now he was assured they'd hold nothing, at all, against him.

Smirking in the twilight, Lean Wolf felt for the knife at his knee. Then he loped away, to hunt down his quarry.

Something From Nothing

Enfolding his wife in his arms, Cecco felt as vulnerable as the driftwood fragments erected by his men for shooting practice. Each gun as it fired brought a burst of sound and a stab of flame that streaked through the night. The sea-weakened wood stood exposed, and the ball burrowed deep to the heart of the target. Just so, Cecco felt, his exposure to Jill could be fatal.

She sensed his disquiet as they danced together, and she pulled back to gaze in his eyes. "Giovanni, I am trying to help. Have I done harm instead?"

"Where there is no help, there is no harm, either. I am simply amazed to find myself holding you."

The fiddler's bow teased out a tune with a circular strain, plaintive, its pitch rising in progression and growing in intensity. Strolling the beach as they played, the musicians, like the rest of the sailors, kindly affected to pay no attention to the captain and the lady. Undeceived, the couple drew together again, keeping their expressions casual however much their bodies delighted in one another's proximity. Their time together, like the tune, grew tenser.

Prickling with electricity, Cecco held Jill's crimson hand in his as he led her through the steps. This point of contact meant all the more to him because, having sworn loyalty to Hook, he had vowed not to touch Jill before she herself reached that red hand toward him. Now, with her coveted hand nestled in his and his arm round her waist, he pressed as close as he dared, reliving their golden moments, and

254

capturing the scent of her perfume. The fragrance charged his feeling of familiarity, reviving those many nights when her passion fused with his. Through her touch, he confirmed that, given a chance, that ardor would re-ignite. As always, his mind churned to find opportunity.

Another pistol cracked, and Cecco glimpsed the silhouette of the commodore, his hook and his hair black against the bonfire, his head bending low as he listened to Lily. The two seemed engrossed, at least until Smee appeared, his red hair like flame in the firelight. He nodded to the commodore, and with a grin shining broad on his face, he was quick to sweep Lily away. Hook stood taller then, and, still just a shadow cast by fire, he turned from Lily's retreat to face Jill's direction. Silently cursing Smee, Cecco led Jill farther from mindful eyes.

When the melody ascended to its end, he did not feel compelled to release her. He acted upon privilege. "Lovely one," he said, his brown eyes growing soft. "I await your pleasure. For a dance, or for ever."

He smiled, he bowed, and, turning her scarlet palm upward, he brushed it softly with his lips. He lingered over her hand, looking up at her. "*Bellezza*. Shall I read your fortune?" This seduction was the one he had employed when he revealed his desire for her, under the eyes of the men who watched now. He'd been a common sailor then. He was her husband now. Everything was changed, and yet the same.

Jill remembered every moment. "No need. You assured me last time that I am adored. What fortune could be better?" Discreetly, she withdrew her hand, reading the disappointment on his face.

Yet she was not immune to the joy he promised. Her pulse beat a cadence not entirely caused by dancing, and even the ring of his bracelets set her tingling. But one of the first tactics she'd acquired aboard ship was the appearance of composure. She raised her left hand, the one where Cecco's wedding band glimmered, and in the gesture he'd often made for her, bunched her fingertips at her lips to send a kiss winging. "Thank you, Giovanni. I will not forget." On the pretext of smoothing her hair in its twist, she stepped back, tucking in tendrils that strayed from the pins. "And now I must play the hostess. Come, join us. I've contrived a way to dance with all of our men."

Had she offered her right hand, he'd have seized it. But now he simply glanced at her left, extended toward him, and asked, "What, all our men at once?"

"As the only girl among a troupe of boys, once upon a time, I learned to maneuver in similar circumstances. I assure you that Wendy's grown-up counterpart is equal to the task. Watch and see."

Cecco watched her, as bidden. He noted that, as always, Mr. Smee hovered near to fulfill her needs. With a brooding look, Cecco backed from the crowd.

When Hook, too, held aloof, Cecco's sensibilities eased a trifle. And when the commodore motioned for the captain to join him before the pavilion, Cecco let go his grudge, and accepted a glass. Few words passed between them, but those words were amicable, and Cecco remembered that the purpose of this feast was to honor his crew and himself. For the company's sake, as he talked with Hook, Cecco tried to ignore the insidious Irishman.

Their conversation concerned Cecco's chore while in port, the refitting of the *Red Lady*. Although her new name had been painted over '*L'Ormonde*' while at sea, the calm of Neverbay allowed for more artistic treatment. Cecco and his men were completing her transformation from privateer to pirate, raking her masts to a more efficient angle, and redistributing her ballast to ensure her best point of sail. Cecco was keen to keep his ship as fleet as the *Roger*.

Presently Hook inquired, "How are you faring with your Frenchmen, Captain? You appear to understand one another."

"Aye, Commodore, well enough. *Monsieur* Guillaume translates for the men, and he is teaching them English. We, in turn, pick up French from them."

"Years ago you yourself felt it necessary to learn English. You've a talent for languages, I find."

Surprised at this compliment, Cecco answered without thinking, "*Sì.*" He and Hook looked at one another, then chuckled. Ever so slightly, the atmosphere lightened.

"If I may make so bold," Hook queried, "your principal language was Italian when first we took ship together. What lingo did you speak as a child? The Romani, I presume?"

"Romani, certainly, but as my tribe roam through Italy and seek their fortune among those people, we all speak fluently in their tongue. It is the language of my homeland, and the one I spoke when forced abroad."

"I see," Hook replied, and he sat back in thoughtful silence, tapping his hook on the base of his goblet.

When at Jill's command the revelers had been pushed and pulled into place by Mr. Smee, they formed two lines on the sand. The concertina gushed forth, and together the lady and the bo'sun led a reel that gave every man a chance to join hands with the few females present. Cecco noted, as a gnawing gall worked at his belly, the heedlessness with which Jill offered Mr. Smee her right hand. The blood-red hand, that he himself had held just the once in these many weeks.

Even the musicians took turns forming the archway of arms. The couples paired off to plunge between the lines, skipping and stumbling, to resume their places in the arch at the end. This bridge of humanity migrated, by jolly stages, toward the bay, so that, at last, the dance ended with damp feet and laughter in the moonlit brine, and with all the four ladies left breathless.

A few merrymakers remained in the waves to assail one another with drenching. Most of the party reformed by the fire. Smee kept his eye on the hourglass, and soon the bo'sun's pipe howled. Those watchers called to duty readied their weapons and headed toward their posts, looking with reluctance over their shoulders. They faded into the darkness, to the strategic sites where the beach met the woods. For the safety of all, the next hour promised no merriment for the sentinels.

As Smee turned the glass to measure out the new watch, two of the lookouts hurried to the rocky end of the shore, opposite the fire. They selected a boat from the waiting craft, and hove it to the water. Once clear of the sand, they jumped aboard. The swimmers heard their oarlocks as they passed, chunking in rhythm along with the low, slow gurgle of the seawater they stirred. Before long, the boat could be glimpsed again in the moon's luminance, returning to the beach. It disgorged two new men, fresh from *Red Lady* and ready to rejoin the fun, which now centered on the victuals.

Yulunga hailed them. "Any problems?" he asked.

They shook their heads, and Flambard reported in uncertain English, "Pierre-Jean, he is dolorous, but not to be trouble."

Yulunga smiled his vast, knowing smile. The mate of Mrs. Hanover's earring flashed against his brown skin. "That's right. Pierre-Jean's trouble is banished to the Clearing."

"*Pardon,* Sir, but how do you know she will remain there?"

"I warned her that there are bats aplenty, and flesh-eating beasts in the woods. But now that I think on it, maybe I should have warned the beasts instead."

They laughed, and Flambard hurried toward Red Fawn, who broke from the crowd and flew to his burly embrace. She teased him, "Your absence works to your advantage, *Monsieur.* I paid my respects to the others while you were on duty." He understood the message, if not the words. From the play of her dimples, it was plain that she now felt free to lavish her favor upon this dark, muscular Frenchman.

Lily and Lelaneh caught each other's gazes, and smiled. They weren't surprised by Red Fawn's fascination for Flambard, whose size and coloring reminded the women of her former favorite, Captain Cecco. Married now, the captain steadily refused the ladies' offerings, and the *Red Lady's* men were more than happy to compensate for their commander's restraint.

Red Fawn served Flambard a drink from the cask and a plate from the table, and before he was sated, she threw her shawl over his shoulders to draw him to her bosom. Twining their fingers together, the couple strolled to the woods where they spread the shawl on the forest floor and enjoyed the intimacy they sought— if not the privacy, for, though their giggles and gasping were drowned by the music and Lily and Lelaneh had long since turned back to the revels, the revelers' weren't the only inquisitive eyes.

As Jill rejoined the officers at the pavilion, she was followed by Chef and Jacquot, who set before them a tray laden with delicacies. Exhilarated from the activity, Jill consumed just enough to gratify Chef's appetite for praise. Once the fingerbowls had been offered and Chef, duly lauded, returned with a pompous promenade to his secret cache of wine, Hook dabbed his damp fingertips on a napkin and surveyed the surroundings. He observed, "You seem contented with the evening's events, Madam. Our men, too, appear satisfied."

"I'm enjoying the party quite as much as they. And I believe, Sir, that you are, too." While she had divided her attention among Hook, her husband, and their sailors, Jill felt the strain between the commodore and the captain waning. So concerned had she been about these two that Cecco's attitude toward Smee escaped her. She was elated by the success of the celebration. "Everyone is relishing Chef's efforts. And the games and the exercise, thus far, have kept drink from befuddling the majority."

"The night is young," Hook quipped.

"And so are my Frenchmen," Cecco riposted, grinning.

"Well, Captain, we shall indulge them. We have all earned a respite." Hook laid his hand upon Jill's, on the armrest of her new rocking chair. "Are you comfortable, my love, on your throne?"

Jill glanced at Cecco, but he bore Hook's endearment with grace. Relieved, she answered, "I am quite at home in my lovely new chair, thank you. As I told the twins, I feel a story taking shape." She knew it would come to her, given time. "The men tell me they're anticipating a tale, tonight."

"Shall you please Captain Cecco by relating his history?"

Jill smiled at her husband as he assumed a guarded expression. "I shall please the captain by keeping it quiet." She turned toward Hook again, "And I extend the same courtesy to you, Sir."

"While I fear nothing from truth," Hook replied, "I agree that the men might prefer a subject with whom they hold more in common."

Just then Lily and Lelaneh exclaimed, and Smee's rollicking laugh carried over the crowd. The tide had come in, lifting the surf, and Jill heard the waves rush the shore and then hiss in retreat. A gust tickled the hair at her forehead. It carried a whiff of smoke from the fire, sweetened with seaweed.

"Aye...a common man." Jill's expression grew vague. The music dulled in her ears. Hook watched her, perceiving that she'd left him for a reverie. Cecco, too, understood, and he leaned toward his wife, protective. Unaware of the source of her inspiration, he relaxed the vigilance he'd employed through the evening. 'A common man' might define any one of this band of buccaneers, and he looked forward to her narrative.

The four of Jill's sons who were present saw her musing, and drifted near to assume posts at her side. Gradually, at some unheard signal, the instruments tweedled to silence. One by one, the pirates felt the mantle of magic. It descended, like a fog, to mute the beach. The little stars ceased winking as if to listen. Turning toward the pavilion, the sailors left the fire to dwindle, and gathered in the sand at Jill's feet. Just like Wendy's boys, they had awaited this moment.

Red Lady's crewmen had not yet experienced a yarn spun by Red-Handed Jill, yet this sense of synchronicity seized them, too, and they gazed eagerly her way. Time had reached a tipping point. Even the little chef, surfeited by his feast, tasted the flavor of expectation.

The men observed her, and their hearts bounded. When inspiration came to Red-Handed Jill, her splendor assumed new dimension. The sailors viewed not only her face, but the intuition that illumined it. Her flesh appeared translucent; the scar that marked her white throat evoked a sense of sacrifice. Even the gems of her necklace donned an aura of offering. She glowed like an image on a high temple altar, though it was moonlight rather than candlelight, and Nature rather than a sculptor's hand, that cast each feature in perfection.

Her jewel-blue eyes looked to the sky. When she spoke, her every word dropped like a diamond.

"A young man holds fast on a vast, wild isle. His is a chill island, dank but noble, where the sea sends winds to stunt the trees, and breakers carve cliffs into hollows. Scattered on its surface, with stones and with hedgerows, communities cling like lichen. Inhospitable though it feels at times, its beauty is nowhere surpassed. Families both wealthy and wanting nestle down here. The rich hail from elsewhere; the lowly ones might come and go. For this fellow, though, born to dwell here, sure— no other island exists.

"Close to the ocean, a hill of emerald rises to mountain. On its heights silence falls, as mist and distance absorb the sea's roar.

The young man is hardy, and he has climbed with his brothers by sheep track up the slick slopes, past a prehistoric tomb, dodging streams screened in heather. He's been rewarded, on clearer days, with a prospect of the ocean as it stretches past the possible, away, and away. Many's the man who seeks to ship out for fortune. But home is home to this son of the Smaoigh clan, and new continents do not entice him.

"Yet, whether here or whether there, all people must eat. The soil of this country is old, and ancient moss yields peat. He works for his living on the bog, his shoes turning black with it. His hands are calloused, his neck and his back and his shoulders ache as he bends to cut and to toil with his spade. He and his workmates strip the turf and lay it down in rows for drying, leaving deep, dark ditches, like scars, in the green. These men slice the turf into bricks. Days later, they turn it to air again, then they foot it like tepees to dry, finally stacking the bricks in a three-sided shelter. The stuff is heavy and dense, like gold turned to dross.

"On shipping days the labor begins all over again, to load the peat onto carts. When that's done, he leads a donkey down the stone-strewn path. The animal chuffs, and the wooden wheels churn, groaning. A dock juts out over the sea, a high timber road— a bridge to nowhere until the vessel hauls up for lading. As the gulls scream and swirl, the sailboat's hull is as much at risk as the island's population, against wind, tide, and rock. The work is arduous, but the young man is proud to claim he earns his own bread, and some for his brothers to boot.

"On the day his fortunes change, he heads over the spongy bog toward his home. The gray sky, puddled with peat smoke, turns suddenly sunny. It shimmers into rainbow— not one, but three at a time. A good omen, he's thinking. But the shadows lengthen before he reaches the cottage. A skylark trills an evening song over the whitewashed walls. The bird perches, briefly, on the thatched roof between double chimneys. One fireplace warms each end of the house. It's made of two rooms, and the south half was once a cow-shed. The shed is partitioned off now to make a *shebeen*, where local men come to drink, the only living left by his father to support the widowed mother. The young man's strides grow quick as he approaches, eager to sup with his family, and keen to put his scheme into play. The creel over his shoulder clinks with bottles, and he slows his pace to preserve them intact. At the door, he hides his pack in a bush.

"His errand made him later than usual. When he lifts the latch to the kitchen, the two youngest lads lie abed in the loft, warmed by the chimney. His mam looks up from her darning to push a lock of bright auburn from her face. Alice could never be stout, but she's not boney either. The dress she wears was new years ago, her bibbed apron a recent creation, sewn from the flax grown here on her island and milled into linen in the village. When she smiles at him, her face radiates the humor for which she was loved as a lass. She spoons stew for him from a cauldron that sits on the embers. The fire, made of the turf he has harvested, smells sweetly of earth and of iron.

"Alice's sons necessitate much in the way of mending, and their mother is never far from her needlework. She delights to 'make something from nothing.' In truth, this homily of hers is the sum of her history. Taking up her darning again, she sits herself down by the table, and asks after his day.

" 'Does your back pain ye, lad? Will I bring ye more tea?'

" 'It hurt for a bit, but the hike home has cured me.' He shifts in his seat to ease the aching. 'Josie's right here, he'll be pouring me a drop.'

"Josie, with hair his own shade of ginger, is a year younger than his eldest brother. He bumps the table as he comes from the fire with the kettle.

" 'Mind yourself, Josie,' says his mam. 'Ye'll be needing spectacles, next. Was Mr. Cavanagh fit to work today, Con?'

" 'Old Corkscrew Cavanagh?' he says, grinning.

" 'Mind your manners, lad. The man's no older than your father would be, had he lived. 'Tis the work makes him crooked.' Alice bites her lip here, not wanting to think how short a time will pass before Con stoops just like his father had. 'Did Mr. Cavanagh last out the day?'

" 'Nay, the old man rode his donkey home, swatting the beast and swearing he'll never be back. I've got tuppence says he'll show up by dinner time.'

" 'Ye'll win your wager, that ye will. I never saw a lad so lucky.'

" 'Mam,' says Con, and he leans toward her over his mug. 'I've lucked onto a scheme that'll prosper us. Let me tend the bar, nights, and ask me no questions.'

"No questions she asks, not when the *shebeen* draws more drinkers, then more strangers, nor does she inquire weeks on, when Josie turns his currach ashore to leave off fishing, for to take his brother's place cutting turf on the bog. She knows little, and says less. But the stew pot fills more easily, and, crossing herself, she starts tucking silver away.

"She says nothing when Con haunts the crumbling Tower House at the Sound, where smugglers are known to glide by. She keeps silent when the constabulary canter down the lane in their low hats and sashes. The officers' vigilance confirms her suspicions. When she tidies the *shebeen*, mornings, she scrubs the counters clean, sweeps, and tends the fireplace, but she neglects the shelves under the bar, where false panels are fitted. No one mentions the *poitín*: Irish spirits distilled in the hills and bottled illicitly, and no revenue paid to the king.

"The widow and her sons prosper now, but take care that the neighbors don't notice. Though Alice no longer dreads the knock of the landlord, she feigns a reluctance to pay him. No goods are purchased that will raise any eyebrows; still, she sews shirts for her family, and a new Sunday frock for herself. A milking cow joins the sheep in the byre. The smaller boys lose their scrawny, gaunt looks, while the older lads take on more muscle. Con, standing straighter now, treats his brothers to days at the horse fair. Alice sings at her chores, and at Mass whispers prayers of thanksgiving. The next Easter, a new cloth appears on the altar from an anonymous benefactor, made of linen according to edict, but fringed with handsome tassel.

" 'Stitched by an angel!' exclaims the good Father, clasping his hands.

" 'But procured by a devil,' jests Con, in private.

"One summer night, as the waves rise to savage the shore, the widow lies on her cot, and the roar of the waters muddles her dreams. 'Tis the roar of a lion, with golden pelt and kingly mane, and the woman awakes in alarm. Easily enough, she reads the meaning of that dream. She pulls her shawl tighter, and sits up to think.

"She and Con have never discussed it, but all their countrymen know the risk that he takes. Arrest means conviction. Judgment means transportation. Few prisoners survive such a voyage, and the ones who fail to die of fever, filth, or seasickness arrive bound in chains on a continent of criminals.

"She binds her shawl about her nightdress. Scooping up a weighty tea towel from the bread box, she hides it at her bosom until, within a stand of rhododendron that blocks out the wind, she gains her vegetable patch. Money won't grow here, she knows, but neither will it be confiscated. If she could conceal her son here, she'd do it. But, whenever the revenuers find reason to return, she knows that only himself can shield Con.

"And that he does. He runs to ground as the need arises. The odd night finds him where the customs officers don't, under the roof of a turf shelter, or in the caves off the coast, or yet, covered with fleece, a specious sheep by the tomb on the mountain. And still he manages business, becoming more wily with time.

"A figure of mystery now, Con is chased by the girls. His new hiding places are warmer than those he'd found in the wilderness, because— unlike the king's men— the lasses are able to catch him.

"All this time, the widow works, stitching and sewing, and holding her family together. Con's luck is fine, but good fortune can't last forever. Alice puts up a parcel to keep for him, filled with essentials in case he must flee. She knows, though, that the most vital item is the one her son carries inside. No matter where he must roam, in the end, he'll always hold love from his mother.

"At last, the crisis arrives. Alice rises up and hurries to the door, where a breathless neighbor pounds. He's followed by the sound of hoofbeats. Torches burn, bobbing over the hill as a company of constabulary descend it. She wakes the boys and seizes the parcel. 'Josie, ready the currach, lad, and hurry!' Alice tears open the door to the bar.

"The buzz of the crowd falls silent. Con turns from the bar, and the smile dies on his face. Alice stands barefoot with the bag in her hand, her auburn hair as wild as her eyes. Just so, Con will always remember her.

"Hurriedly, he gathers the bottles from beneath the counter. Most he tosses to his mates, to conceal in their coats. In a mass, they push each other out the door. The last jugs he hurls to the field. Alice runs behind him, taking his big, rough hand in hers this one final time. Together they race over emerald grasses, the last Con will see of them—dark, damp, and fragrant.

"As they flee seaward, the sound of the surf drowns the officers' orders. Alice grabs the paddles from Josie and jumps aboard. 'Get back to your brothers, Jo. Say I'm sewing a shroud, like we planned, and let the revenuers search the place. Keep them there long as ye can!'

"Josie and Con shove the currach until the sea snatches it, and Con rolls over its side. Josie takes one quick look at Con, then he turns to speed homeward, swiping at his eyes to clear his vision. It's not spectacles he's wanting. It's his brother.

"The lights from the shore fade from sight, leaving starlight to guide them. Con hauls on the oars, watching his mother. He shrugs in apology. 'Mam…' he begins.

" 'No, Con. It's done now. Ye did all ye could.'

"He hears the waves rage in a hollow as the boat passes by it, bellowing as if a beast lives inside. He heaves the craft round to calmer water past the headland, and rows toward the Tower on the Sound. Seaweed lies limp on the sand.

" 'I'll be leaving ye here, son. Ye must pull away. Hunker down now, and wait in the water for your smuggling friends to fetch ye. Don't ye dare set your foot on this island.'

" 'Aye, Mam. I'll be minding.'

"She opens the parcel. 'I've provided ye all ye'll be needing. But here, Con.' She pulls out a woven-flax packet. It holds a thimble, a rainbow of thread, and a needle. A name is stitched on the bag, unknown but familiar, glistening in embroidery floss and worked by her hand.

" 'Remember, lad. With a needle and thread, ye can make yourself anything.' She leans forward to stare at her eldest son, hard. 'Ye can make *yourself*…into anything.'

"She stuffs the packet in the bag, then squeezes Con as fiercely as her strength allows. When she kisses him, she feels the damp on his cheek. Sea spray, and a sweeter kind of salt.

" 'Go with my blessing.' She smiles with the humor he loves in her. Yet next, she shakes her head, as stern as the day his father died. 'But, my dear…Don't ever come back here again.'

"She is gone.

"Then Con, for whom no other island exists, is forced by his fortune to loose his hold on this vast, wild isle. With a weight like lead in his stomach, he pulls at the oars, and watches his home shrink away.

"He must lose his name, too. Con of the Smaoigh clan will soon be transformed into legend. Like a ship cut free of her anchor, his habitat, now, lies afloat. His heart must turn sailor, to wander over other islands, and to voyage upon other oceans.

"Adrift from his homeland, Con smuggles one last commodity: his identity. He'll stitch his soul together; he'll shape a new life. He tailors himself to fit the name his mam fashioned. He is an exile, and he re-makes himself. And now, he's become Conor Smee.

"Over Smee's shoulder, the prospect of the ocean stretches past the possible, away, and away…to an *im*possible place. Another island— host to comradeship, love, and duty— the spot he now knows, as the Neverland."

Jill sat back, her eyes wet with tears. Moved by her story, the men remained hushed. When she felt able to look up, another pair of eyes met her own. Behind spectacles, they, too, shone with moisture.

Smee smiled in sorrow, but said, simply, "Thank you, Ma'am."

Jill reached out to him. With both of her hands.

And then, in the midst of serenity, Cecco's wrath erupted.

A Touch of Irony

Before Smee reached Jill's outstretched hands, Cecco leapt up and seized him by the collar. He yanked the man's face close to his.

"Do not dare touch my wife!"

As big as the bo'sun was, he was too surprised to struggle. He managed to grab Cecco's wrists, resisting, but his efforts to break free proved useless. His new shirt ripped with a screech.

Cecco seethed through his teeth, "I did not stop you before. I stop you now. Not one more finger upon my lady."

The emotions Jill's story had roused in Smee sapped his habit of caution. Feeling the burn of truth in Cecco's indictment, he threw discretion overboard. "Do you fear a third wedding, then? You think she'll be marrying me, too?"

"You disrespectful dog!" Cecco shook Smee, rattling the Irishman's teeth. He jutted his knee into Smee's gut. The bo'sun buckled forward, wheezing, and in a mighty heave, Cecco struck Smee full on the jaw.

The crack of the blow resounded on the beach. The sailors scrambled, the men bellowing while the women shrieked. Noodler was the nearest sentry; at the sound of the ruckus he caught up a torch, abandoning his post by the boats. He came running toward the trouble.

Smee jolted sideways from the force of Cecco's clout. The crowd backed from the battle and Smee landed, dazed, on the sand. Cecco stamped toward him and towered there, his boots astride the bo'sun, his great hands ready to drag the man up, to strike again.

Smee gasped for air, clapping his palm to his jaw. His skull nearly split with the pain. But, as Jill's tale portrayed him, Smee was hardy. He ignored his aching gut. He whipped off his spectacles and tossed them to a sailor, bracing himself to stand.

Cecco kicked Smee's legs out from under him. Smee fell again, spraying sand all directions. He snatched a handful, and dashed it at Cecco's eyes.

Cecco ducked to the side. With a move as instinctive as breathing, he reached for the knife at his belt. As he seized the hilt, he gripped something soft instead. Jill had rushed to his side and closed her hold on his dagger, preventing him from pulling it. She caught up to face him. Pressing his cheek, her stained hand, at last, ministered to her spouse.

"Captain!" she commanded, "You must stop now."

He stared at her, and the torches reflected over the darkness of his eyes. "You are too late, Lady. Your man Smee is dead."

"Giovanni, no." For the moment, the knife remained in his belt, but Jill couldn't fight his grip. She gave up the dagger and threw herself into his arms. As she clutched his shoulders, the vibrancy of his rage coursed into her. "You must listen—"

"I listen. I hear every word you say about him…this man my wife knows— so *intimately.*"

Smee spat blood on the beach. He warned from the ground, "Ma'am, you'd best be shoving off." He was rubbing sand between his hands, to dry his grip. In a practiced motion, he rolled to his feet and crouched, with dagger drawn. "The captain struck me first. Officer or no, I'll be butchering him, with a sharp knife and a clear conscience." Only Jill's presence between the men held back the bloodshed.

Jill had witnessed Cecco's fury before. She knew the degree of his ruthlessness. She was gratified when he applied it, acting as her champion against Doctor Hanover, and she had watched, in cold satisfaction, as he carved her name in letters of blood on Hanover's back. Embracing her own barbarity, Jill chose to live as a pirate, and, still this moment, she thrilled in Cecco's savagery. Even as Wendy, the males who enticed her were adventurers and rogues. She prized Smee as one of them, and she'd realized, of course, that Smee too could be brutal.

But Jill had never seen Smee so alarming. His shirt, like his beard, was streaked with blood; his shoulders— formed early by cutting the turf appeared broad and bellicose. His mouth formed the grim line it held when he'd whipped Cecco raw, and the knife in his hand rode there easily. With his finery in shambles and his spectacles cast aside, Jill understood the ferocity that kept the *Roger's* ruffians in line.

An odor of rotting fish swept up with the breeze from the shore. Within the party of pirates, all eyes aimed at the combatants. Yulunga had moved like a panther to guard Cecco's back— that back scarred so deeply by Smee. Subtly, the other men chose sides, and in the wake of the conflict, the two companies drifted apart. In French and in English, voices raised in support of their shipmates. The battle that threatened wasn't only over the woman. It was the *Red Lady* differentiating from the *Roger*, their new unity decaying, like creatures washed up with the tide.

But the sky flashed in a streak of orange, and a throaty blast rent the air. United in surprise, everyone whipped round to face it.

Hook stood before the gaily striped pavilion, his pistol smoking in the torchlight, his face a mask of displeasure. He tossed his pistol aside and pulled a second from his belt.

"The story is ended."

To Smee he said, "You are banned from this beach. I will deal with you later." To the sentry, he said, "Since you neglect your post, Mr. Noodler, *Monsieur* Flambard will relieve you. Take Smee away." Then his gaze shifted to Cecco.

"The knife: to Red-Handed Jill."

The shock of the shot rang in Cecco's head. He looked down at the blade in his grip, much too close to his beloved. He lowered it, and he gazed into her eyes, admiring. "Jill," he murmured, "so brave."

He'd seen no fear of himself in her gaze, only concern. He now offered her the weapon. With the bo'sun out of his way, he watched, mesmerized, as her blood-red hand closed upon it, and she tucked it in her sash. Once again, he beheld the scar at her throat, the symbol of her courage. He ached, with a terrible longing, to press his lips to it, no matter who was attending, no matter what the consequences. It was the return of circumspection, not a lack of valor, that checked him.

When Hook was at his most dangerous, his manner turned deadly with courtesy. His voice dripped like liquid gold. "If the happy couple would grant me the honor of their presence? In my pavilion."

The tang of gunpowder hung in the air. The woodland night noises, stopped short by the shot, left an eerie vacuum of sound. The lady, the captain, and the commodore entered the tent. With one stroke of his claw, Hook slashed the tie, and the swag fell closed to conceal them.

The Men of the Clearing escorted their women past the bonfire toward the end of the beach, to help Noodler to tend Mr. Smee. Assuming Smee's office as bo'suns, Nibs and Tom checked their weapons and placed themselves outside the pavilion, at a discreet distance. Yulunga waved his arms and urged, *"Allez!"* while Guillaume called, "Clear away, hearties. This way." They shooed the sailors toward the fire, to reintegrate the two ships' companies and to secure some privacy for the commodore.

The men mustered by the casks, their eyes wide with wonder, their throats dry from excitement. Before long, the piles of driftwood diminished and the fire grew hot, while the gossip began again, fueled by the evening's events.

Red-Handed Jill had given them plenty to talk about. In the short time since its telling, the Story of Smaoigh had grown deeper.

Inside the tent, time grew shorter. The bonfire threw light against the pavilion, and its colors bled through the fabric to mottle the inhabitants. In a state of naïveté, the furnishings waited to provide them with pleasure. The plush of Persian rugs masked the sand. Netting on the camp bed draped open to offer its comforts. At the bedside stood a little crystal vial, its golden dust muted in the twilight of the tent.

Hook shoved his pistol in his belt, where a mother-of-pearl inlay glowed on the handle. He nodded to Jill, and she laid Cecco's dagger on the table, then lit the lantern beside it. As its yellow beam changed the atmosphere of fantasy to actuality, she turned to encounter the men— the two very real men— she loved.

"I'll not waste time." Hook eyed Captain Cecco. "This conduct reeks of mutiny."

The breath caught in Jill's throat. "Commodore," was all she could manage.

"The captain struck my first officer. A direct affront to me."

Cecco did not flinch. "I do not deny it."

"No— Sir," Jill kept her voice level. "Captain Cecco misunderstands the situation."

"Madam. No one misunderstands. The facts are clear to every man in my company. Bound by oath, Captain Cecco cannot challenge me; he fights my mate in my stead."

"Giovanni, I swear to you. I saw how you were provoked. But until this evening, Mr. Smee has acted respectfully."

Cecco crossed his arms over his chest. "With the exception of the commodore, I deal death to any man who thinks to touch you. As I warned you from the beginning."

"But *this* man—"

"Will not be threatened again," Hook finished. "*Signora*, I command you and Captain Cecco to come to terms. For the good of the company, no further incident shall occur." He raised his voice to call, "Mr. Nibs."

A moment later, the door flap opened and, with a taut face, Nibs stooped to poke in his head. "Aye, Commodore."

"You will escort Red-Handed Jill and Captain Cecco to the boats. You and Flambard are to stand guard as they hold parley there."

"Aye, aye, Sir."

Relief eased Jill's dread. Hook had every cause to execute the penalty for mutiny, yet he granted one last chance to redeem her husband— if only she could manage the task.

With a flick of his claw, the commodore waved Nibs away. "Fetch me the hourglass."

Nibs plucked the timepiece from its post outside the pavilion. During the uproar, it had run out its hour, and the sand lay slack at the bottom. Hook grasped the brass casing. He held it poised over the table, next to the lantern. His ruby ring glowed.

"Madam. Consider all ramifications. Then decide."

Jill met his eye.

"Remain with me as my consort, or go with Captain Cecco, as his wife."

"Sir, I made that choice before we married."

But Hook stood adamant.

"Captain Cecco deserves complete candor." He turned the glass, and banged it down on the table, beside Cecco's knife. "You have one hour."

The sand began its tumbling descent. Jill turned toward Cecco. A light of hope now burned in the depth of his eyes. With a jangle of his headdress, he inclined his head to Hook, then shouldered his way through the door. After a glance at the commodore, Nibs followed him.

The night had grown chill with Jill's apprehension. Shivering, she perceived that, in the conflict, some part of Hook's mind had closed to her. She snatched up her wrap and tossed it over her shoulders. Uncertain but expectant, she drew herself upright, to stand in state before her pirate king. She bore his blood on her skin; she was Red-Handed Jill. Surely, she believed, he intuited her intention?

Still stern, he opened his arms, and, mirroring her sense of ceremony, he beckoned her to his embrace. As his hold tightened round her, he granted her the security of his strength. Although his demeanor remained even, his corporeal being, like her own and like Cecco's, pulsed at a rapid rate. Tracing the hidden straps of his harness, she smelled the dry, familiar scent of leather. She ran her fingers over his shoulders, then over his chest. His body responded to hers, and with his hook he lifted a loose curl of her hair, exposing her neck to the night.

Her love for him swelled in her breast as she admired his features, and, even more, his mastery of the circumstances. His comportment was impeccable. Yet, oddly, instead of reassuring her, his self-possession left her troubled. Despite their proximity, Jill felt Hook's presence as if one step removed.

Hook studied her, too, while his claw held her hair from her face. His eyes were astute, conning her visage the way she'd seen him at the helm, studying the sea. But soon he bent his head to touch his lips to her neck. He brushed along the curve, his beard prickling her flesh, then roving along her jaw. When he arrived at her mouth he covered it, seeking for her kiss. No self-possession impeded him here. His embrace was heated and deep, a physical rite that embodied the totality of their time together.

His reserve was banished; she wove her arms about him, and once again her soul filled with him. She kissed him as she always kissed him: eagerly as the very first time. Passionately, like the last.

But she remembered the sand in the glass, sifting Cecco's time away. She whispered, "*Adieu,* my love."

He smiled, half-way. In his velvety voice, furred with irony, he answered her.

"*Ciao, amore mia.*"

Blinking in surprise, she drew back to stare at him. She'd heard her lover's own words, couched in her husband's language. But in the next moment she smiled, absorbing through their own channel of communication the spirit of humor, pride, and promise that prompted this form of farewell.

As she tried to slip from him, his hold tightened, and he kept her for one second longer, perhaps ten grains of time. When he raised his arms to release her, he freed her completely, his hand and his hook open, as if the hourglass had turned back to an earlier era, to an age before ever he'd touched her. Before he'd turned real for her: only a story.

With the sense of unreality returning, she felt that, after all, James Hook contained strata so deep that, on certain levels, he might yet be a stranger. She remembered his warning: *do not take our union for granted.* She stole from his tent, almost relieved to depart.

Surrounded by luxury in his hermitage, Hook turned down the lantern, so that the striped light of the pavilion scored his face. As the twitch at his lip signified, he was stirred by the passion of her parting. Always, physical intimacy with his woman overcame any hindrance. Wishing Jill's verdict to be hers and hers alone, he had veiled himself, but now he re-attuned to her essence. Rich in Jill's love, he could afford to be generous.

But, Hook sensed, beyond doubt, the same could be said of Giovanni Cecco.

He sat down— alone again— to observe the granules of sand as they competed to squeeze through their passage of glass.

From the lowest level of his being, James Hook discerned what the ignorant sands did not. There was no need to compete; all contenders would arrive at the destinations designed for them. As decreed, by the Storyteller herself.

Golden Trophies

In Tom Tootle's hands this time, the bo'sun's pipe twittered and shrilled, and the new set of sentries hustled to their posts. Flambard remained where Hook had assigned him, close to the boats at the western end of the beach. He stood watch in his new blue jacket, gazing outward toward the woods or toward the water. Tactfully, he kept his back turned as Captain Cecco paced.

The captain's chest brimmed with joy at the prospect of even one hour in company with his wife. He felt that, at this more private spot, he could open his heart to her. The woods encroached upon the sea, with rocks and boulders cluttering the sand between them. The pirates' boats lined the shore, most turned like turtles with their hulls to the sky. One remained upright, a skiff with oars shipped inside. A pair of *Red Lady*'s sailors could be seen rowing out to relieve their mates aboard, with orders from Cecco for the returning men to beach their craft closer to the fire. Cecco's dim hope was brightening, and he'd ensured that his parley with Red-Handed Jill would not be disturbed.

The revels on the other end of the beach remained subdued since the unpleasantness. Where Cecco walked, the woods sighed behind him. The moon's arching road had led it farther west over the high, forested hill, and its light had grown distant, and cold. As Jill approached, Cecco's heart beat faster. Her garments appeared ghostly in the ebbing moonlight. Nibs, carrying cushions, had linked her arm in his. When they arrived, Nibs placed the pillows on a large, flat stone. He saluted Cecco. "Your knife, Sir," he said, and he presented Cecco with his confiscated weapon. Tightening the orange kerchief about his forehead, Nibs backed off toward the woods, out of earshot, to stand guard as ordered.

Cecco wasted not one speck of time. Quickly, he restored his knife to his belt, then he stood before Jill, his hand open. In his Mediterranean accent, so familiar to her, he said, "I welcome you, my Jill. My wife."

Jill's manner was reserved, but she replied, "Under the circumstances, Captain, I won't deny you this much." She placed her crimson hand in his.

He closed his fingers upon hers, and pulled her close. He pressed his lips to her fingertips. "*Bellezza*, how often, how ardently, I have longed for you." He kissed her palm next, then the tender inside of her wrist, then his caresses wandered. Up the path of her arm he roamed, her shoulder, along her throat, and, finally, across her cheek.

Her senses reawakened to him, and her resistance dwindled. By the time he reached her lips, she was eager to accommodate him, seduced, once again, by the force of his passion. An ache gnawed her heart, and she felt a visceral quickening at her center. She had not forgotten this man's effect upon her; she *had* forgotten to prepare for it. Her body remembered how she enjoyed his embrace. And she indulged in him now, sliding her hands into his hair to pull him nearer, returning his kiss without shame. After all, she thought, once this hour was over, he would not hold her again. He would hold only this memory.

But they each bore in mind that time was short, and the situation called for decorum. Gratified by her response, Cecco relented, then led her to the cushions on the boulder. Here they sat down, side by side. The sea lapped lazily some yards before them, kissing the beach and caressing the rocks, then sliding back to its bed. Jill rested her bare feet in the soft, cool sand. As she moved, the diamonds at her throat made sparks of the starlight. Cecco still clasped her hand, now that she had tendered it. Like Hook, he took nothing for granted. She might never offer so much again.

Jill drew one measured breath, then, in her clear voice, she opened the parley. "The commodore warned me, even before this trouble
arose: I hold your life in my hand."

"This has always been true."

"I do not take your well-being lightly. For the sake of your
survival, I insist that we honor our initial accord. We vowed to be
one, but only until Hook's return."

"Lady, we know what Commodore Hook wishes. As for me,
from the first moment I saw you, I looked to husband you; my
wish was granted." Cecco was guided by Lily's counsel. "Now I
ask, what wish lies deepest within *your* heart?"

"As before, I desire harmony among the three of us." She shook
her head. "But now we have only this hour to achieve it."

"I seem to have driven your hope away. I myself had hope
enough, once, to ask the commodore if we three could reach some
kind of peace."

"What was his answer?"

"He does not feel it necessary to divide his soul with me. He is too
proud to compromise."

"You are more alike than either of you cares to admit. I came to
terms with *that* notion long ago."

Jill heard Nibs cough behind her. When she glanced his way
through the darkness, she made out his shape among the shadows.
He was watching the woods, his hand resting on his dagger.

Cecco said, "Perhaps your hope will be restored, when I say that
I apologize to you, for my outburst tonight."

"Thank you, Captain. Mistakes are powerful allies, our best
tutors. The commodore knows it, and that is why he granted this
parley." Her solemn look emphasized her advice. "Giovanni, you
must erase this mark of mutiny— it is an egregious offense, in
Hook's eyes, and in our men's opinions, too."

"This first point is agreed. If you wish it, I shall offer my regrets
to the commodore."

"Do let it be so."

"And, under certain conditions, I will make amends to your
Smee."

Jill's anxiety relaxed a little. "By all means. What conditions do you suggest?"

"You swore that Smee respects you. But it is obvious to every-one— even to Lily— that he feels a much stronger emotion for you. He, too, adores you."

"I swear it again: I do not allow him the commodore's prerog-atives."

Cecco nodded once, emphatically, and his medallions chimed. "And so, the second point is agreed."

"I am relieved," Jill said. "Yet Mr. Smee will retain all three of his offices, including that of steward of the commodore's cabin. My own stipulation is that you accept that fact."

"He will be your steward only if you remain aboard the flag-ship. *Bellezza*, be my wife in more than name." He smiled, warmly. "I propose to *you*, this time, and beg that you come to live with me, upon our *Red Lady*."

"My dear, even before we discuss my feelings about your pro-posal, I decline, on the grounds of the consequences. Hook com-manded me to consider all ramifications. The first is that if I joined you aboard the *Red Lady*, would not the commodore lose face?"

"On the contrary, the men will respect his magnanimity. It will add to his legend."

"And add to his losses. As you said, I *am* his soul. You know how monstrous a man he became when alone. And this difficulty leads to the next. Not one of our crewmen will support a move that returns Commodore Hook to that vicious state of solitude."

"You underestimate your power. You have changed him."

"My presence changes him, Giovanni. My absence might cause disaster."

A night creature interrupted, its claws scraping as it scrambled up a tree. Some leaves shook, then the animal chirred to its nest mates. Jill took advantage of the interlude to ground her emotions, inhaling the Island's scents, the smells she so cherished. Pine needles, the mulch of the forest floor, the musty aroma of bark, all mixed with the scent of the sea. Strains of the sailors' music reached her, but faintly. She wondered how much sand remained in the hourglass, and, noting the hope on Cecco's face, she resumed her reasoning.

"But let us look farther. Were I so close but so absent from him, Hook might no longer wish the *Red Lady* to keep company with the *Roger*. Separate and unescorted, both vessels would lose their protection, and their mutual advantage against enemies."

"Aye." Cecco angled his head, considering. "Yet our ships are swift, our sailors competent, and both companies are used to sailing independently."

"But," Jill said, "consider a worse contingency. If, soon or late, Hook takes active offense at my desertion, what then? If he should disband the fleet with animosity, how many men would remain to us?"

Cecco looked grave. "I have not thought that my men might be forced to choose between two captains."

"The situation could turn more ruinous still. The *Red Lady* will become the *Roger*'s prey. We might be taken. I'd be restored to Hook; you would be destroyed."

"I fear no man. And Hook takes no woman by force." One look at Jill, though, banished any thought of coercion. "Of course. This event can hold no dread for you."

"Only for your sake, my dear."

"But, my Jill, it is *your* safety that is my concern. Let us look to that matter now."

"My safety? Surely you don't believe that Hook might cause me harm?"

"Lovely one," comforting, he brushed her temple with his knuckles. "I do not fault you for evading the subject. We all know what menace is looming. I will never cease striving to guard you… from Doctor Hanover."

The sea air blew in Jill's face, biting, like the fear that Cecco's words uncaged. She drew her scarf tighter against it. She heard Flambard wheezing, and her imagination magnified the sound to something sinister. She and Cecco turned toward the lookout. Although his silhouette was all they perceived in the dimness, they saw that he'd simply knelt down. Nibs now hunkered near him.

Cecco wrapped his arms around Jill's shoulders, for warmth, and for protection. He explained, "Hanover believes you to be sailing aboard the *Roger*, as Hook's consort. No doubt he thinks me dead. But, we will outfox him. When the time for our rendezvous comes, I will sail away with you. Far away. Even Hook must approve of this plan."

Jill regained her composure, and assumed a resolute expression. "I will confront that danger when it arises. We are talking of our marriage, not of strategy against a foe."

"Do not fool yourself; Hanover will hold to *his* marriage. But I have learned of a further protection."

Puzzled, Jill listened.

"The boy. David. He is more valuable than you may suppose."

With a derisive huff, she countered, "A boy cannot protect me against a man. I learned that lesson long ago."

"We have not time to discuss David now. But you may trust in my claim about him. Come to me, live with me, and I will do all in my power to ensure that you remain there, safe within my arms." With a melodious ring of his bracelets, he placed his fingers under her chin to kiss her, gently. *"Amore."*

She accepted his kiss, drawing in his tenderness, then she pulled back.

"As I told you," she said, "we had first to discuss the practical side of the situation. We have done so, and I maintain that a change in our original accord is too hazardous. But I feel it necessary, now, that we consider our hearts."

Cecco read the affection in her eyes, still lingering after his kiss, and he seized his moment. "You know, lovely one, how much more I offer than strategy. I bring you love. Love to last all your lifetime. I bring pure devotion, with no complications. I am a whole man— whole, that is, when you are by my side. I have nothing to prove to the world, no debt to pay, no vengeance to collect. I have no legend to uphold. I am strong, I am ardent and amiable, and I am yours without reservation." Again, he took her hand in his. "My family is lost to me; your people live far over the sea. The sons you raised are grown. And yet, together we may begin anew. Do you not wish for children, my Jill, for babies? You told me of your delight as a girl, fashioning a cradle to hang in the old hideout here on the Island. You spoke of how you doted upon the little ones. Your sons are going their own ways, now. A daughter, perhaps, might come to us, as beautiful as yourself, to listen to your stories, and grow to womanhood under our guidance. This, *Bellezza*, is the fondest dream of my heart. I suspect that you dream of it, too."

She smiled. "I've certainly brought up my share of boys."

"I would welcome a boy-child, equally, if Fate should deliver him to us. I should welcome any number of boys or of girls. But, lovely one, if you remain on the *Roger*...your arms will hold neither."

"Captain," she said, kindly. "This longing is another reason to release you. I lived my time backwards, raising my family when I was a girl. Now I am a woman, and free to indulge in the life I have chosen. A pirate's life."

"Yet, even as a pirate, as my wife you will be protected while here on your Island. Even the commodore admits as much. The tribe's warriors will no longer hunt you, once it is known that you are not their enemy's mate. We can build a home here, in the land that you love. We will stay as long as you like, as often as you like, and live under truce in the Clearing, without hostility from the natives."

Cecco had described a tempting idyll, and Jill would cherish this dream. But he had also introduced a crucial point. "The natives. Yes, we must speak of them." Jill paused first, to collect the right words. "Giovanni, I request candor. Tell me of your Indian woman. I won't ask if she loves you; she cannot help doing so. But, perhaps, you have come to love her?"

Cecco frowned. "Whatever you have been told of Raven and me, you cannot presume to be true." He remained quiet for a moment, as he thought of the lonely woman. "She has given me comfort— and only comfort— in my grief."

At Cecco's avowal of fidelity, Jill looked away to hide her reaction. She herself wasn't certain whether she felt satisfaction for her own sake, or regret for Cecco's.

He said, "Raven, also, suffers the loss of a loved one. The Island boy killed her husband, some time ago."

Jill's eyes widened, and she pressed her hand to her heart. Suddenly, she envisioned a silver knife, bright beneath a man's red blood. In her memory, she hovered with her young sons above the trees, and the boy was boasting of a trophy. The horror that had gripped her that day clutched at her again. "I know," she murmured. "I was there." Her hand clenched, as if still surrounding the remembered arrow.

Cecco's eyebrows rose. "You were a witness?"

"Worse. I am guilty, too."

"You were only a girl then."

"The brave showed his arrow, and Pan dove for him. As the Storyteller, I made Pan what he was. I carry the responsibility of this woman's— this Raven's widowhood."

"But you retold the boy's story. You made him more wary of the natives, and less of a threat to them."

"I acted too late for Raven. Because of me, Pan robbed her of her lover and provider. Her whole life is altered." She laid her hand on Cecco's arm. "Giovanni, I understand now. Our stories have intertwined." Gazing earnestly into his eyes, she declared, "You must care for this woman. It is fitting that I should give you up, to her."

Cecco looked down where Jill touched him, and beheld his wedding band on her finger, glimmering in the starlight. He placed his own next to it, his strong, warm hand upon hers, their rings resting together.

"*Amore*, I pledged my life to you."

"And when Hook returned to me, I set you free."

"Why, then, do you still bear my ring?"

Jill's lips opened, but she had no ready answer.

He nodded, and smiled, his even teeth white against the night's dusk. "You wear it because you honor our marriage."

She cast her gaze down.

"I am your husband. You will not let me go. Nor will I surrender you."

"You asked for my deepest wish. It is for accord between us. Between you, me, and Hook."

"This ring on this hand, a hand that touches a lover, proves the fact. You could have put my wedding band away. But no. You love me still."

"I love gold. You know of my weakness."

"I have found, I think, that I, too, am your weakness."

Unwilling to confess it, Jill returned to their task, adopting a more businesslike tone.

"Captain, our time grows short. We have reached a degree of accord: you will offer your regrets to the commodore; you will make amends to Mr. Smee; and I guarantee Smee's proper conduct toward me. But my terms demand one more article: that you survive our union. And so, my answer is no. I will not take my place as your wife."

"Is this your heart speaking, or your sense of duty?"

"My desire is in accord with my duty. I remain loyal to Hook." Her grip tightened on his arm. "But I will not be selfish. You may still father a family." She said, formally, "I grant you your freedom to follow the new love that offers."

"I follow only one love."

"An unlucky love. Cannot you see? Tonight it led you to mutiny."

"Now you know how sincerely I want you."

"Another incident will be fatal. I forbid you to die for me."

Cecco only shook his head, and sighed.

As Hook commanded, Jill had examined the contingencies with Cecco, considered all ramifications. Yet her husband remained blind to his peril. To reason with him was useless. She must find another way to sway his resolve, or his constancy could kill him. Truth had always served her before; she had wielded it as her weapon and her shield. Perhaps, instead, like the hourglass, it was time to turn her honesty on end. Jill had never lied to Cecco. Surely he would believe any story she told him.

But, like all dissemblers, she must pay a price for dishonesty. She would be forced to forsake her wish for harmony. How greatly would she suffer for this sacrifice? What would be the consequences for Cecco, and for Hook? Her thoughts churned rapidly. She frowned, and she reached her conclusion: better discord than death.

The lie tasted like brass on her tongue. "Captain, I have done with you. Follow whomever you please."

"I follow she who wears my wedding band."

She shrugged. "I wear a keepsake, no more."

"You tell the world of our union."

"I show off my winnings."

"Both of us won, and the rings on our fingers encircle our hearts."

"It pleased my pride, all these months, to make you believe so."

He no longer smiled.

In the silence that fell between them, they heard Nibs scuff the sand. When they turned his way, his tall frame faced the woods again, and he was tightening his kerchief. Their gazes returned to one another's. Jill's heart spilled over with concern for her husband, while she worked her ploy to save him. In distorting the truth, she believed she'd found the way to protect him, from Hook, from her, and from himself.

"Giovanni." It was a drastic strategy, but effective. "In our intimacy, you challenged me to win your jewelry from you. I earned the right to wear your gold. This ring—" She waved her fingers before his face. "This is just another trinket." Hook's advice filled her head. *Yield to the man one last time...* "Or no, not just a trinket,"...*then slip your knife beneath his ribs.* She drew nearer. She began to smile again, a coy smile, engaging him. It was difficult. It was necessary.

His brown eyes clung to her, in his former, familiar way. Encouraged, he leaned closer. Close enough for the blow.

"I wear my trophy, for all the world to see." She tipped her head to an arrogant angle, and she smirked at him. She set her red hand, proprietorially, upon his jaw. "I won you. I keep you. And as I lie in my lover's bed, I still hold *you* in my hand."

"How do you dare—"

"It is *amusement* that keeps Hook from killing you."

Cecco stared as her words dug into him. Then he batted her hand from his face. He stood. He looked down on Jill. The love light vanished from his eyes, and he glared at her.

"If I did not know Red-Handed Jill to be truthful, I would name you a liar."

"It's the truth. You know my greed for prizes."

"The Storyteller weaves another tale!"

"You feed my vanity. If my tale keeps you alive, it also keeps me satisfied."

"Like your hands, your face now wears two colors."

Jill aimed her final strike, and pitched it perfectly. She sneered at her husband, and jeered, "Take Raven, Giovanni. A woman who *needs* you."

She saw his fists clench. Only once, ever, had he struck her; it was when he'd believed she had betrayed him. Betrayal was the gift she gave him now. She didn't flinch, but she had not forgotten this man's effect upon her— and, unlike the beginning of their parley, this time she prepared for the force of his passion.

But he did not strike. He stood up straight, a pillar of dignity. He turned on his heel, and marched toward the boats. He ignored his own craft, which lay overturned with its several oars beneath it. He chose the skiff that was ready to float, and shoved it into the sea. Within moments, his powerful arms were stroking a furrow toward his ship. Although he faced the Island, his eyes remained averted from Jill. She saw his armbands glinting in the light of the cold, stark moon.

His anger was audible in the clunk of the tholepins, and in the swift swirl of water. She had injured Cecco. She had wounded him, gravely. She felt the agony she caused him seeping, bleeding within her. It sapped the very lifeblood from her heart. Yet, as the hourglass emptied, Jill was assured of the one fact that mattered: the parley had succeeded. Her red hand lay open on her lap, empty, and her husband's life belonged only to him.

Cecco did what he'd never believed he would do. He strained at the oars, pulling with all his very substantial might, desirous to put distance between himself and his Jill. He loved her, and he loathed her.

Neverbay rocked peacefully tonight, in contrast to the storm within his breast. His motions sent him speeding toward the *Red*

Lady. With his thoughts in turmoil, he paid no attention to his surroundings. His mind was too full of her words. His heart was too full of betrayal.

Though he did not watch as Jill's form diminished in the moonlight— for once, did not *want* to watch her— he saw her as clearly as if she sat on the bench right in front of his face. Halfway to the ships, still she plagued him, and he squeezed his eyes shut, cursing her, and when he opened them again, his overburdened heart nearly stopped from shock.

He saw Jill herself rising from the stern, throwing off a wrap that had hidden her. Wraithlike, with her back to the sharp, sinking moon, the woman sat up to face him. A whiff of Jill's light, exotic perfume wafted his way.

"Madre de Dio!" he exclaimed. He dropped the oars and sketched his gypsy banishing sign, down from his forehead and across his chest, believing for this instant that the Jill he'd just deserted, a Jill he'd never known, a duplicitous Jill, had taken on a demon's powers, and materialized here, in his boat, to torment him.

And then he realized what had happened, and he wished with every sliver of his shattered heart that the demon were here with him, instead.

Mrs. Hanover knelt in the stern, gazing at him, her mouth open, her eyes wide with trepidation. It was clear to Cecco that the girl was just as stunned to see him as he was to find her. She wore a yellow tunic, patterned upon Jill's. Her hair was twisted into Jill's elegant knot. With her pregnancy, her slender figure was enhanced to a woman's fullness. And, the most powerful factor at work upon Cecco's vulnerability, the perfume that maddened his intellect, arose from his own skin, the only part of Jill that she'd left in his arms.

When Cecco's astonishment wore off, he plucked up the oars again, and his fury came flooding back, redoubled. "Girl," he warned, "you chose the wrong hour to throw yourself in my way." The knife in his belt reflected a shard of the hard, cool moon.

Mrs. Hanover continued to gape at Captain Cecco. This night had brought several surprises. Much earlier, she successfully made her way from the Clearing to Neverbay. Yulunga had admonished her with tales of man-eating beasts in the woods, but she learned, to her relief, that the sounds of the revelry kept the predators at a distance. Once near the festivities, she had intended to creep toward the beach, waiting for her chance to climb aboard a boat and head for the *Red Lady*. But she'd been delayed by the presence of sentinels, and by the goings-on at the party, both amorous and angry.

Carefully, she'd picked her path through the forest bordering the bay, avoiding the lookouts' range of vision. As she drew nearer to the shore, feeling the way with her toes before each step, seeking soft, safe earth and avoiding noise, she found she needed to beware of more eyes than the sentinels'. Although it slowed her progress, the intrigue of Red Fawn and Flambard had captivated Mrs. Hanover. In the darkness of the woods, she'd spied on the couple's lovemaking, the merry music muted at this distance and the orange glow of the bonfire behind them.

Her eagerness to meet Pierre-Jean mounted with the lovers' ardor. Afterward, the couple forgot to collect the shawl on which they'd lain, and Mrs. Hanover appropriated it in case she was glimpsed. In the darkness, she might be perceived as one of the pirates' women. She'd worn only her shift thus far, stimulated by her near-nakedness in the brisk evening air, and wishing to avoid tearing her new garments in the brush. After the twosome retreated, she had unrolled her bundle and donned her tunic, protecting it with the shawl, then she resumed her vigil for an opportunity to climb into one of the pirates' boats.

Later, the fight and excitement piqued her interest again. But when Mr. Noodler heard the noise and grabbed up the torch to desert his post, Mrs. Hanover snatched her chance to slip to the shore unnoticed, and she'd picked a boat, huddled in the stern, and covered herself with the shawl. She'd chosen the smaller of the two craft lying upright, assuming the next shift of watchmen would soon row it toward the *Red Lady*.

Surrounded by the stale smell of wood steeped in seawater, she felt contented as she crouched. Yulunga was not yet aware of her escape, and by the time he discovered it, her pleasure with Pierre-Jean would be accomplished. In whatever mood Yulunga received the news of her disobedience, whether he'd be amused or turn wrathful, she'd claim his attention once more. Fear of exposure prickled when she listened to Cecco ordering the next shift from *Red Lady* to land farther up the beach, but no one looked in the stern of her skiff. Yet, to her consternation, the lookouts had taken the other boat after all, leaving Mrs. Hanover quivering with disappointment.

Her disappointment didn't linger. With the coming of the parley, she felt her luck returning. While hidden in the boat, she hadn't understood the discussion on the beach; she caught snatches of the voices that she recognized to be Jill's and Cecco's. And she was pleased at the little knowledge she gleaned. Trouble for Jill always led to opportunity for Mrs. Hanover.

Now, as her astonishment abated, she climbed over the bench to sit upon it properly. She observed Cecco as he toiled at the oars. His limbs were tense, his movements decisive. The white moon lit his handsome Italian face, and she read his emotion. But even if she hadn't seen his expression, the cacophony of his jewelry proclaimed his state of mind.

Excited by the evening's adventures, Mrs. Hanover delighted in this new development. Try as she might, she had overheard only a few words of the parley on the beach, but the implication was clear. Jill had cast her husband aside in favor of Hook, and, when Cecco resisted, she made a brutal business of her rejection. Mrs. Hanover had always felt uneasy near Cecco. Now, there was a treacherous edge to him that caught in Mrs. Hanover's hide.

Quite suddenly, her scheme to tryst with young Pierre-Jean, with the bars of the brig between them, transformed into child's play. Mrs. Hanover set her sights on a free man, instead. A powerful man. An *innamorato* whose touch could turn dangerous. This man before her, seething with passion, was bent on vengeance. His intensity was electrifying. All at once, her throat thickened with desire. Anticipation coursed through her womanly precincts, like the arousal she felt when oppressed by her master, Yulunga.

And to this man, unlike Pierre-Jean, Yulunga had offered the solace of her body. Cecco held license to use Yulunga's mistress in any manner he chose. And she could use *him*. The captain. The gold at his ears, on his arms, and at his throat dazzled her senses. The flesh of his chest, the flow of his muscles as he rowed provoked her craving.

Even the sound of him was pleasing. She hadn't realized before how musically his ornaments fed her ears. Taking him in, Mrs. Hanover licked her generous lips.

This night might prove fruitful in more ways than one. The smile that came so rarely crept over her mouth. Jill's husband needed a substitute, and Mrs. Hanover was dressed for the part. Whether he would love her or loathe her didn't signify. Tonight, whatever the risks, she aimed to do something she'd never believed she would do.

Mrs. Hanover leaned forward and, softly, laid her hand on his thigh. His leg jerked at her touch, and he scowled. Before he could object, she spoke. Her voice was rough, but the lie came to her lips as readily as breath.

"Yulunga sent me."

Jill sat on the rock where Cecco forsook her, her head drooping. The cushion beside her, where her husband had sworn his devotion, lay vacant. She did not regret her decision to remain with Hook, nor could she lament cutting Cecco free. Yet she knew that the heartache she had inflicted upon Cecco, even justified as it was for his own safety's sake, would haunt her for her lifetime.

Tears traveled down her cheeks, cold streaks on her face as the breeze tried to dry them. Within moments of Cecco's departure, Nibs stole to her side and sat down. His strong arms clasped her, and, comforting, he drew her to his breast.

Drained by the ordeal, Jill allowed herself to lean against her son. With a corner of her scarf, she dabbed at the tears that blinded her. She relaxed into Nibs' hold, sighing, and grateful to feel his support. As she rested there against his familiar vest, preparing herself to return to the commodore, she inhaled the Island air once more, drawing strength from it. Mingled with the memorable scents of the shore, she caught a rusty aroma. The soggy smell of the beach reminded her of the sands of the hourglass.

Even through her sorrow, she brightened as she anticipated her return to Hook's pavilion. Growing eager to reunite with him, she murmured, to Nibs, "Our time for parley must have run out by now." He nodded, and, still leaning on him, she looked up to his face with the beginnings of a smile. "I am ready to—"

Farther up the beach, the bo'sun's whistle shrieked to call the next watch. Jill's heart screamed with it. Her eyes opened wide with disbelief. The man in whose arms she had taken refuge wore Nibs' vest. He had tied Nibs' orange kerchief about his hair. He was dark and tall and lean, like Nibs. But, to her amazement, Jill saw that her consoler was not her son.

Immediately, the Indian covered her face with his hand. Jill couldn't breathe, much less call for help. As she struggled, he increased his hold, restraining her arms and pressing her body to his. His large hand stopped her intake of air altogether, tightly covering her mouth, her chin, and her nose. Now she recognized the source of the rusty odor she'd perceived. This man was a hunter. His skin smelled of blood.

The more Jill resisted, the dizzier she became. Even if she hadn't left her knife in the pavilion, she couldn't have reached for it. She was unable to move her head to strike at her captor's nose, as Hook had taught her to do, nor might she move her jaw to bite his palm. Colored spots of light danced in her brain. Vaguely, the bo'sun's call came to her, tweedling its last, long notes. Half a minute later, with her lungs hungry for air, her senses went black, and she swooned.

She didn't feel the hunter's fingers unclasp her necklace. She lay insensible as he draped the chain of opals and diamonds in Flambard's hand. He dressed Nibs' limp form in the vest again, hauled him over his shoulder, and left him stretched out next to Flambard's bleeding body. He obliterated his footprints, stepping only on stones to disguise his movements. Then the brave gathered Jill up, and, with the strength of his arms, he carried her through the forest, leaving no trail on the path he'd mapped yesterday. Jill didn't sense how lovingly he cradled her, as he jogged toward the cage he had made for his pretty yellow bird.

By the seashore, the cushions on the rock lay vacant. After so such upheaval, peace was restored to this spot, where *Signore* and *Signora* Cecco, with their matching golden rings, had come together.

Scenes of Dream and Nightmare

Feeling keenly the loss of Mr. Smee, Hook occupied himself in Jill's absence. With one hand, one hook, and the grip of his knees, he cleaned his pistol, then polished it, then loaded it. He glanced at the hourglass, pleased for once that this task took so long to perform.

Looking down at the gun's honey-colored handle, he angled it in the lamplight to watch the mother-of-pearl of his initials shift and shine. With his finger he traced their inlay, smooth and cool, *J.H.*, embedded with a flowing script.

Its partner lay on the table, the pistol with which he'd armed Wendy, hinting to her of her identity as Jill Red-Hand. While pursuing her, he marked her own initials on the stock, a simple addition of one letter imposed upon his: *J.H.* in mother-of-pearl; *R.* burned in black, between and over the first two letters. He had branded her symbol into existence with his own red-hot hook. It was his love letter, written to her in flame. He remembered the odor of char in his lungs, and the smoke curling dark. He remembered those days, darker still, before she was his— a time when hope hung like smoke, insubstantial but tantalizing. Now he set both guns on the table, their muzzles facing one another. Danger-ous and dedicated, they were two halves of a perfectly matched set.

Nothing could change that reality. Both Hook and Jill were free to choose any path that offered; but, always, their story started, and ended, together.

Hook sat back and, with a creak of wicker, laid his head against Jill's rocker. He'd had the chair brought into the pavilion, to await its mistress. In the vial by the bed, a glimmer of gold caught his eye, and for some moments he contemplated calling Jewel to his side. His fairy always proved useful, and often amusing. But the hourglass, busily tumbling its grains, finally came to a halt. Glad that his impatience was at an end, Hook stood to grasp the timepiece, leaving the rocking chair tottering. He bore the hourglass to the post outside his tent.

"Mr. Tootles," he called. "Change the watch."

"Aye, aye, Sir." Tom poised the whistle at his lips.

Before Tom drew breath to blow, Hook stood suddenly rigid. He turned toward the boats, scanning the darkness where he'd sent Jill and Cecco. The bo'sun's call shrilled out. For one brief moment, Hook construed the piping as a scream, a pang of panic quickly echoed by the woods. A fugue of confusion followed, then, abruptly, Hook sensed no more. He felt drained, as if the flow of sensitivity between him and his counterpart had been dammed. Where before, even as he slept, he'd sensed Jill in every hollow, he now perceived nothing. No emotion at all.

Tom's signal faded. Its echo died away. The men were rousing for the change of shifts. Hook darted into the pavilion, and, seconds later, he emerged with the lantern on his claw and the matched set of pistols in his belt. With his blue headscarf flailing, he hurried toward the beach, ordering Tom over his shoulder, "Bring that torch!"

He didn't hear Tom's response, but soon his own shadow stretched before him on the sand, moving erratically as Tom followed, jogging with the flambeau. Jukes and Mullins, the two seaman assigned the next watch by the boats, fell in. All four men sped to the western shore, prepared to find a disconsolate captain.

The sailors weren't surprised at Hook's hurry. They supposed that, under Cecco's disheartened gaze, they'd watch the commodore escort the lady back to his pavilion. But when they arrived, the place appeared vacant. The boats were present, waiting and silent, but nothing else was there to be seen. No couple sat upon the cushions, and no sentries guarded a parley. Hook's haste now acquired a more ominous implication.

"Where is everyone?" Tom asked, staring toward the woods, stepping toward the cushions.

By intuition, Hook was pulled elsewhere. He strode right up to the shore and waded into the bay. He still sensed no sentiment from Jill, no trepidation, no joy; but his own heart was pierced— sharp and hot— as if he'd fallen on his claw. As the cold from the water penetrated his boots, he sighted the skiff. Halfway to the ships, leaving a wake in the bay water, the boat moved away.

The moonlight was merciless. It showed Captain Cecco rowing. It revealed Jill perched in the stern, her topaz tunic pale in the moonbeams, her hair swept up, her figure leaning hungrily toward her husband. No constraint held her there. She had closed her mind to Hook, but his eyes still read her body. In the posture of her form, in the inclination of her head, her compliance was obvious. She didn't call out. She didn't look back. The moon flaunted the fact that this woman had chosen this course.

She had chosen Cecco.

Hook stood watching the boat. As his men followed his gaze, they lined the beach behind him. They gaped as the scene bared its secrets. Hook heard their exclamations, then their whispered, half-expressed guesses. Had his sailors looked, they'd have seen by the glow of the lantern in his claw the disbelief that marked their commodore's face. Stunned, Hook stood like a figurehead, staring, until the skiff rounded the *Roger*. Disappearing behind Hook's ship, it could only be rowing for home— for Jill's husband's home, aboard the *Red Lady*.

Without a word of farewell, Jill had forsaken him.

With one hand, one hook, and the grip of his knees, Hook held himself upright. As always, adversity summoned his strength. Standing tall, he ordered his thoughts.

Tom stood goggling, then shook himself, recalling his responsibility. His voice broke the quiet as he spun. "But where are the others?" Casting his light in a circle to search the vicinity, he bellowed, "Nibs, where are you? Flambard?"

Jukes and Mullins hustled to the boats and muscled them up, peering under each vessel. "Nothing here; and just the one boat gone." They hurried back up the slope of sand, to join Tom at the end of the area, a discreet distance beyond the cushioned seat of the parley point. Tom huffed in surprise as his torch illuminated Nibs and Flambard, prostrate.

"Commodore! Over here, Sir!"

The commodore's jaw had set while he glowered at the bay. When Tom called to him, Hook's habit of authority took precedence. Whatever else he lost, Hook would never lose command.

He turned and stalked from the sea, scarcely feeling the drag of the water. He determined to comprehend this incident. Under no circumstances did he shrink from learning the truth, however undesirable. And he trusted at his most instinctive level: his Jill, his storyteller, had left him a message.

"Sir," Tom was kneeling at Nibs' side. He felt for a pulse at his brother's neck, and relief eased his features. "Nibs is out cold, but he's still breathing." A glance showed no hope for the Frenchman. "But Commodore...Flambard's dead." Tom handed the torch to Jukes, then scuttled to a tide pool to soak his kerchief, hurrying back to daub his brother's head wound. Only vaguely did he register that Nibs wasn't wearing his own favored kerchief.

Mullins shook his head. "We'll have to tell Red Fawn gently. She was smitten with this Frenchman." He spotted a glitter in Flambard's hand. Disentangling a chain from the sailor's grip, he held it up to dangle in the torchlight. Shards of color flashed, brilliant, from the diamonds and the opals. Astonished, Mullins said, "Here be the lady's necklet, in the Frenchy's fingers!"

"*What?*" Tom cried. "Is the chain broken?" Mullins handed the necklace to him. Examining it, Tom answered his own question. "No. It isn't broken, and the clasp's intact. It wasn't yanked off Jill's neck."

Jukes plucked up the knife at Flambard's side, rolling it in his tattooed fingers. "This belongs to Nibs, doesn't it, lad?"

Tom looked, then nodded, gravely. "Aye, it's Nibs'." He dropped his voice. "And the blood is Flambard's."

Mullins raised his gaze to the commodore's icy blue stare. "Nibs killed him, Sir, but it looks like Flambard knocked Nibs on the pate before he died. Seems like they were brawling over the baubles."

Hook viewed the insensible Nibs, tended by his brother, and then Flambard, with a slit severing his throat. The French blue jacket was stained purple, and blood oozed into the sand. A red-speckled stone lay near Nibs. "Where is Flambard's blade? Surely, to end with his gullet cut, he employed something more deadly than rocks."

Mullins rolled the body. Grunting, he swore, "By the Powers, this Frenchy's built as solid as his captain....Here, Sir." A dagger lay beneath Flambard.

"And their cutlasses?"

"There, by that boulder. They must have agreed upon weapons."

Lifting his lantern, Hook searched the sand all around for signs, but found nothing to refute Mullins' supposition. The situation appeared to be as his second officer surmised: a knife fight between sailors, and a severe breach of discipline.

Hook's face grew sterner. "Whatever else happened here, the beach was left unguarded. Mr. Smee shall discipline Mr. Nibs when he recovers."

Jukes kept mum, but Mullins dared to speak for the young bo'sun's mate. "We know our Nibs well enough to judge he was doing his job." The other sailors nodded agreement, and Mullins continued, "Seems he was preventing a theft, of your own belongings, Commodore."

In Hook's mind, no doubt existed as to the circumstances, and it wasn't Nibs whom he faulted. He desired to entertain other explanations. "Say on."

"Well, now," Mullins proceeded, but guardedly, "from the looks of things, I'm guessing the jewelry was...given up, so to speak. Given up to you, Sir. Else, how could the lady come to lose it, and how could Flambard get his chance to filch it?"

Mystified, Tom said, "I know for a fact that this piece is Jill's favorite, by reason that the commodore gave it to her at the start. With Nibs and Captain Cecco to shield her, there's no way Flambard could have forced her to give it up."

Mullins suggested, with reluctance, "Mayhap the lady was *encouraged* to cast it off..." He cleared his throat, "when she, well... when she made her decision." He cocked his head, indicating the *Red Lady*.

Better than anyone, Hook understood Jill's attachment to the precious piece with which he had gifted her. This necklace was his earliest offering of jewels— her first pirate treasure. It once symbolized their joining. Now, Hook knew, it meant something else.

He crooked his fingers, and Tom handed him the chain. Its metal felt cool, as he had anticipated it would feel, yet he was disappointed that it no longer registered the temperature of Jill's throat. He scrutinized it, asserting, at last, "Jill herself removed my necklace. Or caused it to be removed."

At the note in his voice, the three kneeling sailors leaned back. They exchanged uneasy glances.

Yet Tom's anxiety could not stay silenced by the warning. "But why would Jill leave her jewelry on the beach?" He leaned over his brother again, and tamped the gash with his kerchief. "Nibs'll explain everything, once he comes round." He jostled his brother, trying to wake him. "Nibs?"

Mullins tucked his husky thumbs in his belt, still cogitating. He and Cecco had been mates for years, serving Hook. It was Cecco who promoted Mullins to his present position. Mullins felt it his duty to his comrade to put the best face on a bad situation. He ventured, "Flambard dove deep in the merrymaking tonight. He got drunk. After Red-Handed Jill shed the necklet, he started a ruckus with Nibs over it." He reasoned, "When the fight got mean, Captain Cecco led the lady away— for her safety."

Tom gazed at his foster father. Some presentiment prickled his skin with apprehension. Hook's tanned face looked more tawny, and his eyes, so akin to Jill's moments ago, now appeared bestial. Tom puffed out his barrel chest and bluffed, trying to settle his own disquiet along with the commodore's. "We mustn't worry, Sir, I'm sure the captain's just protecting the lady."

"Aye, Sir," Mullins agreed.

"Aye, that's the way of it," echoed Jukes. "Cecco's keeping her safe."

"Indeed, Mr. Jukes. I am *certain* her husband is…keeping her."

To these men, who plumbed the level of Jill's betrayal, Hook's voice sounded strangely civil. They remembered, then, that Hook waxed most dangerous when most polite.

He took a final survey of the area. His lip curled in a snarl, and he commanded, "Carry Nibs to Lelaneh. Tell Mr. Yulunga that I require two Frenchmen to guard this point. Two more to tend to Flambard." At his orders, Tom, Mullins, and Jukes stood immediately to obey. They each felt the lionlike stare of their commodore, and hastened away from his claw.

The matched set of pistols weighted Hook's belt. Jill's absence brought his spirit to ground. The truth had, however, become clear to him.

Jill was free to choose any path that offered. The tale she told, the story of Hook and Jill, had started together. Nothing could change that reality. Hook mused, toying with the necklace in his only hand, deciphering the message she'd sent by rejecting it.

Their story had started together. The end of that story might prove— altogether— different.

Approaching *Red Lady*, Cecco slowed his rowing. "Yulunga sent you," he scoffed. "Are you so much like my wife that you, too, tell stories?"

In answer, Mrs. Hanover dragged her fingertips over Cecco's thigh. She felt sick with fear, and with wanting, but she forced herself to smile.

"Who do you think you are, girl, to tempt *me?*"

"Tonight, I am whoever you want."

The lookout's hail rang across the water, "The boat ahoy!"

Relieved at the interruption, Cecco called over his shoulder, "*Red Lady*. Her captain."

"*Oui, Monsieur,*" answered the sailor, de Lerroné. "Welcome aboard." Then his voice snapped to attention, with a note of surprise, "And welcome to Red-Handed Jill, too, *Madame*." Hastily, *Monsieur* de Lerroné retreated from the rail to resume his watchpost high on the quarterdeck.

Angry as he felt, Cecco was a seaman, and he steered his craft with expertise. In a hiss of foam, the skiff came kissing up to the

Red Lady's side. Cecco shipped his oars and hooked the boat on to the mainchains. This business done, he considered Yulunga's offering where she sat straight and bold on the bench.

One hand rested on her breast, her chin coyly angled. In the shadow of the ship, Cecco couldn't see her eyes, but he felt her avid gaze. Distaste twisted his face, wasted no doubt, for he presumed she couldn't discern his expression either. She simply waited for his decision.

The boat rocked in the bay water, and their bodies leaned in tandem to compensate. As much as Cecco hated to admit it, Mrs. Hanover's audacity reminded him of Jill's. He cursed the nighttime, wanting to view the face of the woman he hated. Instead, he saw Jill— her clothing, her posture, her coiffure…her smile. Her smile, that couched both truth and deception. His heart fell even lower.

How many times, he wondered, had Jill lied to him?

This virago might be no worse than the woman he'd espoused. Why should he detest one of these females any more than the other? Both were liars and connivers.

"To my quarters," he ordered, finally. "Only two sentries are aboard. I will lock you in where I can watch you, to keep you from straying to the brig. For this night, poor Pierre-Jean, at least, is safe from you."

Mrs. Hanover accepted his hold to be helped up the side. His bangles sang, and the tightness of his grip sent a quiver through her system. As they found footing on the ship's deck, Cecco did not release her. His fingers pressed her flesh.

"Pierre-Jean is protected," he said. "But your own well-being, I do not warrant."

Roughly, he pulled her toward his cabin. The lookout kept his distance, but while the bay's breeze caressed him, he sniffed a *soupçon* of exotic cologne. *Monsieur* de Lerroné watched in the half-light of the moon as the captain and the lady sped for privacy, the officer's boots stamping in urgency, *Madame*'s bare feet silent, but fluttering to keep up.

As the door banged shut, de Lerroné saluted Captain Cecco. A true Frenchman, the sentry didn't wonder at the power that had drawn the commodore's lady back to her spouse.

"Alors, l'amour." He shook his head, chortling, and counted the minutes until his shift should be over, and he might find his own kind of love on the beach.

He was curious, too. The commodore's temperament was notorious. *Monsieur* de Lerroné was intrigued to see how James Hook would compensate himself for the loss of his lover.

Staring around him, David sat up fast, seeking the foe. His ears hummed with the sound of war whoops. Were the Indians striking at last?

The attackers' torches soon resolved into flickering orange, from the hearth. Snug in their hideout under the ground, the other boys lay limp, as spread out as they could manage all together in the one big bed. Far from a battle scene, the earthen walls closed comfortably round the children, the roots forming sheaths for their weapons and shelves for their treasures. The loamy smell that was becoming familiar to David pervaded. Warm furs covered him, soft against his skin. He sighed in relief, knowing he and the Lost Boys were safe in their home. And it was no foe who woke David, but Peter himself.

Peter was dreaming again. With his eyes open but unseeing, he challenged some terror. His arms flailed as if fighting, and his fist clutched an imaginary dagger. As David had witnessed another evening, Peter, engulfed in his nightmare, was not afraid, but blazing.

"Have at thee, all seven of you!" he cried. His patrician face glowed with gallantry as he fell to, defending the bed. As far as David could ascertain, not one of Peter's seven adversaries advanced beyond its edge, and the littler boys slept on, unwitting.

During Peter's hauntings, David wondered if he should wake the boy. But Peter appeared so pleased with himself as he struggled that it seemed a shame to deny him his triumph. Further, David reflected, Peter didn't know the difference between what transpired in his imagination and what happened in truth. It made no odds if he woke or he slept.

When the battle was won, Peter crowed and stowed his weapon, as cocky as ever he behaved in the daylight. His life, it seemed, night or day, consisted of fantasies. Depending on your point of view, David thought, Peter was the lucky one fated never to outgrow them. Perhaps Peter's land, the 'Never-land,' was named so for that reason. But dreams might be delightful, or they might just as likely turn dreadful.

David, who had experienced real peril at sea, found Peter's courage appalling. Seen another way, though, Peter took childish risks. The boy wasn't mature enough to appreciate the dangers he faced on a daily basis. So David puzzled: was Peter a hero, or simply ignorant? Either way, he was fun to follow. David grinned. He had picked up the habit of grinning, and he found that fact a little appalling as well.

Without choosing to do so, David discovered the charm of these shores. In his more prosaic moods, he rationalized the Neverland's magic as the lure of a childhood he'd never enjoyed. But when his soul filled with Red-Handed Jill, David pandered to the Island's mystical properties. In those moments, the burn of Jill's blood-mark scored him, and his cheek flamed with her passion. He got plenty of opportunity to adore her, because Peter and his boys were addicted to Island lore; the story-telling girl who as their mother mended socks and pockets remained as large a legend as the Pirate Queen. Even now she ruled their hearts. And, still in thrall to her, David found himself, by extension, beguiled by the enchantment of her Island.

He was old enough, and, owing to Peter, *young* enough, to recognize Jill's wisdom in banishing him to boyhood. Although exiled from her presence, he worshipped her. Yet so many occupations possessed his time and his mind alongside of her that he assigned his hoped-for gratification to a future era. He was, in effect, a child again. His business now was play, with a man's estate awaiting.

Occasions arose when David contemplated the responsibility that had pulled him here. He recalled his conversation with Captain Cecco, and the purpose for which he and his packet wrapped in oilskin were saved from the sea. Like the other boys, David hid treasure.

But unlike the shells, antlers, sling-shots and feathers tucked tenderly in the roots forming the walls, David's artifact seemed too grown-up to enter the hideout. It was too weighty, even, to glorify the mantel beside Peter's trophies. In contrast, David himself *did* belong here. And he did intend to honor his obligation to his uncle and his shipmates. But while he played a Lost Boy, duty's urgency diminished. As for his part to play as Jill's rescuer, he hadn't forgotten, and he cared just as deeply. But the lady was safe with her pirates, for now. His secret would keep.

Peter had lain down again, one arm slung off the bed, and one leg arched. His mouth fell slack, displaying his perfect little teeth. No mother under the influence of a nightlight might resist such a child. The riddle in David's mind was how Peter, who had just fought off a squadron, could lie so seemingly defenseless. Only his victims could fail to love him, when he was asleep.

In all these respects, tonight, Peter's hideout under the ground remained its usual, unusual self. It was the next stage in the dream that caused David unease.

"You can't make me," Peter declared. Then, more piteously, "You can't make me go there. The wind told me— I'm banished."

The only place on the Island that David knew to be forbidden to the Wonderful Boy was the House in the Clearing. Peter himself had escorted David to the area, where only the big house was off-limits. They'd basked in the place, made friends with the native children, and were petted and fed by their mothers. David could think of nothing in the Clearing to affright Peter so. Perhaps the nightmare conjured up something sinister there. But, at Peter's next words, David quailed, too.

"They're not buried." Peter flopped on his tummy, as if turning his back on someone, or some thing. "No...no, I can't go... Halfway...halfway there is the rule!"

It was clear to David that this adventure was no longer fun. He reached out from the blankets to nudge Peter's shoulder, but the boy recoiled from his touch.

"They're only bones on the sacrifice mat...lain in their tomb."

And David got an inkling of the trouble. Peter, like David, dreaded a certain location. A place David had learned he should shun.

This foreboding was one reason David deferred his duty, delaying his return to civilization. The first step toward home lay concealed in the Tomb of the Lost Boys. In spite of the weeks in which David denied the horror of the place, sheltering there, it retained a shuddery aura. Yet if Peter himself— the bravest boy in creation— avoided the grotto, it was more grotesque than David conceived.

As if to confirm the fact, Peter whimpered in his sleep.

Only once more, David told himself. He need only enter that cave one last time. But when?

His toes grew chilly, and he realized he'd stretched out beyond his fur blanket. David shrank himself small again, and stopped formulating the future. He trusted in Jill. When the right time arrived, he'd know what to do, and he'd be grown up enough to do it.

Behind his eyelids, the darkness changed shades, from the warm of orange to the cool of blue. A flutter passed over his head. When he opened his eyes, Jewel was sitting on Peter's shoulder. Her little hand patted the child, and her whispers made music in his ear, as if she strummed a harp strung with his golden hair. The sound was like a chiming of bells, low, and ever so pleasing. Peter's furrowed brow smoothed, and David watched him descend into slumber.

Drowsy again, David grinned. His ears filled with the hum of the lullaby.

Neither boy noticed when Jewel ceased her singing. They were sunk in the realm of Morpheus when she sat up, abruptly. She arched her back. Her wings burst into radiant blue. With her eyes half closed, she smiled a smile of joy. She lingered, languorous, in the pleasure of the moment. And then she tidied her hair, brushed down her gown, and zoomed to shoot up the hollow of the tree chute, flying toward the nighttime sky.

Jewel, too, harbored dreams. Tonight she'd been summoned by one of them.

Monsieur de Lerroné sprang from the skiff and scurried toward the casks, leaving his companion to beach the boat. Sand flew from his feet. *"Mes amis,"* he shouted, "have you heard?" His shipmates handed him a bottle, but he didn't pause to drink. "For our captain this night, a dream has come to life. *Madame*, she has joined him!"

"Mrs. Hanover?" wondered Noodler, taken aback. Then he began to rationalize, "Well, I suppose it had to happen."

Poor de Lerroné couldn't fit another word of English into the hubbub, and the assumption met with mixed emotions. No one but Pierre-Jean cared for Mrs. Hanover, exactly; she'd caused too much trouble for the company, although considering her upbringing, they felt sorry for her. "Aye," Cookson offered, "she be a female, and females be in short supply." Captain Cecco, as the men knew only too well, had been lonesome since the commodore came back to life and came back to Jill. The girl's attention might help.

But Mason protested, "Rumor is he found a native woman. A widow. I thought she'd be his one, from now. Barring our lady, of course."

"Aye, so I heard, too. Are you sure it be Mrs. Hanover, de Lerroné?"

Yulunga overheard his mistress' name as he strode into the crowd. He appeared displeased. "What nonsense are you spreading, de Lerroné?"

He'd just returned from Flambard's death scene, where Tom Tootles confided the news of Jill's abandonment. His first priority was to locate Mr. Smee, confined by the commodore's ban to the edge of the beach. He did so immediately, and one glance at the bo'sun's red, anxious face told him Smee had learned of the development. No doubt Jukes and Mullins described the events in detail to Smee, once they'd carried Nibs back for nursing.

The two first officers exchanged troubled looks. Tacitly agreeing to handle the changes one task at a time, they carried on with their respective duties. At the moment, Smee had the charge of Nibs. It fell to Yulunga to join the men again, and he turned his formidable bulk toward de Lerroné.

Mr. Yulunga was known for his predilection for stirring things up when a ship got too quiet. Thanks to Jill's defection, a shake-up was certain. Before Yulunga became an officer, this turn was just the kind of chaos he relished, but as Cecco's first mate, and even as his friend, he couldn't see a long-term bright side to Cecco's new bliss.

The situation cast Yulunga in a gloomy humor, and his men backed a bit as he lumbered toward them.

He said, "Mrs. Hanover is here, on the Island. She won't bother Pierre-Jean, or anybody else tonight." He only wished it *were* his mistress with Cecco. But reality was dismal enough. The company didn't need another rumor. *Monsieur* de Lerroné's gossip was true, and no threat from Yulunga could thwart it.

"No, no, indeed, *not* the little one," de Lerroné verified. "The Lady herself, Red-Handed Jill. I saw her with these eyes. She and the captain— they locked the door to his quarters."

Stunned by this declaration, the Rogers eyeballed Yulunga for a denial, but the look of reluctance on his broad black face confirmed their fears. Their shoulders slumped, their hands hung by their sides.

The mariners of the *Red Lady*, though, gave a cheer. After the sad story of Flambard, they could look forward to something pleasant— the presence of Red-Handed Jill aboard. The Frenchmen took pride in their Italian captain who, with his persuasion and prowess, had won the lady back. Cecco's mood would be lighter, and his crew members clapped de Lerroné on the back, toasting one another as they anticipated the ship's more amiable atmosphere.

The Rogers, however, saw the situation in a different light. One and all were dumbfounded, not because Jill accepted Cecco— she'd done it before— but because she'd forsaken Hook. Solitude was a curse to him, one that slung round to scourge his crew, too. Once the *Roger*'s sailors found their voices, a few words set the Frenchmen to considering the repercussions.

"Mates," declared Mason, his back to the bonfire, "You're sworn to the commodore. If the lady's choice cuts a rift between captains, be you men of your word?"

At this question, the Frenchmen murmured amongst themselves. Hook was a shrewd commander. He had demanded an oath of allegiance from each of his underlings. Cecco himself had so sworn. Any breach between the two officers placed the crew in an awkward position. No, not awkward. The realization hit them; their position could be fatal.

"See what has happened to Flambard," lamented his tie-mate. "His death, it may be only the start of the trouble."

Mullins, Hook's own second officer, intoned, "You Frenchies, you never knew Hook before Jill. May you *never* know him." His crewmates bore grim faces, nodding. Their dejection cast a pall on the gathering— the shade of Hook's legend, remembered.

The *Red Lady*'s sailors looked to Guillaume, who strove to pacify them in French and in English. "*Attendez, mes amis*, we will learn more tomorrow. Come, let us settle now, and enjoy the last of the kegs." With Yulunga's looming mass to shepherd them, the men subsided into groups, to roost cross-legged in the sand, tossing dice on driftwood, and waiting for sunrise.

Banished from Hook's side, Mr. Smee felt more worry than both crews combined. He was anxious to resume his station, looking after the commodore. The pavilion stood only yards across the sand, its gay, colored stripes glowing from within. It might just as well have been pitched on the moon, so distant did Smee feel from his commodore. On this nightmare of nights, Hook must be needing his first mate and confidant. Smee was all too familiar with Hook's volatility. Jill's coming had restored his humanity. Her departure might bring the reverse: the old days, the old ways.

He waited, hoping for a summons. Alongside Lelaneh, he tended Nibs' wound, and with Lily he comforted Red Fawn. The moon moved on, and Smee's worries only compounded, because Hook's summons failed to occur.

Equally disturbing to him was the idea that the lady's loyalty stood in question. "Lily," he said, once they paired off at the woods' edge, and were able to speak privately, "They say the commodore witnessed it. Red-Handed Jill turning away with her husband— and not a word for himself to soften the blow. I can't be believing it."

With her tender touch, Lily soothed him. "The Lady Jill knows her heart, and the commodore's. All will be well, Smee. We must trust her judgment."

"I'm that vexed about Nibs, too. It's a nasty knock he took. I'm thinking he won't wake 'til daylight." A wail of woe rose up from Red Fawn, where Lelaneh rocked her in her arms near the warmth of the fire. Smee looked their way. "Lelaneh has a job to do, consoling Red Fawn. The poor woman set her heart on Flambard, and she's sobbing as if she'd murdered him herself."

"Come," Lily urged him, "We have done all we can for our cherished ones. Lelaneh is good medicine for Red Fawn, and the Men of the Clearing watch over Nibs. Let us lie on my blanket, until Commodore Hook sends for you. And in the meantime, Mr. Tom attends him. You need not fear for your master."

Grateful for her wisdom, Smee kissed her and, reclining on the blanket, he sank into her soft embrace. "You're a wisewoman, Lily. I've always known it."

Lily smiled for her lover, but she couldn't help feeling troubled. The Lady Jill knew her own heart, but her act of abandonment struck false. Jill adored Cecco, and she deeply loved Hook. Until tonight, she had directed her energies to upholding harmony between the two. And to renounce either one for the other required a parting with words. Jill was a woman of words, a storyteller. Surely she should have spoken before disappearing?

Smee lay silent for a while, and Lily dared to hope he slept. The evening had been trying for him, physically and emotionally. Tomorrow could bring only worse. But, far from slumber, he raised up on his elbow and said, "Look at you and me, Lily. Why can't they be doing like us?"

Lily waited. She sensed what her dear one would say. He was a generous man.

"Why can't they let her love both of them?"

Lily pulled him down to her, and made love to him. She was generous, too.

When their heartbeats had calmed, Lily spoke one more time. "This Island is one of mysteries, Smee." She sighed. "And mysteries may not be trusted. Let us hold close together, my dear, while we may."

As she lay, beloved in her lover's arms, Lily's thoughts flowed to Captain Cecco. How content he must be, right this moment. To hold his wife was the wish of his heart.

For one man, at least, she believed, this nightmare was a beautiful dream, come to life.

Wicked Victims

Mrs. Hanover was receptive to sound. The slam of the door thumped in her ears, and the bolt clicked home. A scratching noise, and light flared at the bedside, growing as the flame in Captain Cecco's fingers licked the lamp wick. In her eagerness, her breaths came panting. He must have heard her because he turned his head her way, and the light danced upon his earrings, swinging.

She braved his gaze. As his face became illuminated, it remained strained and severe. Captain Cecco was a strong man, suffering strong emotion. She was part of the reason he suffered, and his intensity vibrated at her center. At this moment, she felt that she signified. His eyes skimmed from the twist of her hair to her barefooted toes. Then he took his first full observation of her tunic, patterned after Jill's. He turned his back, but she sensed he still saw her.

Ready to insinuate herself in his quarters, Mrs. Hanover glanced around. This cabin was smaller than its counterpart aboard the *Roger*, but nearly as comfortable. Paisley drapes hung long at the windows, which were open to the air. The bedstead was large, the rest of the furniture diminutive, at odds with the captain's physique. He had cleared away LeCorbeau's more effeminate trappings, but the remainder showed quality craftsmanship: ripe polished woodwork; thick-woven fabrics. The rug beneath her feet felt lush, and the air was spiced with leather. His cabin was orderly. She imagined that it had changed since its previous captain's tenure, now allocated to business rather than pleasure. Watching Cecco settle in, she felt just as at home here as he. It was the kind of place Mrs. Hanover found most familiar— it was a man's room.

She listened to the chink of medallions as Cecco tossed his headdress on the locker. Its crimson ribbon pooled on the cushion there, like blood. He took his heavy necklace off next, then his bangles, and after that he stood still, staring at his wedding ring. He clenched the hand that bore it, then dropped his fist.

Where the grip of that fist had recently manacled her, her wrist ached. She rubbed it, to cherish the tenderness. Her next perception was one for her ears again. The captain was swearing, in Italian. She gloried in the sound.

He paced the length of his quarters, then turned to glare at her. "You, lie here." He pointed to the settee against the wall, opposite his desk. It wasn't near his bed but he kicked it, savagely, forcing it farther away. "I know you prefer not to talk. I prefer not to hear you."

Obediently, she stepped to the settee. She draped the shawl on it, then let down her hair, shaking it free over her shoulders. Loosening her tunic, she noticed that her clothes retained a whiff of the woods. She caressed the material, remembering the secrets she'd seen. The vision of Flambard and Red Fawn coupling roused her to a higher pitch, and she turned halfway, to indulge her senses in the captain. Her smile vanished, and she gasped.

Before she could back from him, Cecco was upon her. He grabbed her tunic at the neckline, bunching the yellow linen in his fist. He whipped his knife from his belt, and thrust it, cold, against her throat.

"Never believe that you tempt me."

He pointed the knife down, between her breasts. Its tip bit her skin.

"Only my knife will make love to you." With a scream of renting fabric, he shredded the dress with his blade, from neckline to hem. He yanked it from her body, sending her reeling, and he cast the tatters to the floor.

He caught her, snatching her upper arm, and shoved his face close to hers. "Do not presume to dress like Jill." He pushed her down on the settee. Then he turned away, leaving her blinking. Tramping toward his bed, he tossed his knife on the table. He stripped off his vest and sat down to slough off his boots.

Mrs. Hanover was in heaven. A surge of lust made her salivate. Her left breast pricked from the nick of his knifepoint. Never mind that her tunic lay ravaged. It had served its purpose. She'd bewitched him with it. The force of his reaction set her trembling, but not out of fear. Always, this sensation— the feel of goading a male to perceive her, of pushing a man to the edge— stimulated her. This, she believed, this effect on a man, was the quintessence of womanhood. She lived for this feeling, even if she died for it.

Instead of whittling at her hopes, Captain Cecco, with his knife, had cut them loose. She shed her trousers, never taking her eyes from him. She gazed upon his shape as he re-tied his hair, hair as dark as his eyes. He rinsed his hands and face at the washstand, while she touched her tongue to her lips at the sound— droplets dripping from his chin and tinkling in the basin. Here, at her fingertips, was more man than she'd fantasized. Her impression as she stared was a composite of olive skin, glints of gold, the bulge of muscle...and animosity. Beneath the swell of her baby, her lower parts throbbed. She pressed the score on her breast till it bruised.

Cecco dried his face. Retaining his breeches, he drank from a cup of wine, then lay back on his bed. With one arm he covered his eyes, and he unleashed a sigh of anger.

Perhaps he believed his fight was over; Mrs. Hanover was not so tame.

She judged it best to warn him of her approach, so as not to startle him. She wouldn't object if he struck out again— she looked forward to it. But she desired him to strike out deliberately, as he had just done, and not at random. She asked, "May I sip some wine?"

As she predicted, he jolted at her intrusion, rising up on his elbow with a scowl. He jerked his head toward the bedside table, where his cup sat. He punched his pillow, then he turned on his side, to be rid of her. He only intrigued her the more as his scars came into her view.

She drank, just enough to wet her tongue with the wine's heady taste. She set the cup down with an audible tap on the tabletop. She turned down the lantern so that the slim silver moonlight cast her features in obscurity. Then she slipped off her shift and slid into his bed.

Immediately he turned to her, hostility harshening his voice. "You disobey."

"I obey Mr. Yulunga's command." She leaned in, and kissed his shoulder. His skin thrilled her lips, as hot and smooth as she'd imagined, as potent as his wine.

He didn't bother to shrug her off. "I gave you warning."

"I'm not afraid."

"If you are careless for yourself, are you not mindful of your child?"

"No."

She'd revived his attention. He stared her direction in the half-light, aghast.

Cecco had never really listened to this girl before. He listened now, disbelieving the cool note of her voice as she spoke of her baby.

"I study doctoring. I know the prospects."

He remembered, then, her ignorance of the infant's paternity. No doubt she assumed her womb carried the seed of incest. She did not know that Hook, who forbade Jill to conceive by him, might yet have sired a child there. Cecco's heart stung for Jill, and it ached for himself. A vision of the little ones he'd lost spurred his ire again. "How wanton you are, to risk your blessing." Incensed, he turned from the girl, shunting her away.

Mrs. Hanover didn't shrink from the challenge. "I can soothe your hurt."

"It is not you I want."

"You want a woman."

Cecco snorted. "I have my pick of women. Never the one."

As a result of Yulunga's goading, Mrs. Hanover's speech was enhanced. Only now did she appreciate his bullying beyond its physical stimulus. With chameleon ease, she increased her likeness to Jill: she used words.

"You took me for her before. Look, the light is dim. I am your Jill, if you will it."

"I do not will it. Were she here, I should kill her."

"Kill me, then."

The bulk of his body loomed in the dimness as he sat up, jeering. "I misjudged you, girl. You are not wicked. You are mad. Save your insanity for your master. I know him; he welcomes trouble."

"I dare not go back to him, having failed in my duty."

Melodic to her ears, his accent rumbled his frustration. "I have had a bellyful of duty."

"That's why I'm here. Forget everyone outside these quarters. Tonight, you may do as you will."

Cecco shook his head, exasperated. Desolation must be distorting his thinking. The girl almost made sense.

She felt his resolve diminishing, and she played upon reason. "No love or loyalty restrains you. What will you do, here— right now— to your Jill?"

His thoughts dogged her lead. He half imagined the scene that she conjured.

"Will you punish me?...Love me?"

Against the governance of his intellect, Cecco's heart weighed her suggestions. "Both," came the answer, through his teeth.

The girl was correct, he found. The feeble light shrouded her face. Jill inhabited his mind, and, if he willed her presence in the flesh, it was Jill who now incited him.

But no, it was some wraith, not Jill sitting here, fondling the gold at his biceps. His wife had betrayed him. She had skewered his heart, and laughed. He had fled from her, to stay his hand from the deed he was just about to execute. He raised his arm.

Just as Jill would do, the woman held her ground, unflinching. But a curtain flicked in the breeze, manipulating the moonlight, and now she appeared as Mrs. Hanover— Yulunga's property; the Doctor's doxy; Liza the servant girl...Jill's imitation. Cecco's anger at his wife turned to fury against this female, who sullied his image of his loved one. She disgusted him. She defiled his very memory of his wife.

He struck her, a backhanded blow. Her body snapped back and her fingers flew to her face. "Ah!" she whispered. With her eyes closed, she traced her jaw to her throat, to her bosom. And then her gray eyes opened again, and she reached for his hand, the hand that abused her, and dragged it toward her flesh. Firmly, she held him to her bosom. Her nipple invaded his palm, engorged and rigid, and her heartbeat vibrated in his hand.

"If I am she," she hissed, "I deserve to bear your anger." She squeezed his fingers, making him press the swell of her breast. Her head rolled back. Her eyes closed as she worked his fingertips at her teat. Greedily, she drew his hand down, past her pregnancy, below her abdomen. Already a gloss of moisture had begun, warm and silken, and she gasped when she pushed his hand to stroke her flow. She swallowed, wallowing in ecstasy.

"I despoiled your contentment, Giovanni. Now you must despoil me." She forced his fingers to penetrate her privacy. "Do me damage— dole out to me the hurt I dealt to *you*."

At first, he believed her— as a storyteller, a seer. His gypsy mysticism paid homage to a wise one. Superstition held him captive, as if the speaking of his name must exorcize his will. Her craving fused with his fury, imperative, impossible to deny. He didn't resist as she led his hands, urging him to brutality, turning rough, and rougher. Perversely, the punishment he inflicted seemed to pleasure her.

But, as she writhed beneath his wrath, he remembered. *His* woman was not perverse. His wife used no traps, nor deceit. She served her purpose with honesty. When confronting her husband's anger, or any man's, she flexed, but never bent. This being, who raped herself with his rage, was someone else...something *other*. Her guilt made her craven; it was she who was entranced, and destruction was the devil that enthralled her. No matter how she dressed, or how she undressed, this female was a creature, never Jill.

Disturbed at his own complicity, Cecco jerked away. She followed his body, pressing against him, begging for climax. She seized his breeches, to tug at the ties. On the defensive now, he thrust her to arm's length, holding her shoulders. She slipped his grip and drove at him, lusting for more.

Yet he was mistaken. She did demand more, but her focus swerved to the knife upon the table. She snatched it, then yanked at a corner of the bed linen, to swaddle the sharp half. When its bite was sheathed in the sheet, she cradled the knife by the blade. Looking into Cecco's eyes, she lowered her chin, opened her knees, and thrust the hilt in the center of her sex. She bared her teeth, and, like an imp upon its victim, she rode the handgrip. Her hips worked back and forth, as she ravished herself with his weapon.

"*Malocchio!*" Cecco whispered, appalled. His own utterance, intended simply to intimidate, reverberated in his head: *Only my knife will make love to you.* He was no soothsayer. He hadn't voiced a prediction; he'd cast no curse. The affliction, he realized, resided in this woman, and it worked upon herself, and on anyone who touched her. He must stop it, and he must stop it now.

With one hand, he wrestled her shoulder. With the other he tore the knife from her grasp. He rolled it loose from the linen to bounce on the bed, and then he drove it into the tabletop, deep, so that she could not recapture it. As she lunged for it, he scrambled to restrain her. Reluctant to touch this bawd, he sought the least intimate hold. His stomach pitched while, with both hands, he grappled her throat.

She moaned, and seized his fingers again. As she'd done at the start, she squeezed so that his grasp tightened. Indulging in the agony, she held her body stiff. Her breathing rasped in his ears, gurgling, choking, then ceased altogether.

In horror, Cecco felt her blood mount between his hands, the tension building in her jugulars. He must let her die, or he must let her go. Should he grant her her will, or deny her? Which choice invited least evil? Wild-eyed, he witnessed the contortion of her torso as she suffered. Then she gave a sudden huff, nearly stifled, as she reached her sexual crest.

He let go, recoiling. She slumped to the bed. As her lungs heaved for air, she smiled. One of her hands dug in her vulva, one trolled the bed for his thigh. She found him, and another spasm of gratification rippled through her. Afterward she lay there, splayed before him, exhausted.

Shocked, Cecco remained where he knelt, staring. Slowly, he put her arm away from him. A sense of violation invaded him, as if some demon had possessed him. In his native tongue, he whispered words from his ancestors, ancient charms of expulsion. Then he turned his head and spat on the floor. He sketched his gypsy banishing gesture, down from his forehead and across his chest.

Rolling off the mattress, he stood by the bed. He gathered her body in his arms, holding it out from his skin, and, gently, he laid her down on the settee. He drew the comforter off his bedstead, and covered her.

Three times, he washed himself. And then he lit the lamp, and carried it to her side. For long, he stood gazing. He imprinted her image on his brain. Her youthful face, her eyes of gray, her brown hair, the fullness of her lips. Her lies.

He memorized this woman, who, in truth, was not his wife, and whom he could never, ever mistake for his Jill anymore.

Pity crept its way into his heart. She was a lost girl. As her captain, it was his duty to look after her.

He would find a way to aid her.

As he lay down to sleep at last, the realization dawned. What madness had captured him? His own folly confounded him, long before the girl did. He should have identified, instantly, the act that transpired on the beach.

Cecco's Jill never lied to him. Given the right frame of mind, a trusting mind, any falsehood she attempted to tell, he'd see through. Tonight, Jill had told him a tale. It was simply that, and only that: a story. She made it up, because she loved him. It was a tender duty that she'd paid. A sacrifice a faithful wife would make.

She saved his life.

Giovanni Cecco vowed, that instant, that from this moment he would hear her, truly. He would listen to her heart. He'd be receptive to her sound. Her clear, calm voice, that siren song, would guide him.

Cecco understood, now, the deepest wish of Jill's heart. Empowered with her love, he held the strength to grant it.

Hook's phantom hand burned, though he'd felt no discomfort for months. None at all since Jill joined him. Now his wrist flamed with pain, red-hot, as if freshly severed. He winced, teetering on the verge of his vilest memory.

Or was it the worst? This disjointing from Jill surely rivaled his maiming. He sloshed a shot of rum in his cup, and slammed down the bottle. The table trembled, and her necklace shivered where he'd thrown it. He yanked his gaze from her cast-off, ranging his regard over the tent instead.

Its comforts disgusted him. His thoughts were hard, his surroundings too yielding. The lone piece he appreciated was the brittle crystal of the vial, and the sharp shards of gold it contained. It still glowed from his summoning. Jewel would be on the wing by now, flashing through the forest.

Unlike his woman, his fairy held no options. However Jewel adored him, however willing to submit, she was bound to obedience. He had tamed the woodland creature. The woman he'd created, Red-Handed Jill, by definition would not be domesticated. No doubt at least one of her husbands agreed. Grimacing, he seized his arm as the old wound flared beneath the cover of his hook.

He halted his pacing by the looking-glass. In her untamed nature, Jill mirrored her maker. He snarled at his reflection, and dashed the scarf from his head. Impatient for the fairy's arrival, he set off again, prowling his pavilion. The silk scarf tore beneath his boots. He kicked it aside, then scooped up the drink and drained it.

Fire in his throat; fire in his mind. *Every grain of the glass is precious*, she'd said. More precious than he had believed— few enough to last only an hour. How many grains would spill before he slaked this conflagration?

If he hadn't seen Jill departing with his own two eyes, he'd never credit it. Not the fact that she'd deserted him, nor that she'd gone without forewarning. Be it impulse or no, this trickery wasn't her tactic. For Jill, candor was the weapon. Perhaps, just this once, she dared not employ it. Not against Hook, who read the very etching on her heart.

Throughout her parley with Cecco, the tone of her emotion rolled through him. Passion, compassion. He'd felt jealousy prick her heart, and even the pinch of sacrifice. And, following all, she radiated an ambiance Hook never before felt surround Jill: falsehood.

He had miscalculated. This evening, thanks to him, she'd learned a new tactic. He closed his mind to her tonight, one lone, only time. He'd freed her from his influence, allowing her full liberty of choice. She had always been a quick study. To all appearances, she'd mastered that practice, first try. At the end of the hour of parley, as the couple came to accord, Jill barred Hook from her thinking completely.

He could only hope this silence would continue. If he had to live without her, he'd rather live without the torture of her joy.

"Commodore, Sir," Tom Tootles interrupted, throwing open the tent flap. "Jewel has come."

"Enter, both of you."

The fairy flew in, and a haze of peacock blue cooled the hues of the interior. She looped through his tent, and he held out his hand to her. Fluttering above it, she tossed kisses from her fingertips. Then she settled, and the agitation of her wings blew a breeze to sooth his flesh.

"My Jewel. How fleetly you attend."

His words were pleasing, but she saw, with sorrow, that he did not smile at her, not even his half-smile. His eyes appeared steely, and, lit with Jewel's aura, more intense than before. His long black curls tumbled from his crown, like a lion's mane.

Jewel knew her man. Something dreadful had happened. Reassured to know that Peter, safely slumbering, could not be the cause of her master's disturbance, she uttered her concern in a little, lilting resonance.

"I'll spare no words for pleasantries," he said. "The facts are ugly."

Jewel leaned closer, grasping his thumb.

"My lady has jumped ship. Captain Cecco is the victor." A cadaverous cast whitened Hook's visage. Above everything, he valued Jill. Above anything less, he prized victory.

Jewel's face crumpled in sympathy. Her heart ached with emotion. It was too small to hold both compassion and love. She chose love, and felt better. She squeezed his thumb.

"I trust that you obeyed my order regarding the Indian?"

Growing solemn, Jewel nodded.

"The time has come to make use of it. You will guide Mr. Tootles to the village."

Wondering if he was to be punished for his mother's transgression, Tom sucked in his breath. This new Hook, or rather, this *old* Hook, made him wary.

Yet Tom was not the man on whom Hook intended vengeance. "My errand is urgent; you will fly there, without delay."

Jewel rose up, flickering, to hover over his palm.

Hook clasped a lock of his hair and, with a flash of his claw, slashed it off. He thrust the curl toward the fairy, who accepted it, cherishing it at her bosom.

"Bestow my token on the widow. She will know from whom you come."

Tom's eyes bulged. "Sir, you can't mean—"

"Captain Cecco's Island beauty." Hook's lip twisted, his voice intimate with irony. "Raven."

Tom worried the scar at his temple. He cleared his throat. "Commodore, may I fetch Lily for you, mayhap? Or Lelaneh?"

"No." Hook turned grim again. "Raven tended me once; I was wet and shivering. Tonight, she must put out a fire."

Jewel zipped to Tom's elbow and prodded him. He stood rooted to the rug. "But..." Against the force of Hook's will, he found no words. And from now, Tom reflected with dismay, Jill wouldn't be here to gentle the beast.

"Mr. Tootles, inform the captain's paramour that you will escort her home at dawn."

"But, will she come with us?"

"You will *make* her come. To me."

"Sir, your legend— your reputation—" Tom hesitated. "All your men respect that. We boast about you."

The commodore towered, daring him to continue.

The youth held his position, like a man raised by Jill. "You've never forced a woman."

Tom couldn't believe his ears, next, but he did believe his eyes.

Hook lowered his chin, riveting Tom with his stare. He cocked his hook at his side, threatening, and the flame of the lantern arced across the claw's curve. Through clenched teeth, Hook commanded, "Bring her to me. I don't care how."

Jacquot wended his way down the staircase, guided by his toes. In his hands he balanced a tray laden with remains of the feast. The roast sent its aroma ahead, the wooden stairs squawked, and by the time Jacquot arrived at the bottom, Pierre-Jean was leaning against the bars of the brig, salivating, his china blue eyes alight.

"Bonsoir, mon ami," Jacquot hailed him. "Chef takes pity on you. Enough that you miss the party, he says. He wishes that you indulge your empty belly." He set the tray on the deck. "I have not the keys. Chef did not dare ask permission."

"He is kind, and so are you, Jacquot. But Chef holds the good will of everyone. Why does he fear to ask the captain a favor?"

"I will have the pleasure of telling you all about it. Here, I recommend the roast boar. I cranked the spit myself. See," Jacquot flexed his arms, "the muscles I made! The Women of the Clearing approve me."

"Good for you. And I am glad that you stay. It is not only my belly that is lonely. I've had no company but the cat." Eagerly, Pierre-Jean knelt on the straw and reached through the bars. *"Excusez-moi,"* while I dine before puss comes demanding. She declined my bread and water."

Jacquot settled his bony bottom on the floor. "These pirates... eh, I mean to say, *our* pirates, *hein?* They throw a good *fête.* Food, music, girls. We danced, we drank."

"The ship was quiet. Did everyone attend?"

"Tout le monde."

Through a savory mouthful, Pierre-Jean gabbled the question he'd been wondering all evening. "Mr. Yulunga and little Mrs., too?"

"Mrs. Hanover, *non.* She was condemned to the children, in the Clearing. Mr. Yulunga's command."

"Oh," Pierre-Jean said, trying to sound disappointed. "I pity that she missed the fun." He blushed, grateful for the low light of the brig's lantern. From certain signs she gave, he had been certain Mrs. Hanover would make use of her cleverness, and smuggle herself to his prison. His heart trembled as he imagined what might have happened, had she dared. Despite his captivity, he'd spent the evening in paradise, dreaming of such a tryst. At least she'd had no chance to flirt with other men at the revels. He knew her by now. Behind Yulunga's massive back, she never missed an opportunity to flaunt herself. Just thinking of her wantonness made Pierre-Jean smile.

Suppressing it, he asked, "And did you hear a story from Red-Handed Jill? Was the experience all we've been told?"

"No."

Pierre-Jean gaped, a hunk of boar halfway to his mouth.

"It was *more* than we'd been told." Jacquot grinned, and Pierre-Jean filled his maw. "The most amazing story, though, is not what she said, but what she did."

"Tell me all. I will not interrupt."

Jacquot didn't need to be begged. He narrated the night's adventures in detail, relishing the telling. A calico cat crept up to rub against his arm, her green-eyed stare aimed at the tray. Jacquot restrained her, and when he reached the astonishing conclusion of his tale, he saw with satisfaction that Pierre-Jean had ceased chewing. In triumph, Jacquot declared, "She is here, three decks above our heads, *tête-à-tête* with our captain." He sat back, waiting for Pierre-Jean's awe. But the grin fell from Jacquot's face.

"Jacquot," his listener asked, quietly, "are you certain?"

"*Mais oui!* She was seen in the boat with Captain Cecco, by Commodore Hook himself!"

Pierre-Jean shook his head, and his long, blond braid dragged on his back. "It isn't right."

"Of course it isn't right! This is what makes the amazement. Red-Handed Jill has desolated the commodore. She is ours, the *Red Lady*'s lady, from now!"

"So, Captain Cecco and this woman... They are wrapped in the act of love, at this moment?"

"Two ships' companies are visualizing it."

Pierre-Jean pushed the tray away. His stomach no longer felt well, and the bilgewater smell of the brig beset him. "This cannot be the case. The commodore mistakes." Suspicion gnawed where his hunger used to be.

"*Quoi?*" Jacquot goggled. The cat seized the opportunity to leap on the tray. "What can you know of it— you, who are buried below in this ship?"

"I know women. Two breeds. Red-Handed Jill is one. Mrs. Hanover is another."

"Tell me then. I wish to learn about females."

"The lady is loyal. One can see it; one can feel it."

"And?"

"The other is wicked. Unsatisfied. Perhaps it is no secret to the company; I watch Mrs. Hanover."

"Well, eh…perhaps." Jacquot hid the smirk on his narrow face.

"I know her, I think." Pierre-Jean wiped the grease from his hands on the straw. He pulled the cat through the bars, and, hugging her to his chest, he retired to the bunk by the hull. "Good night, Jacquot. I appreciate your company. Give Chef my thanks, too." He buried his face in the warm feline's fur.

Baffled, Jacquot slowly collected the dishware. "*Bien sûr.*"

"Do one more favor for me, *s'il vous plaît.*"

The ship's timbers groaned, and the lantern swayed on its hook. Pierre-Jean's voice came, hollow, from the shadows.

"Tell Mr. Yulunga, with my apologies, that I suggest he examine the Clearing."

Tom didn't want Indian territory to see him before he spotted it. He ran his finger over the edge of his knife, appreciating Jewel's illumination of the Island. Gliding at her side, he soared over the treetops in the fragrant midnight forest. "This adventure reminds me of our capers with Pan, Jewel." The difference was that Pan, unlike pirates, never went hunting a woman.

Tom himself felt grateful for women. "I'm that glad to have talked things over with Lily. But I'm sorry we troubled Mr. Smee."

The fairy turned up her nose. A believer in strict obedience to her master, she hadn't approved of the delay. But it wasn't just her habit of compliance that motivated Jewel. She had urged Tom to hurry his pow-wow with Lily because she fretted over Hook's misery.

"Don't be angry," Tom encouraged her, "we'll be there in a trice. Hook has no cause to fault you."

Jewel pinched his arm in an affectionate way. They'd been through a lot together, and more work awaited them.

Still, she sighed, and yearned to alleviate her master's grief. Soothing Peter as he dozed this evening was a task, but not an arduous one. Jewel, as Tink, had watched the Wendy accomplish the undertaking a dozen times. The commodore's case was graver.

Hook was no child, sleeping through a bad dream. He walked a waking nightmare. Time, always a trickster here, seemed to reverse itself like an hourglass, casting him back to the days of his curse. Jewel was a believer in the power of Time, and she obeyed it. She acknowledged, though, that the postponement had given her and Tom a chance to refine their strategy. For once, Jewel's job was the easy one.

Tom hurried to keep up with her, glad to feel the night air whooshing over him. As anxious as he was about his brother, and his mother, he hadn't been sure he could fly tonight. But he found relief in ascending the skies over the Neverland; it gave him a chance to sort his thoughts about Jill.

His faith in Jill was too strong to fault her for tonight's upheaval. He'd accepted her decision the first time she'd joined forces with Cecco, yet, at that time, she hadn't simply exchanged one captain for another; on that day, Hook had disappeared. He was most likely dead. But Hook was among his company now, very much alive, more potent and more angry than Tom had ever witnessed him.

Even combatting Pan, who had chopped off his arm, the commodore had never appeared so malevolent. Tom had chosen pirates' ways, had sworn his oath to Hook, and he'd do his duty tonight and always. Until this evening, Jill acted and felt the same. Shuddering, Tom remembered Hook's threat, and he could not fathom Jill's reasons for salting the commodore's wound.

He slowed their journey as an awful notion occurred to him.

"Jewel, why didn't Hook venture out, with us as his escort, to persuade Raven himself?"

The fairy shot him a look of disbelief. She secured the lock of hair she'd belted at her waist, then she folded her arms, folded her wings, and plunged down toward the ground. Buzzing back to Tom's side, she raised her eyebrows in query.

"Aye, I understand. And that's just what I feared." A lump grew in Tom's throat. He swallowed it, appreciating another of the losses Hook was forced to endure, and without Jill's love to succor him. In losing Jill, he'd lost his bliss, and along with it his gift of flight. No wonder Mr. Smee was near frantic about the commodore. Maybe Hook's instinct was correct. Maybe Raven could save him.

Or, maybe, the capture of Raven was just ruthlessness— a ploy to even the score with Cecco. And Jill.

Tom sniffed the smolder of campfires. He and Jewel were mounting the slope toward the Indian plateau. As they dropped to earth, she pointed to an old, knotty oak in the forest that fringed the encampment, and Tom concealed himself behind it. Obviously Hook, with his usual shrewdness, laid his plans days ago, preparing for any eventuality. He'd made Jewel map the topography. She knew which foliage might cloak even the brawniest of Hook's men.

Laying a finger to her lips, Jewel bid her fellow conspirator farewell. She flitted from leaf to leaf, her chiming muted, hiding her glow as best she could as she made her way to the village. At Hook's command, she had followed Raven home from her assignation with Cecco, and marked the way. Scanning the encampment, she found her bearings in the pattern of the dwellings. She identified her target and, looking around one last time, she sped toward White Bear's tepee, to perch upon the interlacing poles at the top. Leaning in, she let her eyes adjust to the dimness. She had to suppress a sneeze as a strand of smoke curled round her nose.

Lit amber by the embers of a cooking fire, two pallets were visible, and a cradleboard hung from a tepee pole. The wrappings hung slack, and the little one cuddled snug between the man and the wife, who were sleeping. All three lay swathed together in a pale, heavy fur. Jewel recognized the other woman as Raven, who lay on her pallet like a shadow, facing the sky. The fairy thought she caught a glitter in Raven's eyes, perhaps Jewel's own light reflecting there. In another moment, she knew it was so, because Raven blinked, started up, and stared skyward through the smoke hole.

Jewel jumped from the pole, and floated lower. She smiled at the woman's astonishment. Human beings were so easily impressed, but Jewel never failed to be flattered by their adulation. She'd have liked to explore the tepee— some interesting pots lay about, and Jewel loved to look into jugs. The furs appeared soft and inviting, too. But her master's orders didn't allow for sightseeing. She hung near Raven's face, looking charming, and gesturing toward the door.

Fairies and Indians rarely communed on the Neverland. The former were too engaged in indulging themselves, and the latter too busy making a living. They shared the fruits of the Fairy Glade's garden, but circumspection prevailed between the two communities.

Raven was, therefore, astonished at this fairy's appearance. Her first impulse was caution. So much had changed in her life of late though, that this turn seemed inevitable— and harmless; fairies were known to be mischievous, but, really...what danger could come of them?

Raven was curious, too. Why had this creature come to call? Raven already broke taboo by befriending a pirate. She hardly need fear the overtures of this tiny thing. A moment later, her scalp tingled as she remembered. The women's talk said one of the Fay had allied with the pirates. Perhaps this sprite was a messenger, from Captain Cecco? No doubt he felt concern for Raven ever since she'd left him waiting on the cliff top. Surely, for his sake, Raven should learn the fairy's errand?

Deliberating, Raven looked toward her brother-in-law. She listened to his steady breath. Then, quietly, she rose from her pallet. She pulled her dress on, smoothed her short hair, and was just about to raise the tepee door when she caught sight of the beaded moccasins. She reconsidered. If White Bear awoke, she'd need a reason for venturing out. Snatching up the basket she used to collect cradle moss, she followed the fairy outdoors.

She paused there, expecting some form of communication. But the creature fluttered away, leaving a trail of twinkles behind her. Reluctant to wander from the dwelling place, Raven beckoned her back. The fairy didn't stop.

Her light dwindled into distance, and night sounds surrounded Raven. She felt alone, then, even while standing near her people. Her arms grew cool, and she chafed them. She judged by the moon that one day was ended, and another new born. Aloneness turned to loneliness. She thought of Cecco feeling the same way, gazing over the ocean from the cliff's edge, awaiting her companionship.

Plucking up her courage, she gripped her basket tight, holding it before her like a shield. She stepped carefully in the gloam of the forest. Feeling the way with her feet, she embarked on the path that left the village to unravel the distance to the end of the plateau. A tinkle of bells sounded, and Raven hastened her steps. Now that she'd started, she felt eager to go on.

Beholding an ethereal gleam up ahead, she hurried past the last of the trees. At the top of the slope, she halted. Jewel hovered like a vision, and Raven spoke to her, gently. "Little One. What secret have you to tell me?"

Jewel dropped a resonating note, and held out her hands. In them, she offered Hook's token.

Slowly, in order not to startle the creature, Raven slid her basket onto her arm and reached for the offering. Immediately, the smooth, silky feel of his curls brought the memory.

She rubbed the long lock between her fingers and envisioned him, his sea-blue eyes lingering over her body, his smile insinuating. On her jaw she felt the brush of his only hand where he'd touched her. And his voice spoke to her, soft as cradle moss, as he had spoken in front of White Bear and all of the People...*May we meet again.*

As her whole being chilled, Raven knew, without doubt, that she *would* meet Hook. Tonight.

When a hand covered her mouth and an arm seized her waist, she didn't drop the lock, and she didn't try to struggle.

She knew, now, what danger could come of a fairy.

Silent Huntress

Jill's mind hovered in twilight, between darkness and discernment. Some grace allowed her a gradual revival, so that by the time she opened her eyes, she had gathered enough of her senses to meet an ordeal.

At first, she believed herself captive in a cavern of the Underworld. A few feet above her, a dappled green glow bridged her vision. The air felt dry, but cool. She shut her eyes again, to gain time to absorb her surroundings.

With a stab of alarm, she wondered if she lay in the old croc's grotto, the Tomb of the Lost Boys. Gratefully, she rejected that idea; the surface beneath her back was padded and warm. It smelt and felt like fur, and the loamy odor of the place was not putrid, but pleasant. The combination of scents reminded her of the hideout under the ground. Unlike the hideout, though, no rush of spirits animated the air, and no sound of children predominated. Rather, the place felt close and constricted, and silence loomed like death— until gravel crunched, and a man grunted.

Suddenly, the juxtaposition of place to sound connected, and in a flash she formed a picture of her situation. She jumped up to rush to the entryway, throwing herself against the rock that blocked it. "No!" she cried. Disregarding the man with whom she knelt, shoulder to shoulder, she flattened her hands on the cold, stony surface, straining to force it outward.

Neither her plea nor her exertion yielded effect. The man glanced her way, but continued his labor, unhurried. She watched in horror as he worked at his task, and the scant slice of night around the boulder grew slimmer.

Steadily, he pulled on two ends of a thick, woven rope. The sinews stretched along his bare arms, his shoulder muscles bunched, and he dragged the boulder backward. When the entrance was sealed to allow only enough space for air to flow, he let the rope sag, and yanked one end to slide it inside his lair. He dropped it by the door. Dusting his hands, he said, "Welcome, little bird."

He rose to a crouch, and she recoiled from him. But he didn't touch her, yet. He moved a few feet deeper into the cavern, where he found headroom to stand. The moss that lined the cave seemed perpetually illuminated, casting a soft, otherworldly glow. It lent his skin an olive tint. As he attained his full height, so tall in proportion to his surroundings, and those surroundings so primitive, Jill got the sensation that he was a Titan from mythic times, born of Mother Earth. But this scene was no fable of another age; Jill recognized the Indian.

"I've seen you before." She whispered, but the closeness of the cave made even her breathing audible. The stone walls echoed with a sibilance that swirled around the two inhabitants, as if binding them together.

"I hoped you would remember."

His voice held a mocking quality. Still, in spite of the circumstances, Jill's intuition told her that he spoke from his core. She read his eager stance. His eyes were deep black, but hopeful under the leather band at his forehead. Half naked and unashamed, he came from a different world, yet something about this warrior reminded her of Johann Hanover.

The comparison made her shiver. Here before her stood a clever adversary. Like the surgeon, he was a foe made more dangerous by a fact that should have protected her: some how, some way, she had engaged his vanity. She must be wary, with this one.

She remained kneeling by the entrance, beneath the limited protection of the roof's rocky overhang. "Now I understand why you let me escape, that day I came too near the village."

"You did not escape." He grinned, wolf-like. "I have caged you, yellow bird." Again, the words bounced around her, as if weaving the cage as he spoke of it.

"You've seen me fly, then. I have seen you hunt."

"Yes, I have seen you. You are the queen from the sea. I am Lean Wolf...the Silent Hunter."

Viewing him on this second occasion, she recognized his hungry expression. And, certainly, she had not heard him stalk her. "You are aptly named."

"As are you, Red-Handed Jill." He gestured toward her scarlet palm.

Jill felt a need to keep her marked hand private, and she pressed it to her throat. Only then did she notice her loss. "My necklace—where is it?"

"It lies on the beach. Your lover, the Black Chief, will find it."

Jill turned quickly away, to hide her distress. Hook must be wild to find her.

She was staggered by the few words Lean Wolf had spoken. Clearly, the man had been watching her. No doubt he'd heard every word of her parley with Cecco tonight, but it was obvious that he'd been spying far longer, doubtless since the day of Hook's capture. What he knew about her frightened her, not because of all he knew, but because of all she *didn't* know, about him.

And then she remembered one thing she did know. She spun around, searching for the single item she'd missed in her first impression. She found Nibs' orange kerchief. Smeared with blood, it hung at the Indian's waistband, dangling over the bare flesh of his hip. Exactly where a scalp might dangle, she realized, with revulsion.

"What have you done to my son?"

"For your sake, I spared him. I cut down only the Frenchman." His smile turned bitter. "Red Fawn will not miss one of her many patrons."

Jill sighed with relief, and, next second, bowed her head in sorrow. Her suspicions were verified: this brave was Red Fawn's former husband, and a man to dread. But she hadn't the luxury to mourn or to fear right now. She must act.

First, to identify his weapons.

She eyed Lean Wolf as he picked up flint and stone, struck a spark, and blew on a pitch-covered pine knot. It flared to life like a candle, and he wedged it in a crack of the cave wall. As its resinous scent pervaded the cavern, its light bloomed, and Jill seized her opportunity to examine her surroundings. Her prison was small, but not cramped. Her embroidered yellow scarf lay limp on the ground. She spotted no arms of any kind, and no exit, just victuals and utensils, the man, and his bed of furs. Nothing she might use against him. Her only tools were her wits.

He said, sneering, "I see you thinking. The storyteller, searching for means to persuade me. But let us make better use of our time." Lean Wolf hunkered down on his haunches, to place himself at her level as she knelt, and leaned toward her. "I will tell you the truth that you love so well. The answer is 'No.' " He shook his head. "I will not hear your words. I will not set you free."

"Then I must free myself." Jill turned toward the stone, renewing her efforts to roll it from the door. The night air that seeped in was tantalizing, the outdoors within reach, but inaccessible. The draft amplified the ghastly feel of confinement. She knew this attempt to budge the rock was futile, but, as her captor advised, she needed to make use of her time. Thinking was her time's most advantageous application, and she'd think better with her back to him.

The lack of weaponry hardly mattered. Resistance was an option, certainly, but at a terrible price; if she injured her abductor, she'd still be trapped in his cage. If she killed him, likewise. He'd played a most intelligent trick, pitting his strength against her. He'd made it plain, also, that her weapon of choice— her wordplay— could not liberate her. Still, her mind was free. She must not allow him to imprison that, too.

She ceased her labors and smoothed her tunic. Not deigning to look his way, she held her head erect, and asked in her clearest voice, like a command, "What do you require of me?" Her heart careened. Only one answer could follow.

Lean Wolf felt swollen with victory. All his plans, all his preparation, had borne bounty. Here, in his dominion, perched his little yellow bird. Now to tame her. Now, to make her sing.

"Do not fear. What I require of you, I will return to you in full."

At his answer, Jill flung herself upon the rock again. Resisting the urge to panic, she poured all her energy to applying pressure. Her hands scraped, her knees dug into the ground, burning against the shale as she pushed. She would not yield without a fight.

He watched the contortion of her comely body, and the bright hair tumbling from its pins. He listened to her gasps as she shoved with all her strength. Her reaction didn't disappoint him; he admired her enterprise. There was plenty of time to persuade her, and even if he didn't guide her to his way of thinking, the only one who would suffer was she. When the woman ceased her struggle, panting from exertion and her crimson hand sliding down the rock, he could almost hear her thinking that exact same thought. He voiced it for her.

"Shall you choose pleasure, or do you choose pain?"

Three times, she had tested the doorway. Now she appeared to surrender. Keeping her back to him, she exhaled, and dropped her hands to her lap. Her shoulders slumped in defeat. Lean Wolf waited, wondering if he'd assessed her correctly. Moments elapsed before he was certain. She raised her head again, and straightened her back. She flung her hair from her face. As Lean Wolf's hopes ignited, he watched the pirate queen he'd seen on the beach, resuming her role. A few heartbeats passed, and then she turned to him.

He expected protestations. But when she confronted him, his spirit leapt up. Jill was almost smiling. Her curls cascaded over her shoulder, and the jewels on her tunic glimmered in the light, conjuring the scales of the mermaid who'd escaped him. He licked his lips, and his lust for this golden-haired girl surged through the branches of his body.

She said, "I am a woman, and I cannot budge this rock. But not many men could roll it, as you have done."

He held his hands out at his sides. "I am known for the strength of my arms." He crooked his fingers, beckoning. "Come, see for yourself." As she studied him, her blue eyes kindled with admiration, and he grinned, gratified. She moved closer, settling on her hip at arm's length. He got a whiff of her scent again, like nothing in nature, European perfume mixed to confuse men's minds…and to stimulate their other senses. He felt its effect at his loins. With an effort, he made himself lower his arms. It wouldn't be long, though, before he learned how much force he'd need to apply with them.

Jill made a show of assessing his physique. "I have never witnessed such strength." Her gaze roamed slowly over his body, delaying his next move. She saw a striking man, narrow-waisted, broad-shouldered, with fine black hair that hung long, sweeping the meat of his chest. He exhibited the same look of hunger he'd worn the first time she'd seen him, when they locked eyes as she lay near the river, drenched and exhausted. Although she'd been unaware of the fact, he had snared her in his net at that moment.

And his net was cinched tight. Jill might never be found, and if she died by Lean Wolf's hand here, who would know? Even Jill could not guess where on the Island he'd hidden her. The chance that Hook would find her was remote. She knew better than to believe this predator left a trail to follow. Hook must wait for daylight to find the slightest clue, and, by then, her fate would be sealed. Like this tomb.

She had to control her trembling, next, as she caught the odor of blood on this murderer's skin. Her belly lurched. To master her emotions was imperative. She must call upon the instincts of her totem, the tigress, to lend her power. Coldheartedly, she dismissed the death of Flambard. For the time being, the transgressions Lean Wolf committed must not signify. Nor could Jill's sensibilities.

She discarded her pride, her dignity, her loyalty. Like Jill herself, they were hostage to her captor's desires. Relinquishing all other thoughts, Jill focused on Lean Wolf's physical attributes. She knew, now, that until he used his brawn to roll the boulder from the door, nothing else mattered.

Her task was clear to her. She must concede to this man what he craved. And her chore reached beyond his simple wants; she must be generous. She must keep him greedy for more— so that he would preserve her, alive.

Little could be gained by procrastination. "Silent Hunter." Her voice mellowed within this womb of a cavern. Slowly, she rose from the rock and moved toward him. She had identified his weapon. She must direct it against him.

Allowing her shoulder to buff his flesh, she walked past the man. When her feet met the shag of the furs, she stopped, waiting for him to follow. She didn't wait long. The hairs at her neck prickled as she felt his presence loom behind her.

He laid his hands on her shoulders. As he did so, he detected only the lightest tremor under her skin. "Have I tamed you so quickly, Jill Red-Hand? Shall we not wrestle a while?"

Over her shoulder she answered, "Such a contest could last only seconds." Biting her lip, she slid from his grip and lowered herself to the pallet. Still, she could not face him. She took a deep breath to steel herself. Remembering that truth always served her best, she put it to use, confessing, "Your strength has confined me, but it is your cleverness that arrests me."

Lean Wolf followed her down, to sprawl next to her on the furs. Grabbing a jug, he offered her a drink of water, and she noted the marriage bracelet on his wrist. Jill was startled to see that he still wore this token from Red Fawn. She accepted the vessel, amazed at the man's composure. It reminded her to cling to her own equanimity. She drank, grateful for the restoring effect of fresh Island water, and returned the jug. Leaning on her elbow, she lay facing him. The water drops rolled down his chest as he satisfied his thirst.

She reached out a finger, and captured one. She touched it to her tongue.

By the shifting of his hips, she knew he'd been instantly aroused. It was her turn to feel gratified, and she smiled. Pressing her advantage of surprise, she slid the vessel from his hands, brushing her breast on his arm in the process, and she set the jug aside. Circling her fingers in the fur on which she lay, she said, "Powerful, and intelligent. Fine looking, too. Truthfully, Lean Wolf, you are the kind of man I admire."

"I knew I would please you. Now let us please one another." He anticipated the delights of her body between his thighs, the gloss of her sun-colored hair beneath his fingers. Now that she was moved to show him her smile, Lean Wolf felt the power of its allure. Drawn closer, he abandoned his languid posture and sat up to lean over her.

Lightly, Jill touched his hair. She began to stroke it, as if trying the texture. The tender feel of this fondling surprised him. He turned his head a little, and next she appraised his cheekbone with her fingertips— the white fingers, not the blood-red ones— and somehow he felt her choice of hands to be significant.

He was seized with a need for the touch of her painted hand. Much ruddier than his skin, it matched the color of the blood that flowed in a stag's veins. The stain on her hand held a story, and its mystery excited him.

He gestured toward it. "Is this paint made of your own blood? An enemy's?"

Her smile turned sly. "You forbade me to answer. No storytelling, you said."

For once, Lean Wolf enjoyed a female's denial. Her daring intrigued him, and his fascination increased. Perhaps magic was at work upon him. When he made her touch him with that hand, might it bewitch him? Would she leave her mark on him, too? As he wondered, captivated now, she laid her white fingers along his jaw. They were supple, they were warm, and the gesture was welcome enough. But how much more would he appreciate her hand of color when soon he demanded it? Jill surprised him again, bending down to remove his moccasins.

He humored her. He was ready to couple with her, but time was of no importance. She couldn't get away, and he had ensured that no weapon was available to her. As he learned of her skill with arms, he had listened also to talk about her fierce fidelity to her lovers— *all* her lovers. Beside her sensuality, it was her contradiction that intrigued him. How exhilarating, to mate with a woman who loved passionately, yet who did not insist that a man be faithful— nor pretend even to be faithful to *him*. He had heard the gossip among the women; rather than berating her husband, the second captain, it was said that the lady pirate encouraged him in his dalliance with Lily.

But even allowing for her reputation, the woman from the sea was behaving in a manner beyond Lean Wolf's expectations. Her conduct was commanding, yet submissive. From the start, she imposed the tension of opposites. She seemed to be two women at once, exhibiting a spirit that promised him battle, yet kneeling on his blankets, almost docile, to serve him. She must have learned to curb her impulses in order to secure her position on that ship. The men she loved were powerful chiefs. At their hands, no doubt, she found it wise to yield, and to do so with that grace so tempting in a woman. He had not believed this grace would extend to her abductor. One thing, though, he expected absolutely. She would not fail to pleasure him.

Maintaining her composure, Jill placed the moccasins on the ground. From Lean Wolf's waistband, she pulled Nibs' orange kerchief. She untied its knot, then extended her hand— the pale one. Willingly, he grasped it. She urged him to kneel, facing her, their knees cushioned on the furs. She laid her ruby hand over his heart, exploring, then caressing, and, soon, sampling the electricity of his excitement. As he moved to grip her, she evaded him, leaning back to position his hands together, prayer-like. Loosely, she wrapped the kerchief around his wrists, and tied it up again.

Becoming impatient, Lean Wolf smirked. "You have witnessed my might. I can tear this tie in two."

"I hope you will not wish to," she cajoled him. Palms together, she slid her hands between his own. Lean Wolf cocked his head, amused. Jill looked deep in his eyes, blacker still within the cave, with flecks of green reflected from the phosphorescent rock.

"Lean Wolf. What name will you give me?"

He squinted, regarding her. As rumor foretold, she was a bold one. Although suspicious of her motive, he saw no harm in this request. He used the time to savor the sensation of her blood-warm hands in his. He noted the scarlet scar along her throat, surprisingly like a knife wound. Taking advantage of this opportunity, he moved his gaze lower to ogle her peaks and curves through the linen of her tunic, recalling her nakedness at the waterfall. After some moments' enjoyment, however, he contemplated her question. Her foreign scent regaled him again, and the trace of the sea on her clothing. When he answered, it was his heart that spoke for him.

"I see depths within, and life within the depths. You are…Red Hand from the Sea. It is suitable for the lifeblood on your hand, and true to your sea-blue eyes. This name is fitting for you."

"Then so you may call me."

He shrugged. "It is fitting," he repeated.

Still her gaze dwelt on his eyes and, unafraid, he hid nothing from her. But when her declaration came forth, he was unprepared for it.

"Lean Wolf Silent Hunter. I accept you as my husband."

Lean Wolf drew back. Mistrusting, he asked, "Do you understand what you are doing? This ritual? Or do you just play house?"

"I have played with other men." She shook her head, once. "With the Silent Hunter, I stand in earnest." *Deadly earnest*, she finished, in the only free part of her— in her mind.

His shoulders relaxed. He felt his heart relax, too, opening just a wedge to let this woman in. Perhaps she *did* own the strength to shift a boulder. "Your spirit moves me. I see that you mean what you say."

"You've impressed me, too. You and I now have an understanding: my life rests in your hands, and yours rests in mine."

He tightened his grip, surrounding her soft, steady fingers. "You have courage. I like it."

"I admire daring. You possess all the qualities I demand in a man. I accept you."

Lean Wolf's primal drive snatched at her willingness. His eyes flashed with humor; who would have guessed such a woman would stand on ceremony! Here was his pleasure, on a platter. He had only to speak the phrase. "Red Hand from the Sea. I accept you— as my wife." His conceit told him he'd been clever in his handling of her, but once he'd said the words, he knew that he might mean them. This female was unlike any other. He marveled, "I have never known a woman such as you."

Although tempered by the moss on the walls, Jill Red-Hand's voice, like that of a prophetess, resonated in the depths of their sanctuary. "Lean Wolf Silent Hunter. You have found your match."

The promise in her words, in her look, made his insides feel hollow and hungry. He was compelled to taste her lips, to consume her. Leaning toward one another, the man and the woman joined together and, with a kiss, a marriage was made. The ease with which it was conceived pleased both husband and wife.

Closer the couple inclined, their knees meeting on the furs, their joined hands lowering in favor of their bodies, and soon the bright bond of cloth became superfluous, and fell away. Jill cast her arms about him, Lean Wolf pressed her against his chest, and their kiss redoubled, a taste transformed to a feast. Scarcely believing how effortless this conquest had become, Lean Wolf took her head in his hand and tipped her backward. His arms assumed her weight and he laid her down, far more gently than he had expected, on the cushioned bed of his trysting place. He eased his body downward to lie upon hers, the spear that was his only weapon in this cave pressing through his breechclout, seeking her woman's own trysting place.

Her hands traveled along his waist, unfamiliar with his garb and searching for a way to free him. He helped her, and, soon after, he enjoyed the interest on her face as she appraised the male endowments between his deerskin leggings. His branch was already upright, but her fervor made him stiffen all the more, and he had to employ discipline to prevent himself from ravishing her now.

But, as he discovered, that pleasure was not yet possible. With surprise, he found his delight in this woman's facial reactions so absorbing that he had forgotten the less obvious response under her garments. He must deal with her clothing first. As he was aware from other encounters, a woman's garb was an obstacle to be removed, a secondary fortress, and no matter how easily she succumbed to his initial assault, not always a simple defense to breach.

But now, with a rush of gratification, he found that clothing didn't matter. Again she moved ahead of him. His bride disrobed, quickly and without a hint of embarrassment, slipping from her tunic, then sliding off her leggings. She slithered his own off, as well. And after that, with the vision of her fair femininity glimmering under the phosphor, Lean Wolf applied his store of force to himself, to compel his eyes to make love to her first.

She was like a moon spirit. Pale and serene, she granted her blessings to a petitioner. Her breasts were like moons themselves, but pliant, trembling as he neared her. Her abdomen was just round enough to prove she was a woman, and her shapely thighs, with that curious, curled fleece in between, parted as though to invite him in. But it was her mouth that seduced him first.

Against her pallid skin, those lips appeared red, and she opened them as her hand— her crimson hand, he noted with a hot spasm of shivers— closed upon his branch. The stroke of those painted fingers proved as erotic as he'd imagined. In another moment, Lean Wolf shut his eyes, and he swore he could feel her color as she held him. Scarlet. It was at the same time a burning and a balm. Her redness worked upon his body, shooting bolts of pleasure to prickle in his scalp. He buried his hands in her hair. His knees sank into the blankets; his manhood sank between her lips, red, ruby, rosy. He moaned to feel the plush of her tongue, and then, with a low rumble, he laughed to think the cold, dry moon, upon intimate acquaintance, should prove so hospitable.

And like the moon, Red Hand from the Sea commanded the tides. She indulged her newest husband, brought him to the crest of a wave, and when his breathing ran shallow and promised to stop, she ebbed away, denying him. Sitting up, she drew him nearer. He nuzzled her neck with affection, her cheek with care, as if his honor might be damaged if he failed to inspire in her a similar thrill. He awakened it when he arrived at her breasts, and her rapture at his touches made his chest burgeon with an emotion unfamiliar to him. Lean Wolf prided himself on sating his women, and now Red Hand more than any other, because she was so strange to him. Mysterious as the moon was she, yet he felt her truth in his soul; once grounded on his terrain, she trusted him.

He kissed her again, running his tongue along her teeth, prodding to open them. He played with her tongue, and then he enveloped her right hand, her bloody hand, and he drew it, too, to his mouth. He kissed her ruby palm, licked it, and remembered that it hadn't been idle; it was flavored with the pungency of his flesh. She responded to his sampling, and he surmised that the paint lent her palm sensitivity. Her back arched, her moans roughened. But, after lingering in the feeling, she freed her hand from his grip. Pressing her palm to her bosom, she shaped her breast so that she held it cupped in offering, as in the village mothers did for their babes. As she waited for his advance, Lean Wolf saw that Red Hand longed for it— the mound of her bosom grew firmer, and the tip of her breast peaked. Obliging, he suckled there, drawing from her childless fount no milk, but another kind of sustenance. An acceptance. And, once again, a trust. It had been long since Lean Wolf was trusted. His heart cracked open, just a mite more, pried by a weapon he had not known she held.

And Jill wielded her weapon with skill. Hadn't Hook done the same when caught by an amorous keeper? Like him when ensnared by the surgeon's daughter, Jill chose to work within her chains. Hook could have easily overpowered the girl, but that girl was the key to his shackles. And tonight, although Hook had taught Jill how to kill a man, even a strong man, with a single strike, Jill dared not employ that knowledge. Silent Hunter had her trapped. No exit could open without his wish. The job for Jill's arsenal was obvious.

He had her now, but she had him too. Willingly or no, it was merely a matter of method. To grapple or to capitulate, either choice was soon over, and the identical fate lurked at the end. Had Lean Wolf lined his cave with knives, Jill would scorn to touch even one. The only tool of use in escaping this prison was he himself. She had seduced this mighty man. With her sensuality, Red Hand from the Sea must overpower him— and wait for his readiness to roll away the stone.

And then, when the moment was ripe, Red-Handed Jill would kill him.

The thought was stimulating. She allowed it to work on her, setting her blood afire. In her trials aboard the *Roger*, Jill grew adept in the give and take of power. The exchange of dominance with the commodore, with the captain, with even the surgeon, was challenging, but bracing. Now, engaged in a duel, she must thrust and parry again. Like Hook's, a passion for winning was indispensable— if she was to emerge, not simply alive, but victorious. What little choice she *could* take, she seized. Red-Handed Jill ravished her ravisher.

Behaving like lovers, the couple linked their limbs in one another's, embracing. At last, tossing his head with impatience, Lean Wolf delayed no longer. He pushed Red Hand to her back, stretched out above her and, with his fingers, touched her tender threshold. Finding the moon's tide in his favor, he smiled, sucked its moisture from his fingertips, and with the spear of his manhood, probed again. She pulled on his hips, to force him closer. In slow anticipation, contrary to the predator he was, he slid the only obvious weapon in the cave deep, in her sheath.

Jill drew him toward her womb. With a sense of fate in her fingers, she skimmed the copper of his hide. Hook had once hunted her too, just as ruthlessly, and with the same single-mindedness of intent. Like him, this hunter roused her, in every sense of the word. Even Lean Wolf's scent, the blood imbued in his skin, incited her totem tigress. But— always— Hook allowed his Jill to choose. As this wolf in human form filled her sex with his vigor, Jill's mind filled, too— with vengeance. And although the prowler held her prisoner, had schemed and succeeded in ripping preference from her grip, she savored the intimacy of these moments. Precious moments, that numbered among his last.

With every lunge, he plunged more profoundly into Jill Red-Hand's snare. Every word she pledged to him was true. His life rested in her hands. Her curse was alliance; all her husbands suffered for her love. In binding him thus, she arranged her revenge, and, for Jill, the spur of power yielded passion. He had found his match, indeed. The bloodlust of the huntress, first evoked as she stained her hand, sought satisfaction again. As Hook once suggested, the prospect of death heightened her experience. Here it came again. A kidnap, and a kill.

Her arms glowed in the eerie light of the crypt. His life force throbbed in her womb as, with manly vigor, he exchanged his seed for ecstasy. Lean Wolf groaned and shuddered, and Jill welcomed the pulsing of his muscles. She exacted his essence, drawing him in. With an exultation unknown to the stoic walls of her cage, she reached a heady height, shouting until the sound beat back against her ears, and with the assurance that her captor lay— all the evidence of his pulse, his breath, his heat, his flesh to the contrary— within his grave.

Jill felt vibrant. Absolutely alive.

The tension drained from Lean Wolf's body. As if already lifeless, he lay upon her. But he was far from the door of Dark Hunting. He rolled from her belly so that she felt the fiery fluid of their union oozing, like blood, to the blanket. "Red Hand," he panted, jubilant with self-congratulation. "I must kidnap you again. I think what they say is true. You thrill to life lived in danger."

Curving her lips, she sighed. When her frenzy abated, when she could speak, the hiss of her whisper bounced back from the boulder that sealed her in her cell.

"Lean Wolf Silent Hunter. My third-time husband." She caressed his biceps, so firm, so alive. Like her own blood, the pounding in the great vein of his arm ran rampant beneath her scarlet palm. She shook her head. "It isn't life that does it." She used her smile again.

It is death.

Lean Wolf's potency proved as robust as his reputation. Twice more that night, he provoked his new white wife to give voice to rapture. The strength of his arms was well known among the women of the tribe. A few of the select had witnessed the strength of his staff. None had kept pace with it. He smirked with satisfaction. Even in the young days of their marriage, Red Fawn had not cried out so often, nor so lustily. Red Hand's words were prophetic. He had found his match.

He tracked his fingers along her figure as she lay on his blankets, wrapped in sleep now, her golden head nestled in the crook of his shoulder. Her body smelled of the musk that manifested between a man and a woman when indulging their lust. Her branded hand rested on his man-place, warm and sultry. His hand, the color of copper, settled on her breast.

His mouth remembered suckling there, and the feel of her nipple, hard on the softness of his tongue. Maybe that was how coupling felt for a woman, he reflected. Hard within soft. Such a notion had never occurred to him before. A woman's view of lovemaking— this woman's feeling, as she shared her fervency with a man who was her equal. Stirring again, his branch began to fill, and he felt her fingers awaken. She encircled him with them, her touch of fire igniting to burn once again. The blanket of sleep fell away, and, like the tide, Red Hand from the Sea rose from her slumbers to pay tribute to desire.

Gingerly, as if she carried poison beneath her claws, Jill's fingernails grazed her husband's skin until he tingled. The man felt every sensation she designed for him to feel. That which the hunter promised her, the huntress granted him. Tonight, she left no wound upon his body.

Above the surface of this cave, up beyond the tree limbs, and higher, in the sky, the Furies raced through the heavens while, trapped within the entrails of the earth, Jill's cries burst upon the rock of her prison, to echo, fade, and die.

Just like her new husband, Red-Handed Jill was a predator. She could move noiselessly, when it served her. She was a silent huntress. On the day she chose to slay him, he would never hear her stalking.

Medicine Women

Tom threw open the tent door to reveal a man as wild as any lion. Raven had heard many tales of the Black Chief. None matched the ferocity she encountered as she faced him this night. She drew back, and her resolution faltered.

Tom gave her no chance to reconsider. He ushered Raven inside, relieving her of her basket, and she felt him squeeze her arm in encouragement. She remembered the young man's promise: he swore that his chief never pressed a woman for more than a woman consented to give. But now Raven read two meanings into Tom's assurance. Seeing the pirate chief before her, she could not imagine refusing him *anything*.

This man was more than the commander who waded ashore to her village. He seemed transformed to a spirit of retribution. His appearance was barbaric, even beyond the claw he held poised at his side. His black curls straggled. Around his beard, dark whiskers roughened his face. His shirt hung open at his chest to reveal the strap of brutish leather that bound it. Jewels glared on the fingers of his only hand, and his golden earring trembled at his jawline. When at last Raven looked him in the face, she could not break away from his eyes. His gaze flamed with intensity. The man who remained so cool when attacked by her tribesmen now appeared heated to sizzling pitch.

Tom came to her assistance. "Commodore, Miss Raven agreed to come to you of her own free will." Tom glanced at her frightened face. He didn't blame her; he was fearful himself. "She's not accustomed to parley, Sir, so I'll just let you know that she's set some terms." He cleared his throat. "As your courier, I took it upon myself to suggest that you might honor her wishes."

Hook raised one eyebrow, and looked Raven down and up. His lip twitched as he observed her. "The lady and I will decide that."

Raven had never felt so vulnerable. Men of the People did not stare as freely as these Europeans, and rarely spoke so straightforwardly. Even Lean Wolf understood that he must at least appear to abide by tradition. Raven knew from Tom and from Cecco that these pirates esteemed their women, even their native women, yet she could not accustom herself to their manner of address. It made her proud, but equally, afraid, to be consulted herself in place of the headman of her family. The loss and the gain struck a balance. She was at liberty to choose her own way, but she had only herself to watch over her.

Camp stools stood by, and a chair made of willow boughs. Raven wondered if women of this tradition were denied the comfort of the ground. To her surprise, the commodore accommodated her. With the barb on his arm, he snared a blanket off his camp bed and flung it to the carpet on the bed's farther side. He gestured to it, and Raven followed his lead. She knelt down there, the fringe of her deerskin dress pooling at her knees. Somehow she felt less exposed with the cot and its hangings between her and the door. Hook settled across from her, one knee up, and his elbow resting upon it so that his hook dangled before her. "Mr. Tootles, bring the lady some refreshment." Tom lost no time in leaving on his errand.

Without preamble, Hook asked, "Have you been informed why I sent for you?"

Still shy of this frank approach, Raven hesitated. As she had done when she walked through this enemy camp and saw the buccaneers strewn over the beach, she realized how deeply she had waded into this foreign world. It was Cecco's world, and she missed his caring courtesy. Indirectly, it was Cecco who was responsible for her presence here. How would she fare without him, at the mercy of his commodore?

Raven lowered her eyes, and answered mildly, "I believe you seek revenge."

"Revenge is mine. I won it the moment you entered my tent."

She considered the truth of his claim. Then she nodded.

"What did the boy tell you?"

"Tom says that your woman returned to her husband. That the chief of the pirates finds himself alone—"

"As you see, I am not *alone*." Hook bared his teeth at the word. Inhaling deeply, he rolled his shoulders. "I pledge safe passage home, ahead of the dawn. What else do you require before…acquiescence?"

Once Tom had convinced her that he meant her no harm, Raven thought hard before agreeing to accompany him here. So much lay at stake, and disaster threatened if White Bear discovered this meeting. By now, Raven knew exactly what favor to request. She had known it all along; she simply never dreamed she'd be given the opportunity to bargain for it. She offered, "I will assist you through your time of need, if you will do the same in mine."

"And your need has to do with the warrior White Bear."

Raven looked up, astonished. "Why do you say this?"

"Captain Cecco did not win you. Whether by fear or by affection, your sister's husband rules your heart."

"I am not as brave as your lady pirate, nor so openhanded. I asked Captain Cecco to carry me away from White Bear, to the Other Island."

"And Captain Cecco had the gallantry to promise?"

"He had the gallantry to deny me, unless his commodore bestows his permission."

Hook shut his eyes, wincing as if in pain. After a moment, he recovered himself. "And you will explain your absence from your tribesmen, how? We only just avoided war. I should prefer to enjoy the peace for a while."

"Some of the elders propose to exile Lily's son Rowan and his companion, Lightly. I would question the elders' decision. Then they must exile, me, too."

Hook sneered. "Ah. Civilization demands conformity. 'Twas ever thus." He grunted, shifting his position. He appeared to have difficulty concentrating. "And if White Bear tries to shield you?"

"To side with Outcasts against the ruling of the council is an offense beyond pardon. Once I am gone, White Bear will resent the dishonor, but he will not believe me to be abducted."

"Ironic, since that is exactly what you *are*, my dear." Hook smiled, half-way.

Raven's heart drummed behind her ribs. Again, she was helpless to deny the Black Chief. She sensed she was a toy in a very large game. Unsure how best to respond, she held silence. The candle on the table guttered, giving off a smell of beeswax, and its yellow light flickered over their faces. Raven watched Hook's pulse beating through the vein at his throat. Surely, it ought not to beat so brutally?

"And you believe Captain Cecco still intends to help you, now that his dream has come true?"

She recognized the pride and the pain in the man's question, and countered it with care. "I have no wish to cause you hurt, but I know the captain better than I can know you. I find him a man of his word. When he had cause to wander, when he held small hope of winning his wife from you, he remained faithful to her. I cannot doubt that he will remain faithful to his promise to me." She gazed at Hook, and her black eyes grew earnest, entreating him, "If you could only—"

"Granted."

Raven shrank back, wondering why the conceding of her desire should make her shudder so. She felt that his barbed hand had snagged her, without ever moving. His next words confirmed that she was caught.

"Will you now prove as generous as I?"

She looked away, her fingers flying to rake her shorn hair.

"Think well. How badly do you wish to leave home?"

Through her mind flashed the faces of her sister, of the newborn baby girl. And White Bear. Raven was a danger to them all. "It is difficult to—"

She jumped when Hook growled, "Enter!"

"Sir." Tom came in, bearing a pitcher of water and a plate of fruit. He arranged them on the table, then flung the stale water from the washbasin out the door and filled it again. He replaced the candle in the lantern and, as its light revived, the jewels in the necklace next to it sparkled. Tom's forehead wrinkled as he looked at it, then he stood at attention to ask, "Will you be needing anything else, Commodore?"

"I need to be left in peace. See that the sentries keep alert, but bar them from the vicinity."

The young man touched his forehead. "Aye, aye, Sir. I'll guard your pavilion myself, and I'll be back for Miss Raven before daybreak."

Tom grinned at Raven, nodding his reassurance. When he left, the bright-striped flap tumbled down to enfold her in the tent with the Black Chief. The space itself seemed to dwindle, while the man loomed even larger. Raven now awoke to her situation. She had gained her future. Now she must live through the present.

Pretending she was safe again amongst the villagers on the day Hook intruded, she prepared to follow the instructions White Bear had issued. Her chore was simple: she must tend to the pirate chief's needs. Now that she was secluded with him, with his men at a distance and all who might protect her beyond call, Raven relinquished thoughts of her own distress. Because there was no help for her, she was free to consider Hook himself, and the reason he sent for her. As she studied him, she began to comprehend his difficulty.

"You are in pain." She leaned toward him, and slipped her hand to his forehead, beneath his tangled hair. The heat of his skin surprised her. "And you are fevered." She poured a cup of water and served him. He swallowed some, but she was alarmed as his lips failed to close, and the liquid brimmed over, spilling on his beard and down his throat. His eyelids drooped.

She found a towel and dabbed at the moisture, then dipped it in the wash basin, to cleanse the sweat from his flesh. She smoothed his hair, next, gathering it from his neck, while with her fingers, accustomed to her own sparse locks, she indulged in its luxury. Raven recalled tending her husband, Ash, in this manner, and the comparison startled her. Like this man, Ash had been passionate. She had matched him, once, in an existence that seemed long ago— in her life as it was, before heartache invaded.

Recognizing his vulnerability— his grief for his lost beloved— she ceased to look upon the Black Chief as a legend, and saw him as a man. As she viewed him in this light, her task became manageable, and she clutched at the hope its performance extended to her. Both she and Hook teetered at the brink of painful change.

"I am sorry," she said.

Hook turned to her, his brow dark and furrowed. The voice that oozed so smoothly that first day now sounded muddy. "The captive, apologizing to her captor?"

"No. A woman regretful of her mistake. I see the meaning of your 'parley' now." She knelt beside him, encircling his one hand in hers, noticing how it shook. "In this agreement, we both receive what we need. Not without cost, but without rancor." She blushed. "I understand, and I, too, say to you…Granted."

Relieved, Hook no longer tried to hold his fervor at bay. He locked her hand in his, pulling her to his chest, and he hissed in her ear, urgently, "I am burning."

Through the bristles of his beard, the heat of his cheek blazed against hers. His heartbeats banged against her breast.

"Oh, Sir, what sickness consumes you?"

"My illness is Jill. To your eye I lie alone, but she drags me with her." He gasped, "She will not let me go."

"You are not a weak man, nor do you imagine this malady. Some spirit must drive you."

"I closed my mind to her, but we are linked by magic." His lip jerked again, in a spasm. He seemed powerless to control it. "In my body, I feel her frenzy."

Raven remembered her own body's responses to Cecco. How much more deeply must Jill's passion run, a wife reunited with her husband, after absence, after turmoil? "I will soothe you, Commodore."

But she balked, and he caught her staring at his hook, reluctant to trust it. He pushed her away to sit up, hauled his shirt over his shoulders, and flung it from him. Shaking his hair from his face, he leveled a look at her. She quailed at the sight of his harness.

"You are not too dainty, I hope." He allowed her no time to reply, but seized the clip on the strap, opened it, and shrugged off his brace. "Jill was my right hand. I feel it sear, as if she slashed it off— again." He clutched his wounded wrist, cradling it at his breast. Then he snatched a tattered blue scarf from the floor and wrapped his stump with it, shrouding the scars from her gaze.

Raven moved close to him again, tying the ends of the scarf to hold it in place. It covered half of a tattoo, too, a lovely painting of a mermaid, whose tail swirled round his wrist. When she finished concealing his hurt, she felt able to breathe more freely. She froze, though, when Hook took her chin in his hand.

His grip was strong, but unsteady. With his iris-blue eyes, he studied her face, appraising. "You are a handsome woman." His thumb brushed her lower lip with an intimacy she'd forgotten, and something fluttered in her middle.

His voice lowered, to turn throaty. "I have been wanting you."

He kissed her.

He handled her gently, to start. Raven tasted sweetness on his tongue, a flavor that matched the smell of the bottle by the basin. Soon, she felt his restraint diminishing. With his one hand round her neck, he forced her lips against his, hauling her down to lie atop him on the blanket.

She now realized the power of the control he had exerted. He was fully stimulated, nearly mad with arousal. He must be feeling every nuance of the lovemaking his woman was sharing, this moment, with another. He dispensed with his breeches, then bustled her dress from her body.

Raven felt little discomfiture; this man's attentions were not of a personal nature. He was a flame, and Raven, the fuel he consumed. His was not the passion of begetting, but of letting go, of getting back, of regretting. He laid her down, he rolled to cover her, his full naked weight pressing her into the sand beneath the carpets. Another convulsion overtook him, and, after that, no trace of tenderness remained. He was wild as any lion.

Many tales were told of the Black Chief. Unlike the pirates' lady, Raven was no storyteller. She pressed her ear to his heart, heard it thunder with his lust, and resolved that, once he freed her, her lips would never part to hint at the happenings of this night.

A seagull cried and Nibs the Knife grunted, waking at last to see a purple sky above him. From the snores of the men on the beach, he supposed the night was nearly over. Discovering that he wasn't alone on his blanket, he looked about to see Lelaneh stretched warm against him on one side, and Red Fawn tucked in the curve of his arm on the other. Careful not to disturb them, he patted at his chest and thighs, disappointed to discover that he was fully clothed.

But no, something was missing. He felt the sea breeze ruffle his hair. When he touched his aching head, he felt a strip of bandage, and muttered, "Curse me for a lubber. I've lost it after all."

Lelaneh woke, and hushed him. "Lie still, man. You are hurt. You must rest until daybreak."

At once, Nibs conjured the scene upon the beach. He'd been watching the woods when a burst of stars filled his brain, and now he lay on the other side of the bay, by the dying bonfire. "Is Jill all right? What happened?"

Rising, Lelaneh arranged her long hair over her shoulder, then stirred the fire to awaken the flames. "The Lady Jill is with her husband. Your brother is tending to the commodore."

"Jill, with Cecco? But she refused to—" A dart of pain interrupted. He closed his eyes and clutched his head.

"Be comforted. We all know you did your duty, and no one blames you for Flambard's death. Drink this, now. It is good medicine. You will sleep." Lelaneh steadied his head and held a cup to his lips.

The herbal mix smelled pungent. It was tepid, but strong. Nibs swallowed it. Once her words caught up to his brain, he fastened his focus on Lelaneh. He exclaimed, "Flambard's *death*? How did he die?"

"Do you not remember? You cut his throat, with your knife."

Nibs blinked, then examined his hands. In the firelight, they appeared to be clean. He held them out to Lelaneh. "Did you wash me?"

As she realized the implication, she looked stunned. "No! The only blood on you was at your head."

"Who has my kerchief?"

Lelaneh thought, then shook her head. "No one here. It was not found where you lay."

The crease between Nibs' eyebrows deepened. "And you say Jill isn't here, either?"

They locked gazes, and stared at one another.

"I will fetch Tom," Lelaneh said, but as she padded through the cool, dry sand toward Tom's post nearer the pavilion, Nibs' eyelids sagged to close. To ease his hurt, Lelaneh had used her most potent herbs. Before the taste left his tongue, Nibs faded into stupor.

He dreamt of a seagull's cry. Or had his mother screamed?

Jill rose from the cave entrance to stand in the clear, cool air. Relief revived her spirit. She wasn't disposed to panic in cramped spaces, but after the long night of captivity, she shed her dread like drops of water. Unwilling now to confine even her arms, she dropped her long yellow scarf on the grass. Behind her, the rock scraped, but she declined to watch as Lean Wolf pushed the stone over the hole again. She breathed deeply, to fill her lungs with freedom. One item remained to be managed, then she could walk, run, and fly toward home.

As she turned to Lean Wolf— fierce and formidable, even in the open air— she masked her urgency to escape. Still, a hint of doubt marred his face. It dissolved as she moved to him and circled her hands around his biceps, where she had tied the orange kerchief that bound them as husband and wife. She had folded it thin, wrapped it round his arm, and knotted it firmly. Nibs' blood upon it, she felt, made the vow it sealed all the more binding— and augmented the curse she cast by marrying him.

"Now you wear my marriage bracelet," she said. "We cannot share our lives, but we can share our hearts. I will send a message when we may join them again."

He scoffed, "What messenger can travel between our camps? A bird, perhaps?" He ran his hands through her hair again, as if enjoying its color one last time.

"Yes, a bird: my son, Lightly of the Air. He will do as I command, and with discretion. None of our two peoples will distrust his presence." Jill raised up on tiptoe, and kissed her brave. "When I can come to you, we will meet at this spot, as the sun sets."

"You are certain you can come away from your pirates?"

"I am no man's slave. I proved that to you."

"Truly, you did." He smiled and touched his new armband. "I am the caged one now. And yet we both walk free, until our next meeting." He pulled her close, his embrace revealing his anticipation, and he murmured in her ear, "Red Hand. Do not make me wait too long."

"My timing will be flawless. You must trust me, Husband." She clung to patience one last time, waiting for him to ease his hold. Then she slid from his side, scooped up her scarf, and turned to travel down the gravel path toward the waterfall.

As soon as Lean Wolf rolled the stone from the door, she'd known where she was. The sound of water informed her, and she recognized the line of hollows in the rock along this forest track. How many times had she passed them on the way to the waterfall, never realizing their depths? This place was another mystery her Island held for her, adventures as yet undiscovered. If her plan evolved as conceived, the secret of these caverns would endure another age.

Lean Wolf watched her go, her topaz tunic reflecting the violet of the sky as it filtered through the leaves, preparing for dawn. She did not turn to him again and, if she had, she'd have seen only the stone, the moss, and the path. He left no visible trace of his presence; his impact on Jill pressed far deeper than the prints of his moccasins in the forest.

Soon the rushing of the waterfall drowned the early morning sounds of the woods. The piping of the birds became subdued beneath it, as were the sighs of the breezes. Jill smelled the fresh scent of water, and the sweet aroma of grass as it bent beneath her feet. These messengers were kindly reminders of home, and of liberty.

Anxious as she was to return to Hook, even urgent as she knew his concern must be, Jill stopped at the waterfall. Last night, she defied the role of victim. She was not about to return home looking like one. With a heart full of joy, she flew up to the ledge, threw off her clothing, and dove into the deluge to scrub herself clean. Jill was mother to six sons; a wife three times over; lover to another. But she was no man's slave.

Refreshed, Jill squeezed the water from her hair and donned her tunic. Her flight home required only minutes, and from the air she smelled the brine, and saw the white line of waves rolling up the dusky beach. The figures of Tom and Lelaneh stood close together in the faltering light of the bonfire. Eager to see Hook first and relieve his anxiety, Jill was drawn like a moth toward the light of his pavilion. Her feet touched down on the pile of the carpet, and she smoothed her hair and skirt. Then, unobserved by anyone, she flicked the door up and ducked inside.

The tent glowed in the warm lantern rays. No one was about, nor had the camp bed been disturbed. Of course Hook had not slept this night; he must be out searching for her. Jill spied a half empty bowl of fruit on the table, and a bottle. After her ordeal, she could use a taste of something strong. She hurried toward it, tossing her scarf on the bed. She poured a tot of rum and quaffed it. The liquid sent a pleasant blaze cascading from her tongue to her stomach.

Her necklace lay on the table, as scintillating as she herself felt in her restored state of freedom, and she took it up and fastened it round her throat. As she stroked it, enjoying its beloved contours, a dear, familiar sound rose behind her.

"Madam."

It was the voice for which she had longed all that night. Her head raised up, and her smile grew radiant. She closed her eyes to savor the sound.

"That treasure no longer belongs to you."

Something in Hook's tone wasn't right. Perplexed, Jill turned her ear his way, to hear him better.

"And nor do I."

The smile fell from her face. As she rotated to view him, shock replaced her joy, and she gasped.

Hook reclined on the carpet behind the camp bed, leaning on one elbow. He lay unclothed and unkempt, his eyes hard as sapphires. The peacock blue scarf wrapped his damaged wrist. Sheltered within his arms, his stump intimate with her skin, lay a woman, exotic, striking, and bare. She appeared almost as astonished as Jill. Jill reached behind herself, clutching for the support of the table.

"Hook...?" A piercing pain lanced her heart. "How— what—" she stammered, and then she gave up speaking, and simply stood there, propped up by the table and panting from the blow.

Deliberately, Hook covered Raven with the blanket. He murmured to her, "My apologies," and he took his time, rising leisurely to stand. As he looked down upon Jill, the air between them felt too thick to breathe.

He saw her hair, dark gold with moisture, and curling. Her face was ruddy from love, as he so often viewed it. Unlike every previous occasion, to witness her this way, now, was maddening. She appeared weary, but he sensed the triumph that radiated from her soul. The sight of his necklace emblazoning her throat incited him the more. He clenched his teeth at her audacity, resentful that she should confront him thus, to revel in his pain.

At that moment Tom entered the tent. His eyebrows shot up, and he exclaimed, "Jill! I knew you'd be back." Remembering Raven, he reddened, and dropped his gaze. "I mean to say, excuse me, Commodore. I'm here for Miss Raven."

Hook's eyes never wavered from Jill. Raven had slipped her dress over her nakedness. Taking up the blanket, she draped it over Hook to shield his own. He surprised her, then, covering her hand to retain her touch on his shoulder. He waited until the lady averted her eyes, and only afterward turned from her to take Raven's cheek in his palm.

"Raven. My dear." His manner was steadier, this morning. "Send word when you have need. We'll not risk more difficulty for the Messengers. Best, perhaps, that we speak through Lily." He kissed her full on the lips. He seemed in no haste to be rid of her, and for this dignity Raven was grateful. She kissed him in return, receiving the affection he withheld from his other woman.

"I thank you," Raven replied, "and I will be ready when you sail." She joined Tom by the door and picked up her basket. Looking back, she braved the fire of Jill's gaze.

"Lady," she said, softly, "I did what I could to heal the Black Chief's wounding. It is not *my* medicine that he needs." She raised her hand to Hook, in farewell, and Tom escorted her from the pavilion.

Hook watched her steal away. When she was gone, he turned, stone-faced, to Jill. Still aching and amazed, she searched for words. Yet now that Hook and Jill stood together once more, as of old their need for speech dwindled. While he glared at his brazen Jill, Hook narrowed his eyes as if he found something unexpected.

She heard her voice shake as she began, indignant, "Hook, what on earth—"

But with his broken wrist he commanded silence, waving her words away. He cocked his head, listening to some inaudible signal. Heartbeats passed, and his face began to clear. He strode to Jill and seized her upper arm.

As their bodies touched again, their sense of estrangement lost power. It sank beneath a new sensation, an intuition that prickled with urgency.

"I did not know." Hook's gaze roamed her face, as if conning for damage. "I could not sense it."

The lost emotions came flooding back to fill his features. For Jill too, the circumstances were sliding into place, and she began to comprehend. She stepped backward. "Oh!" Her hurt surged as it mingled with his, to redouble. "Oh, no....Hook, I never betrayed you." She shook her head. "It was Giovanni I crossed. I spurned him, and I sent him away."

"You lost consciousness, did you not?"

"I awakened in a cave...sealed within."

"I lost my sense of you, and I was alone again. And then my eyes deceived me."

"Your *eyes* deceived you? What did you see?"

"I saw Deception herself, dressed like a queen."

Hook took hold of Jill, and pressed her to his breast. She found harbor in his arms. All barriers tumbled down, and their souls flowed together. They imbibed each other's love, like wanderers finding water in a barren land.

At last, with his wrath washed away, Hook exhaled and said, "Thank the Powers. You are alive." He held her secure, in the protection she had missed throughout the night.

"It is no wonder you did not perceive the danger," Jill answered, "I blocked it from even my own mind."

"Had you not acted as you did, he would have slaughtered you."

"So I believe." She shivered, recalling her peril. "And had you not acted as you did…"

"Raven sustained me, but you, my love, triumphed on your own."

"As did you, Hook, in all the long, long time before we found one another."

"To believe in Time is to trust in a cheat. I allowed you an hour…"

"…and an eon has passed." As they gazed their fill of one another, no time ticked at all.

Hook offered his marred arm, and she freed his wrist from the scarf. Gathering up his harness, he thrust his stump in the base of his hook. Together, they settled the straps on his shoulders, then dressed him. With the tip of his claw, he lifted her necklace to watch the colors flow through the opals.

"Always changing," he reflected, "yet ever the same."

With their thoughts now open to one another, she held up her crimson hand to him. He raised his left, and they pressed their palms together, their blood bond renewed. Then he circled her fingers with his, and, bringing them to his lips, he kissed them, one by one. He led her to the willow-bough chair, he set her on his lap and wrapped the blanket about them both. There they settled, united once more and grateful to be so, enlightening one another as to the evening's incidents, while the ocean wind freshened to agitate the tent, and dawn burst upon the beach. With its gaiety and guile, the old night paled away, and the coming day offered its promise.

"Phallusies" and Fantasies

The sounds of the village reached Raven's ears as she hurried through the cool, dewy grass. Dogs begged for bites of breakfast and women carried water from the river, bantering and sloshing their pails. As soon as Raven entered the encampment, White Bear accosted her.

After her night of intimacy, she jumped to feel his touch on her arm. Her movement startled an unruly blue jay from the bushes. It screamed, and White Bear looked up at it with a scowl, the feathers of his scalp lock twisting in the air as if wishing to fly free like the jay.

"The sun has only just rimmed the horizon. Where did you go, so early?"

Thankful that she had thought to bring her basket, she showed it to her brother-in-law. It was full now, with cradle moss. "The little one must keep dry." She disengaged from his grasp, and kept her head low, hoping her face did not reveal what she felt. Raven wasn't sure what that feeling was, and she needed time to herself to identify it. She knew only that it wouldn't squeeze into White Bear's tepee. In this new morning, her life force burgeoned like the jaybird, boisterous and boundless.

White Bear wore a blanket wrapped around him, slung over one arm, and his battle-marked chest expanded as he inhaled the fragrant morning air. When he looked over his shoulder, though, he seemed distrustful. Raven understood why; Lean Wolf Silent

Hunter stretched out by the tepee door, lolling in a patch of sunlight. He bore an orange band on his biceps, and a lazy smile. White Bear's voice rumbled low so that Lean Wolf would not overhear. "Lean Wolf came from the forest, too. I feared for your well-being, but I see that you have not been careless. Now that you have returned, you can serve us our morning meal."

"Yes, White Bear." Raven followed him home, preparing to hurry past Lean Wolf on her way through the tepee door. Lean Wolf looked more than usually pleased with himself this morning, and Raven's instinct warned her to be wary. His hunter's eyes missed nothing when a woman was near, and she knew that her own color was too high to bear his scrutiny.

As she had feared, her disregard of White Bear's law stirred her spirit. Worse, the Black Chief's rugged lovemaking had shaken Raven from the role she had chosen. The Shadow Woman ceased to exist last night. Her entanglement with Hook, like that first kiss from Lean Wolf, ignited the desires Raven used to feel for her husband. But while her urges lay so near the surface, she could not afford to draw the braves' attention. Since Ash's passing and the shearing of her hair, she had not even a natural curtain behind which to hide. She could not chance finding the Silent Hunter on her trail again. She averted her face from Lean Wolf, and, once she'd greeted Willow in the confines of their home, Raven took a pinch of corn meal from the breakfast fixings and rubbed its grit into her cheeks. She wished she might obscure herself completely, but, knowing that she would soon depart forever, she contented herself in obedience to White Bear.

In the five suns since the baby's birth, Raven was granted a reprieve from her brother-in-law's insistence. The nights seemed shorter, broken up as they were by the little one's hunger. The man's hunger had had to wait, but Raven understood that the hour must come when she need yield to him. Glancing at her pallet, she viewed the furs that still lay scattered by her nocturnal leave-taking. She did not yet know whether her intrigue with the Black Chief would cause her to react more favorably to White Bear's lusts. She did not want to find out.

As she worked to prepare the meal, the stimulus of her venture became muted by the soft sides of the dwelling and the trappings of her family. Raven tried to settle into life in the tepee, if only temporarily. She watched her sister tend the bundle of her baby girl; the child burbled and cooed. Raven's heart swelled with sorrow at how little time was left to share her sister's company. To tear herself away would be agonizing. To stay would be worse.

Cloaking her emotion, she vowed to keep close to Willow in the days that remained. She knew not with which of the lady's lovers Cecco's wife might settle, nor what his frame of mind might be, and she could not risk finding out. In any case, she realized with a pulse of pleasure that she could renew their friendship once she sailed with him. At the thought of traveling over the big water in his great wooden ship, Raven's own boldness jolted her, and she nearly dropped a platter. She must stop thinking of pirates. She must stop thinking of braves. She must behave like the Shadow Woman she used to be.

One day, soon, she could think again outside the boundaries of her village, as she had done last night. She could choose her path. One single thing was certain. After her encounters with Lean Wolf, with Cecco, and with the Black Chief, the role of 'wife' was increasingly difficult to refuse. In recent days, Raven had been touched. She had been loved. Alone again now, just as the Shadow Woman had feared would occur, she felt nearly as bereft as on the day that Ash died.

As she served the meal to White Bear and Lean Wolf, Raven's knees trembled. She remembered the bright-striped pavilion and the raw, carnal coupling, and she could not look at these men. Her husband was dead. She was a widow desired by each of them. If she wished to fly free like the jaybird, they must not witness her wings.

Lightly of the Air skimmed under the canopy of the trees, scanning the forest floor for signs of Mrs. Hanover. Early this morning, he discovered that she had abandoned the Wendy House. Under his arm he carried her dress. In his heart he carried concern. It was his job to watch her, and she had lulled him into trust.

He and Rowan found no indication of force, nor had the twins' sentry shrieked warning of intruders. No one knew how long she'd been loose, but everyone who knew her had a notion of the kind of damage she could do, in just one evening. Lightly sighed, and prepared to be castigated.

Approaching Neverbay, he saluted the lookout, who waved back and shouted to the company, "Stand down, mates, it's the Lady's son. The white Indian."

Lily, Lelaneh, and Red Fawn came walking toward Lightly from the beach, accompanied by his brothers, the golden-brown skinned twins. They were laden with blankets and bowls, obviously on their way home to the Clearing. Upon seeing her son's companion, Lily dropped her burden and rushed forward, trailing her flowered shawl. "Are the babies all right?"

"Yes, we had a fine little party. Looks as if you did, too," Lightly observed, although as the other women came closer, he noted that Red Fawn's eyes looked somber and hollow. "Rowan's giving the children breakfast." Lightly twisted the fringe on his vest and confessed, with reluctance, "The only problem is Mrs. Hanover. She ran away in the night."

The women showed relief for the children's safety, yet Lightly was puzzled as they looked suddenly enlightened, nodding at one another with knowing glints in their eyes. Lightly asked, "So you've seen her?" He hoped that their signals meant good news, but, at Lily's answer, his apprehension swelled.

"No, we did not see her. But the commodore did."

Lightly blanched, and Lily took the dress from his hands. "I will return this to Mr. Yulunga, and tell him what has happened. I advise you to keep your distance for a while." She reached up to Lightly's face, soothing him, and pushed his wheat-colored hair from his forehead. "Please tell the children we will be home with them soon."

"I will, Lily. Thank you."

She kissed his cheek and waved him off, watching as he leapt in the air, lightly, like his name.

Lily took the arm of one of the Men of the Clearing, and said, "You three may go back to the children. We will manage here."

As the People of the Clearing separated, the pirates gathered together on the beach. Although somewhat besmirched, their colorful shirts showed bright in the morning sun. Shading their eyes against its glare on the water, they viewed Captain Cecco's boat as his rowers sped him to shore. A sense of tension prevailed among the sailors. They were curious, naturally, but also uneasy, waiting for resolution of last night's brawl between their officers.

Lily spotted Yulunga stretching himself awake. He slapped the sand off his breeches, kicked a sleeping seaman, then, rising to his gigantic height, he looked up to see her. Even Lily was apprehensive at breaking bad tidings to him, but she didn't hesitate. Best to tell him quickly.

She soon found that words were unnecessary. Yulunga took one look at the maroon material in Lily's hands, and his face set in lines. "What has she done?"

Lily gave him the dress, saying, "Dark Prince, I ask you not to deal harshly with Mrs. Hanover. She is young, and her baby needs your protection."

Yulunga tossed the gown across his shoulder. "If anyone but you made that suggestion, Lily—" Medallions jangled behind him.

"And if *I* suggest it?"

"Sir?" Yulunga pivoted to face Captain Cecco. "Good morning."

Dressed in striped satin breeches, his brown boots shining, Cecco was crowned in his gypsy regalia. He gestured his respect to Lily, then excused himself, steering his first officer away from the crowd of men. Eyeing the garment on Yulunga's shoulder, he said, "Mr. Yulunga, I see that you are aware of your mistress' disobedience."

"Everyone but me seems to know of it."

"Do not be alarmed for her. She is on the ship, where I watched over her last night."

"You caught her?"

"She stowed away in my skiff, no doubt to steal time with poor Pierre-Jean."

"I will punish her soundly. But, Sir," Yulunga's wide smile opened up, "you are looking contented this morning. My congratulations on winning your wife back."

Instantly, Cecco seethed. "You mock your captain?"

"No, Sir." Yulunga stepped back. "I do not mock you. Are you not reunited with the lady?"

"I am not. Why should you believe such a story?" Cecco grimaced at his own choice of words.

"Captain, we all thought—"

"The only woman in my quarters last night was yours."

"I see, Sir. I apologize. I was misinformed." Yulunga's mind worked quickly, seeking, first, a means to smooth the offense he'd caused his old friend. "I hope Mrs. Hanover served as good company for you."

"Not in the way that you offered her to me. But her behavior made me mindful of my duty. Mr. Yulunga," Cecco looked candidly into Yulunga's black eyes. "You and I have been mates for many years. I do not presume to change your customs, but, as your captain, and as Mrs. Hanover's, I advise you to be generous with her."

"She disobeyed my command. We don't yet know what disruption she has caused."

"I was told of Flambard's death. It is most unfortunate."

The degree of disruption that Mrs. Hanover had caused was fast becoming clear to Yulunga. "Captain, as we've learned, when bad luck strikes, Mrs. Hanover is usually at the heart of it. The company had troubles last night— more, even, than you are aware."

"Whatever has occurred, I tell you now. Mrs. Hanover has been served her full punishment."

Yulunga squinted, trying to read his captain's meaning.

"Here is my order: feed her need, rather than starving her. Indulge her appetites. Trust me, my friend." Cecco smiled and his white teeth flashed, a sight that Yulunga had not beheld for weeks. "As you have heard me boast often times, I am naturally understanding of females."

"Cecco. What has come over you?"

"What else? 'The love of a good woman.' " He clapped Yulunga's back. "Enjoy your mistress. In doing so, you will keep her from mischief among the men, and you will make yourself happy, too."

Tom joined the two officers, and knuckled his forehead to Cecco. "Captain, Mr. Yulunga. The commodore requests your presence. I'm to fetch Mr. Smee next."

Cecco's earrings swung as he looked benevolently upon Tom. "Mr. Tootles, you look worn."

Rueful, the young bo'sun's mate grinned. "Aye, Sir. Mayhap I'll take watch aboard ship, next time there's a party." Tom's eyes opened wide as he realized the significance of the dress draped over Yulunga's shoulder. "Oh, no." His head snapped toward the boats, and, in his mind's eye, he saw Mrs. Hanover stealing amongst them under the moon, a little stowaway. He felt for the scar at his temple— the old reward for his kindness to her. "So *that's* what we saw…"

Collecting his wits, Tom straightened up and tucked his shirt in his straining trousers. Inwardly, he prepared for a squall. Tom had learned the hard way not to trust Mrs. Hanover. He pitied his brother, who'd had charge of her. No doubt Lightly acquired the same knowledge, today.

"Well, Sir," he cautioned Cecco, "you'd better brace yourself. She's bollixed us again."

"I warn you, Pierre-Jean. You must resist little Mrs. Hanover." Dressed once more in his red and blue uniform, *Monsieur* Guillaume pocketed the keys to the brig. "This ship has no need for champions, only sailors." He handed Pierre-Jean a broom. "Now you will sweep out the straw, and you may go."

"Oui, Monsieur." Pierre-Jean saluted as his officer left him, then he hurried to finish his job. He'd had enough of this dark lower deck and its fusty odors. Its atmosphere pervaded even his sleep, for, last night, he dreamt he was locked in a dungeon. As if of like mind, his confidant, the calico cat, waited for him halfway up the narrow steps, licking her paws. The chaff swirled upward, and she sneezed. When Pierre-Jean finished, he fingered his long blond braid, picking out stray wisps of straw. He chuckled to imagine the gold of his hair had been spun from it, as in a fairy tale.

As the liberated 'champion' trudged up the stairs toward the crew deck, the cat bounded ahead with her tail held high. The air grew sweeter as he climbed, and the scents of Island greenery sharpened his regret about missing the festivities on shore. *Sans* a visit from the 'princess,' his imagination had not lived up to reality, after all.

Monsieur Guillaume was right. Pierre-Jean felt a fool, pinning his hopes on a fickle girl. Such was his nature. He was a romantic; he had a soft spot for women other men didn't appreciate. But he assured himself he was over Mrs. Hanover, or soon would be. Apparently she *was* appreciated, now— by the captain.

Despite de Lerroné's gossip of Red-Handed Jill boarding the *Red Lady*, Pierre-Jean felt certain of the identity of Captain Cecco's late-night lover. His instinct never failed him. And he was savvy enough to know that, whatever amusement Mrs. Hanover might have planned with himself in the brig, an opportunity to be petted by a higher-ranking man was like catnip for the feral little female. In Pierre-Jean's fantasy, she was the witch as well as the princess. A few months ago, she had thrown herself at the commodore. It was no surprise that she'd target Captain Cecco as the next best prize.

Jacquot had brought Pierre-Jean's breakfast, gruel that turned pasty and bland as the galley mate explained that he'd been unable to deliver Pierre-Jean's warning. Mrs. Hanover's whereabouts remained unknown to Mr. Yulunga because before the message arrived, the massive first mate had dozed off. No one dared to wake him, and certainly not for the delivery of bad news.

On his way toward his hammock, Pierre-Jean passed the door to Mr. Yulunga's cabin. It was usually closed, and was so this morning. Always before, if he was alone, Pierre-Jean paused to lay his ear against the rough wood of its panel, listening for Mrs. Hanover's movements. He never heard her speak or sing, of course— she was no Rapunzel— but if the ship was quiet, he might catch the rustle of pages turning, or the snip of her scissors.

This morning he forced himself to ignore her door, telling himself that he was already shifting his interest. When allowed ashore again, he would set his sights on the pretty, dimpled native lady. Jacquot had lamented that Red Fawn was distressed by Flambard's demise. As Pierre-Jean demonstrated with Mrs. Hanover, he had a talent for comforting. It didn't hurt, either, that his hair was so fair and his eyes so blue. A fetching Frenchman like himself was not often seen in these parts. Cheered, he straightened his back and marched proudly past Mrs. Hanover's door.

And then he stopped dead. He heard a sound that didn't belong in a first officer's quarters. Angling his head toward the door, he listened again. He was sure of it now. It was a rhythmic chink of chains.

Pierre-Jean looked at the calico cat, who stared back at him. No one else was about; *Monsieur* Guillaume had returned to the Island, where most of the *Red Lady's* sailors remained, and the watch were posted topside. Curious, Pierre-Jean grasped the door handle, and gently turned it. Pushing it open an inch, he pressed his eye to the crack. Instantly, his fascination for the little Mrs. rekindled.

She had pulled a paisley bolster off the bunk, and was sitting on it, on the floor. Like Cinderella, she was clothed in a tattered shift. Her slender body showed through the sheer frock, casting her delicate pale skin in an even more vulnerable light. Remnants of Captain LeCorbeau's fabrics and furnishings softened the room, muffling the sounds she was making and lending her an air of gentility. To Pierre-Jean's eyes, she appeared the *demoiselle* of his dreams.

He could see the bump of her abdomen, where her baby grew. She wore an unusual expression on her face. Not, he mused, unusual for a woman, but odd for Mrs. Hanover. She appeared content, sitting there, mesmerized by the length of chain she plucked up and dropped, over and again, on the floor. She seemed spellbound by its music. Pierre-Jean blinked, then understood that he wasn't imagining it; the chain was a manacle, and at the end of its measure it trussed Mrs. Hanover's ankle to the bedstead.

The metal fetter seemed cruel in the context of an expectant mother. His Gallic heart ached as he viewed this tragic scene— fair damsel, locked away in her tower. With no thought for the consequences, her champion flung the door wide, and he ran to her.

She startled at first, gasping. When he knelt by her side and took her in his arms, she smiled and melted against his neck. He felt her shoulders lift and fall as she sighed. He felt her contentment, and he didn't know why he, the hero, felt afraid.

He didn't try to make conversation, English or otherwise. As always, he relied upon his hands. His touch roamed her body, and his fingers settled on the firm flesh stretched over her baby. As he leaned down to kiss it, her chain tinkled again, and even though Captain Cecco was across the bay on the sand, Pierre-Jean caught the resonance of his captain's voice.

Be warned, my boy.

Pierre-Jean shuddered, and pulled away from the girl, only to lose himself in her big gray eyes, that beckoned him back.

She will be the death of you.

Impassive to passion, the calico cat sat in the doorway with her tail curled around herself, purring.

The bo'sun's whistle shrilled over Neverbay, one last time. The men of the *Roger* and the men of *Red Lady* congregated before the commodore's pavilion, milling about and craning for a view of their officers. After last night's upsets, no one knew what to expect this morning.

Alf Mason elbowed Noodler to make room, treading on his toes. "Sorry, mate…but get an eyeful of poor Mr. Nibs. Rot my bones if he ain't peaky."

"At least he still be breathing. Od's my life, he got the best of that Frenchy." Noodler rubbed his aching foot on his leg, and waved toward Tom with a backward hand. "His brother did his best to take bo'sun's duty last night, all by his lonesome."

"There's a good sign," Mason said, catching sight of a familiar auburn head emerging from the tent. "Mr. Smee's back in charge."

"Aye, I'm that glad. Look what happened while he were banished. Flambard's gizzard got slit, the lady jumped ship and— Rip my jib, here she be!"

Smee upheld the tent flap and the pirates murmured in surprise as Red-Handed Jill stepped from the interior into the morning sunshine. Commodore Hook and Captain Cecco followed her. The sailors voiced their approval, smiling widely to see Jill at her customary place upon Hook's arm, the usual jewels gleaming at her throat. The lady hadn't deserted them after all. The rumors that stormed the beach last night became so much hot air. Likewise, the hostility the men expected to feel bristling between the captain and the commodore failed to materialize, and although Mr. Smee appeared somewhat haggard in his torn white shirt, he stood tall at Hook's side, his hands clasped behind his waist and his eyes scanning the crowd as always, alert for any laxity in discipline.

Contrary to the company's expectation, Captain Cecco, dressed head to toe in his finest garb, addressed them first. "Good morning to you, men. I begin this bright new day by clearing the air. I wish for you all to hear." He turned to Smee and declared, "My sincere apology, Mr. Smee, for visiting my temper upon you."

Mr. Smee was prepared for this announcement, as demonstrated by his even demeanor. With his face bruised but devoid of emotion, he nodded to Cecco. "Apology accepted, Captain. And I offer mine to you." Relieved, the men cheered the two officers as they clasped their right arms together and emphasized their accord with a shake.

Mason nudged Noodler. "That's our Smee. He was boiling last night, and not a hint of smug about him now."

"And that be our Cecco. A man what knows when to bend." Noodler's gold teeth gleamed as he glanced around to see pleased looks on the others' faces. Both ships' companies relaxed as their officers sealed the peace. Next, Cecco turned to the commodore. With eager expressions, the mariners observed the two powerful men.

Captain Cecco laid his hand on his heart, saying, "Commodore, once again I swear my loyalty. I stand ready to serve as you command." He bowed, and the sunshine glinted off his armbands.

As Cecco straightened, Hook gripped his shoulder. "A welcome gesture, Captain, and I am gratified." The commodore faced the company. "*Jolly Roger; Red Lady.* On this glorious morning," he raised his hook high, in triumph, "we rise united."

The atmosphere filled with the lusty voices of his men, roughened from their night of carousing, but all the more potent for it. Sailors every one, they understood the magic of their brotherhood. The tempests they weathered bound them more forcibly than smoother waters. They clapped and hollered, stamping their feet in the gritty sand. When the lady kissed Cecco's cheek, then Smee's, and then embraced Hook, their whistles rent the air, more strident than the bo'sun's pipe.

Hook dismissed them, and, setting to work with a will, the pirates cleared the beach, loading the boats to row back to their ships. They sang as they worked, their stomachs growling as the smells of breakfast from the ships' galleys wafted their way.

While the men removed the pavilion's furnishings and its silken sides shivered down, Hook and Jill stood apart with Cecco. "We shall rest today, Captain," the commodore said, careful not to let the poison in his voice be overheard. "But make no mistake. Tomorrow, we three have matters to attend."

With two fingers, Cecco touched his forehead in salute. His eyes smoldered as he looked into Jill's. "Aye, Commodore," he answered, his tone low but vibrant. "Against our foe, we rise united."

Jill linked an arm with each of them, Hook on her right, and Cecco at her left. "Gentlemen," she said, her soul set aglow as she soaked up their strength. "To the ship."

"Good news, little girl. I am back to free you." Yulunga drew a ring of keys from his pocket. He shut his cabin door and strode toward his mistress where she reclined on the bolster by the bunk. Her cheeks were tinged with pink and her shift mussed and torn, one strap hanging off her shoulder. He flung the dress she had abandoned onto the bed.

As if to distract him from her misdeeds, she wasn't watching that dress as it cascaded over the pillows. Instead, Mrs. Hanover gazed up at her master, so high above her, his head bent to fit under the ceiling. As always, Yulunga's quarters constricted around his presence. Her heart filled with that mixture on which she throve— friction, and thrill. Realizing he awaited some words, she ventured, "Welcome home, Sir."

He surveyed her lone earring, seeing it quiver. "You seem frightened." He hunkered down to look her full in the face. His deep voice mocked her. "Not to worry. I will give you what you deserve." The keys dropped from his hand to crash on the floor, and with his huge hands he tore the remnants of her shift from her body. The screech of it filled her ears.

She shrank from him, but he took her in his arms, bodily, and ran his lips along her neck, kneading and biting the tender flesh there. Once she relaxed in his hold, he used his fingers to stroke her, and, as she opened to him, to please her. By now, his hands were expert in her inclinations. As the chain juddered with her response, he smiled and silently agreed with Cecco's counsel. Mrs. Hanover craved his generosity, and to accommodate her stoked his pride. Now that he was free to revel in his mistress, his wicked side savored the rebellion she embodied.

Liking to keep her off balance, Yulunga unhooked the one golden loop from his ear. This piece was the match to her own, and a prize she'd long coveted. He threaded it through her empty earlobe, sensing her excitement as he pushed it into place. When he brushed her hair aside to view it, he felt something stiff among the strands. Pulling it free, he held it up.

He raised his eyebrows. "Well, Mrs. Hanover. You have sprouted a stalk of straw."

The sublime look on her face altered, replaced by alarm.

"You cannot have gone to the brig. It looks like the brig came to you."

Her hand crept up to guard her new earring.

He sighed, and shook his head. Then he bit the straw, holding it between his teeth. He nudged her. "Do you like your chains?"

Unsure what response to give, she stared at her master. The earring tugged with a seductive weight. The iron hold of the shackle, warmed with her body heat, kept her primed on the brink of bliss. Finally, she nodded.

"*Say* it."

"Yes. I *like* my chains."

"I thought so." He smiled, picked up the key ring, and tossed it in a drawer. As he divested himself of his breeches, Mrs. Hanover nearly fainted. The straw bobbed as he worked it in his jaws.

She wasn't watching that.

26

Shades of Promise

In the aftermath of the abduction, Jill spent the day in the commodore's quarters, her body enfolded in her lover's arms and
her emotions whirling within. After their early exchange in the
pavilion, she and Hook remained silent on the subject. Communing
in their own unspoken way, each contemplated the situation.
Hook, too, had suffered an ordeal, and Jill returned his care for
her. Still, the need for action roiled beneath the surface, like the
convergence of river and sea.

Together, they watched the reflection of the sun on the waves
as it shivered and slid on the beams above them. As the day
ended and the moon took its place, Hook played to Jill on his
harpsichord, choosing music to delight her— until she insisted he
should express his own feeling, too. With one hand and one hook,
he discharged such a fury of sound on the keys that Smee made
excuse to knock, fearing for the commodore's instrument.

This following morning Hook had ordered the copper bathing
tub to his cabin, filled by buckets of water that came steaming
from the galley. Behind the crimson curtain, in a world all their
own, Hook and Jill luxuriated together, sponging one another with
tender touches, and toweling their dampness dry. Jill was grateful
that although the adversity she'd experienced brought distress,
it might also render consolation. She sorrowed to consider that
Cecco, too, must need relief from the torments of rage, and she
anticipated their meeting later today.

Serenaded by the sounds of the ship, Jill sat alone now at her escritoire. The water on the hull whispered to her, and the wooden planks crooned, adding their atmosphere to her stories. Jill drew the final flourishes on her parchment, then sanded the ink. As always, the facets of the Neverland endowed her works with an abundance of inspiration. She had captured the story of Smaoigh first, titled 'Something from Nothing,' to add to her tales of the sailors. The second narrative was rather more private, but, having penned it, Jill felt a weight lift from her heart. Her art was cathartic.

As she stowed her pen, Hook's footsteps tapped the companionway. He rejoined her, announcing, "My love, we are honored with guests." Rowan and Lightly entered in his wake. Jill sprang from her chair and hurried to embrace the young men.

"How welcome you are, my dears. I've just set down our most recent adventures. Please, sit with us and tell us of yours."

The two Indians greeted her, and Lightly explained, "We got approval from the elders to meet with you here." He slipped a pack off his back, and gestured to it. "They understand I have a duty to my mother, and also to my brother. While we're aboard, we'll have a word with Nibs and Tom. We heard Nibs was wounded."

"Yes, he was still woozy yesterday, but Mr. Smee has pronounced him recovered. He regrets his lost kerchief, though."

The Indians settled cross-legged on the Oriental carpets. Observing her son, Jill noted that, increasingly, Lightly resembled his native hosts. The fair hair beneath his headband only got lighter with his days in the sun, but soon it would be bountiful enough to braid. Long past the smoothness of boyhood, his skin smelled of wind and woods, and looked to be tanning toward russet. Lightly's rangy arms were banded with leather, and bulged with new strength. Like Rowan, Lightly moved with a tranquil grace that served him well in his chosen calling. Jill felt a rush of pride. As with all her sons, she was gratified by his progress.

"What have you brought for me?" Glad for the distraction of company, Jill perched on the sofa, spreading her skirts of amber satin. Hook was, however, more restless; he refused to be seated. With his mind at work upon their difficulties, he chose to pace behind Jill where she sat on the divan. The rich, shimmering velvet of his long tawny coat matched the leonine look in his eye.

As if to gauge his mood, Lightly studied Hook, then he unrolled his pack. "Rowan and I offer our apologies, Ma'am, which we hope you'll accept along with this." As he worked, the orange-yellow pelt of Jill's tigress was revealed in its glory. Lightly hoisted it to place it on her lap. It was warm and heavy over her legs, reminding her of the lion skin that, as a girl in Pan's hideout, she had treasured. Her son and his partner had tanned this pelt to perfection, and the coat glowed in the afternoon light of Neverbay. The fur felt plush and pliant under Jill's fingers.

"How beautiful this fur is," she said. But as she admired the tigress, Jill frowned. "If she hadn't been about to devour David, I'd have never killed her." She raised her blood-red hand, observing it with an air of detachment. "I am told I made peace with her, although from the frenzy that followed my first kill, my memory is clouded."

Lightly grinned. "You underwent the rite you foretold, long ago in the hideout. It's your Story of Red-Handed Jill. I think that one's my favorite. I told it to the children at the Clearing yesterday."

"It is the *end* of that story that I treasure most." Jill sent a loving look to Hook, and her heart fluttered as she remembered. *The Pirate King fell in love with her...*

He bowed to her. "In this respect, Madam, as in most, we are in accord."

Smiling, Jill turned again to her son. "Thank you, Lightly, and Rowan. I shall honor the memory of this noble creature."

"As for our apology," Lightly explained, "we admit that Mrs. Hanover outfoxed us. We underestimated her courage, never thinking she'd run alone into the night, putting herself at risk from beasts like this one."

Hook scoffed. "It seems no beast is too fearsome for that one's taste. The more dangerous, the more desirable she finds it."

"Lightly," Jill said, growing solemn, "although Mrs. Hanover caused confusion, she was not the source of misfortune last night. The true trouble began with someone else. You must hear what occurred."

Hook stopped pacing to watch her, and Lightly's hide prickled with apprehension. Even as a Lost Boy, he had never seen Jill's pirate king look so fierce.

"Keep it secret," Jill commanded the younger men. "I must ask you to serve as my messengers— to another kind of beast. One who lurks within your tribe."

The Indians sat straighter, exchanging wondering glances. Rowan said, "We vow to help Lightly's mother in any way we can. We know you will not ask that we act against our people."

"Quite the contrary. In helping me, you will preserve the People from a threat. He is a secret predator— a *silent hunter*— whom, I am convinced, few of your kinsfolk suspect they should fear."

"Speak, Lady." Rowan Life-Giver crossed his arms, and his chiseled features sharpened. "We hear you."

Moving to stand behind his Jill, Hook felt outrage boil within his breast, like a storm upon the waters he loved so well. He set his hand on her shoulder.

Jill stroked her tigress' coat, and, word by dreadful word, she revealed her misadventure. As her listeners grew graver, the next chapter of her story took shape. With her son's assistance, and her lover's, not only the crafting of this next story, but its enactment, too, could prove cathartic.

The waves pawed the hull with a low, rumbling snarl. Lightly wasn't certain, but he thought that, as Jill spoke, her gaze flashed green, like the eyes of her tigress.

Since the pirates returned to their ships, the Clearing enjoyed its own noises once more. As if in relief, the breeze sighed through the branches. Grasshoppers sawed on the sward, the creek's burble was audible again, and birds chirped as they bounced in the treetops. Blossoms and herbs in the garden scented the air. The grasses basked under the sun, with a fringing of shade, deep green and tempting, that offered a cool canopy for children's play. Peaceful as the place was, still, Lily knew one who suffered here.

She left her redheaded daughter with Lelaneh and her brood, and lingered outdoors for a moment. The twin Men chopped firewood by their workshop, nearly naked and free as the breeze that buffed their hempen hair. First one raised his ax, then the other; together they followed through in two graceful arcs, grunting as their tools struck and thumped, and their logs split to halves as identical as themselves. Lily loved to watch her men work, knowing that they loved their work as well as they loved their women. She blew them a kiss, then, more soberly, walked to the house they had built to shelter their family.

She approached the grand oaken threshold. Above her, in the windows, green gauzy curtains waved her in, then the interior welcomed her— embraced her, really— with rugs woven by her own hands, and the homely feel she and the other women cherished. It emanated from the low arches of the pine beams and from snug, padded alcoves. Ragdolls and whittled boats lined the stairs as Lily mounted them, playthings for the little ones, fashioned by sailors in long months at sea.

"Red Fawn?" she called, softly. Her voice sank into the house, to become another of its comforting qualities.

Red Fawn remained subdued in the time since the party, keeping to herself in her bedroom as if chary to set foot outdoors. Lily approached quietly, her feet meeting the warm, sanded wood of the floors. The planks didn't creak; the Men of the Clearing were expert carpenters and considerate fathers, and they'd worked to craft a house in which children could slumber without disturbance. Lily hesitated now to disturb Red Fawn, but she and Lelaneh agreed; the time had come to tend to the troubles of their spirit-sister.

As Lily entered the room, Red Fawn raised up on her elbows to greet her. She wore a loose doeskin shift. The silver earrings she adored, her gift from the commodore, lay scattered on the bed table. Usually cheerful, her slender face appeared drawn. "I am sorry I worried you." She peered out from under a cloud of black hair.

Lily plucked up a brush and sat on the bed. "Turn your back, and I'll smooth your hair. This way, you can tell your troubles to the house."

A hint of a dimple appeared at the corner of Red Fawn's lips. "Lily, you are ever sensitive to those you love." She sat up straight, so that Lily could work.

"You loved Flambard. Is he the cause of your sorrow?"

"No. And yes."

Lily laughed, but gently. "Which of those answers was for the house, and which for *my* ears?"

"Both are for you. I loved him, and I shall miss him dearly. But...I am also afraid."

"Not afraid of his spirit, surely? Flambard wished only joy to you."

"No, not of Flambard. It is the old fear, Lily." Red Fawn whispered over her shoulder, "It is my former husband."

Lily stopped brushing. "What? Has Lean Wolf entered the Clearing?"

"No."

"But you have seen him?"

"I may not say that I have seen him."

Lily's hands lay idle, now, and the brush rested with them in her lap, pricking her fingers. "I understand," she said. She too felt the fear that made Red Fawn tremble, as unwelcome as a worm in an apple.

"He spied on us, and he learned that I loved Flambard. He knew it, and out of spite he killed him!" Red Fawn spilled her tears, and, at last, she sobbed openly. Lily leaned against her back, and wrapped her arms around her. When Red Fawn calmed again, Lily listened to her woe.

"I never should have left his tepee. Look what I have done! A good man is dead, and Raven lives in danger."

"Hush, my dear. White Bear holds power within the tribe. He will protect Raven."

"No one knows Lean Wolf as I do. No protection is enough. He hunted me down, and he slaughtered Flambard. The more Raven eludes him, the more eager he will be to catch her. And worse, he must do so deceitfully, behind White Bear's back! What he does in front of the People is hurtful, but what he does in *secret*— it's vile." Red Fawn dabbed at her eyes. "Silent Hunter will punish me if I tell. How can we help her, Lily? What will become of her?"

Lily turned Red Fawn to face her, and brushed the hair from her eyes. "Red Fawn. I, like you, may not say what I know. But I will tell you this: the fairy came to visit today."

Red Fawn's puffy eyes widened. "From the Black Chief?"

"Even so. He sent a message. His message came not for you, nor for me, nor for Lelaneh. But it was intended for a woman."

Red Fawn gasped, and hope dawned on her tearstained face. "I knew that he asked about her, and that he admired her. But now the Black Chief, himself, lays claim to *Raven?*"

"I cannot say. But can you think of any man more capable of outwitting Silent Hunter?"

Now the dimples were coaxed to show around Red Fawn's lips. She shook her head. "No. I cannot. How lucky we are, Lily, that He of the Eagle's Claw is our protector."

Lily smiled, too. "And how lucky is he, to call us his relatives. I will warn our Men to watch after you carefully, and we will wait for the fairy to carry more news."

The women hugged one another, and the curtains waved in the window. On the breeze came the sound of the children laughing, and the babbling of the brook, the Men swinging axes to thunk into firewood, and the scent of the garden that sustained the People of the Clearing with its herbs, and its beauty, and its nourishment. Everything the three women cherished.

"Truly, Lily. I am glad, after all, that I left Silent Hunter." Red Fawn reached for her silver hoops, and fixed them to dangle from her ears. "One bad man is no cause to neglect the good ones."

"No, Jill! You propose an impossibility." It was Cecco who paced this time, back and forth before the mahogany desk from which he once ruled the *Roger*. The accoutrements of Hook's resplendent room closed around the three occupants, and the ambiance grew as dense as the tapestry. Even so, Cecco's boots thumped the floor, barely muffled by the rugs.

"I concur. The act you propose is impossible." Hook sat in state behind his desk, dressed in his tawny velvet. Riled by Jill's proposal, he appeared as ferocious as the creature he resembled. He tapped the desktop with his claw. Through his teeth he said, "If we kill a brave outright, we shall have war."

Jill countered, "The only impossibility is that I might forfeit my vengeance." She attempted to settle on the cushions of the window seat, tucking and smoothing the skirts of her gown. But she was too agitated to find real comfort there. The tiger hide stretched out beside her, its color fierce in the sunshine that drove through the bevels on the windows. "The man is a threat to every woman on the Island. First Red Fawn, now myself. If we fail to act, who may be his next victim?"

"I can tell you who," Cecco rejoined. "He pursues Raven."

Both men watched their lady's reaction to Raven's name, but although she drew herself up, her face showed only concern. "I did not know. I am distressed for her."

Cecco continued, "Thus far, her brother-in-law forbids a marriage, but Lean Wolf threatens that he will have her. His insistence is why Raven seeks to flee the Island."

Hook kept his counsel regarding Raven's reasons for flight, and remained firm in his policy. "To fight the entire tribe for the sake of one man's depravity is out of the question. I keep the peace for good reason. Too many of our company would suffer wounding, or death."

"Not to mention the threat to those whom Lightly calls brethren," said Jill. "And let us not endanger our men in my defense. I know how loyal our sailors are, and I have no intention of informing them of my trouble."

Loath to recall those hours of intimacy with Lean Wolf, she cast her gaze down to view the silver rings on her toes. She remembered another time, when, obsessively, she memorized the details of this very room— the intricacies of the carpets, the nap on the curtain, patterns of pits on a cork— in an attempt to crowd out the violence Pan had imposed upon her. When Hook spoke to her, he drew her back to herself, just as he had saved her, that day, from her shock.

"My love, shall you take something to drink?"

"No, I need nothing save your kind attention."

"You have only to command me. But I must remind you that rumors are rampant regarding your whereabouts on the night of the revels."

"Let the men speculate all they wish. The question of whether I took comfort with their captain or their commodore is immaterial, as long as peace is maintained between us and the Indians."

Raising one eyebrow, Hook looked to Cecco. The captain nodded his agreement, and Hook pronounced, "Conceded, for the good of the company. Let the truth remain sequestered. Only Jill's sons and our first officers shall know what transpired."

"Thank you," Jill said. "To address another problem, which is worrying Nibs, the men believe that he killed Flambard in a brawl, due to some misdeed of Flambard's. He feels this falsehood to be unjust to the murdered man."

"If Captain Cecco agrees, you may instruct Mr. Nibs to say what he knows to be true: an unknown party attacked him and Flambard. The less elaboration, the better."

Shrugging his shoulders, Cecco assented, "I am satisfied. Flambard was an inept gambler, but a good sailor. My Frenchmen will be relieved to learn of his innocence."

In the two days since her abduction, Jill had considered this matter. "The men are always on guard for attack from Pan. They know of course that Jewel works to prevent him from troubling us. Still, no harm can arise from a belief that Pan and his boys are the culprits." Her expression turned guileful. "In fact, Pan himself will believe that story, given time."

Hook exchanged a knowing smile with her. "I shall instruct the fairy to inform Pan of his cleverness."

"And I shall arrange for Flambard's old blue jacket to slip into Pan's hideout."

Cecco snorted. "At last, a good use for the boy's recklessness. The mystery of Flambard's demise is put to rest."

Once again, Hook became stern. "I am, however, displeased that our sentries were caught unawares. First Mr. Noodler allowed himself to be distracted from his post, enabling Mrs. Hanover to slip to the boats. Then Nibs and Flambard were surprised and struck down. I shall not censure Nibs further; no punishment I could inflict is worse than that of finding his comrade dead. The incident is unwelcome, but the lesson learned. The fictitious attack by Pan's band imparts a stark warning to the men."

"Aye, Commodore, we must redouble our vigilance against enemies. As for pursuing justice…" Cecco asked, "might we not seek redress for the insult to Jill through the Indian council?"

"We have no proof to present to the elders. Lean Wolf would surely display his marriage bracelet. Although it proves his defiance of taboo, it constitutes evidence of our lady's willingness, however specious we know it to be."

"And so, gentlemen," Jill insisted, "we return to the strategy I devised. It is the surest method to serve Lean Wolf his due."

Hook's face darkened, and Cecco exclaimed, "*Miei dèi!* I forbid it!"

"Please, Giovanni, we will get nowhere if you vex yourself so. Come, sit next to me."

Incensed as he was, Cecco did not refuse the opportunity to approach her. "Very well. I will sit." As ever, her proximity affected him, yet his concern was sincere and his disapprobation of her plan in no way weakened. "But explain to me, if you will, Madam, why you feel you must meet with this monster."

Hook rested his chin on his fingertips. Deceptively casual, his claw lounged at his thigh. "Yes, my love. A question we both wish to hear answered."

Jill slid closer to Cecco, linking his arm in hers. The sensation of her husband's might, dedicated to her welfare, fortified her resolve. "The first question is this. Shall we three work together, or must I kill him on my own?"

"We honor your determination, of course." The commodore controlled his tone, but the disapproval on his face was eloquent. "Yet to allow you to walk into danger defies every instinct."

"I know that each of you would avenge me, in a heartbeat. I am grateful for your gallantry. But some force within me kept me alive in that cave. I invoked a power. I vowed to myself and to Lean Wolf: his life rests in my hands." Her eyes challenged each of them. "The man is *mine*."

Cecco gathered her hands in his, not hesitating this time to hold both the blood-red one and the pale. His gaze fixed earnestly upon his wife— she who was so powerful in her womanhood, and yet so vulnerable. "I am your husband. I am a man who loves you. I will not watch you place yourself at that murderer's mercy."

"I am no weak woman to step aside for the sake of safety. But, however, I *am* a woman. And I am no fool." Cecco began to speak, but she shook her head. "No, Giovanni, I will finish. Nor is Lean Wolf foolish. I fell prey to his cunning, and I witnessed his strength. While I insist on taking vengeance with my own crimson hand—" she raised it, "*this* hand— I shall not do so alone."

The men reserved approval, yet their tension eased, if only a trifle. Jill noted the fact, and pressed ahead. "I need not hurry. The longer Red Hand from the Sea waits to snare the Silent Hunter, the lower he will hold his guard."

"I cannot fault your logic, Jill," Hook looked as if he'd bitten something sour. "Nor can I say that I like it."

Cecco grunted. "Aye, Commodore. In this opinion, you and I stand in accord."

"I am Red-Handed Jill. What more need I say?"

As if to finalize Jill's statement, the ship's bell tolled. She looked from one man to the other. "And so, I shall set my plans in train." As the lady rose from the window seat, the officers got to their feet. "You will excuse me, gentlemen, while I outline my instructions to Lightly." With her fingers, she stroked the red scar at her throat, and the rings both her men had bestowed upon her glimmered there, golden, and emerald. "This very evening, he will deliver a message to my new husband." Smiling in her regal way, Jill swept from the room in a swirl of amber satin.

" 'Sdeath!" Hook spat the word, then strode to the sideboard. He yanked the stopper from a decanter and tossed it to tumble along the tabletop. "I begin to believe it isn't only the woman's *husbands* who are cursed." Cecco joined him by the board, the glassware clacked, and, in ominous silence, they both downed their drinks.

Hook's lip curled. "Od's blood! To sink my hook in him, and have done."

"I too burn to destroy him. Jill herself must not venture near that predator."

"You know her as well as I. She will do as she must."

"I will not countenance it. I would not allow it for all the gold in Rome! We must keep her from him, however fiercely she insists." Cecco jerked his chin toward the tiger's pelt. "There may be truth in the natives' lore. Surely that tigress is Jill's totem." He seized the decanter to pour out again, a splash in each glass, and although the smell of the liquor pervaded his senses, it did nothing to numb them.

"I have witnessed her blood-rage," Hook said. "It came damnably close to killing her, and led her to the threshold of the Indian village." With his boot, he nudged the tiger's hide. "Indeed, Jill's victory over this animal is the crux of our dilemma. Had I kept her safe in the aftermath of the chase, she'd not have crossed paths with the Hunter."

"Commodore, had I listened to her heart, I would not have left Jill on the beach. Nor would she now crave retribution."

"The trouble spans further than that. Conjointly, we refused to grant her wish."

Astonished to hear Hook's conclusion, Cecco stared at him. "Aye...the day that I asked her what she most desired. Her answer seemed impossible then, even to me."

Hook banged down his glass. "Impossible, for any *other* island."

"It is even as Lily said. Magic dwells here." Cecco gazed landward, brooding. Like a kaleidoscope, his perspectives were shifting. As of today, his single concern was to keep his wife alive.

With his barbed arm, the commodore gestured toward the Island. "Capricious as it is, this place is Jill's homeland." He too gazed through the window, toward the Neverland and its varied hues— the sand of the bay, the emerald of the woods, white rock at the cliff top, a wisp of auburn adrift above the Clearing, and the shimmer of cerulean tinting the sea to share its light with the sky. The enchanted isle stretched before him, as ever and anon he had viewed it: an infinite array of the shades of its promise.

Hook's heartbeat felt heavy, and as erratic as the Island. Grimly, he said, "For her, for *here*, anything is possible."

Birds of a Feather

"This is not the first time the Council of Elders have been called to discuss Rowan Life-Giver, and Lightly of the Air."
Walking Man sat on a blanket before the council fire, with the scented smoke of apple wood swirling up before him. Across his lap lay a spear, its end ornamented with a cluster of feathers. His gray hair hung loose and limp over his bone-studded breastplate. In the pouches beneath his eyes, he bore the burdens of a lifetime. Today, he bore one care too many.

The seven elders had assembled at the meeting lodge, arranged in a half circle with Walking Man on one end, and the Old One at the other. The Old One stood leaning her bony frame upon her staff. Panther, her son and the father of her grandchildren, sat cross-legged at her other side, patient as he awaited his questioning.

"Your words are true, Brother. It is not the first," the Old One answered. "The first time, we chose as one to award Rowan and Lightly the distinction of their status of Messengers."

Walking Man's voice creaked like an aged tree. "And soon after, we censured them, for their ties to the savages from the sea."

"How can blood-ties be censured? We merely advised the Messengers to use caution. A young man, and even a *grown* man," she placed her hand upon the head of her son, "owes duty to his mother, and respect to his mother's people." Demonstrating that respect, Panther disciplined his jovial face to stare straight ahead, and his white-streaked braids lay motionless against his vest as he feigned not to hear the council's discussion.

"Let us not confuse the matters." Seeping through the chinks in the meeting lodge, light fell in stripes over Walking Man's face, like war paint. Walking Man intoned, "Rowan and Lightly do not stand in question *this* time because of filial links to the mother." The elder stiffened, as if to heighten his authority. "On this day, we discuss their ties to one another."

The Old One blinked, slowly. "My son is here at your request. Ask him what you will."

"Panther," Walking Man tapped the man's shoulder with the feathered spear, granting him permission to listen. "Tell the elders how Rowan Life-Giver answered the offer of marriage to your oldest daughter."

Panther stood, and inclined his head in deference to the council members. White Bear held his place among them, attentive, and he gestured his welcome to Panther. Where the others wore their wrinkles as their badges, the bear claw trophies on his necklace and the scars on his chest marked White Bear's importance.

Panther began, "I feel honor to stand before the Council of—"

Walking Man cackled. "Soon Panther, you will sit among us."

The others murmured in disapproval. The Old One waited for silence, then rejoined, "The council choose well to admit not more than one member in a family, and although I journey toward the Spirits, Walking Man, I do not yet tread in the land of Dark Hunting." She turned her hazy eyes toward her son. "Panther is a mighty warrior with many scalps on his belt, but he has yet to match his mother in wisdom." She smiled upon him, and he and the others laughed.

The elders adjusted their blankets, and when all had settled once more, the Old One rapped Panther's arm, to indicate that he should continue.

He resumed his formal posture. "Honor is mine today, Walking Man, and I answer your question. When Rowan replied to the offer of my daughter's hand, he did so with kindness and nobility. Ayasha feels no insult, and my wife and I feel satisfied."

"You have told us *how* he refused her," the elder said. "Now, tell us why."

Panther had learned at his mother's knee. "Can I speak for another man? Is my mouth at one with his mind?"

The elders looked to one another, some nodding, others frowning. White Bear's iron eyes narrowed in disapproval as Walking Man persisted, "Panther, did Rowan not indicate that he and Lightly would admit no woman to their tepee?"

"No, Walking Man, he did not. He said the opposite. He said that they two would welcome Ayasha, if my daughter and I so decided."

As the elders interpreted Panther's answer, no one spoke. After some moments of suspense, the cool, dry fingers of his mother applied pressure to Panther's arm, and, keeping his eyes averted from the council, he left the lodge. When his shadow slipped away, the Old One announced, "Other matters wait for our consideration. Hear me, Brothers: since we named the one who was once called Lelaneh as Outcast, our women lack the remedies and medicines the Outcast provided. I advise—"

"We have not finished with the young Messengers—"

"We have finished, Walking Man. The young men do their job diligently. They do the tribe honor."

"They do defy taboo!"

White Bear broke in, his voice rough but patient. "The council listen, Walking Man. We will hear your proof."

"Well…" The fire hissed, but Walking Man had no more words.

"Then we pass on." White Bear turned his attention toward the Old One, and the others followed.

She lifted her staff to thump it on the ground. "Brothers, the time has come to consider recalling our herbalist."

While the sweet smell of apple wood rose toward the sky, the Council of Elders discussed the Old One's suggestion. For today, at least, Walking Man had been relieved of a burden.

Lean Wolf caught a hint of her exotic fragrance on the wind. Long before he saw her, he knew Red Hand from the Sea was waiting for him.

He was surprised that she wore scent to their secret place, but, as his branch swelled pleasurably against his breechclout, he was not displeased. The mere suggestion of her nearness stimulated his body, as did her zeal to couple with him again. Her early arrival at their trysting place exposed her enthusiasm. His vanity swelled, too, at her impatience to indulge in the searing, sensual rites they shared five nights ago, in his lair.

He did not quicken his pace. Lean Wolf was a creature of the woods, grounded in ways to prevail in its setting. He declined to reveal his presence by haste. Always, he kept surprise on his side. The Silent Hunter held the weapon of stealth. She would never hear him coming.

When he peered through the brush to view the path before his cave, he used all his senses. Red Hand sat upon the rock, inhaling the pure forest air, scented with pine and living green. He smelled the zest of fresh water from the waterfall, a swift arrow's flight to the west. His wife's yellow hair fell curling over her shoulders. She wore a forest-green tunic, with gold threading along the collar and cuffs. Fawn-colored trousers hugged her thighs, visible through the slits at the sides of her garment. Her eyes were closed, and her hands moved across the surface of the stone, as if she willed it to roll open of its own accord, the sooner to slip inside and disrobe for her lover. Lean Wolf smiled, but still, his hunter's instincts warned him to delay. Fiercer prey than his wife may lie in wait for him.

Cautiously, he moved his gaze over her surroundings. He listened for any sound, or lack of sound, that might betray an adversary. Lean Wolf felt a strong inclination toward this woman, but his will to survive was stronger. Her people were his enemies; her chiefs were clever. If she had divulged her ties to him in any way, deliberately or by mistake, his moccasins might even now be stepping toward Dark Hunting grounds.

His lips twisted with irony; death was the very destination to which he had meant to guide Red-Handed Jill when he finished with her. But that was before he named her Red Hand and succumbed to her lust. Whatever his joining with her offered, though, her lust was the only power to which the Silent Hunter intended to surrender.

He scrutinized the treetops, and listened over the water's burble for the birds. Here, as everywhere in the woods before twilight, they piped louder and more petulantly, as if to shame wayward ones homeward. A pair of squirrels clattered up a tree, but Lean Wolf spotted nothing unusual within the branches, high or low, nor did he spy Red Hand's messenger, Lightly, among them. He was certain no pirate prowled this part of the forest to avenge her. No white man moved as noiselessly as Silent Hunter.

Satisfied, Lean Wolf slid from the woods to set his feet upon the gravel of the path. "Red Hand," he murmured, and she turned to him with her sea-blue gaze and her pearl-white smile. Her eyes ate him up; she stretched out her arms, and, with one last glance around him, he entered her embrace. But his hand encountered steel, and, quickly, he backed from her.

"Why do you carry your knife?" he demanded, his handsome face souring. He himself wore his hunting knife strapped near his knee, and his tomahawk hung in his waistband.

"Is your wife such a fool as to enter the wood with no weapon?"

He grinned then, and plucked her off the rock into his arms. "You carried no weapon to our first meeting, yet you managed almost to murder me."

Red Hand smiled, too, and held him to her breast. "Perhaps this time I shall succeed." She wove her fingers into his hair and pulled him down to kiss her. As he pressed into her warm, loving lips, the few doubts Lean Wolf had harbored burned up in her passion. Once again, every nerve in his body ignited with excitement. Still, his senses remained alert to any change in his surroundings.

"Husband," she said, when at last she let him free. "I had to wait these lengthy days, to be sure no one suspects us."

"What did you tell your devil men, to explain where you were on the night of our wedding?" A surge of affection rushed through him as he indulged her dream of marriage. The idea was both absurd and gratifying, and, as he humored her, he delighted in the fantasy.

Besides, he could find no danger in their ceremony. It struck him suddenly, then, that he had not sought Raven in days. Already he thought of Red Hand as his spouse. Ever since their coupling, had he not called her 'wife' in his mind? Never one to feel too tightly tied by marriage, Lean Wolf was further amazed. As on that night in the cavern, she continued to practice some witchery upon him. A spirit woman she was, with her magic.

"Each of my lovers believed I was with the other," she answered, and her eyes sparkled with mischief, like sunlight on the Mermaids' Lagoon. "This evening, I left them both wondering."

Oddly, Lean Wolf felt a pang of jealousy. He asked, with a hope that his words might come true, "Perhaps they will kill one another?"

"Oh, no. The commodore and the captain are too concerned for their treasure. They understand that despite their animosity, when they work together, they reap rich rewards."

"It is not *my* way. But it is a way we can use to outsmart them. Come, let us find privacy."

He released her, and hunkered down before the boulder. Flexing his arms, he prepared for the effort of opening his cave. He felt Red Hand lay her blood-red palm on his shoulder, and in his imagination the crimson color flared elsewhere on his body. Anticipation spurred his might. His throat went tight, the stone budged, then it rolled. He scarcely felt the effort; it meant nothing to him. But he still felt the touch of his wife.

He held out his hand to assist her through the entrance. As she grasped it and knelt down, they heard the sharp, piercing cry of a hawk. Jill whipped around to search the sky. "That's Lightly's signal."

Lean Wolf jumped up, yanking his weapon from his waist. Among the treetops, Lightly flew their way, hailing them. As he touched down to earth, Red Hand seized him.

"Was I followed?"

"Not directly, but a party of pirates are hunting game, and now they're tracking your perfume."

Boots became audible, crushing the underbrush. Weapons jingled, and a shot popped in the distance, followed by a cheer from a number of men.

Lean Wolf commanded, "Quickly, boy, they know you. Lead them away from here." The singed scent of gunpowder came to his nostrils.

Lightly looked to his mother. "Jill, they *know* you're about."

"You must have no truck with them," she said, "They are drunken, they may shoot you." She turned to Lean Wolf, her eyes earnest as she gripped his arm. She slipped her fingers under the orange kerchief she had tied there, and his makeshift marriage bracelet tightened. "I am sorry," she said. She spoke with urgency, but no fear. "My perfume is all over you. You are in danger, too, if they hunt me." She kissed him, imparting the fervency of her feeling. "Hide yourself, Husband. I will send word."

Before he could restrain her, she and her son ran up the path, light as songbirds. Spreading her arms, Red Hand gave a twist of her shoulders and lent her body to the air. It was the most graceful, elegant motion Lean Wolf ever witnessed a woman perform. Red Hand's hair flowed behind her, her green garment rippled in the wind. She looked back, to send a kiss flying, too, then vanished beneath the covering of trees.

Lean Wolf was infused with loss, with disappointment, the same feelings he suffered as a younger man, when that mermaid evaded him. Yet his primary emotion was confusion. How had his pleasure eluded him? He had caged the yellow bird. He had spoken her pledge. And yet there she went, winging away from him. His confusion distorted, then, into anger. If not for Lightly's interference, Red Hand from the Sea would be sheltering here, with her husband.

Another shot barked out, closer this time, and Lean Wolf tossed his tomahawk in his cave and slithered after. He flung his rope around the stone, and heaved to roll it closed. Breathing heavily, he sat on the shale of the cave floor, his eyes adjusting to the dim, greenish light. Soon he rose up again, and started prowling his lair.

Lean Wolf was a creature of the woods, grounded in its ways. Always, the Silent Hunter held the gift of stealth. It occurred to him that, just as she declared at their joining, in choosing Red Hand he had made a fitting match. Like the knives they both carried, his wife held *that* weapon, too— the weapon of surprise.

With her scent on his skin, he knelt before the wall and dipped his forefinger in a pot of ochre. Painting one stripe on the wall, in line with five others, he wondered how many more he must render there, before he would have her again. Her smell on his flesh made him wild.

Frustrated, he drew an image, too. When he banged the paint pot down, two figures of men marked the wall. They stretched horizontal, to signify flight, and faced away from the village. The symbol of taboo marked their backs. They were chased by a shower of arrows.

Lean Wolf wiped the paint from his hands and reclined on the furs of his pallet. Among the intrigues he formed as he waited there with his angry gaze on the phosphorous glow, those for Rowan and his 'friend,' Lightly, took precedence.

As twilight touched the treetops, an eagle perched among them. He looked down to eye Nibs the Knife, Tom Tootles, Mr. Smee, and Mr. Yulunga, all laughing and swaggering as they traipsed through the woodland. They passed flasks back and forth, and the odor of alcohol trailed them. Crunching their boots on the gravel path, they headed away from the waterfall. The party carried no deer nor fowl, but Smee could be seen to hold a pistol, still smoking.

Wary of the verdant surroundings, Smee peered over his spectacles. The men marched in the direction Jill had flown but, rather than returning to the ships, the 'hunters' aimed to end their junket at the Clearing. The pirates tramped until they gained distance between themselves and the caves. Smee noted the landmarks and signaled, and the men paused in their journey.

"Hush, now," Smee murmured. With the eerie feel of being watched, they listened. They waited. Then, at the corner of his eye,

Smee caught a movement in the forest. The other men stiffened in alert.

Something was there, and then it wasn't. Smee felt the hairs rise up on his head.

He blinked to clear his vision, then stared again. "Scuttle me!" he whispered under his breath, and uttered, "If those two Indians aren't magicians…" Smee thrust his warm gun next to another in his belt and, tentatively, stepped forward.

Separating from the background, a lone figure became visible. A permutation of beast and of tree, it was nothing these men had ever laid eyes on before, even here in the Neverland. All the stories Jill had told them converged in their minds, but this tale was a new one, as yet untold.

The creature seemed to walk upright, but didn't look human. Its legs were strapped with leather, the color of tree bark. The upper body was molded of mud, striped in various shades. The texture of bird's nest, its hair was smeared with clay the hue of twigs, plaited to dangle and interwoven with vines. Where the lowest part of this thing touched the forest floor, a pair of leafy clusters materialized, in lieu of feet. It moved with the gentle susurrus of wind through a sapling, approaching with its head cast down, and only when it raised up to confront the men did they register a color not conceivable on a tree.

Collectively, the pirates dropped their shoulders to sigh in relief. None dared to speak. They gaped at the apparition one long, final time, then Nibs, Tom, and Yulunga surrounded Smee and the beast, turning their backs on the two of them to stand guard with their hands on their weapons.

"You put the fear o' Hades in, me, so you did." Smee searched for a spot on which to focus. The jewel-blue eyes of their commodore pierced through his camouflage.

Hook's voice seeped like sap from the tree he counterfeited. "I do hope you have ordered the bathwater."

"Aye, aye, Sir, 'tis all in readiness. Seeing as you left your hook at home, shall I send your sons to fly along with you now, as escorts?"

"Mr. Smee, from your own reaction, I see that no being will wish to approach me. And I *am* armed." With his only hand, he reached behind his back to draw a long, wicked knife from its strapping. "Take these men and move on to the Clearing, and watch over the women. While Jill believes the Silent Hunter will resist calling there, mine is a more cautious nature."

"Nature, Sir! Aye, you're looking natural enough." Smee, too, was a cautious man, and he tamped his humor down. "A quick dip in the bay ought to wash off the worst of it. Then the lady will tend you in your quarters." He stepped backward, waving a hand before his nose. "Woosht! That clay fairly reeks."

"Rowan and Lightly are under strict orders. They are never to reveal to me what this foul substance is."

"A fine job they made of you, too. And what were you seeing as you guarded her, Commodore, perched up there in the treetop like He of the Eagle's Claw, in your eyrie?"

Hook smiled, half-way, and the earth that had dried on his lips crumbled, to tumble back to its source.

"I saw another husband. And his curse."

Water Craft

Battered, barely seaworthy, the boat nosed slowly into the Lagoon. Its crew looked ragtag and tired, its captain grizzled, yet the great man stood proud at the prow, eyeing the waters for enemies. Pointing with his cutlass, he directed his oarsmen toward his destination. Huddled behind him was a prisoner who trembled to see it. Marooners' Rock was a bleak place to die, cold and uncompromising— like the captains who used it.

Before the boat bumped against the islet, the captain hobbled up upon the rock. "Hoist him up," he cried, and his men bustled to obey. They secured the craft by means of rusty rings driven into the rock. Then the ruddy-cheeked bo'sun grasped the malefactor by the shoulders and, without a twinge of pity, delivered him up to his doom. He inspected the prisoner's bonds, making sure his hands were tied behind so that swimming was impossible, and he tethered him, too, to the rings.

The crew were grim, and even the Lagoon looked hostile to them, this late afternoon. Tall moss-covered cliffs enclosed the place, stark and stoic, offering no escape but for birds. With a whiff of kelp, the wind assailed the sea, sending waves to chop the shelves of the shore. Caves and fissures gaped along the coast. To the prisoner, those openings seemed to stare, like hollow, hopeless eyes. No merfolk lounged about the shore to brighten it with color and, even if they had, by their nature they would offer no succor. When the water rose with the tide— soon, at sunset— any creature who could not swim must drown.

"Hath the prisoner last words?" asked the captain. Judging by the look on his face, he did not encourage a statement.

Surrounded by shipmates, the condemned one knelt on the punishing rock. Although he was unable to clasp his hands before him, still he appeared penitent. His voice quavered as he begged, "Please, Cap'n! Show some pity, Sir. I never meant no harm, and that's the truth!"

"Belay that. If ye have no words worth hearing, stow your gab." The captain flourished his cutlass. With it, he tapped the tender underside of the wretched man's chin. "Or wouldst thou rather die by my steel?"

The bo'sun caught the captain's arm. "Begging your pardon, Captain, but this bit of scum ain't worth the work o' wiping your blade." The others guffawed, although nervous quivers ran up their backbones, and they watched their commander for signs of displeasure. None of his men wished to keep his victim company here on this rock. The bo'sun was a brave one, ruthless in his captain's service, and much admired by the seamen, yet even he felt weak at the knees.

"Bo'sun," a suspenseful pause followed. "Ye speak true. Let us abandon this scalawag to justice." So saying, the captain thrust his cutlass in his belt. " 'Twon't be long now, hark ye, before the waters mount to swamp thy gullet." He stood tall, to gaze toward the lowering sun. "Behold, even now the light be changing."

Kicking his men aside, he began to stroll the solid surface of the rock. Back and forth he stumped in his Navy coat, like Nelson on the *Victory*. It became apparent to his men, and to his prisoner, that justice must wait. Deliberation occupied their officer. Before long, his brow unfurrowed, and his weathered face turned nearly youthful.

"By gad, I almost envy thee, ye scug."

The bo'sun's boot poked the prisoner, who grasped that he was expected to respond. "How's that, m'lord?"

"Why, look about thee, boy. Here ye lie, on the rarest of isles, surrounded by sea and sky and the creatures that inhabit 'em. Here ye lie, faced with the great unknown. Rip my jib, boy! If I were thee, I'd have some utterance worth spitting out, at the end."

The crew passed glances around, stymied. Mermaids' Lagoon was, however, a magical cove. As if suddenly inspired, the prisoner flung off his lethargy and leapt to his feet. Turning, he confronted the torchy orb of the sun. He squinted in defiance, and the company gasped to see him twist his wrists to break his bonds. The severed cords fell to his feet; he set his fists on his hips. With his heart pounding as hard as the surf, he said, with flair, "To die…will be an awfully big adventure."

Captain Pan gazed upon his victim, his green eyes wide with wonder. "That's prime, Chip!" He clapped the boy on the back, all thoughts of execution over. Erupting in a crow, Peter jumped in the air and soared to the height of the cliffs, where he flipped and frolicked. Zooming down to the rock again with his golden hair wild, he managed to muster a fraction of his former dignity. "Odds bobs, hammer and tongs," he vowed, "Bo'sun Paleface be brilliant, but Chip triumphs again."

All the Lost Boys whooped, glad the grim scene was ended. They felt gladder still that it won success in Peter's opinion. Chubby Bertie hopped in the boat, nearly capsizing it and causing a drowning after all, and Bingo, with his orange hair flaming in the slanting sunlight and his stomach roaring for supper, followed to fetch out the picnic, before it, too, got deluged. He plunked the basket on the rock. "Marooning is hungry work. Can we eat now, Cap'n?"

"Aye, aye, sailor. Bo'sun, swab up the deck, and we'll have a square meal."

"Yes, Sir!" David Paleface kicked the frayed braids of weeping willow into the sea, the remnants of the condemned man's bonds. They floated around the rock like a derelict Neverbird nest while the Lost Boys devoured their supper. This meal happened to be material rather than make-believe: breadfruit and bananas, with cocoa-nuts to crack noisily upon the rock. As usual, Bingo ate one too many mouthfuls, and, as Wendy wasn't there to hold him back for half an hour, he challenged Bertie, "Race me to shore!" and down he splashed, holding his nose.

Spooked by the mood of the Lagoon so late in the day, Bertie was wiser, and declined to submerge himself. As Bingo's carrot-top bobbed away, he called, "Come back, Bingo, the tide's a-rising!"

Helplessly, he looked through his dark, bushy bangs to the others. Peter and Chip were smoking imaginary after-dinner pipes, reclining opposite one another like diminishing mirror images. They seemed absorbed in watching dragon flies flit through their smoke rings. Bertie appealed to David, who was tossing bits of cocoa-nut shell off the rock to plop in the Lagoon. Neither boy saw the scaly-backed hands that caught those bits, nor the pearly teeth that nibbled them.

"All right, I'll fetch him back." David had mastered flight by now, and felt really quite proficient, but here at the Lagoon it seemed only right to swim, so in he slid, and he ducked after Bingo. Shadows had fallen upon the rock ledge that made up the shore, and its grottos appeared blacker than before. Already, the tide was seeping into them with unearthly gurgles. It was time to turn homeward. Even the Lagoon knew it, and, accordingly, sped its agenda.

Almost to shore, Bingo looked back to shout out his victory. As he opened his mouth, a curl of surf smacked him in the face. He choked and gagged, and, weighted with his dinner, soon he sank down. Some yards behind, David saw him go under. Executing a dashing maneuver, David propelled himself into the air, like a porpoise. He caught up to the spot where Bingo disappeared, then dove down to find him. Had Peter been paying attention, he'd have blazed with pride to see David fly with such style— just like his tutor. But Peter wasn't paying attention. Only Bertie and the lurking mergirl saw.

Spotting Bingo by his flaming hair, David seized the boy and pulled him up to the rock shelf. Bingo coughed, winking the sting from his eyes. Clinging to the ledge, he recovered, but when his sight cleared and he looked for David to thank him, David was gone.

How far gone, even David didn't know. Something held his ankle in its grasp, and tugged to tow him under. When it let go, his surroundings seemed dim and distorted. Through the wavering water, he gazed at a sea creature, and she stared back at him. Even submerged in tepid waves, David felt his cheeks flush hot. The depth filled his ears with pressure. He ignored it. Floating upward, the mermaid's hair was weaving with the currents, and her eyes seemed almost to glow. In the hues of the sea, David couldn't determine the color of her hair, nor her tail, nor the more remarkable parts in the middle. He simply goggled. He'd believed, of late, that he had become accustomed to the Island's trickery. He should have known better. Always, the place offered marvels, and menaces. This time, the opposites met, in irresistible combination.

David wasn't capable of thinking at the moment, but he formed a strong impression: a body— feminine— that fluxed in fluid contours; a soul as old and as young as Peter's himself; and a face whose glory rivaled Red-Handed Jill's. If he lived through this wonder, David knew he'd have a story to tell— and no one to believe it.

At the periphery of his vision, David saw Bingo's feet thrashing, and he was reminded of his mortal need to breathe. With his lungs afire, he gestured to the mermaid, pointing upward, and although he expected to feel her grip on his ankle again, he surfaced. She followed him, bobbing between the sea and the air, her hair now slick against her head, and her indigo eyes curious. If she planned to dispatch him, he figured, she'd toy with him first. The prospect appealed to him.

Spitting saltwater, he flopped on the rock shelf. The surf sloshed in the caves, and he opened his eyes to see Bingo's freckled face looming above him. "Get back to Peter, Bingo," David panted, "And you'd better not swim." He sat up and wiped his eyes, then searched for the mermaid. His pluck returned once he saw she was gone, but his heart submerged with her, and David sagged with disappointment. With an ache in his insides, he barely noticed when Bingo pushed off to fly.

David had glimpsed mermaids from the air, when in flight over the Neverland, but he'd avidly hoped to view one up close. Peter enjoyed David's new nautical games so well that he'd salvaged a rotting boat from the riverbank, and commanded his boys to help David patch it up. Always one for drama, Peter felt that David's first experience of the Lagoon should be staged to reflect its character, and a marooning on the rock seemed such an admirable scheme that Peter bent Wendy's rule about curfew. The other boys were excited to stay out so late, but David's excitement derived from something more potent than mischief. It had to do with destiny. Now, his intuition was confirmed. David Paleface felt it in his bones; Fate meant for him to be here.

He had seen a mermaid! But why should Fate send such a slender adventure? David spent days toiling on the boat, building his anticipation along with the craft. Surely the Island intended something more substantial than a mere sighting? The other boys had assured David that these creatures, so eccentric in their tastes, would scorn him. They might try to kill him for sport, but merfolk made time only for Peter, who played with them, or for pirates, who offered some other form of fascination. Instead, this mermaid deemed David interesting. Perhaps she still watched, even now. As the breeze chilled his sodden clothing, David cast his gaze, like a fishnet, over the Lagoon. The other boys romped on the rock, the amber sun burned low, and still, he detected no flash of fins beneath the water, nor any movement but the waves that crept craftily over his knees.

He slumped. And then every hair on his head prickled up. A sigh sounded behind him, and he felt her breath on his cheek. David turned to behold the beauty, lolling at his back. Her purple lips puckered as she blew on him, then she opened them to smile. He saw now that her hair was so black it shone blue. Like her eyes, her tail was indigo, and she wore only a gem in her navel. In spite of its glistening, he felt his eyes drawn lower, to witness the seamless V where her belly changed from flesh to fishtail. In such an unnatural creature, that place of joining seemed natural. If he dared to touch her, how might that spot feel? Soft, no question. Slippery? Or was it filmed with grains of salt? His mouth began to salivate as he considered how she'd taste there. As he balled his fingers to hold them back, his gaze wandered upward again, and, clammy as his skin was, he felt a feverish heat.

As a sailor, David heard tales of her kind, and he'd heard the warnings. They proved true enough. Face to face with her now, he was dazed by the blatancy of her nakedness. When he'd watched her underwater, her bosom floated, weightless and free. Now, subject to gravity, her breasts swelled heavy at their bottoms, curving upward to peak at their middles. David's experience was limited, but he was certain most females' nipples weren't blue. He flushed, then, as her shining eyes took him in, and he grew aware of his own body. He felt the rigidity that hid in his britches. He wondered if it were not quite polite to be clothed when one's company was not. It seemed oddly proper to cast off his garments and let this mermaid view him, too. But in the primordial lexicon of the Lagoon, no 'polite' nor 'proper' existed. Emotion ruled over utterance, and, with eloquence, David's body expressed what he felt. He knew she understood; she slithered near, smiling, and brushed her breasts along his arm. Wordless, will-less, and helpless against such divinity, David surrendered. He knew he was doomed.

The mermaid gazed at his face. With one pallid hand, she reached out with a touch that felt warm as the air. Midnight blue, her scales glimmered on her forearms and the backs of her hands. He soon understood what aroused her curiosity. She dragged a finger over his left cheek, outlining the mark Jill had made. As her fingertip traced it, thrills trickled up and down his spine, like jets of a fountain. Then, with a knowing shine in her eye, she laid her hand flat upon Jill's brand. She seemed pleased to find that the woman's handprint matched her own. But her interest didn't end at David's cheek.

While her right hand held his face, her left caressed his body. Starting at his shoulder, she traced the length of his arm, then she abandoned his limb to stroke his torso. From there she moved to his belly, and next to his hip. As her indigo gaze confined his eyes, she found his thigh. The tidewater was rising, covering him up to his ribs now, and all David wanted was her touch. He was hyperventilating, growing dizzy, waiting for the ultimate sensation, for the pleasure she promised, in full.

She slid her fingers up his mast, where he pulsed with desire. He thought his passion would burst within her grip. With her blueish breasts, she made it worse, pressing her flesh upon his chest. She leaned him backward, to recline. He lay back, low, and lower, agog at her lovely face as the water came between them. Again, he disregarded the pressure in his ears, manfully striving to hold back the force at his loins. Liquid sea slipped over his eyes, swirling her image but, if anything, enhancing her charms. Her chin joined him below the surface, becoming firm again, her lips slid in, then her nose, and...

She sat up, abruptly, turning away with a hiss. She released her hold on his privates. A fresh grip seized his shirt, and that grip yanked him up, to the right side of the tide. He gulped a breath he hadn't known he needed, and, astonished, found cheeky Peter sitting squat on the mermaid's tail.

"Not this one," Peter declared to the creature, in his captainy voice. "Not yet."

Indignant, the mermaid tugged toward escape. Peter held her down, to show who was boss, finally allowing her to float free. The water lay so high above the shore now that she swam, gliding right into a cave, swishing her indigo scales. Still drawn to her, David saw her bright eyes peering out at him. He launched himself to paddle her way but, with a firm grasp on his belt, Peter pulled him back.

"No you don't, Paleface. I need you to work the ship."

Blinking, David set his feet on the ledge and stood, his masculine glands throbbing, and he stared down to see the tide above the level of his thighs. "Oh," he cried. On Peter, the water came to the waist. Recalled to duty, David looked where Peter pointed, to the boys on Marooners' Rock.

"The little ones are up to their necks."

"Peter, the boat's about to break moorings!" He and Peter joined hands to gain traction, and shoved off, dripping, to recover the others.

The adventure wasn't over yet. Peter's plan was twofold. Now that the salvaged boat had served its role in the playacting, it was destined to sink a second time, as host for diving missions. Dressed anew in his French blue jacket, the captain took up his stance on the prow, commanding his crew to "Heave ho!" At the edge of the cliff, by the northern entrance to the Lagoon, they shipped oars. Here, as ordered, the boys lined up, balancing on both gunwales, and they jumped up and down, alternating port and starboard. The craft rocked, creaking in protest until it gave up, burbled water to its gills, and yielded to the brine. Bubbles rose to the surface while the sun sank at last. In the ragged remains of its nimbus, Peter drew his cutlass once more. He scored an X on the cliff side to mark sunken treasure, and pointed the route to his crew. "Homeward, ye lubbers. To hammocks!"

Up they rose, one by one, to follow the stars, like the ancient mariners they were. The Lagoon lay submerged now, its only sound the slurp of the surf, and a haunted song pouring from a grotto. At the tail of the line, lagging behind, a young man trembled to leave it.

Marooners' Rock was a bleak place to die. Older and wiser tonight, David Paleface left part of his heart there.

Deliberations in council this morning had tested the Old One's patience. Since then, she rested and reflected. Now prepared to resume her responsibilities, she set her staff aside, settling on a log to stretch her toes in the pure, cool course of the stream.

"Thank you, White Bear, for joining me here. I think better with my feet in the water."

Gruff but pleased, White Bear responded, "Old One, you do me honor."

"This river is the source of the People." With her frail hand, she patted the dry, fallen tree trunk, indicating that White Bear should sit beside her in the shade. "The feel of the pebbles under my soles reminds me of the path our tribe travel. Mostly pleasant, but never smooth."

"The same is true today. This very morning, we met with unpleasantness." White Bear looked around to ensure that their words would not be overheard. Upstream, a group of boys prattled as they floated tiny canoes made of birch bark. Birds called from branch to branch, and a woodpecker pounded with a hollow rattle. Above the sloping ground behind White Bear's back, the camp drowsed in the warmth of afternoon. He slipped off the moccasins his wife had so lovingly beaded for him, and he set them on shore. The Old One was prudent to come here, he found. The swish of water over his skin worked to soothe White Bear's agitation.

She observed, "The birth of your daughter; the betrothal of my granddaughter. *These* things bring joy."

"I was pleased to hear you announce Panther's news in council. I have observed Mountain Cloud. He is a quiet brave, but steadfast. He will make a fine husband for Ayasha."

"Yes," nodded the Old One, "in spite of my jests, Panther shows wisdom. I admit my satisfaction in the fact that Panther's name was put forth, however prematurely, to follow me as an elder. And my son speaks well of Rowan Life-Giver and Lightly of the Air. It is, in part, because I trust his judgment that I spoke against their exile."

"Like me, Lightly came from another island to make his home here."

"And like you, Lightly has proven his worth. The service both men render as Messengers is valuable to the People."

White Bear acknowledged the compliment with a gesture. "Although I revere tradition, the safety of the tribe must be our first consideration. The Golden Boy threatens, as always, and the number of pirates increases."

"No one can claim that Rowan and Lightly neglect to keep watch on those dangers."

"Now that I am a father, I see even more clearly." White Bear's brow creased as his voice grew sterner. "As I advised the elders, it is a mistake to compromise the People's safety by dismissing our Messengers from the camp."

"You have heard me argue against taboo in the case of Lelaneh. It is well that the elders chose to accept her again. In both situations, the Outcasts possess skills that work for the tribe. It is my hope that, in time, the council will see sense in accepting Rowan and Lightly, too. Their affection brings them happiness, and causes harm to none."

"I am Lean Wolf's friend," White Bear said, "but I see his hand stirring trouble. I am angry that it is he who brought the evidence Walking Man sought."

"And it is Lean Wolf who is punished for spying on the Outcasts in the Clearing. He deserves this taste of the banishment he brought to Rowan and Lightly. Those two had leave from the elders to linger among the Outcasts that night; Lean Wolf had only the consent of his malice."

White Bear huffed his disapproval. "It is no punishment to Lean Wolf to spend time in the forest. True, he must now earn his way back to the tribe's good graces with game, but Walking Man is the one who will benefit. He has no sons to hunt for him."

Now returned to the subject of family, the Old One smiled. "Tell me, White Bear, how fares our littlest one, and her mother?"

"Very well." White Bear puffed out his chest in pleasure. "In these eleven days since her birth, she has grown to look like Willow." White Bear's pride in his daughter and in his young wife was etched on his angular face. "As I anticipated, Willow is a praiseworthy mother." Grounded in tradition, White Bear of course still hoped for a son, and he looked forward to making more children with Willow. Patience was required until she recovered from childbirth, and, gladly, White Bear granted it.

Sighing, the Old One squinted her cloudy eyes to view the far bank of the river, whence came an aroma of sun-warmed wheat. "I regret that the question of her sister Raven was raised. How do you intend to answer Walking Man?"

In the case of Raven, White Bear could *not* afford patience, neither personally nor in the greater context of the tribe. Walking Man made that fact clear when he questioned White Bear in the Council Lodge this morning.

He growled, "I know who prompted *that* discussion, too. Lean Wolf challenges my decision." Lean Wolf had ceased his demands for Raven's hand, but White Bear knew his old friend. He suspected that Lean Wolf dropped the subject only to scheme for the match in a more subtle way. Today White Bear's suspicion was confirmed. "I will tell Walking Man that I am resolved. On Raven's behalf, I refuse Lean Wolf's suit. It is better for her, and better for her sister, that she remain in my tepee. I will accept her as my second woman."

"And will you offer her a ceremony? Make her your wife?"

White Bear looked mildly surprised. "No ceremony is necessary. I follow the custom. She will want for nothing."

"And is the widow, Raven, ready to walk forward?"

"I allowed time for my sister-in-law to rise from her grief and prepare a new life. Still," White Bear shifted as the log's bark bit into his naked thighs. "I do not believe she understands how her status will rise as she moves from widow to helpmeet. Eventually, she will be respected as a mother herself."

"It is well, then," the Old One confirmed, "I will advise the council not to flout custom. I will contend that the wishes of Raven's provider prevail over Lean Wolf's. But, White Bear," her wrinkled face became grave, "the elders are right to insist that Raven's future be settled. One way or another."

"Old One. Your words show both shrewdness and care. I hear you."

White Bear sat quiet, then, and the Old One turned her face to the sky, allowing him time to reflect. The river breeze ruffled the quills of his scalp lock. The feathers stirred back and forth on his shaven head, mimicking his thoughts about Willow's sister.

In recent days, something about Raven changed. White Bear couldn't quite see it, but he felt it in his gut. He sensed too, that this shift had little to do with Lean Wolf. When she entered her brother-in-law's tepee, the woman carried herself with more presence. Even the scent of her skin was stronger, and her hair took on a sheen it had lacked since she sheared it. When near her, White Bear felt that her being was charged, like the atmosphere after a lightning storm. She tried to hide her new physicality. She cast her eyes down, she kept her hands busy. She even powdered her cheeks. But White Bear was not deluded. Where before her body slept, now, the widow exuded vitality.

On the other hand, Raven's spirit felt more absent than ever. She avoided conversation. She hovered over her sister, but she seized any chance to walk alone in the woods. White Bear felt an urge to overcome her reluctance, an impulse in his hands to drag her back into his tepee. The farther her spirit slipped away, the more compelled he felt to pursue her.

Several nights ago, she roamed abroad by herself, on the pretense of collecting cradle moss. Again, White Bear was not fooled; an abundant supply lay at hand. He now determined that the next time she wandered, he must follow.

Not for the first time, White Bear believed she deceived him. The mistrust she always instilled in him grew. He sensed again that, no matter how his sister-in-law behaved outwardly, at her core she was not obedient. She was careful only to appear so. As he sat by the Old One, pondering his situation, White Bear ground his teeth. This morning's council discussion determined him. In the last five days, Raven's moon-time had lain upon her. Now, as her body renewed her receptiveness, White Bear must undeceive Raven. The very nature of her womanhood warned them both: the time had arrived to conceive Raven's future.

The breeze settled, and the feathers of White Bear's headdress lay still. He turned his hard, gray gaze to his fellow elder. "Old One," he said. "You are wise." He nodded his respect. "I think better with my feet in the water."

On the shore behind him, his moccasins lay vacant.

In the peace of afternoon, Willow sat before White Bear's tepee, humming a lullaby to her baby. Contentment radiated from her face, until a shadow passed over her. Then her sweet smile turned to astonishment.

"Raven," Willow gazed at her sister, who seemed to glow bright in the sunlight. "You are dressed in your ceremonial garb!"

"Yes, Willow. I feel that the right day has come." Raven looked away, unwilling to raise her sister's hopes too high. In truth, she hadn't realized she was ready for this change until she thought to use it as an excuse to visit Lily. A pang of remorse shot through her, but it quickly passed. In her heart, Raven felt that the spirit of Ash approved. He understood what she had to do, and he lent her the opportunity to do it.

Ash's widow had donned her best tunic. Made from the hide of a doe, it was bleached to the whiteness of birch bark, rubbed and scraped until the texture felt soft as down. When Ash passed to the land of Dark Hunting, she had removed all its ornaments. With no beads or embroidery to stiffen it, the dress clung to Raven's figure. She cinched it at the waist with a snowy belt and pouch, to hold the things she would use in her ritual. The sleeves reached her elbows, edged with long fringing. Loose and pliable, the skirt swung when she walked, its trim dangling down to brush her legs. She had first worn this dress the day she married Ash. The last time she wore it was the day Ash's body was burned. It still smelled faintly of smoke.

Willow said, "I know that in making this decision, you must feel both lighter and heavier. But how striking you look, Raven."

"Do I?" Raven asked with indifference, feeling the length of her hair. "It was some trouble to tie these feathers, but I believe that my hair is growing."

"You should have let me help you."

"You have Baby to tend. She is much more important." As Raven moved her head, the three black feathers she had fastened there quivered. "After so many months, this headdress feels foreign."

"White Bear and I agreed last night that you seem to feel better. Do you want me to accompany you?"

Quickly, Raven discouraged the idea. Where she needed to go, she needed to go alone. "No, thank you. I must take these steps by myself."

"I understand, and I am glad to learn that your heart is healing." Willow sighed, and her pretty face saddened. "Every day that I am married to White Bear, I understand better the loss that you mourn."

Raven knelt at her sister's side, taking her face in her hands to look earnestly in her eyes. "I know, Willow. But you must listen to your older sister. Do not let my loss diminish your delight. To do so would deepen my grief."

"Where will you go to cleanse yourself? To the waterfall, by the caves?" Willow smiled again, remembering. "How many times we scampered to those caves, Raven, when I was little."

"You never did catch up with me, but once we got there, you kept very close."

"I was frightened of the creatures that made their homes in them. But I should not have worried. You kept me safe."

Determination rang in Raven's voice. "I will always do what is best for my sister." She smoothed Willow's braid, a habit from earlier days, when both of them, as girls, wore two pigtails. Raven stood then, and dusted her knees. "But no, I will visit another place for my rite, a smaller stream that journeys more gently. It is a place Ash and I went together."

"White Bear will wish to know where you've gone. With Lean Wolf roaming the forest, he is concerned."

"As he knows, all aspects of my rite must be secret. But you may assure your husband that where I mean to go, Lean Wolf most certainly will not."

"Perhaps you will tell him yourself. I see him helping the Old One to her tepee."

Raven stopped herself from turning toward the forceful form of White Bear. Instead, she edged away. She needed every grain of resolve to take this next step. "I must go if I hope to return before day fades. Goodbye, Willow." In a flash of white, she was gone.

Her first impulse was simple: to hasten from White Bear. If he discovered her destination, her danger equaled the risk she took at Neverbay. But as she hurried up the trail— the same she wandered the night she followed the fairy— she felt the lure of adventure.

Attempting to tame her eagerness, she measured her paces. She loped through the wood to emerge from the trees, and trotted down the grassy slope. Redwings threw their sharp, bouncing cries, taking flight in black and red whirls. Raven half wished that they'd carry her with them, then she stifled the notion. Now that the Black Chief had quickened her yearnings, she felt vulnerable to them. To persevere in her plans, she must hedge her impulses. Raven had weakened, once. She now guarded her longings more strictly.

Yet how good it felt to run through this land, as she had done since a child. Surely such innocent pleasure couldn't cause resolution to wane. Released from the village, free from the scrutiny of her brother-in-law, Raven sped from the plain toward the paths of the forest. The mild Island air caressed her flesh as she fled, fingering the fringe of her garb. Her bare feet delighted in the sponge of the turf. When she entered the wood, acorns littered the path. Impishly, she jumped upon them, planting the hard, little nuts with her heels. But when she looked up, the trees leaned in on her, caging the sunlight in their branches. Raven hesitated. The ancient oaks loomed large above, their limbs jointed like arms that might reach down to catch her. Such a foreboding had never troubled her in her youth.

Again, she shrugged off her folly. Today, as always, the forest offered things to fear and things to welcome. She smelled the damp airs of its elements now, both fresh and festering, as foliage sprang from high boughs and dead leaves decayed underfoot. Inhaling their odors, Raven found them symbolic. Like the oaks and the acorns, they called to mind the cycle of life that she meant to mark in her ritual. An old life decomposed; a new hope took root.

And today, Raven's hope lay on the Other Island. She regretted that the path she must follow should cause Willow grief. Raven couldn't know, but could only believe that, in time, grief might render good—in the form of contentment for the wife of White Bear. Like the forest that two sisters once traveled together, Raven offered mixed blessings.

The light was shaded here, and Raven slowed under her more somber thoughts. Preparing her mind for her rite now, she pressed on. As she passed an enormous rock, furred green with lichen, the path curved again. Before long, the ground turned to clay. It felt cool beneath her feet. She knew that, above the treetops, red smoke puffed up from the dwelling in the Clearing. Since the Golden Boy appropriated that spot, Raven had forsaken it. Now she drew closer to the Clearing than she'd ever dared to go without Ash. He attended her in spirit, but something more tangible accompanied her, too: a gift from the Black Chief. Among the tools and herbs for her ceremony, his token rode in her pouch.

With relief, Raven had learned that this token was the lone keepsake the pirate chief gave to her. As she intuited, the passion he spent on her was *not* in the nature of engenderment. Her moon flow began immediately afterward, and she knew without doubt that no offspring could come of their coupling. Their bargain was sealed. Raven's obligation was over, and the Black Chief's about to commence.

The sound of babbling water spurred her thirst. Cautious to avoid the cesspool at the end of the stream, she edged along to her left. A flute piped nearby, and young voices rose in song. When Raven met with the creek, she knelt down to drink. The water was cold in her fingers and sweet on her tongue, with a faint taste of mineral. Once her need was quenched, she walked the stream's bank until the air grew still and tranquil. Weeping willow boughs tickled her arms. Winding her way through the greenery, she found the place that she and Ash had enjoyed. The willows drooped like ribbons, and formed a kind of enclosure, with grass underfoot and the creek flowing through it. Raven emptied her pouch to lay out herbs, a bone-handled knife, and a tool for digging. Between her fingers, she rubbed the black, glossy lock that the Black Chief had cut from his hair and sent to her.

Closing her eyes, she cleared her mind to concentrate. Once her heart felt composed, she brought her being into oneness with the earth. The terrain beneath her toes melded with her legs. She imagined she was planted, like a sapling, drawing nourishment from the ground. Her fingers were leaves. The air that surrounded her mixed with the breath in her lungs. Raven quivered with the vibration of the world around her, its life and its creatures. Touching the sky, her head became part of it. Standing thus, merging with Mother Earth and Father Sky, Raven summoned the Spirits, and she initiated her ritual. She trusted that, when it was done, she would find peace, and hope, and strength. After long months of sorrow, Raven focused on the future. Soon, if she willed it well enough, the past would lie buried, and good things would grow from its forces.

As always when handling magic, truthfulness was essential. Raven opened her emotions. She missed her husband, and ever would do so. Raven feared for her prospects, yet she must trust her own judgment. Her heart brimmed with love, some of which she might pour forth, and some she must reserve. And here, in her circle of willow boughs, Raven's spirit stood naked.

She made the motions, and she voiced the chants. When the rite ended, three black raven feathers, intertwined with strands of her hair, lay on a loose mound of soil. Beneath them, she'd buried her token. All were symbols of her phases. Past, present…and forward. The wind and the earth would take them, would make them of use again. Raven's next steps were her *first* steps— on a journey to the end.

Those steps carried her up the stream bank. They ushered her through an arbor laced with blooms. Her footfalls bore her into the Clearing. In the peace of afternoon, Lily, Lelaneh, and Red Fawn sat before a tepee, singing songs with their children. Contentment radiated from their faces, until a parrot shrieked high in the trees.

The women turned from their youngsters to gaze at their guest. Their astonishment changed into smiles. Then, all three of them held out their arms.

David was different. All the boys knew it. In the two days since Peter saved him from the mermaid, something had changed.

"It's his color," said Bertie. "We can't call him Paleface any longer."

"It's his appetite," said Bingo. "He doesn't stuff himself anymore."

"It's his size," said Chip. "He hardly fits down the tree chute. In another day or so, he'll have to *dig* his way in."

Shiny-bell sounds came from Jewel. She plucked at her chin, fingering make-believe stubble.

"It's time to thin out my band," said Peter, threatening. He turned to eyeball the subject of their speculation. "Paleface," Peter shook his golden head. "You've got to go."

The Lost Boys gasped. On the hearth, the fire snapped in shock. The hideout under the ground seemed to convulse, as if shaken by an earthquake. Jewel's fairy light flickered.

Only David didn't flinch. Peter's verdict instilled a sensation of nerve-jangling panic in the others and, only two days ago, it might have frightened David, too. But he had anticipated Peter's ruling, and he felt prepared to hear it. "Aye, aye, Captain," he answered. The resolution in his response impressed even himself. He didn't so much as blush. In fact, as Bertie noted, David's face was nearly clear again. The brand of Red-Handed Jill was fading.

The captain consulted him one final time. "What's the procedure, Bo'sun? A court-martial? A flogging round the fleet?"

Jewel wrung her hands, but, considering, David pulled a thoughtful expression. He stroked his chin and wrinkled his brow in true officer fashion. The rough hint of whiskers that Jewel had pointed out pleased him, yet he waxed grave. "I believe..." he answered, after deliberating long enough to impress the younger sailors, "I believe we must have a plank-walk."

The boys surged to their feet, shouting with zeal. Those on the bed bounced until its frame groaned, bumping their heads on the earth of the ceiling. With green eyes aglow, Peter jumped up upon his willow throne, one foot on each arm. The sheer volume of the boys' cheers made David smile. At this instant— the very moment that decreed he must leave— he felt more at one with this band than he'd ever done. The irony struck him. It was a paradox he could not have perceived only three days before— before he grew up. He joined in the whooping, no longer fearful that his voice might break.

When the noise subsided, Peter perched on his chair, his brain teeming with plans. The boys leaned in to listen as the fairy whizzed round the room.

"We'll launch the driftwood raft."

The boys nodded.

"We'll sail her into Neverbay."

The boys ooh-ed.

"We'll run out the plank!"

The boys ah-ed!

"Then we'll put the scoundrel at the point of our swords…"

The crew stood on tiptoe.

"And we'll send him down, to drink with Davey Jones!"

A more delightful dispatching could not be conceived. One and all, the Lost Boys stared, openmouthed, in awe of their leader's ideas. Jewel gaped at him, too, but hers was a look of horror.

Peter sat back, grinning in gratification. "Tonight we feast, in Paleface's honor. Because tomorrow…" Dramatically, Peter pointed to David, *"that man dies."* The wicked glint in Peter's eye left no doubt of his intention.

In an act of anticlimax that only he himself noticed, David saluted. "I'll see to the vessel, Captain." He headed for the tree chute, to squeeze his way up to the forest.

"Chip, bear Paleface a hand there. Bertie, round up some rope. Bingo, stop eating and ready the feast." Peter beckoned, and, anxiously, Jewel flitted to sit on his knee. "Jewel, prepare to follow my orders, exactly."

The silver blade in Peter's belt shone sharp in the firelight. Jewel knew her boy. She chimed in a tactful manner, ending with a delicate question mark.

"No, Jewel."

Searchingly, she opened her vivid blue wings, then closed them.

Peter's voice grew stern. "You know the rules."

She cocked her little head, coaxing.

"There's no other way. I've got to get rid of him."

Her wings drooped, and her loving look crumpled.

"I want you to deliver a message."

Holding her breath, Jewel waited, and her little heart banged on her insides.

"To the ladies at the Clearing: I'll abandon one tomorrow. After the plank-walk."

In relief, the fairy exhaled, her sigh trilling like a harpsichord. She smiled again, and her light glowed brightly as she beamed on her boy.

She'd suspected, but she hadn't been sure. Peter was different, too, in the months since Red-Handed Jill retold his story. Something had changed.

At the pinnacle of the Indian mountain, two braves stood on high, looking down. One's eyes were blue, the other's gray as slate. Both men's eyes filmed with sorrow. The whole of the Neverland lay at their feet, yet their gazes reached only to the limits of their loss.

In contrast to their gravity, the river danced behind them, its rapids skipping and shimmering in the sun. A brace of hawks circled on wide-stretched wings. In front of the braves, the forest glowed emerald, and, just to the east, red smoke signaled in invitation. That place was the Clearing— the place these Outcasts must now name as home.

Lightly sighed. "We have family to welcome us, and they make it easier," He sat down to dangle his feet over the precipice. "Your mother and the twins, at least, are happy to have us among them." The wind seeped between Lightly's toes. The air blew chillier up here, and felt thinner in his lungs. Perhaps it was this meager atmosphere that caused the hurt near his heart.

"Yes," Rowan answered, shifting his tomahawk to hunker down at his partner's side. "Our family makes the exile from our village more bearable."

"Last time we came here, I joked of our situation." Lightly's voice wavered, and he cleared his throat. "We walked in two worlds."

"We understood that our path might be stony."

"I'd hoped that the Old One's arguments would win out over Walking Man's."

Early this afternoon, Walking Man had marched through the village, from the Council Lodge to the dwelling place of Rowan and Lightly. He was draped in a yellow blanket that swished on the ground. A dried gourd hung from a strap on his shoulder, and he bore the feathered spear. Grimly, the old man slipped the gourd from his shoulder, to upend it. Water streamed over the remains of the cook fire, and the flames shrank from it, fizzling and hissing. Then Walking Man held up his hand, not in greeting, but in hostility. Taken aback, Rowan and Lightly saw that his fingers were black, smudged with cinders from the council fire. With this residue, he marked the symbol of taboo on the hide of the tepee. Imperious, Walking Man turned to witness the shock on the younger men's faces.

With the last words that their tribesmen were permitted to speak to them, he glared over the pouches of his eyes and decreed in his aged, creaking voice, "Rowan Life-Giver; Lightly of the Air. The council have ruled. Taboo is defied…and you are judged 'Outcast.'" Saying no more, the old man circled his spear to indicate their tepee, then pointed its tip toward the forest. The elder's message could not be clearer: *Take your belongings, and go.*

Lightly felt the injustice. It ran hot and cold through his veins. At first, he and Rowan could only stand helpless, stunned by the blow, while the stench of the wetted fire stuck in their throats. When Walking Man turned his back, they watched him lurch away. Still speechless, they gazed across the encampment. The People went about their business, as always. But this afternoon, no one smiled, no one bantered, and no one looked back at them. Taking a few steps toward the totem pole, the young men drew closer to the villagers' activities, but the people took care not to acknowledge them. Clearly, Rowan and Lightly had become Invisibles. The sensation of non-existence made Lightly's skin crawl.

To Rowan, the scene felt too familiar. It pricked at the wound he received the day his mother was banished. But he understood the constraint laid upon his tribesmen by their elders, and, gently, he had guided Lightly into the tepee, to explain it. "Not a word nor a gesture may be exchanged with us. If we stay, we will be no more than ghosts. Our presence is unwelcome to the People— even frightening."

Lightly couldn't speak, but he nodded. A bitter taste lined his tongue. To worry the women and men was bad enough, but he dreaded lest the children might fear him. With weighty hearts, he and Rowan rolled their possessions into packs, dismantled their tepee, and, bundling it onto its poles, dragged it from the encampment. Exposed and unimpeded, wisps of smoke from the choking fire rose up to coil toward the sky.

As they traveled, the words of Walking Man rang sharp in their ears. Upon their arrival, the People of the Clearing could see what had happened. Kindly, they asked no questions. Accepting help from the twins, Rowan and Lightly erected the tepee in a corner of the Clearing. They positioned it across from the house, at the farthest point from the workshop. It was a pleasant place to dwell, surrounded by woodland and filled with good company, good food, and the love of family. But, blessed as they were, the men were stung by this reversal of the People's good will. So, too, the loss of their status as Messengers pierced their spirits, as if Walking Man's spear had jabbed at them.

They worked quickly to prepare their shelter, then flew here to the mountaintop, their private place, to think on their fortunes alone. "Who, now, will see to the People's needs across the Island? Who will watch for mischief from Peter and his boys?"

"Lightly, you know the answer to these questions." Affectionately, Rowan nudged him. "A man may wander from his tribe, but a worthy man cannot wander from his duty."

"I know. We won't shirk responsibility; we'll still serve the tribe. And, any day they wish, I will welcome them." Lightly blinked the moisture from his eyes. With his hand, he sought his partner's.

Rowan gave it, and his warm, sturdy grip brought comfort to his lover. "Moons ago, Lightly of my Heart, we sat on this very pinnacle, mourning the change in your circumstances. You had sampled the tart taste of truth, and you had outgrown your tribe. It was an end but, also, a beginning."

"You told me then that I would endure, that I'd become stronger. Your prophecy came true. And this time, we're making the change together. I'm satisfied, Rowan. If I'm with you, I'm at home." Lightly lifted Rowan's hand and pressed it to his cheek. Rowan returned the gesture and more, gathering Lightly in his arms to embrace him. As their mouths joined together, Lightly welcomed the strength that the two of them embodied. He clasped his companion, encompassing the firmness of his flesh, and the vigor of his blood. Together, these braves were potent. Whether the elders believed it or not, the might of two men, united in love, was a force for much good for their people.

Rowan's thoughts followed a similar track. Considering, he ran his fingers through Lightly's hair, saying, "We may find this arrangement to be comfortable. No one can question our movements; we may go to the ships, or anywhere else we see fit. We might find, even, that we serve the People *better* than before."

Lightly's burden of hurt lightened at the thought but, paradoxically, his shoulders fell again when he remembered better news. "I was staggered all the more to be cast out *today*— the very hour the elders raised our expectations by restoring Lelaneh to the tribe. The council's ruling gave me hope for us, and hope for Lily."

"That hope can still live. Our actions will prove the elders wrong. But Lelaneh is wise to remain at the House in the Clearing, where she has found happiness. And consider, Lightly; she will be our link to the tribe. With Lelaneh to win them over, are we unreasonable to hope that the elders will accept my mother, and Red Fawn, too?"

"While Lean Wolf lives, Red Fawn can't return to the village." Angrily, Lightly slapped the dagger strapped at his knee. "I believed she was safe at the Clearing, but he sought her out and threatened her. Jill was right when she warned us about Silent Hunter."

Gravely, Rowan nodded. "Red Fawn is another reason for our presence there. Now, the women and children have more men to protect them."

"And Lean Wolf *is* a danger, Rowan. Not just to the Women of the Clearing."

"Yes. We acted discreetly. We did not offend the tribe. It is Lean Wolf's malice that spurred our exile." Protective, Rowan's arm encircled Lightly's shoulders. "But think, Lightly. Why should he so suddenly turn against us? Why now, as he takes interest in your mother?"

Beneath his tan, Lightly blanched. "Only we know that he, too, violates taboo. His connection with Jill is forbidden."

"Our knowledge of his marriage is a threat to him. And because we glide like birds, we are able to track him more easily than the others. As long as we are present and vigilant, we force Lean Wolf to use caution in his contact with her. No matter; we can protect ourselves. Yet today, he closed the council's ears to us. The elders will not hear us if we warn them. In time, Lean Wolf may decide to hide the evidence of his misconduct. As a result of our exile, he is more dangerous to the People...and to Jill."

Lightly's stomach flipped over. "Jill..." Suddenly savage, he jumped to his feet to stand tall against the sky, a light-haired, buckskinned warrior. "You're right. The elders can't stop us now. We must go to the ship, to inform Hook and Jill of the danger."

Rowan's slate-gray eyes smoldered with appreciation, and his carved face softened in a smile. "You see, Lightly? We still walk in two worlds."

"No. We don't." Lightly leapt from the precipice, to coast on an updraft of air. "We glide *over* them."

Lightly offered his hand and, springing like a hawk off the mountaintop, Rowan seized it. Wheeling toward Neverbay, the Indian Messengers broke the boundaries of their losses. They took up their task again, to safeguard the people they loved.

Still arrayed in his yellow blanket, Walking Man sat in state in the center of the encampment. The feather-decked spear lay across his thighs and, with the totem pole at his back, he felt that he personified the People. It was a surprise to him when, contrary to custom, he continued to sit there alone.

Usually, the mothers of the village shooed their young boys from their skirts, sending them to crowd around for his teaching.

At Walking Man's knee, these future warriors learned the tribe's lore and customs. This afternoon, though, they only peeped at him from their doorways, or scuttled to open ground with their game sticks and hoops. Walking Man frowned.

He spotted Panther moving toward him, his easy manner marked by a loping gate. The old man's mood lightened as he anticipated a discussion on the carelessness of young boys today. Panther was an upstanding man. As Walking Man suggested in council, soon he would govern with the elders. Panther was a man worthy to uphold the tribe's longtime traditions. Walking Man raised his hand to Panther, and his leathery face eased to a smile.

But Walking Man's smile turned to stone. Panther walked right past him. The man did not so much as nod in his elder's direction. Strolling on in his pleasant way, Panther passed as if no one of consequence were near.

Walking Man burrowed into his blanket. Such disregard never ventured his way before. No doubt Panther was simply embarrassed, thinking how close he had come to betrothing his daughter to an Outcast. Any right-thinking man would react in this way. Although Walking Man disapproved of Panther's lack of regard toward him, he dismissed it— for now.

Resting from his exertions in the ritual of banishment, Walking Man warmed his old bones in the sun and observed the village around him. A pair of sparrows indulged in a dust bath before him, flapping and chirping. Seeing them made him thirsty, and he tipped the gourd over his mouth to catch a few drops of water. But none remained, and his mouth felt as dry as that dust. He held the gourd high, looking around to catch the eye of some child he might send to the river but, as if he were an Invisible, no one noticed. He missed the children, who not only ran errands for him, but who filled his heart as they sat at his feet, gazing up with their dark, curious eyes to hear his teachings. For the time being, he contented himself in watching the youths and girls with whom he, as an elder, had little to do. Nodding, he approved of their industriousness. Walking Man's work had borne fruit. If the young braves followed in his footsteps, all would be well with the People.

This morning's purge of bad elements worked for their good.

Panther's daughter, Ayasha, scurried up the slope from the river. Walking Man observed how lightly she trod as she gazed under her long black eyelashes at Mountain Cloud, close beside her. On one side, each carried a basket of fish; on the other, they linked arms. This couple made a fine match, and Walking Man approved. Again, his faith in Panther's judgment stood confirmed. He looked forward to the wedding feast, and prepared a few words of encouragement with which to regale the young couple as they passed. The smell of fish came to him, but, however, they themselves did not approach. Ayasha and Mountain Cloud delivered the fish to Panther's tepee, then, circling round the fire pit, they moved on to the dwellings on the other side of the totem pole. Like Panther, they appeared to avoid him.

When the couple reached the barren ring from which the Outcasts' tepee was uprooted, they slowed. Walking Man was too distant to hear their conversation, but he saw Ayasha linger there. Her head drooped. Clasping Mountain Cloud's hand, she restrained him from moving on. She spoke in his ear, as if wishing to keep her words private. Mountain Cloud listened, then looked around at the beaten-down ground. He said something that seemed to reassure her and, gently, he kissed her. Then Mountain Cloud pulled his tomahawk from his belt to test its edge on his thumb. With renewed energy, the couple hurried to enter the woods.

Registering disapproval, Walking Man determined to mention the incident to Panther. According to custom, to take notice of a site of taboo was forbidden. But he was sleepy, and he positioned his spear so that he might lean on it. More comfortable now, he fell into a doze. He roused only when White Bear hailed him, and he sat up with a grunt, his aged joints aching.

"Good day to you, old one." White Bear sounded surly, as usual. The old man appreciated White Bear's aura of severity. The man was tall and, looking up at him, Walking Man squinted to see his scalp lock in silhouette against the white of the clouds. With the light behind the warrior, the old man could not perceive his expression.

"Good day, White Bear. Help me up. I have sat here long enough."

White Bear obliged, somewhat roughly, and the two men turned toward their tepees. Walking Man's voice was reedy from disuse, a condition to which he was not accustomed. "I see that you have finally prevailed over Raven."

"With respect, Walking Man, what is your meaning?"

"I saw her some while ago in her ceremonial dress, heading out from the village. Surely you sent her off?"

Abruptly, White Bear stopped. He hesitated only a moment. "Of course. She will be preparing herself." His jaw tightened, and he rumbled, "But she did not inform me where she would go. Tell me, Walking Man. Which path did she take?"

Walking Man pointed with his spear. "I saw her scamper that way, along the plateau." He smirked. "The elders will be glad when you've settled her, White Bear. That woman has too much spirit. Our fiery one, Ash, seemed to keep her contented, but now that he is gone, your firm hand is required."

They had reached White Bear's dwelling. "Excuse me, old one. I must see to my wife."

Walking Man nodded. Before moving on, he sniffed, enjoying the smell of the stew White Bear's wife was preparing. With his mouth watering, he adjusted the yellow blanket. As he started toward his tepee, White Bear emerged in a hurry. He wore a grim look, and on his lean frame, his muscles bunched tight. In his belt he had tucked a broad hunting knife; at his back he bore a quiver full of arrows. He clutched his bow, and the taut skin at his knuckles showed pale.

Walking Man observed him over his swollen eyelids. "And where do you go now, White Bear? You look fierce, as if you seek to slaughter that albino bear again!"

"No bear today, old one. But I *am* going hunting."

Contrary to custom, White Bear left without paying the respect owed to Walking Man's status. He sprinted along the plateau, and left the old man standing, alone.

Muffled by the tepee, a hungry wail from the baby inside reminded the elder of his belly. Walking Man ambled away. Since no one else had sense enough to listen, he muttered to himself.

In the Tepee of Mother Birch

"**I** cannot stay," Raven said, glancing over her shoulder at the forest from which she emerged. "Soon I must run."

"We understand." Lelaneh's black hair was even longer than the last time Raven had seen it, long ago at the village, but her healer's gaze touched Raven, just as perceptive. The woman ushered her to a blanket before the Outcast tepee. Four children squatted inside, staring at the newcomer with the round, innocent eyes of ones who viewed new and mysterious things. First they'd encountered the tepee, now the face of a stranger. Raven felt a kindred emotion. She stood in a new place, and the world around her was changing.

But when Raven turned to greet Lily and Red Fawn, next, she saw that Lily's comforting manner had not changed, nor had her laugh; "Even our oldest are too young to remember a tepee. Now that Rowan and Lightly have joined us, the little ones are learning how their relatives live." She invited Raven to kneel down, and, crawling closer to her, Lily's infant, the tiny girl with a sprout of red hair, extended a forefinger to touch the soft, white doeskin of Raven's dress. Then she giggled, and scrambled to the cushy lap of her mother.

When the parrot had squawked its warning, the women's twin providers had come running from their workshop. With their muscular physiques, they exuded protectiveness, and although Raven noted their European features, their dress and their ornaments appeared more native than not. They now grinned at Raven, greeting her as a guest. "You are Raven."

"Please, feel welcome here, lady."

Soberly, Raven acknowledged their salutations. At a signal from Lily, these Men of the Clearing rounded up the children. "Into the house, now," they coaxed. "Who wants to try our new sled on the stairs?" With the littlest ones hiked high on their big, bronzed shoulders, the men steered the tykes toward the structure. To Raven, it loomed huge and inflexibly wooden. Soon she would ride aboard a ship, even larger, and bobbing at the wind's every whim on the sea. She shuddered and turned back toward the tepee, appreciating the familiar feel of earth steadying her knees, and the heady scent of the grasses.

Lily empathized with Raven as she gazed upon the symbol of taboo the elder had drawn in charcoal. Lily was too well acquainted with that mark. It was a crude stick drawing of an open hand, fingers splayed in a sign of prohibition. Lily sensed that Raven feared to be marked so herself, and that she was shocked by her own audacity in visiting the Outcasts. No doubt she needed time to adjust. The three Women of the Clearing, better than anyone, understood the trauma of breaking with tribal tradition, even for just a brief errand.

Lelaneh passed Raven a flagon, saying, "Please, Raven, refresh yourself. This is apple nectar, made of fruit from the Fairy Glade."

Grateful for the distraction, Raven sipped the tangy juice. It revitalized her spirit, as Lelaneh intended it should do. The herbalist was an expert in the healing properties of nature, and she was practiced in reading the People's maladies. It was this gift, Raven reflected, that caused the elders to retract Lelaneh's exile this morning, officially overlooking the woman's associations with pirates. Raven held no illusion that her own friendship with Cecco would be dismissed, to say nothing of her alliance with his chief. She drank again to imbibe Lelaneh's comfort, and licked the sweet residue from her lips.

The healer said, "I think you have come for my help, Raven? I see you are dressed for a ritual. I can guess what it is you now require."

Raven blushed, but, knowing that she had no time to spare for modesty, she pressed on with her business. "Yes, Lelaneh, I thank you. Now that my mourning time is ended, I do have need to brew your tea again."

"Never feel shame for this medicine," the herbalist reassured her. "When a woman feels ready to bear a child, she makes the best mother. Nor are you the only woman of the tribe to come to me." She hurried to the house to make up a packet.

Lily took Raven's hand and said, softly, "I am pleased to see you so rosy, Raven. Soon you will sew your beads on this handsome dress again. But you have not come just to see Lelaneh, I believe. Every day, I receive a message for you."

Eagerly, Raven asked, "From the Black Chief?" Lily nodded, and Raven sighed in relief. "So he *will* keep his word?"

"He always has done, for us."

"Oh, Raven!" Red Fawn's dimples appeared, and her silvery earrings flashed. "Does he love you a little? How I envy you."

Taken aback, Raven reddened again. "Oh, no. I only lent him my help, in return for a favor." She turned to Lily. "What is his message?"

"He assures you of his regard, and he instructs you to wait for his signal. The fairy will carry it to you. It may be a few days, at most a week."

"Very well." Raven squared her shoulders. "With Lelaneh's tea to protect me, I can wait with less worry."

"I understand. You wish to leave White Bear's tepee. You wish to leave without making his child."

"Since Ash died, what *I* wish is not important."

Lily's sympathy draped Raven like a warm fur. "Always, you have protected your little sister. Willow will miss you, Raven, and you will miss her. But I know that, whatever each must sacrifice, the love two sisters bear one another will sustain them."

Red Fawn asked, "Are you sure you wish to wander? Won't you dwell here, with us? You heard our providers. You are welcome here."

"No, I cannot find it in my heart to offend my brother-in-law so deeply."

"Then, will you follow Captain Cecco? He comes often to ask about you."

"I will travel with the pirates, but only as far as the Other Island. Once I have gone, you may send word to White Bear of my whereabouts."

"To the Other Island!" Red Fawn's dark eyes grew wider. "Who will provide for you there?"

"I hope that the family of White Bear will accept me, as his obligation. They will know nothing of my trials, and I will work hard to serve them. In this way, I will honor my brother-in-law, yet remain at a distance." Raven looked to Lily, whose gaze fell upon her with maternal concern. "What signal will the fairy send to me, Lily?"

"You may not see her come and go, but you will find a piece of cloth, matching this one." Lily held up a sleek swatch of fabric, blue as the plumes of a peacock.

Raven recognized it instantly. It was a shred of the scarf with which Hook had bound his severed wrist, to veil his disfigurement from her eyes. Raven was moved by the man's courtesy; this token was light enough for the fairy to carry; it was easily concealed, and a not unpleasant reminder of his intimacies. She fondled it, remembering its feel on her skin, cool and silky where he touched her, on that night that his passions and hers formed a storm.

As Raven hid the fabric in her pouch, Lily continued, "When you see this sign, you must hurry here. Be ready to leave forever then, for his men will escort you to the ship."

"To the Black Chief's ship?"

"To Captain Cecco's."

"And his woman? His Jill?"

"You will wish to know that the Lady Jill, too, asks after your welfare each time she visits us. She retains her abode on the *Roger*, under the protection of the Black Chief."

Raven relaxed, relieved to understand that the Black Chief's summons had not led to more discord, and pleased to learn the good tidings that she would sail with her friend— with her fellow in affliction, with the handsome, outlandish Captain Cecco. For the first time in many moons, her blood pulsed with anticipation. At the same time, though, she grieved for his loss. Her heart hurt for someone else, too. "It is unfair, is it not, that a person may love twice, yet may hold only one?"

"Here at the Clearing, we do not limit our love," Lily said, kindly. "And that outlook is why we were banished. But no matter where one wanders, each person shares affection as is his or her inclination. You, I think, are more openhanded than some might assume."

"No, Lily, you are wrong. I am selfish. I am headstrong and disobedient. I run before troubles catch up to me. But here comes Lelaneh— I must run now, or trouble will find me here." She stood and, seeing the packet Lelaneh offered, prepared to place it inside her pouch, by Hook's scrap of silk.

"Remember," Lelaneh instructed her, offering the medicine, "steep a cup every morning, and drink it down warm. When you wish to conceive, you must not imbibe this tea at all, until your little one enters your arms."

Above the four women, the sky burst into sound. It was the lookout parrot, screaming and fluttering in the treetops, fanning its rainbow of wings in alarm. Other birds rose, too, startled from the branches, to soar and to shriek. Immediately, the Men of the Clearing rushed from the house with their wild hair flailing, pulling axes from their belts. The women looked all around them, then focused on a gap in the fringe of the forest.

There, at the place where the pirates' path ended, stood Captain Cecco. With his bracelets gleaming, he raised his hand in greeting to the men. When he saw that Raven stood among the women, his smile broadened. He opened his arms and called out to her, but the parrot kept up a commotion, and everyone stilled to look for the reason. Then the women stepped back, clutching one another, and the twins resumed their stances of alert.

Within the garden trellis loomed the form of a warrior. Red Fawn whimpered, and Lily gasped. The twin men straddled the grass, poising their axes.

The warrior stood tall, and stately as a totem pole. He carried a bow. White streaks crossed his brow and three black lines tilted toward the peaks of his cheekbones. His skin shone like copper, and the feathers on his headdress bent with the breeze.

His stare rifled each of the people, and his expression grew all the fiercer as he observed the pirate. Soon his gaze fell on Raven, and as he glowered at her, his angular face turned to stone.

Raven took one look in those hard, gray eyes. And then she ran.

Even before she ran, Raven's heart started thumping. It was this beat she heard as she darted into the forest. She felt the rush of panic in her head, the nip of fear at her heels. She dreaded what White Bear would do to her, if once he laid hands upon her. Only one sound rose above her heart's disharmony: White Bear's moccasins as he leapt to the wood in pursuit. After that, the drumming of her heart and the drumming of his feet merged to become inseparable.

Raven ran.

She didn't slow her progress to avoid the foliage. Raven ran right through it, stung by low-hanging leaves, her skin scraped by bark. Raven ran like an arrow, straight through the wood. She couldn't afford to lose even a finger's breadth of space between herself and her hunter. She didn't take time to shield herself— she ran.

The wood was not dense here. Tender leaves collided with her, leaving moisture cold on her face. Sunlit patches rose up to meet her. The grasses were kind to her feet, with only a nut or a twig here and there, to press into her soles. But deeper forest lay ahead, both a friend and a foe. There she might be hidden, harder to track. Yet, equally, her path would turn difficult, the old trees less yielding to the plight of the quarry— as unyielding as White Bear, if once she allowed him to catch her. She angled her path to avoid the thicker growth.

Raven was familiar with this forest. Past her panic, she began to design her flight. Young branches swished behind her as his bigger body plunged through the brush. White Bear was as intent on pursuit as she on her freedom. He, too, spared not an instant to dodge obstacles. But now that they'd passed the long grass near the Clearing, his footfalls, like hers, fell more quietly. Naturally, for White Bear knew this terrain too.

For all her anxiety, Raven was certain her evasion had averted conflict with Captain Cecco. Surely he would not interfere with White Bear; the pirates were under orders from their chief to keep peace with the natives. Nor, in his boots, could Cecco catch up with them. Shedding concern for her ally, Raven felt lighter on her feet. She eyed the lay of the land before her: a small uphill incline, a stand of pine. Beyond the pines, sun-speckled wood again, and, farther off, rock-hard ground should signal the onset of caves.

As Raven and her sister discussed this afternoon, they had played there as girls. Their mother had warned of animals that sheltered there, but those openings in the earth were too tempting. The girl Raven wasn't frightened from her playground, and Willow followed her sister. Within those craggy confines, the girls set up 'house,' nursed little fox kits, and fled summer's heat in the cool of the caverns. Now Raven felt like one of those foxes. No matter what lurked within the hollows, just one animal troubled her now.

As her breathing grew harsher, she looked for familiar outcroppings, making ready to duck in between them. Once among the caverns, Raven could hide. She could choose any hollow along the turning pathway, slide inside, and watch White Bear's moccasins fly by. She wouldn't give him the opportunity to find her. She'd slip out to dash off again. White Bear would be sure to believe she doubled back.

But that move was a vixen's trick. Raven's instinct was finer. She wouldn't follow the obvious strategy, aiming for safety. Instead, she'd plunge far ahead. Because White Bear would detect any trace she left in the grass, she'd keep to rocky ground. Leaving no trail, she'd move more slowly then, and silently. She must not cause rabbits to start, or birds in their treetops to cry out in complaint. Already she had heard deer in the brush, their hooves pattering as they hurried from the intruder. But, for the present, speed was Raven's aim. She must gain the caves. She didn't care if White Bear knew where she headed— she need only reach there before him.

Tense and tiring, her legs felt a change. The earth became firmer. Harder terrain lay ahead, and the caves that promised protection. Raven stole one quick glance behind her. What she saw made her heart flutter, like a hummingbird.

White Bear was gaining. He was closer than ever Willow had come during their many races. Nearer, even, than Ash in the vigor of his youth had achieved. White Bear loped on long legs, his face determined, his nostrils flared— and his bow in his hand. Raven felt a need to scream, but she had no breath to spare. She didn't look back any more. Like a deer, Raven ran.

White Bear hurtled on. He knew that few braves of the tribe could match him. He didn't miss a step. His respiration felt sharp in his chest, but his heartbeat stayed steady. His hunter's impulse came fully to bear; he focused on his prey. As he trailed his quarry, his legs pumped, his buckskin leggings shielded his shins from the whip of the underbrush. The air tugged at his scalp lock, flogging the feathers against his head.

Raven ran like the doe; if Willow spoke true, no brave had yet caught her. But White Bear, too, had prowled these woods. He had a notion of where she would run to ground. If once he let her get there, he would lose her. Reaching back, White Bear snatched a dart from his quiver. His arrow would glide straight and true. Raven couldn't miss the point White Bear's barb would speak to her. Without breaking stride, he nocked his arrow, aimed, and sent it winging.

She didn't see his shot, yet she felt it. Just as she came to the pathway— the haven of caves— a whistling sound shrieked past her ear. The draft from its feathers skimmed the heat of her cheek. Her feet trod on the verge of the rocky trail way, the dry path that promised her shelter. But as the arrow streaked by on that side, she swerved. With a new spurt of speed, Raven veered to the left instead, heading for the wood. Shocked by his shot, she plunged onward, relying on raw, visceral instinct to save her.

She'd imagined what his hands would do. She had not dreamt of his weapons. Now, truly, she felt like the vixen. Fear clouded her mind. No new scheme entered her thinking. The only ploy she could conceive was that of a creature, rushing, running. Her senses grew more acute; the predator's tread juddered behind her. The sound of his breathing reached her, and the slap of fringe against his leggings. She smelled his scent. It was sharp, and excited— like her own.

Raven ran.

Gratified, White Bear saw Raven shy from the path. He had headed her off from the warren of caves. His arrow quivered, embedded in a tuft of grass. He didn't slacken his pace as he bent to scoop it up. It felt hot in his hand. Guided by its maker, it had missed her cheek by a wing's width, that fragile, woman's cheek, unprotected by her brief yield of hair. Her shearing had annoyed him before, but now he appreciated it as a victim's vulnerability.

As he raced with her, White Bear broke a grim smile. Exertion enhanced his vision. With the eyes of an eagle, he watched Raven's body move, lithe, limber, hardly struggling in spite of her effort. Her brown legs worked supplely beneath her white dress. Slimmer than her sister's, her hips held a graceful sway. Her neck looked exposed, appearing elegant under her odd crop of hair. Concentrating on this female as he had never done before, White Bear discovered that she grew in significance. Soon, she was more to him than just his wife's sister. She became other than a handsome burden, and more than reward for protection. Now, newly, she was Raven. She was the goal of the warrior White Bear's pursuit.

Through this physical challenge, White Bear gained mental insight. Gradually, he understood that the object of his pursuit was a *worthy* object. As Raven evaded her hunter, she became a greater prize. Her every bound made her more precious.

White Bear found himself committing to this ritual. As with any other creature, a pact governed the hunt. It connected its participants. The aims of huntsman and hunted diverged, but once the contest was over, its opponents must combine. A tradition was followed, with reverence for sacrifice. After he caught her, like a deer to be devoured, her flesh and his would be one. When engaged with a woman, the process amounted to a ceremony. Their two lives ran toward a purpose— they ran to unite.

And, now, in his body, White Bear knew something other than the anger that had set off this pursuit. He felt a spur of stimulation, a thrill beyond that of the chase. Suddenly, he was filled with desire, so strong that his body felt as vital and hard as a tree trunk. The air leaving and filling him served his lungs more efficiently, his legs lost the wobble of fatigue. White Bear was a tree, his element was the forest, and he moved like a master within it. There was no question he would catch her, in the end. He was strong as the oak that held up its arms, heavy with branches, centuries old. He was hardy as the acorn that dropped from its budding. He required fertile earth to receive his seed. Moved now by the urge of his lust, White Bear ran.

With his presence at her back, Raven searched her memory for a place of sanctuary. A second of White Bear's arrows was sure to hit its mark. If she kept straight on, the woods would rise up and up, thinning as they climbed, until they vanished altogether, opening onto a mossy hillside. A slippery hillside, and an abrupt end— the cliff that hosted the waterfall. That cliff was too steep for a plunge in the water, even if the pool below were deep enough to catch her— and it was not. She must seek out a place to hide, before the uphill slope slowed her down, or her weariness.

The woman darted to the left, but White Bear was one with the woods that admitted her. Its growth here was thicker, the trees wider— oak, alder, and pale-skinned birch. His pulse surged as her white dress disappeared behind a tree trunk, then she leapt into sight again. Nearly stumbling on a knot of root, White Bear slowed to pry off his moccasins. The earth was moist beneath his feet, and giving. He gained traction, and quickly regained his speed. A jay screamed overhead, its lonely call piercing through the wood. The noise lodged in White Bear's soul. He was that jay— raucous and urgent— calling to his female.

As the jay cried, Raven recalled the flash of feathers on the arrow that had buzzed past her cheek. Her bones ached now, her breath speared her chest. Afraid she might drop at any moment, she scanned the land ahead, seeking shelter. She became aware of the sun again, beating down upon her face; the wood was thinning. All around her, bright birch bark made her blink. These small, slender trees offered no protection. Raven sought an older one, a mother tree, whose broad base could shield her, could shadow her, until the hunter and his arrows passed her by.

As if in answer to her need, the tree appeared. Raven shot one last look behind her. The jay called again, but the birch blocked her pursuer from view. Raven fought the desire to keep running. Instead, she flung herself before the mother tree. Shoving her back flat against it, she pressed her palms to the chalky bark. It felt dry to her touch, fresh and calm. She took two panting breaths, then ceased breathing to listen. She counted. One...two— White Bear barreled into sight, his bow in his hand. Raven didn't move, didn't blink.

The sun dappled his copper shoulders. He was rushing through the birch grove— away from Raven. But the jay shrieked a third time. White Bear's head jerked toward the sound, to the side, and his long lock of hair whipped with it. He stopped. Frozen in midstride, he listened. Raven heard his heavy breaths. She fought to stop her own. With her heart in her throat, she allowed only the thinnest passage of air to enter her nostrils. She kept her mouth closed, her eyes open. She wished a breeze would rise to rustle the leaves, to mask the throb of her body. But the wood between prey and predator stood motionless. The blue jay flapped to its nest.

White Bear held still, an oak among birches. Only his head moved, as he read the grass for signs, then searched every shadow.

Raven was grateful for the camouflage of her white tunic, the brevity of her dark hair. If only he would turn to look to the right, she could slip to the other side of her tree. She thought of kicking a twig, to make a noise that would send him hurtling the wrong direction. But any movement would catch his eye. She watched instead, as his gaze scanned the trees, closer and closer to her own. Her blood pounded at her temples. She knew what he must do, if he spied her.

When he spied her, for she held no doubt now. White Bear was too skilled a tracker. The trail was dead; he wouldn't move on. Raven's impulse hovered between fight and flight. But she couldn't run any more. Even a doe reached her breaking point. Raven understood: she waited now at the end of her path.

But to fight? How? With what weapon? In the past she used the defense of avoidance. She had eluded White Bear, turned away from him. But always, in the past, Willow was near. No kind of confrontation could take place before his wife. Raven realized, with a plunge of her stomach, that she had been wrong to run. Better to have remained at the Clearing, where Lily and the others were watching. But Captain Cecco stood there too, and his recognition of Raven was obvious. At that instant, diverting White Bear from Cecco had seemed the right thing to do. And, at that time, Raven believed she could outrun *anyone*. Running was her shield. For the first time, it failed her. White Bear used it better.

Submission, then, was her recourse. If Raven played along, she might placate White Bear's pride. If she promised to come with him, to do as he demanded, would he be pacified? Yet he had seen her *seem* obedient many times in the past. How could acquiescence now appease him? Seeing him crouching, his body poised to pounce, Raven doubted if any word or any gesture, save one, could satisfy him today. She had run, and she had run out of options.

After so many moons, her fight was finished.

As she reached this realization, her head drooped, her eyes closed. No escape remained open. At last, Raven's spirit released its stubborn hold. When, finally, she looked at her feet, she saw that they were bleeding.

White Bear's feet bled, too. Raven's tired eyes opened a little wider. He had abandoned his moccasins. Willow's moccasins! Where had he left them? She raised her face to see her sister's husband, and his gray gaze lay upon her, pinning her to her tree. His eyes were hard as ever, and triumphant. As his black-striped face gained a lordliness, he straightened. Slowly, he set the arrow to his bow. He raised his weapon. He dragged back the bowstring. Angling his head, White Bear drew a bead, his eyes intense, lining up along his arrow shaft.

He growled at her, "Make no move."

Raven saw the glint of his eye, the edge of his arrowhead. She pressed against her tree. She inhaled one final breath.

White Bear pulled the bowstring back, another inch. Sure of

his aim, he lifted his head, to observe her. As if pegged to the tree, Raven watched. His fingers opened, slowly, delicately, like a flower coming into bloom. The air parted as the arrow cut through it. It made a sharp sound, like wind ripped in half. Then, ages later, came the thwack of bark at her ear, and the spray of wood chips hitting her cheek. White Bear stood before her, his bow still raised, his chest puffed with pride…and a firm, erect staff beneath his breechclout. Raven knew what he was doing to her— *now.*

He dropped his bow. He shrugged off his quiver and lowered it, deliberately, to the earth. He divested himself of his broad hunting knife, and his eyes never left her.

Raven felt surprise to be still alive. She felt too much alive. She was too much a part of her world, and that world gaped open to White Bear. Tearing her hand from the tree, she seized the arrow. She yanked it from the bark and clutched it like a knife. In a long-denied declaration, she worked her throat in ululation. The resonance of her cry rang through the wood, jeering and jubilant all at once. And then she ran again. But this time, it was White Bear who was surprised because, this time, she did not run away.

Raven ran right at him.

White Bear stared in astonishment. He took one step back. He hunched over, his arms bowed, his hands open to catch her, bending and bracing for the blow. Raven rushed at her hunter, covering the distance in only moments.

She leapt. He dashed the arrow from her fingers. Their bodies slammed together, and her legs locked about his hips. White Bear caught her in the branches of his arms. The impact forced him backward, stumbling, and although her momentum sent him spinning, he held her secure.

He had prepared himself for the force, and he compensated, rocking as he rounded. What he did not anticipate was her next attack. The moment she was in his grasp, Raven launched herself at him again. She seized his head in her hands and, snarling, she crushed his lips with her own.

Hugging her to his body, White Bear didn't try to protect himself. His mouth pressed against her aggression; he returned her embrace.

They both tasted blood before he recovered command, taking her lips in with his to shove his tongue in her teeth.

Like a cornered vixen, she was feral, and she was brazen. At her core, a ferocious joy erupted, and, as she had expected— as she had dreaded— White Bear matched her. A potent emotion, too long untapped, pervaded her senses. Raven let it run.

White Bear carried her toward Mother Birch. He pressed Raven's back to the bark, a living wall, and used the tree to support her. Inflamed by the chase, he had craved Raven. Now, goaded by her hostility, he was just as rough as she. He jerked her skirt up. Beneath it, her skin was heated, and damp from exertion. He scented the musk of her eagerness. Baring her hips, too, he laid his hands there. She dropped her belt, then pulled her tunic over her head to discard it. He felt her tugging at his breechclout next, loosening it to free his vitals to the air, as he had done for her. They stood naked among the white trees of this woodland, primed to combine her flesh and his into one.

But every impulse of this brave lay grounded in tradition. Under Mother Birch, the hunter White Bear ceded to custom. Symbolically, his arrow had lodged in her heart. Acknowledged in his conquest, still he delayed his indulgence. Gazing in her eyes, he murmured, reverently, "Spirit of the Woodland, I honor your sacrifice." The contest was over, proper homage was paid, and, here at the end, opponents must now unite. He leaned closer to claim her.

This act of respect touched Raven's heart. It resonated more deeply than the feeling she had veiled until now. Tears burned in her eyes, and, in a final deed of agreement, she pressed a kiss on his throat, just above the white ring of bear claws. At last, she tasted the skin of the warrior White Bear, the brave she admired, the man she desired. At the touch of her lips, the quest began again but, this time, its participants were both of one mind, and both of one spirit.

And Raven was eager to proceed. With her legs she held tightly to the sinews of his thighs, which pulsed with strength between hers. This man before her was one who fought for what he loved, and the scars on his ribs stood as testimony. She brushed them with her fingertips, felt the rough within smooth of his skin. As, at last, she allowed the indulgence of touching him, she accepted him wholly, as a man, and as a lover. She was impatient, now, for this rite that she'd so long evaded. She took the weight of his branch in her hand, while her woman-place ached to admit him. As his grip tensed on her hips, she denied him no longer. Setting the head of his manhood to the entrance of her womb, she gripped his arm and rose to it, and she gasped as he drove deep within her.

Foxlike, her frenzy pounced again, and it snapped at him, too, and he shoved her up against the birch. Pressed between the rigidity of the tree and the tension of his chest, Raven's soft body yielded. With each savage stab, the breath chuffed from her lungs, and like claws her nails snatched his skin, and she baited him, and she loved him, and their senses scaled the height of the sky while their bodies moved, brutish, below it, in the shade and the shelter of a tree. Like creatures coupling in season, at the end of their race they were panting, rutting, and sore.

When they stopped to breathe, he leaned his forehead on the smooth, cool bark of the birch. He pressed his lips to her neck. Again, he thought how gracefully this neck held her head, and how the shearing of her hair left her vulnerable to his touch. Her hands stroked his back, and her shoulder rose to cradle his face to her chin. The beat of her heart— *his* heart— vibrated against his chest. Gradually, the sounds of the woodland returned to him, the whirr of grasshoppers; a chatter of squirrels. His remembered that his feet hurt, and he looked down to see blood on her toes.

He gathered her in his arms again, and turned his back to receive the birch tree's support. He slid down, easing to sit at its root. With a handful of moss, he dabbed her wounds, and cleaned them. She winced, but he found only small cuts, like his. He mopped the blood from his own feet, too, and when he looked up, her black eyes shone with a wild light again, and his mind turned alert as before, with a warning. He remembered how many times she had dodged him. Wary that she might turn tail to run, he shot out his hand to grasp her ankle.

At the heat of his touch, she felt a thrill of belonging. It was the satisfaction for which she had longed, and which she had wished to avoid, knowing that she must soon reject it. For the moment, though, her throat purled with pleasure. Kneeling over him, she straddled his lap, and set her knees on the soft, yielding earth. Now his hands gripped her face, and, demanding, he kissed her. She joined in eagerly, reaching down to feel his male strength rebounding, and she led him to enter her valley again.

Raven grasped the tree's trunk, as solid as her brave, and its vital aliveness sent a charge up her arms and into her being. She settled upon him. Then, slowly, she raised up, and now let herself down. This time, she didn't hurry, and, with his hands on her waist and his lips brushing her breasts, the passion budded and blossomed. A rumble rolled deep in his chest, and, more leisurely this time but just as intense, bliss burst through the bodies of Raven and White Bear, to surge through their hearts once again. In a flash of white and turquoise feathers, the jaybird rose from its nest to call down at them, circling over the lovers. A single blue plume whirled as it fell to the ground.

Exhausted, Raven collapsed in White Bear's arms. He laid her with care on the grass, and he stretched out beside her. As he let her rest, he saw in the gentle light that filtered through the birch leaves what he'd never noticed before: small beads of perspiration above her lip, the shell-like shape of her ear. Her form was comely and capable, yet some tension seemed to warn of an independent nature. Still, he found peace on her features this afternoon, a contentment invisible before, not just to White Bear, but to all the tribe, since the day his friend Ash left her widowed. White Bear was a practical man, a man toughened by experience, yet the signs of his effect upon Raven caused his spirit to stir, not with pride, but with humility. To hold such a woman was honor.

When her eyes opened to behold him, White Bear rolled above her. She embraced him, welcoming the weight of his body and the earthen bed that supported them. She felt the possessiveness of his hands on her shoulders, and the coarseness of his lone, long lock as it lay across her throat, just as she had imagined. She memorized these feelings, knowing she must indulge them again only in remembrance.

Harmonious as the moment might be, the two halves of this couple still strove at cross purposes. As if to contradict her thoughts, White Bear said, "Now that I have caught you, I do not want to let you loose to flee again." He frowned with the expression Raven had grown used to viewing on his noble face, and asked, "All these moons. All those nights. Why did you turn from me?"

She looked past him, up, into the green, leafy branches etched against a bird's-egg-blue sky. Now that she had risen in his esteem, now that tenderness warmed his tone, she was unsure how to disappoint him. She was unwilling to cause him hurt, for Raven knew a true test of love: causing pain to a cherished one hurt herself even more. She felt that, in answering his question, her voice would be too heavy. She uttered only, "White Bear."

"I hear you. You do not call me 'Brother.' "

"Yet brother is what you are."

"I know, now, to listen beyond your words. I know that when you turned from me, you did not wish to do so. Whether running or yielding, yours are not the actions of indifference."

She countered, "Your actions *were* those of indifference, and rightly so. I did not mean to change them."

"But you feel strongly for me."

"And how do you feel, for me?"

His grip upon her shoulders tightened. Within his hold, Raven felt all the care and protection of a husband for his wife. He said, truthfully, "My feeling is obvious."

"Yet I would be content as before, when it was clear that you felt nothing."

His forehead creased. "Ash was my blood brother. It is right that I should take you for my own."

"I have been a burden to you."

"And now you are a joy."

"But I am selfish. White Bear, I have always wanted more."

"Today, little blackbird, you have won it. My heart lies open to you."

"I want everything." She shook her head, disconsolate. "Yet I want nothing."

"As always, your words bewilder me."

Raven saw the puzzlement on his face, and understood that he allowed it to show only because of the closeness they now shared. She could not recall one instance of White Bear exhibiting uncertainty before his wife. She rejoiced to share his confidence, yet she sorrowed for Willow's loss.

He continued, "You dwell within my family. You are nourished by the fruits of my hunting, and you sleep beneath the shelter of my tepee. For many moons, you requested nothing, but shared in my all."

"Yes." She loved the frankness of his gaze, but she could not bear it. Sighing, Raven closed her eyes. What she had dreaded was coming to pass, and, as she had guessed, the cost to Willow was too high.

White Bear watched the pulsing of the life-vein beneath her jaw. He spoke her name, as if for the very first time. "Raven." He said it again, lower, and as gently as his harsh voice allowed. "Raven. Even when I catch you, you hide from me."

"White Bear, you caught me long ago."

"And still, you ran?"

"I do not flee from you." She opened her eyes, black as her namesake. The sadness ran in them, deep, like a river. "I run from myself. My own nature frightens me."

"You feel so frightened that you run until your feet bleed?"

"I fear what has happened."

"Yet I am certain that you wanted it to happen."

"It will not happen again."

Angrily, White Bear rose to his knees, startling two chipmunks that scampered, scolding, up a tree. He no longer confined her. If she ran from him this time, he thought, she would not stray for long. Now she belonged with him. Still, he echoed the animals' irritation. "Why do you say this?"

Raven read the wounding she inflicted on his heart, and she felt it in her own. She rose up to sit before him, laying her hands on his arm, tense and tough. After the fever of her passion, the cool of the shade chilled her nakedness, and she shivered. "Here is truth. Here is my heart broken open: I feel too much for you, and I feel too much for Willow."

White Bear pulled her near, rubbing her arms and warming her against his chest until he stilled her shivering. "You have been mourning. Your heart was closed to happiness. I am glad now to hear it speak to me."

"At first, my heart was closed."

"But time has passed. As you have said, I am a patient man."

"Ash was rash, and I loved his impulsiveness. But in these months since his passing, I have grown older. I found your patience to be a welcome trait."

"Patience has served me. It can serve you, too."

"I watch you, White Bear. You are a good man. I see your kindness to my sister. To please her, you welcomed me to your home. I feel your pride in her child. I witness the wisdom that earns you a place among the elders. You respect me as sister to your wife. You allow me to tend to you, and you gave me time to mourn. In all things, you are a man. One day, I forgot to look for Ash. I looked at you. On that day, when you got up to leave our tepee, you carried my heart through the door." Raven looked down. "It was then that I knew I must run."

He sat silent for some moments, and then he smiled. "But today, you came to me."

"No, White Bear. You hunted me down."

"This afternoon we celebrate our ceremony. I am now your husband."

"You are my sister's husband."

He huffed. "A double tie then, all the stronger. Why try to break it, Raven?"

"See us now. Would you wish for Willow to witness us, close as we are?"

"You see Willow when she is close with me."

"Yes." The word escaped from Raven in a sob, and one simple sound turned to confession.

Beneath the black stripes of paint, White Bear's features smoothed, and at last he believed he understood. "Raven." He opened his hands, to show their capacity. "I have no need to choose between you. I can provide for both of my wives, and for their children."

Raven's head jerked up. "No!"

"You bore no sons for Ash. Do you fear this, too? That you cannot bear?"

"I bore no sons because I used Lelaneh's herbs. Ash's temperament was not yet settled, and we both desired to run free."

White Bear drew back, but, this time, he waited to hear more before rendering judgment. The council accepted Lelaneh into the tribe again, and with good reason. Raven had the right to consult the herbalist, although White Bear could not approve of her visit today to the Clearing, where the Outcasts dwelled, and where, even as he watched, a pirate was welcomed. As for Ash's temperament, White Bear regretted as deeply as any of Ash's friends the recklessness that had colored his character. It was Ash's rashness that got him killed. White Bear asked, evenly, "And is this why I found you in the Clearing, Raven? You still wish to run free?"

She whispered, "Yes, White Bear." She could not meet his eyes. Having lived beside him these many moons, she knew the shadings of his voice. When he spoke again, his timbre betrayed disappointment.

"You love me, Raven. But you do not want to give me children?"

Now her eyes fixed upon him, and she declared, "For my children, I want a father all their own."

Considering her meaning, he studied her. His hurt disappeared, and his scrutiny mellowed. "Your gaze is green, then— on Willow?"

"Because I love her, I may not show my love for you."

"But Willow's wish—"

"I will not lie with you within her tepee." Raven closed her mouth, determined to say no more.

But White Bear kissed her, and she didn't need to speak. He stroked her face. With his fingers, he raised her chin, more tenderly than she believed his hardened hands could do, so that she looked up into the highest reaches of the birch tree's boughs. He placed his lips against her ear, and his words vibrated in its hollow.

"We do not lie beneath the shelter of my tepee," he murmured.

"We lie alone, in the tepee of Mother Birch."

Raven had known what would happen, if ever he laid his hands upon her. Worn and weary, trembling at his touch, she wilted against him. He laid her down and, gently this time, the hunter loved her, and she loved him in return. Then they rested beneath the canopy of the Mother's sheltering arms.

As the sun began the journey to its sleeping place, White Bear slung his bow and his quiver across his back, and he nestled Raven in his arms. And he ran again, lightly, lovingly, over the path on which she had led him. He ran *with* her, this time, and the two journeyed as one, as husband and his wife, toward home.

When he reached the place where he had kicked off Willow's moccasins, he was pressing his cheek to Raven's forehead, smelling the birch bark in her hair. The blue jay's feather adorned it. Her arms were wrapped around his neck, her lips shaped a smile that this man, who loved her now, had rarely seen. His heart beat steady, and his breathing came easily. He passed his moccasins, and kept on jogging.

He wouldn't stop to set her down; he wouldn't break his stride to pause. Not now, after all the trouble he took to catch her. Not now that her soul reposed in his. She was like a doe. She was strong, yet she was shy and skittish. Even now, he wasn't sure of her. He believed, but he wasn't certain, that she would no longer run.

As he carried his new wife, the hunter's bear claw necklace tapped against his chest. The drumming of her heart and the drumming of his own merged to become inseparable. This afternoon belonged to the two of them. Tomorrow, he would hunt down Willow's moccasins, in a chase not nearly as exhilarating as today's.

To Honor and Betray

When he spied the young brave, Lean Wolf stopped to stand with his bow on his back, clutching a carcass by the scruff. This winter, Walking Man would be warmed by soft fox fur.

"I bear you no grudge," Lightly said. Beneath his leather headband, his eyes remained clear and blue, as if he were telling the truth. Listening at his mother's knee, he had learned how to tell a story. "I understand that when the council questioned you about Rowan and me, you were honor-bound to answer." He indicated the surrounding wildwood, "Even though it led to this, your own time of exile, you were obligated to speak."

Lean Wolf had betrayed Rowan and Lightly, and he applied caution before allowing Lightly to approach. "Then I will listen," Lean Wolf answered, and his suspicious expression turned eager. He gestured, and the two men moved away from the waterfall that frothed noisily nearby.

Lean Wolf threw down his weapons and his kill, and sprawled on a shady patch of pine needles, fragrant in the fresh morning air. Four suns had set since he'd clasped his wife in his arms. One more would be too many. "Well, what word has your mother sent to me?"

"She knows you feel as impatient as she. Red Hand from the Sea will meet you this day. Can you canoe to the Mermaids' Lagoon?"

With a smirk of conceit, Lean Wolf said, "I have been there before. Have you? I don't suppose you find the mergirls to your taste."

"Of course I've been there. I know how to guard myself against them." Lightly measured the man's mood, then returned the taunt. "Do *you?*"

Lean Wolf laughed, "No female has yet turned on me. I never offer the opportunity."

"Then you are a wiser man than most. When the sun is highest, you'll find Red Hand by the caves along the coast. She said you should come hungry."

"She knows by now that I am *always* hungry."

Lightly's fair complexion turned darker. "Lean Wolf, as I told you, I bear no bitterness. But if you break my mother's heart, our friendship will be ended."

"How can we hold a friendship, Lightly? You are an Outcast. I shouldn't even associate with you. Only my love for Red Hand from the Sea compels me to act against the council's judgment."

"I know how well you respect the council. The longer we talk, the better I understand."

"You've grown bolder, young one, but do not push me too far." His gaze ranged over Lightly's frame, assessing the brave's emerging muscles. "Worse things than banishment can happen to a man."

"I hope to learn, soon, just what those things might be." Lightly grinned then, to take the sting from his words. "I will tell my mother to pack her picnic."

"And her pirates suspect nothing?"

Lightly's ribcage swelled beneath his vest. "Red Hand is as shrewd as any of them." This time, he relayed no lie. "She will see you when she wants, and she wants to see you now."

He dodged into the forest, to leave the Silent Hunter to prepare.

"I bear no grudge, Lean Wolf Silent Hunter," Lightly whispered to himself as he searched for Rowan, whose rigid figure blended like bark on the trees as he stood guard among the shadows of the elms. "I feel only pity."

Humbled by his experiences on the Island, David felt that the House in the Clearing was too grand for him. When the ladies offered him a room, he asked if he might stay instead in the Wendy House. The hut had shrunk since last he saw it— or rather, he had grown. Whatever had occurred, the rough-made dwelling appealed to him as the home Jill had once enjoyed, and as a place of solitude for a young man's growing thoughts.

One of those thoughts concerned his duty. Thanks to Jill, his past had crystalized in glorious colors. His future might prove just as brilliant. Yesterday, Peter and his band had performed David Paleface's plank-walk with hubbub and ceremony. Then they escorted David, dripping wet and draped with seaweed, to the Clearing. The residents of this outpost had welcomed him and allowed him to settle in. This morning, Lily had knocked on the little bark door. She entered with breakfast and a sympathetic ear. David devoured a delicious bowl of corn mush flavored with honey, finding himself confiding in Lily, and, fortified by a real meal and motherly interest, he felt that her counsel was sound. Today was the day. Who knew what tomorrow might bring?

Soberly, David nodded to his guardians, the broad and capable twins, and headed for the path behind the house. He passed the stump where Captain Cecco had loitered with Lily while David spied on them, and David entered the woods once again. The brook called out to him, rushing and bubbling, to guide his way to the stagnant pool at its end, and the dreadful cavern that once served David as shelter.

As he approached the pool, the twilight of the trees closed in, the stream flowed more reluctantly, and the scent of the water turned foul. He paused to lean against the brown, wrinkly skeleton tree, to study this familiar spot. Peter avoided this place, but Lily had told David its purpose. Now he understood why Jill had laid flowers here. Their withering remains lay strewn about the entrance, and David felt a queasy uneasiness about entering that grotto again.

Yet no help could be found in delaying. The task could grow no more appealing with time. Resolute now, David paced the final steps toward the rock wall, brushed the willow boughs aside, and, taking a deep breath, dropped to wriggle his body through the hole. He compared today's attempt with his previous efforts, and felt the difference in his own maturity. It was harder to fit through the entrance, today, but easier to face its interior.

In the darkness, he rose to stand quickly, wishing to avoid contact with the bones underfoot. He scrubbed the muck off his hands. The twins had offered him a pine knot to light the way, but something in David's stomach made him refuse it. He didn't want to see more than he needed to see. It was bad enough to breathe the tainted air. David had no desire to witness exactly what tainted it.

Chilled by the frigid atmosphere, he made his way, step by echoing step, to the mat where he had shivered so many nights between damp, muddy blankets. Locating them by feel, he adjusted his path toward the secret fissure where he kept the precious packet.

He found the mirror first. He now held an intimate acquaintance with its provenance, the Mermaids' Lagoon. Once in daylight again, David would check his reflection for the remains of Jill's crimson handprint. Soon he would tender the looking-glass to Jill. It would be one of his parting gifts to her, but not the most significant.

Feeling his way along the cold stone wall, David detected the crevice that held his treasure. He hadn't really believed anyone would find it, but he sighed in relief to know for certain it was safe. He pulled it out, held it secure, and turned to vacate the cavern and its odors, forever. Confident now, he held no fear of pirates or Indians lurking about, this time, to capture him. When he shoved the packet through the hole before he himself slithered out, he was unprepared to see it grasped and taken up.

In a panic, David scrambled on his belly, scratching and scraping into the daylight. His eyes were blinded at first, and then he gasped at what he saw. With the blazing colors of the parrot perched on one naked shoulder, one of the twin Men of the Clearing stood before him, holding David's secret in his hand.

The man's other hand cradled Red-Handed Jill's.

Once again, David felt humbled. As always, the Pirate Queen seemed too grand for him.

Walking Man slept a little later these mornings. His old bones had become slow to rise. When he had adjusted his elaborate breastplate and pulled his feathered spear from his tepee, the camp was alive with activity. In the last few days, the People seemed moody, but the elder's pouchy eyes crinkled in a smile when he saw that parents and children looked cheerful today. The ruckus of games had resumed, and a cluster of smaller boys sat waiting for him by the totem pole. He smelled breakfast on the breeze, and hoped that their mothers had thought to send him some.

The old man hobbled toward them, passing the tepee of White Bear. He grinned again, remembering how White Bear had gone 'hunting,' and, hours later, returned with his quarry. Raven had walked into the encampment, with White Bear close behind. Neither allowed much emotion to show, but it seemed clear to Walking Man that Raven was tamed. White Bear held his head a notch higher, and the tension on his face of late had eased.

Next, Walking Man passed Panther's dwelling. "Good morning, Walking Man," called Panther's wife, with her pleasant face smiling. She looked sly this morning, as if she guarded a secret, and Walking Man heard giggling in the tepee behind her. Her long, beaded earrings flew as she whirled toward the sound to admonish, "Hush, my daughters!"

The elder strolled on toward the totem pole, where he greeted the boys. He was gathering his robe to sit down and lecture them when something unexpected caught his attention. He dropped his robe, he straightened up, and he gaped. The youngsters sat quiet, their eyes rolling as they exchanged guilty looks. A dog howled, but it seemed to Walking Man that the village had fallen silent.

Outraged, he strode toward the offensive sight, stabbing the butt of his spear in the ground with every step. When he arrived at the spot where Rowan and Lightly's tepee had been struck, he halted. He glared, taking in every detail.

Where he had poured water to discourage the fire, a bold orange flame rose in a homey blaze. Where the new-made Outcasts had pulled up their poles, fresh-cut poles were erected. Over the poles stretched a new tepee made of many hides, stitched neatly together. The top was propped open to vent the smoke of the fire.

In his shock, Walking Man fell a step backward. It was then that he noticed the most distasteful detail of all. On the tepee's skin, the paint was still wet. Fresh images shone in the morning sun. The figures were red, depicting two native men. They were winged; they were warriors. One man held a bow, one man held a tomahawk… and, in their free hands, each man gripped the other man's arm.

Walking Man stared until his eyes could contain the vision no longer. Turning, he hoisted his spear to point it at the People. With the exception of the boys, no one looked his way. Oblivious, the village went about its business.

"Which of you did this thing?" croaked Walking Man, as loudly as his ancient voice was able. He moved the spear in an arc. "Which of you defies the judgment of the council?"

Still, no one noticed.

"Answer!"

As if he were an Invisible, the People offered no response. The elder stood his ground, shaking.

Behind him, he heard a quiet cough. He teetered around to see Panther stepping toward him. A smear of red paint stained Panther's leggings. "Walking Man!" he called, as if he'd just sighted him. "You look unwell."

"Unwell? I am enraged!"

White Bear, too, appeared at his side. "Let us help you to your place, Walking Man. Look, there. Your pupils await you."

"Panther, White Bear, can you not see—"

"I see that you are hungry," said Panther. "My wife has cooked your breakfast. Come, sit with the boys, and she will serve you as you teach."

Walking Man's mouth worked, but no sound emerged. Gently, Panther took his staff and made him to lean on his arm. White Bear supported him from the other side. Panther murmured, "Easy, old one. There is no hurry. It is good for boys to learn patience."

"I will not tolerate—"

"It is good for them to learn tolerance, too." White Bear offered these words kindly, patting Walking Man's shoulder. "You are wise, old one. You have said that Panther and I hold wisdom, also. Together, we three will be examples for these young ones to follow."

The new tepee stood, open, warm, and welcoming. Its smoke puffed up, mingling with the smoke of all the others. There was no hurry. The People's point was made. Patiently, it waited for inhabitants.

After all his fears and triumphs, David had grown, but he hadn't outgrown adoration. He beat the dirt from his clothing, glad that he'd taken time to bind his brown hair and club it in the manner of his uncle, the sea captain. Emulating his officers, David bowed and waited for the lady to speak first. In his grip, he felt the ivory handle of the looking-glass.

With her jewel-blue eyes, Jill, his enchantress, greeted him. Indicating that he should join her beneath the skeleton tree, she settled on a quilt and smoothed her skirts. Her golden hair flowed on her shoulders, and she seemed to glow in her emerald green gown. It was the same gown she wore when David first laid eyes upon her. He was jarred to be reminded of the *Unity* and its pillaging, but soon he realized that Jill's instinct was correct. The two of them had journeyed full circle; the time of parting pressed upon them.

The parrot squawked, and David suspected that this creature had carried the message of his whereabouts to Jill. The Man of the Clearing whispered in the bird's ear, then sent it fluttering home to resume its duties. David felt that Jill was about to do the same thing with *him*.

David hung back as Jill's son laid his packet at her side. Wandering farther up the stream, the man kept his distance. As he lounged about with his feet in the water and his ax shining bright at his belt, he kept guard for Jill. While he waited, he appeared to inspect the area, as if thinking of ways to improve it. Perhaps, soon, the stagnant pool might be freshened, and the Tomb of the Lost Boys sealed shut.

Jill drew David from his speculations. "I have a gift for you, David."

It felt so long since he'd heard her speak, David drank up the sound. Clear as the brook, the voice of his patroness quenched his longing.

She opened her hand. Gleaming in the green of the forest, his shamrock charm lay in her palm, silver on crimson. "Thank you for sharing your luck with me. Now you may take it back."

"But...I meant for you to keep it."

"I think you have something luckier to give me in its stead. Am I right?" She smiled. As he accepted the talisman, she offered him the packet, as well.

It wasn't as heavy as he remembered. The oilskin felt damp from the cavern, but he trusted it had preserved its priceless contents. Keen to confirm its condition, David no longer delayed to unwrap the package. Carefully, he untied the bindings, then peeled away a triple layer of oilskin. His throat thickened with emotion as he remembered how he and a dead man had wrapped it, panicked by the bucking of the ship in the swells, but determined to preserve the vessel's history.

On David's lap, the *Unity's* logbook lay revealed. He felt Jill lean closer. Her satin dress whispered with her movement, and she gave a gasp. Obviously, she recognized this relic, and she grasped its full significance. The two of them looked at one another, and, contented, David witnessed her happiness.

"Captain Cecco told me how much it would mean to you, Ma'am, to register this logbook with the shipping office."

"Oh, David." For once, words deserted her.

"You can count on me. I'll hand it to the proper authority myself. Your marriage will be recorded, in London...Mrs. Cecco."

The leather-bound book was dry enough now, but rumpled by past exposure to moisture. Jill took it into her hands and, gingerly, turned its wavy pages to the last list of entries. The date, the latitude and longitude, the ship's surgeon's authentication as witness, and the names of the couple the captain had married were confirmed in the palsied script of David's ailing uncle. Cecco's signature, and her own— both more tenderly rendered— finalized the entry.

Jill blinked to clear the mist from her eyes. A burden of worry was lifted, and her shoulders felt lighter. She rejoiced in the re-collection of her wedding day; her dread of the monster, Doctor Hanover, did not disappear, but it diminished.

"I am grateful, David. Thank you."

He smiled. "At last I've found a way to serve you."

"How clever of you. This, then, is the defending you pledged to perform for me, and the duty to your family's honor...your uncle's honor."

"I'm glad to be of use. I can't give this logbook to you, but I'm pleased to deliver to you its security." David set the book aside and said, "Here is a token I *can* leave with you." He presented Jill with the looking-glass. "I found this trinket at the Mermaids' Lagoon. Please accept it, with my respect. I know of no woman whose reflection compares." The heat of a blush suffused David's cheeks, and he wondered again if Jill's branding still marked him.

With her bloodstained hand, she accepted the mirror, then she beckoned him near. As their shoulders pressed close, she angled the glass to reflect both their faces. "See, David."

Inhaling her hypnotic scent again, he beheld her image. He memorized the picture of his face and hers, together, like a painting, to treasure forever. Then he examined himself, curious to see how he'd changed. His face was longer now, his cheeks slimmer, his eyebrows darker brown and thickened. Shaded with stubble, his chin was firm. David's left cheek no longer burned scarlet, nor yet even pink. His flesh was tanned, like the sailor he understood he must soon become.

"How handsome you have grown. Your face is all your own now, David. It's a fine foundation, on which to form any future you desire."

"Thank you, Lady." Too soon, she set down the glass. David ventured, "How do you intend to send me home?"

"I am told that you have mastered the art of flight. It's a long journey, but I know you'll enjoy it. I'll ask Cook to pack up some food. The birds you'll meet will be none too generous."

David didn't understand, but he trusted Jill to know. "How will I find the way? Do I follow the stars, like navigating a ship?"

"Jewel will guide you. You have only to keep up with her, and follow her light. She'll get you to London much more quickly than Pan. That boy does show off so dreadfully." She frowned then, and assumed her regal demeanor. "But David. You must understand. The commodore, the captain, and I have discussed the situation. It is imperative to the welfare of our men that you mention nothing about us. For your sake and ours, no one can know that you've consorted with pirates. Never divulge what you've witnessed, or we will be hunted— and you will be hung."

Taken aback, David was horrified. He hadn't thought of this complication. Somberly, he nodded his understanding. "I'll not place you in danger, Lady, and I know better than to admit that I've mingled with buccaneers."

"Never speak of the fleet, nor the men, nor the Island. You must pledge to me, David, upon your mother's life."

As he considered, David's expression relaxed, and finally he gave vent to a chuckle. "My Lady, even if I told the truth in every detail, who would believe me? I'll keep my mouth shut, or find myself locked up in Bedlam."

"Swear to it, David."

He sobered, and placed his hand on his heart. "I swear, on the life of my mother." He shook his head, once. "I'll never reveal what I've seen."

"And what will you tell them, when you suddenly appear there in London?"

"You're the Storyteller, Ma'am. What do you suggest?"

Delighted by a challenge, Jill sat back to strategize. She looked charming with her hand on her chin, her emerald ring dazzling with sunlight.

While his gaze lingered upon her, David listened to the sounds of the woods, so familiar now. The pair of mourning doves reminded him of their presence where they nested in the skeleton tree. They burbled their lugubrious song, and David's heart welled up with sorrow, as dismal as the pool beneath their roost.

Surprising as it seemed, he would miss this Island, after all. Whatever he promised Jill, it wouldn't matter if he told the truth at home. London lay so far away. He had the feeling that he'd never, ever find his way here again. Not if he searched for the Neverland forever.

He clutched his shamrock in his fist. It was only a piece of metal, just a slice of silver. It held no power. David knew now that his luck came from Jill. The woman, like the Island, possessed the property of enchantment. During David's adventure, those two entities, the lady and the land, had combined to work together. Their magic had managed him. Their charms had changed what was left of his life. With difficulty, David swallowed the lump that had formed in his gullet. By choice or by guile, he'd never see Jill or the Neverland again. His magic must lie in remembrance.

Jill beamed with inspiration. At the sight of his goddess, David's heart broke again.

She narrated: "Your ship, the *Unity*, was scuttled in the storm. Your officers feared that they themselves were doomed, but they set you adrift in the dinghy, hoping, for your dead uncle's sake, that you'd float your way to safe harbor. This much, of course, truly did transpire."

David gazed at Jill, absorbing one last story. He understood now, from experience, that at some time that the Storyteller designed, the tale would turn real. Jill always spoke truth. Truth fueled her powers.

"Tossed by the tempest, you drifted in your craft, lost at sea. Days passed, nights rolled over, then weeks. Rain and wind and sun beat upon you. As you suffered from hunger and thirst, delirium seized your senses. You will claim that your memory is hazy, David, but that you believe you were picked up by fishermen. As your fever raged, you might have imagined fantastical dreams— until you awoke, wandering the streets of London with this packet in your hands. The fishermen searched the book to learn your destination, and they delivered you safe. These impressions are all that you'll say you recall, and you are grateful to be back in your homeland, alive, and ready to put your experience to work on a worthy merchant ship. And, David..."

Jill gazed directly in his eyes, without the filter of the mirror.

David's spine shot hot jolts through his nerves, right down to his fingertips. Jill's aspect seemed to alter, and she assumed the severity of her counterpart. Through her ruby lips, it was Hook's words he heard:

"While you keep your promise to our company, the commodore vows to protect you. Through Jewel, who will communicate with you, you will send word. Name your vessel, and we shall never attack any ship that you sail."

David's trembling trebled as he digested this vow. He sensed the threat that it veiled. *Break your promise, and your ship will be taken.* And, terrible as its consequences would be, once more a truth lay revealed to him: one way remained to meet Red-Handed Jill again. It was the way of betrayal.

He had simply to tip the authorities.

But David was a man now. Paradoxically, like gentlemen, these pirates had taught him good form. It struck him then, how generous his renegade friends had proven. From this company of rogues, David learned honor, and love, and loyalty.

Luck no longer haunted him. His adventures had disproven it. But as for Enchantment— be she harsh or be she gentle, he'd burn incense at her altar. *This* mistress was the idol David served.

The morning had passed, and Hook lay flat on his belly. As the sun glided up to its zenith, the Neverland sparkled in its radius. Hook's posture seemed that of a casual sightseer, but every weapon he prized lay on the sward, within reach.

Beneath him stretched a scene that had often seduced him. He had, however, rarely viewed it from this angle. High upon the cliff top, he peered past its edge at the Mermaids' Lagoon. A flock of seagulls circled on the same plane as the pirate, piercing the sky with their calls. In the cove, no merfolk were apparent at the moment, but even in their absence the place was breathtaking. The rough rock coast lined an arching curve, hosting tide pools reflecting the heavens. Hook's eyes delighted in the stretch of sea before him, its jade-colored curls lolling toward shore. His senses reveled in the deep green moss that cushioned the cliff sides, and, of course, in the woman lingering in the Lagoon: his magnificent Jill. The setting was perfect, but for one flaw. Hook was *not* the man Jill was seducing.

Wind from the north rushed up the cliff side, tossing Hook's locks round his head. It brought the smell of the sea and the softness of moisture, but the breeze could not waft Jill's words to his ear. This circumstance mattered little; Hook could guess what she said. As for the native brave to whom she said it, *his* thoughts were obvious.

Lean Wolf's canoe shot through the surf, pulled toward shore not only by the power of his arms, but by the force of his inclination. The appointed hour was noon. Shrewd as she was, Jill was prepared as her husband arrived well ahead of time. Hook sneered when he watched her greet the man. She'd tossed a kiss when she sighted his canoe, she held the prow as he jumped ashore. She pressed a hand to her breast as, with just one arm, Lean Wolf flaunted his strength, hoisting his craft from the water. Hook noted Jill's token, the orange kerchief, tied in a band about the biceps of that arm. Lean Wolf left the canoe lying at a slant, petrified on the rock shelf, waiting till tide bestowed motion.

Apparently, the Indian took issue with Jill's gown. He pointed, questioning, and she twirled to swell her emerald skirts. Next she presented her back to him, gathering her hair that seemed gilded by the sun, and Hook smirked as Lean Wolf picked at her lacings. This chore was an onerous one, a job that Hook, with only five fingers, most often handed to Smee. Once or twice Hook had simplified the task, slashing the ties with his claw. But— for unambiguous reasons— the man indulging Jill, now, persevered. When he pushed the bodice from her shoulders, the satin fell away, shimmering down her body to form a pool of green. She waded out of it to be scooped in the man's bulging arms.

Revealed in the sunlight, Jill's frilly shift shone white. She embraced her brave; Hook, with his lip curled, looked away. While the couple kissed, he opted to sweep the bay with his spyglass. He suspected that merfolk observed, too. Sure enough, he counted three slick wet heads, yellow, auburn, and indigo, bobbing at the opposite end of Marooners' Rock. No doubt the creatures watched Hook himself as well. The prospect did not concern him. The Lagoon had long served as his source of amusement. His mermaids knew his secrets, and they kept them submerged.

Yet, vigilant for the safety of his treasure, Hook soon resumed his loathsome lookout. Now Jill drew her brave toward the picnic hamper, where she stored a repast bountiful enough to sate all three of her husbands. The Indian squatted beside her on the quilt, but he looked reluctant to settle. Clearly, he felt hungry for another kind of sustenance. Hook tensed as he saw Lean Wolf seize Jill by the waist. Quick as lighting, Hook's pistol filled his grip.

One moment...two moments...three moments later, Jill was feeding the man berries, sharing their sweet taste from her lips to his. Hook's pistol returned to the sward. Conversation carried the two through their picnic, with Jill speaking earnestly at times, beguilingly at others. Lean Wolf's expression alternated between fascination and gratification. Whatever the subject, the couple appeared to agree, at the end. At this distance, Hook felt removed enough to evaluate Jill's skill. He must never underestimate this woman. Like the berries she shared, the words on her lips could be sweet, yet her meaning acidic. Only fools took her tales at face value.

And now Hook's time of vigilance came to ripeness. Pulling a rope anchored at the water's edge, Jill drew a net from the brine. Lean Wolf caught it for her, and grinned at the sight of the bottle. He yanked the cork to sniff the liquid inside. The brew would be tangy and tart, and here was the moment toward which Jill's art aimed, and when Island magic began.

With defiance in the toss of her head, Jill removed a napkin to reveal a glass. Already, it cupped the amber wine. Her glass was half empty. *You see, my husband,* she seemed to say, *your wife can't resist a temptation. I indulged myself while I was waiting.*

And her husband believed her. With no further invitation, he brought the bottle to his lips, and imbibed. Jill watched as if counting his swallows. Presently she claimed the bottle for herself. She refilled her glass and resealed the cork. Laying the vessel in its net, Jill bid him chill it again. As it sank in the sea, Hook nodded in satisfaction. Were he that man below, he'd believe in Jill, too. This picnic's purpose was nearly accomplished.

But Lean Wolf had partaken enough of the victuals. Clearly, he felt the urge to devour his wife. Rising to his knees, he gripped her in his arms. Responding in kind, she pressed against him, opening her lips as she drew his down to hers. Soon she shrugged her right shoulder, slipping off one strap of her shift. Eagerly, her husband followed her lead, nestling his face in her neck. This time, Hook did not decline to witness their kisses. He bared his teeth, counting his heartbeats.

Shoving the food to one side, Lean Wolf dragged his wife down, to lie with her on the quilt. As if in accord with Hook's sensibilities, a gull cried out. Hook beheld Jill's arms at work, stripping the vest from her lover's body. Her jewels flashed on her fingers, and her crimson hand clawed at his breechclout. Naked as the merfolk, Lean Wolf lay full upon her, the russet skin tight at his backside. More than ready, he was, to feast at her banquet. Distasteful as Hook deemed this scene, yet he elected to let his gun lie.

Already, another weapon was at work.

Invisible Visions

Thigh deep in clear, cool water, Raven and Willow dug their toes in the grit of the riverbed, to steady themselves against the rushing current. Together they rinsed a blanket, then dragged it toward shore. With her little one swathed in the cradleboard on her back, Willow took care with her footing. She was surprised when White Bear appeared at her elbow.

"Let me help you, Wife," he said, hefting the weight of the wet cloth for her.

"But this is my work, White Bear. You need not concern yourself with washing, especially when you have business with the council."

"Our business is done," he answered, "and this work is heavy for a woman who gave birth half a moon ago." Although he appeared self-conscious about the task, White Bear helped the two women as they hauled the waterlogged cloth to the bank and wrung it out, spattering the pebbles. The scent of clean, damp wool pervaded the air, and, like the village around them, its colors burned bright in the sunshine.

Willow's sweet smile graced her face. "Your strength is welcome, Husband. You make our chore easier."

White Bear grunted his acknowledgment. When the blanket was stretched to dry in a sunny spot of the river bank, he addressed the other woman of his household.

"Raven," he said, in the strangely hushed tone he used for her, since their union. He spoke as if guarding his gruff voice, so as not to place too much emphasis on her name. "Your visit with Lelaneh was interrupted the other day. On the council's behalf, I must go to the Clearing. I will escort you there this afternoon."

"Thank you, White Bear," Raven said. Her only sign of change in her relations with White Bear was the blue jay feather she wore in her hair. She had allowed Willow to believe that it symbolized only the rite of passage she had undergone, her end-of-mourning, but in fact it held dual meaning for its wearer. As always when Willow was watching, Raven avoided the intimacy in White Bear's eyes. She wondered if doing so only made her feelings more obvious. To counter that impression, she ventured a glance at White Bear, and immediately regretted it. Raven saw by the man's intensity that their sojourn to the Clearing was meant to be more of a tryst than an errand. In spite of her resolve to discourage him, a pang of desire surged through her, and Raven's heart leapt with eagerness. Managing to keep her voice level, she said, "I will prepare."

White Bear donned the moccasins he had retrieved from the woodlands yesterday, and settled farther down the river's edge to talk with Panther, leaving the two women to finish the washing. Only when she and Raven were working alone again did the other explanation for White Bear's attentiveness occur to Willow. She stood up straight, almost forgetting to move slowly for the baby's sake. Gently, she jostled the baby with a soothing rhythm, and she smiled.

"Now I understand White Bear's behavior. Raven, he comes to the river to watch you. And not in the old way, with a crease between his eyes. He looks at you softly, the way he looks at Baby."

"You are imagining it, Willow. Your husband helps us because he considers your welfare. You must not overdo. He knows that Baby takes her nourishment from your body, and that you must keep yourself strong."

Willow nodded, wisely. "My sister, you are too shy or too head-strong to admit the truth. I understand that when White Bear found you after your ritual, he won your trust at last."

"Yes, Willow. White Bear won my trust." Two days ago, after declaring her love to White Bear and consummating it so ardently,

Raven was grateful to accept her lover's consideration as he bore her weary body home. But she had roused at the edge of the encampment, insisting that White Bear set her down. She sensed that his pride might be pleased to show off his new wife, but, wishing to spare Willow the gossip that would ensue, Raven could not allow her sister's husband to carry her farther. She had walked into the village, a woman accompanied, but not acquired.

"Raven, you may confide in me. You know I wish for you to find contentment."

"I told you when we returned home, Willow. White Bear and I came to an understanding that day, and now all is well between us. Your husband and I talked of our care for you and for Baby, and as we talked, my respect for him grew even deeper."

"Well, respect makes a smooth path for a man and a woman to walk. It is the ground on which White Bear and I stood, when we began our lives together."

The women gathered their baskets, and turned to climb the slope toward their tepee. Raven felt relief when her feet left the pebbles of the riverbank for the soft grass of the dwelling place. She breathed more freely, too, as Willow seemed to accept Raven's evasion concerning her feelings for White Bear.

Yet Willow had not finished with the subject. Raven's steps faltered as, delicately, Willow continued, "I know that, even after your end-of-mourning, you can never forget your life with Ash. No man can take his place in your heart. Not even White Bear, who to me is the only man worthy of my love. Of course my husband cannot replace yours, but you may find in him a helpmeet. Even though you may share little passion, he will be an ally upon whom you may rely."

Thus expressed, Willow's outlook made Raven more determined to sail to the Other Island. Willow's happiness lay at stake. She must never learn of White Bear's new attachment to Raven, nor of Raven's true feeling for White Bear. "Willow, I..." But Raven possessed no words to prepare her sister for her departure. To disappear without explanation would be too cruel. Raven must think how best to warn Willow of her intent to leave— and she must do it quickly.

Willow saw her sister's struggle, and her eyes offered comfort. "Please trust me, sister. You will find contentment once White Bear gives you a child."

In her distress, Raven's arms gave out, and she dropped the basket she was carrying. Grateful to hide her face from Willow, Raven bent to haul it up again, and kept her back turned as she brushed imaginary debris from the bottom.

Willow did not know of Raven's determination to evade pregnancy, but Raven knew that White Bear remembered. Three times she had caught him gazing at her, his gray eyes puzzling. As she had done long before they made love, Raven avoided closeness with the brother-in-law who thought of himself as her husband. Yet she knew White Bear to be as stubborn as herself. Although he ceased to press her to allow him between her blankets, she had suspected that he hoped for secret time with her elsewhere. After his offer to escort her to the Clearing, Raven was keenly aware that, unless she resisted, today's walk would lead to the raptures they'd enjoyed two days before. And, perhaps, to the entanglement of a child.

Gazing down to the river bank where White Bear sat straight and proud, a finer figure than any of the other warriors, Raven doubted her will to forbear. Even now she longed to caress his copper skin, to soothe the scars his past battles had earned him. Forgoing her feelings had been easier when White Bear held so little esteem for Raven. How long could she deny her yearning, now that he reciprocated it? How much damage could the emotion she felt for this man— this love fully shared by her loved one— inflict on her sister's marriage?

Raven was certain of one fact. Only her absence could ensure her sister's serenity. Within days, Raven expected the signal from the Black Chief. Whether with child or no, she must vanish from her sister's home. Raven must leave Willow here, secure in her position as White Bear's only wife, as the only mother of White Bear's children, and as the single recipient of her husband's love.

In the same way she had steadied herself against the rushing of the river, Raven tried to fight the tide of her emotion. She labored up the slope, lugging her basket of washing, grappling, too, with her very nature. Raven knew herself. She knew her passions still flamed as brightly as they'd burned for her husband Ash. She knew that White Bear had succeeded him.

Should she— and could she— deny herself just one last hour of ardor?

As Lean Wolf stirred, he sensed the cold and closeness of a cavern. Dim light greeted his eyes, but instead of the earth-scent of his cave, he detected an odor of fish. He recollected that he lay by the seashore, at the Mermaids' Lagoon. At his side, where Red Hand's voluptuousness should warm him, he viewed an empty place on her quilt. Rubbing the cloth, he found that it, too, was cool. Red Hand had returned to the sea.

He had slept soundly after their tryst, awakening with a tangy taste on his tongue and the memory of her touch at his loins. He couldn't recall moving from the water's edge to this cavern. Woozily, he half wondered now if he'd dreamt their encounter. Raising a forearm to his nose, he sniffed his skin. Red Hand's perfume prickled into his nostrils, confirming that he had, in truth, held his wife in his embrace. Along with the pride of his conquest, he felt a sense of shame at his memory lapse. But he would never let on to Red Hand that the drink she served him befuddled his mind. Wife or no, no woman would laugh that he might be weak against firewater. Sighing, Lean Wolf let her scent fill his mind instead, and he felt the resultant urges swell his branch. He stroked it, surprised at how promptly his hardness formed again, so soon after sating his wife. No matter how many times he enjoyed her, it seemed she just left him lusting for more.

He rolled to sit up. His vest and breechclout awaited, neatly folded. Peering out the cave's entrance, he saw the glimmer of waves as they licked at the rock shelf, green and luscious. But, except for his canoe, the shelf itself lay unoccupied. No sea creatures basked there. Lean Wolf felt a rush of disappointment.

His need resurged. It was urgent; he hadn't the patience, today, to fish for a mermaid. His yellow bird had flown. His old friend White Bear had appropriated Raven's interest, for now. Where was a man to find comfort with a simple, warm-blooded woman?

The answer was obvious. Smirking, Lean Wolf drew on his clothing. He rolled up the quilt and left it for his next opportunity. For a moment, he paused to allow his foggy mind to remember what Red Hand arranged for their coming encounter. He envisioned her, brazen in sunlight, her shape barely veiled by lace on white linen, her eyes the blue of blossoms that bloomed in a crevice by his cavern. And she'd spoken, with a mixture of offering and authority: "I'm to sail again soon, Husband. But don't think I'll neglect you. We shall have an afternoon of adventure together. Watch for me, with the third sun from now, at midday. Open our cavern, and I'll come to you— soon."

"Not soon enough, Yellow Bird," Lean Wolf muttered now, flexing his biceps to feel her kerchief stretch tight on its bulge. Walking stiffly, he strutted into the afternoon. He set his canoe on the water. "And *I'll* decide, Wife, if you'll sail, or if you'll stay in your cage."

White Bear was guarded as he approached the Clearing. For the People of the tribe, two of its residents remained outcast and Invisibles. He judged that he and Raven might enter here without violating taboo, but circumspection required that their visit be restricted to the corner where the tepee of Rowan and Lightly stood. As an elder of the tribe, he, more significantly than anyone, must uphold its customs.

Accordingly, when to the accompaniment of the parrot's shrilling he and Raven presented themselves, he waited under the garden trellis, unresponsive to the curious gazes of Lily and the children until the twin men greeted him. In order to avoid undue offense, White Bear also ignored the other inhabitants, including Lelaneh, who, seeing Raven, entered the house and returned with a packet. The third woman, Red Fawn, did not show herself.

White Bear bore white paint on his face this afternoon, a crescent notched like an unstrung bow, outlining his face from eyebrow to chin, indicative of diplomacy. Also in white, a bear paw print, claws downward, was painted on his other cheek. As usual, his arrows hung at his back, and he'd strapped his knife at his knee. He carried a long, thin buckskin wrap, thickly fringed and elaborately beaded, like his moccasins, but darker and more pliable, showing its age.

Standing proud, he announced to the men, "I bring word from the Council of Elders. I seek pow-wow with Rowan Life-Giver, and with Lightly of the Air."

Astonished, Rowan drew nearer. He hadn't expected any member of the tribe to look at him or his partner, far less to ask for them by the names the elders had bestowed and then denied. But Rowan's sharp, carved features remained stolid. The first Man of the Clearing asked, "Do you welcome this warrior?"

Rowan said, "The warrior White Bear is welcome. Lightly of the Air is not present, but I will hear the council's words." Indicating the tepee, he stepped back and lifted the door flap. Beside it, Walking Man's mark of taboo showed stark on the hide.

Before White Bear moved to enter, he spoke again to the Men of the Clearing. "My second wife, Raven, requests counsel from the herbalist."

Ignoring the sensation that his claiming of Raven caused among the women, White Bear turned to Raven and pointed to a grassy spot near the tepee. She followed him there, unfolding the blanket she carried and spreading it out. The two braves then entered the tepee. Discreetly, Lily gathered the children to play along the stream bank in the woods behind the house, but Lelaneh joined Raven, as requested, folding her long legs and sweeping her hair to one side. The two women settled just out of earshot of the men.

The area was pleasant. Now that she had permission to enter the Clearing, Raven took time to understand its appeal to the Outcasts. The flowers at the edge of the green lay open in the warmth of day, spreading their essence. Shade trees arched high overhead, filling the air with the buzzing sounds of summer. A work shed provided occupation for the twin men, and the house stood sturdy, a welcome shelter from weather and predators. The red-tinted smoke that rose from the smaller dwelling's chimney gave a cheery, welcoming feel. Still, Raven was struck by the quiet, and by the lack of village activity.

With a spur of pain, Raven felt herself to be a kindred spirit to the Outcasts. She recognized the alienation she must endure, once she sailed away from her tribe, and her sister…and from the husband who offered to fill her lonesome heart with love. In the depths of her soul, the reality resounded: however pleasant her next dwelling place might be, her first home would haunt her forever. These thoughts were too melancholy, and she narrowed her thinking in order to accomplish the tasks she must tackle before taking leave of her family.

Soon a cloud of tobacco puffed from the tepee, bringing its mellow smell, and Raven and Lelaneh understood that the men passed the peace pipe that White Bear had carried. They looked at one another, Lelaneh's smile all-encompassing, and Raven's bittersweet.

Lelaneh said, "First my status is restored, cleansed of taboo. Now, I gather, Rowan and Lightly are accepted, too! Tell me Raven. How came these good things to happen?"

"White Bear is reserved, but from what he does say, we learned that the council have yielded to the will of the People. In the night, the villagers sewed a new tepee for Rowan and Lightly. Before dawn they erected it over fresh tent poles, and rekindled their cooking fire. This gesture made it clear even to Walking Man that the People overlook an old custom in order to honor these braves. White Bear speaks for us all. We wish to welcome our Messengers home."

"So the People, too, hold good judgement, and now teach the elders to change. I wish Red Fawn had not stepped out to collect her Neverlilies. She has missed the moment. But still, this news brings wings to the hearts at the Clearing."

"As I have learned, most changes are difficult, but some may bring joy."

"I see a new light on your face, Raven. Whatever change has

come to you may be a fortunate one. Two days ago you ran from this very spot, in dread of White Bear. Now he calls you wife, and you speak of him with pride."

Raven fingered the jaybird feather that dangled at her collar bone. She had added beads to its clip, and more jay plumes she had found in the forest, white and blue with stripes of black. Her short hair felt smoother to her now, balanced out by the beauty of this headdress.

Lelaneh respected Raven's hesitation to speak. She offered the packet. "If you still wish for it, here is your tea."

"Of the changes that have occurred, nothing has caused me to alter my resolve. Yes, Lelaneh, I accept it, with thanks." Raven tucked the packet of herbs in her pouch.

"Then you still wish to leave aboard Captain Cecco's ship? We expect the pirates here the last few evenings of their stay, to say their goodbyes. We will miss their company." Lelaneh chuckled, adding, "But we expect some happy nights before they sail."

"The village will host a celebration, too, before Rowan and Lightly's return. It will be a feast in tribute to Walking Man. He has been persuaded to retire from the council."

"And the old man will be treated with honor instead of humiliation. It is fitting." Touched, Lelaneh sat back, and tears glistened in her eyes. Her voice faltered with emotion. "Another good change on the part of the elders."

Raven, too, was moved by the People's kindness, and by the role her brother-in-law played in encouraging it. Behind his iron eyes, she had always sensed the strength of generosity. She hoped that Lily and Red Fawn would soon be welcomed home, too. "Lelaneh, should all three of you be restored to your status, would you then return to the village?"

The woman observed the bounty of the Clearing around them and, wistful, she answered, "It is a funny thing, Raven. Much as we three Outcasts loved our lives among the People, we love our independence more. Nor do we wish to separate the children from their new fathers, whom we love, and who care so well for us all."

"Is Red Fawn truly happy here?" Raven remembered her own

difficulty in evading Lean Wolf's maneuvers. Judging by the panic his presence imbued in herself, she could easily believe that his former wife, who had fled here to seek safety from him, felt compelled to shun him still.

"For reasons I think you understand, Red Fawn will never rejoin the tribe. Lean Wolf ever hounds her, and she has good grounds to fear him. She ventured abroad this afternoon only because we have assurance that he is occupied at the Lagoon. But what of your own plans, Raven? It is clear that White Bear is not yet aware that you intend to leave his tepee."

"I will tell him this afternoon." Her shoulders sagged, and she sighed, "Somehow."

The underbrush crackled, and sharp sounds of panting came from the edge of the Clearing. The women whipped around to see Red Fawn tearing her way through the bracken. Her lower body was naked, and, below the swinging fringe of her blouse, her slender thighs showed scratched and bruised. Through the tangled hair across her face, her wide eyes searched for her companions. Once she gained the grassy circle, she herself remained silent, shivering; it was Raven and Lelaneh who cried out.

From their workshop, the two Men of the Clearing came sprinting. White Bear and Rowan bolted from the tepee, Rowan clutching his tomahawk, and White Bear gripping his knife.

The men took one look at Red Fawn. Then, in the manner of trackers, they hunched low to slip through the bracken. In uncanny quiet, all four vanished to search through the wood.

Lelaneh rushed to gather Red Fawn in her arms while Raven brought the blanket. Draping it around Red Fawn, Lelaneh turned to beg Raven, "Please, fetch Lily from the stream— but do not frighten the children!"

And, once again, Raven ran from the Clearing. This time, the focus of her fear was not her brother-in-law, White Bear. She remembered the reason for Red Fawn's troubles, and she, too, feared a silent hunter.

Another taboo had been broken. Like the custom itself, an Invisible was violated.

"I intended for Lean Wolf to lie insensible till sunset." Horrified, Jill stood with her back to the Island, the slanting sun casting her figure in silhouette against the beveled windows of the commodore's cabin. In agitation, she twisted her opal and diamond necklace. "I should have let him swill that green-apple wine."

Hook's teeth were set, and his nostrils flared in fury. "Another attempt to despoil a woman— another woman I pledged to protect."

"The man has the strength of an ox," Jill exclaimed. "Lelaneh could only guess how much of the draught to administer. Unlike my second husband, she never before prepared such a potion."

Lightly, who had delivered the bad tidings, went on with his tale. "I knew Lelaneh had doubts about the dose, so when my instincts told me Red Fawn had been gone too long, I went after her. I found her just in time. She was struggling with Lean Wolf. He'd ripped her skirt away, and he was warning her to keep silent. He struck her, too. It was obvious what was going to happen next."

"And you stopped him? How?"

"He and I exchanged insults earlier, and I thought it best not to let him see me. I shot an arrow his way, but kept hidden in the trees. When he loosed his grip to look for the witness, Red Fawn seized her chance to run. A few more arrows kept him from the chase."

Hook gave a brisk nod. "You judged well not to challenge him." He turned a severe look on Jill. " 'Red Hand' would be wise to do the same."

"Say what you will, Hook. I have won Lean Wolf's trust."

Her son asked, "Then your picnic at the Lagoon went as planned?"

"Indeed. Lean Wolf has no cause to doubt my devotion. He took the bait, and collapsed as soon as I got him undressed. I had to wait for Hook to free me, and Lean Wolf was senseless as we dragged him, on the quilt, to the cave." She sighed in relief, taking Lightly's hand in her own. "I am grateful to you for ensuring Red

Fawn's safety. She is a friend to me, and I'd hoped by my actions to help her, rather than hurt her."

"She didn't want to concern you, Ma'am, but I told her that in order to keep ahead of him, you have to be informed. She's still badly shaken."

Hook snatched up his black velvet coat. "I shall speak with her." His blue eyes turned icy, and his stare penetrated Jill with its cold. "Since I swore I'd not kill the villain, lending comfort to his victim is the least I can do." He strode to the door and wrenched it open. "Mr. Nibs, Mr. Tootles," he called. "You shall accompany me to the Island."

Jill stood firm. "My revenge advances. The man will collect his reward."

Hook scoffed. With one boot over the threshold, he demanded, "Have you any more of Lelaneh's concoction?"

"By the Powers, no! I poured it out as we passed over Neverbay."

"You should have preserved a measure, to dose Captain Cecco. He shall be infuriated at the risks you insist on taking."

Jill stepped forward from the window, where Hook could clearly see her face. She had gone paper pale.

His tone froze her blood. "I leave *you* to deal with Cecco, my dear. If I may employ so crude a cliché, you made your bed. Now you may lie in it— with your barbarous husband."

"I have long suspected that Lean Wolf keeps some secret shelter. I believe that he has retreated there now, and we need not fear an interruption from him."

Raven was relieved to hear White Bear's reassurance. So little time remained to share his company, and to inform him, at last, of her impending departure. Only now did she realize that the threat Lean Wolf posed to her had been eclipsed by her efforts to guard her sister's happiness. Today, though, with Red Fawn's fright, the Silent Hunter rekindled Raven's dread with a vengeance.

As the four men had backtracked along Red Fawn's path to

search for her assailant, they met Lightly winging his way toward the Clearing with a precautionary arrow nocked in his bow. He hurried back with them, to see how Red Fawn fared. After hearing his account of the attack, White Bear and Raven took their leave of the Clearing so that its people might comfort the woman, and restore a sense of calm for the children.

Without the sanction of the council, White Bear made no promise of justice to Red Fawn, nor, after the first glimpse of her in her distress, did he appear to see either Red Fawn or Lily. Although he was bound by tradition not to speak to the Outcasts, nor to speak *of* them, his face set in grim lines as he and Raven departed, and Raven believed he was deliberating on the proper action to recommend to the elders. Lean Wolf himself was still a member of the tribe. He might confine his worst impulses to Outcasts— or he might be a danger to any woman on the Island. Raven's worries for Willow gained more urgency.

As a token of the elders' good will, White Bear left the peace pipe in Rowan's care, until the two formerly outcast braves should be prepared to resume their places among the People. Naturally, the couple refused to leave the Clearing until they could be certain that the predator who preyed upon a member of their circle was restrained. The pipe would be warmed again only when order was restored, and the young men reunited with the tribe.

Raven's resolve to leave the Island did little to reduce the anxiety Lean Wolf instilled in her. His abuse of Red Fawn, an Invisible, proved that the man was not only ruthless, but lawless. Who knew what malice Lean Wolf felt for White Bear, who had destroyed his hopes of marriage to Raven? What harm to White Bear— or to White Bear's family— might Lean Wolf contrive? These questions caused Raven to shudder.

White Bear, too, was thinking of the welfare of the village and its inhabitants. "It is proven, today, that the tribe has need of the Messengers. I do not begrudge them a few more days at the Clearing. In guarding their charges, Rowan Life-Giver and Lightly of the Air show themselves worthy of the People's confidence."

"The People will feel safer once our Messengers return—" The words 'to us' hovered upon Raven's tongue. They remained unspoken. White Bear looked at her, questioning, but restrained his curiosity until they reached the destination to which Raven guided him.

White Bear was pleased that Raven remained levelheaded during the rush of trouble. He sensed her uneasiness, but she did not interrupt his thoughts while they hiked. Like him, she desired this time together, and she had requested that he accompany her to a special place on the Island. As they gained distance from the Clearing, his musings turned more pleasant. He followed Raven along a trail in the wood, wide enough for one pair of moccasins and barely visible in the grasses. Just as he'd done the first time he pursued Raven, White Bear studied her grace, finding himself captivated by this woman's form, by her movement, and by the mettle that led her in directions so divergent from other wives of the tribe. Her sister Willow had never challenged White Bear's convictions, nor had she engaged his mind as fully as this woman. White Bear's heart swelled again to think of her as his. With both his being and his body, he anticipated the end of this trail.

Gradually, the path sloped upward, and the air held the scent of pine. The footpath squeezed between tall conifers, and Raven beckoned White Bear to follow her through them. He did so eagerly, now knowing their destination. The pine needles pricked at their arms, and then, as if by magic, the forest disappeared, and a magnificent vista took its place before their eyes. White Bear smiled.

The white rock of the cliff top warmed the soles of their feet. A breeze sent gentle gusts against their faces, scented by the water that lurched far below. To the left, the lines of the two pirate vessels appeared clear and sharp against the oncoming evening. The ships rose in the gentle, sheltered swells of Neverbay, illuminated from the west by the orange light of sunset. To the right lay a sight that, in the days of his youth, White Bear often came here to contemplate: the wide greenish sea, seeming vacant from this vantage point, but leading, surely, toward the home of the tribe of his birth. The Other Island.

He stepped forward to stand near the brink, the long single lock of his hair blowing back from his shoulders. Breathing deep of the open air, he surveyed the view. He thought before he spoke, employing his resolve to allow scope for his new wife's complexities. He said, "I thank you, Wife, for reminding me of my origins."

Raven's spirit took courage from his words, yet she was distracted for a moment, as she noticed movement aboard the larger ship. She recognized the brawny build of Cecco, his headdress glittering as he stamped up a set of steps. He disappeared into the many-windowed cabin in which his wife dwelled with the Black Chief. A bang, delayed by distance, indicated that the door had shut hard. Raven felt for Cecco, who was clearly disgruntled. Once she joined him aboard his ship, she would do her best to console him, as a friend. For now, Raven's concern could encompass only Willow and White Bear. Encouraged by White Bear's stillness, she held her peace as he considered the memories to which she had led him.

"Raven." He kept his coarse voice to the gentler tone he now reserved for her. "If you bring me here to honor me, I am honored. If you bring me here to remind me that I, too, have not always seen eye to eye with the traditions of my adopted People, I stand humbled, acknowledging your wisdom."

He turned to Raven with a subdued expression she had not witnessed before, and, knowing that this change came of his care for her, she ached with love for him. When he opened his arms to her, she stepped into his hold. His strength and protection surrounded her; his newfound insight touched her heart. She would find it difficult to step away, when the moment of parting arrived.

Resting her head on his chest, she savored the feel of his hand in her hair. He fingered its ends, as if still wondering at her choice to cut it. His skin retained a hint of the tobacco he'd smoked in the peace pipe, a masculine smell that, since Raven's earliest days as a child in the village, bestowed a sense of safety. Much as she wished to prolong the peace she found in her lover's arms, Raven reminded herself that time was short. She must not delay. Steeling her nerve, she confessed, with her lips brushing his skin, "You say I am wise. After this night, you may doubt my judgment, just as you used to do."

The cording of his muscles tightened as he held her, but he listened.

"White Bear. Before you loved me, my spirit moved me to leave this Island. An opportunity to do so opened to me. Very soon, I will travel away from this shore."

After an agonizing moment, White Bear pushed her to arm's length, and he glowered at her. This face, she knew, was the sight that enemy warriors beheld, when cringing at the edge of his tomahawk. The bear's paw print on his cheek matched his aura, while the white line curving down from his eyebrow, endorsing diplomacy, seemed too civil to linger there now.

To forestall his anger, Raven held up her hand. "I undertake this journey for my sister. It is my last, and lasting, gift."

White Bear's eyes, which had turned hard once more, narrowed. Again, he strove to make allowance for his skittish new wife. His wrath turned to bafflement; surely he misunderstood. Taming his impulse to chastise, he waited to hear her next words make sense.

"Saying farewell to my tribe and my family seemed a heavy burden before. But now that I have earned your esteem, White Bear, my task is harder still. Yet go I must, for, if I fail, the hurt to Willow will redouble."

"What are you saying, Raven? You can offer Willow no greater gift than your presence."

"No. Full of knowledge as you are, I know Willow best, and I know myself. The greatest gift I can bestow…is her husband."

Taken aback, White Bear searched Raven's face. He answered with a shade of indignation, "Already, Willow rests secure in our marriage. I will never abandon her."

"Think. Which of us has occupied your thoughts, these many moons past?"

"Indeed, Raven, you have done so. Because of your widowhood. Because of your need."

"And my widowhood has passed. The question of my status is settled in your mind. Now think again. In which of your wives do you hope to seed your next child?"

White Bear shook his head. "Raven, these questions are unnecessary. As I told you before, I can provide for the happiness of both of my wives."

She pressed on, relentless. "Which sister brings serenity? Which brings your blood to the boil?"

White Bear pulled back. Too honest to answer, he sealed his lips.

"I know my own nature. Willow is openhanded with her affection." Frowning, Raven admitted, "I am not. As I have always known, the role of second wife cannot suit me. If I remain in the shelter of your tepee, I will not yield my hold on you. Instead, I relinquish my claim to you now. I will not stay to see Willow diminished."

White Bear studied Raven, assessing her sincerity, yet he knew her too well by now to doubt it. She was no teaser to toy with his emotion. She sought no power. In truth, she did intend the opposite. This declaration meant, simply, and with no guile, that she chose to release her husband from all obligation. He must concede that her intention was genuine. And he could not deny her description of his feelings for his wives. The words came grudgingly, in a growl. "I hear you."

"As you honor me, White Bear, do not press me with questions. My path is marked out. Trust my instincts, and send me on my quest— if not with your blessing, then at least with your love."

"No questions! If only as your brother-in-law— and you know how much more than a brother's affection I feel— my responsibility is to see to your safety. I am your provider. I must protect you, I must oversee your welfare—"

"You must give me a message to relay to your relatives. I go to your homeland, White Bear; I voyage to the Other Island."

"Voyage…" White Bear shot a glance at the pirate ships. His forehead filled with furrows. "You cannot mean to— Wife, what you propose is forbidden!"

"It *was* forbidden, when I was a woman of the People. Soon, I will be a woman of the Wider World."

"Those men are enemies, Raven! Only Outcasts consort with the wild men."

"Yet the elders have learned that their laws might be faulty. By their own admission, they were mistaken to banish the Outcasts. Lelaneh is recalled now, and Rowan and Lightly forgiven. Perhaps you will help the elders decide soon that, just as proved true with the

Outcasts, it is wiser to know one's adversaries than to battle them."

Against even his own wishes, White Bear turned his back on his loved one. This woman, whose thinking was so mysterious to him, had become his wife. With a sense of duty, he had accepted her. With a sense of surprise, he had learned that he loved her. And despite his hard-won devotion, grief and anger were her bride-gifts. The notions she proposed were outlandish. The woman had wandered so far from custom that, as of this moment, White Bear believed he could never guide her back. The pain of this realization was sharper than any arrow he'd received from an enemy. He staggered one step closer to the sea.

"Please, White Bear, do not be concerned for my well-being. I have made certain of my safety on the voyage. And once I arrive, I will work hard for your family. As your sister-in-law, I will find my place within your tribe."

Facing the watery way to his homeland, he spoke to her over his shoulder. His voice carried more sadness than wrath as he murmured, "I made you my wife, Raven. No matter what occurs, a good man cares for his family."

Raven laid one hand on his arm. The tension stretched beneath his flesh, proof that his grief was genuine. "The man I see before me is a good man. With the love this man bears for me, I have gained self-assurance. I am confident, now, that your kinsfolk will care for me, too."

"This, then, is the reason you once asked me to speak of my people. To teach you of the Other Island."

"Yes." Raven spurred her courage again. Turning him to face her, she tried to hold her gaze steady. "I ask you once more. Tell me, please. As my provider, provide me with knowledge."

"Headstrong woman," he said, remembering his impatience on the night of which they spoke. Some sense inside him had known, even then, that this woman could never be wholly his own. "The Other Island lies far from this place." He took her hand in his, and held it to the side of his face, along the curve outlined in paint. "Until the day that you walk on its shore, it lies even farther from my thoughts."

White Bear kissed her palm, then he lifted Raven up and into his arms, and he cradled her. He pressed his forehead to hers, and he heaved a great sigh of sorrow.

Raven whispered to him, "My yearning, too, is not there, but here. Lay me down, White Bear, and let us follow tradition."

"I know of no tradition that guides us down the path you propose. It is entirely strange to me." Yet, lacking another direction to take, White Bear bore her toward the soft, mossy ground and set her down beneath the tree of ardor, the alder.

"Can a husband and wife not craft their own custom?" Raven held his face close to hers. "Can we not love in any manner we declare?"

She kissed him, her lips warm and full, her touch so present and so full of feeling that he felt his heart bound like a stag. Her body was here, was his, seeming in her fervor so far from departing that hope danced within him afresh. But when their kiss ended and she pulled her lips away, he heard her begin her goodbye.

She asked, "Are there no customs for parting?"

"Of course." Trying to find footing in this strangeness, White Bear relied, as always, upon his reverence for tradition. "When a brave leaves for war, his son will sharpen his weapons. His brother warriors paint his face, and his wife will dress his body and weave ornaments into his headdress."

"And when a woman's husband dies and leaves her alone with her memories, may she not observe her loss by cutting her hair?"

Again, he touched her hair. "As I learned from your example, Raven, such is an ancient tradition with the People, so old a practice that it is rarely followed now. My first tribe did not observe this custom. According to the people of the Other Island, for a man, his hair is his fortitude. For a woman, her constancy."

"You have enlightened me, White Bear. But here is another practice that you *do* acknowledge. When a woman leaves her tepee for the birthing lodge, does her husband not follow some rite?"

"He cleanses his tepee with the smoke of sweet grass, to welcome the spirits of life. He holds vigil in his doorway until his wife's return, with his back to darkness and his face open to the sun."

"We can hold vigil, tonight." Raven gestured to the sky. "See, it is the proper hour for this rite. The sun, like me, is departing." Its radiance was lost now, and the shadows of the evergreens stretched across the chalk of the cliff top to cover the lovers.

Reclining together on the earth, they were bedded by the roots of the fire-tree, the alder. The scent of evergreen spiced the air, and they were blessed by the faded rays of day. Water washed the cliff side, singing of the sea.

"This cliff top marks the point where your island and mine lie the closest. Is it not right, then, that we should make our ceremony here?"

"Yes, Wife. All this is right." As they faced one another, White Bear touched her shoulder. His hand wished to restrain her, tightly, yet he made himself caress her instead. "What is not right is parting. Our hearts are one. If you go, only half a heart remains to each of us."

"Willow's heart is whole, and beats solely for you."

He bowed his head. "Again, Raven, you humble me."

"It is Willow who humbles us both, by her bounty. What step is next, White Bear, for this rite of passage?"

"Truly, Raven, I do not know. I see only that, in trying to do what is right, I have done what is wrong, for you." His hurt was etched upon his face, and his copper chest rose and fell with emotion. "Difficult as it is for me, I will allow you to guide me now, just as you guided me through the woods on the day of our union, and today on the path to this parting-place."

"I thank you...Husband."

He looked upon her in wonder.

"Yes, White Bear. I do think of you as my husband. This leave-taking is as painful to me as I find it is for you. In order to separate, we must acknowledge, first, that we are one."

Somberly, Raven rose, and she disrobed her body. Standing with her back to the alder trunk, the dusky half-light rimmed the fullness of her breasts and the dark tint of their points. The curve of her waist led White Bear's gaze downward, to the swell of her hips, and the black veil before her womb. She reached down to lift him up and, as they stood together by the end of the land and the edge of the sea, they bared his body, too, in preparation for their ceremony.

He slid his hands along the turn of her breasts, and bent to kiss them. He wondered, as he touched his tongue to their tips, if one day soon his own son might feed from this fount. If so, he thought, as he closed his eyes to envision the image, with a mother so thoughtful, so giving, this son must grow strong and wise. When she raised her knee to his, opening her thighs to proffer herself, too, White Bear pulled Raven into his arms. With his branch engorged in longing, he pressed his body to her offering. Her arms received him, her bosom pillowed his, and, pressing toward his man-place, his wife invited him.

White Bear lifted her up. Circling back to their beginning, he made love to her in the manner of their first time. With his hands below her hips, he supported her, pushing up and into her softness, feeling her warmth draw him in and surround him. To steady himself, he pressed her back against the alder. Gentle at first, White Bear moved slowly, trying not to drive her too harshly against the bark. But she urged him with energy, pulling him nearer, rhythmically, as if indulging two sensations— bark at her backside, and the man's branch working within.

With his teeth, he nipped at her ear. The plumage of her head-dress brushed his jaw, and he glimpsed the blue of the jaybird. He almost heard it cry, its caw an admonishment. It was the message Raven herself must be heeding. *Run!* it seemed to shriek, in a frenzy of feathers.

And White Bear remembered what this ceremony symbolized. As his heart filled with anguish, he reached his crest. Groaning, he gave to his love his emotion. Her body arched and shuddered as she, too, shared her all. Their ardor sparked, burst to flame, and burned beneath the alder. Because this bonding might be the last, it grew all the more vigorous, and even as the fire sank, it seized heat again. Raven's fingers became brands, pressing like embers on his skin, goading for more and receiving it. Thus they joined, poised on the cliff top— both in pain and both in pleasure— in this coming together that must lead to division. Reluctant to end, they extended the rite, conceiving a bridge of remembrance to share through their lifetimes, a pathway, reaching from this Island paradise out toward the Other.

When at last White Bear laid Raven down beneath the alder, they lay spent. White Bear understood, now, the manner in which this magic worked. As close as they were, physically, they would remain in each other's souls. Their bodies would move forward, to working, and loving, and growing old. The heart they shared would endure, here and in spirit, fixed upon this ghost-white cliff. Their parting was a joining, part of the past, and part of forever.

White Bear held his wife while he might. "Raven," he murmured, "So that I may keep you, I take leave of you now."

"Husband; White Bear," she answered, low, "I take leave of you. And I bear you with me."

"When you fly from me, Raven, I ask for two things."

"I will render what I may."

"I well remember my journey here. The sea between islands is too perilous for a single canoe to venture. I myself undertook the passage as a rite of manhood. As a man now, my obligations are such that I cannot accompany you to see to your acceptance by my people. Allow me to send our Messengers, Rowan and Lightly, as your escorts. They will watch over you, and when you are settled, they will fly back to me, bringing word of your contentment."

Only a moment's hesitation delayed her response. "Yes, White Bear. As you wish."

"And, Raven…you will not slip away in secret. When you find it is time to depart, I will bring you to this place, for our final farewell."

"It shall be as you say." Tonight, Raven lay wrapped in his arms. Tomorrow, and in the time left to her here on this Island, she would make her preparations. The first task she dreaded; she must break her news to Willow. After that trial, Raven, too, must make a last entreaty. The need was urgent, the answer a hazard. It was a plea she could not beg of White Bear. Just one man held the power to meet this necessity.

With her mind decided, Raven turned away from tomorrow. She thought not of the challenge that lay before her, but of this hour that she shared, in love, with her husband.

The sun had not yet set when boots stamped up the companion-way. Hook's rebuke still rang in Jill's head, and she leapt up from the daybed. In her agitation, her foot caught the emerald hem of her gown. With a ripping sound, a seam parted at her waist. She ignored it as the door was shoved open. Cecco burst into the cabin, his gypsy ornaments blazing and his temper aflame.

Jill's chin rose in fury. "How dare you enter in such a manner?"

"I was wrong, Jill." Cecco slammed the door closed behind him.

"You are wrong, indeed!"

"Raven was not his next victim. But I was *not* wrong to demand that you have no more to do with him."

Her eyes flared, bright like the diamonds in her necklace. "Not one of my husbands commands me."

"Truly?" Cecco sneered. "When you tempt him into that cave again, do you think he will let you escape?"

"Giovanni—"

"And once you manage to kill him, how shall you handle the blood-rage?"

"This will be the last of it."

"This will be the *worst* of it."

"I've managed twice before."

"Your third hunt is more dangerous by far. You do not inflict a wound, this time, simply to symbolize death. Nor do you sacrifice your totem tigress. The life you would steal is a man's life, Jill. You cannot know how fiercely you will feel it."

"Hook will help me, if you won't."

Cecco struck the knife that hung in his dashing red sash. His bracelets jangled discordantly. "I will slaughter Lean Wolf myself. I will kill him— for you, for Raven, and for Red Fawn."

"No! I insist that we follow the scheme I've begun. Lean Wolf is a crafty adversary, and his strength is uncanny. If any part of this plan goes amiss, we are all three at risk. We may even incite war with the Indians."

"Jill." Cecco bunched his fists. "He will not touch a single hair on your head."

"You are far too late to make *that* vow, Giovanni. And he will touch me at my invitation."

Cecco's brows lowered. His gaze traveled over his wife, down and up. "You wear your wedding gown, and I see that it is torn." His eyes smoldered as he stared at her, accusing. "Did he rend your dress today, 'at your invitation'?"

"You overstep your privilege, Giovanni."

"Then I step again." He strode closer. "To Hook I grant privilege. But how should the man who raped you receive what your husband is refused?"

Jill backed toward the daybed. "You forget yourself!"

"No. *You* forget, *Amore*. You forget that I am the first man you married. It is I who will fight to defend you..." He strode right up to Jill, he seized her waist in his two hands, and he pressed her to his chest. "And I am the man who shall hold you."

They stood face to face, their jewelry ablaze in the rays of sunset, the woman gazing up to him, the man with his dark, clinging eyes, staring down. His insistence disarmed her, but only for a moment. From his sash, Jill pulled his wicked knife.

Holding it up, she bared her teeth in challenge. Just as quickly, Cecco gripped her wrist, overhanded, dragging her arm out and down. In the same motion, he tugged her forcibly toward his body so that she stumbled against him, and with his other hand he clutched her dress, tightening his hold on her waist.

"*Vi maledicono!*" he cursed her.

And then he kissed her.

For Jill, who loved her husband, this reminder was too much. The day that was ending had been tumultuous. The tryst with Lean Wolf, his assault on Red Fawn, Hook's condemnation— all prodded her toward a storm of emotions. Impassioned as she felt, Cecco's embrace pushed past her limits.

At first, she returned his kiss. She opened her lips, she stood on her toes to press him the harder, wild with the mix of sensations. Only far too late, when her judgment returned, did she yank herself back. As she did so, two more events transpired.

With a shriek of rending cloth, the fold of Jill's skirt in his hand ripped free from her bodice. At the same time, but silently, the door of the cabin swung open.

Hook stepped into his quarters. He saw his mistress and his rival entangled near his daybed. He observed as Jill struggled, restrained by the arms of her husband. Foreign oaths flowed from Cecco's throat. In her captive right hand, Jill wielded a weapon, and Cecco's grip crushed her garment. Through the gap he had torn in her gown, her filmy shift revealed her womanly figure, from the waist down.

Hook stood stiff at the threshold. His lip twitched. After a full observation, his chin lowered, and he turned away.

The click of the bolt in the lock caused the couple to freeze. Aghast, they twisted to blink at the door. The tall, dark form of the commodore confronted them.

Hook sauntered forward, his boots meeting silence on the Oriental carpets. Moving to stand behind Jill, he established himself at her back, and, casually, he lifted the blade from her fingers.

Cecco didn't trust Jill's crimson hand with his knife. Only after Hook appropriated it did he dare to let her go. On edge for any action that offered, he watched as Hook flicked the weapon at the wall. It stuck there, angling out of the woodwork, brutish by the brocaded curtains.

Jill stood with her head held high and her back to her lover, her shoulders heaving. She did not deign to draw her gown closed, nor to open the lips she had just shared, so heatedly, with Cecco.

From his stance behind her, Hook peered down at his woman, on the disarray of her golden hair, and the fire of his diamonds. Resting the curve of his hook on her shoulder, he reached his arm round, and slid his hand through the gash in her garment. Beneath the lace, he found the silken skin at her hip. His touch sidled to her thigh, slipped to the inside, then higher, to glide toward her belly. Pulling her back, he made her lean against the pile of his black velvet waistcoat.

"Am I wrong?" he asked, his voice as soft as her satin. "Or are we engaging our 'unity'?"

Giving Ways

Cecco stood taut but silent, preparing for whatever might happen. With every muscle charged, he waited for Jill to respond. She did react, and dramatically— but not to Hook's words. Hook used other weapons instead. One old, and one new.

Hook remained temperate. "Here we stand, all three together." He manipulated his iron hand as if it were devised not for destruction, but seduction. "You appear uneasy, Jill, but consider." In delicate motions, he teased at Jill's sleeves, plucking and shredding them with his barb until he bared her fair shoulders. "Your loveliness cannot hide. Not even from the meanest observer." Next he toyed with her tresses; "How freely the light plays upon these." Leaning close, he inhaled her perfume. "The very air shares your scent. Why then, when you charm the world with your presence, should you shy from the two men you love?"

Jill remained silent, as before, but her posture eased a bit. Cecco was struck by the incongruity. The claw that men dreaded seemed to instill a sense of safety in Jill, however dubious. Yet Hook's conversation posed a challenge to her, and to Cecco as well. As his hackles raised, Cecco noted that, beneath her skirt, Hook's hand still held her captive, and captivated.

Cecco had expected anything but this beguiling. His foreboding increased, and although witnessing this intimacy between Hook and Jill provoked him, he quelled his impulse to abandon his wife to her *innamorato*. Instead, he stood on guard for her as she leaned back against Hook's chest. Cecco sensed she was trusting in both of them. Cecco, though, was more skeptical than she, and when Hook poised his claw at her throat, he balled his fists. This time, however, the commodore employed the hook merely to draw a lock of hair from the scar at her neck.

"We know the pride you feel in this mark of experience, Jill. You must never veil it— not from us." As he uncovered the scar, he stooped to kiss it.

As his own mouth longed to do the same, Cecco recalled her sensitivity to just such attentions, and how these touches entranced— no— how these touches *entrapped* her. He himself had once used this very means to enthrall his Jill. In the months since he seduced her, such fondling had not lost its allure for her.

Because Jill *did* feel entranced. Cecco watched as, with the tip of his tongue, Hook worked the tender territory of her throat, inducing her to close her eyes and tilt her head. Her husband knew that her skin must be tingling. Gooseflesh rose upon her bare arms. He understood that after her difficult afternoon, Jill was susceptible. Only moments ago, Cecco, too, had played upon her distress. He could easily imagine that Hook's hot breath at her shoulder melted what little reserve the trials of this day had bequeathed to her.

"Hook," she gasped, pressing his hand to her abdomen. Jill cast a glimpse at Cecco, and he knew that she witnessed the indignation on his face. Her eyes did not plead with her husband. Rather, she averted her gaze, granting him choice in whether to stay or to go. Neither she nor Cecco was certain what Hook had seen pass between them, but she behaved as if she discerned what Hook sensed, and as if she deemed it safest, for them both, to allow Hook's attentions to flow unopposed.

And Cecco understood that, as always, Jill was acting in honesty. At this pitch to which her two men had roused her, to pretend modesty would, in her opinion, be disingenuous. Clearly, she was exhilarated by each of them, right at this moment. A yen for both of her lovers had stolen upon her, evidenced by her hands. Her left still pressed Hook's to her body, and her crimson hand turned upward, open, as if she wished to offer it, at last, to her husband.

Like Cecco, Jill seemed intrigued by Hook's test of harmony, and with her movements she encouraged him, seeking to please herself as she did so, and showing no shame.

Cecco was astounded by this turn of affairs. For the moment, he stood considering his wife's empty red fingers, and what he should do. Unabashed by his company, Hook brought his hand wandering low again, to the home of his delectation. Cecco could not turn away from the sight of Jill's body as she followed her lover's motions, her hips angling to enhance her sensations. When Cecco forced himself to move a step backward, his exit was barred by a look, cool but uncompromising, from the commodore himself.

With barely a shake of his head, Hook commanded Cecco to linger. As his heart jumped and pounded, Jill's husband discovered that, although his manhood stood up and ready, he himself was as yet unprepared for impending events.

While his whiskers tickled along her collarbone, Hook caressed Jill's most sensitive sites. Now her breath turned to sighs, and Cecco watched the hook come into play again. Following his instinct to protect his wife whatever the circumstance, he felt pulled to move before her. Here, he braced himself against the shifting of the ship, observing the claw to guard against its tricks. Circling one hand round Jill's upper arm, Cecco steadied her where she stood, and he kept an eye on the hook— even as it came for his throat.

As if charmed by a serpent, Cecco followed the point with his gaze. It reached for him. In two iron taps, the backside of the curve struck the flesh of his chest. Chilled by the cold touch of metal, Cecco twitched, but he did not retreat. Nor did he fear that Hook's gesture was a warning. Instead, the hook caught his vest. When Jill's blue eyes opened to engage her husband's, he was persuaded to let the commodore tow him nearer.

As he came close to her, Cecco knew what to do. He did not ask permission. Released from the strictures of his exile, he caught his wife in his arms. As if Cecco was not in the room, Hook disregarded him. He returned his ministrations to Jill. With both lips and one hand, Hook pandered to her passion, while Cecco, with the dignity of one who claimed his rights, initiated his own amorous measures.

Cecco's body remembered; he tended his wife in the manner she loved. With his hands he caressed her torso, with his mouth he kissed her throat. In a miraculous action that set his soul soaring, she touched him with her scarlet hand. Her fingers roamed over him, fondling his face, his chest, the gilt of his armband, and, beneath his breeches, the stalk where his gold ring grew tighter.

At length, the hook manifested again, to slide under her chin, coaxing her face upward, an offering, so that Cecco leaned down to kiss her lips, now— as avidly he and she had kissed when alone only minutes before— while Hook himself breathed in her ear.

At last, the iron touch nudged Cecco backward, and Hook took possession of that kiss, covering Jill's mouth with his own. Cecco held her, and he held her crimson hand as she stroked him, and he watched her free fingers adore Hook's body, too, sliding upward to rake through his hair, down, to knead his thighs behind ebony velvet. As Hook ended his embrace, Cecco's body throbbed with wanting. He was certain Hook must feel the same. At her backside, Jill had to know Hook's awakening, too. Among the two men, however, an agreement seemed to hang. This moment was Jill's. Attending to her desires, each man set his own drives aside.

Between them, Hook and Cecco sustained her. Surrounding her, front and back, her attentive men pleasured their mistress. She trembled, her agitation increasing, her body twisting. Through the rent in her dress, Cecco pressed his hardness to her valley, so filmily defended by her shift, and, moments later, she exhaled in long, husky moans, while the rapture they engendered together heightened, lengthened, and declined. The three remained thus in the dusk-darkening cabin, listening to the murmur of bay water, and the cries of a gull, while Jill basked in the joy of their proximity.

"Jill." Hook looked down at her, and his voice seemed to emanate from the shadows. "For obvious and pleasing reasons, you shall never forget what we have shown you."

Cecco stepped back, to discern his expression. But Hook reached out with his barb, jarring Jill and snagging her husband by his sash. Hook tugged Cecco closer, so that he leaned in again, and so that, again, the lady felt her two lovers encompass her.

Hook cupped her chin. He raised her gaze to meet his eyes, his lips a mere whisper from hers, and her cheek just inches from Cecco's.

"When the madness of the blood-rage descends, this, my love, is how your men will protect you. One at your back, and one of us, always, before you."

Cecco recognized Jill's look. He understood that her heart stretched full. She seemed unwilling to employ the commonplace use of words to answer. Instead, each man's hand felt the pressure of her touch as, with gratitude, she squeezed them. Cecco was more gratified by the pledge Hook made on his behalf than he was surprised by the seduction Hook had performed to underscore it. Long ago, its truth had taken root in his soul.

"*Sì, Bellezza,*" he affirmed in his most loving accent. Resolutely, he kissed her crimson palm. "I swear my oath upon it. Your men stop at nothing to defend you."

"My Giovanni; Hook, my love." Her eyelids fluttered to clear the moisture that collected. "I am grateful beyond measure. For my own self-respect, I shall do as my judgment commands me. Yet even the strongest woman may long for protection. This paradox, perhaps, is the riddle of my being."

Hook raised one eyebrow. "And to think I had believed it to be your storytelling." He smiled, half-way.

Cecco added, smiling, too, "And I believed it to be your gypsy virtues: courage and loyalty— and a decent disrespect for the law."

"I presume," Hook continued, lightly, "that the discussion that led to this interesting episode concerned our strategy against Lean Wolf."

During his abstinence from Jill, Cecco paid little heed to the closeness of her connection with her lover. He recalled now, with a taste of bitterness, that Hook claimed to share her soul. Of course Hook intuited her emotions, and he knew that Cecco's jealousy caused their clash. Cecco stilled, then, as the implications of this circumstance occurred to him. Hook might not have witnessed their first embrace tonight, but by his bond with Jill he knew of it. By the same token, on some level Hook discerned, and he always had discerned, whatever— or whomever— Jill wanted.

She had wanted Cecco. The first kiss, the one Cecco provoked from her, had proven it. And Hook, without reservation, had granted Jill's wish.

But Cecco was no fool. He recognized that Hook's act was not born simply of liberality. Without question, Cecco had received heightened standing. But, in the giving, Hook's bounty increased his own power. As when he rained jewels upon Jill, the more he bestowed, the more securely he bound her. Once again, Cecco's ally was his adversary.

His emotions whirled in circles. He managed to stow his discomfiture while he assisted Hook in seating her on the daybed, by Hook's side, and then his legs buckled and he knelt at Jill's knee— at his commodore's knee— not ungrateful for the gift he'd been given. Cecco made love to his Jill tonight, but was he any closer to keeping her?

"Yet at last," Hook went on, once Jill nestled beside him, "we three have reached an accord, from which standpoint we are sure to prevail. You may strike the final blow to your foe, Jill."

The imminence of Jill's danger turned the current of Cecco's thoughts. As fear for her safety resurfaced, he considered the wreck of her wedding dress, and the violation she endured at the hands of her abductor. Throwing his shoulders back, he rose to stand before her.

"We shall give our all to protect our beloved, *Amore*. Not only from Lean Wolf, but from anyone who threatens. I dare to speak for the commodore, as he dares speak for me: we stand in accord in another matter, too. We both revile the menace you invite with your vengeance." Cecco strode to the wall, yanked his knife free, and posed before her once more.

"I held true to my vow when Doctor Hanover plagued you. I will keep it again." Point down, he held his dagger aloft. "The man who handles you will not die before my weapon handles *him*."

Looking upon her with his deadly brown eyes, Cecco slid the knife home in his sash. Where in the past he might kiss his fingertips in farewell, this time he took her face in his hands, unhesitating, and kissed her lips until his kiss was complete. When he stood again, he nodded to Hook, then turned the key in the lock and opened the door. Before he descended the companionway, his wife's parting words, uttered softly, stroked him like waves on the sand. He did not turn to acknowledge them.

"Addio, amore mio."

Cecco's body felt tortured, but, for long, ecstatic moments, the heart in his chest had beat close to Jill's. He sensed two emotions tugging at his insides. One old, and one new.

"It's strange how these merfolk know whatever happens on the Island," Tom remarked to his companions. "Makes the hair rise on my scalp. There's Zaleh, looking like he expected us."

Guillaume turned from his rowing to view the merman. Although the *Red Lady's* second officer was now confident enough in his swimming to navigate the Island alone, today he'd brought Nibs and Tom along. The time of the pirates' sojourn on the Neverland was drawing to an end, and the three companions sought one last bask at Mermaids' Lagoon. Guillaume smiled and hailed his foster father. *"Salut,* Papa!"

"Greetings, my son!" With powerful thrusts of his tail, Zaleh surged to the boat and, clamping the cable in his strong ivory teeth, he towed the sailors to Marooners' Rock. Once the craft tapped the stone, Nibs and Tom jumped out to tie it to a rusty ring, then prepared to enjoy the scenery.

Guillaume shed his clothes for a swim. With a new sense of pride and barely a splash, the slender Frenchman entered the cool, blue-green water. He and Zaleh sped away, racing, trailing brown hair and silver braids behind them, like seaweed.

Shading his eyes, Tom peered under the translucent surface. "No sign of his daughters, more's the pity."

"As you say, Tom, the mermaids are well aware that we'll be shipping out soon. They'll be here." Sliding off his breeches, Nibs displayed a golden chain around his waist. As it glittered in the sun's rays, he launched a sly look toward his brother.

"You dog!" Tom bellowed. But as he tossed off his shirt to bare his barrel chest, he, too, revealed bait, in the form of a necklace.

Tom's lure was studded with pearls. He shrugged. "Guillaume has *his* foster father to teach him. We have our own. Hook's example never yet steered us wrong."

Nibs' more serious nature darkened the mood, and the skin creased between his eyebrows. Out of habit, he reached up to tighten his orange kerchief. His frown grew deeper as he remembered that Lean Wolf had robbed him of it. "Don't forget that Hook's advice included a warning. What we yield here, we yield freely. What a mermaid yields carries a cost."

Tom considered the commodore's caveat, rubbing the scar at his temple. Then he grinned again. "I'm feeling generous today." Stretching out, he found a comfortable position with a good view of the environs. Even Nibs couldn't remain serious this afternoon, and soon he too relaxed in the luxury of the Lagoon.

Zaleh and Guillaume dove and swam, then flipped up to rest on the rock shelf. The surf lapped the ledge, and Guillaume dangled his feet near Zaleh's fins. The silver of the merman's scales was tinted green where his tail trailed below the waterline. Guillaume's feet appeared golden. Both creatures leaned back on their hands, their shoulders warmed by the sunshine that glinted upon the plaits of Zaleh's hair. The air smelled of moss, fish, and brine. Here and there, sleek sets of heads and shoulders rose up in the waves, to peep at the sailors who seemed to doze on Marooners' Rock. Guillaume noticed that, inch by inch, they drifted closer to Nibs and Tom— and their trinkets.

"You no longer ask me to protect your friends," Zaleh observed in his musical voice.

"*Non.* They know the chance they are taking. I believe that *mes amis* enjoy the risk as part of the challenge."

"Such is the nature of sailors, my boy. And because the sea, like its mariners, can be perverse..." Zaleh slithered into the water again, leaving Guillaume alone, to feel the kiss of waves against his legs, and to listen to cries of birds hovering over the cliff top. Within minutes, a strange new noise sounded, bringing with it a bevy of beauties.

Nibs and Tom sat up, looking around the Lagoon. Clearly they, like Guillaume, were astonished by the notes, and by the sudden appearance of what looked to be Zaleh's entire tribe. Guillaume spotted the merman, bobbing at the break of the bay. At his lips, he poised a seashell as big as his hands. The silver scales on his forearms glittered in the light, reminding Guillaume of Captain Cecco and his bracelets.

Once again Zaleh blew through the shell, to sound a high, hollow tone. It carried across the Lagoon, then bounced against the walls of the cliff, echoing at Guillaume's back. Both alarming and alluring, the sound resonated inside his heart.

Zaleh gestured reassurance to his family, dispersing them, then made his way in leaps and dives to Guillaume. Huffing with the exercise, he offered the shell to the young man, and with a flourish of his tail, his muscular arms hoisted his body from the brine to recline upon the ledge.

"A gift for you, my son," Zaleh said, "to take with you on your voyages."

Guillaume turned the shell in his hands. It was smooth on the inside, like one of LeCorbeau's bone china teacups, where it curved to turn inside out. Its exterior was knobby and ridged, striped with pink and the lightest of browns. Where the peak of the spiral should be, a hole was cut instead.

"That aperture is where you blow," Zaleh explained. "See," and he took the shell back, to purse his lips and wind it again. As he blew, Guillaume watched his hand slide in and out of the open curve, modulating the pitch. This time, the reverberation from the rock wall came sooner, and louder. "Now you try it."

"*Oui*, Papa." Guillaume tried, and tried again. Before long, Zaleh had taught him how to shape his lips, and the proper rhythm to use for the call. Obviously this signal meant something to the mer-people, because the waters of the Lagoon had come alive with their presence. Over on Marooners' Rock, Tom was beaming, and even Nibs cracked a lopsided smile as their attention was plucked this way and that by the abundance of curves and of colors. Soon the two men were mostly immersed, surrounded by a surfeit of sea women. Thanks to Zaleh's gift, the afternoon that began with modest hopes now appeared bountiful with promise.

His silver-gray eyes shone down on his foster son. "I give you this horn, Guillaume, in hopes that you will never need it. But if you find yourself on the water, and in peril, you must sound this conch, exactly as I have instructed you."

"Papa, you have taught me much."

"You've learned much on your own. Like me, you are an observer of your people's behavior. Not long ago, I watched the woman your friends call their mother. She worked her wiles as naturally as one of my daughters. At the end of the day, I was interested to see her victim rise up, alive, and paddle away in his canoe. But it is not only here, in our Lagoon, that your humans show their true colors. And I trust that I need not remind you that the males as well as the females of your race are quite capable of treachery."

"Aye." Guillaume glanced at the scar on his hand. "It is a lesson I have learned. But, Papa, knowing the tendencies of your own race, your kindness overwhelms me. I shall value this gift, as I treasure your friendship."

"Since the beginning, I have treasured your trust. But remember this caution, my boy. I can't promise that my kindred will help you when you blow the signal, but I can promise you that they will come."

"You grant me a chance of survival on the sea. It is more than most sailors can harbor."

"Men are such foolish creatures," Zaleh shook his head, "forever delving into mysteries they cannot hope to comprehend."

"And merfolk are deeper creatures, Papa." Carefully, Guillaume set the conch down, swiping its salty residue from his lips. "But we mortals are not so foolish that we forget a favor." Sliding into the sea, Guillaume displayed his new prowess, gliding through the water to the dinghy, and swimming smoothly back.

Treading water, he raised his hand from the sea, and opened it. Over the mark on his palm lay a bracelet of beaten silver, inlaid with dark blue lapis-stone panels. Zaleh took it to examine it closely. Each panel was carved like a cameo to display a different symbol of the sea— a shell, a ship, a fish, an octopus, a crab, and a whale. Zaleh stopped turning the bracelet as he stared at the seventh and final carving: a three-pointed spear.

"My trident," he marveled. "Exquisitely rendered."

"I purchased this piece from my captain. He prefers gold over silver."

Zaleh laughed, a sound more melodious than the call of the conch. "My boy," he said, "deep as I may be, it is strange that I did not expect to feel this affection."

"But you may expect your new son to return to you, once our voyage is over." Guillaume was smiling, delighted that his gift and his gratitude had so pleased his foster father. He turned his eyes toward Marooners' Rock. "But whether or not my friends will be fit to sail, this question lies beyond my experience."

Lightly touched down on the stony heights of the Indian mountain, with Rowan at his side. "I'm happy to be trusted once more, but this is one task the council handed us that I find disagreeable."

The air felt brisk and fresh up here, and they both looked forward to kindling a fire in their tepee, once they hiked down to the deserted mountain camp. Having searched the Island and encountered no sign of their quarry, the pair would welcome a rest to warm up some supper.

"Soon dusk will blanket the sky and put an end to our searching," Rowan observed. "Perhaps we should camp here tonight."

"Look, Rowan, there's smoke rising. It must come from a cook fire."

Rowan's gray-glass eyes grew alert. "I believe we have found him." He drew his tomahawk from its home at his hip. Its heavy, weighted head lent reassurance to his spirit. Lightly shrugged his bow from his shoulders, glad of the new, swifter arrows his twin brothers at the Clearing had crafted to fill his quiver.

Descending the path, the men avoided its stumbling points, half leaping, half flying over rocks and crevices. Within minutes they crouched to view the Indian encampment, deserted for summer moons, its cluster of tepees tucked up snug and waiting for winter. From the long wooden lodge-house, a feather of smoke drifted upward. Lightly sniffed, detecting a roast of venison he guessed to be Lean Wolf's lonesome dinner. Hungry as the young men were, the aroma made their mouths water.

Always cautious, Rowan proposed, "Let us call to him. I know better than to enter the den of a wolf." When Lightly nodded, Rowan took up a stance as steady as the tree of his namesake, and cupped his hand to his mouth. "Lean Wolf, Silent Hunter. We come to you bearing news."

Moments later, the rangy form of the hunter emerged, bending to exit the lodge, then straightening to his full and formidable height. He wore leggings and a long sleeved deerskin shirt that stretched tight over the muscles of his arms. During his time of expulsion from the tribe, he appeared shaggier than usual, his narrow face more feral. "Well," he said, licking the grease from his fingertips, "here are the young lovers. Have you come to find warmth at my hearth? Sorry. I do not welcome your kind of heat."

"Nor do we welcome yours," retorted Lightly. "I look forward to the day my mother abandons you."

"Ah!" Lean Wolf raised his eyebrows. "Such a woman is my kind of kindling. What makes you think she'll turn cold to me?"

"Your first wife Red Fawn did. Why shouldn't your second?"

"Red Fawn is the only female who ventured to run from me. She believed she was done with Silent Hunter, but now she knows better."

"Do not dare to try your bullying with Red Hand."

"Strictly speaking, I don't know what you're talking about. No man of the People associates with pirates, or with Outcasts." Giving his words the lie, his first wife's marriage bracelet appeared at his wrist as he cocked his head and held a hand to his ear. "In fact, I am not certain my ears perceive *you*."

"You call yourself a man of the People. A brave of the tribe would not attempt to rape Red Fawn."

"So it *was* you who shot at me. You may regret that your arrow missed my heart."

Rowan stepped forward. "Threaten us if you wish. But if you harm a woman again, we will make certain the elders learn of your transgressions."

Lean Wolf jeered, "The elders do not hear you any more than I do. Not only are the pair of you invisible to us, you are inaudible. Now go away. From this moment, I will follow the council's ruling and ignore you."

"You will hear us." Rowan stiffened, and intoned, "Lean Wolf Silent Hunter. We bring word from the Council of Elders: 'Our Messengers are restored to the People, and all quarrels exhaled with the smoke of the peace pipe. Further, the warrior Lean Wolf is deemed to have served his time of solitude, and may return to the tribe with his tribute of meat and of furs.' "

As Lean Wolf listened, both displeasure and satisfaction crossed his face.

Lightly added, "Walking Man has retired from the council. We feasted to his honor two suns ago. Wherever you skulked on the Island, you must have heard the celebration."

"Do not look so smug, Lightly of the Air. This news that you welcome brings bad tidings, too. It means that only one deed will make sure of your silence." Reaching behind his back, Lean Wolf produced his broad hunting knife. Its shine was dulled by the blood of the deer whose roasting flesh filled the atmosphere.

Rowan and Lightly still gripped their weapons. Neither moved. Lightly asked, "How do you hope to catch us? Though much like a wolf, you are only a man. Rowan and I are like birds."

"Did your mother not warn you? I know how to bring down a bird." He raised his knife as if to hurl it at Lightly, then, suddenly, aimed it at Rowan. "How far will you fly, fledgling, once your lover lies dead?"

The color drained from Lightly's face.

Lean Wolf sneered. "I see that I have hit my target. A blow to one bird is a blow to you both."

Heavy with dread, Lightly backed from him. "Remember what we told you. The council's outlook has altered."

"The Messengers have delivered the elders' words. Unless you prefer that I kill you right now, I'll go eat my dinner." With a malevolent stare, Lean Wolf bent and entered the lodge, flipping down the blanket that covered the open door.

Rowan and Lightly glanced at one another, then shoved off to take to the air. Lightly's knees shook, but, thanks to his partner's presence, he did feel able to fly. Instinctively, they soared upward to their private place on the mountaintop. Once their toes touched its rock again, Rowan turned to clasp Lightly to his breast. He sensed Lightly's emotion, and shared the hollow feeling in his stomach. He kissed Lightly, and laid his head on his shoulder. "Let us return home," Rowan urged. "Your mother's men will watch over her, but, more than ever, Red Fawn needs our protection."

"Yes." Lightly's heartbeat lagged. Tightly, he embraced Rowan, and when he spoke to his lover again, his voice was unsteady. "Although I would have understood such a fate, I did not lose you to the love of Ayasha. But, Rowan…never could I bear to lose you to the hatred of Lean Wolf."

"Lightly of the Air, you are my wings."

The two held together, chilled by the breeze, gazing over the mountain's edge at the dimming landscape of the Neverland below them. A yellow glow danced in the Clearing, showing that their kin prepared for another night of revelry— perhaps the last until, months hence, the pirates might sail in to Neverbay once more.

Rowan said, slowly, "I agree that it is good to be trusted again. White Bear and the council honor us beyond our best hopes. Yet it is clear to me that, while Lean Wolf prowls this land, we cannot travel to the Other Island on White Bear's errand."

"You speak truth, Rowan." Lightly sighed. "For everyone's sake, I hope Jill knows what she's doing."

From the green of the woods, Raven stepped lightly into the pavilion. Its gaily striped colors lit her features, and she appeared as handsome as the first day he'd seen her on the sun-splashed banks of the river. Her raven-black hair had grown a little longer, and in it she now wore a cluster of beads and blue jay feathers that dangled down her neck. Hook could not fail to see that something else had changed, too.

Raven appeared more vivid, somehow, her flesh more full and her eyes more alive. To Hook's gaze, her body revealed the sensuality she had previously subdued. He recognized the amorousness that he himself had quickened in her, on that night she came to him in this very tent, to guide him through his pain. The twitch tickled at his lip. Apparently, both parties had gained from their exchange.

He swept forward to greet her. "I welcome you, my dear." Also welcome to him was the familiarity of a friendly female, and the earthy, outdoor scent she brought. The air around her evoked his memories of Wendy, before Jill replaced them with perfume. Eagerly, he bent to kiss the woman, but straightened as she shied away.

"Commodore, I consider myself now to be a wedded woman." As her dark eyes gazed upon him, Hook identified a hint of who he knew her to be. A rule breaker, like himself.

He smiled, half-way. "Those who know me understand that I never hesitate to embrace another man's wife." Raven did not appear distressed by his statement, but at the moment he chose not to press her. "Yet, naturally, your wish shall be respected." He took her hand instead, and brought it to his lips. Her fingers returned his clasp.

Gratified, Hook prolonged the moment, watching as Raven waited for him to release her hand. The woman was such a charming mixture of self-assertion and self-denial. The last time they met, Hook had damaged that denial. The result, this afternoon, made her fascinating.

"Sir, I find that you have recovered your spirits," she ventured, "and I understand that your happiness is recovered, also."

"Indeed, as, in some measure, your own happiness is restored. My ships are prepared to sail. As agreed, you shall be advised when to make your escape." He raised one eyebrow. "Unless, that is, you no longer desire to do so?"

"I do, yet I no longer look upon my leaving as escape. I confessed my plans to White Bear. He agreed to let me go, provided that the tribe's Messengers accompany me. White Bear himself escorted me here—" she blushed, "although I must thank you for your discretion in choosing this secluded spot, so near the woods. My husband waits for me at a distance there, and I did not tell him who I intended to meet."

"A wise decision." Hook's chest warmed with admiration. "I can imagine the courage required to speak truth to a man of White Bear's stature. It is enough, perhaps, to have gained his acquiescence in your plans."

"Sir, what you have promised is enough. And yet I fear I must ask for your help once again."

Hook stood silent, observing her. In her accustomed sign of agitation, she dragged her fingers through her bob of hair.

"Even White Bear, as my husband and as a member of the council, cannot assure me of the safety of my family— his family."

Hook frowned. "The terms of truce between my men and yours have held firm. In the time since my 'visit' to your village, no spark of war has flared between us."

"You mistake my meaning. I do not fear hostility between our peoples. I dread revenge from the warrior, Lean Wolf." As Hook's eyes narrowed, Raven spoke more quietly. "He whom we call the Silent Hunter."

Hook set his jaw. The humor vanished from his voice. "I have heard of him."

"Lean Wolf asked that I should be his wife. As headman of my family, White Bear refused. Lean Wolf is a vindictive man, and I feel I have brought danger upon my husband, upon my sister, and even her baby. I cannot leave the Island without seeking some way to protect them."

"Can your elders not control this brave?"

"He is too clever. By the time they learn of his treachery, it will be too late."

"And so you come to *me*." Thoughtful, Hook tapped his claw upon the thigh of his boot.

She said, "Nor will the elders act in defense of the Outcasts. I know you undertake to protect those who dwell at the Clearing. I must give you warning: while Lean Wolf hunts, not one of those women is safe."

"Your council understand that I will deal justice to any member of the tribe who causes trouble at the Clearing. Lean Wolf has never shown his face there. As you say, he is clever. I cannot touch him unless he misbehaves within my domain."

"Can you not confront him, privately? Can your pirates present some threat to him?"

"Not in the time I have allotted before departing the Island." Seeing her look of pain, Hook laid his hand on her cheek. She tilted her head, ever so slightly, to accommodate him. Her skin felt velvety, and the feathers of her headdress brushed his fingers. "Raven. I regret that I can make no pledge, this time, to succor you."

"Is there nothing I can do to prevent his harming my loved ones?"

He withdrew his touch. "Other than giving yourself to him?" At her look of horror, Hook shook his head. "No. Nor should you trust him even if you did."

She squeezed her hands together, whispering, "I wish I held the courage to kill him."

"It is no wonder I esteem you, my dear. Yet you are not the only woman of spirit on this island."

Hook stepped closer, and viewed her puzzled face gazing up at him.

"No man of my company, including me, may lay a finger upon Lean Wolf." He allowed a note of promise to play in his voice, and it held her captive. "No *man* of my company."

"But…your company does not contain only men."

"I feel that I may send you away in the confidence that those you love shall be shielded."

A moment of astonishment, a quick intake of breath, and Raven forgot to consider herself a wedded woman. As if her gratitude elevated her, she rose to her tiptoes and flung her arms around his neck. Hook held the lushness of her body in his arms, and, pulling back just a bit, he smiled down upon her. "As promised, your wish shall be respected." This kiss they shared might be their last.

Beyond question, this kiss matched their first.

When, at length, Raven pulled away, Hook raised his claw to her headdress. A quick cut, and one long, blue feather flew free from her hair. As it whirled to the ground, they both watched it fall, to settle on the colors of the carpet. It lay between his black boots and her bare feet, beneath the dangling fringe of her dress. Hook picked it up. He did not offer to return it to Raven, nor did she reach out to take it. Over the feather, a look passed between them— a deep look, and a longing one— but nothing more, and then she whirled to run from the pavilion, late to meet her husband in the woods.

Hook touched the tip of the feather to his lips, intensely aware of its tingling. Then he strode to the table, where his hat and his weapons lay waiting. Employing the point of his hook, he pierced the brim, and, painstakingly, he worked his few fingers to seat the feather securely. When he finished, he donned the hat, cocking it at an angle to sport his prize. Yet he knew, as most of those who knew him did not, that this token meant more than a trophy.

It meant that Raven's flight to the Other Island was a decision for the best.

Still, he reflected…he knew where to find her.

Island Offering

Wittles the carpenter hung up his tools. He stretched and sighed, glad to be done with his tasks. The ship was clean, careened, and seaworthy, and stocked with the materials needed to keep her afloat. The only missing properties were the commodore and his lady. Rumor had it that they were off to the Fairy Glade, for one last evening on the love seat the carpenter had crafted to order. Because no taverns or shops were established on the Island, Hook's coins of payment still reposed in Wittles' pocket.

Soon he'd join the lads on deck for a mug of ale under Neverland skies. These last days had been filled with cramming the holds. Timber, hemp, kegs of fresh water. The smith and the cooper turned out dozens of barrels, stuffed now with foods gathered by the men and preserved by Cook, Chef, and their galley mates— fish, fruits, greens, and game. Though the sailors felt well fed, they were ready for a rest.

This afternoon saw the final fest at the Clearing. The rain showers hadn't dampened the merriment, but, rather, made the party more fluid. Mr. Smee got some groans when he announced the commodore's order to remain aboard on this eve. Smee admonished the hands to keep watch against mischief from Lost Boys, and stay strictly clear of the natives. No footprints on shore tonight, muddy or dry. That was the order.

The sailors grinned, though, when Smee called for casks to be rolled up. Even better, they cheered to see the *Red Lady*'s boats hook-ing on and her Frenchmen scrambling aboard. The combined ships' companies would drink to the Neverland stars that rose over the yardarms, big and brassy, and they'd keep their eyes primed for mermaids. Tonight might be the last they'd see of the Island's allures, until the next time the fleet sailed for home port.

"And which of us knows if he'll sink, swim, or swing first?" Wittles scratched his head with his uneven fingernails. "Best to invest in the dice." He patted his pocket, and whistled his way up the stairs.

This last night in port, Nibs straddled a cannon at the *Roger's* rail. Lanterns illuminated the ship's deck behind him, radiating a liquid yellow light to waver on the bay. An air from the fiddler soared to crescendo, then hauntingly came to an end. Like the company's sojourn here, the melody was done.

Nibs breathed in of the fragrance of Island air. He knew that the other men, even those who hadn't grown up here, felt the same wistfulness. Half of his heart was anchored on this isle; the other half hankered for open sea. By tomorrow night, these shores and their residents would live on as fantasy. Someplace to dream about, someplace to boast about, and someplace to long to return.

Warned to be wary tonight, the sailors saw nothing alarming. As yet, although the men watched eagerly for mermaids, no seafolk thinned out the crew. Jewel had orbited the Island and reported to Smee early on, indicating that the natives did not menace, and no mischief seemed a-brew from Pan's boys.

So the sailors laughed and talked, threw dice to go clattering on the boards, and the coins they lost and won clinked in their hands. Nibs gazed up to the crow's nest, where Noodler and Jewel shared the watch. No doubt they shared Noodler's flask, too. Nibs roused from his musings when Jewel dove from the nest in a streak of gold to make a beeline to the bo'sun. She must have sighted something.

Casting his gaze about the waters, Nibs spotted the craft as Jewel pointed it out to Smee. The bo'sun craned to examine it, then waved to it. Soon Nibs' brothers, the twins, shot alongside in their canoe, floating swiftly by with Lily aboard. She and Smee exchanged greetings. She blew a kiss to him, but glided past the ship. The Men of the Clearing hailed the *Red Lady*.

Captain Cecco must have expected Lily. Having sent most of his men to the *Roger* to carouse this last night, he himself hurried down the gangway to escort Lily aboard. Nibs saw the flash of Lily's bracelet as Cecco pulled her up, reflecting the lights of the party. The *Roger*'s glow also illuminated the wild, tawny hair of the Men of the Clearing. Just like Nibs and Tom, they had their own means of boarding. They stowed their paddles, tied their canoe to Cecco's vessel, then floated up as if swimming with the breeze to join their brothers for one last evening.

Nibs felt a kind of melancholy tonight, and he delayed the reunion. Instead, he watched Smee as Smee watched his Lily. The bo'sun's fingers flexed and fisted, but once she disappeared from his view— inside the captain's quarters— Smee returned to his duty, overseeing the *Roger*'s festivities. Yet Nibs noted that Smee kept vigil on *Red Lady* as keenly as the sailors kept vigil on the bay. Lily, it seemed, was Smee's 'mermaid.' And, like a falling block, a realization struck Nibs. He needed a mermaid, too. He had friends; he had lovers and brothers; he had officers whom he respected and a mother to guide and advise him. But what Nibs wanted was a woman of his own. A lady whose love was all his.

Nibs was astounded by this revelation. As he perched there considering the idea, he felt suddenly off balance. And this time, he was startled by something more ethereal, even, than his thoughts. An unearthly sound emerged from the surf, and the flesh crept up on his arms. Had his wishing made it happen? Had Nibs' hungry heart called a sea-maid from the depths? Staring about him, he saw the other men stop their gaming, to listen. Each man's eyes began searching, too, and a hush fell over the ship.

Seeping through the boards, beneath the decks and through them, the eerie song entered their ears. All around the *Roger*, bubbles burbled up, and, as they met the air and ruptured, the sleek, seal-like heads of sirens came to surface. Sailors lined the gunwales now, their jaws hanging open, and the breath arrested in their lungs. Like a parting gift from the Island, the mermaids had circled, to bid the pirates goodbye.

At first Nibs felt a twinge of disappointment. But through his ventures on the sea, he'd learned to be skeptical. His common sense returned. Suspicious now, he glanced toward his friends. His hunch was correct. Most of the officers, like Smee and Yulunga, stood braced and ready to hold their men back. They navigated the deck, on guard to seize any jumpers. Yet among the officers and crew, one man appeared unsurprised and unconcerned. Dressed in his blue and red uniform, Guillaume stood beaming beside Tom and the twins. Now that Guillaume had won an alliance with the merfolk, no doubt he'd suggested this treat.

The sailors, while enraptured, made no move to desert. The song resonating round the bay was plaintive, poignant. The female voices combined, in harmony, to rise and to fall like the sea, unceasing— to crest and recede, and never to let a man rest. This time, Nibs sensed, the song of the sirens was meant not to lure the men's bodies, but to hold the men's souls. Not unaffected himself, he rubbed his nose. Another look round the ship showed Nibs that he wasn't alone. His mates shared his feeling: these songs were less treacherous than those crooned at the Mermaids' Lagoon, yet this music felt so heartrending that it, too, might turn deadly.

Smee could be seen to heave a deep sigh, and look once again for his Lily. He wiped his spectacles on his kerchief. Nibs sympathized with Smee's sentiment. All of a sudden, it seemed that to part with these females, or the Indian ladies, or any other element of the Island, was impossible. But Nibs soon forgot about Smee. Like the others, he leaned on the gunwale, he looked to the sky. From the very stars that whirled round the Neverland, the song shimmered back like a cloudburst of musical light, until, betwixt masts and yards, between heaven and sea, the atmosphere quavered with heartache.

How long did this enchantment last? Nibs couldn't guess. Here in the Neverland, time was dicey. Just like the mergirls, it couldn't be counted upon. One by one, their voices diminished, their lovely heads sank away. The mermaids' chorus dwindled to solo. When the sound ceased, sinking beneath the waves, the sailors blinked, and looked around, each man surprised to find himself in company, amazed by the gift, and feeling fortunate to hear it through to its end— still alive.

Before the song, the men had been wary, on guard against those mermaids. After it, they reckoned they understood. They were sailors, taking port call on the Neverland. Every stay here offered its wonders, and every incident posed its warnings. No precaution could protect them. And yet…what other island could compare?

For Nibs, now, the search had begun. His was not a quest to find a place to call home. Home was here. His challenge was to seek someplace new to him. What Nibs sought was the island of his true love's abode. Somewhere, she bided, waiting for him. His heart beat quicker as he thought of her, just as cruelly as it beat while the mermaids sang their serenade. The crinkle between his eyebrows deepened. Nibs was determined. He'd win her heart, and then he'd carry her home.

The fiddle sang again, inspired by the sea's song, but paling in comparison. Nibs joined Guillaume, and his brothers. His brooding features brightened. After all, this night was the last night in port.

As the woods fell to dusk, the fairies weaved and bobbed above their hollows, their lights illuminating their circle in spurts, like the flicker of embers at the death of a bonfire.

But the night had only begun, and as the birds nestled into the forest surrounding the Fairy Glade, peeping their sleepy last, the fairy musicians could be heard, tuning their instruments. Their strings produced a sound very like the noise Jewel made when she stamped across the keys of Hook's harpsichord.

Lovely as a fairy herself, Jill glided into the circle to alight on the grass. Hook settled beside her, his hair somewhat mussed by the breeze, but the blue plume secure on his hat, pinned in place with an opal brooch. Their feet were bare, damp now with the remnants of the rain, yet the couple displayed their best garb— Jill in a full-skirted taffeta gown, golden, Hook handsome as he flaunted his best blouse, tawny silk trimmed in lace and tucked into brown velvet breeches. His waistcoat was rich with embroidery. Jill's jewels glimmered like fairy dust at her throat, arms, and ankles. Hook's five fingers glowed with gems, and the filigree gleamed on his earring.

Jill gazed at her lover, taking pleasure in his appearance, as always. But this time, a new element entered in. "Your feather looks jaunty, Hook."

"A feather in my cap, and, if rumors bloom of my dalliance with an unnamed native lady, it offers another reason for our enemies to doubt our devotion."

"It is a token to protect me, in the way that my wedding band does." Jill's demeanor remained pleasant, but she struck a serious note. "And, to you, your liaison with Raven is as meaningful as my marriage to Cecco."

"I have learned never to endeavor to hide an emotion from you. Yes, my love. Raven aided me, in much the same manner Captain Cecco aided you." He smiled, ironic. "If, unfortunately, more briefly."

"Well and bravely stated, Hook. Your liberality is tried. As in all things, I am your counterpart, for I, too, find myself tested."

"You bear it well, my dear. And you, at least, hold the comfort of knowing that your rival will soon depart for what seems to be forever."

"I shall ensure that you do not miss her."

"Begin at once." Hook took Jill in his arms and they entered into a kiss, surrounded by the emerald woodland, among the magical creatures who flew about them, shimmering in the shining light of the Fairy Glade, under the stars.

Clinging to Hook's substantial shoulders for support, Jill caught her breath. "Perhaps it is only the fairies' activity, but I believe I must sit down."

The couple took their places on the loveseat, careful not to block the mirrors on its backrest, so that the fairies could primp before the music commenced. Hook and Jill acknowledged the creatures as they came to admire their reflections, nodding their compliments to each.

"An excellent choice, Hook, to spend our last evening here." Jill inhaled the moist air. "How fresh the rain made the atmosphere." She surveyed the fairy garden, its clusters of blooms full and fragrant. "I can almost hear the flowers drinking it up. And I never witnessed such brilliant rainbows as this afternoon provided."

"Our Mr. Smee claimed the same. It seems that even the isle of his birth cannot match this paradise."

"The rainbows fairly bounced about the sky this afternoon, just as our hosts are doing now." Jill's eyes danced as her gaze followed the fairies. But soon her observation left the Glade itself, and delved farther, into the forest. "But are we not at risk, in the open here?"

"My love, we are safer here than anywhere else on the Island. The fairies will sense any malevolence that approaches, and they will hide away before I can draw my sword." His weapon stood propped against the bench, in a niche specially commissioned from Wittles to hold it within easy reach. Jill herself bore the weight and the beauty of the gem-studded dagger in her sash. Hook drew Jill closer. "But I sense you are not yet at ease."

"Aye, Hook," she said, and hesitated. "Of course I'm delighted to enjoy this lovely place, and to spend this quiet time with you."

"And yet?"

"Yet I am desolate that this night is the last of our sojourn here."

The lovers dropped their voices as the dancers took their places. The orchestra's tootling turned to a melody. The listeners held contentment, and yet they were saddened. Hook and Jill felt the tug that each of their sailors was experiencing, back in the bay. Jill murmured under the music, "Island magic cradles us, in the same way the sea's will soon do. The gifts of each place are generous, but it is impossible to enjoy them both at once."

Hook observed, "Have you not discovered by now, Jill? In all aspects of life, grief seasons gladness."

Jill nodded. To gain one blessing was to lose the other, and some regret lay in the choosing of either setting. In this frame of mind, it seemed, those mortals who indulged in fairy music were most profoundly affected by it. Bolstered by Hook's loving presence, yet Jill felt her heart lower, and the tears pricked her eyelids.

And, for Jill, the evening held another source of tension. Tomorrow, at midday, she must end her marriage to Lean Wolf.

Hook shared her unease, sensing it with his soul as well as through his nearness to her body. His cares were simpler. Where Jill was anxious to prevail in her battle, her lover feared more for her safety. And one other unknown loomed over them. Jill was thinking of that aspect, too.

"Jill." Speaking low, Hook pressed his single hand to her knee. "As promised, I shall attend you. Cecco, too, has sworn to be your protector."

"You know that I trust Cecco implicitly. But, Hook, what if his jealousy should interfere with his judgment?"

"You assured me that in his handling of Doctor Hanover, Cecco plied his gypsy skills. He kept his head, even while you seemed to desert him."

At the mention of the doctor, Jill's anxiety tautened, like a knot, and crimped in her stomach. "It is true. And yet, after all, Cecco lives under the same curse as my other husbands. Supposing that, for all the care I've put into it, my scheme misfires? Supposing not only Lean Wolf, but Cecco, too, falls victim to his passions?"

"Jill, the moment is not too late to change your plans. Both Captain Cecco and I await your command. My sword is at your service." Eager, Hook's eyes took on a tint of crimson. "Shall I have the pleasure of killing Lean Wolf?"

His intensity thrilled her, but her good sense prevailed. "What of the war you believe his murder might provoke?"

"Murder is one thing. Protection is another. The Silent Hunter's actions threaten every female on this Island, and all your sons, too."

"Greater reasons for me to deal justice to him myself. I was a child here, with childish dreams. I am a woman, now, with other women to defend, and other children to protect." Jill shook her head. "No, Hook, this task is mine."

"On one single subject, Captain Cecco and I agree with no reservation. We both wish to preserve you from violence. And Cecco is correct, Jill. You intend, tomorrow, to kill a man outright. You cannot know how such an act will affect you."

"You tempt me to take the easy course. But I must honor the power that inhabited me in Lean Wolf's lair on the night he abducted me. I employed that power to save my life, and I made a vow to follow through." She raised her bloodstained hand. "I am Red Hand from the Sea. I am the wife of the warrior Lean Wolf." She declared, "I shall slay Lean Wolf. And I will lay him to rest in his tomb. Through its passages, he may wander the Dark Hunting grounds."

Hook's features sharpened. "I have every confidence in you, and I have faith in Captain Cecco's intentions. But in the event that his emotions rise to interfere with your plans, even so, you and I must be prepared."

"Aye," Jill asserted, her teeth setting with determination. "I am prepared." The mass of the dagger weighted her sash, and, absently, she toyed with her wedding band. As the fairy pageantry unfolded before her, Jill saw, in her mind's eye, another rite. Not a fest of frivolity, like tonight's display from the fairies, but a different dance. A sacrament to perform with her husband.

A dance of death.

Like the death of a bonfire, Jill thought. Lean Wolf, the Silent Hunter, had sparked a flame within her. No one but Red-Handed Jill could slake this conflagration. It was up to Jill, alone, to feed this fire, until it burned down to ash.

Cecco and Lily stretched out upon his bunk, gazing at the Neverland through the windows of the *Red Lady*'s stern. The Island's trees and beaches lay silvery in the starlight, mysterious, yet familiar even at a distance.

Sounds from the *Roger* drifted in, sounds Lily was used to hearing, but that after tonight she would miss— men's voices, raised in game and in song, accompanied by fiddles and pipes. On the bedside table lay Lily's earrings, their polished copper reflecting the brilliance of the stars. She took a sip of wine that left spice on her tongue, and then set the cup on the bed table, too, next to two pistols and Cecco's notorious knife. His cutlass hung on the hard wooden wall. A boarding ax hung there, too, kin to Lily's tribal tomahawks.

Lily chuckled to think of her daring in coming aboard. "Although the life I chose requires independence, this adventure has swept me beyond my ken." After the initial sensation that her feet could find no security, she had learned that the rocking of the decks could be soothing. Lying now on the captain's bed, Lily was enchanted with the motion, and delighted with the sense of novelty to be found upon Cecco's ship.

Although she had boarded eagerly, she had done so at Jill's request. Her visit was a gesture of reassurance, not just to steady Raven before her travels, but for the Women of the Clearing, too, who would feel concern for Raven as she sailed. Lily knew what conditions a woman of the tribe might seek, to achieve some degree of comfort on a voyage. She had also made one last check on Mrs. Hanover's health, bringing Lelaneh's remedies for the baby's well-being. The little mother seemed satisfied, and prepared for this passage. Lily herself considered the ship large, stark, and disorienting, but she discovered that the captain's quarters, with its padding and privacy, would feel welcoming enough to Raven. Now cozy and at home here herself, Lily nestled against the captain's shoulder, inhaling his masculine scent and enjoying the feeling of being anchored in his arms.

Cecco said, "You have become an adventuress, like my Jill."

"I am complimented. Even more so now that I have viewed her image on the figurehead of the Black Chief's ship, up close."

"Indeed, Lily. The only change I would make upon my lovely *Red Lady* is to place that mermaid at her prow. And, of course, to bring her inspiration to live here with me, too." Cecco smiled, somberly.

"Perhaps Raven will enjoy watching out this window as much as I do. I have lived here all my life, and never fully observed the Island from the sea. How small the land and its natives must seem to you, Captain, who travel the Wider World."

"Not small, Lily, and not insignificant. We sailors have forsaken our homes, and turn to this one. To most of us, you and this place are our haven. We do not love to leave it."

"And this time, you take one of us born here away with you."

"Only a short way, and only at her request."

"Captain, will you not ask Raven to voyage on with you, instead of settling her on the Other Island? You say she called you 'Man of the Lonely Winds.' I know you both. The two of you are kindred spirits."

"No, Lily. I welcome Raven, and I am gratified to be able to help her through her difficulty. But however much I care for her, I understand that she is honor-bound to her husband to follow through with her promise. Nor do I think it wise to keep her among pirates, whose ways are so strange to her." Neither did Cecco wish to keep Raven among the *one* pirate— other than himself— whose ways were not just strange to her, but attractive. Cecco grimaced at the thought. Enough rivalry existed between him and his commodore without adding fuel to the fire. To allow his feelings for Raven to develop could not cheer Cecco significantly, and might cause a great deal of hurt to Jill.

"So you leave the Island as you came here. Alone." Gently, Lily's fingertips followed the firm curve of Cecco's jaw. "And the Man of the Lonely Winds remains solitary through his own choice."

"It is by remaining solitary that I hope to win back the woman I love."

"You have won those you don't love, as well. You cut a romantic figure, Captain, with your devotion to your wife. The very quality that keeps you distant keeps you fascinating. Out of respect to your feeling, I will not urge the offer I made to you that first day you visited. You know that I will always welcome you in my arms. But, Captain, are you as determined as you were at the first to remain true to your lady Jill?"

"More than ever, Lily."

"And tomorrow? I know nothing of the details, and we of the Clearing are sworn to keep silence. I wonder, though, if you will follow Jill in whatever battle she plans against Lean Wolf?"

"I love her, but I will act as I believe to be right. I trust my own weapons, and what I do may not jibe with what Jill thinks best." As he lay on his back, Cecco felt the rough skin of the scars there, and he recalled the one time he was moved to strike his wife. "I have paid for our differences of opinion in the past, and so has Jill."

"Such trials make our loves more rewarding. So I have found."

"I hold another assurance, from Jill's own lips. At a moment of crisis, she told me that I will never be finished with her. Whether she speaks curses or comfort, Jill's prophecies come true."

"I would not choose this gift. To hold such power is frightening."

"Well you may say so, Lily. Jill may have cursed even herself with her gift. Doctor Hanover waits for the day he can claim her."

"No! What words did she speak to give him this hope?"

"At the peak of her victory, she mocked his conviction that she'd come away with him. She meant only to taunt the man, but I believe that the phrasing she used might commit her to follow him." Cecco's teeth clenched. "Hook and I will do all in our power to thwart that blackguard."

"Captain, I am sorry I led you into the dark forest of these thoughts. Please, put them away from you, and do not be distracted from tomorrow. Once the sun rises high, you, the commodore, and the lady must stand united against the Silent Hunter. I fear for the women here, if Jill's strategy fails."

"Your advice is good, Lily. Yet my wife and I have been divided in our strategies before. Whatever happens in our hostilities with Lean Wolf, Jill and I may manage to agree, in the end."

"You and I disagreed, once. Tell me, Captain. Have you and Smee truly buried the hatchet?"

Cecco's body tensed within her arms. They both listened to the distant fiddle on the *Roger*. Lily was relieved, moments later, when Cecco sighed and relaxed.

"Yes, Lily. My apology to him, witnessed by our men, was sincere. In the matter of your beloved Smee, my wife and I reached accord." Sharpened by the starlight that pierced the dusk of his quarters, his deep brown eyes gazed into hers. "As I lie here with you, so tempted, how can I not trust my Jill to honor her word?"

As if to affirm Cecco's point, Lily took his face in her hands and touched his lips with her own. Her kiss was kindness itself, and Cecco warmed to it. The feel of her comely body in his arms, the scent of the woods in her hair, the pregnant air of his cabin on the eve of a dangerous game— all these elements entwined to snare his senses. He closed his eyes and indulged in her comforts.

And as the couple pressed together from their feet to their foreheads, a sense of melancholy merged their spirits, too. From the keel of the ship, seething upward, the song of the sea-maids arose, slowly and irresistibly, penetrating the decks. Those notes crept from all quarters, to lodge in their hearts. As the sound swelled, Lily clung to Cecco, gasping with pathos, and, this time, it was he who comforted her. In one who had never heard the strains of the sirens so close, the sound infused heartache, and heartbreak. Tears rolled down Lily's cheeks, and Cecco chased them with his fingers.

"Poor Lily," he murmured, and smiled as well as he could, under the burden of that music. "You came aboard for adventure, and found it."

They listened to the longing in that song. It shot through them like arrows. As the mermaids' farewell lodged its barbs in the hearts of the sailors, the two in the captain's quarters, like the others outside, ached with an anguish that tightened their throats, until the creatures, at last, sank away. The very air seemed to quiver, long after the melody drowned.

"Poor Cecco," Lily returned, sniffing, "I am recovering my spirits now. But for you, my dear, a siren's song never ends."

"I will not *let* it end. I know that my mermaid loves me. Whatever Fate holds in store for each one of us tomorrow, my Jill will haunt me." Cecco's gaze left Lily's face, to settle on his weapons. "Alive, or in death."

Thorn of the Rose

L ean Wolf's heart stopped beating. Red Hand had made sure of it.

She arrived ahead of him, before the sun soared to its height, and now she was gone. The pain he felt upon missing her tryst was excruciating. Unless he compelled her plans to alter, today her ship must sail away with her. Would she return before then, to salve this wound she gouged into his spirit? He could only wait, and see.

She had left a basket full to overflowing with flowers. It stood abandoned on the gravel path, not far from the door of his cave. Obviously harvested from the Fairy Glade, the blossoms were large and varied— mums, iris and lilacs, daisies, roses and carnations and tulips. Their colors glared garish against the gray of the stone, in hues of purple, yellow, scarlet, orange. If those blooms had voices, Lean Wolf thought, they must cry out to the forest, alerting the Island's inhabitants to the location of his secret place. Like her absence, the idea maddened him at first. Then, crookedly, he smiled, thinking how Red Hand's voice exulted, like these flowers, every time he led her to a similar frenzy. Absurdly, she had aroused him, and she wasn't even here.

He slid off his bow and his quiver and set them down, crouching to roll the rock from the entrance. As he did so, the tie of Red Hand's marriage band tightened on his biceps. Filled with anxious energy, Lean Wolf gained relief in exerting the muscles of his arms to their fullest abilities. A man who could move an implacable rock had no cause to fear a woman's neglect. Once the cave lay open, Lean Wolf shoved the basket inside, inhaling its scents, and he lit a pine knot to illumine his lair. He pulled his weapons inside, too, setting them just within reach. Anticipating her arrival, he kept only his knife on his body, strapped over his leggings, below his knee.

Soon, though, his restless heart lured him out again, where he could watch for Red Hand's approach. In a curious state of sureness and uncertainty, he trusted that she'd come to him. He was tentative, too, about whether he'd let her loose again. Either way, he had prepared. Moments passed, in which even the rush of the waterfall seemed muted to listen; then she materialized as if she'd only been waiting for his reappearance. Floating down through the trees on a current of wind, she lit on the gravel path, a few feet from her husband. His heart, which before this marriage he believed to be so jaded, settled down to a more seemly rhythm.

She had dressed her hair differently this time. She had tied it in a plait that snaked over her shoulder. Her braid reminded him of the women of the village, but, to Lean Wolf, it looked more odd than familiar, because of its sun-color. A pang shot through his body as he realized how— if he allowed her to leave the Island— he'd crave that heady height he reached when he plunged his fingers through it.

She had changed her clothing, too. Instead of the flowing garments to which he'd become accustomed, today she wore only a man's tailored jacket, and breeches. The cloth was a faded brown, old and fraying. Most likely that jacket was made for a youth, since it wrapped her small figure like a husk on an ear of green corn. She had fastened the coat with a belt, the rounding of her belly appearing more pronounced below the cinching. No weapon hung within the grip of the belt. Beneath the coat she wore no blouse, and Lean Wolf's mouth watered to think of unbuckling that belt. Very soon, he'd let that garment fall open and taste the rosebuds on her breasts. He wondered if by her costume she'd thought to fool anyone as to her sex. If so, Red Hand made the first blunder he'd seen her commit. This garb failed to hide her womanhood, asserting her curves instead, and her feminine attributes were enhanced yet again by the smile she wore when she greeted him.

As if the first basketful of blooms wasn't enough, Red Hand carried a bouquet. It was another sign of celebration, he supposed, and despite his broad shoulders and his capacious chest, his spirit ballooned in ridiculous joy, like a boy's. Directing another glance around the forest first, alert for intruders, Lean Wolf stretched out his hand in welcome. He kept his voice low, jealous of their privacy.

"Red Hand."

"Husband," she said, in a whisper, "I bring you a surprise." She stood where she landed on the path, joyful, but venturing no nearer.

"I find that whatever you do is surprising." He beckoned to her, his fingers curling, insistent. "Come, Wife. Our pleasure awaits us."

"Indeed, it does." Soberly, now, she set the flowers down on a stone, then walked toward him with her arms open in welcome. "I have longed for this day." She moved close, her footfalls silent. The birds in the foliage fell quiet, too, as if they wished to witness this reunion. Halting only a hand span away, so that her lover sensed the excitement of her body, his new wife raised her scarlet hand to burrow in his hair, thence to draw his lips to hers, for a kiss. The heat of her redness seared again, seeping from her palm to the back of his head, and on his mouth, through the blood-red lips that matched the flame of her touch. Lean Wolf, too, had longed for this.

As they pressed their bodies together, he pulled her toward the cavern. She followed, yet, disappointingly, she broke off the embrace. Smiling, she twisted from his grip, pushing him to arm's length. Now that he stood this close to her, he saw that her jacket was threadbare. Strings dangled loose from the fabric.

She laughed at the puzzlement on his face. "Never mind the sad state of my clothes. You won't have to look at them long. But wait, Lean Wolf. I must fetch your roses." Turning back, she retrieved the flowers and started to return. But her footsteps halted.

Through the trees at her back floated an unexpected noise. Lean Wolf stilled, too, listening. No birds made that kind of sound, but it might be a fairy. Lean Wolf knew Red Hand trusted one such creature; perhaps it carried some message to her. With her blue eyes, Red Hand signaled a caution to her husband, then he and she turned to the forest, toward the source of those musical tones.

They both startled as, from the shadow of the branches, twenty paces away, Captain Cecco strode into sunshine.

His body looked solid, harsh against the glossy green of the trees. Lean Wolf had seen him before, but this time the gypsy left off his headdress and vest, so that he appeared primitive, his chest and his shoulders naked and powerful. His hair was tied back; a rose-red sash bound his waist. The reason for the noise became apparent. He had raised his forearms, and his motions had set his bracelets jingling. Their merry music belied the smolder in his eyes, and denied the omen of his stance.

But the captain's bangles hung quiet now. In each of his hands he gripped a pistol. One pointed to Lean Wolf's heart, and one aimed at Red Hand's. Both targets knew better than to move.

The pirate spoke in his outlandish accent.

"So, *Amore*, you have run to another lover."

Lean Wolf's pride fired as he watched his woman. She did not falter. "Yes, Giovanni."

"You do not trouble to try to hide him from me?"

"You know me." Red Hand turned to the side, as if to deny the pirate's importance. As she did so, she placed herself between the muzzle of Cecco's gun and the bulk of Lean Wolf's body. "I rarely flinch from the truth."

Lean Wolf's every sinew tautened, but he never stirred. From beneath his headband, his sharp eyes shone, yet, an experienced warrior, he only watched, and waited. Clearly, Cecco rode upon the edge of strong emotion. Lean Wolf would hold patience until the moment the pirate's passion made him reckless. The warrior's arms hung ready at his sides, and his hand dangled only inches from the knife at his knee.

He wished he dared reach for his bow, but even so, this Cecco should be easy to defeat. Lean Wolf was quick and lithe. His blade would find a way to dodge those guns. Secretly, he sneered at the clumsiness of this European. The gypsy had come barefoot, to muffle his steps, but he neglected to stifle his jewelry. Unlike Red Hand's first husband, Lean Wolf was a silent hunter. He bore no noisy bracelets to alert his prey to stalking.

Cecco snarled at her, "I warned you."

"Yes." She raised her chin. "And I warn *you*."

Lean Wolf expected a forceful reaction. Instead, Cecco smiled. He shook his head, maybe feigning amusement. "Ah, my Jill. You stand and defy me, as I have enjoyed to see you do before. And still, you hold no weapon but your charm."

"Will you gamble your life upon it?"

"I gamble nothing. As I have sworn, the man who touches you must die." Cecco's grip on his pistols held steady. "And I found that kiss you shared to be *very* touching."

"I have sworn, too, Giovanni, and you vowed to honor my wishes. This brave is *mine*."

"That kiss will be his last."

Red Hand squeezed the stems of her flowers. Lean Wolf saw her knuckles go white. "You must listen to me," she urged her pirate. "The fleet sails today. I promise you that I will be aboard."

A moment of silence, then Cecco's voice grew grimmer. "No. I do not think you will."

Hearing this threat, Red Hand appeared shaken. Yet, once more, she dared to move. She took one step toward Lean Wolf. Distrusting Cecco's tone, Lean Wolf commanded, "Clear the path, Red Hand. I guard myself." Uneasily, he watched the pirate from over her shoulder. Her position was too vulnerable.

"I fight for my rights," she declared.

Cecco retorted, "There is nothing right in your obsession with this warrior, Jill." With his gun, he waved her to one side. "I will deal with him, and then, if you are fortunate, I will take you back."

"No. We have an accord."

"You have stretched it to its limit. Our accord is done."

At this declaration, she swayed, as if her balance was disturbed. Lean Wolf braced to catch her, but she hesitated for only a moment. "Where is Hook?"

"Hook is here."

The arrogant voice rose behind Lean Wolf, and the hairs stood up on his scalp.

Red Hand whirled to find him, and Lean Wolf followed. He of the Eagle's Claw stood rooted on the gravel path, ten paces behind them. He posed, sword in hand and hook at the ready, dressed simply, in shirtsleeves. In his three-cornered hat, a jay feather glowed brilliant blue, caged in a shaft of sunlight.

"Hook..." Red Hand uttered. "I should have known you'd spy on Cecco."

"And why not? The two of you offer such entertaining displays."

"You're a fine one to talk. Look how you flaunt your conquest! Raven would blush to see you sport her keepsake so boldly."

"Raven?" Lean Wolf wondered, aloud.

Red Hand said with disdain, "A gentleman would have the decency to hide his doxy's token."

In a flash of memory, Lean Wolf saw Raven in her new head-dress; she had taken to wearing a cluster of blue jay feathers in her hair. With his lip curling, he also recalled the fascination the chief of the pirates dared to show for her, even as the People held him captive on the shore of the camp. Lean Wolf felt an old stab of jealousy. "What has the widow to do with the Black Chief?"

"What, indeed? She has more to do with Hook than she lets on."

The Black Chief shrugged. "You speak in temper, Jill. But, at the moment, it is not I who signify trouble. For that, you may look to your husbands." So saying, he lowered his weapons. "I shall retire from the fray, and merely revel in the spectacle." With an ironic smile, he assumed a casual stance.

Resentment bled through Cecco's words. "It is well that you leave my wife to *me*, Commodore— as you failed to do with Raven." He aimed a malevolent stare at Red Hand. "Come, Jill. I offer you one chance. And *only* one."

"Red Hand, woman who tells tales," Lean Wolf said, sternly, "you will tell me this story."

"The widow deceives you, Husband. While she shies from you, she entices my pirates. Even now, she means to sail with us— this very day."

"That is not possible!"

The blaze of Red Hand's eyes gentled. "Lean Wolf," she urged, solicitous, "do not concern yourself for Raven. Your cares are at an end." She turned on Cecco, "As is my marriage."

Deliberately, she strode toward the captain. Clenching the flowers in her right hand, she raised up her left, the colorless one, to exhibit her ring. A thread from her ragged clothing snagged her thumb, but, regal, she ignored it. "And I mean to keep my golden trophy." Before Cecco's eyes, she flaunted his wedding band. She sneered his endearment, *"Amore."* Kissing her hand to him, she turned her back.

Lean Wolf guessed the significance of Red Hand's gesture, because Cecco's shoulders fell, and his expression turned tragic. As if hypnotized, he gazed at her over the barrels of his guns. He responded, *"Amore."* His voice sounded low, and listless; *"Amore,"* he murmured, once more.

Red Hand left her first husband behind. Gazing triumphant into Lean Wolf's admiring eyes, she strutted toward him. She paid no heed to the Black Chief, who seemed to lounge benignly behind him. But she stopped, dead, at the sound of Cecco cocking his pistols.

Slowly, the woman rotated to face him. She watched her pirate's eyes as he drew a bead upon her brave. "No!" she ordered him, and flung herself toward Lean Wolf.

The gun discharged. The blast resounded through the woods, scattering birds, like shot, to fly into the sky. Its impact propelled her forward. Red Hand's arms flung outward, her eyes flew wide. She exhaled in a grunt of pain, and, while a bloom of blood began to seep and stain her belly, she fell into her Indian's embrace.

Lean Wolf caught her, shocked, and stared down at her agony. With the strength of his arms, he sustained his new wife's failing frame.

Cecco leveled the other gun. Another shot exploded, another ear-gutting roar that pounded inside Lean Wolf's chest. And, again, Red Hand convulsed. She turned her face up to his. As he braced her bleeding body in his hold, it slackened. Still gazing up at him, she moaned, then dropped her head. A liquid trickle flowed from the corner of her mouth. It became a crimson stream— a stream that matched her blood-red hand.

Lean Wolf groaned beneath his breath, "Red Hand..."

In disbelief, he stood immobile before the entrance to his cave. Caught in concern for her, when he should have run, he hesitated. This woman had blocked the pirate's shot. She made herself a sacrifice, and, for that act, the pirate murdered her. Cecco, whose passion had finally made him reckless, remained where he stood, his dark eyes defiant, his guns outstretched and smoking. Lean Wolf's nostrils filled with the stench of black powder— the breath of the beast that had killed her. With his arms full of Red Hand, bleeding her being away, he couldn't turn to look at the Black Chief, but he detected no sign from him— another ruthless brute.

How many times, side by side with White Bear— as youths, as hunters, as men who'd earned their names— had he knelt to murmur his respect in longtime tradition? He was unaccustomed to revealing his feelings but, in this grisly hour, Lean Wolf did so, and handsomely. With a reverence he had not observed for years, the Silent Hunter spoke the age-old chant:

"Creature of the woodland. I revere your sacrifice." In his eyes he felt the scald of tears, which for so many moons abandoned him.

When Red Hand's lips moved, her third-time husband bent close. He listened to the language of the Storyteller, the utterance that had to be the last words she would speak.

"Lean Wolf," she said, her voice no longer clear, but straining. Her hands crushed the flowers, and from their broken stems a sweet, moist smell arose. He also smelled an odor more familiar to a huntsman. It was the essence that clung to his own copper skin: the scent of blood, newly drawn, and warm. With effort, she spoke again. Her voice was guttural now.

"Lean Wolf, Silent Hunter."

It was the voice of a predator.

"Your wife is a silent huntress, too." The flowers fell from her grip. "You never heard me stalking."

He felt a movement of her arm, and then, suddenly, a piercing needle-prick of pain. He thought she'd caught a thorn among the roses. The pricking sensation sharpened, and Lean Wolf became aware it was a dagger.

Before he could stop her, Red Hand jammed the dagger deep, beneath his ribs. She plunged it upward, until it pierced his lung. Red hot jolts of pain bolted through his body. He squeezed his fingers, he opened his mouth in protest, but he found he had no breath to curse her. The blade, driven by Red Hand, gouged his innards, a spearing torch of fire. In a final, lethal thrust, she twisted it. Like the love he bore his wife, it tore the inner workings of his gut. With that cut, Red Hand disappeared, and, in her place, Jill Red-Hand made her kill.

"Hear me, Husband. I grant you all the choices you gave *me*."

Lean Wolf gripped her, unable even to wheeze, and he sensed her men drawing near to guard her. Her wicked smile, made savage by her teeth, was tinted with crimson. Her eyes glowed green, like her totem tiger's. In a final burst of instinct, he reached for the knife at his knee.

Jill Red-Hand got it first. Leaving her dagger embedded in his entrails, she counted coup, slapping the flat of his own knife, once, upon his cheekbone. As his skin stung and his vision dimmed, he reached out his scarlet hand to cup her jaw. When his arm went lax and dropped, her feral face was daubed as if with war paint. Surging all over his body, now, was the sensation he formerly craved: he burned in the heat of Red Hand's redness. His legs went weak with it; his knees struck the ground, and he fell down at her feet. With one hand he groped the gravel path and found the boulder, but the strength of his arms, well known among the women of the tribe, had finally failed him.

Lean Wolf's heart stopped beating. Jill Red-Hand had made sure of it.

Eyes of the Tigress

Red-Handed Jill looked down upon her victim, his hunting knife hot in her hand. She spat the crimson liquid from her mouth. It formed a blot upon the gravel. Next to it, condensed by the height of the sun, her own shadow lay across Lean Wolf.

A rush of satisfaction coursed through her spirit. Savoring the moment of victory, she breathed deeply of the lush forest air. She had stalked the beast; he lay before her, tamed.

As she anticipated, she was possessed by the urge to shout her triumph aloud. The shout felt like a bubble under water, forcing its way to her surface. Out of caution, Jill delayed it. To free her cry now might prove dangerous, drawing observers to the fate of Lean Wolf. Yet, when she could loose her voice, it would resonate all the more savagely for the wait. The force of its rising made her heart thump in double time.

Two larger shadows joined her third-time husband where he lay. Jill did not look up. "We must work quickly," she said.

But the men already knew it. None of the three was certain what effect this kill would have upon Jill, nor when. Still, Hook and Cecco spent a precious moment to survey her, assuring themselves that the dead man, so much larger and stronger than she, had not injured her in his last desperate seconds.

"*Amore mia*...you are magnificent," Cecco stated, simply. His deep brown eyes were alive with emotion, but he said no more.

Hook set his hand on Jill's shoulder. His voice was fierce, and gentle. "Madam Red-Hand."

Jill raised her gaze to each of them, but no reply came to her lips. She registered the concern on their faces; she sensed their wish to intervene on her behalf, yet the moment had not come to give herself over to their care. As Jill's limbs began to tremble, a sense of urgency prodded her. She knew that, in a very little time, her madness must overtake her.

She beheld the Silent Hunter, fixing the sight in her memory. Dwarfed by the mass of his musculature, the grip of her jewel-studded dagger protruded from beneath his ribs. It glared with sunlight, and the colors of the gems blurred in her vision. The dominant hue, the hue that continued to bloom, was ruby. With her lip twisting, she pulled her weapon from his wound. The drag of her blade through his flesh repulsed her, yet her wilder self thrilled. One of the men— she didn't look to see who— took both of the blades from her hands. He replaced them with a kerchief, and she dabbed at the wet on her face, and wiped her hands. Then she dropped it, to stoop before the entrance to the cave, and slink inside.

She had not entered this cage since Lean Wolf first carried her in. Today, Jill reversed their roles. Now the Silent Hunter was the captive to be carried in and trapped here. The thought sent another wave of victory through her core, and then and there her triumph nearly brought her blood-rage to the boil. Determined on her purpose, Jill tamped it down again and made herself move on, to pass the rocky overhang and claim this place as the spoils of her conquest.

But in her unsteady state she was assaulted by the smells— the pine pitch, the animal musk from the furs on his pallet, the primordial air of the cave's own loam, and, not least in its potency, the rusted-metal scent of blood on her body. All these odors combined to evoke the night of her abduction. In this atmosphere she detected, first, her own former helplessness, and then the scene conjured the man who caged her here.

Deliberately, she moved to step on the soft bed of pelts, where the sense of weakness vanished as she revisited the moment this vengeance was conceived, in heat and in seed, like a child born to go bad. Jill closed her eyes, and, holding fast to her wits, purged her being of all impulses but the actions that lay ahead of her. She began by gathering up a blanket, to toss it out the door. *One task at a time*, she told herself. The hardest part was past. Jill had killed her husband. Now she had to learn to live with him.

All around her danced the figures that Lean Wolf painted on the wall in her absence. Under the greenish glow shed by the moss on the ceiling, the men and the beasts appeared mythical, as otherworldly as the warrior himself had seemed when she first saw him towering in his underground realm. The figures became nearly real as the flickering light of the pine knot lent its motion.

Jill looked closer, and her hot blood ran chill. In the painting, two winged braves flew, hounded from the village with arrows. Awaiting them in the forest, a wolf crouched with its fangs bared. With a twinge of horror, Jill realized that her act of viricide had come none too soon. As she had feared, Lean Wolf had slated Rowan and Lightly to be his next victims. Had Jill simply sailed away from him today, her son and his lover would have suffered slaughter, or something worse.

But Rowan and Lightly were only two whom Lean Wolf threatened. These walls were alive with the Silent Hunter's thoughts, and the intrigue of his dreams. He had painted a blackbird on the wing, which Jill now knew to represent Raven, and a doe, for his first wife, Red Fawn. She saw herself, too, her scarlet hand distinctly rendered, a fair-haired woman wading in the sea. Jill shrank back from the wall, and gasped as she trod on something rough, another new element here in Lean Wolf's lair. Lengths of hempen rope curled next to his sleeping pallet. Her imagination filled in the facts. Entering here with her new husband, she might never have escaped from his snare. Who knew what fates Silent Hunter had planned for each of the people whose effigies he depicted? It was well, Jill thought, that, with two strikes of two knives, she had severed his hold on their lives.

The men spoke low, tending to the scene outside. A scraping sound told her that one of them was turning the gravel to bury the scarlet stains. Jill opened her coat to tug the bladder of blood from beneath it, still oozing down the string she'd yanked to pull its cork.

She tossed the contraption in a corner, where soon her blood-soiled clothing would join it. As she gathered Lean Wolf's weapons, Hook and Cecco scuffled in with their burden, hauling the carcass on the blanket. Once inside, Hook with his one hand and Cecco with two, slid the body onto the furs. In the bed where he might have cut off Jill's life, Lean Wolf himself now lay cut, and lifeless.

It was strange to see him inert— he, whose every muscle had coiled with the vigor of a snake. Lean Wolf's ribs were bound up with cloth, the gouge stanched, but his blood, still creeping, seeped through the material. Jill knelt down beside him, her knees sinking into the furs. The green-glowing light tinged his skin. She straightened his limbs— such weighty limbs— so that this man might lie in what dignity death could render. With her scarlet fingers, she closed his eyelids, blinding forever those black eyes that had watched and spied and connived. As in his life, so in his death, Jill arranged his bow and his quiver within reach of his hands, and she strapped his hunting knife in its sheath at Lean Wolf's knee. Smoothing his hair, she laid his long locks over his shoulders. When she gestured, Cecco brought the flowers, and she directed him to set the basket of blooms at the warrior's feet. Their sweet scents mingled with the smell of his lifeblood. As still as the dead man lay, Jill herself felt a tremor that mounted in her muscles, minute by minute.

"Lean Wolf Silent Hunter: my third-time husband," she mouthed, uncertain if she spoke aloud or whispered. Susurrating, her voice flowed back from the walls that surrounded them, weaving its spell of binding. This time, the spell ensnared only one. "Red Hand from the Sea delivers your restless spirit to a place of passage. The Dark Hunting ground lies open to you." Jill raised her empty hand, and felt Hook settle her dagger in her grip. "As you wander your way toward the ancestors, I, a woman and a wife, free you from the Land of the Living." With a slash of her dagger, Jill cut the strap of Red Fawn's marriage bracelet. It fell from Lean Wolf's wrist. Finally, Jill pricked at the knot of her own wedding token. As the tie loosened, she drew the orange kerchief from Lean Wolf's biceps. Her marriage-curse had done its work. Her spirit bounded free of her burden, and she shed this husband as a serpent sloughs its skin.

Jill teetered on her knees. While she worked, she'd felt increasingly light-headed. Her dizziness deepened now, into trance. The dagger was removed from her hold, and her crimson hand gaped suddenly empty. Someone took charge of the bracelet and kerchief as well. Her arm was seized and supported. Hook's velvet voice came to her, and his warm breath coursed in her ear: "Never fear, Jill. Your men attend you." Cecco loomed at her other side, and the men raised her up. With tearing fingers, she plucked her jacket off, and then the blood-encrusted breeches, and she kicked them away. The cave's interior distorted, as if she viewed it from the wrong end of a spyglass. She lost her balance and stumbled. She was not allowed to fall; her upper arms were gripped, and her bare feet dragged in the dust. She smelled the air of outdoors and, soon after, the thunder of the waterfall throbbed, like the beat of her heathen heart.

The men lowered her to the earth, leaning her back against a scratchy tree. Some kind of garment covered her, but she shivered. She still inhaled the odor of blood, rising from the heat of her flesh. When she spread out her hands, they were splotched with it— not just the inside of her right hand, her distinctive feature, but the back of it, too, and crusting under her fingernails. Next the boulder crunched over gravel, sealing the tomb, and her shaking turned into a shudder. She panicked, remembering the feel of entrapment that sound stirred in her the first time she heard it. Her stomach lurched, and when she turned her head to wretch, supporting arms returned, ushering her into the woods. She saw red in the grass, and tasted the cherries she had crushed in her mouth, to imitate blood. She no longer remembered; why should she *mimic* blood, when so much of it sprang from her husband? Her belly writhed again, but this time in hunger. Her hand was ravenous for the dagger.

"The frenzy has begun in earnest." Hook watched Jill's gaze roving. "The eyes of the tigress burn green, and she seeks for her claws." He slid his hook behind his back. "You must carry her, Captain."

"Aye," Cecco answered. "I have never seen her more abandoned or beautiful." With reverence, he lifted Jill up and into his arms. "*Bellezza*, we are with you." He could not tell if she heard him. Her fingers trailed along his sash, questing for the knife he had already laid aside.

They inspected the scene before forsaking it, to be certain no sign of the killing remained. When Lean Wolf failed to return to his people, the braves who tracked him must find no trace. Jill had told them that he kept his lair a secret. Their hope was that, as independently as he lived within the tribe, his disappearance would not be marked until a day or two after the pirates set sail. Jill had laid these plans far in advance with Hook and Cecco, knowing that she would be incapable of thinking clearly now. As she had guessed, her impulse at this moment was to *cause* harm, rather than conceal it.

When her quest for Cecco's weapon went unsatisfied, Jill wrestled to break free of his hold. He undertook to soothe her agitation while Hook seized a cluster of leaves and smudged the markings on the gravel path. Hook took up the canvas bag in which he and Cecco hid their weapons from Jill's scavenging glances. It hung misshapen over his shoulder, holding the spade they had used to turn the gravel, along with Hook's sword, Cecco's knife, Jill's jeweled dagger, and the four pistols Hook and Cecco had borne— the two Cecco discharged in blasts of powder without shot, and the one each man had hidden from Lean Wolf, loaded and potent and tucked at their backs. Thus Jill had seen to her own protection. The next step in safeguarding her lay in her men's hands alone, and, in her present state, she would not make that effort easy.

They strode the short path toward the waterfall. Hook had covered Jill with his shirt, and, except for his leather harness, he, like Cecco, was bare-chested. They were both streaked with blood. In the past, Cecco carried Jill with ease, but she hadn't fought him then. He staggered when she kicked and struggled, then he stopped to set her down and gather her wrists in one hand, protecting his flesh from her fingernails. She did not articulate her objections when he bundled her up again— at this stage of her lunacy, even a scream would be too human an act— but she grunted her frustration in heaving, feline hisses. With his hand full and his claw in hiding, Hook could do little to help.

Both men were relieved when they reached the pond. Hook laid down the bag and concealed it, with his tricorn and its blue jay feather, in the foliage at the water's edge. He levered off his boots. Even as Cecco gripped her wrists, Jill tore at the blouse with her teeth. On it she smelled the leather of Hook's harness, associating it with his weapon, and she craved it. Holding her fast, the two men stepped from the grass and waded into the water.

The pool's temperature was tepid, not cold enough to shock her, and not warm enough to calm her ferocity. At its center it was shallow enough that the men could stand, but when Cecco set Jill on her feet, the lake rose to her ribs, and she swayed in it. As a precaution, Cecco unwound his gypsy sash and retied it, tethering Jill's waist to his. Between them, Hook and Cecco towed her toward the falls. Hook slashed the tie of her hair, and her long braid floated on the surface, the strands loosening as the current tossed it about. Swirls of red rose up all around her, where the lifeblood of her husband lifted from her skin to drift away. The falling water grew louder as they neared, drowning the sounds of the woodlands, smothering the huffs of Jill's panting. Despite the temperate surroundings, her teeth began to chatter. Hook touched her cheek to measure her fever. Instantly, she turned on him, and he drew his fingers away before she could bite them.

As the stream fell from the mountain above, its force broke on an outcropping, then it formed a gleaming green curtain. Fed from that flow, behind the ledge where Hook and Jill often sported— accessible only by flight— the cavern pooled with sun-warmed water, an ideal enclosure for bathing. Jill had hidden towels and clothing in a dry spot there, for use once her turmoil came to an end. The overflow poured from that ledge into this pond at its base, and, in its own kind of turmoil, the waters roiled noisily about the three waders.

Too well, Hook remembered Jill's recklessness in the wake of her triumph with the tigress. As the turbulence of the falls pushed and pulled at him, threatening his balance, he stepped with care, feeling the way with his feet through the pebbly bed at the bottom. Hoping to avoid another twist of an ankle, Hook was grateful for the security of Cecco's presence, and for the hand he'd missed when tending Jill's madness before. This time, there was no need for the cruelty of binding her with a belt. Cecco's sash was gentler. Yet the woodlands encroached on the farther shore of this pond, and, even with Cecco's hands and sash to hold her, Hook dreaded lest Jill, the most adroit of deceivers, find a way to slip from her men's protection and disappear in the tangle of the trees. The memory of the river rushing his beloved away kept Hook's teeth on edge. If she escaped to the wilderness, the huntress was sure to be hunted herself, by man, boy, or beast. Amid the many quirks of this Island, even the girl who'd grown up here might be swallowed up and lost to him. The commodore's pirates could not row to the rescue this time. Hook and Jill and Cecco must prevail against Jill's own nature, and they must overcome her impulses on their own.

His own impulses must remain submerged as well. As before, in this, her latest triumph, Jill transformed into the embodiment of victory. The feline gleam in her eye provoked her lover's every sensibility. As she'd torn her antagonist, Hook had felt the blending of their souls. The weapon in her hand became, in his eyes and in his intuition, the claw that her storytelling caused him to bear. No wonder she lusted for it now, and no wonder he returned her lust. Jill, in her victory, was the pure incarnation of power. Body and soul, Hook was hers.

So also was Cecco. He glimpsed the fascination on Hook's face, and knew it mirrored his own. He had listened as Hook warned him what to expect from Jill's blood-rage. Today, that prediction played out. As Hook foretold, Jill's beauty burgeoned as the spirit of her totem possessed her. Her victim's blood striped her face, her body moved with the litheness of the predator. The wild light in her eyes, the radiance that shifted her blue eyes to green, reflected the sensuality of her most intimate passions. Cecco was captivated, and inflamed. Had the Silent Hunter made love to this tigress, on the night he coerced Jill to couple with him? Cecco, too, burned inside as he envisioned her copper brave intertwined with her. He understood Jill's madness; he likened it to the monster that ruled his jealousy, the brute that, like hers, turned his own gaze to green.

But this time, Cecco controlled that monster. Jill needed her husband. Overwhelmed by a yen to kill again, she was devoid of desire to protect even herself. All she required was a weapon, and a victim's flesh to tear with it. Cecco took care that she should find nothing sharper than her nails, but, always, she was aware of Hook's claw. Jill had already searched Cecco's body for a blade. Now, with certain instinct, she glided through the water, closing in on her lover. Cecco saw her clutch at the bands of Hook's harness and press her feverish flesh up against him. The commodore held her close, but he had his own kind of brute to control. He hoisted his hook out of reach.

They had all three agreed that Hook must not divest himself of his barb. It would be another form of madness to defend her without his hook in this situation, with their weapons hidden, all of them naked or nearly so, and one who required constant watch. With Cecco here this time to restrain her, Hook kept one flesh and blood hand for Jill, and an iron one to guard her. Both men knew that, even now, some enemy might be nearing, whether man, Pan, or animal.

But the animal drawing closest was Jill, and her bloodlust was reaching its peak. She gripped the straps at Hook's chest like ropes in the rigging, climbing, reaching, for his claw. The tether strained as she dragged Cecco with her. Hook held her in the crook of his elbow, and stretched his empty arm through the water, for balance. As the current surged around them, Hook urged her under the waterfall, half swimming, half tumbling. The spray misted in their mouths. With relief, Hook felt Cecco's grip, firm and supportive, holding his elbows, keeping his head above water. Jill thrashed between them, grunting and spitting, her hair wild, her cheeks flushed beneath the blood there. And still, she longed to draw more.

Once he'd steadied Hook, Cecco performed the next task. He gripped Jill's hair close to her skull, to secure her and, with the tail of her shirt, he wiped the blood from her face. He tried to be tender, but gentleness proved impossible. She shied back from his hands, twisting to the side. Trapped between Hook's ribs and Cecco's grip, she gritted her teeth and kicked at Cecco's ankles. The water slowed her blows, and he endured them, but when her knee struck out at his groin, he sidled back to stand behind her.

Working together, the two men disentangled her fingers from Hook's brace. Cecco wrapped Jill in his arms and restrained her, bracing her back with his chest. With his hands full of Jill, he was unable to sketch his banishing gesture, so he simply murmured, "*Bellezza*, lovely one. Be purged of this bloodlust." He and Hook raised her up, into the falling water; then, as Hook had done that day in the river, Cecco bent his knees to submerge her. Once, twice, three times, the men immersed their woman in the font of the pond. Each time her face surfaced, she sputtered, and Hook pushed the hair from her forehead. Each time, she fluttered her lashes to blink them open, and the eyes of the tigress fixed upon his. The tint of emerald endured.

The rite was half done; Jill's body was cleansed. Her shirt appeared to have soaked up the residue. It clung to her, dingy and thin. Yet her divine spark of savagery lingered. Where once her lips matched a ruby, her mouth now looked hungry for blood. And still she struggled— grasping at nothing, grasping at everything— reaching out with the arms Cecco pinned above her elbows. She tore at the tails of her shirt first, she raked Cecco's thighs and, finally, as her wrists crossed in front, she caught his bracelets. She curled her fingers into them, and held fast. The bangles bit the flesh of Cecco's arms, and he was glad for it. The grip seemed to satisfy Jill, and her thrashing subsided.

Hook stood before her, his barb submerged and lost to her vision. "Jill, my love. I remind you that you are a woman." With Cecco holding firm behind her, Hook gripped her chin, bending down to lay a kiss upon her. As the water foamed all around them, he touched her lips lightly with his. He was wary of her reaction, but, calmer now, she accepted his embrace. The rush of the falls deafened the three of them; they each grew numb from the noise. Whether because of the din, or the chill of the spray, or because of Hook's human touch, Jill's demon began to loosen her claws.

Hook pressed her lips more heartily, and she responded to his kiss. The tension of his fingers at her chin relaxed. Cecco too, eased his stance. Still intent upon holding Jill steady, he allowed her own legs to sustain her. Neither of her keepers released her, but both felt fresh hope. As she leaned toward Hook, opening her lips to him, she wrapped one ankle around Cecco's leg. Her toes caressed him, including him in this embrace.

The three of them stood thus, lost to time as Jill indulged in her men's attention. Cecco's hold became a hug. Hook's lips were cool; hers still felt feverish. She trifled with Cecco's bangles...and without warning she yanked her head back. Cecco evaded the blow, but Jill had unsettled his balance. She hooked his knee with her foot and pulled, and he pitched backward into the water with her body falling on top. Her hair floated above him, spreading like tentacles. She clung to his bracelets, trapping his arms, and she didn't let go. As he worked to keep both of their bodies from sinking, this instant became an eternity.

Jill seized a breath before she submerged, but Cecco was caught unawares. Inhaling in surprise, he'd gotten water in his throat. The momentum of their fall pressed them down to the bed of the pond. Choking, he convulsed, and he had to let go of Jill's arms. Water stung his nose and burned in his lungs, but she refused to free her hold on his bracelets. As he tried to shake her off, the metal pinched the skin of his arms again, and only as black spots blotted his vision did he feel her grip slacken.

While the waters churned before Hook, he couldn't see through the disturbance. He plunged below to look for them. In the muted world underwater, he saw Jill searching for footing and slipping on the bottom, her arms stroking to ascend to the air. Tethered to Cecco by the sash, though, she was trapped as if by an anchor. Cecco was flailing, stirring up clouds of sand with his heels. Bubbles streamed from his mouth. Clearly, he was panicked to get to the surface, and neither one of them would breathe until he reached it.

Hook shot up to catch a breath, then plunged under water again. He seized Jill by the elbow and hauled her up until the tie between the two stretched taut. Jill didn't fight Hook as he pulled her, but when she reached the end of her tether, she clutched at his arm and scrabbled toward the surface. Inhibited by her grip, Hook grappled with the sash, then slashed at it with his claw. He repeated the motion, slicing at the fabric until the sodden weave parted, and, finally, it broke.

Jill soared to the surface, and Hook followed her. He couldn't stop to watch her now. He had time only to exhale and inhale, then he dove down to fetch Cecco. Free of the tether, the captain rolled to his knees. His head hung down and he pushed at the bottom as he tried to raise himself up. With a single hand to save him, Hook grasped the leather wrap on his hair. Slowly, with Hook's help, Cecco stumbled to his feet, and his heavy body rose. As soon as his face broke the surface, he suffered a paroxysm of coughing. His eyes stung and his lungs heaved, but once Cecco stood, Hook abandoned the man to seek Jill.

Hook shoved the trickling hair from his eyes. Jill's half of the maroon sash undulated on the pond, but Jill herself was gone. From the corner of his eye, Hook glimpsed a flash of white. Like a vengeful siren, Jill rushed up from the water to seize his wrist and take command of the hook.

And this time, Hook allowed it.

Once she clutched the claw, he made use of her grip. Steadily, he pulled her up against his chest. With his good arm, he encircled her. His right arm he held at the level of his face, while she fingered the carving on the base of the hook. Her eyes were wild again.

Cecco, red in the face, finally ceased coughing. He took in the scene; he saw what had to be done. Snatching up the shred of his sash, he approached Hook and Jill, slowly, trying to calm the wheeze of his breathing. Jill's back was to him. She didn't spy him closing in, and soon the two men surrounded her. Carefully, Cecco draped the sash over the hook, and wound it round. As he disguised the claw, it seemed to lose fascination for Jill. Her brows drew together as if she was puzzled, then, miraculously, she let it go. She set her hands on Hook's chest, melting into his hold.

Neither man trusted her surrender. Just as they had done in Hook's quarters, they pressed her between them. Jill was no stranger to cages, but, this time, her imprisonment seemed to free her. She sensed their protection; she warmed to their affection. Her panting steadied, and the tension of her muscles eased. She rolled her head back to rest on Cecco's shoulder.

Hook bent close, speaking to her over the sound of the falls. His voice swam in her ears.

"Your men defend you, Jill, just as we pledged."

"Your two men protect you." Cecco's chin rested on her temple. "One at your back, Jill, and one of us, always, before you."

And Jill steeped in her protectors' presence, tranquil in the whirling world around her, their figures firm as they supported her, fore and aft. Cecco caressed her shoulders. Hook's hair set a dew of droplets on her cheek. Their skins smelled damp, but familiar. Each man's warmth soaked into her, front and back, and— standing nestled between them, sheltered, cherished, her tiger's eyes closing and her woman's heart beating— deep down in her center, Jill felt the fulfillment of a wish.

Each member of this pride restrained a beast; none were tamed, but all survived. And all of them thrived— in unity.

Bigger Games

As happened one hour before, while Jill was beguiling her victim, a series of musical notes hit the air. Although the music tried to be noticed, this time it wasn't perceived. The spatter of the falls overpowered the sound. Jewel flitted above the bathers, doing her best to be heard. With her peacock-blue wings aglow, she chimed and she chimed, and, at last, desperate to catch Hook's attention, she seized a hank of his hair, preparing to deal a sharp yank.

While Jewel gathered her strength, a new sound rang out. This one was more hearty than hers, and it rose above the rush of the waters, to echo round the lake. Hook turned toward it, catching sight of Jewel wringing her hands in distress. He gathered that his fairy had tried to warn him. Incensed at the interruption, he glared at the other intruder.

Pan perched on the rocks above the western bank of the pond, his hands cupping his mouth as he shouted, "Belay, there!" Engaged in a game of Royal Navy, he wore a sword in his belt and the French blue jacket Jill had sent to the hideout. The coat was made to fit Flambard, and it was so large that it gaped at Peter's wrists and flapped about his body. The three boys of his crew stood in the long grass behind him. Each of them clutched knives in one hand, and balanced cutlasses in the other.

Peter's eyes were charged with adventure. Little Chip, crowned with golden hair, posed with his sword in the air and one foot braced on a boulder. Like Peter, he looked eager. Bertie and Bingo appeared pale, and somewhat less enthusiastic.

Peter cried, "If you think to sail today, Hook, think again. Thy doom lies…*at hand!*" Peter tried to keep a stern, captainy face, but his own joke tickled him so irresistibly that he laughed. Heartened by his levity, his boys hopped about the grassy slope before the ferns that bordered the forest, brandishing their swords.

Hook lowered his chin. "I'll *handily* thrash you, should you dare come within reach."

At the familiar ring of Peter's voice, Jill's pleasant reverie broke. Her eyes blinked open, and she swiped the moisture from her face. After some moments, the mother within her awakened and recognized the boys, and once she did she didn't waste a moment. Whether thinking of kids or of cubs, she took advantage of the distraction. She sank beneath the surface and slipped from her keepers' sides. Hook spun to plunge his claw in the water, attempting to snag her by the tail of the shirt. His barb was still masked by the sash, and she wriggled away. Cecco swore and leapt forward, splashing, to recapture her.

Both men moved too late. Her creature cunning prevailed. Like an eel, she swam to the bank; like a mermaid she slithered up upon it. The grimy blouse clung to her figure and her hair fell in ropes down her back. Her eyes burned green again. And now, she felt a swelling in her lungs. The bubble she'd tamped down inside herself, when Lean Wolf lay bleeding at her feet, bobbled free of her control. She threw back her head, opened her throat, and, drawing deep from her diaphragm, Jill piped a bellow to the woodlands. Her holler radiated outward, throaty and visceral. At once her spirit lightened, unfettered from this dreadful force.

Peter listened as he looked down on Jill from the slope, gaping with admiration. When the reverberations died away he exclaimed, "I hoped we'd hear a story from Red-Handed Jill, but that was almost as good."

Jill only sat curled on the bank, smiling a secret smile. It reminded Peter of the tiger's face that the twins had carved on the totem pole at the Clearing. He opened his mouth to remark on it, but stopped, leaving his jaw hanging open.

Another bellow rose up behind him. It was a harsh, feral roar, and an answer to Jill's. All the children's eyes stretched wide, and, apprehensive, they rotated to look over their shoulders.

The tigress padded through the foliage, emerging to stand in the grass a few bounds from the boys. She was a young cat, compact but powerful. As her striped sides heaved with her breathing, her eyes shone emerald in the sunlight. Stretching out her great paws before her, she popped her shoulder blades up on her back, and dug her claws in the soil. When she opened her mouth wide to yawn, her pink tongue curled between teeth as long as Peter's fingers, and thicker. Five members of the present company were reminded of the crocodile.

Jewel zoomed to Peter's side, frantic, to tug at his jacket. The boys, too, crowded round him, hampering his motion, but Peter himself remained keen. He'd come for the glory of dueling with pirates; a fight with a tiger would do just as well. But, however, "Bertie, Bingo, stand aside. You lubbers aren't bold enough to battle pirates *and* lions, both. Chip, which foe do you choose? I'll challenge the other."

By this time, Hook and Cecco had swum to shore and hurdled from the pool. They stood dripping at their stations on either side of Jill. The rag of sash lay huddled at Hook's feet, and neither man held a weapon, save the claw.

Jill did not acknowledge the men. She was looking up the slope to the level of the boys, locked in a stare with the tigress. Eyeing Jill, the cat prowled three steps closer to Peter. Jewel's chiming, inaudible over the waterfall before, became a shrill and sure warning now.

Chip didn't need Jewel's alarm to alert him. He was thinking fast. "Let's play your game of changing sides with them, Peter. I'll be the tiger today, and you be the pirate captain…*if* they agree to switch places, of course, and fight as Lost Boys."

"One of my best ideas!" Peter said, happily. He looked down on Hook, and the boy was immediately immersed in his role. His voice deepened in a skilled imitation. "Brimstone and gall! Well, ye scug, dost give thy word to fight as a Lost Boy?"

Dryly, Hook commented, "It would seem prudent to inquire of the tiger first." He observed Jill, whose gaze still commanded the animal's. She seemed to sustain some mystical connection with the beast. Was she holding it at bay, or was she prodding it on? Through the link Hook himself shared with Jill, in his gut he felt the primal pull of the wilderness. As before, he dared not grant it its head.

As if in answer to the boy's proposition, the tigress purred. The sound was oddly loud, like little drums beating in her throat. And she padded nearer. As she huddled into a crouch, Chip raised his sword and pushed Bertie and Bingo behind him. Peter, in turn, jumped in front of Chip. The creature's black-tipped tail twitched.

"What does she say?" Peter asked Jill, in all innocence.

Hook was unsure whether Jill would speak. Her teeth were bared, and she looked more inclined to snarl. For the sake of expediency, he interpreted for her. "The tigress will oblige you...if young Chip consents to join her for dinner."

The tiger slunk closer yet. Peter smelled her frowzy fur; the heat of her breath warmed his toes. Unafraid for himself, still he got the nagging feeling that Chip stood in peril. Jewel's pinching accounted for a goodly part of that feeling. His decision came suddenly.

"Avast, lads! Time to up anchor."

The boys were only waiting for his sanction. Like arrows, they shot straight up and away from the danger. As they hung high in the azure of the Neverland sky with its white, downy clouds, waiting for him, Peter himself lingered one moment longer. "Too bad," he taunted Hook, "I could have shown you a trick or two about pirating."

Leisurely, the boy floated up to lead his crew seaward. Jewel jingled with relief. She acknowledged a signal from her master, then followed Peter, waving farewell.

Hook and Cecco glowered as they watched Pan's pack disappear. After this harrowing day, a day spent protecting the Island's inhabitants, they stood aghast at the boy's carelessness. The tigress' ears flapped as she shook her furry head. The motion signified to the men that Jill had broken off her stare. The cat threw a look of suspicion at them, then, warily, turned to pad toward the forest. As the curl of her tail slipped between fern fronds, the men were jolted from the day's grim events by the sound that followed. It was the sound they least expected to hear. Hook and Cecco exchanged startled glances, then looked down at Jill, sitting between them.

She was laughing. The merry sound burbled up from her throat, much more easily that the roar of some moments ago. She offered her arms to them, and, staring, they raised her to her feet.

"One act of humanity, and I find I'm a woman once more." Her eyes had turned blue as the sea again; she looked cleansed and refreshed, her fair hair curling. They all woke to an awareness of how unserviceable her shirt had become in its function of covering her figure.

Her mouth no longer seemed hungry for blood. Now, it beckoned like cherries. Her lips held kisses for each of them, husband and lover.

She was Red-Handed Jill at her fittest.

Widows' Wings

Like the time remaining to Raven, the afternoon had half slipped away. Tending Willow's baby, she sat in the tepee. The little one lay on the plush white fur of the bear skin. Through the supple sides of the dwelling, the light filtered in, warm and swaddling, like the wraps of a cradleboard. As Raven sang to her, the child's eyelids lowered, and soon she slumbered. Raven smiled and kissed the tender cheek. For the first time in months, contentment settled into her soul. Like ashes after a fire, it covered the site of the flame that had so consumed her.

Not since her first husband lived had she known this kind of peace. She closed her eyes, and, tilting her head back, soaked up the comfort of White Bear's dwelling. The sounds of the village seeped in, voices of children, the breeze in the leaves of the oaks high above. Sniffing, she appreciated the cozy smells of cornmeal, of firewood, and animal hide. With these scents, she inhaled a sense of oneness with her home. The tepee nestled in the center of the village, surrounded by friends and family and fed by a bountiful land and its life-giving river. Most of the river's gifts were welcomed by the tribe. The one exception was its bringing of the Black Chief. Of all the men Raven knew, he was the most like her Ash.

For Raven, fearsome as the pirate was at the beginning, like the river itself he had proved— unexpectedly— to be giving. If not for Hook, Raven might have found no means to ease her worries, and no way to leave Willow the life she deserved. Now, her sister was assured of the lifelong love of her husband. She would retain the status of an elder's only wife, and the joy of mothering all of his children. Most important, White Bear's loved ones could live without fear. Raven could not guess what trick the Black Chief planned for Lean Wolf. Strangely, Raven trusted the 'white wild man' far more than the boyhood friend of her husband, the Silent Hunter who had been born within her tradition.

In this quiet present, Raven sat snug on the prized white fur won by her husband's valor, living not in the past, nor yet in the future. With sadness balanced on either side of this moment, she dwelt in the now. Thus she sat, unstirring, until the two opposites appeared, presenting themselves simultaneously.

Wings fluttered at the top of the tepee, a sound Raven had heard once before. As she looked up, a strip of silk came spiraling down, blazingly blue. It landed in her lap. At the same time, the flap of the dwelling pulled open, and White Bear stooped to enter. Raven raised the ribbon. She turned her eyes to meet her husband's. He stared at the silk, and the glad expression on his noble face altered. All at once, the sorrow beset them. The Black Chief's signal had come.

Their time, together, was ended.

With many questions on their minds, Rowan and Lightly waited. They applied their anxious energy to preparing for the journey to the Other Island, trying not to allow doubt to weigh down their spirits. Their canoe lay beached on the shore of the bay, their packs rolled and ready. Each kept his weapons at hand. All they needed now was good news. For everyone's sake, Jill's venture must succeed.

The young braves watched so keenly that before the Clearing's parrot could shriek its alarm, they were loping through the garden trellis to hail the visitors' approach. Relief soared in their hearts when they saw Jill hiking briskly between Hook and Cecco. The two pirates were armed to the teeth with swords, knives, and pistols, but Jill, in her forest-green tunic and fawn-colored leggings, looked like a nymph of the wilderness. Clearly, she had come through her trial unscathed. When she saw the young men, she disengaged her arms from her escorts and reached for her sons, smiling.

"My dears, the hunt was successful."

The group trickled into the oasis of the Clearing to be greeted by its people. While the parrot fussed and the children clamored, Lily, Lelaneh, and Red Fawn flocked around Jill, chattering their greetings and shedding good wishes for her voyage. Lily and Lelaneh, who had an inkling of the ordeal Jill had endured, clasped her hands and measured her up, assuring themselves of her well-being.

Rowan and Lightly ushered Hook and Cecco into the tepee, where the two Men of the Clearing joined them. They held a brief pow-wow, saying little and saying it low, then those who were about to sail made their farewells to the ladies. Their embraces were fervent and earnest, but quick. The sea and her intrigues lay waiting.

"I bring a parting gift for Red Fawn," Jill announced in her clear, storyteller's voice, "and one final tale for you all."

The children nestled at their mothers' knees, and, as they all settled on the logs by the totem pole to attend, Jill knelt down beside Red Fawn. It felt quite like old times to her. The lattice of branches cast shade and grace on the circle of friends who gathered beneath it, and the little leafy house that Jill loved so well when she was Wendy seemed to lean in to listen. Its chimney puffed dreamily, just as Peter had puffed on his pipe when pretending to be Father, while the Lost Boys sat sleepy at their feet. Jill smiled at her memories. Catching Red Fawn's inquiring gaze, she returned to the present, enchanted to be here, at this time, and in this place.

"A black, shaggy wolf roved this wilderness. He was a hunter, hungry and lean. As he grew stronger than the others of his pack, this wolf shed his regard for his fellows. He roamed and foraged, gobbling up any tidbit he found. Yet in all the abundance of the forest, he was never satisfied. Even the most wholesome fare might grow stale in his mouth, and he'd spit it out, ungrateful, when he grew tired of the taste.

"One day, as he prowled near the sands of the seashore, this wolf leapt high to catch a bird on the wing. Because he deemed the bird beautiful, he didn't grind the creature's bones between his teeth. He made her sing to him, and when her song ended, he swallowed her whole. But, as the little bird entered the hungry wolf's throat, her beak pierced the beast's gullet. He tasted his own blood instead. The bird flew free, but the wolf, who always before saw himself as the hunter, sensed death itself stalking, behind him.

"Crawling into his den, the mighty wolf rested his muzzle on his paws. The little bird fluttered near, just out of reach. She lulled him to sleep, and with the sound of her song in his ears, the wolf closed his eyes, to see the land of Dark Hunting."

Jill slipped something into Red Fawn's fingers. Red Fawn looked down to find a familiar leather band, beaded by her own hands. When she looked up at Jill again, her large, dark eyes reflected her astonishment.

"Where did you find this bracelet? Has my former husband cast it away?"

Jill did not answer. She kept a warm, steady hold on Red Fawn's hands.

The woman paused, turning over Jill's story in her mind. Her voice grew tremulous, and her silver earrings quivered.

"Jill...am I a widow?"

Jill kissed her friend's forehead. "You may have many questions, Red Fawn, but I have only one answer: the Silent Hunter shall stalk you no more."

In the stillness that followed, Hook, Jill, and Cecco savored the quiet of the Clearing. The nearby brook babbled in contentment; the scents of Lelaneh's garden sweetened the breeze. But another breeze called to them, and these creatures of the sea needed no urging to answer it. Hook rose and made his bows to the ladies. "Come shipmates, our next venture awaits us."

Cecco kissed his fingertips in farewell. "*Ciao*, my dear friends. If Fortune follows us, we will see you again."

The pirates and the Messengers struck out on the sun-speckled path toward the bay, leaving the People of the Clearing waving them off from the foot of the totem pole. For this family, the pole's carved wooden figures evoked a sense of protection. The lion stared proud and fierce from his post at the crown, and below him, the sly tigress smiled.

Red Fawn linked each of the twins' arms in hers. Her eyelashes were damp, but her dimples had started to dance again.

"Is it not time to carve another image, my darlings? I think, perhaps, a lovely pair of bird's wings."

For Raven, relief could come only with departure. These last moments with Willow were agony. Raven was dressed in her ceremonial garb, the white deerskin dress with its long, swinging fringe, made especially for changes. Her bundle was packed and tied, waiting at her feet.

"No, Raven!" Tears seeded Willow's eyes. They fell to the beautiful beads on her tunic, rolling to join them. "Please…change your mind. Do not leave our tepee."

"Be strong for me, Sister. Since I must go, do not make it harder."

"I cannot understand how White Bear allows it. Always before, he has acted to protect you."

"Your husband knows what is best for me, Willow, and so do I. You must trust our judgment. Now hold me, dear, and give me a hug to remember."

"Raven— I am grieving."

"Be glad for me instead. White Bear's people will welcome me, I am certain, and I will find my place on his island." She stooped to pick up her pack. "As much as I will miss you, Willow, this day is one of happiness as much as a day of sorrow. And you who helped me through it know better than anyone…" Raven shook her head. "I have had enough of sorrow." Raven, like Willow, felt the tears burn her eyes.

"Only now do I appreciate your grief, Raven. Today, I truly feel the heartache that caused you to cut off your hair." Again, Willow wept, covering her face. When she recovered her breath, she cried,

"Once you leave, I must live in mourning." Willow halted as the thought came to her. "Raven— I, too, will shear off my hair!"

At Willow's words, Raven froze. Unblinking, she moved, at last, to set down her bundle, as carefully as if it were Baby.

"Willow." Raven gripped her sister by her shoulders. "Listen to me." She waited for Willow's eyes to clear of tears. "Here is the last counsel your older sister will speak to you." She leveled her gaze directly into Willow's. "You must mourn me with all fitting custom. But do not cut off your hair." Raven held her voice steady. She understood the ways of men so much better than her sister. This point was too important to state with a quaver.

"Willow: when White Bear looks at *you*, he must not see me."

Raven pulled her sister to her breast, and held her. She bestowed a kiss upon her brow, and then she let her go. Gathering up her pack, Raven nodded to Willow, flung open the tepee, and smiled her goodbye.

She would try, forever, to remember Willow wearing her sweetest smile. From now to eternity, she would endeavor to erase the face she just witnessed. She was leaving Willow, for the very purpose of preventing the emotion that caused Willow's look. But Raven knew, already, that she could never forget that expression.

Willow's face, at last, revealed understanding. And, moments later, her relief became evident, too, as she sensed her sister's sacrifice. Like a jointed wooden doll, Willow lifted her hand to her lips, and, awkwardly, she gestured farewell.

Always after, when Raven smelled the scent of pine, she was reminded of this hour. It held both her gladdest and her most painful moments. She and White Bear brushed through the stand of spruce trees to emerge on the bright, chalky rock. They had run together, their feet pummeling the earth of the path, wishing to hoard the little time left to them, to spend on this cliff top. On one hand, the familiar waters of Neverbay sparkled in wavelets. On the other lay the ocean that must soon stretch between them, unfamiliar, and unfriendly. It was here that they had conjured the bridge linking their future lives, spanning time and conjoining places.

White Bear slid Raven's pack from his shoulders. She stood catching her breath, watching him, confiding his every detail to memory. She did not glance at the ship rocking at anchor as it readied to sail her away. Instead, she stored White Bear's image, to last her forever: his height, his regal posture, the long black tail of his scalp lock and the feathers she had clipped in it this morning. His iron eyes had softened, and never questioned her, now. Her fingertips would forever remember the bumps of his battle scars. The bear claws resting on his chest belonged to her like her own fingernails, and even his moccasins, beaded by her sister Willow with love, would, in remembrance, ever be part of her warrior. His skin, that smelled of sun and of muscle, and the fleecy feel of the albino bear fur— all these fragments molded together, like clay to shape a jar, and she would carry it just as carefully as she'd bear an earthen vessel— because it held her very heart.

She smiled at him. "You will never grow old, my husband." She took his hands, and they strolled, leisurely now, to sit upon the patch of moss beneath the shifting shade of the old alder tree. "I will keep you just as you are, here, in my being." She pressed his hand to her breast.

"And you, Wife, shall remain always fresh, like the touch of a summer's wind tangling the grasses." He ran his fingers through her brief strands of hair, and stirred the jay feathers that nudged her neck. "Even so has your spirit tangled in mine."

"I would ask you to take good care of my sister, and her children, but I already know your custom. A good man cares for his family. Be assured, White Bear, that I will care for your Raven."

"My Raven." As was his habit now, he gentled his voice on the syllables of her name, and he called her so again, while he could. "Raven. I bear a new weight on my heart, after today, because I will speak your name only *about* you, and nevermore *to* you."

"Every day, I will whisper your name to you, White Bear. Will you hear me?"

He nodded then, gravely. "I hear you." He gazed over the sea, south and east, toward the Other Island, where he envisioned her standing among the tepees of his people. "And also, I see you." His gaze traveled the miles again, back to her face. "I will wait anxiously, to hear tidings of my Raven. But do not send our Messengers home to me too soon. I would hear that you are settled, that you accept my people, and that you are satisfied."

"I will obey your wish, my husband. And I remember the message that you taught me. Your words will be spoken through my lips, as if you stand on the Other Island before your relatives."

"I have a gift for you, Raven. Will you accept my offering?"

"I never made you a marriage bracelet; I have not given you anything."

"Indeed, you have. Although you deny it, you are as open-handed as your sister. Many moons moved around me before I understood your offerings. Today, I hold more wisdom to counsel the People; I make a worthier husband." White Bear knelt before her, the mossy ground soft beneath his knees. He pulled her up to kneel before him.

"What I have to present to you, Wife, is a thing that is worthless by itself. Only when many of its kind are woven together can it be useful, or beautiful, or strong. You are all these things, Raven. I revere you for lending these qualities to me. Now, as you go from me, never to return, I return to you what is yours."

White Bear drew his hunting knife from its sheath. His eyes remained fixed on hers, gray and solemn. The two lovers faced one another, kneeling at the brink of the cliff, encircled by the roots of the flame tree, the alder, and caressed by the sea-scented breeze. White Bear bent his head to the side and collected the hair of his lock. As he gripped it, he worked the knife back and forth, slowly, reverently, cutting it strand by strand, to fall free. Several inches of his black hair remained, prickling upward at the top of his skull, eked out by its feathers to form what remained of his scalp lock.

Raven gasped, covering her mouth with her hands. When she saw the moisture standing in White Bear's eyes, her own tears tumbled down her cheeks. She recognized the act her husband was performing. It was a ritual she herself had observed, moons ago, in mourning. This rite was a sacred ceremony. Attended by earth, by air, by fire and by water, White Bear was making a sacrifice, to sorrow.

Her husband was cutting his hair for her, just as Raven had shorn her own, grieving for Ash. Touched, she could not hold back a sob. White Bear had not approved of this custom, before he married her. Raven's shearing was strange to him, so archaic a compulsion that even her own people had nearly forgotten it. Never, not even in dreams, had she thought to earn this depth of devotion from her sister's husband, her provider, her lover, the man who journeyed to this island from afar: White Bear. He stood on his knees before her, his second wife, and surrendered to her his most prized possession.

When his lock was cut free, White Bear offered it in his two hands to Raven. She regarded it with reverence, then accepted it into her fingers. Warm and vital, it filled Raven's grip with his substance. Their eyes met above it. Nothing more required to be said. In this single ceremony, White Bear imparted a lifetime of loving. The couple held one another then, pressing their beings together, her cheek nestled at his throat, and they remained thus, their hearts drumming like the surf down below, until two birds circled and alighted beside them, on the bright white ledge of the cliff.

Rowan Life-Giver bowed his head in respect. "White Bear. At your request, we disturb your serenity. Word comes from the *Red Lady's* chief that his ship stands ready to sail." He and Lightly stood impassive, affecting not to notice the shortened tail of White Bear's scalp lock. Far from diminishing his authority as a council member, the mark of his bereavement enhanced the man's gravity.

White Bear nodded to the Messengers, and they stood back to render privacy to his last words to his loved one.

"Raven, I set you free to fly. Know that I hold you only here," he held his clenched fist at his chest, "here, my wild bird, in my heart."

"My husband. White Bear." Raven blinked the tears away so that she could gaze clearly into his eyes. "I hear you."

He touched her cheek, and they took one last kiss, tenderly this time, in fear that their grief might betray them. Too soon, White Bear rose to his feet and drew Raven up beside him. She coiled his long lock of hair in her pouch, carefully, and secured it. With his arm around her waist, he presented her to Rowan and Lightly.

"Messengers of the People, deliver my wife safe to the Other Island. I look for your return only once her welfare among our relatives is assured."

"Yes, White Bear," Rowan answered. "Our canoe lies aboard the ship. When we near the island of your birth, we will paddle the final miles, as you instructed. Your people's scouts will not see us in company with pirates."

Rowan and Lightly each clasped arms with White Bear, and Lightly of the Air said, "White Bear, we owe you our gratitude for restoring us to the elders' esteem. We pledge to honor your trust."

"The People spoke with their actions," White Bear replied. "I have learned to listen."

The two young men collected Raven's pack. Then, bending down, they made a chair of their arms, and White Bear settled Raven into it. He touched her hair; her fingers lingered along the ivory of his necklace. White Bear stepped back. Raven spread her arms to weave them around Rowan and Lightly, and, for this lone occasion of her life, she took flight like her namesake. Upheld by the Messengers, the raven in white winged her way homeward.

White Bear watched as their figures soared away, growing smaller. He heard the ships' lookouts cry out. Over the distance, he saw Raven with her black hair and snowy dress, touching down to stand at the stern of the *Lady*. Rowan and Lightly supported her, one on each side, as the vessel bobbed free of its moorings. He saw her hand rest on the pouch, where his lock traveled by her side. Her other arm rose up, in one final gesture— farewell.

From her stance at the ship's rail, she saw White Bear standing straight and tall on the cliff top, with green pines behind him. Below his feet, the pale rock glared and the cerulean sea teemed. Above his head, the wind tugged the feathers of his scalp lock. He raised his right arm, the arm that should have borne his second wife's marriage token but which, in truth, only moments ago held much more. As the ship's peculiar motion pulled her backward, Raven steadied her legs and kept her gaze upon White Bear. He remained there, watching, his hand upraised in answer to hers.

In the sky above them, sea birds swarmed. The man and the woman acknowledged only each other. Neither witnessed the larger ship heel to the wind in her brilliant, gilded glory, nor did they notice the way her sister craft bloomed as she followed, uncurling her sails to flutter them open like wings. In rapid succession, dual guns boomed goodbye to the Island, and the shouts of the sailors bounced over the waves.

The figures stood steadfast, dwindling in one another's vision, a streak of copper and a dab of white, ever smaller, and greedily seized. Within minutes, the two ships deserted the arms of the Island. The lovers lost one another, and the depths of the bay lay wavering and vacant between them.

At last, when the colors of the Neverland faded from her horizon, Raven let down her arm. She closed her eyes. She murmured to his memory, "I see you, Husband."

Far and farther away from her, drawing back from the cliff top, White Bear bowed his proud head.

"I hear you, my wild bird. My Raven."

He turned back toward his family, shadowing her footsteps through spruce that shed redolent scent.

The Wider World

"**C**ommodore Hook is most gracious to offer cigars, but you may have mine, Jacquot," Chef's plump fingers doled out the largess. "Smoking dulls the palate."

"*Très bien.*" Jacquot held the stogie under his nose to inhale its rich tobacco scent, then stuffed it in the pocket of his apron. As he heaved the silver tray with his scrawny arms, he made a show of teetering a bit before lugging it down the companionway toward the *Red Lady*'s galley. The sister ships lay at anchor, side by side in a balmy sea, and as a mid-ocean wave pitched the deck, he nearly missed the first step in earnest.

"Watch your feet!" Chef steadied the tray, then cuffed his galley mate. "I spied you draining the dregs of the wine, you cur. Next time the captain entertains, I shall serve the guests myself!"

"*Oui, Monsieur,*" Jacquot agreed, not reluctant to shirk any duty.

But Chef smiled once again, reliving his triumph. "This banquet was a grand success, another culinary *coup.*" To Chef's delight, Captain Cecco's appetite remained in full flower, and he had ordered a celebration. This afternoon, the captain was regaling Commodore Hook and the Lady Jill in his quarters. The royalty of the fleet had feasted in good cheer, and not a morsel of Chef's effort went to waste.

"Yet I must be modest," he allowed. "I alone am not the genius of today's success. It is *l'amour,* Jacquot, that extracts the superior flavors."

Jacquot wobbled again, causing the china to rattle, and Chef himself seized the tray to balance it on his generous belly. Nimble from years on the sea, he glided down the stairs, his stodgy body moving as fluidly as the waves. "But why do I waste my advice upon you? That Indian widow with the blue feathers, she stole your heart away with one glance of her sad, black eyes. Now she is planted on that other island, and you shall never see her again."

"Do you think the rumor is true?" Jacquot asked, intrigued, "That she bestowed upon the commodore the blue plume he exhibits in his hat?" The sailors' gossip had not ended with their shore leave.

"Ah, who can tell? No gentleman would admit to it, but," Chef's eyes twinkled in his doughy face, "what female can resist our dashing, romantic officers? It is said that Captain Cecco, too, inspired love in her heathen heart."

"And Red-Handed Jill commands the hearts of both commanders! Is it possible that you will be creating another wedding cake, for our lady and Commodore Hook?"

"Non, non, Jacquot. The man is too shrewd. He hides his affection from his enemies."

"It is said any man who marries Red-Handed Jill becomes cursed."

"C'est vrai. You saw what happened to her first husband— or is he her second? Before he could glory in the wedding night, the woman stole his diamonds and drugged him with his own potion. Then she sent him packing back to Austria, to bring her more riches."

"La femme fatale!" Jacquot exclaimed in admiration. "I saw her steal even his watch."

"Captain Cecco, strong man that he is, suffered cruelly from this marriage curse. I judge by his appetite, *hein?* For the sake of my art, I hope today's happiness lasts."

The two men and the crockery docked at the galley without mishap. Before tending to the dirty dishes, Jacquot lit his cigar, and Chef ignited his imagination with more musings on the subject of romance.

L'amour was the inspiration behind the captain's door as well. "Another toast, Captain, to your love and mine," Hook proposed. "To our Beauty. Our Red-Handed Jill."

The two men had indulged in a feast for their eyes as well as their bellies. Jill appeared radiant in her best black silk gown. Rubies glowed at her throat, and her bosom rose above the spare, square neckline. Her fair hair flowed over bare, rosy shoulders. Jill had, however, given thought to the Indian women's more earthy example, and left off her perfume today. The scent of sea and sky on her skin, she found, made a headier impact on her seafaring men's senses.

The men, too, were attired in their formal best, Hook in black velvet, Cecco in his headdress of medallions and his bright gypsy silks. As the men raised their crystal goblets, Jill acknowledged the honor. "Gentlemen, your sentiments are reciprocated." She, too, was enjoying handsome company— Hook with his neat black beard and patrician features, and Cecco's deep brown eyes, his smooth olive skin. Each of her lovers stole her breath away.

"And another," proposed Cecco, lifting his glass once more. It sparkled in the sunlight that came slanting through *Red Lady*'s port windows. Before Raven's stay, Cecco had ordered the former captain's dull paisley drapes to be replaced with gold curtains. The rugs and cushions were changed to suit his Italian tastes, and where once the room suppressed its guests' moods, it now buoyed them up with lighthearted cheer. The *Roger* lay in view, rolling in tandem, and Cecco smiled, well pleased with this wider world. "To our beloved's revenge."

"To justice," said Hook.

This time, Jill sipped the light white wine, too, but as its zest tingled on her tongue, she became contemplative. "The line between revenge and justice is a fine one. In the matter of Lean Wolf, I feel that I achieved both."

"Your instincts are exquisite," Hook agreed. "Although Captain Cecco and I loathed to allow it, your ploy raised a malcontent's emotion to the highest pitch. You won both his love and his trust at the exact moment in which you betrayed him."

Cecco declared, "To destroy his faith in Raven was the *pièce de résistance*, as my Frenchmen would say. By the time your quarry died, his Red Hand from the Sea meant everything in the world to him." He laid his hand on Jill's. "May I never earn your enmity, *Bellezza*. I too, would die a tortured man."

She smiled at her husband. "And you, my dear, played your role to perfection. I myself believed you were about to murder me. But Giovanni," Jill asked, "what of your oath? You swore that the man who handled me would not die before your weapon handled *him*."

From their seats on either side of her across the crisp linen tablecloth, Hook and Cecco exchanged knowing smiles. "Lovely one," Cecco answered, "do you not yet understand?" He raised her scarlet fingers to his lips and kissed them. "You yourself are that weapon."

Hook concurred. "A weapon we are wise to keep secret. The impending menace is as yet ignorant of your powers." At his words, an uneasy silence descended. None of the three celebrants wished to dampen the festive mood just yet. For now, the name of the next threat to contentment remained unspoken.

Hook leaned back and tapped his glass with the point of his claw, striking pleasant little pings from the crystal. "Our sojourn on the Island proved delightful in some ways, exhilarating in others. Our forces have been tested against the Indians', and our opposing powers remain in balance."

"I am satisfied," Jill said, "that I leave my Island sons thriving, and I see my sailor sons happy, in their positions as bo'sun's mates." Jill chuckled, "Even Nibs seems content. His old kerchief is restored to him." But her brow creased as she considered her moody young man; "Yet I've noticed a change in Nibs. Ever since we sailed, I've seen a faraway look in his eye."

"My love, you of all people should recognize that look."

"Ah. You believe he is in love, Hook?"

"Nibs is a man in search of a woman."

"Then I shall not feel concern. Whatever Nibs sets his mind to do, he achieves. I hope the same holds true for dear David."

Cecco snorted. "All I hope for 'dear David' is that he succeeds in registering our marriage in London."

Jill dropped her gaze from her husband's. She had prepared herself to impart the course she felt obligated to choose, but surely the three conspirators had earned a few more minutes of this bliss? She began to fidget with her wedding ring.

Seemingly unaware of the pain awaiting him, Cecco continued, "Before long we shall be relieved of another youngster. Next time we drop anchor on the Island, Mrs. Hanover will pass from my care into Lelaneh's."

"Your care, Captain?" Hook ribbed him. "Do your talents now circumscribe those of a midwife?"

"I have simply learned more of an officer's duty to his crew." Cecco shrugged. "A captain's burden."

"Indeed. And, depending upon the paternity of the child, my own burden will increase or diminish." Hook's lips twisted in distaste, and Jill set a soothing hand on his elbow.

She said, softly, "I am confident that the child's sire is its grand-sire."

"A prediction, my love, or a story?"

"Both, perhaps. Yet Lelaneh believes that the babe is not well, and the birthing will be troubled. Surely this is a sign." Jill felt a knot in her stomach. Content with the family she had already raised, yet she could scarcely bear the thought that another woman might mother Hook's only child. As always, Hook sensed her emotion, and, just as she had comforted him, he laid his hand over hers where it rested on his velvet sleeve. His loving touch warmed her heart.

He admitted to Cecco, "I too gained fresh insights from our Island adventures. I watched a raging river drag Jill away from me. Soon after, our lady suffered abduction. With each disappearance, I imagined my life turned back like an hourglass, to a time without Jill. I now hold more sympathy for her husband, whom circumstance has caused to endure a similar torment." Hook held his glass high. "I drink to you, Captain Cecco."

Moved by his rival's magnanimity, Cecco bowed. "Commodore."

The toast was drunk, and Jill set her cup carefully down, unwilling to cause a sound or a vibration to disturb this pivotal moment. Three times now, the unity that remained her deepest wish had been granted by her lovers. This harmony might prove fragile, or it might endure for three lifetimes. Jill closed her eyes and held her breath, listening to her soul as it sang in celebration.

It was Cecco himself who braved discussion of the state of affairs. Jill had steeled herself against the necessity of wounding him, again, yet Cecco's speech made her love him the more.

"I thank you, Sir. After the crisis Jill survived all alone, I see how love clouds my judgment. My selfishness cast her into danger." With his hand on his heart, Cecco vowed, "Jill, my lovely wife, from this moment, I release my claim to you. You must use our marriage for your protection, but you yourself must go as you will." His accent softened as he finished, tenderly, "I ask only that you act, always, to ensure your safety, which is far more dear to me than my own."

The tears smarted in Jill's eyes. Clearly, Cecco anticipated her intention, and he had moved to make her burden of separating from him easier for her. She searched her heart for proper words to respond, but she jumped as Hook slammed down his goblet. He became their commander again, and he spoke through bared teeth.

"Let me understand you, Captain. It is your intention to abandon our lady?"

"Commodore?" Cecco drew back in astonishment. A glance at Jill showed him that she, too, was startled.

Hook leapt to his feet to tower over the dining table. The curve of his claw reflected the sun's rays. "Soon we must face a most dangerous foe. Jill will require the both of us, and both of our companies, to conquer this monster."

Hook's pronouncement resounded through the room, and then the silence of dread fell again. This time, Jill determined to face the demons that drove it. She listened closely as Cecco countered Hook's challenge.

"No! *È impossibile!* I shall never abandon my wife. But see how pale she grows! Take some brandy, Jill, and we will speak later of this distasteful subject." He fetched the decanter from the sideboard, bringing three crystal snifters, once the pride of Captain DéDé LeCorbeau.

Jill accepted a glass, but her color had already risen. "Do not tread lightly for my sake, gentlemen. I triumphed in the ordeal of Lean Wolf. I chose to brave that monster, just as I chose to brave Doctor Hanover when I stole his wealth instead of his life." At last, she had uttered the name of her enemy. As the words left her lips, all she felt was relief.

She squared her shoulders. "Let us not delay any longer. We have only months to prepare for this battle."

"Well spoken, Jill." Hook settled into his chair again. "As I advised from the first, our best advantage lies in confronting the trouble."

"Agreed." Cecco leaned forward where he stood, to rest his fists upon the table. "I too have been considering our strategy. Commodore, I propose that you steer Jill far away on the *Roger*, and allow me to conduct the rendezvous with our treacherous partners. The *Red Lady* carries the cargo Doctor Hanover requires, two crates of the lotus flower for concocting his philter. LeCorbeau will make us all richer with it, but it is I, after all, who struck the bargain with these devils."

"Dismiss the idea from your mind, Captain. Jill and I will not seek safer waters."

Jill was bristling. "Nor will I run from this challenge."

But Hook shook his head, and his golden earring bobbed with his vehemence. "No, Jill. This time I refuse to allow you to endanger yourself. By the time we meet him, the good doctor will have suffered a full year without you. We can be certain that, in that year, he shall have constructed a scheme to bring you under his power."

"I do not fear him."

"You *should* fear him. The man has money, influence, and intelligence."

"No wonder I married him," she said, slyly. She won a smile from her lover.

Her husband frowned.

"Commodore, everything you say persuades me more thoroughly

that Jill must flee from Hanover. Shall you allow me to sail her to safety on the *Red Lady?*"

"I will not. Since we crippled our enemies' fortunes, we may presume that they will manage to fit out but one single ship. Far better to meet them with two."

"Commodore, with respect—"

"Attend my words well, Captain." Hook's eyes turned as hard as the diamonds Hanover once hoarded in his medicine bag. "The danger that entangled Jill on the Island occurred because we two worked at odds. Our division led to disaster."

"And so, we must work together to shield her from Hanover." Cecco's fist hit the table. "I agree."

"All three of us must work. No matter how skillfully we wield our respective weapons, we need one another to accomplish our ends. Jill, your wit and charm must serve again. Captain, once more, I shall require your hand."

"You shall have it." Cecco pledged, offering it, and, heartily, the two men clasped arms. Cecco's face waxed fierce as they reached this accord. Hook wore a look of supreme satisfaction.

Jill watched their interaction with interest. "But Hook," she asked, "out of loyalty to you, my first love, I feel compelled to disavow my marriage in all but name. Surely we must begin this next endeavor with a clear understanding?"

"Did you not marry your Giovanni for the good of the company? For protection? For love?"

Jill turned her jewel-blue eyes from Hook's, to gaze into Cecco's. Her voice vibrated with emotion. "Aye...for all that." With a melancholy smile, Cecco returned her loving look.

"What has changed?" Hook demanded. "Upon sand or sea, no other woman is created for me. Selfishly, I must insist that you cleave to your husband."

Mystified by Hook's contradictions, Cecco stammered, "But I— I have set my wife free to—"

"The threats to Red-Handed Jill— those with which we are familiar, and those we have yet to meet— are formidable. Your union is essential to our collective success."

"The lady is yours, Sir, and always has been."

"*You* espoused her. I expect you to behave like a husband."

"A husband thinks first of the wishes of his wife!"

"Then do so, Captain, and demonstrate your love for her."

"Next you will order us to fill the ship with our children!"

"I should never presume to impose my own will in that quarter."

Deliberately, Jill rose from her seat and threw down her napkin. In grand fashion, she pronounced, "At last!"

Yanked from their train of thought, the two men blinked at her.

"Did you believe I placed myself in peril merely for vengeance?"

Still, the men said nothing. They listened to Red-Handed Jill.

"I should be a fool, indeed, to act so imprudently. No, gentlemen. Satisfying as my retribution upon Lean Wolf is to me, there is much more depth to that story. I risked my own safety for yours."

Cecco's face darkened with displeasure. "Jill...such an act was unnecessary. How many times have I proved my loyalty to our commodore? How often did I show you that your well-being is *primo*, the first care of my heart?"

Hook, too, glowered at her. "Had I grasped to what extremity you would go to preserve your husband, Jill, I should have—"

"You'd have done what, my love? Killed him first, or given me up to him?" Swiftly, Jill raised her bloodstained hand, forestalling them. "No, don't answer, either of you. I solved the dilemma quite nicely. I had only to enter hell itself to do it."

Hook raised one eyebrow. "A tidy little trap, Jill. Baited with your life."

"I was confident that no matter how resentfully you opposed one another, my champions would rush in, together, to rescue me. And here we are." She spread her arms, encompassing the company. "The three of us, all in accord."

Cecco absorbed her smug smile, and he heaved a sigh. "I cannot approve of your actions. But, my magnificent Jill, I am touched, more deeply than I can say." His bracelets chimed as he raised his fingertips to his lips, and he sent a kiss flying her way.

"Magnificent, indeed." Hook's voice seeped from his soul, low, and velvety. His gaze appraised her. "My mistress of manipulation."

Jill smiled, half-way. "I studied a master." She flounced her black silk skirts and sat down again, between her men, offering one hand to each of them. "And now, since, as the master advises me, our best advantage lies in confronting the trouble, let us hear his strategy against Doctor Johann Hanover Heinrich."

Hook smiled with gratification. "Perhaps I should consult the mistress before beginning, Jill. You appear to have outwitted me."

"I do thank you for the compliment, but my deliberations have been devoted to the overthrow of Lean Wolf. If you please, Commodore, impart your own plans to us."

"Very well." Hook's countenance became grave as he began. "This situation is simpler, yet more far-reaching than our previous challenges. I have, therefore, a simpler design in mind to defeat it."

Cecco gestured liberally, "Please to describe it, Commodore. As Jill has proven, we are all of us together in this effort— and in all things."

"Captain Cecco, my plan begins thus: from today, I forbid you to speak to Jill."

In an instant, accord went by the board.

"What madness is this?" Jill exclaimed, and Cecco glared at Hook, his eyes wild with incredulity. Jill looked Hook up and down, indignant, while Cecco sputtered,

"*Miei dèi!* How is it that—"

The commodore raked the air with his hook, demanding silence. When he spoke again, his tone was smooth, but unswerving.

"I forbid you to speak to Jill, Captain…in English."

Hook allowed a moment for his words to sink in. The couple continued to stare at him, but Jill and Cecco subsided into thought, trying to decipher his meaning. Hook reached to his vest pocket and withdrew the crystal vial, full of sparkling gold dust.

"Captain, I shall summon my servant, and you will meet with her this evening. You are to tell her everything you remember of your homeland and its contours."

"Jewel is to learn of the Italian countryside?" Jill frowned in bewilderment. "But why?"

"Ere long she shall fly to the mainland, in quest of a certain gypsy troupe. She will not rest until she finds them."

"My family…" Cecco murmured, with wonderment. "Our fairy is to locate my family?" He shook his head to clear it, and the many medallions on his headdress jingled, a reminder of home.

"By the time Hanover pays his call to the *Roger*, Jill will be settled in Italy— hidden within the bosom of your tribe."

Jill gasped, clutching her glass. After some moments, she raised it to her lips and drank the brandy down. It burned in her throat, and she did not try to speak. Cecco, too, had fallen wordless.

"Surely your mother will welcome her daughter-in-law? And your brothers— I understand they are legion— they will undertake to protect her?"

"*Sì…sì,* yes, they will do this. But…I had not considered it. I have not hoped to see my tribe, not ever again in this life."

"Nor will you, I am afraid. The bounty still rests on your head. But Jill may go. And Jill *must* go."

She mused, "The one place on the map where Doctor Hanover cannot find me."

"Your single port of shelter. Yes."

"I can vouch for my people," Cecco said. "They will not abide strangers, but once they learn that Jill is wife to their long lost Giovanni, they will welcome her with open arms. *Che bello!* To be there to witness it: my mother's joy, my father's pride, my brothers' celebration! To my people, our Jill will bring sunshine." Cecco's even white teeth gleamed in a smile.

"But Hook, I don't wish to leave you. Nor you, Giovanni. I refuse to flee like a coward."

Cecco declared, with pride, "No coward can walk into a gypsy camp uninvited."

"But to run from my troubles…"

"You shall merely be obeying an order, Jill," Hook reasoned. "I command you to go."

"Much as I long for adventure, I feel I'll be missing a greater one, here."

"It cannot be helped," Hook returned. "This first meeting with our two untrustworthy partners will be the most critical. I shall feel less apprehension, in regard to your presence, in our subsequent appointments."

"You have considered this scheme from all angles, Sir?"

"I have, indeed. Jewel will guide you on your flight. Mr. Nibs and Mr. Tootles shall escort you. One of them will remain with you, and, once the danger is past, I shall send the other to fetch you both home."

Still reluctant, Jill nodded. "Aye, Sir. I am disappointed on one account, and excited on the other."

"Bellezza," Cecco exulted, "although you have shown yourself to be the most courageous of women, this plan relieves our fears for you. I am certain that my family shall make you welcome. And, in turning to my tribe in a time of trouble, you will pour joy in my heart."

"As I am to learn the language first, I shall be able to banish what worries your mamma holds for you. But, Hook," she said, archly, "this scheme is sure to test our hard-won unity. To become fluent in Italian will require hours and hours of study." She looked at him sideways, and smiled.

"Then the sooner you begin, the better." Hook gathered his long legs and rose from the table. Jill stood, too, as Hook pulled out her chair for her. He turned to Cecco. "Captain, I thank you for your generosity. I relished the feast as well as the company."

Cecco opened his hands. "Commodore, you will trust me, trust us— a couple who loves one another, thrust together— all that time?"

"Time means less than nothing to me. It is Time itself I have learned not to trust. If you will, Captain," Hook gestured to the hourglass that sat on Cecco's desk, another gilded relic from LeCorbeau. Cecco retrieved it, and, trusting, passed it to Hook.

"Jill saved her own life from her third husband's bloodlust, by wielding one night of passion." Hook upended the hourglass and held it at the level of his eyes, watching the sands rush down to pool, performing their function of futility. Then he pitched the piece out the window, to mingle with the free sands of the sea.

"Jill and I are bound by rites more sacred than marriage. If a few hours of intimacy are the price of her safety, I'll not begrudge them."

He shook hands with Cecco, who stood in amazement, staring out the window after his timepiece. It was not the loss of the instrument that held Cecco immobile. What he lost with the hourglass was nothing; what he gained by its loss was inestimable— time with his wife.

Hook turned to Jill, whose eyes adored him. "My love, I leave you to your tutor. But, *prima*…"

He caught her close to his velvety chest, and lifted her chin. As she wound her arms about him, with his sapphire eyes he gazed deep into hers. Despite the cool trend of his discourse, all along she had sensed his intensity. He now affirmed his feeling with a kiss, heated and hungering, and Jill returned it with fire of her own. Between his embrace and his edict, she felt herself sway to seduction.

Hook set her free and drew her arms from his shoulders, one by one with one hand. He swept up his hat and donned it, he strode to the doorway. His half-smile slid to his lips. *"Addio, Signora,"* he purred, rolling his wrist in a graceful salute.

He left the door open, so that the couple in his wake stood at the threshold, watching him stride down the steps and stroll over the deck. He called for a cable and seized it, hailing a sailor to throw open the gangway. Then he turned and, assuming Cecco's own gesture, Hook kissed his fingertips to Jill, in farewell. Leaping across the waves, he swung toward the *Roger*, his black coattails flying behind. Jill stood, exhilarated, her heart throbbing in her ribs, and her lips still swollen with his kisses.

She parted them to murmur, "Of all the sailors on the Seven Seas, James Hook has to be the most dangerous."

Cecco drew his beloved close and looked down upon her face. Imparting his first teaching, his tongue trilled with his native language. *"La frase italiana* for your lover is… '*innamorato.*' And, *sì, Bellezza.* Yes, Beauty. He is also the most generous of men." His soft timbre sharpened. "And the most shrewd."

He slid his wife's hand into his, wedding band to wedding band, more enamored than ever of her courage and loyalty, but believing she did not feel his touch. The grip to which she held fast at this moment, he supposed, was not the captain's, but the commodore's. She seemed to cleave to Hook's hand— the hand he'd asked Cecco to lend to him. Yet Cecco believed that, by choice or by guile, some kind of enchantment was acting.

Cecco's guess wasn't wholly correct. Jill's wish was at work, due to him and to Hook, though he could not yet fathom the magic. As her fingers wove into his, Jill felt three lives intertwine, in alliance. She sighed, and smiled, spellbound, and watched the fine figure of her *innamorato* as he boarded his glittering ship. Commandeering the steps toward his quarters, he entered without her, a single man, yet one who was never alone.

Red-Handed Jill belonged with that legendary pirate. And she thanked the Powers, for the usual, unusual way that he loved her.

Author's Note

Because Red-Handed Jill favors frankness, I confess my offense. To make my point in *Other Islands*, literary truth and historical fact had to part ways.

In the same way that I understand that real pirates didn't run their ships like the Royal Navy, I recognize that American Indian tribes don't operate on the same principles as the natives who populate my re-imagination of J.M. Barrie's Neverland. Hook is the exception, always, and he models his ship's company after the British Navy because to do so succeeds. The structure is useful to him. Likewise, the structure of the tribe called "the People" in my novels is useful for my purpose of portraying "people" in general.

For instance, I've turned epithets typically wielded by whites, such as "demons" and "devils," against the white people in *Other Islands*. For another example, homosexuality is generally accepted by the American natives on whom Barrie based the Neverland tribe. In both cases, prejudice is a matter of perspective, and where entrenched thinking is involved, I like to turn that perspective like a kaleidoscope.

Over the arc of a novel, an author strives to bring the characters to new levels of understanding. The work's job is to demonstrate this growth, and, further— as every Jane Austen devotee knows— a literary novel must present commentary on the society in which we live.

In the *Hook & Jill* Saga, each communal group represents some aspect of society: the Lost Boys represent children; the pirates are adults; the mermaids are sensuality; the fairies, hedonism.

Individual people and things also symbolize archetypes: Smee is the faithful servant, Jewel the true believer, the crocodile is the fundamentalist. Lily is the genuine mother on the Island; Time— which makes a bold attempt at the rank of "character" in my series— is, for Peter, the god of the Neverland; and the sea itself is rebirth.

Thus, in the *Hook & Jill* Saga, the tribe called the People stand for society overall. And in order to make my points about society, these characters must experience conflict, and reasons to grow.

Although my writing is researched, it is literary fiction, not historical fiction. My purpose is twofold. First, to re-open the Neverland to grown-up readers who wish to revel in its wonders, in adult context. Next, and no less importantly, to inspire respect for all brave hearts who, like Hook and Jill, Jewel, Lily, Rowan and Lightly, and all the rest, find that they must flout tradition in order to pursue their happiness— which act in itself, is, conversely, a tradition on the grandest of scales.

And so, with the candor of Red-Handed Jill, I quote another fictitious pirate. As Captain Jack Sparrow declares:

"Me? I'm dishonest...honestly."

Acknowledgements

*In bringing this Island to life, I enjoyed the help and support of my tribe.
My heartfelt gratitude goes out to the beloved ones who inspire, require,
and feed the fire…*

Jolene Barjasteh, Lady Scarlett Blue, Mrs. Ruth Brauch,
the Rev. Timothy T. Buenger, Catherine Leah Condon
Guillemette, Stacy DeCoster, Alice Gallagher,
Joseph Guillemette, Erik Hollander, Maureen Holtz,
Celia Jones, Jonathan Jones, Mary Lawrence, Admiral
Morgan Ramirez, Ginny Thompson, Peter Von Brown.

May applause never end for…

J.M. Barrie

"This ought not to be written in ink but with a golden splash."

About The Author

Andrea Jones enthralls us with her award-winning literary series, the *Hook & Jill* Saga. As a "pirate author," Jones breaks the rules, and her stories leave readers rethinking convention.

Jones is the editor of classic restoration projects, beginning with Alexandre Dumas' *Prince of Thieves* and *Robin Hood the Outlaw* (Reginetta Press). Jones' objective is to preserve the original wording of beloved manuscripts before time and re-telling corrupt them.

Jones' debut novel, *Hook & Jill*, is a serious parody of *Peter and Wendy*, questioning the premise: is it desirable to remain a child, or is it a greater adventure, after all, to grow up? In gratitude to J.M. Barrie, Jones included *Peter and Wendy: The Restored Text* (Reginetta Press) in her restoration program. Modern publishers have tampered with the story, and Jones has returned Barrie's novel to its 1911 first edition text.

Graduated from the University of Illinois, Andrea Jones studied Oral Interpretation of Literature, with a Literature minor. Her earlier career was in television production. Jones is known around the world as "Capitana Red-Hand" of Under the Black Flag, a web-based pirate brotherhood.

The first two books of the *Hook & Jill* Saga, *Hook & Jill* and *Other Oceans*, won a dozen literary awards and the hearts of their many readers. This volume, *Other Islands: Book Three of the Hook & Jill Saga*, explores forms of generosity, both usual and unusual.

Within these novels, Jones deepens and explores J.M. Barrie's famous and infamous characters, and re-imagines the Neverland for grown-up readers who long to return there. Five books are charted for this series.